FEAST OF FATES

✱ ✱ ✱

CHRISTIAN A. BROWN

ISBN: 1495907589
ISBN 13: 9781495907586
Library of Congress Control Number: 2014903202
CreateSpace Independent Publishing Platform
North Charleston, South Carolina

For Cynthia

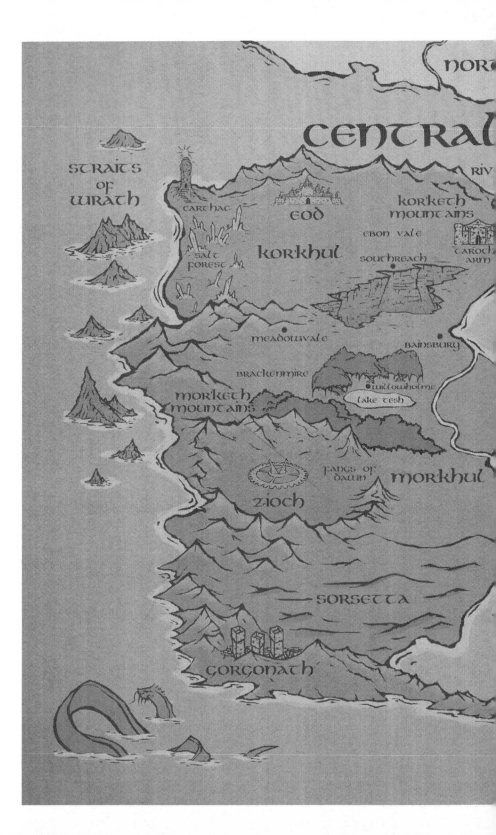

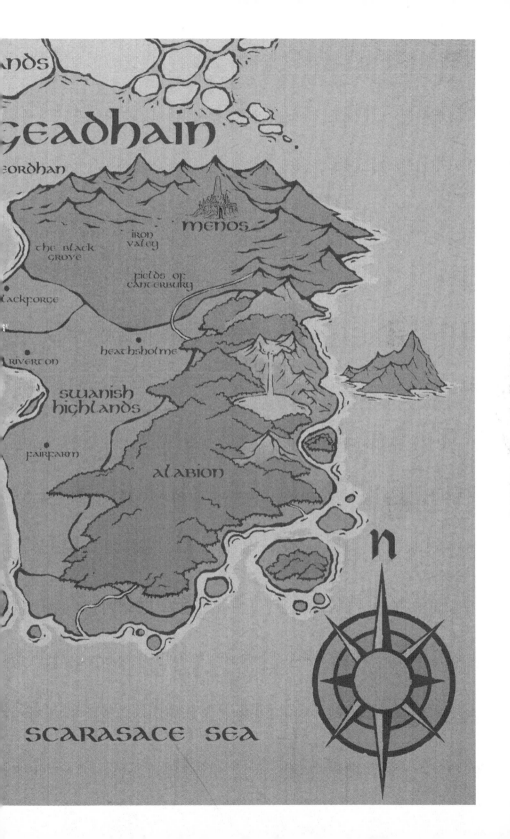

ON GEADHAIN (GLOSSARY)

I: Paragons, Wonders, and Horrors

The Sisters Three—Ealasyd \\\'Ēl-ə-sid\\, ***Elemech*** \\\'El-ə-mek\\, and ***Eean*** \\\'Ē-en\\: From youngest to eldest in appearance, they are Ealasyd, Elemech, and Eean. The Sisters Three are a trio of ageless witches who live in the woods of Alabion. They are known to hold sway over the destinies of men. They can be capricious, philanthropic, or woefully cruel. One must be careful when bartering with the Sisters Three for their wisdom. There is always a price.

Morigan: A young woman living a rather unremarkable life as the handmaiden to an elderly sorcerer, Thackery Thule. Upon a chance, perhaps fated, meeting with the Wolf, a world of wonder and horror engulfs her. She learns she is an axis of magik, mystery, and Fate to the proceedings of Geadhain's Great War. In the darkest days she and her companions must face, her heroism and oft-tested virtue will determine much of the world's salvation or ruin.

The Wolf, Caenith \\\'Kā-nith\\: A smith of Eod. His fearsome, raw exterior hides an animal and a dreadful wrath. Caenith is a conflicted creature—a beast, man, poet, lover, and killer. Caenith believes himself beyond salvation, and he passes the years making metal skins and claws for the slow-walkers of Geadhain while drowning himself in bitter remorse. He does not know it, but Morigan will pull him from his darkness and make him confront what is most black and wicked within him.

Thackery Hadrian Thule (Whitehawk): An old sorcerer living in Eod. Thackery lives an unassuming life as a man of modest stature. However, he is a man with many skeletons in his closet. He has no known children or family, and he cares for Morigan as if she were his daughter. Morigan's grace will touch him, too, and he is drawn into the web of Fate she weaves.

Magnus: The Immortal King of the North. Magnus is one of two guardians of the Waking World. The other is his brother, Brutus. The Everfair King—the colloquial name for Magnus—rules Eod, the City of Wonders. He is living magik itself, a sorcerer without compare, and the master of the forces of ice, thunder, Will, and intellect.

Brutus: The Sun King. Brutus is the second of the Immortal Kings and ruler of the Summerlands in southern Geadhain. Zioch, the City of Gold, shines like a gold star on the southern horizon and is the seat of his power. Brutus is the master of the wilderness and the hunt. His magik has dominion over the physical world and self. He is victim to the Black Queen's whispers and falls far from his nobility.

Lilehum (Lila): Magnus's bride. Magnus sought her when learning to live as a man independent of his ageless brother. Through the sharing of blood and ancient vows—the *Fuilimean*—she is drawn into the mystery of the immortal brothers and imbued with a sliver of their magik. She is a sorceress and possibly eternal in her years. She is wise, kind, and comely without compare. However, she is ruthless if her kingdom or bloodmate is threatened.

The Black Queen, Zionae \'Zē-ō-'nā\: A shapeless, bodiless, monstrous entity without empathy that seeks to undo the Immortal Kings and the world's order. Her actions—those who perceive these things sense she is a she—are horrific and inexplicable.

II: Eod's Finest

Erithitek \'Ār-ith-ə-'tek\: More commonly referred to as "Erik." He is the king's hammer. Erik was once an orphaned child of the Salt Forests and a member of the Kree tribe, but Magnus took him in. Erik now serves as his right hand.

Rowena: She is Queen Lila's sword and Her Majesty's left hand. Rowena's tale was destined for a swift, bleak end until the queen intervened and saved Rowena's young life. Since that day, Rowena has revered Queen Lila as a mother and true savior.

Lowelia Larson: The queen knows her as the Lady of Whispers. Lowelia seems a simple, high-standing palace servant, yet her doughy, pleasant demeanor conceals a shrewd mind and a vengeful secret.

Galivad: Master of the East Watch. The youngest of Eod's watchmasters, he is seen by many as unfit for the post because of his pretty face, foppish manner, and cavalier airs. He laughs and sings to avoid the pain of remembering what he has lost.

Dorvain: Master of the North Watch and Leonitis's brother. He is a brutish, gruff warrior tempered by the winds of the Northlands. He is dependable and unflappable. He is an oak of a man who will not bend to the winds of change or war.

Leonitis: The Lion. He is thusly named for his roar, grandeur, and courage. He is the Ninth Legion master of Eod (King Magnus's personal legion). Once Geadhain's Great War commences, he will play many roles from soldier to spy to hero. Leonitis's thread of destiny is long and woven through many Fates.

Jebidiah Rotbottom: A flamboyant spice merchant from Sorsetta. He sails the breadth of Geadhain in a garish, crimson vessel—the *Red Mary*. Currently he uses different aliases, for reasons no doubt unscrupulous and suspect.

Tabitha Fischer: The sole magistrate of Willowholme. She has assumed this role not by choice but through tragedy.

Beauregard Fischer: A waifish, lyrical young man lost in the Summerlands with his father. In his past and soul lies a great mystery. His cheek is marked with the birthmark of the one true northern star.

Devlin Fischer: A seasoned hunter and Beauregard's father. He is as gruff and hairy as a bear.

Maggie Halm: A descendant of Cordenzia, an infamous whoremistress who traded her power for freedom from the Iron City. Maggie—Cordenzia's granddaughter—runs an establishment called the Silk Purse in Taroch's Arm.

Talwyn Blackmore: The illegitimate son of Roland Blackmore (since deceased). Talwyn is a kind, brilliant scholar and inheritor of all the virtue that escaped his half brother, Augustus. Talwyn lives in Riverton. His thirst for knowledge often makes him cross boundaries of decorum.

III: Menos's Darkest Souls

Mouse: More of a gray soul than a black one, Mouse is a woman without a firm flag planted on the map of morality. She knows well life's cruelty and how best to avoid it through self-sufficiency and indifference. As a girl she escaped a rather unfortunate fate, and she has since risen to become a Voice of the Watchers—a shadowbroker of Geadhain. Mouse's real trial begins when she is thrust into peril with Morigan—at that time a stranger—and Mouse is forced to rethink everything she knows.

Adelaide: Mouse's childhood friend from the charterhouse. The girl's fate is the cause of much torment for Mouse.

Gloriatrix: The Iron Queen and ruler of Menos. Gloriatrix single-handedly clawed her way to the top of Menos's black Crucible after her husband, Gabriel, lost first his right to chair on the Council of the Wise and then his life. Gloriatrix has never remarried and blames her brother, Thackery Thule, for Gabriel's death. With her family in shambles, power is the only thing to which she clings. Gloriatrix has ambitions far beyond Menos. She would rule the stars themselves if she could.

Sorren: Gloriatrix's youngest child. Sorren is a nekromancer of incredible power who possesses the restraint and moods of a petulant, spoiled child. He shares a pained past with his (mostly) deceased brother, Vortigern.

Vortigern: Gloriatrix's second son. This pitiable soul lives in a state between light and dark and without memory of the errors that brought him to this walking death.

The Broker: All the black rivers of sin in Menos come to one confluence: the Broker. Little is known about this man beyond the terror tales whispered to misbehaving children. The Broker has metal teeth, mad eyes, and a cadre of twisted servants whom he calls sons. He inhabits and controls the Iron City's underbelly.

Elissandra: The Mistress of Mysteries. She is an Iron sage and the proprietress of Menos's Houses of Mystery—places where a wary master can consult oracles and seek augurs regarding his or her inevitable doom. While she is wicked, she is also bright with love for her children, and she fosters a hidden dream and hope no other Iron sage would ever be so bold as to consider.

Elineth: Son of Elissandra.

Tessariel: Daughter of Elissandra.

Moreth of El: Master of the House of El and the Blood Pits of Menos. He traffics in people, gladiators, and death.

Beatrice of El: Moreth's pale and ghastly wife. After a glance, a person can tell this ethereal woman is not wholly of this world.

Alastair: A mysterious figure who acts seemingly in his own interests. He greatly influences certain meetings and events. To all appearances, he is the Watchers' agent and Mouse's mentor. He almost certainly, though, serves another power or master.

Lord Augustus Blackmore: Lord of Blackforge. A deviant powermonger with grotesque appetites.

IV: Lands and Landmarks

Alabion: The great woodland and the realm of the Sisters Three.

Eod: The City of Wonders and kingdom of Magnus. Eod is a testament to the advances of technomagik and culture in Geadhain.

Zioch: The City of Gold and kingdom of Brutus.

Kor'Khul: The great sand ocean surrounding Eod. These lands were once thought to be lush and verdant.

Mor'Khul: The green, rolling valleys of Brutus's realm. They are legendary for their beauty.

Menos: The Iron City. It is hung always in a pall of gloom.

Carthac: The City of Waves.

Ebon Vale: The land around Taroch's Arm. It has fiefs, farmsteads, and large shale deposits.

The Black Grove: The forest outside of Blackforge. It leads to the Plains of Canterbury.

Plains of Canterbury: Wide, sparse fields and gullies.

Iron Valley: One of the richest sources of feliron in Geadhain.

Blackforge: A city on the east bank of the Feordhan River. It was once famous for blacksmithing.

Bainsbury: A moderate-size township on the west bank of the Feordhan. Gavin Foss lords over it.

Riverton: A bustling, eclectic city of lighthearted criminals and troubadours. The city is found on the east shore of the Feordhan River, and it was built from the reconstituted wreckage of old hulls and whatever interesting bits floated down the great river.

Fairfarm: The largest rural community in the East. With so many pastures, fields, and farms, this realm produces most of Central Geadhain's consumable resources.

Heathsholme: A small hamlet known for its fine ale.

Southreach: A great ancient city built into a cleft in Kor'Khul.

Sorsetta: In the South and past the Sun King's lands. This is a city of contemplation and quiet enlightenment.

Taroch's Arm: The resting place of a relic of the great warlord Taroch: his arm. The city is also a hub of great trade between all corners of Geadhain.

Brackenmire: The realm outside of Mor'Khul. It is a swampy but pleasant place.

Willowholme: A village located in Brackenmire and famed for its musicians and anglers.

Lake Tesh: The blue jewel glittering under the willows of Willowholme.

V: Miscellaneous Mysteries

Fuilimean: The Blood Promise. It is a trading of blood and vows and a spiritual binding between two willing participants. Magnus and Brutus did this first in the oldest ages. Depending on who partakes in the ritual, the results can be extraordinary.

Technomagik: A hybrid science that blends raw power—often currents of magik—with mechanical engineering.

The Faithful: Worshippers of the Green Mother. They exist in many cultures and forms, and the most sacred and spiritual of their kind, curators of the world's history known as Keepers, often lead them.

The Watchers: The largest network of shadowbrokers in Central Geadhain.

Ode to the East

A weeping sky, a sea of trees that eats,
what foolish hands and little feet
Do poke and tread upon its fright
Do dare to brave its darkest nights
Those who enter, go alone
Bare as babes, chilled to bone
No steel or magik will save one here
From the wildest things that prowl
—the Lords of fang and claw
Nor the Oldest that do howl
—in their cairns of loam and age
Or the leaves themselves that whisper, tease, and hiss:
lost, so lost, and never found,
hope and blood shall feed our ground
You have entered, and now are gone
Into the shadows of Alabion

PROLOGUE

The sky was black over the evergreen sea. No moon, no stars, as if the heavens did not exist in this realm. Creatures sang to a moon that was unseen, each cry more unrecognizable than the last. Elegantly these monsters stalked one another; hunting down in the prison of tangled trees, bracken, and thorns, the serpents' nests and clutching roots that only the maddest ranger might call a forest. Amid the skulking killers, a solitary woman glided through the darkness.

She heeded the whispery winds, which did not lure her into snares as they would other travelers, but told her where to step truly. She asked the tortoise-skinned, ancient trees to move their branches from her path and thanked them as they complied. Many a time, fanged things leaped from the foliage, snarling and slavering for her flesh, and she banished them with the softest whistle or a reproachful shine of her green glass eyes. With her branch of timeworn yew, she prodded her way over stone and twist. When the wind started to natter, she pulled tight her threadbare shawl and kirtle. And if the hike threatened to exhaust her, she would pause, think of her sisters waiting for her, and then push on through the shadows with renewed and ruthless determination: the final resolve of a soul soon to die. She could sense her end in the brittleness of her bones, the fluttering of her heart like a hummingbird's wings, and the snotty rattle in her lungs. Death was such a familiar friend to her that she could time its nearness within a sand or two of the hourglass. She knew that she still had time, but also that she would not live to see another dawn.

Onward she plunged, culling kindness from the vicious woods, taming what those who did not listen to the true voices wrongly called the Untamed. As she went, she basked in the beauty of Alabion; her eyes drawn to dewy leaves glittering as if scattered with diamonds, her ears to the music that echoed through the pines, her nose to the earthy pungency of the mulch beneath her toes. She drank in every sight, sound, and scent; missing none of it, adoring all of it. Soon, the trees thinned to brambles, which rustled themselves apart like kindly doorkeepers for her, and she came to a rocky basin and a steeply rising bluff. Difficult the climb would be, yet she wasted not a speck. Stone was not something that one could sing to in the hope of courtesy: it was stubborn, it wouldn't listen, and it broke in half before it bent to another's Will. So she did not bother asking the stone to accommodate her, but steeled her way up the bluff, not once crying out from the scraping of her hands, knees, and feet. Besides, the journey and struggle of life was half the joy, and she reveled in the toil, pain, and sweat of her decrepit body, for it was to be the last rush of life she would know for a while.

Surely the moon admired her spirit, and it peeked out in a sliver of whiteness. As she stopped, huffing, to look up at its loveliness, she saw that she had nearly reached the slyly tucked escarpment that was her destination. A ghostly female figure with billowing black hair and a gaze that glinted green, even from strides away, leaned over the edge: her sister. Hurriedly, the traveler clambered up the cliffside. But she had reached the limits of her strength, and at the end, her sister's strong, pale arms helped to pull her onto a plateau soft with grasses.

"Eean, the paleness of a death is upon you," said her sister, hovering over her.

"Help me up, Elemech," demanded Eean. "I feel like a boulder on two spring twigs, and we have precious few sands left."

Stoutly, Elemech hauled up her sister by the armpits. They walked over a lush meadow of clover, ferns, and flowers, heading for a cavern draped in vines. In the morning, butterflies and birds would play amid the lea on the cliff, though tonight only evening moths were about. Eean indulged in the study of their dances and one longing look to the sliver of the moon until she was pulled into the cave. Illumed patches of nocturnal fungi spotted the walls here, and it was easy for Elemech to find her way deep through the winding dark, into their refuge. For some time they wandered, deeper, farther into the belly of rock, Elemech never unsure of which branching road to take, even when the fungi dried up and they were panting together in sheer darkness.

Much like Eean was at one with the great wilds, so too could Elemech steer through the unseen. She could find a light in every shadow, a meaning in every casting of the bones, or feel the drop of a tear from spans away in the ripples of her pond.

"Here we are, sister," said Elemech at last.

Not a sand too soon, thought Eean, hanging her head; her breathing was a rasp, and she was mostly being carried now. Eean opened her heavy lids to the brightness of their home, snapping bits of recollection here and there. She saw the crystal-studded walls, glimmering as a geode's violet guts. A flash of the pool where Elemech would often dip her hand and sing of faraway lands to them; of the places they would never see. The limestone table, rusty with blood, where they would eat and read entrails together. Their third sister's cluttered workshop and the stone shelves filled with herbs, skins, jewels, fabric, bones, and knickknacks rummaged from the forest or the cave. Finally she felt the familiar relief of her fragrant pine-and-moss mattress caressing her flesh. In and out she drifted; her pulse and vision ragged. The sand of her death was nearly upon them. She heard small feet running up, and a tiny hand clutched her gnarled one.

"Oh, Eean," cheeped the sweet young voice. "Do you have to go so soon? The season while you're away is so gray. You know how somber Elemech can be. Staring in her pool, reciting all the sadnesses of the world. She is so glum without you."

"My dearest Ealasyd. Let me look at you. At both of you before these eyes fail me," grunted Eean, and forced herself to see.

Both her sisters were kneeling by her. With her honey-gold hair and innocent gaze, Ealasyd was as beautiful as sunshine. Ealasyd had the same green eyes as her sisters had, tawny skin, and the finest features of the three, yet only because she was the youngest. Come a point, when the cycle repeated itself and Eean was young again, Ealasyd and she would be fairhaired twins. She delighted in those years, when the two of them could play as siblings. Just as many, many seasons past that childhood, she would take on the wintry beauty of Elemech, with her mystery and darkness, and they could brood and sing as one. As the crone, her final lap of life was always the most tiresome, for she could not play with Ealasyd or contemplate as adeptly with her failing mind as Elemech could, so she was lonely despite all their intimacy.

So, in that season of her life, she would leave, not to be a burden, and would forage the Untamed, gathering gifts for her sisters to use in their craft. A task to which her hardy, dispensable body was better suited than those of her delicate sisters. And she had been lucky this time. She had one parting gift for them.

"Such lovely mothers and sisters you each have been," praised Eean. "If one of you would reach to my pouch, you will find a few treasures of Alabion."

Ealasyd clapped her hands and rummaged about in her sister's garment. She came away with three things: an animal fang crusted in blood, as if ripped out during a hunt; a handful of crimson grass; and a polished black stone, like the scale of an ebony lizard.

"Oh! These...these are perfect, Eean!" Ealasyd clapped again, and scampered off at once, without allowing her scowling middle sister to have a look.

"Bring those here!" snapped Elemech.

"The gifts are for both of you," reminded Eean, and her sister nodded and took the hand that Ealasyd had left, kissing it.

"She is right, you know. I am colder without you. As harsh as the Long Winter," confessed Elemech with regret. "I hope that I am to bear you this time. A kick inside my ribs might force some kindness into me."

"Perhaps. It is so hard on Ealasyd; she is so small, and my head and shoulders are so large," Eean said, smiling.

The sisters shared a laugh.

In a wind of excitement, Ealasyd was upon them again. "Look!" she cried, shoving her arms over Eean and scattering her with items. First, Ealasyd picked up a rudimentary, four-legged clay figurine, which had the bloody tooth jammed into the bottom of its head. *A wolf*, thought Eean. Then Ealasyd claimed the second toy: a rag-doll woman made of pale mouse skins with a mane of red weeds. *A maiden*, decided Eean. The third creation lay on Eean's stomach while Ealasyd had the wolf chase the maiden around it, and

Eean debated how to classify the thing. What was this ball of nettles and the bird husks—a skylark and a crow—that shared a black stone between their beaks?

"What...is that?" wheezed Eean, curious.

Ealasyd looked to the talisman and shrugged. "I'm not sure."

Elemech's face waned with shadow. "Give those to me," she demanded, and snatched the playthings from Ealasyd and the talisman that lay on her sister, too. While Ealasyd protested, Elemech raced off to a still pool that glimmered with soft light. Although Eean could not turn her head to see, she heard the splash as her sister tossed the items into the water.

"It took me so long to make those! Hunting rats isn't easy, and neither is scraping clay! Do you see, Eean? Do you see what I shall be left with?"

"Hush, my sister. You made your toys well. It is Elemech's turn to play with them," said Eean. A wave of pain suddenly ran through her, and then the cold hand of death gripped her spine. "I love you, sister...I shall see you soon."

Ealasyd nodded her golden head and then placed it on her sister's chest. She listened to the slowing heartbeat and wept. A few heartbeats later, Eean's eyes fell shut, and that sorrow-sweet vision of Ealasyd was the last thing she saw in this life. However, even if muffled with cotton, she heard Elemech's chanting, a rhythmic and fading echo, as she drifted down a swift river that her sisters could not follow. At the pool, the waters ran black, the discarded relics whirled deeper and deeper, and although her body remained upright, Elemech felt herself tip and flounder after them.

First comes the tearing of her immaterial flesh: pins and needles stabbed into every nerve, a thousand mouths nibbling at her tenderest bits, a thousand whispers that hiss every weakness and failure she has ever known. Such magnificent torture should not be, for she is a ghost in this vision, not bone and meat that can be harmed. This is the Hungry Dark, and it has swallowed her utterly. But even as a watcher she is strong, even against the greatest of evils.

"You shall not have me today, Black Queen," she declares.

She steels her Will and cuts through the clinging darkness like a blade of sunshine. In an instant, the blackness splits, and she is free of the Hungry Dark. As a bird, or a wind, she now soars over a scorched and fiery wasteland toward a grand city. A city once golden and now as red with the presence of murder as the great moat of fire that encompasses it. Coiled about the city's spires are black serpents of smoke. This is Zioch, the Golden City, and it has fallen to evil. She does not need to contemplate the fate of Zioch's Immortal King, for she can hear his tormented howls echoing through the haze. Amid his madness, she senses his sadness and knows that he has done something terrible to his brother.

"Fair king..." she says with regret, and then her wind is borne upward, and she sees a white moon, bright and full, bathing the rich woods of Alabion. A pair of birds flies past the moon, one pale to the point of being silver and the other black. The black one is chasing the other; she knows that he wishes to kill it, just as she knows the men whom the birds represent. Suddenly, speedily, she is pulled downward through the netting of trees toward a campfire and an oddly laid scene. Beside the sparking fire is a weathered corpse; its grimace could be interpreted as a smile, and a magpie is pecking at its yellow teeth.

"A kiss," she thinks. "How sweet." For these shapes do not hide the true selves of these beings, and she knows them for who they truly are. It warms her that they will find each other.

A growl commands her attention elsewhere, to the shade outside the campfire's reach. She sees him prowling the darkness there, a great man or beast—a bit of each, she thinks—and he is not hidden in allegory as with much of her vision. He is clear, this enormous, grumbling creature who walks on all fours and snaps his teeth to the night. The man's bearing is defensive, protective. "Of what?" she wonders, until the glimmer of ivory and red courts her eye from the circle he paces. Again, there is no couched meaning to be found, and what he guards is as clear to her as her own name: a maiden. Elemech's heart twists with emotions—excitement, fear, joy—and the vision twists with it and shatters.

"The one lost," Elemech mumbled, paler than cream.

She was still gazing into the pool, which had returned to its clarity and had no more secrets to share with her. She had enough to deal with anyway. Instinctually, she called for her elder sister, whose wisdom would be needed for this matter.

"Eean," she whispered.

"Eean is dead; come mourn with me," pleaded Ealasyd.

Elemech went to join her small sister over the body of Eean, and they huddled together and cried. Elemech's tears came from sorrow as much as from what the pool had shown her, which neither she nor Ealasyd had the power to face alone. If only Eean were with them now, she would know what to do. How to grease the wheels of possibility without breaking the machine.

"We are lost without her," sniffled Elemech, unusually emotional. "What an inconvenient time to die."

"She'll be back soon," said Ealasyd. She started undressing the corpse. "We should return her flesh to the forest, as she likes us to do. Come help, sister."

The sisters stripped Eean's body and neatly set her garments and staff aside on a shelf; these items wouldn't be used again for many, many years. Using the water from Elemech's pool, they washed her, and then anointed her skin with badger musk and animal fats so that she would be a sumptuous-smelling meal for the beasts of the woods. For Eean's dignity, they placed a crown of dried ivy about her head. Carefully, with Elemech carrying the shoulders and Ealasyd lugging the feet, they dragged the thin carcass of their sister down the labyrinth of dark tunnels and out of the cave. At the edge of the meadow they stopped, taking a breath before finishing their task, as poor Ealasyd was spent from the haul. A handful of stars had joined the shy moon to watch Eean's passing, and the night was crisp, windless, and calm.

"I don't feel anything yet. In my belly," noted Ealasyd.

Come to think of it, neither did Elemech; the candle of new life had not been lit in her womb. Eean was not returning to life. *What is she waiting for?* wondered Elemech.

"Do you think?" said the sisters together, and bent over to examine Eean.

As if on a spring, Eean's mouth popped open and a gasp escaped. For such a tiny breath, it roared past the sisters' faces like a monster of air and thunder. The sisters stared up at the sky for a while, trying to guess where Eean's breath, this wind, had gone. Their souls and faces were bright, knowing that Eean had not forsaken them, that she had held on to her flesh for as long as she could. She had given them hope. Elemech was more mirthful still, for with that final breath the miracle of new life had stirred within her; she would bear Eean this time.

"Where do you think her breath went?" asked Ealasyd.

"Exactly where it was supposed to," answered Elemech.

They tossed Eean's body from the cliff.

PART I

I

WHERE THE WIND WENT

I

A RMSMAN, the sign read, in script so fine that it appeared penned on the swinging board, not wrought in twists of metal. Morigan squinted and could decipher that the original lettering of the sign had been erased. WONDERS OF THE ARCANE was there no more, which left her with few options to find a sprig of fireroot for her particular master. If she hadn't been all over Eod today, she might have been less inclined to pop in and ask the proprietor of Armsman if he knew what had happened to the last merchant to set up shop here. But she had paced Eod's hot white streets since first light, wandering from tent to stall to shanty in the Faire of Fates, and finally to the smaller workshops in less commercial districts. From counter to counter she'd gone, almost pleading with the proprietors for a maddeningly rare herb that they simply did not carry. She was footsore, sweating, aching in her bladder, and ironically, quite thirsty, too, and the reaching shadow that fell off the tall pale building was inviting, even if its bricked-up widows, smoking rooftop, and pitted facade leaned toward menacing. The iron-banded door was opened a tad as well, as if a wind had pushed it ajar, and she took this as fate's final invitation.

As light as a dancer, Morigan was up a few steps and had slipped through the crack of the entrance.

"Hello," she called boldly, for it was dark inside the hallway in which she stood.

Morigan was hardly a timid girl; she had watched her mother die, and the dark or any other anxieties since then were minor to her. So she called again and went farther into the dimness, following the sound of a hammer on metal.

What an odd shopkeeper, to have no lights inside. I can only imagine what sort of strangeness I'm getting myself into—all for a glass of water and a piss.

Quickly it brightened with the glow of a fire, and the hammering rang louder. The short hallway ended, and she was in a heat-congested space. When last she had been to this store, before its conversion to a forge, the room was set up from floor to ceiling with shelving and jammed with all manner of baubles, crystals, bundled spices, and animal heads. Now the room was stripped bare to its white foundation, with its casements filled in and its second floor torn out to create a lofty ceiling. A hole was carved in the roof for the smoke to escape. Whoever worked here also lived here, and she could tell he was a humble person, for in one corner lay a dingy straw pallet. Nearby was an undignified lavatory, lacking so much as a screen for privacy. Gleaming weaponry was heaped along the walls and scattered around a grated pit of fire dug right into the floor. Bellows, tongs, molds, and other smithing instruments were laid about in disarray.

Nearly every smith in Eod used the cold flames of magik for his forge. *Not this one,* she cursed as she daubed herself. Indeed, most of Eod was so cultured and proper. From its pearly streets to its sandstone bricks that were shaped into orderly, elegant towers, gabled courts, and even quaint byres for the poor, everything was crafted with symmetry and meaningful precision. The Everfair King would have no less than perfection in his city. In contrast, this forge, with its raggedy roof and its proprietor who lived as meagerly as an escaped slave from Menos, was surely the messiest place Morigan had seen. She knew messiness. She spent her days tidying up after a sloppy and forgetful sorcerer, running his errands, and arranging his life. A bit irately, she called out to the hammering man—it had to be a man to make this sort of chaos—for a third time. A shape was veiled behind the thick smoke of the pit; she thought it was a standing suit of armor and gasped when it moved.

The Wolf had heard the woman enter his shop—not a dropped pin or the nightly bickering of his drunken neighbors escaped his notice—and her light tread, as if a deer was stepping upon grass, was no exception. He held his breath when he heard the noise, for it caused a queer feeling in him: a quickening of his heart that for once was not the thrill of chasing, hunting, and tearing. He continued to hammer, working the kinks out of an already flawless shield. He continued to ignore the other signs of the stranger's entry. Signs like the sweet onion and honey scent of her sweat, a smell that made his mouth water. Or the sweep of her perfumed hair, silkily swishing in his ears and surely as soft to touch as it sounded. He knew that her locks were the deepest shade of red, for she smelled of autumn. The Wolf wasn't afraid of this stranger, for he feared nothing but a cage in which he could be kept. Yet this confusion of emotion persisted nonetheless, and waffle he would not. He was a creature of absolutes, not one for questioning his nature. Finally, he stood and strode through the smoke to meet her.

Morigan gasped a bit more as the man emerged, immediately disarmed by his size and the surety of self that allowed him to walk in his brass-fitted boots through lightly flickering flames without a care. She had never known a man so large, and he carried his immensity as naturally and weightlessly as she bore her slenderness. Likewise, they were in many ways contrary to each other. She was pale as milk, while he was tanned to darkness and shimmered like the coppery metals that his enormous hands might squeeze. She was as delicate and smooth as any woman would desire to be, and he was as knotted and veined as an oak, with thick-black hair on his chest, upon his naked arms, and over his stony chin and chops. Their faces were each beautiful—if again polarities of soft and hard—with her supple angles and pink pout of a mouth and his hewn cheeks and wide red lips. If her hair was a mane of fire, then his was an unkempt flame of darkness, almost as long as hers was, but somehow suiting the man.

With all their opposing aspects, their stares bore an eerie similarity. Morigan's eyes held a flash of silver, the legacy of a bastard father she had never met. Whereas the Wolf's eyes gleamed with the cold gray indifference of an animal peering out in the darkness.

He is like a man sculpted from the earth. Am I dreaming? Have I hit my head? Passed out in the street from the heat of walking all day? Get your wits together, girl! What in the king's name am I doing in this ratty forge with a man who watches me as a beast would its supper and from whom I cannot look away? Morigan cautioned herself.

Sands fled, and they stared and stared, unable to remove their gazes from each other. Morigan had forgotten why she was here, yet she was unafraid, if uncertain of the hungry way in which the large man watched her: his nostrils flaring bullishly, as if he could smell something that she could not. Uncomfortable, she pulled her summery shift tighter about herself despite the stifling heat, and the Wolf noted the teardrop outline of a breast against her damp garment. Her clothing was almost transparent to his cutting eyes, as if she were wrapped in mist, and his heart raced harder. In his head danced thoughts of chasing her through a field, of drinking in her laughter or cries as he nipped at her flesh.

Morigan was not prone to flighty indulgences. She had been offered her share of fair-weather romances; she knew the promises that men made only to break. She recovered her sensibilities first.

"Pardon my intrusion. The door was ajar. I...I am Morigan. Morigan Lostarot."

How strange, thought the Wolf, for he never left the door to his den open.

She went down into the room, which had a small step, and stood outside the circumference of the grate. She offered her hand for him to come forward and shake. Curiously, he beheld it. The Wolf operated by requisition only. Slips were left under his door, with orders for weaponry and no face attached to the order. He had his meat delivered in the mornings by a meatmonger, whom he never welcomed in. Rarely did he see a two-legs. He needed to think about how mortals greeted one another. After dusting off his hands on his blackened apron, he walked off the grate and put forth a calloused paw that engulfed Morigan's hand entirely. As they touched, her arm hummed like a tuning fork, and being close to him, she noticed his queer smell. Underneath the stringency of iron shavings, body odor, and charcoal were more enticing scents of woodland ferns or silky pelts. Morigan couldn't explain any of it, or why she was so captivated.

The enchantment was shared by the Wolf, and he struggled against the urge to rub her satin skin or even lick it, knowing that such practices were frowned on by slow-walkers.

Following a much-delayed introduction, he said, "Caenith. My name is Caenith."

His voice was raw, deep, and cracked, like a stone bounding down a chasm in the earth.

"A pleasure to meet you, Caenith. No promised or family name, I take it?"

Promised name! For the love of the kings, Morigan, it sounds like you're throwing yourself at the man like a common tart!

"No blood or bloodmate that I would answer to, no."

Nervously, Morigan continued with a smile. It was as beautiful to Caenith as the sun dancing over the water of the deepest springs in the oldest forests; it was an expression of true purity.

"Bloodmate! There's a term from the ages. In any case, terrific to meet you! If I could have my hand back, that would grand."

"Yes, of course," said Caenith, and released her.

Feeling a touch more at ease, Morigan asked the curious smith for a glass of water (she decided against asking to use his toilet, however, as it was not ladylike to squat in an exposed corner). Caenith went off to rummage through his den for an object to use as a cup. A particular quandary, as he tended to fill the sink or tub with water when he needed to drink, bathe, or otherwise refresh himself. While he was away somewhere in the smoky chamber, Morigan wandered to the wall and perused the smith's wares. At once, her breath was taken away by their exquisiteness, and she drifted with an open mouth, sighing at each item she passed and was afraid to touch out of the delicacy of its construction. If she had her say, these pieces would be displayed above a great hearth, mayhap even in the golden halls of the Everfair King. She ahhed over foils decorated with metal leaves to look as though they were entwined in ivy. She oohed at blades with thorns run down their haft and embossed with flowers. While she said she would not, she dared to trace her fingertip on the cold shields of steel roses, the iron shillelagh made as a grayish leafed branch, and the gauntlet that had the seeming appearance of marble with streaks of gold, platinum, and silver. Each piece bore some element of the natural world, as if flora had miraculously survived the smith's fire and grown on inside the metal. Every artifact could have been chiseled from the land itself.

What artistry! Eod's sorcerers were its artists, gardeners, and architects. Here in the City of Wonders, you could not escape their ostentation. The watersculptors, firecallers, earthspeakers, and windsingers created fountains of ever-flowing water, statues of heatless flame, orchards from plots of dust, and skies free of the deadly sandstorms that swept the desert around Eod. Their grandeur was undeniable. But for Morigan, the smith's work embodied the denotation of *art* better than any sorcerer's spell could. As she was reaching for a butterfly unfurling its wings on a helmet of netted vines, half expecting the insect to leap onto her fingers, a shadow—and the smell of man, woods, and beast—dropped over her. She jumped and did an about-face.

"Water," said Caenith.

What she judged to be the broken end of a hollow metal staff was thrust before her, dribbling water. How or why the staff had been snapped was a question she never thought to ask, but probably should have, and she was instead amused by the crude charm of the gesture.

What an odd bird, this one. I swear he's never had company before. Here I was worrying that I might embarrass myself to a man who doesn't even have a cup in his cupboard. Or a cupboard for a cup, even.

She drank the water, thanked the smith, and passed back the makeshift cup to him, which he tossed to the floor. Again the heaviness of his stare, as if his eyes alone could consume her, shivered over Morigan's flesh.

"Your work," she said, striking at the tension.

"What of it?"

"I am not a warrior—in fact, I've never held a blade—but the craftsmanship is...extraordinary. I've never seen anything like it. I feel that I should ask if you have cast some magik into the metal, even though I am inclined to believe that you have not. I simply cannot imagine how hands by themselves can make such beauty."

The smith looked at Morigan, or through her, as if envisioning another space. "Hands and patience...*Geadhain*—if you don't know the old name of our world—has secrets that she speaks to any creature, but only the most willing hear her. The sorcerers of today do not bow to the Old Laws, they scribble over them instead. They do not ask the skies to rain; they rip into it with their Wills, and the tears fall. If we listen to the metal, if we hear how it wants to be made...well, then true beauty can be found. To touch is as much a pleasure as it is a gift. I honor that gift. I honor what I touch."

Morigan noted that the smith's attention had returned from its faraway reminiscence and was upon her again, burning off her clothing, sniffing her presence, eating her right up. Other than his flowery, compelling words, there was something about this man that was as off as it was alluring. There was a quality to him that was unlike any person she had met.

"What of you, Morigan Lostarot?" Her name rolled off his tongue like a slow song. "What do you speak to? What voices do you hear? What do you touch?"

Touch? she wondered. He seemed to be asking about her vocation in his outlandish way. Suddenly, her responsibilities and sensibilities rushed over her, and she recalled that she had a purpose before wandering into the dreamy forge and talking with a strange, talented man who smelled like a beast—pleasingly so, a dog she wanted to pet—and spoke like a philosopher poet. Waving her arms apologetically and rambling in staccato, she fumbled to leave, nearly tripping over helmets, poles, and whatever else cluttered her path. Yet the smith followed her closely, stealing touches of her softness as he moved her around these obstacles or kicked them out of her way.

"Oh shite! I'm a handmaiden to a sometimes-cranky sorcerer! I daresay I've been here far too long! How long has it been? An hourglass? More? If it weren't so dark in here, I'd have a better idea. I'm sorry, Caenith, but I really must be off. My master is quite helpless without me. Old, very old. He doesn't soil himself, but I don't think we're that far off. Oh, thank you, thank you, I didn't see that. I never did find that firewort, or wormhazel, or whatever I was supposed to find! Where is my mind today? I didn't get the address of the last shopkeeper that lived here, either. I meant to ask you that, funnily enough! That's how I ended up here. You probably have no idea where he's gone. Oh, thank you once more, forgot about the stair. Here we are, then."

They had reached the door, and Caenith opened it wide to the day. Sunset was upon them, and light poured from the metal roofs of the buildings in the street behind Morigan and lit her in an aura of crimson. Right then, she was a woman of fire, and Caenith was overcome by her loveliness and her honey-autumn scent that a breeze blew his way. His heart hammered as though it would shatter the bone that restrained it, and a revelation split his skull. After so long alone, after wandering a world where the wind only sang when it was whipped to obedience by the new magik, and the true beauty, the old magik, was a whisper when it had been a roar...here was a miracle. Something of the past, something that should not be, unaware of who or what she was, of how precious a dream she represented. Akin to the pack he had lost, a thousand howling beasts of emotion tore through his spirit. He thought of hunting amid pine forests or loping over golden meadows. He dreamed of tasting freedom and breathing life. He felt the rush of blood in his mouth, the splash of water on his snout, the crash of lightning in his ear. In that instant, the Wolf felt it all: every forgotten beauty of his soul. The realization of who this maiden was or what she could be paralyzed him, and he dumbly sensed his hand being shaken and her bidding him farewell without finding his voice.

He sprinted out the door and into the street and was upon Morigan in a whirl of speed—somehow in front of her when she hadn't even sensed him coming from behind. The smith had a desperate enthusiasm to him that was misplaced on such a large imposing man, though Morigan found it endearing, as she did with so much of this relative stranger.

"I never said farewell. That was rude of me," said Caenith.

"Oh, well, I suppose you didn't."

"Will you come back again?"

"Why?"

The answer was plain to the Wolf.

"To see me," he said.

Brazen. Kings be damned, I think I like this man, thought Morigan. If she was honest with herself, she felt more than a simple budding interest; she felt a gravitation toward his being, as if he could pull her right inside himself. A terrifying experience this was, for a woman so used to being alone. Collecting herself, she spoke.

"You've convinced me. I shall come again. Another staff tip of water, another day. Now I really must be off. My master will be worried sick. It was...an unintended pleasure meeting you, Caenith."

Politely, Morigan bowed and took her leave.

"Safe steps, dear fawn," Caenith shouted after her—almost in a roar, which garnered the attention of many passing folk. "Perhaps when the Gray Man is ripe and full with beauty, we could stalk the city for a bite!"

A bite? chuckled Morigan. *Dear fawn? Stalk the city? Gray Man? Is he talking about the moon? I certainly pick the wild ones. If I don't find a toilet soon, I may just wet myself from laughter.*

Long after Morigan left, the Wolf stood in the street, as immobile as stone, and a source of much elbow pain for whatever folks attempted to nudge past him. He could see the maiden well beyond the time she would become a dot to a slow-walker's eyes; she was breathtaking at any distance. And when he could no longer spy her, he could smell her still, or at least the memory that he had captured and never let go. The fragrance of the old magik, of earth and spice, of sweat, honey, and nuts: a bouquet of life.

What the Wolf did not know was that Morigan could feel his hungry sight upon her for almost as long as he held it there, and she smiled, knowing this was the case. Traversing Eod's dusky streets, its usual wonder seemed dull. She passed under spidery bridges and through extravagant, ornately molded gatehouses. She felt the shadows of sky carriages soar over her head, walked by street sorcerers conjuring birds of fire, or took shortcuts through Eod's many gardens—great expanses of nature, with tree mazes and trellises of fruit and flowers—and stopped not a speck to dawdle. She even forgot how badly she needed to pee. Her heart, her mind thought only of the smith. Of when she would next take the trip to see him.

II

WHAT THE STONES WHISPERED

I

M origan could not stall her interest in the smith for more than a night. Her sleep had been restless and haunted by dreams of running through a dark forest while being chased by a growling animal presence. A nightmarish plight she oddly enjoyed, for she woke beaming and bright to the day. During her charwomaning at Thule's silver-topped tower, she lost herself to distraction often and continued to ponder the dream. In it, she was certain that she recalled scents, woodland scents—primal smells of earth, leaf, and fur that she had smelled the previous day at the Armsman. Fancies surely, as dreams were never more than gasps of the subconscious, but all were indications that she had unresolved curiosity toward the smith. More than that, she thought him to be exceptionally handsome, and the further she dwelled on his rough curves and frightening musculature, the hotter her collar became. And yet for such virility, his manner appeared as soft and profound as that of any poet, and that, too, was enticing, for she had not known a balance of those qualities in a man before.

In the very least, I could help him tidy up his home—hovel, lair, what have you.

"Where are you, girl?" croaked a tired old voice. "You were like this yesterday, and I sent you home for it."

"Me? Right here, of course. Cleaning, cleaning. What a mess you are."

She removed the books from the footstool near her master's chair and patted it, coughing from the dust. Master Thule set down the scroll he was reading and watched her. Wrapped in a charcoal robe that drowned his tiny figure, he looked very much like a swaddled, frowning, and immensely wrinkled child, baldness and all. In his youth he was trim, and a spryness remained with him even as he grayed, regardless of his tendency to sit more than walk these days. His eyes, sharp as winter frost and the same pale blue, belied any sense of age, and they read her befuddlement as patently as any book.

"Physically you are present, yes. However, your mind is elsewhere," said Master Thule.

Morigan ignored him and collected the volumes she had set upon the floor; she didn't ask if Master Thule needed them, for it was his habit that when a piece of knowledge was no longer of interest, it was dropped—quite literally. Following this custom, she filled her skirt with scattered treatises and sheaves of parchment, then walked over to one of the bookcases that walled her master's quaint study. Really, she wasn't sure how Thule did it, but for an old man who barely left his chair, he managed to cause a fantastic mess on the few hourglasses of the day she was away. She went to the least crammed shelf and slipped the books into whatever narrow spaces she could find. After dusting off her hands, she assessed the place again. In the moony glow afforded by the pale globes rocking on tables or teetering on bookshelves, she saw books, books, and more books, piled atop stools and stepladders, all in varying states of order. For the study, she had given up on any complex system of organization—those always fell apart during Thule's midnight rampages—and she did her best to keep the different heaps from spreading.

Good enough, she decided. *Maybe a bit of air for the old fellow. This place has a fusty smell.* She went to the chamber's only window, threw back the heavy curtain, and invited in the warm golden air from outside. Such a beautiful day greeted her that she leaned out the window to welcome it back. King's Crown, where Thackery Thule and many of Eod's masters made their homes, was as resplendent as ever. Beneath her, brightly garbed folks and their entourages strolled down polished flagstone paths or beside clattering horse-drawn carriages. *Happy, happy you must all be, in your blissful lives. You have so much, and yet you couldn't even save a woman dying at your feet.* She considered spitting on them, but she had been caught by Thule and chastised for doing that before, so she looked away from Eod's privileged, as there was much else to catch a wandering eye.

About Thule's white-and-silver tower rose many more spires, like trees in a woodland of ivy-grown villas and gated gardens, all so small and delightful from her vantage point that they could be miniatures. Past those lay other, less impressive, yet still pristine properties and houses, and surrounding Eod, protecting its beauty, was a grand pale wall, crested like a frozen wave and tall enough to repel any of nature's or man's advances. Past King's Crown, she saw the craggy russet flesh of Kor'Keth Mountain, its peak scraping the heavens. There, carved in ivory tiers into the mountain, was the city's heart: the palace of the Everfair King. Today, as always, its many-layered magnificence, its boldness of life against rock, took her breath away. Forests flourished on many tiers of the palace, and glistened with dazzling tributaries and flocking birds for Morigan to admire. Other tiers were different aviaries, where flocks of silver sky carriages buzzed to and fro. Some of the king's technomagikal armada were seen ascending to the higher plateaus of Kor'Keth, for the fortress was thousands upon thousands of years old, as ancient as its ageless king, and had been built far up and within the mountain.

At night, the palace would illuminate the surroundings with starry lights along its balconies and within its woods. *The City of Wonders* was an apt name for those who came to Eod and gawked at that sight among all the others. When alone in her humble apartment, far from her second home at Master Thule's, as the taps played their drippy jig in her ears, she could stare at the palace for hourglasses on end. Its grandeur captured everything that Eod stood for: the Nine Laws of freedom that allowed common men to rule as masters, and not only those with sorcery or brutality, as many of Geadhain's other nations allowed; the triumph of magik over nature, for here was a vibrant, fertile realm, raised in the middle of dust and nothingness. On days when her mother's death weighed the heaviest, she would look at the star-dappled palace and remind herself of how fortunate she was not to be some sewn-up third wife to an Arhad chieftain, a sex slave in Menos, or subjected to any other miserable fate.

And now, she smiled, she had met a man—a superbly strange one, but a superbly charming one, too. Unconsciously, she leaned out the window, sniffing the sky for his woodsy musk, as if he were upwind from her.

"What in the king's name are you doing? If you're not careful, you'll fall right out," cautioned Thule.

Morigan retreated from the window and turned to her master, who wore a dash of worry. She apologized.

"I was merely enjoying the day."

"Where is your head today, Morigan? Are you well? If you're coming down with something, I can make you a tincture." He began to shuffle up out of his seat like an old dog, groaning and cracking. "Urgh...let me have a look at you."

Before he righted himself, Morigan was at his chair, helping him to settle again.

"I have no fever or illness. I am fine. A little distracted."

"I'd say," scoffed Thule.

Morigan handed him back the scroll of interest for the hourglass—some officiously printed document with grand lettering and a seal that seemed important, which Thule quickly rolled up. Then she pulled a blanket off the back of his chair and draped it over his legs. Thule, who liked.to pretend that he did not enjoy being doted on, when in fact he enjoyed it rather much, frowned at her nannying. Certain gesture of hers—the lightness of her touch, the flick of her wrists as if she were a stage dancer—reminded him of her mother, Mifanwae, his previous handmaiden, or even of his wife before that, and his scowl melted.

"Thank you," he said. "You do take fine care of me, and I am not easy to care for."

"No, you are not," Morigan said, grinning.

"Would you like to tell me what has been bothering you now? Or will you keep me in suspense?"

"Bothering me? I'm not bothered."

"You certainly seem as if you're in a twist over something. You've always been a dreamer, Morigan, ever since your mother brought you here, clinging to her apron strings, and you'd stare at a wall or spot of air, seeing pictures and patterns that no one else could. But today is worse than most. I feel as if you're a thousand spans away." Thule pinched his face. "Is there some scoundrel sniffing around after you? I got rid of Master Simms and I'll get rid of the next one even faster. No man should behave so basely. The next man who dishonors you will be shipped off as a milkmaid to those filthy lizard-cows of the Arhad, pulling their teats till his hands crack and bleed."

"No, no, it's nothing like Master Simms." Morigan shuddered from saying the name. "Well, it is about a man, I suppose."

Thule's face fired with redness, and they each chewed on a silence.

"I'm going to get you some tea," she declared suddenly, and left the room.

A man, thought Thule, and rage continued its slow kindling inside him. Morigan was so innocent of her comeliness, so careless of her charm, that he was often the champion of her virtue. Once, a few years back, she had come to him distressed about the holes she had found drilled behind her headboard, bathtub, and toilet—*of all the sickest places*—and shown him the crystals of farsight that were stashed in each. He had mustered his considerable clout with the Silver Watch for an investigation, and the culprit was found to be her very own land baron: Master Gregor Simms. Upon his command, Master Simms was cast out in the desert by dusk, exiled forever from Eod, and on a caravan to Menos, where that breed of man belonged. Morigan knew not the extent of his influence, any more than she knew the other details of his past. He was a private man in the winter of his years, and he did not wield his sway unless it was called for. He cared for Morigan as deeply as any father would. A fitting role, as she had no father, and his child was long ago in the ground. What serendipity that Morigan and Mifanwae had chanced into his life, turning a relationship of convenience into one of love.

All it took was a topple, he recalled. A nasty fall down the stairs, as all old fools eventually do, and he suffered an injury to his spine that not even the master fleshbinders could efficiently mend. After their sorcery, he was left trussed up in casts with a prescription for bed rest while time healed what magik alone could not. In his helplessness, he had commissioned a manservant to assist him. Several, actually, though the first batch were either incompetent or incompatible with his temper. Either way, they fled from his tower. When all seemed lost, fire-haired and fire-tempered Mifanwae had come with her quiet silver-eyed daughter in tow. That was an unbreakable part of the arrangement, as she had no husband or family to care for Morigan.

Mifanwae proved impervious to his ranting and diligent with every task. When he had recovered, his life was so organized and comfortable that he had asked Mifanwae to stay on indefinitely. He even invited the handmaiden and young Morigan to take residence at his tower, but the woman dished him one of her sailor-born laughs at that.

Ha! The job I'll take, as you're not too kind and not too mean. You're just the sort of man I can take orders from. As for the offer of a roof, I already have one for Morigan and me. If we're being honest, I haven't had a prick in my house since my daughter came around, and I don't intend to break that blessed arrangement, she had said.

Thule was snickering at the ghost of Mifanwae's pluck when Morigan returned with a clanking tray. She set it down on the footstool that she had earlier cleared and prepared his tea, fitting the porcelain cup into a familiar groove on the armrest of Thule's chair. With the same nursing care, she then handed him a smoked-fish sandwich—a rarity in the desert and Thule's favorite—to nibble on. The old sorcerer spent his nights restlessly, distracting himself with knowledge to escape the nightmares that sleep brought with it, and he rarely ate during these periods, so he was famished as she presented the food.

While he ate, smacking away like a child, he spoke to Morigan, whose gaze was again drifting off somewhere.

"There, you're doing it again. Mooning. Over a man, I take it."

"I am not mooning," snapped Morigan.

"You certainly are. And it's about time that you said who has snared your attentions so, because you're not a girl given to idle fancy! I know that much. Should I be worried? Is he some vagabond? Some foppish troubadour with a feather in his cap and a pretty smile? Will I have to keep my eye on this one? Is he honorable? Or when he's done with you will he be chasing the next skirted, titted thing that he sees?"

Morigan contemplated these questions with a frown. Her success with courtship was embarrassingly scant. In many ways, Mifanwae was a shining aspiration of womanhood and self-sufficiency, proof that any woman under the Nine Laws could eke out freedom enough for her and her child, and Morigan inherited many of the same skills. Well after Mifanwae's passing, these lessons persisted, and she heard her mother's voice as she trudged through the day. *Work for what you need; don't ask for what you can't earn. You never need someone else's hands if you have two of your own.* For better or worse, she had grown to be a woman both as strong and as flawed as her mother. Sadly, there was no room in Mifanwae's life for love. She wondered what had wounded her mother so, what it was beyond an absent lover, for as iron as Mifanwae's spirit had been, she often wept in the night. Terrible muffled sobs. The sound of broken love. These cries lingered in Morigan's memory, deterring her from the same fate. She scowled at every handsome smile. She treated her suitors as unwanted visitors in her time alone. She refused to experience the same pain as her mother had. Until the smith. For him, she had the wild urge to welcome pain if that is what it came to. Simply for the chance to hear more of his poetic allegories, or perhaps even to taste the redness of his lips.

"Witches teats! Get a hold of yourself. You can't even hold a conversation today!" Thule exclaimed, and then proceeded to gobble up what remained of his sandwich and sip his tea.

Morigan moved the tray and sat. "You're right. It's this man..."

"So you've said, twice now. Glad to see that we are getting somewhere. Over nine hundred thousand souls call Eod their home—mind-boggling, I know—and I'd say about half of those have a bit like mine under their britches. So you're going to have to be a touch more specific about *which* man, if you would." Master Thule helped himself to a few sips of tea, waiting for the hand-maiden to answer. Eventually, after much hand-wringing, she did.

"He's a smith."

An honest trade, a man who toiled with his hands. Thus far, Thule had no objections; he nodded the girl onward.

"Well," said Morigan, "he's a smith, but we've covered that. I wandered into his shop the other day—quaint place, beautiful sign—looking for your damnable firesprig. Which, I think we can agree, is nowhere on Geadhain. I think you made it up, but that is neither here nor there."

"I did not."

"If you say so. The smith. His place isn't the most welcoming at first, dark and warm, without windows, and only a great forge, but it is cozy in a strange way. He was working when I arrived, and he walked through the smoke like...like a dream."

"Does this dream have a name?"

"Caenith."

Caenith, the onomastics were ancient; the name was rather unique and would prove an interesting diversion for later. Thackery set down his cup. The girl was entranced by what she was seeing, and he felt a similar magnetism to her excitement, for he had never seen Morigan so absorbed. As she delved into the memory, the words tumbled faster and faster from her mouth.

"He is large...the largest man these eyes have ever beheld, with hands like cinder blocks and eyes that pierce right through bone and into soul. There is a wildness to him, but also a tenderness. He lives like an ascetic, like those men you once told me of who abstain from worldly vices and live in caverns, or the quiet monks of Sorsetta who hear the beat of the earth and live by what they catch and need nothing else. I get the sense from him that he is whole, or complete, as a man. I don't know how old he is. I mean, he looks a few summers my senior, but he bears himself like a man much older. His weapons! By the kings, he has artful hands! Swords and spears and all these cruel things that are so beautiful you would not know their purpose is to kill. And his words, Master Thule! Oh, they are poetry itself! They run into the head like wine. That one awkward parting remark aside. But that's just how he is, I think. Crude and cultured at once. He speaks like a highborn master, but lives like a pauper. It really is all so strange." Morigan looked over, full of doubt. "Don't you agree? Shouldn't I be wary?"

Thule steepled his fingertips and carefully weighed a response. Morigan's silver eyes were flickering with a spark that Thule remembered, distantly. He was old, quite old, and he had seen that spark but a few times in his years and once in himself. A fire that bloomed in the chest like a drink of brandy. An inescapable yearning from the toes to one's twittering fingertips to be with another. He had loved Bethany like that once; loved her in the instant that he had seen her, even turned from him, even from afar. If Morigan spoke of this same ember of possibility, he would be a shameful man for not fanning it to a flame.

"I think that you are a wise young woman...chary and headstrong. As capable as your mother, if not stronger willed. I've never known you to absently cast your affections about, so there must be something to this fellow that has captured you so. All I ask is that you are careful. Men can wear many masks, and behind any of them can be a wolf."

Suddenly it came upon Morigan. A wolf, yes, that is what chased her in the woods of her dreams.

"Amazing, I've lost you again! Barely a speck that time!" Thule said, laughing. "Go on, child. I think I know where you want to be today, and it is certainly not here. Take today, and no longer, and go and see this Caenith with the huge hands and odd customs. I expect you will be here a few sands past a seventh of the glass, no later." Thule tapped a spot near his breastbone where Morigan knew that a small chronex hung upon a chain, one that he pulled out and showed her whenever she was tardy. "I shall spare you an ominous warning about what will happen to this smith if his intentions are impure."

Master Thule never did explain to where Master Simms had mysteriously vanished. Shortly after his disappearance, the Crown had seized the property, and Morigan now paid her monthly dues to Eod's coffers. At a price substantially decreased by some clerical estate-holding trickery about which she never inquired.

He waved her out of her seat. "Be off with you, then. Keep your wits high and your chastity higher! No one buys the spinrex when he gets the milk for free."

"Master Thule!" She wagged a scornful finger, but wasn't able to maintain a stern face, for her excitement bled through. She thanked the old man for his advice with a kiss upon his head, which he shied from like a poison but took anyway. After that, she was gone faster than a fair-weather breeze.

He had planned to get up and shuffle about, tearing up the shelves to find what he could on the peculiarities of the smith's name, for he felt that there was a kernel of scholarly intrigue there, but fatigue was creeping into him. The tea was warm in his belly like a nightcap, and a ladling of sunlight was upon his head, making him sleepier.

He was slumbering a moment later.

Until the sun ran red and the first stars pricked light in Eod's heavens, he slept without incident, wandering gray spaces with gray shapes and muffled sounds. Then the nightmares took hold.

He is on a field of grass, soaked in blood and rain, and holding the mangled pieces of his wife and child. An eye, a twist of hair, a hand fused into a foot, an empty bag of rubbery skin that is a face without meat to fill it—the disfiguration is so monstrous that he cannot even tell if it is Bethany's or Theadora's.

"They were already dead," he pleads with himself. "Already dead. This is not your fault."

His sorrow does not agree, and the cries tear themselves from his throat.

Thule woke screaming in his seat. With the gory nightmare fresh in his mind, it came to him where the name Caenith derived itself. In the oldest of tongues, the ones spoken before words were words, when men chattered in songs or warbled like animals to one another, three syllabic noises stood out to Thule. *Kae-eh-nyth.* Or *Caenith*, if strung together, had associations with blood, death, and hunting, respectively. A curious name for a curious-sounding fellow, he considered.

Rather interested in the object of Morigan's affections now, Thule poured himself a cup of cold tea from the tray that the young woman had left behind, Willed it hot with his magik, and set to work.

II

It was quite a jog from King's Crown to Fates Row, the modest, middle-class district where Caenith lived on the outskirts of the Faire of Fates, and Morigan took an earthbound carriage for part of the trip. She wasn't a spend-thrift and saved almost all of what she worked for, as Mifanwae had taught, but the urge to see the smith again was a weight as heavy as stone, drawing her in his direction. Her unburdening to Thule and his approval emboldened her further, for he was a father and friend—the only one she had, lonely as that might seem—and his opinions were valued. Never did she forget the cautious side of his encouragement, however, of his unusual but apt warnings of a wolf. The more she dwelled on the idea, the more she found that a wolf was a fitting match for Caenith's character: wild, noble, and dangerous.

Once settled with her fare, she was deposited amid squat white houses and tall white shops, with roofs that glittered in the early evening light and streets filled with weary working folk headed home for the day or into noisy taverns, of which more than a few were around. Caenith's house, she remembered, was in quieter environs a few blocks ahead. She stayed off the road and along the path, asking strangers to pardon her as she strode at a hastened pace.

Slow down. Get a hold of your wits or lose your knickers, like Thule said. I'm paraphrasing, but still, she warned herself. She didn't know much about men. She had kissed a few, groped some of the hardness that they kept behind their trousers, but wasn't impressed by much of it. In recent years, she had given up on courtship entirely, for men weren't interested in courtship with handmaidens living in less respectable neighborhoods, even though she was sure that they had other uses in mind for her. Perhaps that was what intrigued her about Caenith so much, his biding patience or surety. She knew that he desired her in a ravenous way, and yet she felt none of the frantic insistence that her other suitors had expressed toward her. None of that childlike need.

You say that, but let's see how he behaves tonight. This whole thing is silly. You're acting as if you know this man when you spent maybe an hourglass with him. Therein was the rub: that for a stranger, it seemed as if she knew him so intimately. Or felt as if she grasped the most fundamental aspects of him: honor, bestial pride, and the beauty and destruction of a wild rapid. All that remained was to mine out the details. *Why do I trust you? Of all the men I have met, only Thule has earned that right through burying my mother's body with me, through sheltering me when I was alone. What right have you to command my trust as you do, Caenith? What right?*

She proceeded down the lane with a fury in her step, her riding cloak billowing, her dark skirt sweeping the ground like a black ghost. She was a startling vision to those who saw her, and they moved out of her way as if she was a mad but exquisite queen. A few roughnecks, red in the cheeks and leering from a tavern porch, did not heed her stormy expression and whistled at her from their chairs. *Pigs!* she hissed with such righteous indignation that the fools pouted into their ales, feeling as if the Everfair Queen herself had shamed them. Night was hungry for the day, and sterling lamplights, their starry magik trapped in hanging glass spheres, were winking on alongside the lane. She arrived at Caenith's run-down property even angrier from the catcalls, stomped up the stairs, and went to knock on the door. It was wrenched open before her knuckles touched the wood. There was the smith.

Some civility had found its way into his comportment this evening, though he wore it awkwardly, like an animal stuffed into clothing, and haphazardly, as if he had just dressed himself and not with great success. His highwayman's shirt was a mess: its laces loose, a sleeve up, the other down, and the hem half tucked into trousers. The boots she recalled from yesterday. He wore a plain ebony ribbon in his hair, which was pulled back from his face. While he had certainly made the effort to be more trimmed than yesterday, she could only call him shorn, not shaved—she didn't think he could ever be stripped to less than stubble. Still, he was no less disarming or enticing with his cologne of steel, sweat, and the deeper aromas of woods and silky fur, and what portions of his sinewy strength burst against his clothing took the remainder of her focus. She found herself completely drained of her anger and fumbling for words.

"I...I am sorry. You seem as if you are dressed and on your way out."

Caenith stared but did not speak. Distantly and with sorrow, he remembered the Daughters of the Moon, victims of the New Age, with their milky skin and coats of nettles, raven feathers and black leaves: garments with haunting similarities to the lacy bodice and sweeping train that Morigan wore. She was as magikal as these phantoms of the past, but paler and prettier still, and her bust and cheeks were flushed from rushing. He could taste the salty-sweet sweat of her on his palate and hear the pounding of her blood as a rousing tribal drum in his ears.

"I was waiting for you," he said.

Morigan looked around suspiciously. "You...you were?"

"I—" *Smelled you down the street and hurried to make myself presentable.* "I felt that you would return today, that the winds would bear your sweetness my way, and I see that Geadhain has granted my wish."

"I see. How very...strange," replied Morigan.

Caenith welcomed her with a grin; his canines were unusually long, they glimmered in the lamplight. "Cups! I have been working on cups! Come inside, dear fawn."

Cups? And there's that "fawn" talk again. I think he's some manner of a lunatic, thought Morigan, and against what little sense prevailed in the company of this man, she went into Caenith's shop. Inside was brighter than she remembered, and small lamps had been lit in vases on the floor. She had to blink to understand them, these twining metal flowers, their petals opened and stigmas made of flame. She stopped to admire one, seeing the wick inside the fire, amazed that this was not magik, but more of the smith's work, impossibly detailed and manufactured by enormous fingers.

"Resilience and beauty," said Caenith, breathing over her neck. "The strength of steel and the beauty—and power—of fire. I was inspired to create them this morning. The metal's song was clear with how it was to be made. Do you like them?"

"Yes, they're...lovely."

"I agree," muttered Caenith, and he placed a hand upon her back, leading her farther into his den. "Cups," he promised, but said no more.

Silent and torn, Morigan's heart raced, and she wondered if Caenith could feel the fear hammering through her ribs. *Who is this man? Who is this man who can reach into me and twist out my hidden sentiments? Stop walking and think! Think! This would be your chance, Morigan! To escape this before...* Before what? Something terrible? She did not sense a dark end ahead, but a precipitous cliff, and one that she wanted to leap right off. Images of wolves and sharp-toothed smiles, of metal flowers and moonlit forests flashed in her head. Before she knew it, she had leaped off the cliff, for it was only Caenith and she surrounded in the soft orange shadows of his forge. Only their gazes appeared to shine in the dimness, and those found each other like swords, clashing.

Her scent had soured with panic. More than anything, he wanted Morigan to be at ease. He apprehended how confused she must be by the mesmerism between them. By the calling of old blood to old blood. He sought to appease the fawn with the clumsiness of words instead of the language of sniffing, biting, and howls.

"I sense that you have reservations about me. About being here in the dark with a stranger. Please, do not fear me, as unusual as my manners might appear. I am an antiquarian, you could say. I honor customs that modern minds do not. I assure you that you are safe, that you have never been safer. What happens between a man and a woman should be as natural as the first kiss of frost on a lake. Close your eyes and imagine." Morigan complied and was swimming in the dark honey of his voice. "Hear the first breath of winter...dry gasps punctuated by stillness. A song, should you listen, sung by Mother Winter. Tenderly, she hums the life beneath the water to sleep and slides a glittering blanket over her tired children. Mother Spring dawns, and she sings a different tune. One of tinkling water and cracking freedom, and the fishes and reeds stretch and celebrate their nourishing rest. Would one break that frost before Mother Spring does in her gentle way, would he smash at the winter skin and shatter it with ugly passion, the harmony of the music is corrupted. The purity is lost. Look at me, dear fawn."

Morigan rose from her imagining of chiming ice and wriggling lake children.

"I would know you, I would chase you, and then I would claim you—should you allow it. That is the way of the Great Hunt," said Caenith, bowing his head.

The Great Hunt? she wondered. Still more of his eccentricity, but she understood that he would not force himself upon her. He would not *break the ice.*

"So this is a hunt?" she quietly asked.

"What else would it be?" said Caenith plainly. "But in the Great Hunt, we must each choose to submit to our roles. A Wolf is nothing without a chase, without forest to overcome, or a fawn to catch. Will you be my Fawn?"

The woods, the running, and the Wolf in her dreams came back to her. That sense of fleeing from a beast, yet giddy from the pursuit. If the animal had caught her, would she have screamed or sighed? wondered Morigan, and she had no answer. Caenith watched her silver eyes darken and wondered if he had overstepped his bounds or spoken too freely. She was a slow-walker, after all, or at least had lived as one and did not know of the gift she carried.

You need to act more like a man. You are confusing her, he cautioned himself.

"Cups! Forget my request for the moment. I was to show you cups."

Caenith hurried off, and gingerly Morigan followed, stepping around the warm grate that her host walked over. They met on the other side of the room, past a set of large bellows. She saw a worktable, covered in tools, and a sitting bench, also strewn with implements, molds, and partially completed armaments. Balled and discarded waxed paper was strewn hither and thither about the bench, and she assumed that Caenith ate while he worked. She wasn't sure if there was an indecipherable organization at work here, but the man lived like a savage. Caenith cleaned the detritus off the bench with a single sweep of his arm and then led Morigan to sit, ushering her down most elegantly. She noted rusty stains on corners of the trash at her feet and assumed it was anything but blood, for she was already fretful enough about being here and still quite preoccupied with the congruence of her dream and the elements of her host.

"One moment," said Caenith, with that sharp smile of his, and he darted off to a shelf along the wall stacked with smaller gleaming items that she could not identify in the dim light. *By the kings, the man is quick on his toes*, thought Morigan. He rummaged around for a speck, and then moved to the lavatory and fidgeted in the shadows there. Patiently Morigan waited. Soon her attention drifted back to the bloody parcel wrappings—yes, she was certain it was blood now—and she jumped in her seat when she looked up and Caenith was in front of her. He was holding two silver chalices, inlaid with the most intricate designs; pictographs perhaps, though his large hands covered most of the cups. He extended one to her, spilling some of the water inside in his excitement.

"I thought of these as well, when making the flowers. I do not entertain, and my hospitality on your last visit was lacking."

Thoughts of bloody parcels fled her as she examined what she was given. Like the rest of Caenith's work, the chalice was exceptionally crafted; his ability to coax beauty from metal was unparalleled. She turned the object in the light, and it moved as a sorcerer's illusion would: this forbidding scene of a dark wood, a full moon, a maiden, and a wolf. The two figures were especially captivating, and though she only looked into the mirror once each day when she finished her bath and was not prone to preening or vanity, the lines and lips of the etched woman she saw were her own. To the humongous wolf, all shaggy fur, darkness, and fangs, she did not draw many equivalents. Nevertheless, the eyes were familiar, for they were upon her this instant.

"Does it please you?" asked Caenith.

Morigan was aware that something immeasurably strange was occurring between her and this man, that these symbols and warnings of moons, wolves, chases, and hunts all bore imperative meanings. But in that moment, with Caenith's heat and smell all about her, her head was syrupy and free of sense. She didn't care what it all meant.

"Yes," she said.

"A toast," said Caenith, his stare sparkling, as if he knew of her yielding.

"To?"

"To awakenings."

"Awakenings," repeated Morigan, and greedily drank the water in her chalice, for her throat was very dry.

Caenith lapped his down like a beast, and it trickled over his beard. He collected their cups, brushing Morigan with the soft fur of his chest as he leaned over her to set them down on the bench, and then offered his hand to her.

"It will be a white moon tonight. Half full. The moon of the witch. Tonight, the old magiks can be tracked by those who listen, and my ears are sharp." Morigan thought she saw Caenith's ears twitch. "Come; let me show you the secrets of this stone forest and whatever secrets sing themselves to me. Will you run with me?"

"Yes."

Bewildered and enthralled, sweating and shaking, Morigan slid her soft fingers over Caenith's gritty palm; they each shivered from the sensation. He smiled then, his sharp and beautiful smile, and swept her into his arms; she instinctively hugged his thick neck. Abruptly they were moving, fast enough for the shop to disappear in the bat of an eye—perhaps she heard a door slam shut—and then they were out under an ivory fingernail of the moon.

The Wolf and the Fawn had begun their chase.

III

When Morigan thought back on her first night with Caenith, her memories would take on a dreamy consistency and she would have piercing spikes of imagery, yet no clear picture of events. Caenith had promised to show her the *old magik*, a term she wasn't aware had a meaning until that evening. For Eod was the pinnacle of sorcery and arcane thought on Geadhain, a realm ruled by an ageless king, where even the harshest elements failed to stymie life. But the magik contained in the City of Wonders was not what Caenith meant. Beneath the glory of the city, under the stone foundations, the pipes, and the sewer labyrinths, was where the true secrets, this old magik, was to be found.

Quickly, quicker than anything imaginable, they were off the streets and in these dank spaces. Scenery smeared by them. Her cloak was torn off from the speed and sent spiraling into the night, but neither of them was interested in its rescue, and she was nowhere near cold. In truth, Caenith was carrying her, surrounding her like a warm wind, and she felt utterly safe. She did not raise an alarm at this uncanny mobility, did not plead the question of *what are you?* that any reasonable person would. For she didn't want her disbelief to shatter whatever spell this was. A sorcery that she, born in Eod and exposed to magik all her life, could not classify. His breath and heartbeat were heaving about her, and she could not sense much other than the faintest odor of where they were or a hint of metal tubing. Shortly those signs faded to perceptions of depth and darkness. They had gone farther underground. She shut her eyes and felt the rise and fall of his legs, moving like pistons in a technomagikal engine, and was lulled into a daze by his rhythmic grunts.

She became so calm that it was almost a sleep, and when the cadence stopped, Caenith ever softly said, "Open your eyes, dear Fawn."

Morigan was set down, and she nearly swooned from the sight before her. For she had never seen a wonder in Eod that matched the yawning chamber of rock teeth, their tips crystallized in garlands of pure clear ice. Or the diamond lake upon whose shore they stood, which was as still as glass and wafting her face with breaths of cold misty air. From the depths of the water, lights played up in a kaleidoscope of blues and greens, and the back of the cavern seemed to stretch off into an indigo darkness. Fathomless, timeless, she felt as if she had stepped into another world.

"By the kings," she said, and then clasped her hands over her mouth, for her voice echoed and caused the placidity of the place to tremble, the ice to chime, and the lake to quiver.

"This is not of their making," whispered Caenith into her ear, so lightly that only the smallest ripples took the shore. "But another magik. Older than them, even. I think that is what drew him here to Eod, the Everfair King, however many ages ago he settled. He felt this pull, like the calling of the moon to a lonely wolf. I wonder if he even realizes what lies beneath his palace. I do not know what purpose it serves, this place. Or how deep those waters are. But there is a presence here, sleeping and calm...a peace. I come here when I want to listen to the old songs. Or to remember who I have lost."

"Who you have lost?" whispered Morigan.

She could feel Caenith grow heavy behind her, and she turned in his arms to look at him.

"Everyone. Everything," he confessed. He lifted a lock of her crimson hair to his nose, sniffed it deeply, and then let it fall from his fingers.

"You have lost someone, too. A precious heart...someone important to you."

Morigan did not ask how he knew this, or what followed.

"A she-wolf...a mother."

Caenith tilted his head back and howled: a guttural, animal warble as deep and fluid as a baritone singer's voice. The cavern went mad with crystalline music. Ice cracked and fell, showering them in diamond dust. They held each other in that spinning moment and grieved together, she for Mifanwae—her laughter, her rustic wisdom, her strength, and her beauty. She missed her mother more than she had allowed herself to admit in many years. The Wolf grieved the Moon Maidens and Changelings, the death of the old magik, and the birth of the new.

The howling stopped, the glittering rain drifted to a stop, and they held each other still. When the silence had thrummed for many sands, and he could sense the Fawn calming again, Caenith pulled back from Morigan and brushed the slivers of ice from her.

"I feel that I should ask her spirit for its blessing. Before you tell me your answer."

Ask her spirit? My answer? Morigan was confused.

Caenith dipped and cradled her in his arms again. *We're going on another trip*, thought Morigan giddily. Another trip indeed, and in specks, the hidden kingdom of crystal and ice had disappeared, and there was just the warm, panting wind that bore her through darkness. The transit was less disorienting if she simply shut her eyes and surrendered herself to the journey. If this was only a delusion, she never wanted it to end. She wanted to stay mad forever.

Silver cups and maidens...the smell of pine and sweat...a black wolf hunting in the night. I am riding the wind. Is this real? she would wonder. Then she would chance a glance at Caenith, with the sky whirling past him; they were back in the city once, and then under a black star-dotted swath of night. Each time their eyes met, he flashed his carnivore's grin, telling her that yes, this was *real*. Soon a cold wind was blowing, and she sensed the openness of the desert, though not as harsh. She listened to Caenith grunting and springing up rocks, and could only imagine the phenomenal athletics he was performing, but she did not look.

Finally, they slowed, and Caenith's footsteps were heard scuffing on hard earth. She asked to be set down. He obliged; again, with exacting care, as if she was made of glass. Morigan stretched her arms, sore from clutching for so long. When she realized where they were, she leaned on Caenith and somberly asked, "How did you find this place?"

"It wanted to be found. It had a song unsung. A lonely melody, crying on the wind like a nestling in an empty nest. You have not been here in some time."

"No, I have not."

Once and only once had she visited the buttes of Kor'Keth, had she climbed the steep terrace of red clay, and that was to bury her mother. Thule had accompanied her, and it was branded in her memory as the most grueling trial of her years. For although Thule was a master sorcerer, one who could evoke incredible powers in moments of crisis, he was stubbornly averse to using magik for anything except the most menial of duties. So they had climbed, and shared the dead weight of Mifanwae's corpse between their scrawny arms. She was a wee sprout of a girl at the time, though she ached as terribly as the old sorcerer did. All day it took them; sweating, scraping themselves, and weeping, until the cold light of the moon shone over a place high enough to suit Mifanwae's rest.

I want to be able to see the moon, clear and bright over my grave, Mifanwae had told her on many an occasion. Grim conversations to have with one's daughter, but Mifanwae had a sickness of the heart that sorcery could stall yet never cure, and she had long ago accepted it. *We chose well, Mother*, thought Morigan. For the stone cairn that held Mifanwae's remains had soundly withstood the ravages of time and the elements. It had not fallen down, as she had often worried might have happened. Nature had been kind and had filled the stones with a grout of dust. It had softened the appearance of the monument into a seamless rise, as if that lump in the land, on that solitary outcropping of rock, had always been. Caenith and Morigan stood downhill from the cairn and then followed the watery white path of the Witch's Moon up the slight incline to the monument. As Morigan approached, the worst of the memories assaulted her. She might have fallen if Caenith had not had so firm a hold on her, if he was not leading her as a shepherd leads a lamb while she wove in and out of the world—remembering.

She is in King's Crown; the tall white spires of buildings are casting black shadows today. She remembers this moment as dark, as gloomy as if the sun had gone away, which, in Eod, is impossible. She is upon her knees. She feels so low, poor, and stripped. She has never felt so useless. What else could she feel, as her mother gasps and clutches her throat? As the tincture to ease her attack lies broken in the street—dropped before it could reach her mouth.

Faces are around them, but they are as black as the shadows of King's Crown. They watch but do not intercede. A city brimming with sorcerers and learned men and not a fleshbinder or physician among them who will speak out. Perhaps it is because of her shrieking, because of her fingers bloodied from her attempts to scrape her mother's tincture off the cobbles. Surely, she looks like a rabid thing and screams just as frighteningly.

She has managed to haul Mifanwae's head into her lap. Mifanwae takes a breath and sees her clearly, looks straight into her face, and the moment silences her. There are no final words; there is nothing more to remember her mother by, just that look.

Rather suddenly, and peacefully, Mifanwae dies.

Her mother is there one sand, and then she is lighter. A sigh that leaves for the heavens. Mifanwae's head rolls sideways, watching that breath float off, chasing it.

At last the cairn was before them, and Morigan awoke from herself. She knelt and touched the sandy stones, caressed their graininess, and reached for Caenith's hand, which had an identical feel.

"No one helped her. She died. In the greatest city in Geadhain...the City of Wonders." Bitterly, she laughed. "My master arrived, but not in time, and I think he punishes himself for that, as unjustly as I do for my ineptitude."

"You were a pup; there is nothing you could have done."

"Perhaps that is true."

They were easy together in the silence of the night. Caenith knelt behind Morigan, drawing his arm about her, pulling her to his hardness, tickling her with his beard and fur. As sensual as his every gesture was, Morigan did not feel any insistence of desire. He was the perfect companion to her grief—tender but hard, giving and requiring nothing.

"Thank you," she said. She wasn't sure how she had ended up at the rocky base of Kor'Keth, staring at her mother's grave, on a cold desert night with a man who was not quite a man, but she was grateful for it.

"I know that the hunt tonight has saddened you, but often the quarry is not what we seek. I listened to the song of Geadhain, to what honeyed praise it sang for you, and this is where I was led. It is good that you have come here. We appreciate life if we treasure death. I think this was Geadhain's gift to you tonight." Caenith concentrated, hearing the whispers of the stones, the scratch of sand over rock, the shift of grit over the bones beneath. He listened for a name. "*Mifanwae.* She would be glad that you have come here, even if only her shadow remains."

A tear rolled from Morigan's eye. Before her sadness could deepen, a fierce cold breeze stole over the pair, and they huddled closer to weather it. On the wind, Caenith could smell the scent of dawn, like hay, along with spicier scents—moss, herbs, and loam—of the East. Was this a blessing? For as he looked, he saw what the wind had brought to Mifanwae's cairn: a thin-stemmed white flower, borne from who knew what distant wood. The flower lay at the sandy base of the stones like an offering.

"Brighten yourself, dear Fawn, and look." Caenith slipped an arm over her, pointing to the flower. "I wanted to see if the she-wolf would bless my pursuit of you, and it seems that she has. Life amid death. I shall take that as a sign."

They watched the flower for a time as it fluttered on the sand but seemed content to stay. They remained in their embrace even though the elements no longer demanded it. Eventually, the flower was taken by the wind again, and Morigan's head began to droop as shadows started to lighten in the sky. They prepared to leave, and Morigan was up in his arms in an instant. She bid her mother a sleepy farewell and then shut her eyes. The warm wind that was Caenith was moving once more. How long the trip to Eod took, she could not say, for weariness drained the last of her adrenaline, and this time she dozed off in the arms of her carrier. Now and again, he would stop to adjust her position as her arms dropped from his neck. Nonetheless, she might as well have been riding upon a mattress, so well was her comfort assured. In the flowing darkness of her dreams, she visited forests and ran with wolves; she flew over a cairn in the desert and there was her mother, standing atop the stones, pale and smiling.

"Morigan."

Caenith's stone-grinding whisper stirred her gently. She was quite hot, and he was slick with perspiration, too; he must have been running for a while. They slid off each other as she was set upright. Along with her cloak, Caenith's ribbon had been lost to the night, and his hair was a tumbled mess.

The sun was fingering the sky with red, and sleepy folks and lazy carriages were starting to appear in the neighborhood of less kempt houses with eggshell-colored facades, dulled roofs, and pockmarked sidewalks—Morigan's district, was she paying attention. A coach master and his gray-horned steed trotted past them as they stood in the middle of the road; he shook his fist at the couple before taking a second look at Caenith and quieting himself. They ignored him, as they did all of what was going on around them. Morigan felt as if Caenith was waiting for a command from her. She could sense it in his wistful gaze and the distress on his brow.

"My question," he said.

She tried to remember what Caenith was referring to, but there were so many memories already blurring in her head that she couldn't think. She was relieved and elated when he simply asked.

"Will you be my Fawn?"

"Yes," she said.

Caenith leaned in, his wicked smile cracking, his teeth sharper than ever. His hands came to Morigan's tiny waist, fitting it like a corset. She wandered her fingers into his hair. An hourglass might have passed as they breathed into each other's faces, as she pressed into his heat and he sniffed her and curled his lip. At last the tension broke. Caenith licked her lips before he kissed them and then swallowed her tongue. She tasted sugary and he tasted harsher: like wood-aged brandy and smoke. Their hands pawed the other; touching ivory skin, tanned skin, the tender meat of a breast, and the hard rod—nothing like the puny muscles Morigan knew—of a prick. When it was over, however many specks or sands she could not say, Caenith traced a wet line to her ear, bit the softest part of it, and then slid a promise inside. *The Great Hunt begins...until tonight,* my *Fawn,* he whispered, and then his warmth vanished like a cruelly pulled blanket.

If Morigan's eyes had opened fast enough, she might have seen the man bound into the nearest alley and leap tens of strides high over a startled cat and onto a roof. She heard the animal hiss, but when she looked about, Caenith was nowhere to be seen. On the street, there were only two witnesses to their impropriety: an old woman who was clutching her kirtle as if she had seen an assault, and a younger lad standing on the walkway, whose long face was even more afflicted from slack-jawedness. Morigan smoothed back her hair, checked that her breasts were in place, and made her way over to the young man.

"Good morning to you, sir," she said, and checked the sky to make certain. "Yes, it is morning. I was wondering if you had the time."

With shaky hands, the young man extracted a chronex: a small tempered hourglass tied to a pocket chain that was marked with larger and smaller lines. Regardless of how it was carried, it wouldn't tip over or otherwise shift the pale sands inside beyond its prescribed loop, as these devices were synchronized by magik. Which meant from reading the glass that Morigan was well past tardy for her master.

Fuk! Fuk! Fuk! I'm late for work! "Thank you!" she shouted, startling the man, and ran to hail the nearest coach.

A speck later, she was jostling against the interior of a carriage, without any coin to pay for it. Not that any of that was important. Grinning like a simpleton, she pressed her face to the window of the coach and watched the sun rise with the joy of witnessing it for the first time. She watched its red and gold fire light up the cloudless sky as if it were the most profound experience of her life. It wasn't, however, and she laughed and sometimes giggled maniacally all the way to Master Thule's district. For she knew what a *true* mystery was. A wolf...a man...a race on a living wind through the night. Grief, loss, passion. For the most incredible thing that had ever happened to anyone, had just happened to her.

III

AWAKE AND DREAMING

I

Thule's unadorned white tower was as much of an eyesore as you could find in King's Crown, and the neighbors were always filing futile complaints with the Crown. The disrepair and neglect manifested clearly when compared to the flowered lattices or ever-flowing fountains of fire that could be spotted in adjoining properties. No grand metal gate did Thule have to fence his holdings, just a rock footstep that seemed pulled right out of Kor'Keth, and a plain but heavy iron door. This simplicity spoke to his lack of pretension.

Thule seemed fine when Morigan whisked into his study, out of breath and asking for her day's wages in advance to pay the coachman waiting outside. He maintained a chilling silence as the young woman threw a hasty meal at him and saw little of her after that. Once done with her master, Morigan hurried about his tower from floor to floor, trying to make up for the hourglasses she had missed with an industriousness exceptional even for her hardworking self. Thule had a large tower with many unused rooms in need of a good airing out, which gave Morigan plenty to keep herself busy with as far as chores went. While she scrubbed, fluffed, and polished, her mind was a million spans away, running through the incredible adventure she had been on last night. She could still taste the smokiness of Caenith on her teeth, and when she was finished with each room, she thrust herself out the window, wondering if somewhere he was catching her scent.

A wolf. A man. A man who is not a man. I don't know who I met. I can't say what you are or what you mean, but I like it. I want it. I count the sands until I see you again.

Caenith consumed her thoughts. She saw his sharp smile flash in every wet sweep of the mop, his dark hair in every shadow; she heard his whisper in every breeze; she caressed his hard chest with every stone tile she washed. And yet, she felt alert, in great control of her faculties, brimming with mental energy, and as much as she accomplished, she never tired. The strange salutation that began last night circled often in Morigan's head.

"A toast," said Caenith.

"To?"

"To awakenings."

Awakenings. She would ask him tonight what he meant. She would ask him many questions, she decided, and tried to reel some sense back to into her body. Later in the afternoon, when it was time for Thule's tea and she had enough self-possession to face her master, she went into the study. Master Thule was not reading today, but staring off at menacing shadows drawn by the red hand of dusk on the wall.

It will be night soon, she thought, and her heart began its pitter-patter. What instincts she had about Caenith told her that night was his hourglass.

She removed Thule's mostly untouched brunch, and he did not look at her directly, though after Caenith's attentions, she was quite familiar with the sense of eyes crawling over her flesh and knew that he was furtively watching. She slipped away and down several winding flights of stairs, noticing the little blue spheres of sorcerous gas that lit the walls as she went and thinking of the sapphire kingdom she had visited last night. Shortly, she arrived at a dreary kitchen that was lit by a lonely slat of light like a prison window. She deposited the old food and made up some soothing white-thistle tea and one of Thule's favorite fish sandwiches, hoping that would appease him. When she returned to the study, Thule was sitting up and alert in his chair.

"Put the tray down and have a seat," he said.

How lucky I've been to avoid a scolding so far. Looks like my luck has run out, thought Morigan, sighing.

The study was messier than usual, and there were piles of books in many places, as if she had not cleaned yesterday or for many days before. She chose the least teetering, lowest pile and placed the platter there, and then found another stack for herself to sit on.

"This is about my lateness. I do apologize," she said.

"I am worried about you," confessed Thule.

"Worried? About me? Why?"

"You are not yourself today."

Morigan contested this with a frown and silence.

"You are acting strangely. What is going on with you?" asked Thule.

Inside Morigan that effervescence persisted, like bees buzzing in her head, though not in a distracting way, for their song was a harmony she felt she could listen to, music that enlivened her. While her body was exhausted, her mind felt as if it would not sleep for weeks. She wasn't certain if this was just a symptom of her fixation upon Caenith. She could not shake impressions of him from her mind any more than she could slow her brain's endless whirring. She felt as if her thoughts were cast into a thousand seas at once. To the streetlamps that winked on as she went to see Caenith last eve, or how many books were on the floor about her toes—four, she noted, as well as their names. To crystal caverns and chores. To the sound of a child crying outside. Into the hot vision of a red kissable mouth, then another of Mifanwae's grave glowing in the moonlight. Into memories of the past or fantasies of the future. Now that she had stopped working for the moment, this velocity of thought had not eased, but continued relentlessly. Still, she had no difficulty in sorting through each and every bit of it. Within her skull was a new presence: a churning machine, a pervasive awareness, and it showed no sign of slowing. As she sat, in that moment of quiet assessment, she was struck by the revelation that there was something going on in her head that she didn't understand.

From an outsider's perspective, Thule had observed this change as well, progressively worsening through the hourglasses. Already, he had been worried about her associations with this smith, this Caenith. His night's research did nothing to allay his fears and only uncovered vague myths of brutal, bloodlusting barbarians who shared the same rare name—though hopefully not the same heritage or inclinations as Morigan's gentleman. But when she had arrived today in the state she had—disheveled, demanding money, wild, and speeding about the tower—he was suspicious that she might be involved with dangerous recreations, be that sex, narcotics, or some mixture of the two. She was definitely not herself. Nor had she even answered him. Instead, she continued to quiver in her seat as if she were receiving a current and stare through him as though he were made of air.

By the kings, there is something wrong with her. Something is very, very wrong, he thought. He had lost a wife, a daughter, and Mifanwae. He'd be damned if he would allow Morigan's health to slip away as well. Thule shuffled out of his chair and clapped his hands to get her attention.

"Morigan! What's the matter with you?"

He rushed over and took her hands, which were vibrating and humming like struck metal. Suddenly, she seemed to focus on him, her pupils as sharp as two silver spears. Her gaze skewered him to silence—peering, peeling, piercing his head. Thule had the sense of the room fading away, fringed in gray mist, and that was the last he knew before blinking into elsewhere.

Now, when Thule appeared before her, Morigan came out of her fugue a bit. On his face, written in wrinkles deeper than his skin, she saw his desperation. She felt his fear rolling off him in a stagnant black cloud. A terror of losing her. *Why so much sorrow?* she thought, and wanted to understand. In her head, the bees buzzed louder, and the cogs of her brain slowed on one flash, a single window in her mind. Only this was not a window that she had ever looked through, not a memory that she knew, not one of her own.

She fell into it anyway.

She is in the tumbledown stone cottage. A place comfortable with its disrepair; its small bird-pecked holes in the roof that let in strands of sunlight and the songs of their makers, its grass-patched walls stuffed with an errant flower or two. All day the hearth crackles here, and it warms the stones and fills the air with the aroma of meat and peppery herbs of a meal that boils in a pot over the coals. Every sign of tender maintenance tells that the folks who live here care not for material things, that love is their wealth. Through a corner of the window, she can spy the tangled thicket, the spidery trees, and beyond that, the shadows of a forest like a black mountain range. Beyond the safety of these walls lies the Untamed, Alabion, where all wicked and evil things dwell.

She recognizes that this is her home. But she has never seen Alabion. She knows it only from the tales her mother used to read to her. And yet, she knows it is Alabion that she sees outside the window.

A door behind her opens. She looks, and there is a woman as beautiful and earthy as a spirit of the woods, with chestnut hair, the eyes of a doe, and a trim figure. She is carrying a basket filled with roots, berries, flowers, and seasonings, all cleverly harvested from the safest, thinnest reaches of Alabion. At the sight of this woman, a flush takes her chest and loins, and she feels the faintest tug of meat between her legs.

("Who am I?" thinks Morigan.)

"Come help, Thackery," says the woman.

("Now I see.")

Thackery moves to join the woman at the hearth. She is unpacking her basket in a stone sink beside the hearth, and Thackery slips behind her, whispering, "Theodora is asleep, Bethany. Dinner can wait."

(A memory within a memory then, and Morigan sees Thackery's young hands and lean arms tucking a dark-haired, blue-eyed darling of a child under woolen sheets. She is no older than a handful of years, this child, and with the gentle beauty—and nature, she feels—of Bethany.)

Thackery kisses his wife (the sword between her legs rises). She returns the kiss with passion and then unexpectedly pulls away.

"My handsome Whitehawk," she says.

(Bethany's name for the man who has helped many of Menos's caged birds fly to safety—including his wife. Morigan understands this without reason.)

"Did you ever think you could be so happy with me? I was blessed once to find freedom. Blessed twice with your love. And blessed thrice with our child. I worry that the world will take away this dream that I have no right in living."

(Bethany has feared this before, remembers Morigan, and always with the same sad coyness. Beneath every word is a betrayal of deeper sentiments. Of what it means to live close to Menos, City of Wisdom. City of power and hate. Where masters rule and all others obey.)

"We all have a right to life. From the lowly spider to the master who would step on him. I shall never allow our dream to end," he replies, placing one hand around her waist and joining their other hands together. "A dance, my lady. It has been so long."

Bethany smiles (she is so close that Morigan can smell the leafy perfume of whatever she washes her hair with). "But we have no music," she says.

"Music is all around us. Listen, my love."

(What happens next is extraordinary. The swell of heat that rises in her host like a breath of pure summer air. Magik. Thackery has called a spell. He has distilled his love for those in this cottage into its purest form and thrust it into the world. Effortless for him, but a gift that few possess, to paint their desire so forcefully across Geadhain as if it is a canvas for their Wills. He could do more, so much more than the illusion he summons, Morigan feels, as the door to his Will creaks open. He is a storm in a rickety cage, a sorcerer far beyond what she suspected him to be.)

A peek of his power, his condensed love shines from him and the cottage lights up as if it were a glass wind chime held to the sun. The magik tinkles as if it were glass, too, making music. Together they sway, dance, and quietly laugh. They are careful not to become rambunctious and wake Theadora. They are surprised, then, to see her standing in the doorway to her bedroom, rubbing the sleep from her eyes and clutching the tattered patchwork wolf that Bethany crafted for her. She is not as delighted by the glimmering, tinkling room as she should be; in fact, she looks afraid.

"Father...I think I saw a man. A man outside my window," bleats Theadora, and runs to bury herself in Bethany's skirt. Her mother clutches her.

"Thackery?" questions Bethany.

Thackery looks to the bedroom.

The darkness is thick there. Too thick for the day.

"Sorren," he hisses.

(Abruptly the memory is slowing, moving as if events are underwater. It does not want to be seen, it does not want to be remembered. Morigan senses herself being pushed away from this space, senses a body that she had forgotten, hands that are actually her own, being separated. The memory is breaking apart, and only shards of it come to her.)

A figure of blackness—bent, thin, and shrouded—he reeks of death.

A flash of shadow, like an ebony flame, and a wave of white light.
Herself (as Thackery) doubled over, sobbing—
A blue eyeball floating in a shimmer of rain and blood—
Sorrow. Black, all-consuming—
"No! No, no, no, no, no!"

Morigan gasped. She was back in Thule's study. Her head was still buzzing, but the bees were less restless, and she could concentrate on her surroundings, at least. She noticed that her master was sprawled and weeping on the floor. Instinctively she reached for him, the vision still clear in her head. *By the kings, his family, they're all dead.* She knew this, she had seen it, and she had little idea how.

Thule slithered away from her, knocking over books, carving a trail across the floor carpeted with papers.

"Don't touch me!" he shouted, and the hand he warded her off with fumed with golden light.

Morigan stopped her advance. The dream state had mostly abated, while the images and sensations she had returned with had not. If she wanted to, she felt as if she could reach right into Thackery's head and pull out more. That is what she had done, as unbelievable as it was. She'd sniffed out his sorrow, his deepest, purest grief, and sucked it into her consciousness. Questions of identity and *what am I?* halted her steps as much as Thule's fear did, for she was terrified and in awe of herself. Remorse soon followed. She was steeped in emotion as she said, "I am sorry, Whitehawk—"

"Thule!" roared the sorcerer.

He had wormed his way back to his chair, lowered his threatening hand, and clutched at one of the lion-pawed legs. "Y-you will call me Master Thule! That name is not yours to use! And you will never, *never* enter my head again, witch!"

Morigan sloughed off the insult. She had assumed that Thule was a contented bachelor, mayhap even a happy whore-lover, for in all their years together he had never once mentioned kin. Certainly no wife or child.

"Not once have you spoken their names," she whispered. "Why? What happened to them? What happened to your family?"

Thule could not answer her. Not from the heaviness of his head, which felt as if he'd drunk a cask of wine, but from the weight of his soul. What

Morigan had seen, so had he. Through whatever diablerie, she had towed up the darkest memory in his abyss and replayed it for them both in flawless clarity. In such granular detail that even he did not recall. *What is she? How? How did she break into my head, my soul? Is this the smith's fault? Has she always been this way? Her silver stare...deep as a pin to my heart. Who was the father that gave you those eyes, Morigan? What have I invited into my home?*

The bees were growing excited again, filling the honeycomb inside Morigan's head with more information than anyone needed. She had a flash of a woman kissing her child while they sat watching a leaping water fountain that Morigan recognized from her daily walk home; she felt the love of that gesture as well, sweet as a warm river of sugar. With a spin, she was at a firecaller who sprayed the air with pinwheels of flame before a cheering crowd. She could feel the onlookers' delight shivering her bones. Then came the memory of Caenith biting her ear, and a waft of his musk, and she swatted her head as if his lips were there. All of these pictures played within her, and she was distracted but not undone by the chaos of it. Though how long that equilibrium could sustain itself was questionable. Yet it wasn't only slices of sensation that she hungered for, but voices now, too, if she heeded them. Secret voices of lust: *I'd stick her like a hog on a spit and paint her tits with my seed.* Chattering insecurity: *I can't wear this, it looks as dumpy as a dress over a sow.* Or vile bigotry: *Bump into me, you lowbred filth! If we were in Menos, I'd buy you just to flog you in the streets!* The sort of statements that would never be uttered aloud in polite society. The hidden voices of Eod were storming, and she was their lightning rod. While the conversation was a burble now, she felt that it would rise to a cacophony, and she dreaded the moment when the sights, sounds, and smells that weren't her own drowned her.

She wanted to tell Thule everything, about Caenith and her strange evening, about the theater in her head.

"You were right...something is wrong with me. So much has happened... in but a day. I don't...I don't...," she stammered, scratching at her head as the buzzing intensified. "Voices. Sounds. Places and people I do not know. Things that are as close as if they are mine! Feelings. Passions. Fears. Please... please help me, Master Thule. I fear I might be unraveling."

As eerie and unexplained as these events were, her appeal stirred Thule. He wobbled his way to stand and then across the room, reaching Morigan just as she released her first tears.

"It—it's all right, Morigan."

Warily, as if she might burn him, Thule dabbed at her tears. No sooner did he touch her face than the bees sang loudly, and she was whisked away—

To a candlelit room in a cozy cottage. She is snuggled in blankets, cold even though layered in warmth, and wet with the sweat of a fever. A lurching monster is in her belly, and over the pleasantness of minty herbs, she can smell her own sick in a pail somewhere. How small and helpless she is, as frail as a featherless nestling. (I am a child.) A handsome man, his face angular, his nose sharp, and his eyes blue and wise as the deeps of the ocean, is above her. This is her father, Thackery.

(I am Theadora, she realizes.)

Thackery tends to her tears, kissing them away.

"Shhh," he whispers. "Hush, my doveling. A little fever is all. I shan't leave your side. Myself and Ruftus are your guardians tonight, and we are tireless."

He takes her raggedy canine toy and makes it bark and play on her blanket.

"Papa!" she cries joyously.

Morigan woke to Thule recoiling from her; it wasn't so much that she had called him her father, it was the songbird's pitch she had used to say *Papa*. Morigan had siphoned another memory from him, of the day Theadora got into blackbriar berries—deliciously sweet and toxic—and nearly gorged herself to death. Rage poisoned him, and he could not stop himself from screaming.

"What torment is this? That you would conjure the ghosts of my family! Get out! Begone, silver-eyed witch!"

Morigan fled.

By the time Thule shook off his anger and realized what he had done, how he had sent that poor, confused girl away, it was too late. Too late to catch her; though he shouted her name out of his tower until his lungs gave out and he crumpled beneath the window frame, huddled and miserable in the bloodred light of dusk.

✳ ✳ ✳

II

The scrape of steel echoed through Caenith's dim shop. To inspire himself, he had kept the lights he made for the Fawn burning while he worked. Often, he placed down his graver and mallet and would watch the fires for a speck or two, to contemplate Morigan and her mystery and the fate that had drawn them together.

I came to Eod to watch the winter rust and the summer die. To watch the slow rot of all that I cherish in peace. I did not think that I would find true beauty again. How many lifetimes has it been? he wondered. How many years of solitude had passed without him seeing another creature of the old magik? Especially one so close to his own kind. Granted, other old things were out there, yet they either hid as he did, were of species unlike himself, or sulked in pits and stalked as monsters. Geadhain's two Immortal Kings, one in the north and one to the south, were the exception to this decline. Their existence was a defiance of the new magik, for they were men who could not age or die: not even the most diabolical sorcerers could claim such enchantment. They were ancient beings, but good men. That is why he had come all the way north to Eod, for King Magnus's city was a sanctuary. He might have retired in Zioch instead, the kingdom of the second Immortal King, Brutus, which lay far to the south of Eod. Yet those lands were lush and green and reminded him too much of the forests of Alabion. Memories he wanted to forget. So in Eod he had settled. To make metal claws and shells for slow-walkers. To wash the innocent blood off his paws in the ash of his forge. Mostly, he sought to ease his mind of the ghosts of Alabion. Bitterness would consume him if he followed these final bread crumbs of thought too much, so he jumped back into his work and thought again of the maiden. Her smell, grace, and pure spirit, and these fancies brought him joy as he crafted.

He was working on a bracelet for her. A loop made of gold filigree, which had the appearance of a twist of oak leaves coiled with holly and berries. The bracelet was to be his offering to Morigan in the ritual of the Great Hunt. Symbolic of the pardons one should make to the Green Mother for every life that is taken. When he hunted for flesh, he would leave the prey's bones buried beneath a tree and laid with ivy, and then mark the site with his urine so that no creatures would disturb its peace. These were customs that any slow-walker would find repulsive, and he understood this. Thankfully, the rituals for the Great Hunt were more refined, and the offerings were tokens of adoration made by the hunter and given to his prey.

Wolves mate for life. Once and once only had he made an offering for the Great Hunt and taken the most sacred of vows that came after. Aghna was her name. She was a paragon of her kind, a wind of white fur and fury, and his heart never tarnished her memory. Thinking of Aghna as he made an offering for a new mate was, in many ways, honoring her wishes. She wanted him to find another mate one day, she had said as much with her final breaths. He could not ask Aghna for her blessing, not as he had asked the spirits of Morigan's ancestors, for the she-wolf was well and truly dead and in a place unreachable to him. Thus, he would remember her instead. He would think of how he loved her and honor her with that truth. With a mind as old as his, the vision came over Caenith in a mirage. It brightened the room with the glittering frost of a winter day, transporting him to a place deep in the wilds of the Untamed.

All he can hear are the exertions of his body, the thudding of his prey's heart, and the swish of the fearful trees he rumbles past as they quiver and dump their snow upon him. He is pounding through the snow with paws of stone and thunder. Overhead, the sky is gray and withdrawn. On land, all animals shiver in their burrows. A lethal tension has hushed the woods. For the land is watching the hunt, waiting for the snow to run crimson so that it might untense itself. As it should be, for he is power, he is a lord of fang and claw. He is to be anointed in the iron-tinged blood of lesser beasts. When he hunts, he is death, which all life fears.

He has left the pack behind—they are too slow—to deal with his bold prey, and he chases the great elk alone. The wily creature has lived and bred and eluded him for many more years than it should have. Through the falling snow and white-muffled trees, he sees a darting silhouette of gray and follows the reek of fear that streams behind it, leading him like a leash. Bravely, the elk dashes, spraying cold sweat and snow to the air, but still it cannot outpace his hammering paws. Under a jagged cliff lined with sad, snowless trees they race. Nearer and nearer he comes, for each of his bounds make for two of the elk's. Soon the mist of its fear, the snow and sweat, splashes his face. He licks it off and snaps at the air, announcing death. Above them, a white shape moves along the cliff. It is sleek, nimble, and smells of wolf. It makes no impression on him, for his attentions are narrowed on the kill.

They are racing down a slope now, and the forest is opening wide into a grand white desert that he distantly approximates as a lake blowing with chill. He hopes to drive his prey into one of the winter dunes, and it seems to be where the animal is headed. Until it surprises him by leaping over the bank and skidding onto the lake, which is clearly frozen. Logic does not rule him in this moment, and he leaps over, too. Only despite his tremendous agility, mass has a greater authority, and as he strikes the lake, it breaks like a crystal plate, plunging his haunches into the frigid water. He scrabbles on the ice, shattering more with his granite paws and complicating his situation further. Sense would allow him to sort out his predicament, but the animal, not the man, has control; and all it wants to do is howl, froth, and rage at its prey: the laughing elk, which skates away.

The ice cracks and cracks, and he sinks deeper and deeper into the hungry lake. As the heat in his loins flees, so too does the bloodlust, and the man inside him suddenly grasps the inconvenience that they face. Before a decision can be made on how to extract himself, she is before him like a white lightning bolt: a lean ivory wolf. She makes the choice for his survival for him, bites his meaty forepaw, and drags him from the ragged hole he has made. Widely she stances herself, like a four-legged spider, and this spread of her diminutive weight allows her to haul him out without too much collapsing of the ice. When the man inside himself realizes her logic, he stops any struggling and sprawls himself, allowing the unpredictably strong she-wolf to tow him to safety.

Once they reach the snowy shore, the she-wolf releases him. He shakes off the icicles in his fur, and they pace each other, sniffing beneath their tails, nipping at what is tucked there. He recognizes the smell of the young she-wolf from his pack, though he had never taken note of her, nor could he have guessed at the strength that lay in her willowy limbs and foxlike snout; this power that could pull at a body larger than the largest bear in these woods. During his jeopardy, he could have slipped back into his more nimble skin and crawled from the ice with his five-fingered hands, or even allowed himself to drown and dream until he woke again—for death does not come to him easily or at all. But she has saved him the indignity of a failed hunt. She is canny and quick; he will see what more she can do.

He howls across the lake to the great elk that thinks it has found freedom in the weald on the other side, and he catches the sweet musk of its fear again. They have wasted too much time already, and he thanks the she-wolf by leaving her to follow him as he plows through the banks of snow, circling clear of the ice. Within specks he is in the weald, cleaving up the rise through thorny bushes and trees that sting and lash, but break like tinder. She is behind him, the speedy she-wolf, as near as his own tail. United, they bark as the gray shadow of the elk is spotted, moving with painful slowness through entanglements that do not hinder its enormous pursuer.

Nearer.

Nearer.

The musk is stronger, putrid with the soiling of death. The air is crackling with the music of the chase: snarls, huffing, thrashing trees.

He leaps—

The silence hangs.

SNAP!

The elk's neck breaks; the succulence of bone, blood, and fur is flowering in his mouth, across his jaws and onto his coat. He rolls with his prey, tenderly as a lover on a white sheet. He chews and suckles the animal while it dies. The she-wolf has joined him, and as they pick at the corpse, their wet noses touch, their tongues lap together; they share the viscera coils with playful grumbles like two pups fighting over sausage links. He notices that she has pretty eyes, a shade of violet that reminds him of the flower so named. He is curious now about what other loveliness she conceals beneath her stained ivory pelt.

Once they have eaten the elk to its bones, they hunch and howl to the night, while they shudder back into their two-legged selves. As a man, he looks upon her, and likewise as a woman does she upon him. Under her red paint, she is as white as frosty birches that stand outside the circle of blood—her hair, her nipples, even her eyes. She could be Mother Winter herself, and though he knows that he has seen her, first as a cub and then as a member of the pack, he has never truly seen her as a woman, for she is beautiful.

After they bury the elk's bones, drape the grave in pine as no ivy is about, and piss upon its rest, they stay in their skins. As if they are still beasts, they pace each other: sniffing, nipping, licking. Quickly their dance turns aggressive. He bites her shoulder, and she bites his chest, they each draw blood. In the *snow, next to the grave of their kill, they make love as people, then as wolves, and occasionally as something of each. Many hourglasses later, when they are spent, they track the hidden sun as it moves toward night. Because he is so warm, neither of them are cold, but he holds her as if warming her still.*

Calmly, for he is so sure of the question and its answer, he asks her to be his Fawn. She accepts by smiling, standing, and screaming into her four-leg shape again, then racing off into the woods. For weeks, they hunt together; they sleep in hollows of the Untamed; they bathe in the hot forgotten springs that creep in hidden cracks in the forest. They laugh as people and howl as wolves. When they return to their pack, he forges the ring that she is to wear in her ear until she is interred with it, and they swear their promise together in blood.

"Goh an deireadh." (To the end.)

Caenith's craft was now finished. He held up the bracelet, fingered it to make certain it would not harm his Fawn. Overall, he was impressed with its construction and likeness. As beautiful as the circle he made for Aghna, if for a different part of the body. One to pierce the flesh, the other to surround it, for what he felt for each woman was as unique as the way he had chosen to express it. He was never much for words or sentimentalities, so he did not profess to understand his nature more than the wind or thunder could understand itself. He knew only that he wanted Morigan, from her fragrances to her taste to her soul, in the instant of their meeting. She was a cool wind to his fiery beast, which, after ages of nursing on blood and then sadness, was in need of a soothing touch. She made him want to be a man, which was an urge he not often felt.

Solemnly, he prayed to Aghna.

I think you would favor her, Aghna. You bade me to rip apart and devour my grief and to choose a mate and leader of our pack once you were gone. For all my strength, I failed in that. You cannot ask a seedling to grow in blighted earth, which is what my heart has been since your passing. Yet she has done just that. She is special. Special in ways that are mysteries to me. A mystery in this dying age? Can you believe it, Aghna? Can you believe that this mystery has found its way to me of all the wounded beasts in Geadhain? Her magik is sacred. Her presence as lulling as a full and misty moon. Aye, there is surely a spark of Alabion's wonder within her. And so far from home...a thousand spans away, you lay sleeping beneath the yews, but perhaps you hear my whisper still.

I have found someone who can move me again. Someone I want to protect and bite and warm with my fur. Someone whom I shall share the bond of blood with, should she have it. I hope that you rejoice for me, Aghna, just as I release myself from you.

He howled until he was sure that the Silver Watch would be called, and then kissed the bracelet and set it aside on his bench. *Time to work on being a man*, he coached himself, noting his nakedness in the forge light. He started with a quick splash in the tub for once, and then trimmed his facial hair with a knife and the reflection of a shield. To his rack of curios he went next, rifling through the more artistic pieces of his craft—a set of caltrops that looked like thorns, chains, unbonded hilts, his and Morigan's chalices—for a black ribbon to tie back his hair. On the bottom shelf was his meager wardrobe, and from it, he selected the pants and boots from yesterday, but picked out a black hunter's vest. It was free of sleeves and as free of constraint as clothing could be. When all was said and done, he inspected himself in the shield he had barbered with and saw what could, at the most casual glance, pass for a genteel man. He took the bracelet, stuffed it in a small pouch, and tied it to a loop in his trousers. Anxious now, with nothing left to occupy himself, he paced, as restless animals do.

He did not have to wait long.

Over the stink of the city, a ripeness of spoiled ale, Morigan's particular smell came to him as even more sour. She was scared, perhaps even terrified, and not far away. The Wolf inhaled her fear, sprang to the hole in the ceiling, and swung himself by a single arm out through the opening and into the orange skies of dusk. Up on the rooftops and dressed all in black, he moved unseen, unheard, but maybe felt as a shadow of menace, like the black hand of death falling upon the lesser creatures over which he leaped.

III

What's happening to me? Shut up! Shut up! Shut up! Get out of my head! Get out!

But the bees were in control of Morigan's mind, not she. And they were busy. Busy with harvesting the thoughts and soul-secrets of every person in Geadhain; that is how it felt to Morigan. Opening her eyes made the experience worse, for then she saw images atop images, clippings of their lives like phantasmal picture frames, and memories—warm, foul, grand, or sensual—of what those moments were like. Throughout the carriage ride to Caenith's district, she rocked in the back against the cushions, muttering to the bees to just *shut up*. As if she'd poked the nest, the transmission of consciousness increased with every denial she threw at them. When the coach master finally stopped, he wasn't concerned about payment, only about getting the madwoman out of his carriage, and she was dumped on the street—hopefully near to the Armsman, as she had requested.

She stumbled down the walkway like a drunk, with her hands upon whatever walls or railings were near to keep herself upright. She knew how she must look, she could *hear* it. Every piece of verbal filth smeared right into her immaterial ear.

Pretty girl like that, sodded beyond her wit, and it's not even supper. Shame, whispered one old woman she passed. A woman named Agnes Coldlily, the bees said. Her maiden name, reclaimed after her husband's death. Once, Agnes had been married to a Hernest Borvine.

Want to see him?

No!

We'll take you there, buzzed her silver wardens. What a fine ceremony the bees showed her: a sticklike woman and a boorish man in a white hall punctured with sunshine. Every night after their wedding, Hernest took Agnes violently, smashing the headboard with her head or sometimes beating her beforehand. *No more, no more, please stop*, begged Morigan. But on the bees went, to happier times at least, for now Hernest was dead, and Agnes celebrated with celibacy and animal comforts. Hernest hated cats, so Agnes had seven. She slept with them in the bed and let them make nests out of all of Hernest's old clothing. Surely, Morigan could have gone on with the details of Agnes's entire life, but thankfully, the bees buzzed elsewhere. So many minds to wander to, as Eod was a veritable field of succulent pollen, an endless feast of knowing.

Something wrong with her. Still sweet enough to fuk, said the randy, eel-faced man leaning outside a pub whom the bees found next. She had a few glimpses of what he wanted to do to her, and none of it was pleasant. He smiled, and she worried that he was going to follow her, for she was in no state to defend herself.

Too much noise. Too much for them to feed on. I need...quiet, realized Morigan. Whatever had happened to her, it was thriving in this environment. A city as condensed as Eod was probably the worst place in Geadhain for her to be. The images and voices were spearing her now, agonizing and blurring her sight, and when she tried to see, she could not differentiate between the real and the immaterial.

She was in a schoolhouse, listening to a tight-faced woman scold her and feeling shame, and then she was on a beach of rocks and blue water, breathing in calm, salty serenity. She wanted to stay there, but was pulled into the grunting pleasure of a man so obese that he could barely see past his belly while he pulverized whatever was underneath himself. The vision was nauseating, down to the smell of his unwashed skin, and she doubled over. She tripped and her head struck something hard, making the bees buzz angrily, filling her head with vengeful waves of clairvoyance: squealing births, fists striking noses, flashes of rage, terror, and violent passion.

As she crawled, she called for the only man that she knew might hear her. She called for Caenith.

At once, the warm wolf wind was upon her, sweeping her up and away. The bees attacked her rescuer, but their hungry stingers seemed not to penetrate his skull. In her swooning darkness, she knew nothing except that it was Caenith, and then only by the smell and feel of him. She could sense her distance from noise and traffic below her, and a slight wind. Was she on a rooftop, perhaps? She guessed as much. Away from the crowd, her mind was clearer. A few of the bees continued their futile assault on Caenith, who was armored, somehow, against their intrusion. The rest were already sparking off and flying toward new targets for inspection. They were voracious; they would not stop.

With what breath she had left in herself, she gasped, "I...I am all wrong... since...since last night. Bees. Bees in my head. I need to be away from people. Far away. Please...help me."

"You are safe, my Fawn," swore Caenith, and never had Morigan heard a voice so strong with conviction. "If silence is what you need, I know where to take you."

He did not ask his Fawn to hold tight, for her arms were like rubber, and she was almost immediately unconscious. He fit her against his chest like a babe and noiselessly vaulted across Eod's roofs. Few on the streets saw them, for he was a flicker of darkness, ivory, and red, and those who did had no idea what they had seen. In sands, he had skipped across half the city and was nearly to the palace, aiming for the mountains beyond. Unexpectedly, from nowhere a buffeting wind kicked up, offsetting even his imperturbable balance, and he stopped for an instant on a noisy tavern roof to steady himself. The strangest instinct came over him that he had been subject to this wind before, as there was an earthiness to it, a note reminiscent of ripe woods of Alabion, which was quite out of place in Eod.

He paused a moment longer on the roof to examine his charge, and he noticed her twisted expression and that her beautiful face was dewed with tears. Impulsively, he licked at them and made a sour snarl when the salty taste did not match the Fawn's. A man's tears. Even stranger than the wind. He looked around for where they might have come from, but was given no answers save the dazzling nightscape of Eod or the looming facade of the palace. Perhaps someone was crying up there, out of whatever sorrows could be scrounged in Eod, he scoffed.

She needs silence, he thought, and shrugged off the experience. He continued sprinting along the rooftops, not straying too near to the unfriendly brightness of the palace. Soon he came to the great ivory wall of Eod. He made a loping climb of the bricks and ivy trellises, using only one arm, as he would not endanger or relinquish his charge in the slightest. Over the ramparts he passed, smooth as a shadow of the Silver Watchmen patrolling the heights, and vanished into the desert.

IV

The bees drink in the tears like honey. Digesting their secrets, hunting their tale.

In the space between here and there, the grayness that is neither waking nor sleeping, Morigan travels, led by the bees. She can see them now, as little flecks of silver light that are indeed like a cloud of metal bees. She has no hands or feet, no face or otherwise mortal features, but she is quite aware of who she is. More aware than she will be when she wakes, for here in the Dreaming, all things are clear to her. The silver bees fly through the obscurity, never unsure of their destination, and suddenly Morigan feels herself halt in the amorphous currents. Bright as firebugs, the bees shine, piercing the area with light, chewing away the scenery in a flaming curtain, and she is elsewhere. Her sight balloons into a new set of eyes. Into a new host.

She bobs in this head, up and down, up and down, as if riding something. A woman is beneath her, writhing and screaming, and she realizes what her host is doing. If she were to wipe away the blood, ice the black eyes puffed with terror, and ease the swelling from the woman's face, she would be beautiful, as there are shimmers of golden hair and tawny skin, hints of stunning symmetry. Only now, any loveliness is distorted by the foulness of this act.

"Magnus...please...stop."

But Magnus does not stop, and he strikes her with a pale hairless fist. With each plea, he increases the tempo of his thrusting, at times missing her slit and sliding into her other hole without a care. Scratch as she might at her intangible prison—the skull of her king—Morigan cannot escape this witnessing. She is condemned to watch. What confounds Morigan is that as trapped as she feels, an even bleaker condemnation fills her host. He is loathing this act, reviled by himself, as battered in spirit as his victim is. At times, he turns his head to vomit on the cold stone where he commits his crime. Yet he does not stop his pumping; as if he is a vulgar sexual machine. He cannot stop. The revulsion that they each suffer—victim, witness, violator—at the insanity of the act, at the stench of sick in the room, is so utterly nauseating that it will curdle in their souls for eternity. It is a wound that shall never be healed, and the victim, witness, and violator all understand this.

"Forgive me, Lila," grunts Magnus, and there is a shimmer of empathy between the golden beauty and her violator before he hits her again.

A black beast is driving him, a monster, and Morigan can sense it in Magnus's skull. The bees are intrigued by this, by the wildness of the black beast's presence and its raw, unadulterated urge to hate and consume. The evil is delicious and they chase it, wanting a deeper taste. With that, the king and his victim fade into silver sparkles and Morigan is freed from the agony of watching. Fast as shooting stars, the bees travel, soaring through the gray mists of the Dreaming as if it were the canvas of space, and in instants, they have tracked the smell of the black beast and torn into another head.

She needs a moment to adjust to the senses of her new host, as they are incredible. First to his vision, which sees with telescopic clarity in the bloodred luminance: the gothic curves of the architecture, the tapestries of stretched mortal skin hung as hunter's trophies, and the glistening garlands of entrails wrapped on the pillars of the vaulted chamber. Then with her nose, which is as acute as a hound's, she can smell the fresh death, the iron of blood, the manure and methane sourness of shite, piss, rot, and sex. And lastly, with her ears, which beautifully capture the screams and sighs and grunts of a sadist's orchestra of sex and murder.

Bodies are everywhere: males and females, young and old, some living, some dead, some unknown in their states. They spill beneath her host in a carpet that rolls down a regal flight of steps and into the grand hall. The ones that certainly live groan and clutch their groins, mouths, and anuses. Others that are mobile walk about, but they are altered, unclean. They have been wiped of expression, and there is a redness, a bleeding, and a blackness to their stare, as if their eyeballs were scooped out and replaced with tarry eggs. The black-eyed things—for Morigan does not feel that they are men or women, not anymore— walk around mechanically, inspecting those who have fallen, or herding stumbling, pleading victims into a corral at the base of the stairs.

At random, one is chosen; a lad, scarcely old enough to have a beard. He drops to the ground and wails as he is dragged by his feet by two Blackeyes up the sloppy steps. He grasps the bloody appendages of those he slithers over, but his strength is no contest for the Blackeyes' relentless grips. Closer and closer to the top he comes, to a throne where Morigan's host, the king of this gory nightmare, the monster of all monsters, sits.

The king stands to meet his meat.

Come this point, Morigan has been holding her thoughts as still as she can. Even the bees buzz low and cautiously in this host. For she can feel the passions of this monster, his thirst to breed and conquer, to rape and devour. It is the same gruesome desire that poisoned Magnus, only infinitely stronger, infinitely more pure, and it rises in an animal musk about her: the rage, virility, and supremacy. She is aware of her host's power in that moment and of her own insignificance. Of how he could hunt her and crush her like all those who fill his hall, and she dreads even the slightest awareness of his that she exists. The bees whisper what he intends to do to the boy, how he will trap him under his extraordinary mass and impale him with the horselike hanging of meat between his legs until his seed spreads like a poison, changing him to a Blackeye or a corpse. There are only two results. Just as the king has done or will do to all the others that enter his breeding ground. A gift, as he sees it.

The lad is thrown at the massive feet of her host. He tries to scamper off, but a bronze hand as large as a foot grips him, encompassing his whole back, pinning him to the slippery ground.

"My gift. May it change you, as it has changed me," says her host, and his voice echoes thunderously in the chamber and in his skull. What size is this creature? she wonders. As her host squats over the boy, lowering his obscene shadow and dripping rod, Morigan loses her restraint and shrieks for freedom from this depravity.

No! I shall not watch! I shall not watch this! No! No! No! No more!

The bees are not marshaled by her demands; they have their own agendas. Still, her outcry has poked a different nest. What rises amid the mad-dog rage of the king is a blackness and a bleakness all the more terrifying: a voice. So powerful is the speaker that although it whispers, it has the menace of an earthquake happening far enough away to feel the tremors and imagine the screams: a grace with death that is barely escaped. Morigan has no flesh, but her soul shivers anyhow.

Begone, little fly. This is not your place. These children are my flesh, my puppets, my slaves. Come to my Dreaming again and I shall trap you in my web and suck out your insides. Flee, little fly. Flee and await the coming of my reborn son, the Sun King. Await your turn with his gift and worship me as I rise eternal to the throne of Geadhain.

Flight is wise, agree the bees, and in a flash of brightness, the rocking grayness of the Dreaming is around Morigan again. She pleads with the bees to lead her nowhere else, to see no more grisly sights. She sobs in the emptiness between here and there, wishing she could wake.

V

"A popped lock, a flower, and a gift of tears...not bad for a single breath. She always has such hearty lungs, our Eean," praised Elemech, as the image of

Magnus's tears caught on Eean's breath faded in her pool. "I still don't know how much any of it will help. We've done all we can, I suppose. Anything more and we've overwatered the garden, and the roots will be too drowned to grow. It is time to see what the seeds of possibility bear."

"Hmm?" said Ealasyd, who wasn't listening to her sister. She was instead at her workstation, sticking her tongue between her teeth in concentration as she whittled away at a piece of wood. The older sister stood, her feet protesting—already swollen from the alchemy of pregnancy, though her belly had yet to change—and wandered over to Ealasyd. She took a seat on the bench where Ealasyd crafted, and saw other wood figurines already carved and lying beside her sister. The child inside her was encouraging her motherly nature, and she stroked Ealasyd's golden locks while she asked her about her creations.

"I feel that these three scoundrels should have proper names. Something sinister, Elemech, as none of them is nice."

"Oh?"

"Rotten as fall fruit and just as smelly. This one here, in particular." Ealasyd held up the doll she was fashioning: a replica of a grinning skeleton in a robe made of feathers. She sniffed it and made a face. "Stinks, he does. Can you smell it? His soul has gone bad. We shall call him the Rotsoul, then. I would have done a dark sun around his head, because of the hidden light that shines and whispers to him, but I'm not that talented, sadly."

With her bone knife, Ealasyd pointed at a wooden carving of an emaciated man. He had animal whiskers scratched into his face, and his mouth was opened and wailing. He was naked and tied in chains. "The Bloodmerchant suits that one. Yes. For he buys and sells, buys and sells, like a rat with a hole in its belly scurrying mindlessly for food. He is an empty, sad thing that knows only to eat, eat, eat. And I shan't tell you what. But it's certainly worse than those grubs Eean would bring home now and then."

Ealasyd seemed unwilling to talk about the third figurine. It was a bit gruesome: a woman who looked quite slim and graceful, but as Elemech picked the figure up and turned it around, she saw that an ebony cave spider had been pinned to its back.

"Oh, her." Ealasyd frowned. "She might seem like a woman, but within her is a crafty she-monster with a thousand legs and eyes. Too many legs and eyes to do, really, so I felt that the spider would suffice. In fact, let's just call her the Spider and leave it at that."

"Rotsoul, the Bloodmerchant, and the Spider...interesting," said Elemech. But they were much more than that. Each of the three relics resonated with vibrations of fate, and she hungered to throw them into her pool and see what secrets they held. Her matronly kindness won over her craving, though, and she kissed Ealasyd's crown instead.

"When you've played with your toys awhile, I'd like to see them."

Ealasyd didn't fancy this notion, as she never got her crafts back from Elemech, but she made no outcry and continued shaving bits from Rotsoul. He was nearly done, and she liked him the most out of the three vile dolls, for he was the wickedest and had an extraordinary tale to tell, she felt. Meanwhile, Elemech returned to her pool to sweep her fingers through it and watch in the ripples the pictures that only she could see. Once or twice, she made a *hmm* of curiosity, and Ealasyd asked her what for, but she did not offend Ealasyd's innocent ears with the scenes of craven sickness and madness that she saw. The crimson orgy and spreading of a toxic seed. The birth of a new vile race of mortalkind. The Sun King was no more, but hollowed out to become an unholy vessel, and the shadow that drove him would soon thirst for the blood of Geadhain.

IV

THE BLACK QUEEN

I

In the pale milk of moonlight, he leaned upon his balcony. He was a creature of contraries held in balance: his hair was a tumble of the blackest blackness, his skin the pale and polar opposite of that; his mouth was a feminine pout set in a masculine jaw; his nose was a slash of crystal between two hard cheekbones; his brow was a cut block of ice; and he had enchanting emerald eyes, with long, luscious lashes that belonged on a temptress. The manner in which he held his chiseled athletic body was a pose of perfect surety. A carriage of superiority not come from arrogance but from an inherent greatness. The bearing of a king.

While it might seem as if Magnus were stargazing, he was in fact speaking. Silently shouting across the vastness of Geadhain to his brother, who had fallen quiet and would not answer in their mind-speak for either of their sins. Nor could he feel any longer the fire of Brutus's spirit: that gut-warming, purring beast of flame. Since the yawning ages of the world, that fire-beast had nurtured him, had flushed his cheeks against the bitter wrath of the Long Winter, had been the comfort to cling to while Brutus hunted the tundra for their survival. Brutus was his courage, just as he was his brother's temperance; a cold wind to soothe a wild, flaming animal. Now he was empty.

Brutus had shut him out. And Lila, his queen, his precious desert flower, was cowering elsewhere like a whipped animal. All he had left to echo in his head were the words of that vile monstrosity that had claimed or influenced his brother, and therefore himself, to such despicable heights. Words that were the coldest of comforts.

In an instant, the repellent passion that has consumed him ends, and he is viciously aware of the slickness of vomit, semen, and blood that he swims in; he sees the battered beauty of his queen and knows exactly what his hands have done to her. Even worse, he feels the pain of her body and the misery of her spirit—for they are all connected through blood. Brother to brother, brother to wife. A circle of suffering and guilt. Only Brutus has no more to say. No more grotesque appetites to pollute him with, no feelings of guilt to share. Nothing. It is just Lila and him and the ruin of their love. He tries to speak—not with his mind, but in words—and all he can retch out of himself is a shapeless moan. She slithers out from under him, sobbing. He can only claw the air and then the wet stone as she lurches from the room. He will not pursue her. It would be unthinkable.

When he is alone, well and truly, with no voices or emotions that are not his own, when he does not think it possible to feel more contemptible than he does, the voice comes to him. He seizes as it speaks from nowhere, blasting into his head as if a door within had been shattered by a hurricane.

See the blood, smell your sin, and revile yourself, for you are as pitiful and disgusting as you are weak. Soon you will know a loneliness that scrapes you raw with despair. Soon you will know a sadness that devours you to the bone, one that rips love and honor from you. When you are empty, then you will understand my pain. Then, only then, will you be filled. You have taken what I value, and so, too, do I take all that you love from you. First your brother, then your love. I shall eat it all. Fear your doom, for it shall be an end so mournful that the stars themselves will weep before I eat them, too. Fear your doom, for the queen of Geadhain rises to claim her throne.

That threat was the last of what he was left with. From his brother, who would not speak, from the mysterious whisperer that had poisoned them each, and from Lila, who hid for days and nights now, somewhere within the maze of the palace and would not reveal herself. He did not send for his queen or seek her out with his emotions. He cancelled all matters of state and retreated to his chambers. Before being king, he was a soul of ice and reason. He was the man who had lived the Long Winter, who had made fire with his Will when there was only ice. He would find a solution to this impossibility of events. He would create another flame in the darkness. After days of somber meditation, of putting aside the trivialities of grief and regret, the coldest side of his intellect had arrived at a solution. Where he hesitated was in taking that final step toward action.

Enough, he told himself. *The time has come. Cut the cord.*

He shed a single tear for what he was to do, weeping as a statue would—immobile, expressionless. The droplet was swept away by a sudden and hungry wind. Magnus summoned his Will, and the space about him wavered with an aurora borealis of emerald and white light. Deep into himself he went, to build magikal and mental fortifications, to shelter his soul from an enemy that had ingress into any stratagems he would make. Resolutely, he sealed each memory of his brother away, turning it over in his mind's eye like a favorite picture before locking it inside his deepest vaults. Brutus's golden beauty, his wild hunts, his nurturing songs. Flashes of campfires, chanting, and walking with the first tribes across a glacial and unformed land. Memories of calling saplings from the cracked plain beneath Mor'Keth, which would one day be the green, sweeping kingdom of Zioch. Or the remembrance of gritting their faces against the sands of the screaming desert and choosing what slate from the red mountain of Kor'Khul Brutus would haul for Eod's foundation. Such intimacy they had shared. As two children within a womb that never separated, so too did he and Brutus live together. He walled it all in, their love, and slid the final brick into place. When the magik ended, his sorcery drifted off him in glimmering gusts, and he felt colder and emptier than before. He had only his fury. He brooded on dark voices that called themselves queens and filled himself with plots of revenge.

A presence entered him—a cozying sensation, like a glass of hot brandy and a crooning minstrel by a fire. It prickled his smooth chest. He called her his Spring, for she was the soft season that melted his iciness.

"My Spring," he said sorrowfully.

Magnus turned to greet his queen, a woman as pleasing to the eye as her spirit portrayed. In the thousand years that they had been together, the sun-soaked nature of her Arhad heritage had never left her and she was as sultry and tinged as honey, and just as delicious to consume with his eyes. Her hair was golden-threaded spun sugar, her lips red and plump as an apple, and her stare fluted and yellow as two candies of amber. The whiteness of her wrap was nearly transparent against her curvaceous figure. He could trace the heavy teardrops of her breasts and see the faint shadow between her thighs as she walked through swaying curtains to join him on the balcony. As long as they had been together, his desire had never waned for her, but he felt none of that now. He felt only shame. The fleshbinders had healed her well in their time apart; only hints of bruising about her face could be spotted, and the necklace of welts had softened to green. Disgusted with himself and quite naked in a mere throw about his waist, he quickly faced away from her.

She came up to him, and there was a painful hesitation as he waited for her to either strike or embrace him. She chose neither, but stood with him instead, and they watched the city and the stars together. Every moment he thought of reaching for her hand as it lay trembling on the balcony near his, but he knew it was too soon to touch. Undoubtedly, she would look at his hands, those that had loved, embraced, and caressed her since Eod was young, as instruments of violence for many months to come. Perhaps forever. In all their years, she had never been *afraid* of him. Not once. As they stood beside each other—conflicted, horrified, and yet yearning for the other—Magnus grasped how broken his relationship was. He discovered his own black beast then. He was not only angry with his brother, he wanted to harm him. He had discovered the monster of hate.

"Punishment will not be enough," spat Magnus, and his form illuminated with noxious, pale light. Lila stepped back. "I should have known from his secrecy these past few months. We cannot hide truths from each other. Or so I thought. But my brother has kept a secret, a terrible one, and it has nearly destroyed us. Perhaps it already has. I dread to think what he was doing when that sickness overcame me. I have allowed him to make a fool of me. I can never be forgiven, but I shall whip penance from him. Blood for blood, bruise for bruise. He will bleed as you have. This I swear."

The bitterness of her king's remorse and rage chilled Lila into gooseflesh. A similar wrath had summoned her here, an expulsion of great power that she could not ignore, and she had questions regarding it and the rest of her horror that she would no longer chew on in exile. With the same steel that Magnus loved her for, she brushed off the oily shivers of revulsion and clasped the clenched fist that had beaten her.

"I cannot hide from the shadow that looms over us, nor can I let you face it alone. I need to understand what has happened to you. To your brother. I need you to tell me about the voice."

Of course she had heard everything, he cursed. Magnus's anger broke, his chill aura faded, and he allowed himself to be led inside.

For a king, he lived as simply as the others in the palace: a four-poster bed billowing with pale netting, two birch chairs, a corner fountain and basin for cleaning, and a sandstone hearth. Lila deposited him in one of the seats near the fire and then quickly sat in the second chair, which was how they would relax and talk the long nights away. Such fond memories she had, though none of that fondness was present in her eyes that day. Magnus shrank farther and farther into his seat, the flickering fire's shadows creeping long and forbiddingly across his angular face. He could not glance at her; it was like glaring into a scornful sun. She was stormy and unreadable. Once more, she demanded answers from him.

"That poison that whispered to you. The one that infected your brother—for I have felt his bestial urges in you before, and that was not it. What was that evil?"

"How can you be so collected?" Magnus asked, sighing.

"Because I must be," snapped Queen Lila. "There is no time for pity, not now, not when so much is at stake. The peace of a thousand years or more has ended. The kings of the North and South speak no more to the other, and madness has taken them each. You and he rule the greatest kingdoms on Geadhain and there are lives, countless lives, other than our own that balance on your fates. I shall have time to grieve for you or loathe you later. In fact, I have all the time in the world. For now, I need you to focus. Separate yourself from your anger, and think. Tell me who seeks to undo us, who can enter the minds of the Immortal Kings and twist them to wickedness. That is what we must discuss, not whether I love you, or whether I can, in time, forgive you, because the answer is yes to each."

Magnus trembled in appreciation.

"Is it the work of the Iron sages?" she asked.

Magnus waved off the thought. "No, something darker, more insidious. Something older."

"Older than you?"

"Yes."

Queen Lila was at a loss for a moment, as she knew no living thing that could attest to that.

"Whatever it is, this whisperer, this poison, as you say," hissed Magnus, "it will not harm you again. I shut Brutus out. I sealed off our brotherhood with sorcery and vengeance. His impulses, or this vile spirit that calls itself queen, will not invade me again." She pondered the gravity of his statement. The brothers and their unique bond of emotion, thought, and *Will* had existed long before she joined the fold—prior to Magnus's invitation to her to drink each other's blood in the ancient ritual of the Fuilimean. Unwillingly, she wed two men that day, not simply one. A reserved intellectual, a philosopher, and a tempestuous lover; and Brutus, a beast of pure fire and instinct. Even hundreds of years later, as their strange blood changed her into a creature more like them, she never fully understood the brothers' bond or their makeup. *If you drink from a mystery, you become one yourself,* an old and only friend once said. And he was correct, the sage, for the brothers were a mystery. Things that should not be. A fragment of her always had felt isolated by her choice. Not quite an immortal, not really a mortal, but a third and unwanted creature that was neither.

Despite Magnus's love for her, she had always maintained certain insecurities that she was superfluous to the greater connection the kings shared. For as close as she and her king were, he spent much of his time in some otherworldly commune with his distant brother. The moments she had with Magnus in which they were truly alone, absent of Brutus's wild passions, were what made the loneliness of their union bearable. Those were the moments when he spoke to her in one voice, not two. Or when he lay her down in passion, and it was as if she straddled winter, for his cold was not punishing; his chills were shivering and clenching but titillating, and there was no telling where their bodies met or ended. In those moments, she did not doubt or regret any of the choices she had made. She was his and he was hers, and they were *perfection*. Now Magnus was entirely hers, with no threat of Brutus soiling the bed, although what a bleak and hateful road it had taken to gain that freedom.

She wandered in and out of her thoughts, as the oldest minds do, until Magnus's speaking roused her.

"I have been living in a dreamer's paradise. With my golden queen and my glorious kingdom and all the wonders of creation around me, like a child drowning in a bed of toys. I have been asleep to the world while the waking cry out in pain. How long my brother has been plotting this betrayal or the extent of his bargaining with these dark forces that assail us, I know not, but he must be stopped before word of his madness spreads. There have been murmurs of unrest in the simple mountain clans around Zioch for months. I have ignored them, thinking not to assert myself over my brother's domain. I am sure that there are other signs of disharmony, if I were to look for them. You are right, my Spring, we are the axes of this world. We have appointed ourselves as such, and if we are to fall, then order will follow. I cannot imagine a world under the reign of the iron hands of Menos."

Queen Lila clutched the arms of her chair. "What will you do?"

The king's mind was a ceaseless machine. He had already considered a plan. Two of them.

"I shall smash him into submission. I shall beat him back into the man I love and snuff out this dark whisperer, should it dare to reveal itself. Tonight, I rally. Tomorrow, I shall leave for my brother's realm of Mor'Khul, along with nine legions and those who curb the elements to their Will, so nearly a thousand men. I shall not take more from Eod than that, for our city must be secured from what other threats might strike in my absence."

"A march? You are speaking of starting a war."

"A battle so swiftly and silently decided will be no such thing, my Queen. For all appearances, I am marching south to help my brother with the unruly savages in the Mor'Keth. My brother has superior arms and numbers, and legendary sorcery of Will over the physical self, but I have the strongest sorcerers in Geadhain and Will over the immaterial. Though he moves like a bitter wind, I am the wind itself. If it comes to a trial of might against the unseen, my magik will prevail—unless Brutus has some other feint to play, which we must not rule out. While I am gone, there are two grave tasks that fall on you to execute."

Before her blood-union with King Magnus, Lila was a rebellious spirit, a renegade daughter to the Arhad, and after the ritual that bound her and her Immortal King, her flame of independence grew brighter still. For a sliver of his cold pride and magik had entered her heart along with his devotion. Thus, she was a sorceress, too. A woman of courage, power, and composure enough to serve when her nation demanded it. A noble bride and complement to her king. A true queen. She did not shrink from whatever was required of her, but walked to her king and formally bowed upon a knee.

"What would you have me do?"

"Your first task is to keep the ruse behind my absence afloat," instructed the king. Lovingly, he played his fingers over her face and touched her golden tresses. She did not rebuke him. "I have never been able to give you, or any of my past and forgotten lovers, the gift of children. That shames me as a man and has always been a regret of mine. A shared sorrow of yours, for I see how you look at the smiling faces of the children that run these stone halls. But together we have come to love Eod as if every life here were a child of our own. Now more than ever, these lives need stewardship. They need to know that they are safe despite what darkness or wars might rise. Functions of the nation must continue as if nothing is amiss."

She was not a silent monarch; she ruled more of the kingdom than Magnus did, for he was too often preoccupied with metaphysical matters or meditations in the Court of Ideas. The responsibility was easy and as good as done. No harm would befall any man, woman, child, or animal behind Eod's white wall.

"What of my next duty?" she asked.

Magnus frowned. "My mind's creativity works against me, as it arranges probabilities and outcomes. We must consider the possibility. We must think of what our next course of action will be should I fail."

Lila caught the hand that was tracing the light bruises on her neck, kissed it—wincing at the memory of her blood on that very skin—and held it tightly.

"You will not fail."

"Not if my love for you alone determines it, no," promised Magnus. Her soothing Spring was glowing inside him, and he took the liberty to kiss his bloodmate for as long and as hotly as he could. When he had raped her, he had not kissed her, and his cool tongue was not instantly offensive to Lila. Magnus would not assume the freedom to pursue more than a kiss, however, and he was the one to end their small passion.

"I shall never harm you again. I swear I shall end myself before I do."

"Stop it," said Lila, as smartly as a slap to the face. "You will not leave me alone and everliving in this world, like a tormented ghost. If I am to haunt Geadhain, it shall be with you. We shall endure whatever this storm is. The only promise you need to make is that you will return to me. No matter how broken, how bloodied, or how lost. You will return to me."

"I swear."

Never had he treasured the day he had learned of his bloodmate more than this moment. The journey that he had taken to find her, the arduous climb through the wildest deeps of the world, reminded him of what he had yet to say.

"What I would ask is that if my return is *hindered*, if there are walls to surmount before I reach you again, you must find the bravest souls in this age and set them upon a quest. A most dangerous journey. Find men of courage, strength, and cunning, for all such traits are needed where they will tread."

Most dangerous journey, she thought, knowing *where* but unable to accept it. Her king had undertaken a similar quest once, and it had come close to claiming his immortal life. He whispered what she feared.

"Those charged by your hand must seek counsel with the only three known creatures in this world older than me. From the women who know the names of trees that I do not, for they watched those first saplings grow. They surely understand the dangers we face. The oldest and wisest on Geadhain...you know of whom I speak."

"I do."

Lila's soul was turbulent. It circled his ribs like an angry bird. He tried to calm it. "A last resort, is all, if I do not return as soon as we might hope. I do not believe there is a mystery in Geadhain toward which the Sisters Three have not tended a hand, eye, or ear. They will know the true nature of our clouded enemy."

Magnus lifted Lila's chin and his emerald gaze bore into her. He said, "I was once lost and seeking...restless with all that I had done...weary of the achievements of mortalkind. Of the empire I raised, or the lovers I took to my bed. None of it satisfied me. I believe Brutus felt that restlessness, too, and it can become like an unfed monster. Time and distance did not heal it, for we can never be apart. Not until now, at least. How can either of us be a man with nothing that is truly our own? I wanted that, Lila, my Spring, my golden, glorious Spring. I took the journey; I found the myth that was not myself. I asked the question, and you were the answer. Without the Sisters' hand, without your face reflected in the witch water of that one with the mournful stare, I would not be here. I would not have found what made me a man."

He is there again, in the crystal-studded cavern that bleeds unearthly light. Three figures are about him: one large, one medium, and one child-sized. They have not told him their names. They do not feel he needs to know them, yet he knows who they are. The eldest one found him in the woods, slung him up like a bag of turnips, and through blinking and inky memories—brambles, bobbing up rocks—he ended up in this cavern. And he sleeps, lightly, while they dress his wounds and sing old songs, like the ones he and his brother made up while pretending to be animals.

It is a wonder that he is alive. Although he does not recall much of the sleepless, deadly trials that brought him here. He has flashes of hunting animals with spear and wit; as magik, even his great magik, works as it wants in Alabion, which is often not at all. He remembers the whispering trees that would lead him astray, off cliffs or into thornbushes, or try to lure his feet into serpents' holes. He remembers running, panting, and shivering in trees as grotesque, shaggy terrors sniffed for him below. He remembers hiding from his brother, too, lying about his whereabouts and concealing his intents. For this is his journey, his alone. It is more difficult than the Untamed's lethal wilds. It is the fight against the fire-beast within that cannot live without him.

I want to live without him. I want to be myself.

Onward the chant drives him, bloody-kneed and ragged, until he falls.

Now he is here, with the three women who hum with magik, even though he does not. When he is good enough to stand and not much better, he is hauled up and brought to look into a pool. All or one of them speak; he cannot say. But voices echo in the chamber.

"Outside these woods, you are a king. Within, all truths are bare, and we see the boy in the skin of a man. You seek what will fill your emptiness. What

you will rule as yours and yours alone. All life is a circle, and you have come so far only to return to where you left. A flower, a golden flower in the desert. Show him, sister. Show him what he seeks."

In the water, a vision ripples forth, conjured by the sad-faced sister's hand. He sees her, this golden flower, wrapped in the sheets of an Arhad bride. Only her eyes are revealed, which are all that is needed. For the iron in them, the determination to be more than her fate, is as striking as his pale countenance that shimmers alongside her reflection.

"A queen. A love to last one thousand years before it is tested. Go, boy. Go and play at being a man, until that happiness must end," command the Sisters.

Lila allowed Magnus to float back to her, knowing that he was off in a memory. She saw wisps of it in her head—glimpses of grand, haggard woods, yellow-eyed beasts, and three eerie women in a glowing hollow.

"I shall arrange for this quest, should you"—she hung on the words until spitting them out—"be delayed in your return."

"Good," he said.

A thick silence hung between them, but they did not disengage from each other. They relished their contact. She, in his smooth strength, as if she hugged pliant marble; and he, in her lemony perfume and the tickling of her hair against his cheek.

"I must soon prepare our soldiers. Would you lie with me awhile? Nothing more than our bodies entwined on the bed. Nothing more than my arms around you, if you trust them."

"I do," she replied.

They wandered over to the bed and came to rest. Forehead to forehead, they lay, with Magnus's arms and legs slid between hers, and he murmured his love to her in words or with bursts of his winter. Through that embrace, as they passed passion into the other, lovemaking without the crudeness of their bodies, she pardoned her king for a crime that was not ultimately his. As he left the bed, kissing her upon the shoulder, she was so calm and sleepy that she didn't reach out to him when she should have. For without any magik, but merely in her heart, she knew that this was the last she was to see of her bloodmate, her immortal and beautiful king, for a long, long time.

V

THE MOUSE

I

If Eod was known as the jeweled crown of the desert, then Menos was a black crown of iron forged from the chains of a slave. Where one was built of white stone, clean magik, and honest work, the other was a grim metropolis of dark metal towers that stabbed at a polluted sky as if in hatred of its existence. A city whose foundations were smudged in filth and steeped in the blood of forced labor. Look closer and the handprints of slaves could be seen on the poured stone of Menos's gray roads, all slippery with oil or alchemical effluences that ran in rainbow trails into rusty grates. Mirthless folk glanced up to the overcast clouds, hoping that it would not rain today. For in Menos, the sky was filled with technomagikal contamination, and when it wept, it burned enough to give one a case of *stinkeye*, as the locals called it—an unfortunate malady that made the eyes weep with cheesy encrustations. Those not walking rode the streets in carriages, with metal-and-meat horses that carried the faint herb-and-formaldehyde waft of preserved flesh. Beasts animated and repurposed from dead parts were these; enhanced with plating, pistoned legs, and nictitating eyes so that they could navigate farther and faster than a natural of their species. Jealously, the masters in these coaches sneered out at the rows of steepled, iron-gated manses, and with disdain upon the dilapidated, filthy quarters of the city—some of these homes no better than shanties piled alongside and atop one another. Scarce was the smile that was seen on the cheeks of a Menosian, for it was a society that valued mind and power over empathy and weakness. It was a hierarchy of predators, where the weak were food for the strong.

Spare the rod, sell the child, was the quintessential Menosian proverb. How true that adage rang in the markets of Menos, where anything could be bought and sold, from death to life to sin. Under a girded metal wall that encircled the city—the Iron Wall—commerce flourished in a raucous marketplace. Here abounded a sea of black tents, clanging metal smithies, and magikal workshops that looked like chapels with tin chimneys—*ateliers,* the locals called them. But at these chapels, a man would not pray to the lost spirits of the land; rather, he would procure elixirs to poison, confuse, or incapacitate. Were the tools of treachery not of one's interest, Menos's greatest trade was on display upon bloody stages, where chained folk shivered before barking crowds; or in even less savory arcades deep under the streets, where the nameless tribesmen stolen from their homes were sold in beaten, naked herds.

II

Mouse didn't care for the Undercomb, the second city under Menos. It wasn't the sweat-thick, pissy air that repelled her, however, or the cringing sobs of mongrels trapped in barred pens, or the masters shouting bids over one another, or the constant cracking of whips, or even the porridge of blood and fecal matter that ran down troughs along the cell-lined hallways. Mouse simply pinched her nose as she passed. In truth, these atrocities were nothing to her. She had known the kiss of a lash and the thrust of a knife to places meant to bear children. She had crawled from the indentureship of a Pleasure Maiden (what a wholesome name for such a despicable torment, she thought). These wretches could break free of their fates, too—if they were lucky, vicious, and determined enough.

She was as hard as a dagger, just as warm in bed, and twice as deadly. But that was the means to survival in Menos. You were strong or you were used and shortly dead. She would never be used again. She wasn't opposed to taking *paid* instruction, however. Her shadowy overseers were kind and absent, and she was essentially the freest that any lower creature of Menos could dream of being. And she had her measure of power, for she assisted in the dispensing of information—a currency of its own in Menos, and as valuable as flesh. She was a runner in the shadows, an ear to heed, a mouth to whisper: a *Voice*, as her kind were known. She was an agent of the Watchers—the curators of all secrets, lies, and half-truths in the civilized lands. For the most part, being a string to the puppet masters of Geadhain was a satisfying vocation. The only regrettable part was that she did not choose her clients, or the messages she conveyed. Which brought her to the Flesh Markets this afternoon, for a visit to a man more terrible than any of the surrounding atrocities. She had an appointment with the Broker.

While the Iron sages were the masters of Menos, the Broker was the master of the realms beneath them. He was the keeper of the trades in which they were too haughty to dirty their hands. The choicest slaves—those who spoke, performed the best coitus, and looked the most desirable—were handpicked by the Broker and sent to the pleasure houses above. Trafficking, assassination, witchroot peddling, whoremongering, blood sports, and every other criminal pursuit was at one point acknowledged or approved by the Broker. The Iron sages knew that it was better to have these unpleasant elements united, contained, and controlled than to leave such crimes unregulated—and possibly used against them. Besides, as an Iron sage, it was easier to know who among the Council of the Wise was plotting to kill you if you all visited the same man, the same *Broker*, to arrange for your assassinations.

That day, Mouse carried a message for the Broker from one who did not want a direct meeting—possibly a member of the Council of the Wise. Although she was a woman who feared next to nothing, the Broker was the exception. She had encountered him once, when she was still an owned woman in a house of pleasure, and the impression that the Broker left did not fade.

The master of the house has summoned all the pretty ladies and gents in the foyer before a great staircase. They are all powdered, their bruises concealed, and slick smiles hide the terror that so often consumes them. A special client has asked for his pick from their fold, and he passes each pleasure slave like a shadow of death; he is grand enough to dim the air around himself; it is as if he eats light. She could believe such a fiction from the silver-capped teeth—filed to points—that he bears as he curls his mouth while making his selection.

She remembers these teeth most of all, for they belong on a predator, and dares not look deeper in case he chooses her. Never in all her days has she been so relieved as the shadow moves by her without a silver snarl. Her meek stature has saved her, it seems. For the client has chosen the thickest ladies and the most strapping men. They are herded off, and their strained smiles shatter as they see the heapings of coin being given to the master of the house. For a price that steep, the client has paid for delights blacker than sex.

"Poor sods," whispers a tired old whore, almost drained of use. "If they've been picked by the Broker, we shan't be seeing them again."

Mouse glances up to note that the man she so feared isn't large at all; he is a short limber being who moves like a swaying willow, though the shadow he casts is grand indeed, and that she does not forget.

Perhaps I'll see your face this time, and see if you still command such ter-ror. I kept the name, but this Mouse has teeth of her own now, she thought, and was a bit bolder in her step.

The Undercomb was a second city in its own right, with trapeze-like bridges and ratty apartments strung up in the towering halls and over wide arcades. In these larger spaces, the slavemongers staged their trade, with rowdy ale gardens clouded in the sweetness of witchroot to ease whatever conscience might peek out in this sinful realm. Mouse bypassed these bus-ier intersections and stuck to filth-slimed corridors lit by sorcerous orbs of sickly yellow light. Or she slipped through the pen-halls, dodging the des-perate hands that reached through the cages. Along her path, ruffians lurked in dark places. They eyed her and once or twice followed her, until a flash of her daggers and the stylized iron eye dangling by a chain against her tunic stopped them. The Watcher's eye was familiar to anyone who beheld it, and to harm a Voice, however surreptitiously, would be seen, heard, and direly punished.

Without incident, then, she soon came to the Broker's domain, which was darker than elsewhere in the Undercomb. *As black as sin,* she thought, walking up a metal ramp to enter a cavernous chamber that dripped and hummed like the inside of a giant's sink. The few yellow lights that sputtered here against the distant walls showed a curving architecture with bolted struts, so perhaps this had been a reservoir at one point. She was not even a foot off the ramp when several armed men, their faces swaddled like assassins of the Arhad, bled from the darkness at once.

She speedily shone her mark in their faces and said, "I bear a message for the Broker."

One of the shadowmen nodded and led her ahead while his companions melted away into the gloom. Their stealth was impressive. Silently, she and her guide stole across the reservoir, neither of them making the slightest splash in the stagnant pools spotting the floor. She could smell the iron paint of blood somewhere about her, and she mused idly on how many bodies lay outside her circle of vision. As far as Mouse could tell, they were aiming for a massive, irregularly shaped mound; something like a heap of spiny garbage. As they reached the heap, she was taken aback by the grandeur and oddness of it. It was a mountain of cycle-wheels, gears, pipes, sheet metal, bits of stone, cloth, and wire. Pleasingly, she sensed no organic material or accompanying rot in the mix, though it stank of oil and other steely scents. She was contemplating the genius and madness in its creation, wondering why one of Menos's most influential figures would live no better than a rodent, when she noticed that her guide had not stopped moving. She hurried ahead. In the garbage mound were numerous dim and ragged openings, as if chewed right through, and her guide went into one. She followed not far behind.

A woman less brave than Mouse would have found the narrow passages, the feeble lanterns, and the whistling resonances of the Broker's nest unbearable, for it was as uncomfortable as treading the throat of a giant metal monster and just waiting to be eaten. On many an occasion, she pulled in her cloak to avoid catching herself on any of the sharply jutted walls—if one could call them that. Once, her shadowy guide stumbled over a metal tooth and cursed; it was good to see that he was a man and not some magikal, reanimated thing, as high-ranking Menosians tended to favor. After a long while, Mouse knew that they had traveled far beyond the confines of the heap that they had entered. Air and noise blasted from a few of the tunnels they passed, and she wondered if under all the spackle, these passageways were not part of the aqueducts running through the city. *Ingenious*, she thought. *A maze within a maze. He's using condemned or blocked pipelines to go even where the Undercomb cannot. I bet he could reach right up through the shitter and grab a man's balls. Not even the Watchers use these paths. Not even the Iron sages are safe from him.*

Eventually, space opened suddenly to a wide hollow, and Mouse was washed in the putridness of spoiled meat and urine. The dingy miners' lights continued here, but they were higher up, and the room was therefore darker than the dimness she'd been traversing. With no assistance from the light, she could still spot the limber thin man in the mantle and cowl of blackness. She caught glimmers of his metal mouth as he whispered to himself or to a shape slumped against the wall. Tables, dully glittering with metal—be it coin or weaponry—and shelving stuffed much the same lined the darkness of the chamber. Apprehension clutched her as they approached the Broker, and more so when she saw the withered, chained figure before him: a man so emaciated that she wouldn't have guessed him to be alive until she heard a hiss pass from him—the final noise that he was to make, for he slackened against his restraints after that. The Broker crossed his arms with dissatisfaction.

"As weak as they are dumb, this lot. That was the last. We shall need more," fussed the Broker, his inflections feminine and lisping. "All these years and so few have succeeded. You did, Twenty-two. Wonderfully so, as I recall."

"Thank you, Father," said the shadow guide, bowing to a knee.

"Crunched every bone in your wri—"

The Broker noticed that they were not alone. He moved so quickly that Mouse wasn't sure if she had blinked for too long. A leering face was abruptly in her vision: olive-toned, ringlet-framed, sleek-bearded, and pensive-browed, with cold brown eyes so dark they could be black. It would have been a handsome countenance if not for the mouth and its jarring assortment of needled and picketed teeth, all capped in silver. His lips appeared mangled as well, as if he had chewed on fishhooks, though his facial hair disguised most of the damage. Mouse was quick to react, too. She had one of her daggers out and pressing against his abdomen. Considering the fear that she had held for the Broker, the man wasn't nearly as terrifying as she remembered. Or she was much more daring herself. He was a lunatic, certainly, but she had dealt with those many a time.

Regrettably, her action didn't seem to deter the Broker. He studied her for a speck.

"Who...are you?" he asked.

"She bears a message from the Watchers," answered Twenty-two.

As the Broker withdrew, he snapped at Mouse once, and she almost stabbed him. Having seen her twitch, he was grinning with amusement as he stood across from her.

"Such pluck," he commended. "You would do well at The Binding, I'm sure."

Mouse could deduce enough of what The Binding was from the corpse fallen in the shadows behind the madman.

"I am not here for games, only to deliver a message. Will you have it, or shall I be off?"

The Broker placed a hand on his kneeling aide's shoulder. "A private matter, Twenty-two."

"Yes, Father."

Obediently, Twenty-two rose and slipped into the darkness. Mouse didn't think that the Broker was really the man's father. That being said, there was a respect to the cutthroat's manner, a sincerity to his exiting bow that was uncommon in Menos, where men cared only for coin. Mouse guessed that this numberman, and perhaps the other digits of his brotherhood, were true devotees to their master; though whatever perverse rituals or punishments bred such fealty she didn't care to know. When they were alone, the Broker waved at her to speak.

"I am told that this will make sense to you. We do not decode, only transmit the whispers of our clients," she said.

The waving became agitated. "Yes! Yes! Go on! Go on!"

"A raven flies to the west to pick clean the whitest, oldest bones in Kor'Khul. Follow it," recited Mouse.

"A raven," muttered the Broker, pacing the chamber.

Mouse waited for the madman to excuse her; however, he seemed to be in no rush to do so. Possibly, he had even forgotten that she stood three paces away.

"Do excuse me, but our business is concluded, and I have other tasks that require my consideration," Mouse said most courteously. "If you can tell me which way to go, I can find the exit."

The Broker's attention whipped to her, his dark eyes manic. "Oh, I doubt that. But maybe...oh, maybe you could. So crafty...I can see it in you. Are you certain you wouldn't like to try yourself at The Binding? I think you could be a fine Thirty-three. Wait, we lost Thirty-two, so you would have to be him. He didn't like to listen to his Father, so we had to cut his ears off and let him wander about dumb as a boxed mule. What dreadful bleating the deaf make. I do wish he would shut up." The Broker harked as if hearing a cry that Mouse could not and then shook his head. "I doubt he's found the way out, and neither will you."

A trickle of fear ran down her spine as she realized how alone she was, down here in the darkest pit of Menos with this silver-fanged lunatic.

"I am certain I shall stay no longer. Just as I am sure that my masters"—she despised trotting out the word, but it was necessary to stress in this instance—"would be concerned if my business was delayed. Quite concerned."

"Eight! Eight!" shouted the Broker, and his cry echoed into the passageways beyond. While they waited, the Broker made the unsettling silence even worse by pacing around her like a hunting cat. He concentrated intently upon Mouse. She fondled her weapons in plain sight and waited for Eight to make himself known. Finally, her new guide arrived. He looked exactly the same as Twenty-two did, though a bit broader and shorter than his "brother."

Disgusting little family you've made for yourself, Broker. May the Watchers never send me here again, she silently bid. Eight seemed to understand the reason for his summons and started moving from the chamber, expecting his charge to follow, which Mouse eagerly did.

"Wait!" hissed the Broker.

He did that curious trick where he was suddenly before Mouse again; it wasn't magik, but it wasn't natural, either. He leaned in close, squinting and clacking his teeth. She prepared to stab him if necessary.

"I never forget a face. Delicious—every one," said the Broker. "Such warm hazel eyes. A little sadder...a little weaker...a little more scared. Yes.

That was you, all right. I passed you over for The Binding, but I should have taken you instead. We've never had a sister; not for long. The boys tend to break them quickly. But you...you would be a fine daughter. How did you do it? How did you buy freedom when all that lay before you was death? You have conquered your own Binding once already. Clever, clever."

Great fuking kings! He knows me! Mouse had not endured the harrowing and generally short life of a pleasure maiden without knowing how to conceal her surprise. Through wit, will, and self-preservation, she had survived. She had a stunning mind for observation, too, and did not fail to notice even the smallest particulars, as it was often such details that kept one alive. Like the dimpling of scar tissue around the Broker's clavicle that she spotted as the madman stretched his neck out to inspect her—sniffing her, too, it seemed. She slid her dagger up his chest. He smiled until she tapped the chain of scars with the weapon's tip.

"Some memories fade with time," she whispered. "Such as the details of a face, so perhaps you are confused about what you have seen. Other things, like the scars we bear of shackles that once held us, never fade and are never forgotten." The Broker's smile warped into a grimace and he distanced himself from Mouse as she continued. "Sometimes we defy our destinies for lesser ends and rise to something greater. It is best not to look back."

Not waiting for a response, she turned and shoved Eight into motion again.

An ominous farewell chased after her.

"I shall see you again."

Not likely, she thought, scowling, and chose not to resheathe her daggers until she was free of the Broker's filthy pit. Seeing the markings around his neck, the brand of a long-worn chain, did not excuse the man for his madness or brutality, though at least it helped her to understand it. *So, you too were a slave before you became a master? Good for you, I suppose. Though there's not much left of you to fill the smallest glass after. I may be dark, but I am not broken.* Or so she tried to convince herself. Down here, in the unholiest of places, she wasn't always sure.

III

The instant that she was out of the reeking underground and into the flatulent streets, the skies gurgled with upset and then unloosed buckets of rain. Hastily, less she be smitten with stinkeye, she leaped for cover under the tiny awning of the nearest stoop, and warded off fellow huddlers with her knives and promises to gut them if they came close. The sincerity of Menosian threats was not to be taken lightly, and she was left in peace. She managed to hail a carriage by running into the street and holding her Watcher's sigil before the coach master, which got him to stop. In typical Menosian gratitude, she ordered the sourpussed master and his concubine from the carriage—leaving them to flail for cover in the sizzling rain—and was soon on her way to her next appointment.

At least this meeting was to be in finer surroundings than the last. To Blackbriar Lane in the Evernight Gardens of Menos she was headed, a neighborhood of prestige and influence. She reclined against the warm leather seating of the carriage, still fresh with the concubine's vanilla perfume, and watched the city roll by. People scattered in the streets; it was pandemonium whenever the skies decided to weep. One poor fool wasn't watching his step as he raced across the slick road. He tripped, cracking his head on the cement, only to be trampled by a speeding reborn horse a moment hence. Those nekromantic animals were no better than machines, so they couldn't be expected to stop—or so Mouse told herself. She didn't even turn to watch the rain wash the blood away or to say a passing prayer for the man.

She ruminated on the austerity of her city, and to a lesser degree, herself. How unusual it was to live in a city where so much life held no meaning. She knew of other places in Geadhain, nations that promised *freedom* and *equality*, and as an agent of The Watchers, she had been to many of these libertine states. But no matter how prettily they dressed up the virgin for the slaughter, she was still bound to die. There were still unbreakable authorities, clandestine maneuverings, and subterfuges in place that ensured that the strong presided over the weak—that the natural order was preserved. Eod and its eternal king, who only loosely governed and left men to deal with themselves under the Nine Laws as laid out by him and his sages, were the only exception. As if the wickedness of men could be so easily curbed, the desire to overpower, pillage, and harm, by nine small statements. She recalled hearing one of the Nine Laws once, in a tavern here in Menos, before the drunk shouting it was punched free of his teeth for his unwanted rambling.

No man shall live as a king. All kings shall live as men. To be revered only if their honor demands. Only if their deeds are worthy of worship, which the voices of all who witness them will decide.

What a faery story you live in, Everfair King. With your noble sages and their laws, your golden queen, and your nation of riches in a land where there should be none. How effortless for you to preach from your ivory palace, you who have lived for thousands of years and would tell us the virtues that we mortals should aspire to have. What would your kind know of mortal suffering? Of what we do or do not need? You, who have never suffered or known fear, scoffed Mouse.

The rest of the Nine Laws sounded just as misguided, and she could not fathom a nation of simpletons that would obey them. Yet King Magnus's realm prospered, far more gloriously than Menos did. As did Zioch, the Sun King's wooded domain in the South that bowed to the same Nine Laws. No wonder the people of Menos loathed these pristine princelings, these half-men who declared themselves kings, but lived by rules that mortals did not. For centuries now, the three countries had been engaged in a covert warfare with one another. Well, to be fair, reasoned Mouse, the aggression was mostly on the side of the Menos. Though who could blame the Iron sages and their covetousness toward the stores of wealth, magik, and elemental power that these kings had amassed in their eternal existences. Dangle meat in front of a starving dog and it might bite your hand off to get at it. The diplomatic relations between Menos, Eod, and Zioch were strained and delicate, with Menos ever anxious to bite the meat, the hand, and the throat of the master, after having been denied it for so long.

No war yet, dear kings. But soon, if the Iron sages have their way, she reflected.

The Crucible rose over the black peaked roofs of the city, catching her attention. The fortress of the Iron sages never lacked for intimidation, this ebony edifice towering from the heart of Menos as if it were a pillar supporting heaven and earth. Taller than any building in the city, almost as tall as the peaks of Kor'Keth, which Mouse had seen, the Crucible's majesty was humbling and unquestionable. And with a smooth, rain-slicked, windowless exterior and the emanation of an insectile hum of the sorcery that could be felt vibrating in Mouse's groin even this far away, it made one think it was truly an artifact left by giant creators and not of this world. Dark metal sky-carriages—Menosian Crowes—buzzed over the Crucible, disappearing into the clouds to docks that could not be seen. She watched their transit, wondering what they ferried, before turning her eyes back to the neighborhood her carriage traveled.

She had reached the Evernight Gardens. Appropriately named, for the carriage fell into the sudden dusk of the Crucible's shadow. The estates of Evernight Gardens were among the fanciest in Menos: rambling properties and black manses fenced in ornate thorny gates. Real thorns, she knew, which made them even more interesting to stare at; thinking on the magik that grew such plants to monstrous dimensions, sculpted them, and then transmogrified them into metal. There were few people on the streets here, but many carriages, and traffic slowed to a crawl.

She didn't have far to go, however, and the carriage turned into a gated drive hung in metalized willows, which made steely music on the carriage roof. The carriage stopped outside a peaked iron gate, and two dour guardsmen, unhappy at being pulled out of their cozy booths and into the rain, came knocking on the windows with blunderbusses and scowls. The men backed away as Mouse pressed her signet to the window. A moment later, the coach master was whipping his dead mount forward, through the opened gates.

Quite a master lives here, thought Mouse, as she eyed the dark splendor of the grounds.

Twisted hedge-mazes, with settees and bush-monsters and shrubberies of blue flowers, rolled by on either side. In the middle of each maze—and she glanced quickly from side to side to catch them—were macabre statues of naked women and men twisted together like wire and vomiting water from their mouths amid slate fountains. "The beauty of Menosian art," she snidely remarked. But there was more, and her snideness became awe as the carriage trotted into the forbidding shadow of a keep ripped straight from a fireside tale. With its sooty bricks caulked in dark moss, its tall draped windows, its grand belfries, and its sharp parapets, it was easy to imagine that an undying evil presence called this place home. About the roof and corners of the manse, freakish gargoyles clustered, baring their fangs and claws to those who would approach. A roost of faceless stone men holding downward spears stood atop the arch over the entrance and watched the circular court beyond where the carriage slowed to a halt. Lightning dazzled the gloomy day as Mouse stepped out of the carriage—not paying the coach master—and bolted through the downpour. The inanimate gazes of guardians and gargoyles were more chilling than the weather, and she debated if this haunted castle was indeed more hospitable than the Broker's rotten lair.

A city of madmen, schemers, and diabolists, each trying to outdo the vileness of the other. Oh, well, let's make this quick.

Fleetly, she was up many stairs and under the protection of the stone wardens' awning. A luxurious set of mahogany doors faced her. They were giant, and no rungs or handles were present to tackle their mass. So she chose to knock. Not long and a churning of gears echoed, and the entrance rattled open.

A reborn manservant greeted her. He was less decayed or patchworked than any of his kind she had seen, and could even have passed as alive; the inkiness of his eyes, the unusual fishy paleness of his skin, or the small surgical scars about his pouty, sad mouth notwithstanding. The rest of him appeared to be a fine, proper gentleman, and he was positioned with poise, clasping his hands and puffing out his broad chest, his three-piece, black satin suit and goose-gray cravat free of wrinkles or dirt. Even the dead man's hair was immaculate; combed and slicked into a horse tail away from his handsomely hawkish face. *What a queer master to keep his dead things so prim,* thought Mouse. Reborn were incredibly expensive playthings, treated no better than reanimated beasts of burden and certainly not dressed up like serfs to an Iron sage. She talked slowly so as not to confuse the reborn, whose partial brains were so often childlike and whose tongues could not wrestle with the intricacies of language.

"I-am-here-for-a-meeting-with-your-master."

"I see. Follow me, if you would," said the dead man, huskily but with complete fluency.

"Gah!" exclaimed Mouse.

"I'm so sorry," said the dead man. "It was my speaking, wasn't it?"

"Yes."

"My master is talented at his craft. He can work miracles with dead flesh. Please, come inside."

"Talented" at his craft, contemplated Mouse. The master of the house was certainly a nekromancer, and one of such efficacy that he could achieve what those in the blackest ateliers of Menos could not: a reborn creature with more than an ear for instruction, but a will. She wasn't of an arcane mind, but knew enough of magik to apprehend that she was witnessing a singularity.

"Dear Voice, please, we should not keep the master waiting," said the dead man, and beckoned toward a black-and-gray-checkered foyer dominated by a huge branching staircase. Mouse had been standing still like a fool and jumped to motion. While the dead man fiddled and shut the door behind her, she dripped a wandering trail over the clean floor, admiring the velveteen furniture and softly glowing chandeliers of the chamber. An instant later, the dead man caught up to her and led them up padded steps to the right, and down a hallway. Mouse perused the surrounding artwork: depictions of dissection by dark wraithlike figures; images of drawn and quartered men; busts with snakes wriggling through their skull sockets; and a line of masters' portraits in various centuries of dress—all pale as death, blue of stare, and wickedly inscrutable in manner. Shortly thereafter, she passed an oil painting of a nude woman splayed on a shingled roof, smiling as blackbirds picked at her gaping red chest. *Ravens. The raven flies west,* she thought, and wondered whom she had come to meet. She was drawn to the image, and lingered at it before the dead man roughly ushered her ahead to a vestibule arranged with lavish chairs and an ebony mantel.

"A moment," said the steward, and he strode to a nearby door and slipped through. As he did, she glimpsed what was beyond: electrical flickers of light, arcane conical shapes charged with currents, swinging meat hooks, and a grim figure twisting his hands on a wet, writhing shape upon a metal table. Hastily she looked away, but the stink of scorched meat and a scream, imagined or not, persisted. A blue fire crackled nearby, and was more inviting than anything in that room was; she went to it, took off her gloves, and warmed her hands while the miniature gargoyles on the mantelpiece spied on her. The color was starting to creep back into her hands when she heard the entrance to the buzzing laboratory open. She turned.

Standing beside the tall, dead man, the strong-featured master of the house could have been his twin but for eyes blue and sparkling with mad wit and the slighter angles to his unshaven face. He wore a bloody rubber apron and black elastic gloves that ran to his elbows, and he held the latter out so that his immaculate attendant could strip the unwanted things from him. The master then lifted his arms and tapped his foot impatiently while the steward removed his apron. When the tasks were done, the master nodded to the dead man, who gathered the items in a pile and made an exit.

"Do excuse the mess," said the master, not really looking to his guest, as he picked and fluffed at the gentlemanly blouse he wore. A strange shade of midnight-blue it was, the color of the petals on an evening rose, but it suited him well. Mouse might have found him attractive if no other elements had preceded their meeting. The master fished in his pants for a kerchief and began to dab what blood he felt on his face; abruptly, his manner became cross.

"I was interrupted, and I'll presume it was for a good reason. Don't hold your tongue, Voice."

Mouse wasted no time. "I was told to find the master of Blackbriar Lane and deliver a message to him. One of a pair. I apologize, but this message may be out of turn."

"How so?"

"My first message sent a man to follow the Raven." She chanced an opinion. "I would guess that you are he?"

The master let out a dry laugh. "Making assumptions is not part of your profession. But yes, for the purposes of this dialogue, you may call me the Raven. If your original message was to a certain bottom-dwelling lunatic, then I wouldn't worry; the order is correct. Steering the deranged is akin to herding cats on fire. It's a disaster, trust me, nowhere near as entertaining as it sounds. Not even in the throes of youthful enlightenment. 'Tis best that he received instruction before I. The man takes woefully long to do the simplest of things."

Mouse wasn't confident that the Raven was sane enough to deem anyone mad. She cleared her throat and hurried to finish the meeting. "In any event, this is the second whisper. Make of it what you will. *The skies above the desert are bare, free of the guiding star of the north. In the darkness, the*

Raven flies, and the Hound follows. It is hungry and it will feed. Weed out the blackbriar root, if you can."

"Oh," said the Raven, smiling, and his perfect teeth and charismatic grin were somehow rictus and horrifying. "Thank you for the message. This was a welcome interruption." The Raven clapped his hands. "Vortigern!"

As silkily as one of the Broker's numbermen, the dead man materialized behind Mouse. He didn't breathe, and she was only aware of his presence from the slightest ruffle of clothing and the floral potpourri of whatever he had been preserved with—not altogether unpleasant.

"Good day to you," she said to the Raven with a bob of her head. In the motion, the Raven must have caught a flash what her hood concealed, for his unpleasant smile deepened, and he asked her to stop.

"Wait. Wait a speck. Come here. Let me look at you."

An odd request, and Mouse wasn't obliged to entertain it. She flapped her hand at the dead man to move.

"Come here."

"I have appointments to keep. Our business is done—"

"Come here," demanded the Raven, without kindness.

Few actions provoked a reaction from Mouse, with all her composure. Being ordered about was an incivility that she suffered no longer, and she stormed toward the hall.

Whoosh!

A wash of glacial wind prickled her back, and a power rudely seized her, holding her still as ice. She could breathe wintry breaths and dart her eyes about in horror—seeing the dead man looking on, vexed, even compassionately—but she could not move, nor could her tongue wag to intimidate her captor with reprisal. It lay dead as a slug in her mouth. She then remembered her weakest moments in the charterhouse in which she grew up, those times when the masters would beat her, chain her, and leave her in a basement beneath a drainage pipe because of her disobedience. The water that drummed on and numbed her skull was always cold, and soon the poison of Menos that it carried would get into her eyes, gumming them. Soon she could see nothing but darkness and knew nothing but the locking of her fingers, spine, and jaw, or the coughing agony as her body took each gasp. And yet that coldness was never as cold as the ice in her bones now. Momentarily, the nekromancer was in front of her; he was nonplussed, there was not even a drop of sweat on his contemplative brow from maintaining her complete paralysis. He robbed her of her hood and examined her face with his cold bloodstained fingers. He was pleased with what he found, for another sick smile broke over him.

"The perfect shade of brown, like the first of the autumn leaves. But the notes of a golden summer are still there." The Raven caressed Mouse under the eye. "Nose, as fine as a sliver of silverwood. The redness to your cheeks, the sharp and noble chin." He stroked her jaw and neck sensually. "And the rest... you...you could be her. What is your name, Voice? Your true name?"

The Raven snapped his fingers, and a wintry cloud blew from Mouse's mouth. She could use it again to speak, or to threaten, in this case.

"The Watchers will hear of this!"

This neither fazed nor offended the Raven. Disinterested now, he walked away to sit in one of the posh chairs near the fire. His face was etched in profound thought.

"Yes, yes, the Watchers *will* hear of this. At the moment, I am not equipped to deal with the development you present. You may go. We shall see each other again soon," declared the Raven, and snapped again.

In a sigh, the magik was off Mouse, but the blood had not yet returned to her tissues. She fell, only to be caught by the dead man. More chivalrous than Mouse would ever have assumed, the dead man carried her from the room and set her down when she regained enough strength to slap at him.

How dare he touch a Voice! I'll gut the bastard! she raged within. However, the likeliness of her being able to stand against a man able to stop her with a thought was the wildest of delusions. She took a few breaths, and then several more after that. Along with her sense, she was reminded of the nekromancer's foul promise to see her again. Suddenly her legs were moving—not running, but almost—and her heart was pounding with the red rush of fear. How long had it been since she had felt so bare? So crippled and powerless? In one instant, that man had revived every weakness and terror that she carried in her heart—emotions shoveled under years of discipline and coarsening of her virtues. She was a Voice, an instrument of the Watchers. She was supposed to be beyond fear, just as she was outside the reach of law. Yet she was afraid of the nekromancer, and rightly so.

For all my achievements, I am still nothing more than a commodity to be bought and sold. That man will use me if he pleases, and there is little I can do to stop it.

"I summoned a carriage for you," said the dead man, keeping pace.

Mouse might have given a reply—snappy, grateful, or otherwise—but the painting on the wall that had earlier caught her interest claimed it once more, and she tripped to a halt. She stared at the woman and her banqueting ravens, and was agog at how she had not seen it before: who this woman was. Even if she only glanced in the mirror to see how low her hood fell each day, she could recognize her own face. The Raven's words fluttered back to her, kissing her ear. *The perfect shade of brown, like the first of the autumn leaves. Nose, as fine as a sliver of silverwood. The redness to your cheeks, the sharp and noble chin.* The woman in the tapestry had longer hair, but their faces were similar enough to make them sisters. In his sad, watchful way, the steward observed the moment of epiphany.

"Your carriage, dear Voice. You should *go*," he stressed.

Ravens, gory experiments, sentient reborn; she didn't know the black game in play and wanted no role in it. She thanked the dead man with a nod and hurried along. At the doors, which loomed grand and frightening, she paced while the steward flipped a lever beside the entrance to grind it open. She did not say a farewell, but ran out into the burning rain, her hood flapping to the wind and welcoming a case of stinkeye—a pittance to pay for freedom from the black manor. Once inside the coach, she huddled into the cushions and did not glance back. If she had, she would have seen two pale men, almost identical, watching the carriage roll down the lane. One from under the arch of stone guardians; the other from a tall window above, his hand pressed to the glass as if waving or longing.

IV

All the pieces are in play. The Raven will fly, the Broker will follow. Mayhap we shall at least bring vengeance to my brother. The whispers howl like holes in your sinking ship, Everfair King. Our ears have heard of your leaving. The City of Wonders is ripe for the picking with only its golden queen to protect it.

We shall finally see what treasures of the ages lie buried in Eod's vault, and once the two kings have destroyed each other, we shall harvest from the ruins of Zioch, too. My success in this venture should at last silence the tongues that I have not yet cut.

Reflected in the black glass of the Crucible was a woman's hard, lined face, once sharp and comely, but ruined by frowning and age. A deep-purple and black gown hung off a similarly wearied frame, and her hair was pulled tight into a gray coronet. At least her stare maintained its vitality, cruel as sapphire daggers and sparkling with a frightful passion: a well of ruthlessness, of skipped kindnesses and unwavering choices, of a woman who feared nothing, not even death itself. She had not celebrated her name day in decades and had lost track of her age. Age was a triviality in Menos, anyhow, to those with power and access to the most potent and dark alchemies of the Iron City that could cure all but the gravest of illnesses. She was over two hundred at last count, whenever that was, and had outlived the oldest of her enemies on the Council of the Wise. She had outlived her husband. She endured because there was no one else who could fill the role she had made. She had no real heirs. One of her sons, the one with a mind to rule, was taken by tragedy before he could provide a successor. Her other child lived on in the old Blackbriar estate, crippled by madness. He was a genius and a ghastly sorcerer without compare, a liniment inherited from neither she nor her late husband—though his accursed uncle shared a similar talent. She wouldn't want a child from her son's loins anyway, as tainted as they were. Now the game was all that she had left. Not that she had ever wanted anything else or could reverse any of the damning decisions that locked her to this path.

Would I? she thought whimsically. *Would I ever have chosen differently?*

In the dawning of her youth, she had loved her husband, Gabriel, as deeply as a woman could. This was before she had learned of his other lovers: men and women, for his appetites knew no bounds. Even after these discoveries, her love had persisted, though it grew as dark and perverse as Gabriel's did. If he wanted to have lovers, she would see how many he could keep. One by one, they met with neck-snapping tumbles, tripped carelessly off bridges, or fell while leaning against the loose doors of skycarriages. When at last Gabriel realized what was happening, he came to love her not just as a dowry bride, but also as a true wife and equal to a Menosian master.

My Spider, he would say whenever they engaged in violent passion. *What a beautiful web you weave.* After that, it became a game, and the first of many that she was to play and master. For each new lover that Gabriel fetched, she devised a creative demise, and with each passing, her husband would storm to her, feigning rage when his prick spoke otherwise. She could see now how her dalliances had sharpened and shaped the tools of her mind, how inescapable this path was once she had placed her feet upon it. In making these deadly arrangements for others' ends, she met the mad Broker of the Undercomb, and she had learned the essentials of subterfuge: the secrets of how a woman could sway life and death even within her gilded cage. With that, she began to dream of what she could do if she was free of her bars.

I got that freedom. Though not as I wanted. At the cost of you, Gabriel. I never loved another man after you, if that sick passion we shared ever was love. I think it was, it hurt and broke me like it was. I never took another name for myself, only stole those of my children. I am a Blackbriar now. I have fulfilled our promise together. I miss you. The face in the glass twisted with bitterness as she thought of why he was gone. *I hope it was worth the cost, brother. The destruction of our old name and honor. The death of my Gabriel. I hope you rot in misery till the end of your days. If I ever catch you, I shall string you up for all of Menos to see, just as my husband was. I would have you die in shame as he did.*

She remembered the day Gabriel had been taken from her.

In this one rare moment of Menosian accord, the rabble has been let onto the grounds of the Evernight Gardens and into the opulence of the Crucible's plaza. The filthy masses are penned on the wide black arcade, away from the steps and terraces holding masters and their tidy slaves. All have been summoned to witness the cost of betrayal, the price of defying the basic Iron Rule to never curry the West. She and her children do not watch with the spitting masters, but huddle in rags—concealing themselves among the throng of lessers. For as of today, they are no longer those who rule. Such a right will end with the life of her husband: a battered, flayed figure, as red as a fresh cut of meat, who whimpers in the stocks ahead.

She has pushed herself through the rabble so that she and her children can be at the front of this spectacle of her husband's death. Firmly, she holds the squirming hands of her boys and demands that they watch. They must learn the cost of failure so that they will appreciate the rewards of success. They must see the men who have done this to their father and hate them, as she does. Hate and its blossoming thorns, cut as they may, are the only weapons one needs in Menos. Little Sorren is broken by the sight of his father, she can tell, though her other son, the stronger one, has a face of steel.

He will be the back of our family, then. He will be the one to rule the Iron City next, once we have rebuilt ourselves, once we have a new name, she thinks. For however dark the hourglass, this is still another of her plans. Gabriel's, too, their final game together. When they learned of her brother's mutiny against the Iron Rule, they knew that the Council of the Wise would not let such a slight fall harmlessly away—particularly not when the criminal was linked through blood to the wife of the First Chair. Surely, there would be retribution, and if her brother could not pay, then all who shared his lineage would. They would have killed her and her boys. 'Twas then that Gabriel proved himself the man and father she had loved, despite any of his vices. He offered himself as penance, including his coveted chair on the Council: vacancies that only occur alongside a death, and his would be no exception.

"I love you, Gloria," he told her. "See that you and our children survive. I have never known a woman so canny or beautifully complex in her soul. You will use what wealth I have bargained for and take this city back. Make it bleed; make it yours. You will honor me with your survival."

"I shall," she swore.

Yesterday they had made that promise and sanctified it in furious lovemaking, even cried for the first time together. In the evening, the Ironguards came to their estate and dragged Gabriel away. At least his punishment was swift, for here they were, and his life could surely be not more than a gasp from leaving Geadhain.

"Watch," she commands her children again.

Which is the time for such orders to be given; it is the gasp for which she has been waiting. The bloody meat that was once her husband slumps and dies. The rabble have been given stinking produce to throw and are commanded to do so. While the corpse is splattered with rot, she studies the shadowy masters in their terraces, counts the faces of the Council she sees and makes note of who smiles the most: he will perish first. Against the screaming crowd, that is all she has—her vengeance—and it will be her new love now that Gabriel is gone.

She had done it, too, finished their dream. Along the way, her sons had failed her, and so the plan had to be rewoven. If a man could not take the First Chair, then a woman would. *The Crimson Spring* was what the historians called her rise to power, for never had so many of the Council of the Wise fallen in one season. Between the Broker's bloody contracts and her son's black sorcery, six Iron sages were culled in a week. The remaining six were true to their mantle of *wise* and voted for her ascent to Council.

I should thank you for your death, Gabriel, for that pain nursed me on the iron milk. It taught me to be strong, to push beyond what a woman can achieve. The Iron Queen of Menos pressed her hands to the cold glass, as if clutching the murky streets below. *Mine. All mine. I cannot have family, so I shall have the world. The white and green kingdoms of the immortals, too. A mortal woman, not even gifted with magik, shamed by her family, and about to claim the eternal kingdoms of the North and South, which no conqueror in history has so much as dreamed. Look at what I have earned.*

"Iron Sage Gloriatrix," said a young man's unsteady voice, interrupting her thinking. "The Council awaits you."

Gloriatrix turned from the wall of glass and saw a fancily suited lad kneeling on the oval rug in her office paneled in dark wood. She stepped around her commanding desk—a slate of polished rock mined from nameless ruins of the East—and asked the courier to follow her. Outside her office were many Ironguards, the armored elite of Menos, with their techno-magikal rifles cocked and blue fire licking at their muzzles. The men joined Gloriatrix and the courier as they strode echoing hallways laden with gold and onyx wealth: portraits, busts, tapestries, and embellished weapons (from a smith in Eod, if she recalled, and was always struck by their beauty). The entourage stopped in a domed antechamber gleaming from tile to pillar in black marble and lit along the roof by sorcerous stars. Wonder claimed none of them at the splendor, and Gloriatrix tapped her foot while the courier rushed to operate a switch hidden in the darkness. Gears groaned, and the floor under Gloriatrix and her party puffed with the sound of an unsealed naval hatch and began to rise. Gloriatrix's destiny was not to be crushed, and above her, the ceiling folded away in sections. They were traveling upward through a black glass shaft toward the Crucible's highest offices: the Iron Crown.

Gloriatrix enjoyed these moments of relative silence and authority, safe behind armed men, staring out over the maroon cloud cover that smothered the ugliness of her city. She found the purple toxicity of the stratosphere enchanting, the way it folded the red evening sunlight in a stain of oil-shimmered rainbows. Other transit shafts were about her and lean ebony skycarriages zipped around. These Crowes reminded her of mastless metal ships twisted with the thorny aesthetic of Menosian craftsmanship. Listening to the hum of the technomagikal platform, she slipped into a meditative state, preparing herself for the maneuvers she was to face in the Iron Crown, where every meeting was a sparring of wits and deceptions. She was still quite dreamy when the transport stopped, and she was led through passages and finally into a grand hall like the star-chamber below. Yet here the lights pulsed on smoky glass, not marble, and the entirety of the bleeding sun warped the chamber in forbidding hues. Under a pillar of red light from the cupola, twelve seats were present; ten filled with ominous figures and two that were empty. The Council of the Wise was waiting on the First Chair to be filled only, as the Eleventh Chair belonged to the last man who made a play against Gloriatrix, and the Council had not yet voted on his replacement. Baleful glares followed Gloriatrix to the largest of the iron seats, and she drank in the Council's malice with delight. Once her Ironguards were positioned about her chair, she called the session to order.

"Keepers of Menos, wise of Menos, I welcome you."

"This meeting is unscheduled. What is this regarding?" huffed a portly red-faced man a seat over from hers. He adjusted his lank, spotty hair while waiting for Gloriatrix to respond. As always, Gloriatrix eyed the man with disgust, wondering why the richest whoremonger in Menos couldn't even be bothered to get a proper scalp from some thick-haired savage and five sands in a fleshcrafter's studio. His slobbery speech and sweat-stained, strained clothing were measurably repulsive.

"It is scheduled as *I* have called for it, Third Chair. Since you'd like to jump right into it, what this meeting is about, Horgot, I shall tell you. *War.* This is about war. The hourglass is nigh for Menos to strike the kingdoms of the immortals." Gloriatrix waited for the chatter to die down after her announcement before continuing. "The hourglass is *fated* even, as Elissandra will attest."

Gloriatrix waved a hand across the way from herself, and all attention shifted to the quiet woman sitting there. She had not taken part in the eruption. At first glance, it was obvious that Elissandra was not an earthly master but a mystical one. Her pale-gray robes, her drawn, bloodless face, and her mane of frost-white hair gave her an ethereal air. When she spoke, it was hardly a whisper, and her silvery eyes saw past the room, as if she was a conduit for forces beyond and not speakers on this plane of existence. She was an astromancer, a sorceress who dealt in cosmology and heavenly portents; her Houses of Mystery and their divinings were among the most profitable ventures in Menos—for every master wanted to know what knife to watch for next. She was also the only other woman on the Council and a silent ally of Gloriatrix. For some time, Elissandra had been working on a project for the Iron Queen. Now the time had come for Elissandra to announce her findings.

"Sixth Chair, tell us what you have discovered," urged Gloriatrix, snapping her fingers to rein the astromancer's wits.

"Yes, First Chair," said Elissandra, rising from her seat. Like an eclipse, she had a dark and ruling presence when she chose to exercise it, and the others gave her their rapt attention. "Gloriatrix, through channels unknown to me, recently came into possession of a relic. A highly significant relic. A key piece of Menosian history that is tied to the destiny of our nation. The Sixth Chair's scroll."

"Bullshite!" roared Horgot.

"Quite the opposite, I'm afraid. And the wise in this Council would heed its words, for they are dire and meaningful," replied Elissandra.

Seventh Chair, Septimus Sortov, youngest and freshest of the Council, had a cheery face and warm red hair that belied his devious proclivities as a nekromancer. He had only heard fireside chatter of the Sixth Chair's scroll before and made that known to the sages. He also tended to argue or stand against anything Gloriatrix overtly had a hand in, as he despised her talented son.

"Sixth Chair's scroll? I know that we live on the borders of the Untamed, but surely we are beyond the folklore of savages?"

Gloriatrix stabbed him with a stare. "You are young, so I can excuse your ignorance. Before the accomplishments of Menos, before our glorious achievements, we were a weak and pervious nation that had not yet found its footing. In our darkest days, we were stricken by famine and plague—a sickness spread by rats that no shaman could cure—and we reached out to the greatest kingdoms on Geadhain for aid, thinking the Immortal Kings to be the keepers of our land. But they spurned us, for they found our culture distasteful. They did not agree that some men should live in chains and others not, while what we do is no more perverse than any natural order of the greater over the lesser. Our founders grew ever more committed to survival then; they learned to take what they needed, to poison their enemies, to spy, and to trust only themselves. We have *never* forgotten the insult of the Immortal Kings, they who would have seen us die. And we have imbued our bodies, cities, and sky with iron, waiting for the moment of retribution when we, as one great weapon, as a nation of iron, can strike."

"Thank you for the lesson in history. Bravo," mocked Septimus, clapping.

Elissandra was upon him at once, uncommonly zealous. "You should understand the past to comprehend the importance of the Sixth Chair's Scroll. Gloriatix's illustration of our history is important, for it speaks to how deeply our hatred of the kings runs, and of how dearly we would see Geadhain rid of their fickle influence. We are not the first generation, though we are certainly the most lax in our hate when that very flame is what defines and unites us as a people. Our ancestors, the man who sat in my very chair some six hundred years ago, was more passionate and true to the soul of our nation than any in this room—Gloriatrix aside. My noble ancestor, Malificentus Malum, was not content with the piddling espionage of his peers. He sought a way to undo the balance and end the reign of the Immortal Kings."

"What did he do?" asked Septimus, who was now listening intently.

"He looked for something older and more powerful than the rulers of North and South. A weapon or wisdom, which can be much the same if wielded correctly. He went east into the Untamed. He did what no man dared and met with the Sisters Three."

While the more learned of the Council were aware of the ancient hags of the East, their merest mention evoked childlike shivers of wonder.

"To reach the Sisters took what strength Malificentus had, and his attempt to return home with his prize ended his life. A nameless grave in the Untamed and a legend to tell the young masters of Menos were all that was left of his legacy. As the legend goes, he wrote his last testament, and the words imparted to him by the Sisters Three on a scroll torn from his own flesh and preserved in blood sorcery." Elissandra paused. "I can tell you that much is true, for I have seen and touched my forefather's skin."

"You have the scroll?" exclaimed Horgot, who was suddenly quite interested.

Elissandra nodded.

"May I see it?" he asked.

"No," both the First and Sixth Chairs said together.

Horgot grumbled but made no further protest, and the rest of the Council mulled in silence. Sly workings were twisting inside Septimus, who now grasped the magnitude of this event.

"This scroll, then...it has the power to undo the kings?" he asked.

"No," declared Elissandra. "Material power was not what the Sisters gave him, as their gifts are never quite what one desires, but what suits a purpose of their own. They gave him the invisible sword of information, instead. Three small utterances, or at least that is all Malificentus was able to share."

Elissandra floated off, perusing the stretched gray parchment in her mind, recalling the leathery tackiness under her fingertips. Salivating with anticipation, the Council shifted in their chairs waiting for Elissandra to finish.

"Brother will rise to brother. A black star will eat the sky. The old age will crumble to—"

Gloriatrix interrupted the Sixth Chair, who had almost said too much. "*Brother will rise to brother.* That, fellow sages, has come to pass. My ears in the South talk of the creeping madness of the Sun King. They say he herds up the young and strong and takes them into Mor'Keth for blood rites that would turn a nekromancer's lunch. And in the North, my ears in the palace speak of the Everfair King at last leaving his ivory fortress. For the first time in more than a thousand years, he is away from Eod! Only his queen will remain. One king is mad, the other races to stop him. If ever there was a time where the heart of Eod was exposed, this would be it. This is the hourglass of Menos's vengeance! By the Sisters' own words, brother will rise to brother, and the old age will fall. *We* shall be the new age."

Murmurs of accord ran through the Council. So rare it was to see so much agreement. Nevertheless, Horgot raised a concern.

"Wait, wait. What was that about a black star, and that third proclamation of the Sisters, which sounded unfinished to my ears?"

"It was quite finished, I assure you," said Gloriatrix. "Should you need further convincing of the Sisters' omens, have your astromancers look to the heavens, to the darkest, farthest reaches of space, and you shall see a phenomenon that shatters your perception of what we believe is grand in our universe. Show them, Elissandra. Show them how small their minds truly are."

Nonchalantly, the Sixth Chair swept her hand as if ridding herself of a fly, and a wrinkle of darkness appeared between the circle. With a fleshy rip, the slit widened to a tear, through which the Council could see the star-spun darkness of space. Dwarfing the misty planetoids, however, was a pulsing sphere of shadow: a sun made of ink and curling with smoke, and as extraordinary and humbling a vision as any of the wicked sages had seen. Bored after a moment, Elissandra waved at the image, and it sizzled away to nothingness. She took her seat and added a bit of commentary.

"That is a phantasm of what we captured using our astroscopes. None in my houses have ever known so queer a phenomenon. It is unexplainable. And it is on course for Geadhain."

"On course? How...how long?" asked Moreth of El, a lanky, trim-faced gentleman in less ritual attire—a suit, bowler hat, and cane—than that of the other sages.

"At its velocity, we should see it in our skies come winter. It should not strike our world as other stars have, but hang above like a black moon. I can only imagine what dark wonders await us," replied Elissandra, who appeared quite enamored with her doomsaying, while the rest of the Council paled. Except for Gloriatrix, who was riding the bull of change and power.

"As you can see, two omens toll, and the third comes as surely as the cock crows. The tides of our world are shifting and ready to be steered by brave captains. We shall be those captains. Or I and Elissandra shall be, at least. Will you join me in this war? Shall we unseat the ancient kings, which the fates themselves have deemed unworthy of rule? Whose deaths the stars send a herald to proclaim?"

"Aye," promised Septimus. The rest of the Council followed suit around the circle, with Horgot holding out until the end.

"Aye," he snorted. "Though let it be known that I say the titted members of our Council are keeping secrets to themselves. I wonder, how did you even acquire such a prestigious relic? I would like to see the scroll for myself," he said, and folded his arms atop his belly.

All fair suspicions, but ones which neither the First nor Sixth Chairs would answer. Gloriatrix would never tell the Council that the most important piece of Menosian history washed into Menos through an underground channel that drew from Alabion's sweet waters; that it bobbed its way to the Drowned Shore and could have been lost forever amid the trash. Somehow, the Broker's clever hands found it there, outside his lair; he said it *smelled like old magik.* He gave it to her during one of their meetings regarding the expulsion of her recent enemy on the Council. He often gave her gifts, thinking that they were friends or some other grotesque relation, and was utterly ignorant of what he had discovered. Gloriatrix would never announce this association or how she got the relic. Elissandra, on the other hand, was content to keep quiet on the incomplete verse of the Sixth Chair's scroll out of whatever esotericism muddled her stare, and due to arrangements discussed between the two women during previous private meetings.

"I have given you my answer on that. Do not ask again," spat Gloriatrix. "The Sixth Chair's scroll may one day be on display in a hall dedicated to our glory as heroes in the Great War. Even then, should you survive it, you will never lay your greasy fingers upon it, as it will be enshrined in sorcery and dedicated to *my* name."

Anger gurgled in Horgot's throat, and Gloriatrix's guards dropped their flame-tipped rifles in his direction. The Third Chair quickly ceased his outburst. Gloriatrix smiled, which looked painful on her face, and gave her last instructions to the Council.

"With your approval, I shall set a handful of my forces into motion," said Gloriatrix, having already set many, many wheels turning, which they knew nothing about. "When we next meet, I expect that each of you will have gathered a substantial calling of your own for a march."

The Iron sages, including Horgot, bowed their heads.

"Excellent. Our meeting is adjourned," declared Gloriatrix. She remained in her chair, stroking the cold metal of the armrests, while the

Council drifted off into the shadows. She spoke aloud, mostly to herself, as they left.

"Remember, Iron sages, we shape the future of Geadhain. A world without kings. A world ruled by those of iron hearts and wills." *A world ruled by the Black Queen,* she thought, and turned over the unsaid third verse of the prophecy, which was of little interest to nine of her fellow sages, for it could never apply to the ones with sausage between their legs. *Brother will rise to brother...a black star will eat the sky...the old age will crumble to the rise of the Black Queen.* An Iron Queen wasn't enough, she decided. The Black Queen had more appeal.

"Iron Sage?" inquired one of her guardsmen, for she had been still for sands.

"A moment longer," she said, and looked up to the darkening sky and starry roof, imagining her reign as the queen of all Geadhain.

VI

THE BREWING STORM

I

K ing's Road, the snaking strip of buffed white slate that wound all the
way to Eod's Palace, was clear of traffic this morning, and sparkled
in the sunshine as brilliantly as a vein of gold. Today was a day of great cel-
ebration, where all of Eod, from the workmen to the masters, would have a
glimpse of their reclusive king. Such was not an occasion to be missed or left
uncelebrated. And though the King's Road was bare, the sidewalks were not,
and people clustered like eager spring flowers on shop steps, tavern awnings,
or rooftops. Masters of the elements, minstrels, and entertainers roused
the masses to a frenzy, filling the skies with glittering explosions of magik,
crooning ballads of Magnus's glory, or awing the crowds with funambulists
treading invisible ropes of air.

Thackery Thule was at the railing of an inn's porch, being elbowed by
tankard-clanging oafs and generally affronted by the spectacular spectacle.
He was as surly as those about him were joyous. Too many thoughts occupied his head for this to be a happy occasion, though he knew that it was one
of paramount importance, and not to be missed, no matter how perplexed he
was over his vanishing handmaiden and her mysterious lover.

I do hope that bloody pigeon flew safe and true, he fretted.

After two days with no sign of the girl, he had made contact with The Watchers. A missive sent by carrier bird was all it took. Rather archaic compared to farspeaking and other technomagikal advancements, and never guaranteed to reach its recipient, yet this was The Watchers' way. Timeworn and honored traditions, predating modern conveniences. A Voice would come, sooner rather than later, he supposed, but the waiting was agony.

If I could take it back, Morigan, all those cruel words I threw at you, I would. Please...please be safe. If this Caenith has harmed you, I...I shall kill him, swore Thule. Without warning, the noise around him became riotous and drew him from his thoughts. The mania of the crowd meant one thing: the king approached. As distracted as his insides were, Thule was magnetized by the silver-shod army that came trotting into sight.

Knight and beast alike wore the spiny pearlescent armor of Eod, as if they were creatures marched from beneath the most enchanted reaches of the sea. *The Silver Watch come riding, riding, from under the Great Desert's waves. Lay down your swords, spare your lords. Ere dawn comes, the battle is won, and you have not mercy, but graves,* went the old soldiers' tune, which captured the essence the king's army. While Eod had not warred in the last century, its soldiers prepared as if they were under constant attack, and the will of the king's army was a legend across Geadhain. Thule noticed it in the confidence and bearing of knight and steed, in their absolute focus, distracted by none of the glitz surrounding them. From his visits to the palace, he recalled the precision of the watch as they sparred in Eod's golden courtyards, waltzing about like ribbons of silver, lethal in their precision. The pale-hooded masters of the elements who rode amid the knights held themselves with identical pride and poise, yet without armor, and wove their spells with the same sophistication as their brothers and sisters slung steel. Also among them were Eod's thunderstrike artillery, with their crystalline, electrically twined bows; their darting, hawklike heads; and twitching gauntlets. They needed no further announcement of their threat. He remembered a day when he was taken with a rare moment of sky gazing; he had witnessed the mystic archers strike down a fleeing Menosian skycarriage. Still he remembered it, for it was as if a storm of lightning had launched itself from the ramparts of Eod's great wall, instead of from the sky above. He had covered his mouth in awe and doubted that anything but the smallest scrap of seared iron drifted down into the desert afterward.

All this to quash an uprising of savages? pondered Thule, who had heard the rumors of troubles in the mountains of Mor'Keth. A curious story. Although the revelers around him might be too enamored to delve deeper into suspiciousness, Thule was not. He had seen military assistance, and then he had seen marches of war. This force wasn't large enough to be the former, though it was certainly well ammunitioned enough to be the latter. Surely, a strategic misdirection was in play. *Where are you* really *going, Magnus?*

No better a time to ask such a question, for the first through eighth legions had passed and the king appeared among the final. Last out of the city, but first upon the field of battle if the legends sang true, and the crowd first hushed and then roared at the king's inspiring presence. King Magnus was humble to their noise, stiff in his saddle, and he nodded to his people and caught as many stares with his striking green gaze as he could. Dressed in pearl armor and silver-chained furs with a thin crown caught in his loose, wind-kissed hair, he was as fair as his name described. He rode upon his mythic black mare, Brigada, a horned beast, thick and tall as a Northman's ox, with the face, mane, and tail of a mare. Queen Lila rode alongside the king on a comparable creature, only white and more slender—the male of the species, oddly enough. Not many but the most learned knew of her origins as an Arhad bride to be what gave the queen her caramel and gold beauty, and it was impossible to believe that so youthful-looking a maiden could be older than many of the stones in the street.

Thule waved to them both, more spiritedly than the rabid masses about him, hoping to catch either of the royals' notice. Age had shrunk his shoulders, and he barely rose high enough to stand out among the children. He would have flashed a bit of magik to make himself known, but there was already such a spectacle that whatever he attempted would hardly be seen. Fate would have it that the queen's serpentine attention weaved through the crowd and somehow found him on the porch. She was hailing and smiling at every face that beheld her, but she lingered upon Thule a speck longer than most, and gave him a nearly imperceptible nod. *Old friend,* she seemed to say, and in that eerie, synchronized manner that Thule had noted between her bloodmate and her, the king's emerald awareness was suddenly upon him, too. Thule couldn't quite read that stare, though it was longer and sharper, as if assessing him for his fitness to a duty unsaid. As though the king could read his mind, Thule silently called out to him. *King Magnus, my friend. Why do you go south? Who is the true enemy that you face? With these hands, I have touched old magik. A girl that bears the wonders of the East. Arts of the Moon, a gift that not even the House of Mysteries could touch. Is she an omen? A sign of a rising tide? Why do I feel as if Geadhain is waking to a fire in its house, or plunging into a nightmare?*

An elbow from behind interrupted Thule's connection, and when he looked to the royals again, he saw merely the flapping white banners of Eod, with their crest of a silver fist shaking at the sun. Thule shook his own fist at the pennant, and then grumbled his way through the crowd, unsettled by the instinct that the world was facing tumultuous changes, and that Magnus, Morigan, and by association, he, were all somehow involved.

II

Eod's grand mercantile, the Faire of Fates, was bustling with bodies and gossip that day. The ladies were gabbing about the fairness of their king, the men guffawing with respectable lewdness about the curves of their queen, and all were equally blithe about the peril brewing around them. Or at least the peril that Thule suspected. The Faire of Fates was distracting enough without the chattering, and Thule found himself missing the utility of his handmaiden more and more with every sand, particularly when it came to the contemptible task of *shopping*. Ask him to fetch a bloodroot from the shrieking groves of Alabion, and he would oblige, even at his age. Yet the Faire of Fates was a different and hostile wilderness of its own that he was terrible at navigating.

Thus he slunk along the shadow of Eod's white wall, weaseling through the crowds, tents, and platforms thrown up with seeming abandon; staying on the outskirts of this massive jumble of commerce as much as he could. Delights of every imaginable configuration called to him, deterring him from his task. He dawdled once to gawk at a stage with a watersculptor riding a viscous steed of mist, then again at a wind-flutist whose notes lifted him into the air. The stalls of succulent meats, fruits, and savory vegetables were what he had come for, but he was as helpless as a child with a shopping list and had no idea what to purchase without Morigan present. So he overpaid for a few loaves of bread, cheese, and some coils of smoked swine, and told himself he would make do until Morigan returned. Which she *would*, he promised. While caught up in that sentiment, he did make one final purchase at the Faire. He stopped at a table laid with elemental baubles, and he bought a pair of liquid-fire earrings, molded in two loops, like the symbol for infinity. *Those will look lovely on her*, he thought, pocketing the item and giving a much unused smile to the burly merchant who had sold them.

He was leaving the entrapment of the market, walking among sparse crowds and breathing in the sweetness of freedom, when he noticed the reflection of a darkly shrouded man in a glass window on the other side of the street. Thule stopped to read the menu board of a quiet eatery, and then popped in to have a sip of tea and a bitter stone meal biscuit—he preferred the savory to the sweet—while watching traffic from the coziness of a wicker chair. In the shadows of an alleyway across from the café, and mostly hidden by a lamplight or moving carriages, was the same man in black. Thule was certainly being followed. Against the better instinct that one should show when being tracked by a suspicious stranger, Thule finished off his snack and scurried between people and moving wheels into the alley. The man in black was leaning on a pile of filthy kegs, waiting for him. Very little could be said about the man beneath the cloak, other than that he appeared to be thin, and the red beard that protruded from his hood was sparse. He hailed Thule with a casual wave without unfolding his arms.

"We have heard much about your request."

"Morigan, did you find her?" asked Thule.

"The girl? No, we did not."

"The smith? Did you find the smith?"

"I was not clear," corrected the Voice. "We have *heard* much, though we have seen nothing. It is as if the two have vanished from Eod."

Distraught, Thule sank onto the nearest object he could find, which was a creaking crate that moaned his feelings for him.

"What have you heard, then?" he sighed.

"Of the young maid that you inquired about, there is little history that you probably aren't aware of. Dead mother, a runaway father—a nameless tramp, as far as we know. She is as boring as the average charwoman."

So you would think, snorted Thule.

"The gentleman that we looked into, this Caenith of Eod. He was rather interesting," cooed the Voice, pulling at his beard thoughtfully. The Voice seemed to be contemplating his findings.

"I'm not paying you for silence; I'm paying you to speak," spat Thule.

"I do apologize," said the Voice. "The information seduced me for a speck. It really is among the more"—the Voice wiggled his fingers as if to conjure the word—"grisly of whispers that have passed these lips."

"Grisly?" Thule was on his feet again. "Grisly?"

"Indeed. The trail leading to Menos was cold and old. Older than your passage here—"

"You should know better than to mention that," threatened Thule, looking about with suspicion, as if they were heard. "That shadow is well behind me. You will know your place in not mentioning it again. The smith. He is from Menos?"

The Voice gave a deferential nod as he continued. "I regret that my tongue has spoken faster than my mouth can contain it. There are few with such a unique name as the one you shared with us. Yes, there is a smith in Eod named Caenith—no familial name beyond that, strangely. More importantly, there was once a man of that name from Menos with that same name. He worked—killed, rather—for the house of El."

In Menos, the blood pits where two men entered and one man left were notorious for their profit and allure. Any man of serf status or higher could submit himself for trial by combat, and in doing so was severed of any previous bondage and property of the house of El. An enticing proposition for freedom, as it could be bought with only a month's worth of winnings. Though rare was the man who lived long enough to extricate himself from the webs of the house of El, and rarer still was a master of El to honor the oaths of service and free that man, should he kill his number.

"He was a dog of the pits, then? A bloodbeast?" exclaimed Thule.

"Oh, no, no, no," twitted the Voice. "The story is one of Menosian legend. I wouldn't expect you to be kept abreast of such tales, all things considered."

Thule sneered, and the Voice held up a finger. "Muzzle your snarl, you might find it misplaced with what I have yet to say. This warrior with the uniquely similar name was no steelworker. In fact, he didn't carry a weapon with him in the ring, though that hindered him little. He could kill a man as quick as a blink. He was said to be so vulgar in his sport that he would drink the blood of his torn victims while they screamed their last screams—their limbs ripped off as you or I would tear up a child's doll. Bloodbeast, as the vernacular you are familiar with for the house of El's sportsmen, did not suit so magnificent a monster. The masters of El called him the *Blood King*, in mockery of our Northern and Southern immortal sovereigns, from which all good wit in Menos seems to derive itself. The Blood King was the house of El's favored pet, kept on a tight leash and fed sickening things to keep him happy—sweetmeats, organs, and not the sort that the meatmonger sells." The Voice gave his audience a black smile. "The Blood King scarcely spoke his name, but it was there, in the shadows, remembered by one whisperer or scribbled down by another. And the description of the man you gave, as interpretive as it could be, describes no other. A beast of a man, towering, feral, and radiating power. So either it is this Caenith, a descendant, or a grand impersonator."

"He is a murderer and a villain, or a liar and villain. Is that all?" spat Thule. He was repulsed that Morigan had involved herself with such an unscrupulous charlatan as well as terrified for her safety.

"No, that is not all. Not nearly," said the Voice, bemused. "The records of what happened next are...dusty. The whispers of that era are weak. We do know that Caenith decided to end his contract with the house of El, and it was not through the elusive and unfair breaking of the bond. He killed Mordencai, the father of El. Dozens more, too. Then the Blood King fled Menos and has never been seen since."

Mordencai? puzzled Thule, and had to reach deep into his memory to discover the name. Not surprising that he did not recall it at first, as Mordencai was the father of El several generations before Thule was even a seed in his mother's belly.

"Mordencai?" he mumbled, still grappling with the notion.

"Yes," the Voice confirmed energetically. "The fourth father of El to Moreth, who rules the house today."

"Which means..."

"That this Caenith is either a talented pretender, or he would be five and some centuries old."

Thule rubbed his head from the ache of his thoughts and tried to arrange what he knew about blood kings, girls who read minds, and the move of great powers to war. He didn't care for any of the speculations his mind could conjure. Life, it appeared, was tipping toward disaster.

"Is that everything?" Thule asked, sighing.

"Mostly so," said the Voice, and began slinking around the kegs. "Not out of personal courtesy, but out of satisfaction for our services, I should warn you that the girl you seek is in danger so long as she is entangled with this imposter. More so than merely being in company with a dangerous, delusional strongman. As you know, the houses of Menos have memories as long as the list of their sins. The house of El is no different, and the contract for information regarding the injustice of Mordencai's murder remains unpunished and preserved to this day. Therefore, I am obligated to see that the house of El knows of this Caenith, regardless of who he is. You of all people should understand the slipperiness of honor when it comes to our dealings."

Thule did, for they had betrayed him once. Or he had betrayed his sense in trusting liars. He would not abide with them threatening Morigan, though. He leaped from his box, his eyes flashing with the dazzling light of his Will, and the kegs in the alley were blasted to cindery smithereens. People screamed at the noise. But beyond the clouding dust, he saw nothing. The Voice was gone like a terrible dream. He had done his job, and surely, another Voice spans away would do his: alerting the house of El that an ancient blood hunt was soon to begin on this fool or monster that called himself Caenith.

III

In the emptiness, wherever she has been taken, there is nothing for the bees to feed upon. Hungrily, they buzz about her.

"Go away," she thinks. "Go find something to do." Perhaps it is her absolute calm, her absence of fear in this numb state, but the bees comply. Off they crawl

into the hollows of her mind, extracting delicious thoughts from her stems of memory and bringing them back to their queen, their host. She understands an element of this process as it occurs, that she is indeed the master here, that she has somehow commanded the bees. She cannot contemplate long, however, for they have brought to her the strangest nectars—memories so old that she has not recalled them in years, if ever.

How young am I? she wonders as the memory envelops her. For her limbs are stumpy and soft, her words a gurgle, and she is held in a bouncing backpack in a realm of terrifying green shadows. She knows who carries her, though, whose strong back she is strapped to; she would never forget the fragrance of rosewater and Arhadian myrrh that was the scent of her mother. If she could weep here, she would; she does not shed tears, but pulses with love and longing.

Happily the bees buzz now. They are pleased to have served so well. She doesn't need to ask, only Will it, and they are gone into the honeycomb of her head again, seeking further nectar of that taste: the taste of Mifanwae. The obedient insects are back sooner than the request is sensed. They wash her in another memory.

"The job I'll take, as you're not too kind and not too mean. You're just the sort of man I can take orders from," declares her mother, who is standing between herself and a grumpy-looking old man.

Thule, thinks Morigan, though her young self is still quite leery of the sorcerer, even though he was kind enough to give her a book to read and occupy herself with. While her mother and the old man engage in that marginally bickering way of theirs—bartering on price, hourglasses, and duties—young Morigan examines the book, which she has had much fun with that day. The book. She had forgotten about it, shoved it away in the dusty closet where childhood memories go to die.

Young Morigan, who has just begun to pen her first letters, struggles over the writing on the chewed-up brown cover.

"T-uh-ee...Uh-uh-un-tammied. Thee Untammied. The Untamed!" she cries in success, and the adults in the room are each taken with a smile.

The bees buzz louder. They like this memory, and they crave more of its nectar. Morigan, who is calm and in control, bids them to do so. Fear, she sees, works against her in this place. She must not stumble through the streets in terror of herself, but demand that the bees do what serves her. Like any magik, the *bees will do as she wishes so long as she steers them with confidence. This is an important lesson, and she vows not to forget it when she leaves the Dreaming.*

Soon the bees return, bearing their sweet memory, and Morigan is transported once more. She is about the same age as last time and tucked under boiled-wool blankets. Creaky floors, hanging pots, a nicked-up table, and other details of a modest apartment are seen, but not really paid much attention to. Mostly, she stares at the ceiling and relishes the butterflies of excitement uncaged in her chest. A person shuffles up to the bedside and snuggles into bed with her. The two of them bump noses, and young Morigan gets a kiss on the head. As Mother pulls back, Morigan sees her face clearer than she could ever remember her when awake. They don't look as much alike as her anamnesis would paint it, but more like red-haired cousins of the other. Mifanwae has not her daughter's softness, but a face carved of stony beauty, and hair less coppery than her child's.

"Let's see what wicked tales want to be read tonight, eh?" clucks Mifanwae, and pulls out the book that she has fetched. Young Morigan has improved with her linguistics and can read the cover perfectly now.

"The Untamed," she says.

The two crack the book open, each taking a side of the cover, and begin as they always do, by reading the poem inside. The prose is still a challenge for young Morigan with its complex, rolling sentences of hungry trees, graves made of piled stones, and lords of fang and claw. Much of what lies inside the book is equally as mysterious, though eerily enticing to young Morigan. The freakish pictures and Mifanwae's narration do much to illustrate the stories therein. One night each week, they read farther and farther into The Untamed. Grim tales of wisps of light that guide men to their deaths in bogs or off cliffs; of women who are glorious maidens by day and fanged, scaly hags at night; of spirits that live in trees, rocks, and streams. Or of small beings of light and shadow with the wings of insects or bats: faeries, as the book says, which get up to the meanest kinds of mischief. To young—and old—Morigan, it sounds like a phantasmagoric ecology too incredible to be real, which Mifanwae assures her these tales are.

The bees have harvested this memory for a reason, though; it has relevance to their queen, and shortly she sees why.

"That one looks interesting," says little Morigan, as the page flips.

She points to a highly contrasted image of a gigantic black wolf standing atop a stone heap. The wolf's head is tilted up, his jaws gaping as though howling, and even young Morigan, without her adult sensibilities, can see that this is some portrayal of sadness, grief, or rage. The text opposite the picture is quite flowery, with certain letters grand and curlicued and the rest of it quite small and spidery to her eyes.

"What does it say, Mum?" she asks.

Mifanwae is quiet as her eyes devour the script and does not answer until Morigan asks again. "Nothing, my love. Let's find a different story. This one is too sad for your tender ears." Mifanwae begins to flip the page, but holds her attention on the picture for a speck. "There is one pretty bit to this, though, my love. How he buried her. That is so much kinder than the rituals we have; so much more natural. I think...if I am ever to leave you, I want you to have a place like that where you can go to see me. I want to be able to see the moon, clear and bright over my grave. Sorry, dear, listen to me go on so glumly."

Morigan can sense her young self's confusion, and there wriggles the first seed of doubt that her mother will be with her forever, as she always has been. "You will get your wish, Mother," thinks Morigan.

Mifanwae kisses the concern away and flips the page. Now Morigan—the real Morigan, not the ghost of her past—sees why the bees extracted this memory. For one of the embellished words catches her eye, something that would have had no meaning to her as a child, yet is sharp with importance to her presently. "Caenith," it reads, and her head swells with implications of finding the smith's name in a book of faery stories. A singular name, one she has never heard of before, and she knows that this is no coincidence.

Now that the bees have served their queen, the scene clouds over in grayness. Morigan floats in the Dreaming, pondering. The kings, the wicked voice, Caenith, tales of yore, and strange bees, all these things are connected. At least here, she can sense that correlation. She is sure of it.

"I need to speak to Caenith. I need to understand why this is happening," she demands.

The bees obey and hum louder.

IV

Calmly as a leaf on a spring stream, Morigan bobbed her way back to consciousness. She felt fingertips of soft grass upon her cheek. She heard the music of flowing water and the songs of birds or other small-minded creatures that the bees in her head had no interest in harvesting. Nor did she suspect that her servants would do so without her command anymore. Quiet. A perfect peace that she had not felt since…

Since my mind exploded into a net for all of Eod to swim through.

Trying to stand resulted in a nauseating spin. In a whoosh, a warm, man-spiced wind was upon her, holding her waist and arm; his powerful heart pounding against her like a surf.

"Caenith, I need to talk to you."

"Ssh, my Fawn. You are still waking." Water was trickled into her mouth from what felt like a flute of bark as she clung at it. "You have slept as the bear does come winter. Stretch before you run out into the world again."

He did just that for her: moved her arms and legs, and rubbed the pins and needles from them while Morigan focused on where she was. A sun-wet, soothing plateau faded into view, with finches hopping bushes, wildflowers swaying, and a babbling pool tended by mossy-stone guardians. Slowly, while whispering appeasements into her ear, Caenith turned her about on the rock plateau, and she saw the vista of pastel-blue skies, tanned steppes, and the chalkiness of Eod laid out beneath them as if it were all a distant picture. They were near to the edge of death, only a few strides off, but she felt safe with Caenith's arms around her. They dawdled in that dreamy moment. She didn't allow herself to relax too much, but held fast to the wisdom and terror of her dreams.

"Where are we?" she asked.

"You wanted quiet, and I would not take you to the hollow cavern under Eod again. Who knows what you would hear there. This little nook is where I come when I want to forget the things that trouble me."

Little nook? A cliff on the path to nowhere? What troubles do you have, Caenith? Are they as unbearable, as unusual as my own? worried Morigan. She turned in his arms, frowned at his disarming handsomeness, and what first seemed like a caress of his sensuous lips ended in a prodding examination of the sharp canines that hid behind them. Caenith did not protest her poking. When she was done, she spoke without reservation—what was the point with one so strange as Caenith?

"I was hearing voices...voices that were not my own. Thoughts of...well... everyone around me. Not only thoughts, but pictures, feelings, and passions both fair and foul. I could not plug whatever well had opened in me. After I fell, I remember you catching me. And then I dreamed. Two dreams that I remember. Though I have never dreamed so clearly in my life before. I would call these visions, not dreams, for they were as crisp as you are, here and now."

Caenith nodded, as if he understood perfectly what she meant.

"I want to know what you have done to me," said Morigan, with the forcefulness that her romance-heady head had squandered lately.

"My Fawn," murmured Caenith, and reached out to touch Morigan's neck and shoulders ever so delicately with his fingers, as if she might break. "I am as amazed as you are that we have found the other. For I thought that the old magik was mostly lost."

"Old magik?"

"The spirit of Geadhain. The voices in the leaves. The song on the wind. The power that flows within all things. I am a creature of this power, and so, I believe, are you. When two children of Geadhain meet, just like the raw flint to stone, there is a spark. I believe that I have had the honor of awakening that spark in you," said Caenith, and he resisted the urge to nip at her, for in the breeze she smelled of all the ancient and wonderful herbs of Alabion.

"You have such a hold over me," he continued. "A yearning that is as fierce as the song of the Gray Man himself. I did not know I could still feel so deeply. Yours is a pull stronger than anything I have tasted in my long years, and certainly a power greater than any of your kind."

"My kind?" Morigan pulled on Caenith's collar. "Please, Caenith. The voices, the dreams. Do you know what sort of magik this is? What you have awoken in me?"

"My mind is always racing, chasing smells and memories, and I have hunted the question of what you could be, Morigan. In the East, when the forests were young by men's years, there were once children with powers similar to yours. Perhaps one special child each hundred seasons would be gifted to the woods, and these children were wonders even in Alabion. Enchanters and enchantresses were they, of dreams, futures, pasts, fates. All the unseen workings of Geadhain were at their command—energies that not even the greatest sorcerer can tame. Each of these wonders was born under the fullness of a new moon, and always to a lonely woman and without a father: save for the gray lord of the night—the moon, that is. Children of the Moon, they were so named. Your mother has passed, and I smell no other males upon you except an old element-breaker who is not of your blood."

Caenith let the statement hang, allowing Morigan to digest his information. *I am a creature of old magik...a Daughter of the Moon...an enchantress of dreams and fate.* Acceptance was astonishingly easy. It was a relief, actually, finally to understand the whirlwind of events: the bees and voices in her head, the strange and intoxicating man-beast whose name she saw in faery tales and who ran like the wind. Which brought to mind the matter of the man himself.

"What...what are you, then?" she asked.

Caenith grinned, baring all his sharpened teeth, and bowed her to the ground, pinning her tiny wrists under his massive hands with the gentlest of force and sniffing her up and down her body. Though her heart was throbbing, she wasn't afraid. She understood that this was an animal behavior not meant to harm and more likely associated with mating. In a moment he was in her face, huffing. His eyes were gray and swallowing as storm clouds, and his beard had the sheen of a fine black pelt; when he released her hands, she petted it and it felt much the same.

"Do you not know?" he asked.

"You...are...a...wolf," muttered Morigan, in amazement of the answer so clear to her. The bees in her head suddenly sang, and her words continued to flow. "You are two *creatures*, yet one spirit. A man and a wolf."

"Correct, Daughter of the Moon," growled the Wolf.

In that moment of truth, of her seeing him for what he was, the Wolf was snared by the beauty of the daughter. Morigan felt his passion engulfing her; his warm, stone hands squeezing her tender thighs; his body stiffening to rock—she had never been so eager to be crushed. They rolled on the grass. His mouth wandered her body, tasting, nipping, and licking her swanlike neck before finally meeting her mouth, and they kissed as if the other was the very air of survival. How easily they could have lost themselves, ripped off their clothing, thrown away all their worries, and fit together as a puzzle of flesh. Both the animal and the man in Caenith lusted to tease and eat the maiden's delicacies until their bodies collapsed in sweaty exhaustion. But he had made a promise to himself and to Morigan, and that responsibility pulled him back from the brink.

"No. I must be a man," apologized the Wolf, and withdrew himself to an arm's length as if for her protection. "I have thought long and hard about how I am to pursue you, about which customs honor the woman you are. As a man, I shall honor your virtue. If we are to be together, then we must complete the Great Hunt. I would not disgrace you by taking your innocence. You, who are as white and pure as the spill of moonlight upon a silent lake. I shall not bathe in that wholesomeness before we are bound. I shall not rudely take what you have chosen to give to no other. I must earn that."

Morigan blushed and stood up. She didn't ask how he knew or smelled her virginity. Twenty-six years had passed, and she found the company of men a spectacular disappointment. Aside from some disinterested manual handling or heavy petting ending in his wetness and her regret, she was, physiologically speaking, a whole woman who did a much better job at keeping herself entertained on lonely nights.

"I have embarrassed you," muttered the Wolf, and he was behind her again, surrounding her in a strength that she wanted to caress. "Please, look at me."

When she turned, the Wolf was upon his knee. Between his fingers he held a shining circlet that was so lovely that Morigan forgot her shame.

"I offer you this," declared the Wolf. "Part of Great Hunt is an offering to one's mate. That much can never be changed. Nor should the ceremony that binds us be."

"Ceremony?"

"An oath of blood. The same that our ageless kings were once said to swear. But that is the end, and this is still the journey of our knowing the other. Every choice you make will take us nearer to that end. Now you must decide if you will accept this offering: a symbol of the sacrifices and contemplations that come with every choice. As a Wolf, this would be for the taking of a life as food. Today, it represents the loss of some of your innocence, and my respect for you and the Green Mother for making that choice. What say you to my offering?"

A million questions lay unanswered, a heaping of troubles lay ahead, and yet Morigan only paused because she was so taken by the poignancy of this moment: its absolute importance in the future of her life. Indeed, there were nightmares of kings doing terrible things. And yes, pledging her soul to a man—who was not even a man—whom she had known for three days was a recipe for madness. But the bees were buzzing with contentment. They knew that this was natural, that it was meant to be, and she trusted these arbiters of all truth and intuition more than she ever trusted herself. Morigan took the bracelet.

"I accept your offering." The Wolf's face lit and she thought that he would leap at her. "Yet first, I have a request."

"Anything, my Fawn."

"I would like to see...what you are. The second body that shares your soul. Show me your fangs and claws," she commanded.

Perhaps it was the steadiness of her voice, how she ordered him to bare himself as if he belonged to her, or that animal impression of ownership that made the Wolf's heart roar to comply. He did not shed his skin but for the whitest moons of the year, and even then, so far from the city and never in front of another. In a sense, he was as much a virgin as she. With an unaccustomed shyness, he found himself undressing before the Fawn, confused for a speck as to who was the hunter. The flare of her nostrils, the intensity of her stare that ate at him for once.

I have chosen well for a mate. She is as much a Wolf as I, he thought, kicking off his boots and then shimmying his pants down to join the rest of his clothing. No bashful maiden was Morigan, and she did not look away from his nakedness, but appreciated what she saw: every rough, hairy, huge bit of him.

He howled and fell to all fours. Bones shifted and snapped, rearranging under his skin like skeletal gears. From his head, chest and loins, the soft black hair thickened and spread over his twisting flesh. His heaving became guttural and sloppy, and when he tossed his head up in a throe of agony or pleasure, his beard had coated his face, and she noticed nothing but white daggers of teeth. Wondrously Morigan witnessed the transformation, watched him swell with twice the muscle he had possessed as a man, saw his hands and feet shag over with fur and split the soil with black claws. Another howl and a final gristle-crunching shudder (his hindquarters snapping into place, she thought) signified the end of the change.

Her dreams did not do Caenith justice. Here was a beast twice the size of a mare with jaws that could swallow her to the waist. Here was a monster that had stalked and ruled the Untamed. A lord of fang and claw. The birds and weaker animals vanished, knowing a deadly might was near. Around her, the Wolf paced; making the ground tremble with power; ravishing her with his cold gray gaze; huffing and blasting her with his forceful breaths. While the scent of his musk was choking, it was undeniably Caenith's, if rawer and unwashed.

Morigan was not afraid, and was flushed with heat and shaking as she slipped the bracelet on and knelt. She did not flinch as the Wolf lay behind and about her like a great snuffling rug and placed his boulder of a head in her lap. No, she stroked his long ears and his wrinkled snout. A maiden and her Wolf. Soon the birds returned, sensing this peace and chirping in praise of it. And neither Morigan nor the Wolf could recall a time—if ever there was one—where they had felt so complete.

V

Menos was darker than usual: its clouds as black as the shadow of fear that haunted Mouse. The city felt more menacing to her. She saw shadows in every corner, noticed the glint of every ruffian's blade or slave's chain as though they were all intended for her. The warning of Alastair played inside her skull on a loop of nightmare theater.

A hand over her mouth startles her awake, and she twists for the dagger in her pillowcase until she recognizes the shadowy apparition atop her, who hisses at her to calm.

"Alastair?" she gasps.

The hand unclenches and the willowy shadow retreats to more of its own; she can only see the scruff of his red beard in the dark.

"Get up, Mouse. Get dressed."

Her mentor sounds annoyed or confused; she is each, but finds her garments quickly enough anyway.

"I don't like good-byes, so let's not call this that," Alastair says with a sigh. "But it will be a parting, nonetheless. You need to go low. Lower than you've ever been before. A new name won't be enough. You'll need a new face. I don't know how or who, but the sacred contract of our order has been broken. Your safety has been bought."

Mouse knows the who and how, and as she glances up from her boot-lacing to explain to her mentor her predicament, she sees that he is gone. Just empty shadows, echoing words, and the sound of her heartbeat drowning out all the rest.

She expected the dead man and his icy master to emerge from the dim nooks and doorways of the buildings she passed at any instant. With a hand on her knives and a fury to her step, she swept down the sidewalk; no carriages for her today, as they were essentially cages on wheels—too easy to trap oneself in. With its sooty storefronts and their wrought-iron windows, its black streetlamps that rose about her like the bars of a prison, Menos was constricting itself around her, and she had to get out.

You've survived worse than the nekromancer, she coached herself, though she wasn't certain that was true. She hurried through the grimness of Menos, dodging pale faces and quickening her step with every sand. By the time she arrived at the fleshcrafter's studio, she was sweating and stuck to her cloak. She looked down the desolate sidewalk and up the long sad face of the tall tower with its many broken or boarded-over windows. When she was sure she wasn't being pursued by the phantoms that her paranoia had conjured, she pulled back a rusted door that did not cry out as it should have, given its appearance, but slid along well-formed grooves through the dust. She raced through the door and hauled it closed.

It was dark and flickering with half-dead lights in the garbage-strewn hallway in which she stood. Mouse picked through the trash with her feet, tensing as she passed every dark alcove in the abandoned complex. Hives, these places were called, and used to house enormous numbers of lowborn folk under a single roof. In Menos, even the shabbiest roof was a desirable commodity, so the building's ghostly vacancy meant that it likely was condemned by disease at one point. Soon the stairwell she was seeking appeared, and she tiptoed down it, careful not to slip on the stairs, which were slick with organic grunge.

Couldn't have picked a nicer studio, she cursed. *I'll be lucky if this flesh-crafter leaves me with half a lip to drink with.* Lamentably, speed and discretion were her two goals in choosing where to have her face remodeled. Such stipulations cut the more promising fleshcrafters off the list and left her with the dregs. She hadn't put much thought into what she would have done, or even if she would end up hideously disfigured. Monstrous disfigurement could even work in her favor, as she bore an uncanny resemblance to that crow-eviscerated woman whom she suspected was the object of the nekromancer's dark desire. *I'll take ugly over dead. Over whatever he has in mind for me.* Consigning herself to whatever face fate had planned for her, she went on to think of other matters, such as where her flight from Menos would take her. As unpleasant as the notion of seeking refuge among a libertine state of do-gooders and royal lapdogs sounded, Eod might not be such a terrible idea. It could even prove a marvelous hideaway with its Nine Laws, virtues, justice, and all the other shite that Mouse only cared about as a hunted woman. *Eod it is*, she decided. Mouse reached the bottom of the stairwell. A path cleared from foot traffic led to a metal door that bled yellow light around its edges. She rushed to it, tested the handle, which gave, and went in.

The fleshcrafter's studio was immaculate compared to what preceded it. The room was small, tidy, and had clean metal walls. After so much murk, her eyes stung from the lights overhead, but she squinted out a row of steel chairs over by a set of swinging doors and made her way to a seat. Her only other company was a bald man dressed in leather, who gave her a mercenary smile with a jaw that had been fleshcrafted with iron teeth and bones. There was nothing friendly about his greeting. Mouse let her cloak drop open, and the hand on her weapon hung out in a greeting of her own.

In Eod they have fleshbinders, not fleshcrafters. So I'll never see another thing like him again, she thought, as if she was a child being told a nursery tale. Waiting, waiting, waiting. She tapped her foot to make a bit of music while the sands dripped by as if coated in honey. She sensed that the man in the room was in some sort of distress, for he paced and nattered to himself; sometimes twitching or slapping his head. *Or just crazy*, she concluded, and felt this to be the truer supposition. Eventually, she gave up her foot-music and slouched in her chair.

No sooner had she reached a certain calm than the man came barreling toward her. The double doors flapped open before she threw her knives, and she quickly thrust her hands back into her garments as she realized that she wasn't the target. Instead, he ran past her to lift a buxom blond woman straight off her feet and spin her around as if she were his bride on their wedding day. The chesty blonde laughed huskily, and asked if he fancied them: her breasts, surely, which pressed over the man's shoulders. Several not-so-subtle glances were needed for Mouse to absorb that she was seeing two pairs of breasts, bundled like grapes beside the other, and after another instant of comprehension, it dawned on her that the throatiness of the bald ruffian's partner was actually the hoarseness of a man.

A four-titted whore with a prick. Maybe two pricks, for all I know. Well then, I don't think Menos could have given me a finer send-off, Mouse decided, watching the happy couple kiss and fondle their way out of the studio. The fleshcrafter who stood holding one of the swinging doors was so silent that she didn't notice him until the couple had left.

"I am paid by the hourglass, as well as by cost of parts," he said.

Mouse turned to the man, whose dark-circled, hooded eyes and pinched, generally unimpressive face was common among fleshcrafters. Mouse's theory was they couldn't be bothered to fix themselves up, doing what they did on a daily basis. The fleshcrafter wore the cotton gown and rubber apron of the more medically minded members of his art, though Mouse was not here for healing today, but a rebirth. Casting off any second thoughts, she followed the man into his workshop.

Inside the studio, Mouse was pleased to see that the fleshcrafter kept his workshop as sparse and clean as the waiting room. Immediately, Mouse spotted the steel physician's slab where she was to lie, with its large waterspout above and pink-stained grates below. She wondered how much of her would be washed through that drain that day. By that were a small wheeled stool and a tray of surgical and magikal implements: crystals, scalpels, drills, vials of foul-colored alchemy. Floor to ceiling, the walls were fitted with lockers, and Mouse felt a chill coming off them and whitening her breath. While she removed and folded her cloak and tunic, she played guessing games as to what sort of meaty contents were preserved within the lockers. When she was done, she placed her clothes on the floor and walked to the still-wet slab to sit. The fleshcrafter rolled up to her on his stool; he had put on a pair of gloves and clapped his hands together.

"What are we to craft today?"

"My face," replied Mouse.

The fleshcrafter reached out and turned her head from side to side. "Your face is decent, pretty enough. I'd recommend what I gave the gentleman that was just in here. You seem to be lacking in what men like."

"I don't need a bundle of tits. I need a new face," spat Mouse, crossing her arms over her chemise. "As different as you can sculpt. Pretty is fine, though plain will suffice, too. Whatever you choose, I don't want to look a thing like this when I leave. I hear that you are among the best and most *discreet* of your trade, and I have coin to pay for such discretion."

Even though Mouse could have intimidated the man to service with her Watcher's sigil—it lay securely in her boot cuff—she wanted to live as a shadow, which meant leaving no distinguishing marks of her passage. Revealing herself as a Voice would not be a fact easily forgotten. He appeared content enough when she handed him a purse thick with crowns—the black stamped chips of Menos's anticurrency to the *fates* of Eod. The fleshcrafter tucked the purse under his apron and set to work at once. He took a metal basin from the tray of many instruments and wheeled over to the lockers. Mouse lay down and looked away after watching him pick out a disembodied nose from the frosty storage.

She could still hear his muttering and the crack of each locker as it was opened, or feel the chill gasps come over her, and she bided her sands as patiently as she could. *A few more hourglasses and you'll be away from this.* The weight of that notion struck her rudely. The concept of freedom, real freedom, with hunters, yes, but no masters to serve. *Kings be fuked, this could be the best thing that's ever happened to me.*

Mouse was grinning when the fleshcrafter rolled back into her field of vision.

"Stop smiling," he ordered.

She obeyed, but found it difficult to hold down the corners of her mouth, particularly as the fleshcrafter drew lines upon her face with a ticklish quill.

He tilted her head around, checking his markings, and then reached to his tray of curiosities and brought a vial of ether-smelling liquid to his patient. He helped her up so that she could drink it. The elixir tasted as harsh as it smelled, and she gagged it down.

"That should put you out until I am done," said the fleshcrafter.

He assisted her back to a lying position. Already the slug of a substance had crawled its way to her stomach, where it wriggled sleepy nausea into her flesh. It was the sort of dizziness that Mouse had experienced when she had drunk too much to pass out, yet not quite enough to vomit. Her eyes were flickering up and down like shades, and the elixir was having a profound effect. In mere specks, the psychotropic properties of the drug had transformed the hovering fleshcrafter into a putty-faced caricature with great silver hands, which the soberest part of her knew was a scalpel. The freakish man was counting backward from one hundred, and in the midseventies when he suddenly stopped.

"I am with a patient," he shouted—a muddled sound to Mouse, as if her ears were stuffed with fat.

"She is not to be touched," replied another.

She recognized this voice. Its sinister articulation, the way it addressed a person's insignificance with every barbed inflection, could not be mistaken.

No! she screamed, yet what came from her mouth was a garbled sound and a dribble of spit. Pathetic as her resistance was, she managed to slump her lead-limbed self on her side and tried rocking her useless flesh off the slab. How she would save herself, or squirm to freedom past the blurry figures standing in the doorway, was the most desperate of dreams. Three or more abductors were present, though she knew only two—even if she could not clearly identify them. Two lean shadows, one paler than the other: the nekromancer and his dead twin.

"I say, you can't be here! I don't care—"

Then came a quick flash of white power and a breath of frost, as if all the lockers had opened. She couldn't make out what was happening until the fleshcrafter dropped to his knees before the table, thrust clearly into her view, and she watched him shrieking and fighting against the hand that held the scalpel for a speck before plunging the tip swiftly into his eye. The instrument struck his brain, and he did a quick jig and then fell on his heels.

Upon his death, Mouse struggled harder, despite the reality that she would not escape. Not with this poison slowing her body; not against a man who could command flesh and bone. The Raven wanted her, and she had been marked to be his since their meeting. Nonetheless, her spirit was admirable even in defeat. *He will not have me!* she raged, tragically hopeful that the narcotic paralyzing her flesh made her impervious to the nekromancer's magik; this might have been true, yet she was ultimately at his mercy. She was nearly at the edge of the table.

"Vortigern! She will fall, you worthless corpse!"

One of the shadows near the door moved so fast that her faltering eyes saw only the smear of black. Suddenly she was in the cold spicy embrace of the dead man, looking into his sad face, which was drooped with an expression that she sensed was regret.

That was the last Mouse knew before the darkness.

VII

THE BREAKING OF LIES

I

Dusk ran in purple streams across the sky, and the Wolf heard the rumbles of hunger in his Fawn's belly. Morigan did not ask where he was going. She just watched him with wonder as he leaped over the precipice and carelessly skidded down the mountainside. Straightaway, she missed the heat and throb of his body and noticed how cold it was so high up in Kor'Keth. The magik of Eod kept even the hint of winter away, trapped as if behind the wall of these mountains, though she could sense its insistence to be free in the hollow howls from above.

What would happen if King Magnus and his great magik were no more? she pondered, and the dream of the brother kings and the black voice was scratching at her insides with fear again. In the bliss of these past hourglasses, she had neglected to tell Caenith of her dreams. She certainly should and would make a point of it when he was back. She decided to make the most of her time alone and shuffled off to find a bush to pee in, offering pardoning smiles to the finches as she soiled their home. Once that was taken care of, she found the bark flute that Caenith had used earlier and went to the pool to wet her throat.

By the kings, you look like a bush witch, she thought as she caught her unkempt reflection in the water. She undressed herself and slid into the pool, which was covered in smooth stones and deep enough to rise to her breasts. She washed the leaves and grass from her hair and floated on her back, watching the stars pop out in the sky. Although her hearing was muffled in the water, she sensed the Wolf's return: a wave of heat, a wash of bestial odor. She walked from the pool, beading with sensuous trails of water; a glistening ivory treat for the huge monster that panted on the shore. She felt no more embarrassed about her nudity than the Wolf did as he snapped and stretched and moaned his way back into a naked man. The transformation was no less interesting to see a second time. When he was back in his skin, heaving on all fours, she noticed the blood on his chin, neck, and chest and the large dead lizard in his shadow. The corpse had long fore and hind legs, a crest of sharp ridges to its face, and looked quite like a scaled, horned colt.

"Spinrex meat," barked Caenith, his voice still throaty and not yet completely a man's. "I shall make a fire to cook it for you. I have had a few young already." He hiccupped, coughed for a speck, and regurgitated what looked to be a bone onto the grass. Even at this, Morigan was not disgusted, only intrigued. Caenith wiped the drool off his bloody beard. "Do pardon me."

His eyes began eating the Fawn, who was as lovely in the evening light as a spirit of moonlight and fire. He resisted the call of the beast to nip her dewy breasts or kiss the shadow between her legs, though it pained him.

"You should dress yourself. I shall wash up. Make myself presentable, as they say."

He lumbered into the pool. While he splashed and shook water from his hide, Morigan slipped back into her garments. Morigan had stoked many a fire and she picked some of the larger stones from the pool to make a pit for the flames, and then gathered leaves and dry twigs. By the time Caenith joined her, civil in his pants and boots, she had sparked the fire to life. He settled behind Morigan, fencing her between the mountains of his legs, warm and clean smelling if with a hint of damp hound. Quickly he set to cooking the stick-speared spinrex he had brought, abstaining from a spit and turning the beast himself. He held Morigan to him with his other arm and she ran her hands over the veined limb that entrapped her; she felt so at ease with him, despite there being so much unsaid.

"You built a strong fire," said Caenith.

"Thank you."

She indulged in their intimacy, in the night songs of insects up in there small slice of nowhere, before speaking of her dreams.

"I need to tell you what I saw. In my dreams."

Caenith nudged the nape of her neck with his nose. "I had not forgotten your mention of these visions. Please, my Fawn, go on."

Arranging the details was not difficult, and the bees seemed eager to help, filling her memory with flawless recall of blood, rape, and ritual sin. The words fell from her.

"When you found me, I drifted in nothingness for a time. In this strange place that I think is called the Dreaming." Caenith inhaled as if from surprise, though shared not from what. "These things in my head—*bees*, I call them, for they buzz and hunt for information as those insects do pollen. In the Dreaming they are silvery, a swarm of lights, and they led me to terrible memories. Ones that were not my own. I think—no, I *know*—whose heads I was in. First Magnus, and then Brutus."

Caenith did not conceal his shock. "The immortals?"

"Yes, yes. I am sure of it. I felt them, this bond that they share like a mother's cord that had not been cut. Brutus's rage was bleeding into his brother, making him do the wickedest things. I don't...I won't repeat the worst of it, not that you couldn't stomach it, but I doubt that I could again." *Queen Lila is pleading, her beauty distorted with swelling and bruises, her golden hair matted in blood.* Morigan pinched her eyes and willed the bees to stop their harvesting. They could have gone deeper into recall if she chose, but she was afraid of how vividly she would remember. "The Everfair King raped her, his own queen. Against his will, I feel, for there was such a twisted sorrow between them. That's all I'll say."

"My Fawn," said Caenith, placing the smoking spinrex on the grass and trapping Morigan with both his arms. "I am sorry that your gift brought you such horrors."

"That's not the last of it, nor the worst," replied Morigan. "The cord that connects them. The bees wanted me to follow it. I didn't have much of a choice and I was taken to..." *A blood-sluiced hall of organs, sex, and writhing flesh.* She swallowed her bile and continued. "Brutus's court, I think. I always believed the Sun King to be a noble man, a keeper of nature. Or so it is told. He's become something else, Caenith. Something *evil*. Or there is something evil that has twisted him to that end. A shadow over his soul. Black and ageless. I have never felt so small. And it spoke to me, this shadow. Threatened me. It *knew* that I was there."

"What did it say?" grumbled Caenith. His coddling had hardened, his heartbeat quickened. He wanted to kill this thing, whatever it was.

The bees had no problem reconstructing the words of the Black Queen; Morigan echoed them as if in a trance. *"Begone, little fly. This is not your place. These children are my flesh, my puppets, my slaves. Come to my Dreaming again and I shall trap you in my web and suck out your insides. Flee, little fly, flee and await the coming of my reborn son, the Sun King. Await your turn with his gift and worship me as I rise eternal to the throne of Geadhain."*

Morigan, trembling, took a breath afterward and did not want to speak. Caenith held his silence, too, though his twitching body betrayed his agitation. Slowly, his ire cooled, and he hugged his Fawn. He purred into her ear.

"History does not teach the West the oldest legends of Geadhain, and even in the East there are few who remember, or remember more than myth. The oldest tales of the land speak of a time of an endless winter and before that endless darkness—a nothingness where life was *dreamed* into being. I find this curiously similar to your wanderings with your bees and your insights. As for this...*thing* that would claim the throne of Geadhain and who—rightly or wrongly so—calls the immortal brothers her children...she is a monster I have not heard of. For the kings have no mother to speak of. At least none that is known. And my memory is long."

"About that, Caenith," whispered Morigan. "I had a second journey in the Dreaming. Much nicer than the first. The bees took me to see my mother, to walk among memories I had forgotten. There was a book that she and I would read together. A book of Eastern tales. Stories from the Untamed, stories of Alabion. One story, I never read. Mother would not have it, told me it was too sad. But the picture stands out. A black wolf, larger than any bear, standing atop a cairn and howling—I think with sorrow—at the moon. I saw a single word, too, a name, before the page was turned."

The Wolf flinched as she uttered it. "Caenith."

Morigan said no more and gave Caenith time to sort out a reply. The fire was dancing bright, and she turned her glorious bracelet in it, watching the leaflets come alive. Caenith's hand spoke first, stopping her admiration by clasping her wrist.

"An offering, like this that you wear, I have given once, and only once before."

"To whom?" asked Morigan.

"To my bloodmate, Aghna. She-wolf of Pining Row. A hundred lifetimes of men have passed since her death, and I did not think that I would ever forge another gift for the Great Hunt."

A hundred lifetimes, thought Morigan. *Is he an immortal, too?*

He answered this question ere she could voice it. "Most of our kind age slower, as magik things do, but they still fall to wrinkle and time. I...do not. I am condemned to see those that I care for waste to bone. It is my curse to lay stones over those I love and sing to the moon," Caenith said with a sigh. "When Aghna passed, I swore—against her wishes—that I would never run in the Great Hunt again. Until the wind of fate, you could say, unlocked my door and blew you into my den."

Morigan could not find her voice; she was consumed with doubt. *So that's it. We are doomed before we even begin. What are you thinking, girl? Running amok with an ageless wolfman. Bees in your head. Kings and dark voices. This whole world is going to shite, and you're along for the ride. I don't think anyone has ever been so magnificently fuked.*

"I can taste your soft despair, my Fawn. It is like sour currants on my tongue. Do not think me hasty, or merely feeding the beast in my pursuit of you. I pondered, deep and long as a mountain spring, about what I was to do with you. Could I build another cairn? Or should I merely walk the night alone, as I have for so long. In the end, I could not resist your pull. For it was stronger than Aghna, stronger than my spirit to resist. I am a lord of fang and claw. I rule; I am not ruled. And yet I submit myself to you." Caenith released her hand, swept her hair away, and kissed the back of her neck, and her cold composure steamed away. Between kisses he continued. "The well of old magik is bottomless within you. It is a power that will not be denied. Do not fear that you will walk this world alone. Do not fear the kings or nameless monsters. I shall stand with you, and you will stand with me. I do not think that even death could separate us once we have chosen to be together."

Not a line on your face, nor a freckle to your skin, remarked Caenith, and started to lick and bite in passion, moving from her neck to her ears and shoulders. *You could be ten years younger than you are. I can't even place your years, and my nose never lies. I would not be surprised if the world worked slower for you, so that it might savor your beauty, as I am. I would not be surprised if the lifeblood of fate itself keeps you youthful as I at last grow gray. You are a wonder, Morigan Lostarot. The world has never seen such a creature. And you are mine, and I shall never, ever surrender you.*

Caenith did not share his deepest thoughts with Morigan. She had enough surprises to deal with; these other lessons would be learned in time. Turning elsewhere, to the needs of his Fawn, Caenith warmed up Morigan's spinrex and then tore off pieces of it for her to eat—stringy, salty meat, she found, and not altogether horrid. After she ate, they discussed what was to happen next.

"We need to warn Eod," she announced. "I don't know how, but we must get word to the palace. They will think me mad, but if even one person believes me, that will be a start."

Caenith studied the sparks thoughtfully. "Perhaps they are already aware of a threat. There was some kind of commotion echoing from Eod: music and light and noise. A formal ceremony with the thrum of marching hooves and clattering metal. So loud that I could hear it even while I hunted the dunes spans away. I have heard armies move before, and the noise was not dissimilar, if happier."

"Well, that's good!" cheered Morigan. She crept over to Caenith and threw her arms around his neck. "I did not think I could have a more magikal, peaceful, or strange time than any of the hourglasses you have spent with me, but I think that I am ready to return to Eod."

Caenith nodded.

"I believe that the bees and I have an understanding, too. That they will stay quiet so long as I am master of myself. Regarding masters, we should speak to mine, Thackery Thule. He and I didn't part on the best of terms, but he is a father to me, and I imagine he's feeling as regretful as I am about how things played out. Thule is quite connected, too, though I've never known how far or high that goes. Perhaps to the palace—or at least to an ear in the palace, we can hope. At least then my part shall be done."

Thule? Caenith frowned. He knew Menos and its history better than he cared to. *That is an old powerful house from the City of Iron. And your part, my dear Fawn, my darling weaver of fates, will not end so shortly. Though I am here, with you. Walking together until whatever end.* Caenith crushed his mood with a smile.

"To Eod, then," he said.

Caenith stamped out the fire, left his vest for the birds and mice to nest in, and was back in a blur to gather Morigan in his arms. She knew what to expect and held on tight, and soon the warm wind bore her down a near vertical drop. She laughed at the thrill of it, cackling like a wild-born witch of Alabion.

II

"M-morigan!" cried Thule.

The old man threw himself out his door and into the arms of the young woman. He didn't care what her strange magik did to him; he wanted to hold her. In his enthusiasm, it took a moment for Thule to sense the towering shadow beside them. At once, he pushed Morigan behind himself and glared at the enormous, shirtless barbarian on his doorstep. Coldly, the brute stared back with a wildness that was as dangerous as fire. A deceitful villain, or a ruthless, ancient killing pet of the house of El—Thule hadn't yet decided which this man was, though it was surely one or the other.

The bees hummed Thule's fear to their mistress, and though they could not penetrate Caenith, no prescience was needed to sense his huffing crossness. *Old man,* said the Wolf, *you stink of sadness and death. I know your family: Thule. Monsters like I can be. Only I was greater than they. You should ask the spirits of El. I watch you as a hawk waits for the mouse to show its head from its burrow, so that I may swoop and chew it off.*

Morigan quickly intervened, stepping between the two men.

"This is Caenith, the man who I told you about."

"I know *who* he is. Do you?" sniped Thule.

At this, the bees buzzed their interest and flew off into Thule's skull to see what they could find. They returned with scraps of a conversation about blood pits and hundred-year-old debts, stuff that made little sense to Morigan in the context in which it was delivered. She shook it from her head and addressed the men.

"Enough, please. Caenith and I are...well, together." Thule threw his hands in the air. "I came because of how unpleasantly we parted. I came because I missed you, Thule. I would like to think that you have missed me, too."

Petulantly, Thule shrugged. He had missed Morigan, worried for her for every speck and with every fiber of his being. Morigan took his shoulder and leaned in for a whisper.

"I have dark tidings that we must speak of together. In private."

"Very well," said Thule, defeated. Inquisitive faces and strolling masters were beginning to spy on the activity on Thule's doorstep anyhow. "He's not welcome, but I doubt you'll listen to my wisdom at this moment. Don't dent my door frame, you giant thing."

Caenith snorted and followed his Fawn and the son of Thule into the tower. At the threshold, a tingle washed through him, and he sensed that he had just been granted passage through a warding: he wondered how big of a shock he would have received had he not. They climbed stairs that circled the curving walls; the place had a ghostly brightness from the many sconces and their blue spheres of sorcery. Occasionally Thule or Caenith grumbled to himself, but for the most part their climb was silent and moody. The bees continued to feed Morigan with wafts of Thule's unease; nothing excessive or unbearable, only whatever drifted her way. By her Will, the bees did not seek his secrets, and she was impressed at how behaved her magik was now that she was back in Eod. She and Caenith had entered the city cautiously at first: slinking on rooftops, sticking to alleys, worried that she might suffer another attack like the last one. And while the sea of whispering minds still hissed like so many rustling blades of grass in a meadow, she could filter out most of the noise and simply concentrate on what—if anything—she wanted to sense. By the time they reached King's Crown, they were bravely walking in the streets together, and she was able to tune out the slanderous or salacious gossip that the masters were casting their way. *Keep thinking your nasty little thoughts, but be careful that I don't peek into your head and pluck out your nasty little secrets,* she thought, smiling to herself, feeling more empowered with every mind she restrained her buzzing magik from examining. Slowly, her awakening was beginning to seem less of a curse and more of a blessing.

I still haven't figured you out, Caenith, she thought, sliding a glance over her shoulder at the Wolf. *What are you keeping in that head of yours? And why can't my bees get in there?* Thule appeared to have a rather negative impression of her lover, and Caenith seemed to reciprocate the distaste. Once her own business was in order, she would sort those two out, as they were the most important people in her life and she couldn't have them hating each other.

Every so many twists of the staircase led to a landing, which they had to cross to reach the continued ascent on the other side. They passed a sparse, sunlit scullery and several rooms filled with must-peppered documents that made Caneith sneeze. On the second floor of the tower were sleeping quarters and an airy lavatory of polished metal and shining basins. *Where are the shrunken heads, the bird's feet, the stinking elixirs?* wondered Caenith. He was familiar with witches' lairs from the cold iron ateliers of Menos to the stone circles of the East, yet this magik maker lived as a common scholar would. For a son of Thule, there was a definite absence of blood or suffering—the piss and chemicals of fear that men excrete when tortured. Mayhap Morigan was not entirely unwise in trusting this man, even if she was unaware of her employer's dubious lineage.

The third floor housed a small alchemical laboratory that continued to defeat Caenith's expectations of their host as a wicked conjurer. The beakers were gray with dust, the shelves sparse of reagents, and there wasn't a smidge of blood that the Wolf could smell ever having been dropped there. Surely, the place had been unused for ages, and it was doubtful that it had ever been used for anything sinister.

Morigan noted the Wolf staring at the workshop as they neared it and fought against the happy memory of Mifanwae cackling as Thule singed off his eyebrows at a burner yet again. Thule's passion for potioncraft had died along with Mifanwae, she knew. Across from the workshop was Thule's study, which they entered, Caenith ducking to make passage. Thule went directly to his seat, and Caenith squatted nearby as if he might pounce. While those two scowled at each other as a pair of old tomcats, Morigan went to open the window to let out the staleness.

"That's better," she said as the golden breeze of day rushed over her.

She walked to Thule's footstool, removed the clutter he had heaped it with, and sat, placing herself between the two men. A bit of her mother's prudence entered her, and she gave each man a stern look. "This is going to stop, right now. I care for each of you too much for it to continue, and there are graver events to focus on."

"We can sort out our differences later, I suppose," said Caenith.

"Yes, we shall," said Thule.

Each man sounded as if he was still making threats, but an uneasy alliance was good enough for Morigan. She sealed the peace by offering out her hands, which they took, one apiece. She pumped her arms, acting as their handshake, and held her fellows as she continued.

"You remember, I'm sure, how I got into your head," confessed Morigan, and Thule looked away from her. "I promise never to do that again—intentionally, at least. The problem, it seems, is that there are things that *want* to be seen. And kings be damned, I've been chosen as the conduit for that. While I was away, while Caenith took me somewhere quiet so that I could calm the voices in my head, I had a dream. Very dark and very real. In fact, I'd say that I wandered off into someone else's head. You need to know what I saw there, as horrible as it was. Perhaps, Master Thule, whatever shadowy connection you have in Eod can get this information to someone of authority who can use it. I don't know, but I have nowhere else to turn."

Concerned, Thule leaned to the edge of his chair and cupped another hand over Morigan's; Caenith did the same, though from jealousy of this man's affection for his Fawn.

"My poor child," said Thule, his eyes watering. "I never should have forced you to leave. All the weight of Geadhain on your shoulders. What is it? What did you see? Tell me *everything.*"

Everything, considered Morigan, who had not yet faced those black thoughts, not even with Caenith. Morigan shut her eyes, and the minutiae of King Magnus's savage rape and his brother's impeccable sin welled up like the tears of her master. The bees had found a task, and that was to remember and *share*. Down the pathways of her mind they buzzed, seeking the nectar of their mistress's memory. What Morigan did not sense was the flash of silver light from her face or the charge that ran down her arms and into the bodies of those attached to her. When the energy entered Thule, he was suddenly elsewhere. Even the Wolf, with his mystic protection, felt the steely stingers of Morigan's magik pierce him, and his head wavered with images. He was not so lost as Thule, but captivated still.

"I was in a gray, formless mist," said Morigan.

Thule is not with her, not in his study, but among billows of nothingness. Alone, he thinks, until a cloud of silver midges appears about him, a thousand glints of light, and then he is swiftly moving and just as jarringly inside another's mind. He sees his friend, the fair and kind Lila, under him. She is covered in blood and mauled of her beauty. He has done this. He is doing this. No, King Magnus is doing this, he realizes, and strikes her again. Tears, so many tears. And so much blood and sick.

"The bees, they followed the link between the brothers," continued Morigan. Both her listeners appeared glued to the tale, not even blinking.

Another whirling journey, ending with a brightness that fades, and Thule is deposited into a new horror. He knows Brutus's Court of Roses, he has seen their beauty once, and this horror cannot be it: the squirming crimson bodies, the stink of waste, seed, and evil, and the sense of power and foul lust in the body he inhabits.

"And then I heard the voice."

As it whispers to Thule, he shrinks. His soul hides like a snail within itself. For the Black Queen speaks the truth. He is the gnat on her skin, the meal in her web. She will rise to claim Geadhain. She will eat the moon, sun, and stars, and, finally, the darkness that remains.

"Thule? Thule, please say something. You are pale. You, too, Caenith." Morigan had finished her account a sand ago, and neither of the men had said anything. She pulled on their hands, which seemed to stir the two from a waking sleep.

"My Fawn," muttered Caenith, and bowed to her side.

Caenith had not seen everything clearly; Thule had been thrown right into the memory. Worried that he might be sick, he wrenched his hands free and covered his mouth.

"What is going on?" asked Morigan.

"You...urp—" Thule paused as the bile fought to come out instead of words. "You did...urp...I can't...I can't...urp."

"You used your magik, my Fawn," explained Caenith in a whisper for her ear alone. "I felt it, which is saying much, as my kind are slippery when it comes to the craft. Magik cannot affect what it cannot find, and being of two natures acts much like the spots on a toad. You are very strong; the greatest hags in Alabion couldn't do what you have done to me."

"Magik? Oh, Thule, I am so sorry!"

Morigan tried to reach for the old man, but he crawled back into his chair as if she had the plague. Caenith softly restrained his Fawn while Thule gasped and heaved himself back to normalcy. He could never carve what he had been shown from his mind; however, once he was settled as much as he could be, he sat up again and patted the distressed witch on her knee.

"Your gift is a dark wonder, child. I would not have believed the horror myself if you had not shown me. Across Geadhain, there are farcasters, far-seers, and other adepts of the mind, but not even the mistress of the House of Mysteries could pull me into her inner self like you did. You are...tapped into something, Morigan, something beyond me. At least now, I understand how you have suffered. I shall put aside my differences with your...gentleman for now, as we have far greater perils to attend to." Thule drew a hand over his face; he was still quite ashy. "What you did there. That spell or trick or what-ever it was. I shall need you to do it again for someone else."

Morigan nodded. "I can try. For whom, though? I'd prefer it if the secret of my strangeness didn't get about."

Thule quashed the idea with a flip of his wrist. "I wouldn't worry about that, my child. She can keep a secret as tightly as a whisper to an oak."

"Who can?" asked Caenith.

Thule answered as if they had asked a trifling question.

"Queen Lila."

III

Mouse was good at pretending, and right now, she was feigning sleep. At her first glimmer of wakefulness, the survivor's instinct shot into her like an ampul of adrenaline. She recalled the studio, the dead fleshcrafter, her abduction. As her head bounced about, she sneakily gathered glimpses of her surroundings. She saw the black-metal-and-buttoned upholstery of an expensive carriage, and through a grubby portal, she spied wisps of clouds so cottony that she did not need the humming of her seat to confirm that they were airborne. Persons came and went. Once the Raven came over to her, kissed her on the cheek, and called her Lenora. If she had her knives, she would have gutted him without pause. However, her hands were bound and her possessions had been stripped from her, even her clothing. Someone had dressed her in a lacy ladies' gown. So she stomached his kiss and continued playing dead, until she heard the lisping chatter of the Broker, and she realized that she was in the company of more than one monster.

The monsters left after a time, and one less frightening creature remained. She could smell his sweet-tobacco cologne nearby but could not say exactly where he was, for he didn't breathe or cause the tiniest sound.

"They are gone, for the moment, if you would care to open your eyes," said the dead man quietly.

Fuk, thought Mouse. Cautiously, as if it could be a trap, she did the slightest of squints; she still could not spot the dead man.

"Let me help you," he offered.

Opposed to any of these fiends touching her, she shrugged off the cold hands that reached for her and twisted herself up; her face peeled off the leather with a painful slurp. She was in a cabin with long couches and small circular windows, the sort that a seafaring ship would have, crossed in iron. On the other side was a turn-handled portal to another area of the skycarriage. Now that she was upright, she could see her silent companion a few paces down the couch from herself. He sat with gentlemanly leisure, his arms and legs crossed as if he were watching a fire and sipping spirits. He appeared sad, though he had always seemed that way to her, or perhaps that was merely her despair projected onto the creature. He was one of her captors, after all.

"The Watchers will have all your heads!" she swore, and pulled at her restraints, which she realized were metal, and she cursed her situation all the more.

"No, they won't, and I think you know that. I don't know that taking my head would do more than inconvenience me, either, so save your threats. I would urge you to keep your voice down," cautioned the dead man. "Metal walls can carry sound like a shaken tin sheet."

Mouse could hear echoes coming from elsewhere in the ship, and she took his advice. She couldn't understand why he pitied her. Still, it would be best to assess the extent of her danger before attempting to extricate herself from it. She reminded herself that a long-lived mouse knew when to listen for the padding of a predator's paws. She would listen, then. *I'll be quiet for now, dead man, but not so much once I get a hold of something shiny and sharp. I'll play whatever damned game this is, and I'll win, too. We may just find out if taking your head does the trick after all.*

"Why? Why are you doing this?" she whispered, as ordered, with a genuine note of hopelessness.

The stitched lips frowned further. "I am following the master's orders. As much as all living—or reliving—things might wish to pursue their own lives, that is not my purpose. My purpose is to serve. I do not question the commands that I am given. If I were the master myself, and not the servant, perhaps your fate would be different."

Mouse swallowed a lump of fear. "My fate?"

"We needn't talk about that. Mayhap you will be different from the others. Yes, there is a spark, a newness to you. As if..." While swallowing her with his profoundly black gaze, the dead man trailed off.

"The others?"

"The other women," replied the dead man, fading back to his guest. "They weren't suitable. They weren't right. Granted, Master hadn't perfected his experiments. His work was still rough and unformed: quite messy." The dead man shook his head with regret. "Success is much more in your favor than those that came before you."

Experiments. Other women. Mouse remembered the thing flopping on the master's table like a fish in a lake of blood, and her stomach began to roll. *I'm as good as dead. It's merely a matter of when.* She attempted to control her hyperventilating, and unexpectedly, it was the dead man's large cold grip of support to her naked shoulder that calmed her. Looking to the hand, she finally saw what she was wearing. She had been dressed in the evening wear of a master's wife: an onyx-beaded bustier, a crinoline-and-lace skirt, and a necklace of dark pearls. In any other situation, she might have gasped in delight. Presently, she made a whimper of shock.

"That...," said the dead man, and he slid his fingers over her shoulder and down the side of her bust—the gesture was not sexual, though certainly intimate, "that was her favorite dress, so I am told."

"Lenora's?" guessed Mouse.

When she said the name, the dead man's hand faltered at her waist and he withdrew it. He folded his arms and turned to watch the clouds whisk by in the purpling sky.

"Yes, I believe that was what Master called her."

I think you know more than that, dead man, thought Mouse. *Or some part of you does. The part that reached out to me a moment ago. I might have considered it, too, if you weren't dead and hadn't kidnapped me. You're not a reborn, not as I know them. And you look so much like that nekromancer that it's uncanny. I don't know how these black threads all tie together, but if I intend to live, I need to find out.*

Mouse shuffled down the cushions toward the dead man. "Who was she?"

"Someone very close to us. Very dear."

"Us? You mean your master?"

The dead man's face wrinkled with compunction, and he clutched at his head. Mouse knew that she had found a crumb, a crack, possibly with the sweet wind of freedom blowing through it. She asked again.

"Close to *us*? What did you mean by that?"

"Close to...to the master...to us. I don't...I don't know," grunted the dead man, as if in pain.

Right up to his ear Mouse leaned, as if to suck out the secret. "What is it? What don't you know? What can't you remember?"

"Ssh!"

Abruptly, the dead man slapped a hand over her mouth, and she thought that she was about to be grievously harmed. She heard the spinning of the hatch, though, and went from biting her captor to collapsing against him as a maiden fainted in the summer heat. When the Raven entered, Mouse was, for all appearances, asleep on his servant's shoulder.

"Get her off yourself. It's unseemly for such beauty to rest on a corpse, you disgusting creature," spat the Raven.

"Yes, Master," replied the dead man.

Mouse was gently laid upon her side. The Raven came over to inspect her, blanketing her in men's flowery perfume and the iron tang of death, which was on his hands, skin, and probably in his mouth at some point. No cologne could erase the rot that had infused his body.

"Did she wake?"

"No," lied the dead man.

"Shame, we have so much to catch up on, Lenora and I. She is the one, I can feel it."

Feel it he did, with his greedy, caressing hands and then his kisses along what skin she had exposed—neck, collarbone, and shoulder. Mouse kept her eyes closed and went to that place she visited when men used to put their slimy pricks inside her: an endless golden plain where the wind was warm and swept all worries away. She only noticed the Raven's cloying shadow when it was off her.

"We should be in Eod in a few hourglasses. I'll be sending some of the Broker's men in to keep you company. Can't have them buzzing about my head like blowflies. Insufferable cretins, all of them, for men who don't speak. Don't touch her again unless she's about to roll off and crack her pretty face," ordered the Raven, slamming the hatch closed.

"Yes, Master."

Mouse didn't have long before more captors arrived, and certainly not enough time to chip away at the dead man. She did the next best thing and watered the seed a bit more, out of genuine gratitude and not entirely a desire to manipulate.

"Thank you, Vortigern," she whispered.

As the dead man took his seat again, in defiance of his master's command, he laid a cold touch on Mouse's skin. A fleeting comfort gone as quickly as it had come.

✳ ✳ ✳

IV

No sooner had Thule mentioned Queen Lila than he had pulled out the chronex that hung around his neck, twisted off one end and dropped into his palm a small stone similar to an opal. After discarding the sand, he cupped the stone and whispered between his thumbs as if he was making a birdcall. His observers heard no call. Not a single sound escaped his hands, not even to Caenith's ears. Thule seemed just as odd when he held his hands up his ear, nodded several times, and then dropped what looked like a black pea to the floor.

"Farspeaking stone. It is all used up now. I was given one in case of these sorts of emergencies. The Silver Watch should have a skycarriage along shortly. Go freshen up if you need to." Thule cast a withering look to Caenith. "Put on a shirt, perhaps."

Morigan held up a finger to her lover's lips as Caenith began to snarl a reply.

"I know you've pulled a few strings here and there," she said, "but are you going to explain how you know Queen Lila?"

"Not at the moment." Thule shrank from Morigan. "And keep those magik hands or bees away until I've said my piece. A man should have safety and some privacy, at least in his own head."

"I've shared enough for a lifetime with you, and you'll need to do the same eventually," warned Morigan, and she took her finger off Caenith's lips and tapped it on her nose. "I've never met a queen before. I should give myself a once-over."

Morigan smiled at the men, asked them to *behave*, and went to use the lavatory. Morigan's footsteps were barely down the first flight when Thule looked to the shirtless man in his study as if he were an animal that had defecated on the carpet and dragged its arse around the room. He asked, "What's the sport, then? What are you after with her?"

Caenith wasn't a liar and did not hide the truth of his feelings. "I wish to make her my bloodmate."

"Pardon me?" said Thule.

"You spit at me as if I have made some offense in proclaiming my intentions with the Fawn. Do not question me, my honor, or my virtue. Your ears did not deceive you, son of the house of Thule," snarled Caenith.

"It seems that we each know a bit of the other," tossed Thule right back—deterred only for a speck by the dredging up of his ignoble heritage. "I cannot change into which family I was born, though I have done much to prove myself a man not cut of the same wicked cloth as my forefathers. What penance I have done, too, were you to know. How deeply I have paid, a thousand times over for the crimes of my ancestors. Can you say the same, Caenith? Shame on you to speak of honor and virtue. You, who plays the role of the pet of the house of El. At least I hope that you are pretending, for the implications otherwise are as damning as they are preposterous. In either case, you've drawn a mark on yourself, and likewise on Morigan. Revenge for the Blood King's murders has not been forgotten by the masters of El."

Caenith held the old sorcerer's stare, unwavering. "A Wolf does many things when he is without his pack. Loneliness is its own terrible beast. It can claim even the strongest man over time, as water rubs away the hardest rock. When we are lonely, we do not listen to the voice of reason or civility. We do not hear the Green Mother. We are the animal. We are instinct. The animal, now he can be as wild as a river of blood, and in Menos, there are many who would feed that sort of urge. Many who would set it loose and watch it destroy for profit or black amusement. I have my shame for what I have done. I pretend to be nothing, element-breaker. Let the masters of El come. I shall feed them to their ancestors."

A Wolf? Is he mad? Does he believe what shite he is spinning? wondered Thule, yet could not assemble a retort for this convincing con man, who was so fervently assured with what he had said. Which left Thule to consider the second, less palatable truth, wherein this great hairy thing with his cold-metal eyes and confessions as a killer of hundreds was somehow older than all the sorcerers Thule had known, notwithstanding the Immortal Kings or Queen Lila. Indeed, as Thule engaged in his contest of wills with Caenith, the unblinking stare, the musk, and the shadow of the man seemed less worldly and more otherworldly, and he broke the stare and retreated to his seat, as if hiding from a yellow-eyed predator in the woods.

"You can't be," rambled Thule, unable to hold his thoughts and skeptical of what he was saying. "Are you...are you the Blood King?"

"I have given you my answer," declared Caenith.

Having said his piece, Caenith dropped his hands off his haunches and spread them over the floor, posed as a waiting, tail-thumping hound would be. The cold gray eyes lost interest in the old man and made lightning glances elsewhere in the room: to motes of dust dancing in ribbons of sunlight, a spider spinning its web in a corner, a bird flying past Thule's window, or a dozen other instances of life in one precious speck. Caenith's nose was just as active in honing in on Morigan's wet, sweet scent above the usual alchemical farts and industry of Eod. All the while, Thule watched Caenith and his strange behavior and faltered ever more in his theory that this man was a fraud.

An ageless warrior? References to animal behaviorisms. What strange idioms he uses. A bloodmate? Does he mean an ancient ritual of union? Dear Morigan, what have you invited into your life? What am I looking at? Thule sweated. He leaped a little in his seat when the cold gray eyes suddenly found him again.

"Morigan is coming," warned Caenith. "I shall not have you speaking of my sins before I have had a chance to confess them to my Fawn. I shall afford you the same courtesy to speak of your cursed bloodline at a time when you see fit. A pact of silence between sinners, then. Do you agree?"

"Fine, yes," said Thule, though he would have agreed with whatever the man had proposed to get that stare off himself. Caenith put on a slightly fanged smile, which chilled Thule with its hungry gleam, and rose to meet his lover. Into the room, Morigan flowed like a breath of fire and excitement. She warmed each man with a grin.

"You two appear to have sorted out your differences," she noted.

"For now," replied Caenith.

Thule gave a contrite smile and stayed in the security of his chair while the lovers huddled together, whispering sweetnesses to the other. Watching them made Thule's stomach crawl with nerves, for he felt as if Morigan—the daughter he had known better than his own, dear Theadora—was a stranger to him, or had matured into something else, and in so short a time. As for the man, no longer a smith or a deceiver did he see, but a creature more concerning than either. *A Wolf. Yes,* Thule thought, now that Caenith had planted the word in their conversation. Thule was so swept up in the storm of his thoughts that it took Caenith barking at him twice to tell him that a skycarriage was here.

As guests of the palace, they would want for nothing, so Thule abstained from grabbing any personal effects and hurried down the stairs with his companions. He did not lock his door, as magik would see to that, but shut it and turned to see Morigan running wonderstruck toward a silver vessel that dazzled in welcome, with Caenith loping after her. There was a definite animal heaviness and grace to the man, observed Thule. He caught up with the others as they were introducing themselves to the half-dozen Watchmen assembled aside the skycarriage's elegant silver-and-tempered-glass stairs, which had been folded from the vessel. The skycarriage was a remarkable achievement in artistry and technomagik. A vessel nearest in shape to a mastless ivory skiff, with a sharp prow, a thin bow, delicate metal struts that bore the weight of the craft, and wavelike curves and platinum embossing about its windows and portals. Compared to the sky terrors of Menos, this was a dove to their Crowes, and Caenith was impressed at the craftsmanship even if he was apathetic at man's overall desire to conquer nature. As far as Caenith was concerned, the sky belonged to birds, which had the right and the tools as given by Geadhain.

"What a *beautiful* ship!" cried Morigan, clapping her hands.

"They are with me," Thule stated, for the six stoic Watchmen had their hands to their hilts and were eyeing the excited maiden and the half-dressed brute through the crosses in their helmets. One of the Watchmen was a Watch*woman* and was absent of her helmet, though not immediately identifiable as female with her deeply tanned, block-jawed, broad-nosed face. A handsome woman, observed Thule. The impression of masculinity carried through in her tall and strong build, her cropped sandy hair, and the armor of a male soldier that she wore. She was seemingly unfussed by the inconvenience of a breastplate not tailored to her sex—which did exist, so this was a choice, then. A suggestion of femininity could be noted in the warrior's soft brown eyes, flush with lashes, and there a glint of kindness lay, if buried under duty. Honorably, she bowed to a knee as if each of the three were a master.

"Rowena, sword of the queen." She nodded to Thule. "Sage Thackery of King's Crown, I am told that we must escort you to Her Majesty at once. Please."

Rowena swept an arm toward the stairs, and Thule hustled up them, hoping to escape the questions surely raised by Rowena's statement. However, not even the narrow, light-bending chamber they entered, as disorienting for an instant as a house of mirrors, could distract Morigan from what she had heard: *Sage Thackery*. She bit her tongue, though, and Rowena entered behind them and led their company through an oval portal into a room with white padded benches and long windows through which they could spy the city. Once her guests were settled, Rowena politely excused herself. Thule sat across from his companions and stared out the windows, pretending as if the others were not dissecting him with their eyes, and a tense sand of silence later the technomagikal engine gently purred to life. Their stomachs did a small dip as the craft left the ground, and another dip as it bobbed unsteadily for a speck before finding its wings. As soon as the ship discovered its balance, they were off, the ground reeling away beneath them, flying as free and smooth as a bird would glide on currents of wind.

"Sage, hmm?" said Morigan. "I don't follow these things, but I'm hardly dense. Isn't that the highest honor awarded to those in the service of Eod? I can't say that I'm entirely shocked. What with Master Simms and all the other little strings you've pulled over the years. Don't think that I haven't noticed. What is it, then? What did you do to earn the title?"

Thule continued his cloudwatching.

"The sprite is well out of the bag, Thule. Go on, what's the story?" she pressed.

"Allow the man his silence, if that is what he wishes," interceded Caenith. "We each have our burdens to speak of in time."

What is that supposed to mean? debated Morigan. As much as the old sorcerer kept his pouting face to the window, Morigan saw a similar guilt in Caenith's eyes. Both of her men were nursing secrets. She wondered how dark those truths were that they thought that she, who had witnessed rape, murder, and genocide, could not handle them? The possibilities of that revelation made her slide down the couch and take a gloomy seat at the window herself.

"You two have only so long to tell me what this is all about, and then I'll send the bees to find out," she threatened, and then said no more.

Caenith did not reach for her, as much as he wanted to.

VIII

THE HEART OF THE KING

I

From the moment that Morigan watched the sky carriage land upon a vast anchorage of sanded stone, so polished that it gleamed as white as a band of moonlight, she felt as if she had entered another world. She forgot how angry she was at her two insouciant companions, and she found much more to divert her frustration once she was down the transparent steps and out onto the landing strip. High up in the mountains of Kor'Keth, even the lightness of the air lent itself to a certain euphoria, and as beautiful as the palace had been from afar, true justice was not given until one stood near its loveliness. Awestruck, Morigan stared about. First at the fleet of sparkling skycarriages and their silver attendants arranged along the anchorage in orderly rows, or lifting off as if they were rising stars; then at the vine-wound colonnades, bustling cloisters, and further tiers of the palace rising up the mountainside to a summit haloed in sunlight, at which she could only squint. Of all the sights, this one struck her the most, the clawed peak of Eod blocking the sun.

As if the powers here hold the very bodies of the heavens in their hands. How deep down the well you've fallen, girl, thought Morigan.

Someone had spoken in her daze, and then Caenith was pulling her by the hand down the anchorage as he followed the lead of Rowena and the sage up ahead. Morigan pondered what was being said between the two, for Thule was bent on her arm like an old maid. *Sage Thackery,* she scoffed, and then turned her scorn to Caenith. *And you.* Him, she found it much harder to muster any rage for, as twisted with fluttering emotion for him as she was. *Bloody love. Is this what it feels like? Recklessness and total forgiveness for the man who lies to you?* Still, she did not remove herself from his touch, and secretly they were each appreciative of that.

Rowena guided them through an opening in the mountainside guarded by two grand pillars as much vine as they were stone. Into lofty corridors they entered, finding more of this fusion of nature and magikally sculpted stone. Within the palace a brightness permeated the halls, not only from the sheer whiteness of the sandstone architecture, or from the strands of verdure with little buds of light that tumbled from the high reaches of the space, but from an intangible element of divinity that was felt, if never seen. Hallowedness was sensed in the small vestries, libraries, and sitting alcoves that she passed, with white-garbed folks who could be mistaken for peaceful ghosts wafting about each. To speak felt as if it would shatter this fragile contemplation, and the Watchmen or folk whom they passed greeted them with nods of wordless respect. Now and again conversations, soft laughter, or plucked melodies carried through the halls, though these noises were always muted, at times so low that they could be imagined, and little appeared to disturb the hum of silence other than their own clacking footsteps. In her peacefulness, Morigan quickly forgot that she was inside a mountain and was not paying attention to the wending of their travel. Whether they were moving up or down, left or right, she could not say. They were simply moving ahead through white, silver, and green spaces, surrounded in brightness and the ethereal presence of other travelers in this tranquil realm. *This place...I could be dead,* she mused without alarm.

On and on they trod, until Morigan's sedation was interrupted by a climb up a flight of steps so grand that they were surely made for the feet of giants, where every stair was akin to a separate landing that required many paces to cross. At each end of step, a Watchman stood, motionless as a metal golem.

The chamber that awaited them beckoned with light, and the final landing rolled out to become the floor of a grotto trickling with watery music. A whole kingdom within a kingdom was around them, and amazement captured each of the three travelers, even Thule, who had been to the Chamber of Echoes before. There was too much to see at once: the rock teeth of the ceiling overgrown in bolls of starry flora; the patchy gardens of transparent bushes, crystalline grasses, and rainbow-scattering flowers clustering around the stalagmites below; or the distant wall of water that poured from a hidden vein in Kor'Keth and thundered down the walls of the grotto and into a misty abyss. Somehow, they were on an island of land within the earth, and a drop that they dared not contemplate awaited them if they were to walk to the edge of this expanse and gaze over. Thankfully, Rowena's path did not lead them there, but straight on, toward the land's end. A sprawling garden was ahead, pierced by a great leafless yew as twisted and white as a tree of bones. As they approached the tree, gaping from its size, the grinding noise of the water swelled and then suddenly reduced to the merest musical echo, like a chorus of whispering carolers. Morigan knew then how this place had acquired the name Thule had muttered upon entry. Hidden in the calm shadow of the tree, kneeling in grass of glass, was a slight figure with gold skin and pale clothing. It looked almost as if she was praying.

The woman picked herself up and flowed toward the company, as graceful as a ripple of sunlight on water. Everyone, including the brazen Wolf, bowed upon a knee, for they were in the company of a true queen. Once close enough, she drifted from member to member, examining each of them with her inscrutable amber stare. Morigan could not settle on an age for the woman; as young as she appeared, she seemed as ancient as the tree behind her. First, the amber gaze narrowed upon Morigan and then clashed with Caenith like two snakes in a pit, and broke that instant of conflict to settle on Thackery.

"My Queen, I bring you the sage," announced Rowena.

"Thank you, my sword," said Queen Lila. Her use of Ghaedic carried a lilt to it, made heavier by her smoky voice. "Sage Thackery. How long it has been since you joined me in the Chamber of Echoes? The palace is colder without your wisdom and duller without your wit. I am glad to see you again, even if the situations are so ill-tided."

"Your Majesty," nodded Thackery. "It is an honor. Thank you for seeing me so shortly."

"Our meeting could not be delayed, from the sound of it."

"No, it cannot."

The snake eyes flashed to Morigan. "The farspeaking stones do not allow for nuanced discourse. What is your name?"

"Morigan Lostarot."

"And this man?"

"Caenith? He is my..." *Wolf? Hunter in the Great Hunt? Man I met less than a week ago with whom I've been all over Eod and seen wonders untold, and to whom I want to offer my heart? By the kings, Morigan, spit something out.*

Caenith answered for her. "I am her bloodmate-to-be, should she choose me. I am Caenith as declared."

"Bloodmate," repeated Queen Lila, and if their Wills were visible, there would have been fire and thunder between them. Caenith showed but a minor tremble as his nerves screamed of one predator in the presence of another, for as pleasant and golden as the queen was, magik leaped off her like sparks, raising his hackles. Only the slightest quiver of a lip told of the queen's surprise at this barbarian who spoke with olden terms and who, with his puffing strength and sinew, reminded her so very much of a man whom she could not think of without fantasies of murder or a painful rape of his own. Morigan picked up on a bit of this, as bees sang an alarm in her head, but the moment was over and the queen appeared satisfied. She then cast her attention back to Morigan.

"Thackery has informed me that you have information vital to the safety of our kingdom."

"Well, yes. I have seen something," confessed Morigan.

"You've seen something, have you? Thackery would not have wasted a farspeaking stone to request an afternoon tea—as much as he enjoys those. Please, seat yourselves, and we shall speak," suggested Queen Lila, and rested upon the ground straight-backed and with her shins parallel, as perfect as an artist's portrait. Morigan didn't think that this was intentional, but an inherent elegance. The company settled near the queen, with Caenith a pace or two farther back, and the watchful Sword Rowena standing next to her mistress as grim and towering as the ancient yew.

"What have those strange silver eyes of yours seen, child?" asked Queen Lila.

"Not with her eyes, with her mind!" blurted Thule, unable to contain himself.

The queen squinted in disbelief or amazement. "She is a prophetess?"

"Much more than that," continued Thule. "What she can do shames the black readings of the House of Mysteries."

"I don't know who they are," confessed Morigan.

"The black prophets of Geadhain," muttered Queen Lila.

"Fallen children of Alabion, twisted Daughters of the Moon, gone from their virtue," mumbled the Wolf.

This was the second time that this brute had referenced the old powers, and he drew the queen's cutting glance. "An unusual association to make for a man who does not have the bearing of a scholar. That is a tie to the past that few, even Sage Thackery, are learned enough to recognize."

"One should never assume whether a man is wise or unwise, strong or weak, given only a glance," replied Caenith, his lip curling as he spoke to show his canines. "Even the thinnest sapling may withstand the strongest wind. Even the dullest mind can shine now and again with wisdom. I am twice-natured in many ways, and you should remember to judge me so."

"Judge you? Pray tell, how does one judge a man who arrives shirtless as a tavern-brawler to the court of his kingdom?" The queen was not sneering—not with her face, at least—though venom laced her words.

"The wise observe before they judge, then observe thrice more before they speak. And this is not *my* kingdom."

Rowena's hand itched on the crystal hilt of her weapon, a lethal sword likely quick as lightning once unsheathed. While the deeper conflict between the queen and her lover was intriguing and surely worth examination to Morigan, that wasn't the reason they had come to the Chamber of Echoes. Whatever was happening between the two was veering the conversation well off its course and toward a dangerous end. Mifanwae's prudence reared in her daughter once again, and Morigan sharply took charge of the situation. She placed a hand on the bristling flesh of the Wolf.

"I would like to hear more of this House of Mysteries and its connections to my gift. I really would, as there is much about myself that I know nothing about. That said, my Queen, in the interest of Eod, you really must see what I have seen. Not all of it; I believe there are parts from which you should be spared."

With a deep breath, the blush of rage had left Queen Lila's caramel cheeks and she smiled to Morigan and Caenith. The expression was so lovely that the hate toward her lover was only noticed by Morigan's bees.

"Do pardon any offense, yourself in particular, Caenith. You remind me of someone, is all. A man I would rather not be reminded of. We have matters of far graver importance to focus on than my personal torments. Now, Lady Lostarot. Your vision, yes. What have you seen?"

"I think it might work better if I showed you," proposed Morigan.

She came forward on her knees and offered her hands to the queen so that she might take them. The queen studied the invitation, as circumspect as she was curious.

"Show me? How?" asked Queen Lila.

"In your head!" exclaimed Thule. "It's like nothing you've ever known! Quite safe, quite safe! She won't scramble anything too badly, far as I can tell."

As Thule was no longer the subject but the chronicler to this process, he appeared more enthusiastic about Morigan's gifts. He shuffled nearer to the queen to watch the magik unfold.

"When you are ready," said Queen Lila, taking Morigan's hands without pause.

Morigan had already begun. In a flicker of thought, the bees were off and harvesting from their mistress. She was careful about *what* brain-nectars they were to bring back: as fearless as the queen might be, she did not need to relive her king's crime. The bees returned with their droplets of memory, each a tear of the sorrow and suffering that Morigan had experienced in the Dreaming. Before the queen could blink, the static of Morigan's magik had crawled up her arms, and a dazzle of silver light from the young witch's face was her final vision before the horror of the crimson-drenched court of the Sun King swallowed all that she knew. Admirably, when the queen gasped and tore her hands from Morigan a sand hence, she did not scream, cry out, or shed a tear. If Morigan were to guess, her puffing breast, rosy cheeks, and slitted eyes showed anger, not distress.

The queen reached for her sword, who was at her side as quick as one's cane, helping her to stand. Together the queen and her sword turned away from the company.

"What is it, Your Majesty?" asked the sword, hushed, though the Wolf still heard it.

The queen did not speak and only shook her head ruefully. Morigan and the others knew too well the Sun King's evil. What the queen had seen required rumination; she would speak when she was ready. While they waited, Caenith crept over to sit behind his Fawn, his legs rising aside her like two mountains over a canyon with his comforting strength pressing into her back. She could feel him inhaling and cautiously nuzzling her hair. They hadn't touched all that much since she deduced that he—and the old sorcerer—were concealing things from her, and as she watched the silently torn Queen Lila, thoughts of what she had seen in the heads of Magnus, Thule, and Brutus pronounced themselves, and she understood that dealing with darkness was a battle, and one not won in an instant. She would give these men time, more time than she had angrily declared, to draw their darkness out into the light. Such could not be an easy task to submit oneself to.

Consumed in these sentiments of forgiveness and compassion, Morigan reached out to hug one of Caenith's knees. *I am sorry, my Wolf. Share your darkness with me when you are ready. I shall not stir the monsters of your past from their lair.* She meant what she said, with the whole of her heart, as an expression that wanted to be shared, and mayhap that is what stirred the bees and sent their silver stingers flying from her head. Caenith tensed behind her. As she looked over her shoulder and saw his toothy grin, followed by him mouthing the words *thank you,* she made the calm if unsettling realization that he had somehow just heard what she said—without words, and using only her mind. Was further confirmation of this feat needed, Caenith gave a slow, approving nod at the astonished expression of his mate.

"Morigan Lostarot," said Queen Lila.

"Hmm? What? Pardon?" Morigan shook her head free of its fog and peeled away from her lover. "Sorry, Your Majesty. How may I serve?"

The queen strode to her and knelt as close as if they were girlfriends; she smelled of spices and sweet things and was not afraid to reach for Morigan's hands again. "This gift that you have, it is as Thackery has said, only all the more extraordinary, for words fail where experience shines. I have lived many lifetimes and I have never heard of one who can see what you see or weave it so deftly into the head of another. I wonder how far and how deep those silver eyes see, or what else you might be capable of."

I could stab my words right into your head it seems, if I Will it badly enough, thought Morigan, and had to rein the bees not to follow this impulse.

Affectionately, the queen tucked a strand of Morigan's autumn hair behind her ear and then rubbed her pale skin with a thumb—a gesture so fundamentally mothering that Morigan was reminded of Mifanwae. "I am sorry that you had to see this," said Queen Lila. "And I thank you for what you did not show me. We both know where that dream began, though I did not know how it ended until now. I cannot question you or your promised bloodmate's honor, for were you an enemy of Eod, you would not be a friend of Sage Thackery, nor would you have come to me with this information. You would have found a more compelling reward for what you witnessed."

The queen rose, and Morigan with her, as they had not yet relinquished their grips. Warmly and unexpectedly, the queen embraced Morigan, holding her tightly and then releasing her. The gold pools of the queen's eyes glittered with melancholy: a sadness that the bees wanted to inspect until Morigan restrained them. In such a short time with her power, she was already weary of sifting through people's sorrows.

"Now, Sage Thackery and I have many a matter of state to discuss. I welcome you—and Caenith—as guests to the palace. Rowena can show you to your suite."

"Guests of the palace!" cried Morigan, and quickly embraced her hostess once more. "Thank you!"

Caenith would have preferred the open air to this bastion of rock and magik, though he could smell the citrusy-sweet scent of Morigan's exhilaration and knew that there were limits to courtesy that not even he should press. He bowed and thanked the queen, and she bowed in return. Stoic Rowena then led them through the Chamber of Echoes, and Morigan's giggles of delight could be heard echoing back to the two who watched them go.

"She seems excited," commented Queen Lila.

"Aye, she has had a hard life. I doubt she even knows how to enjoy the finer things that the masters of Eod see as commonplace," said Thule, nodding.

"We shall make certain to spoil her," promised the queen. "She has the look of one whose hardships have only begun."

Thackery agreed with a frown and reached for the queen's elbow, which was ready for him. Decades apart from each other had not dulled their familiarity, and the pair strode slowly around the great yew and into the roaring mist that ruled the precipice beyond. They did not go too close to the edge, but found two flat damp stones hidden in the back hollows of the tree and planted themselves upon them. Here, the roots muffled some of the noise, and they could hear each other speak.

"Too long, too long it has been, old friend," sighed Lila. "Rowena is doting, but loving in her manner, and she and I so often go back and forth between mother and daughter that even I get confused. The problem with never having children, I suppose, is that you're never certain that you aren't one yourself."

The queen and Thackery laughed.

"And my king," she smiled, and wistfully looked off to the falls. At that very moment she could feel him grumbling away like a gray winter's day in her heart, consumed in the staunchness of the march. He hadn't whispered in her mind in many an hourglass, and the communications were becoming less and less frequent, even as his storm was building. She sighed again. "You know how he can be. As distant as he is beautiful. Sometimes I feel that I have married a dream. Only recently, a nightmare."

Thackery patted the queen's hand.

"Which leaves you as the only friend I have," she admitted. "And you haven't come to see me in thirty years. One might take offense, you know. I remember when we used to bump into each other, shy as sinners, in the quietest nooks and corners of the palace. You, to contemplate what Laws a fair nation should abide, and me to contemplate how a woman who had all the wealth and wants of Geadhain at her fingertips was still eluded by certain joys. Once we'd gotten over our shyness, we came to trust each other." Her chuckle was throaty and uncouth, with a bit of snorting. Thackery had missed it. "We told our stories—a sad man with a dark past, and a daughter of the desert. And they became bonds between friends. Almost as intimate as the man with whom I share my bed, my soul. Would you say, too, Thackery, that you've never had a friend like that?"

"I would," he confessed.

"Even Magnus, as unquenchable as my love is for him, was never a choice. He is elemental to me. He cannot be denied, and much as I hate myself for it, I would not want to. Now here I am, with my old and not-so-faithful friend. Where have you been? I have missed you. Dearly so."

Thackery took a while before he answered, and when he did, it was a tired wheeze. "If we are breaking truths today, then I would say that after I finished the charter with our king, I had felt that there was nothing left for me to do. No more for me to achieve. No more distractions while I waited for the end, where at last I might see my Bethany and Theadora again. When I saw you and Magnus together, your harmony reminded me of a love that had been ripped from my heart, and it brought me as much pain as it did joy."

The queen came off her rock and held Thackery; her arms were as warm and golden as sunlight. "Thackery, what are friends if not comforts to your sadness? Do not feed your darkness selfishly. We have seen what can become of a man once that path is taken."

"Brutus."

"Yes."

They separated, the queen returning to her seat, and their friendliness hardened to steel.

"I shall assume that our king is not dealing with the mountainfolk of Mor'Keth," said Thackery.

"You are correct."

"He has gone to face Brutus, then?"

"Yes."

Heavily, Thackery pondered this. It was what he suspected, but hard to accept. A battle of the immortals; the end of a peace that was thought unbreakable.

"I'd have him castrated and chained for a century, were the choice mine or the fault wholly his," she continued. "However, there is the presence inside him to consider. I was not convinced until the young witch showed me. I would not have thought to absolve him of any of his darkness. I think it is controlling him, or has incited his natural brutality. I shall have to tell Magnus. But I worry that it will give him mercy toward his brother, which is not a quality he can afford in the circumstances we face. I have seen Brutus... what he has become. Before, he was a king among beasts. Now, he is a king among monsters. He will not share the same pity as Magnus does for him."

"Then you haven't told him yet?" Thackery tapped his head.

"No," replied Lila. "Though I felt his cold concern wend its way through me while the witch and I were together. He will ask soon, and I should have an answer ready for him."

"You sound as if you are unsure as to what should be said."

"I have never lied to my bloodmate," she asserted.

"There has never been a situation so dire that would require a careful application of the truth," countered Thackery. "A king must be strong and free of doubt. A king at war must be an unstoppable wrath. He cannot question; he must only conquer."

The queen did not or could not reply.

"I mean not to salt the wound," continued Thackery. "But you haven't had the opportunity to ponder the details of the Black Queen's threat to our young witch. The fiend is in the fine print, they say, and I would draw your attention to how the dark voice referred to our kings. Well, one of them, as it were."

Not wanting to hear it, the queen turned her shoulder to the sage. Thackery came off his rock and brought it to her ear anyway.

"*My son.* It called Brutus its son. I know of no father or mother that bore them. They are a gift from Geadhain herself. Or so the world believes. Have you been told different, Lila? Or do we all share the same *truth?*"

Again, she kept silent. Thackery placed his weary leathered hand on Lila's trembling shoulder. "While you debate what single small truth to keep from your bloodmate—this very thing that could well be the pebble that keeps all the rocks of Kor'Keth from collapsing into ruin—I would ask you, as your one true friend: consider that your faultless king may indeed have been keeping secrets from you."

With a tender squeeze and those hard words of truth, Thule left the queen there alone, perhaps the loneliest woman in Eod. A woman whose faith in a love of a thousand years was cracked and seeping with doubt.

II

Morigan is aware that the Wolf is curled around her, in that place where her body is kept. An echo of his heat she carries with her, wearing it like a knitted blanket. Tonight, the Dreaming is warm and the bees are jubilant, dancing as on a summer's eve. They are obedient now, trained as pets, and they do not rush off but wait to be led or whisper places where they could take their mistress. The bees can still taste the sweetness of the one who earlier embraced them.

"You like love? We can show you love," they promise, with their speech of tinkles and chimes.

"I do," agrees Morigan.

The silver bees swarm and sparkle around her, and then she is funneling through the grayness as a current of ether. In moments, the bees have traveled eternity and deposit Morigan from the Dreaming in a flash of light. Her tongue is a dry rock in her mouth, as parched as the scorched and sandy waves around her. She smells the stink of sweaty hides, both mortal and beast, and sees herself in a throng of half-naked men riding four-legged equestrian lizards, and hundreds of veiled, shrouded women, of which she is one.

(I am a daughter of the desert. I am one of the Arhad.)

"You like this, Mistress? We shall show you the nectar of this one," coo the bees. Morigan's pets celebrate by warping the desert with folds of silver light, and she is in and out of many places—many histories and dreams of this woman—in a single blink. Suddenly, she is inside with the cool wind of a desert evening rippling the tent in which she and the other veiled women and bawling children hide. So much noise, for the children scream like broken instruments, and her fingers are cracked and bleeding from the weaving of baskets.

(These tanned hands are familiar, thinks Morigan.)

"Fine work," says one of the elder wives, and she hates the woman for even speaking to her and more so for commending her on this dreary task. "Do you want nothing more? Is this all you are, a slit for breeding and hands for nursing and mending?" she wants to roar at the elder wife. Instead she smiles and nods in thanks, loathing herself a little.

Another ripple in the Dreaming, and she is around a shadowy campfire on a night when the desert is not so harsh. Tonight it is her turn to teach the half-truths of her people. She is telling a gathering of grubby urchins—men not yet warriors and women not yet brides—of their place as the curators of Kor'Khul, and of the ancient pact with the land that they honor.

"Once the sands were woods and streams," she tells them, "and today much of that beauty remains. But only the Arhad can find it; only we can claim the harvest of the sands. We hunt the hidden life; we search for the forgotten springs. We find the forests of cactus and papyra that remain in Kor'Khul's sacred glades. We shepherd the flocks of noble spinrex and grow strong men on their milk and meat. Those who hide in stone-walled villages fear us, for we can survive in what they cannot."

(That voice, I know that voice, thinks Morigan. Even if the guttural words—like a language of spitting and hacking—are unfamiliar, though understood by her supreme awareness in the Dreaming.)

A third silver ripple, and she is squatting in sand while squeezing the udders of a spinrex, which squirt a dairy-scented, buttery fluid toward a pail, but mostly onto her cumbersome dressings.

"Lilehum!" barks one of the tenders—men who watch and guide but do not help with common duties. He follows up his reprimand with a slap across the back of her head that cascades her sight with stars. She apologizes and takes greater care while milking; it is easy to weep unnoticed behind her veil, and she does so.

With the fourth ripple in the Dreaming, the vision within the vision is over, and Morigan is back and marching in the desert, knowing almost everything that one could know about her host. As muses to their tribe, the women rattle the dusty air with their songs while the march goes on. Odes to the greatest shepherds, hunters, and chieftains. Songs that praise the strong and brave. Hardly a mention is given to the wives who wean and raise small children and the larger ones that think themselves men, she only hears of her place as a number, a footnote to the glory of a certain Arhad. The greater the hero, the more wives he is granted to proliferate his wonder. For her people wed to breed, and they breed to thrive, as many are lost in the desert.

"We are the flowers of the desert, wombs to the strongest seed," sing the elder wives with pride. "The rivers of life through which our people flow." She joins them in their harmonious indoctrination, cursing herself for feeling so different. "If I am so unimportant, why would I be missed? Why can I not make a life or a choice of my own?" she has always wanted to ask. Yet she knows better, and joyously sings of flowers and wombs and the red miracle of life that she is destined to bring, enslaved by the music and beat upon by a vengeful sun. The elder wives have chosen this rare, woman-honoring tune for a reason. Tomorrow there is to be a wedding, and her stomach curls and bites as if there is a lizard trying to chew its way out, for the marriage is hers. She is woefully watching the dunes, wondering how far she could run before a spear found her back when her ferocious husband-to-be caught wind of her from his spinrex, far ahead at the chieftain's side. He is a man as bushy as a black-maned sand cat, all size and hungry teeth; he wholly repulses her.

"He will be the one to throw the spear," she thinks, and seriously considers taking her chances. In the end, the stumbling, whipped-along ghosts of the shamed wives who have attempted her very fantasy before shock her into submission. She would rather live as a slave than as a beaten, circumcised, and sewn-up thing: a creature that is given the lowliest tasks that the Arhad can arrange; for a society of shepherds and nomads, there are surprisingly many ways to generate the filthiest of wastes. Besides, she will be her husband's sixth wife, as he is a mighty warrior, and once he has sweated himself inside her a few times, he will surely tire or look for another. At least, that is what she hopes.

Come the cold kiss of night, the Arhad camp in a cleft between two buttes that protect them from the wind while howling with a forbidding music. She falls asleep with the squealing whelps and finds a single happiness in knowing that she will soon have a larger tent to be shared with fewer, regardless of the price. Her sleep is bitter and filled with dread, and she is awoken before the sky is tinted orange. The elder wives wash her and dress her in white; this morning her face is exposed, and they comment on how lovely she is—many are surprised, as they have never seen her features before. "Your husband will be proud to own you. Be sure to give him many children," beseech the elder wives.

Before the dawn or ceremony can begin, before she is even led outside the tent, a storm begins. A wrathful manifestation of sand, wind, and thunder that flaps the fabric of their shelter like a sail on wild seas. She hopes that it will tear the tent down and sweep them all away. At worst, she prays to the old spirits of the land to delay the ceremony, to allow her one more day of this pretense of freedom, this small bit of herself that she has as an unwed woman. But the spirits do not hear her—they never have—and the storm passes as it came, clearing to golden skies.

(This was an omen, the bees tell their mistress. A sign of things to come. All is not lost. Love, we promised. Love to last a thousand years before it is tested.)

She is dragged out of the tent and into the desert. Many have gathered for the ceremony. Without her veil, she feels bare. She is not used to attention, to the famished stares that the men she is not to marry give her, though she knows enough to see it as lust. Her husband-to-be wears the grin of a pleased man. He is naked to the waist and has painted himself with the striped markings of a male spinrex today. She feels that he could be the lizard-stag itself was he only on four legs, not two. At his side is the gnarled chieftain of the Arhad and his flock of wives and sons. No other women are present, save these elder wives and those that brought her: this is a sacred ritual, and once they are sworn, they will celebrate the river of new life as her new husband takes her before those who matter. As if it is an honor to lose one's flower before a council of perverse watchers. In that moment, the sickness of what she is about to endure crawls up her throat like vomit. Perhaps she could run. Perhaps a spear to the back would be a better end. In that moment, her nameless husband smiles as if challenging that thought.

My fate, then, she thinks. I surrender to you. I have lost.

She bows in the sands before her husband, trying not to gag on her fear or from the stink of spinrex musk that he has coated himself in, and waits to repeat the words that will bind her to her new master. As the chieftain speaks, she knows nothing but the incessant reek and the shadows of the great buttes growing longer and longer in the sun; a rank darkness swallowing her, a hopelessness without compare. It is her turn to speak now, her turn to repeat the vows, and she pauses for an instant thinking that she hears something. A rumble.

Her husband-to-be glares at her and prepares to strike her, until he, too, hears the noise.

Suddenly, a whistle of warning cuts the day. It comes from the riders camped in foothills they cannot see. The chieftain's wives scatter, and she is grabbed by the ones that escorted her and pulled back in the direction from which they came. She is younger and stronger than the wives are, though, and she digs her heels into the sand and makes their job difficult; they slap her to obey, and she slaps them in turn. Her wriggling and fighting takes the wives by surprise, and they drop her as if she is an adder, unsure of what they are dealing with. She isn't certain herself what she is doing, or pausing to consider the consequences of her misbehavior. With every tingling intuition she has, with every flickering hope, she feels that this moment is special, and she will not miss it.

Chaos has broken out. The Arhad men are scrambling, the women who dropped her have run off like headless birds. A cloud of sandy thunder is rising over the valley between the twin buttes, and just as she thinks she sees shapes, they emerge: fantastic, beautiful beings, so white that they could be spirits, and upon enchanting beasts that are every softness and grace that the spinrex are not. One of the chargers is not like the rest, and her sight is drawn to him instantly. He is as dark as the others are pure, a shadow upon a midnight mount. He sees her as well, and shouts her name—or enough of it, all rolled together in a flowing way: Lila. The dark rider aims his steed and the wave of warriors toward her.

The tribesmen spot her, too, as drawn as hunters to a rustle in the sand, and they grab their spears and turn to her as if she is a demon who has summoned this army with witchery.

"You have brought the king of the North!" they cry.

The wiser among them grimace and bow to the ground, only her husband-to-be keeps his rage. She has ruined the tribute to his glory, she has corrupted her offering to him; sewing her up will not be enough. He hefts back his feather-rattling spear and snarls as he throws it—he is one of the tribe's best arms, he will not miss. Staring into death, she realizes that she is not afraid of it and wishes that she had known that about herself sooner. She ignores the angry man and looks for the king of the North, and in that languorous instant, as life slows before its end, their eyes meet across whatever distance and clash, spark, and kiss.

CRACK!

A fork of sizzling white power careens from the sky, incinerating the pro-jectile that her would-be husband threw before it had hardly left his hand, and the ground erupts in a sheet of emerald flames. In the bosom of the inferno, her wailing husband-that-will-no-longer-be writhes, and the other tribesmen— miraculously unharmed—scurry away from the pocket of fire, throw down their spears, and plead for mercy with their faces to the dirt. The death is so spectacular and the adrenaline in her so high that her knees buckle.

Through the dust and smoke, trotting over prostrated tribesmen, her sav-ior emerges. He is the most frightful and beautiful man she has known. He does not seem real to her. She sees no weapon, and she isn't sure how he has pro-tected her, though his body is cooling with a white steam, and her skin prickles from being near to him. Magik, she grasps, and thinks of all the legends she has heard of the Immortal King, whom her people loathe and revere like the forces of nature that destroy them. She is shaking with wonder as he glides off his mighty mount and is abruptly before her. He helps her up with his cold hands. At once, the world fades, and she falls into the well of his green stare. She does not know how or why, but he is as doe-eyed and spellbound as she is.

"Lila," he says.

"How do you know my name?"

"I journeyed long and hard to find you. Your name was a gift from the three wise women," he replies. His Arhadic is so delicately said, like a poem in how it unfolds in his mouth.

"Who are you?"

"Magnus of Eod."

"A k-king, yes?" She stutters on the word not because she is timid, but because she does not wholly understand its meaning—only the intimations of extreme power.

"Yes."

"What is a king?"

"A man who rules. A man who tries to sow virtue and justice through the mirror of his actions."

No direct translations exist for many of the words the king has spoken, and she smiles at her fumbling comprehension. The king smiles, too. He offers her his hand.

"Will you come with me, Lila? I shall show you my kingdom."

She looks to the pale strong hand and hesitates; his intention is unclear. Is this a choice? A genuine choice? Or is it merely another road to subjugation? she worries. She refuses to be taken or owned. Not by him, as magnificent as he seems, as powerfully as she wants to surrender to what he offers.

"I shall not force you to remain. I shall never force anything upon you," he promises.

Simply said, and she believes him.

She takes the king's hand, and he brings her to his mount. As they ride from the smoldering camp, she can hear the hissing of her terrified tribe, penned up like snakes in their tents or wriggling on the earth. She says farewell to no one. She leans into her savior, holds on to his firm body, feels her heart racing against his, and knows that she is free.

The bees shine and slice up the desert in silver rays. Momentarily, Morigan is again in the gray tides of the Dreaming: bodiless, buoyant.

"That was love. True, great love," she thinks.

"Your fate will be grander," declare the bees.

From the Dreaming they hurry then, sensing their mistress's keenness to return to her mate. The bees, too, are eager, for a feast of fates awaits them with their mistress as its host, and they hunger for what sweet nectars—what lives, dreams, stories, and ends—she will lead them to next.

✳ ✳ ✳

III

"Good morning, my Fawn."

Morigan awoke to the sight of Caenith's face, and she alarmed him by kissing it, and he quickly returned the passion. On the softest sheets, they wrestled: tongues, hands, and limbs tangling. They stopped when Caenith's fangs protruded. Excusing himself, he rolled to the edge of the bed and huffed for a spell. Then he wandered to the corner of their sparse but luxurious white-walled room, where a stone lip burbled a thin veil of water down over a grate. He doused his head in the shower and shook it like a wet beast. Beside that was a toilet, which he made use of, grunting as he peed. Morigan blushed and grinned at his crudeness. When he returned to bed, he saw his Fawn shrouded in lacy netting; her dress hiked, half off, and her body reclining as if she was prettiest of the autumn nymphs of Alabion. Morigan was acclimating to his moods, and she could read his sniffing desire as plainly as his nose-wrinkling anger. She wondered how much longer they could chase each other; she wanted to be caught. As he passed through the hangings and into the bed, crawling over her until their noses touched and their heats mingled, she spoke her mind.

"What remains in the Great Hunt, Caenith?"

"First, you accept, which you have done. Then, I chase you through woods to show you the truth of yourself, the truth of your feelings for me. You must be cleansed of the ghosts of the past if you are to move forward with another."

"You have done that for me. I see my mother almost every day, in the smallest of ways. I have never felt lighter," replied Morigan.

"I am pleased that you are pleased." Caenith smiled. "I have given you my offering, symbolic of my devotion to you and a token for the sacrifices you are making. This, you have accepted, which completes the second task. Finally, there is one thing that both the hunter and hunted must do together that does not involve a role of predator or prey and represents the step toward unity."

"What? Name it," demanded Morigan.

"We must create life or death together, only then have we proven ourselves partners and mates worthy of being joined in blood and promise."

"You're not...I mean, I'm not ready to have a child." *And what would it even be?*

Caenith laughed and rolled off Morigan, bringing her with him so that she rested on top of his chest. "Worry not, my Fawn. I've never had much success with children, not even with those closer to my kind. I can smell when the bleeding or fertility is upon a woman, too, so we should never fear for accidents."

Playfully, Morigan slapped his chest. "Caenith, you really have no shame. For the most part, it's as refreshing as it is honest, though I must draw a certain line. The peeing I'm fine with, but I won't stand for dropping a cracked stone loaf in front of me, should that thought ever cross your mind. Or talking about my monthly cycles. I am a lady. I do need a shred of privacy to hold on to. Only a shred."

To her surprise, the Wolf could be embarrassed, and his cheeks flushed red. "I...yes, I shall respect your limits. I shall never speak of those things again, my Fawn. The third test. When I say we must create life or death, a child is but one literal interpretation of the challenge. Another is making a song that the bards would praise for lifetimes, or a house as sturdy as our commitment that would stand as long as the woods around it. *Death* is one end of the challenge that has fewer possibilities attached to it. We could hunt and slay an animal of suitable might, but I would not suggest so dangerous a pursuit, for the strength of our kill must match both mine and yours combined. Or we could hunt one of those who took our heart and wronged it, though you are too fair and kind to be a creature of that sort of vengeance."

"Oh, well then, making something together sounds nice."

"Now we must ponder *what*."

But no ideas presented themselves to the Wolf and his Fawn, and as the starry trellis on the ceiling brightened, as did the world outside, they decided to explore the palace to see if inspiration awaited them elsewhere.

IV

Even for a tracker like Caenith, the labyrinth within Kor'Keth was troublesome. He made do without asking any passersby for directions, as his senses gave him enough of a map to follow. The spice of books and knowledge lured him first to a library, which was a good place to start when seeking answers. Not just any library was this, either, but a temple dedicated to its worship. Morigan gawked as they entered a pearlescent antechamber spindled in the brilliance of a skylight to nowhere. They were surely still under rock, though one would never know from the illusion of day above them. Hallways ran off from the chamber, and from higher up in their ornate loggias—carved with motifs of monsters, battles, and other scenes of legend—a few scholars stopped what they were reading for a speck to peer down at the pair scuffling and whispering beneath them. With no books in the antechamber, Caenith and Morigan wandered down one of the hallways, fingering tomes and treasures of knowledge spanning languages and eras. If there was an order here, Morigan could not uncover it. She knew, though, that this was a wonder of its kind and was awestruck by the excess of lore: histories, calendars, astromancy charts, journals, scrolls, diagrams, and random sheaves of arcane theory. Surely, Thule had walked these halls, and she whimsically wondered how much of a mess he had left after himself. She was so amazed that she simply had to know more about this place. So she interrupted the reading of a spectacled lady scholar, who jumped on her bench once at the disruption, and then again as she laid eyes on Caenith.

"Excuse me," said Morigan. "I was wondering if you could tell us where we've ended up."

"Ended up? You're in the Court of Ideas, and clearly lost."

"Not lost, *looking*," replied Caenith, and the woman clutched her book and shrank back onto her bench.

For a court full of ideas, they didn't find any to help them. All around they wandered, interested for a time in the ancient accounts, which they inspected as indiscriminately as their fancies directed. Morigan discovered that Caenith knew many tongues, for he could read nearly all of what they pulled from the shelves. She wondered idly how old he was to have learned so much. She remembered his counter to the queen's reprimand and noted that there was indeed a man of wisdom beneath the animal. There came a point where Caenith was reading to her an Orcelean text on the migrating habits of bonesparrows—tiny hairless birds, white as bone, which fed on the offal of the dead. The subject matter was boring, but Caenith's mastery of the information was not; it was admirable and attractive. She pushed aside the book and kissed him.

"You make me feel like I am a pup," muttered Caenith, when they came up for air. "All spry, short-furred, and rubbing myself against the nearest warmth I can find. I've never desired a creature as much as you, Morigan. We must not forget our purpose. You are more to me than my desire. Besides, I hear men around the corner, and I don't think we are supposed to be here."

Indeed, this area of the Court of Ideas was quite abandoned—by scholars, at least. But another wall away from them, he could hear a shuffling of metal feet and hissed commands to *check out that noise*. Caenith didn't consider what so many armed men were doing—or guarding—this deep in the Court of Ideas. Instead, he scooped up his Fawn and sped them through the hallways so quickly that the startled scholars who looked up noticed nothing except a ruffling of papers and a musky wind. He placed Morigan on her feet once they were out of the court, and they continued hand in hand.

Food was next on the Wolf's mind and his nose guided them to a banquet hall, a place where hundreds could eat on long tables draped in green, white, and silver, the colors of the king. A place as lavish as a king's feasting hall should be, with Magnus's gauntlet and sun banners hung from the walls and chandeliers of floating lights. Cobbled arches led off the chamber and into glowing kitchens, from which salty, spicy drafts spoke of the culinary delights being prepared. Serving staff were abundant in the hall and a bit chattier than elsewhere in the palace, so it took a moment for anyone to notice the two of them. Soon the whispers reached the ears of a stocky, aproned woman laying runners and issuing orders to the maids and porters. She dispatched herself to greet the visitors standing at the entrance to the hall. She had a motherly and natural air, expressed most sharply in her face, which was round, red, and pleasant as an apple; and noted in her sturdy frame and large hands, which were used for rolling, cooking, and fluffing—perhaps spanking, too, Morigan wagered. The woman's hair was frazzled and wild, and her smile of welcome about the same.

"King's mercy, you're large! I've seen smaller warhorses!" exclaimed the maid. "And what a rose of a thing you are, my dear. Never have I seen a girl so lovely, besides our Queen Lila! My name is Lowelia Larson, mater of the White Hearth, and you must be the two guests of our sage that everyone is chattering about. I'd ask what you're here for, but that one looks like he needs an ox to sink his teeth into, so follow me, and let's see what we can find that's red, dead, and ready to be eaten!"

Caenith liked the woman at once. Even more so when he strode through one of the nearby arches into a hopping scullery and witnessed the symphony that she commanded: the clattering of knives on wooden blocks, the dancing butchers, the sloshing sinks, the singing maids, and the clanking stoneware. What a marvelous, harmonized performance it was—no slips or bumps to be seen—and it was little wonder that the king's army was so daunting when even his cooks were masters of their domain.

"Quite incredible!" shouted Morigan.

"Ha! Hardly!" laughed Mater Lowelia, and prodded them over toward a corner where a handful of tables were set aside for resting. A few servants were about the tables, sipping ale or steaming drinks, and they scattered at the mater's approach. After seating the pair, Mater Lowelia rushed off through a sizable archway from which enticing fragrances of smoke and seared meat billowed. Caenith twitched in his seat, sniffing the air. He didn't have much of a wait to test his hunger ere the mater and a shy maid returned, each carrying a platter of steaming food and a flagon of watery mead.

"You poor thing, your eyes beg for food like a starving mongrel!" Mater Lowelia joked.

Caenith cracked off a mighty clap at the kingly feast arranged before them: shanks of hog, lamb, and ox, quail, potatoes, and greens dressed in spring herbs and brandy, from the scent of it. Even if Caenith wasn't a man who needed to flavor what went into his stomach, the taste was as excellent as its scent, and he was asking Mater Lowelia for bread to sop up the juices on his plate and then quickly diving into Morigan's helping.

"Quite the appetite," noted Mater Lowelia.

She had decided to use her guests as an excuse for a well-deserved break and was soon nursing a mug of watery mead herself with her feet up on an empty chair. Simply by studying the matron in her moment of repose—relaxing as if this instant was life's greatest pleasure, seeming to sigh from every part of her, shoulders to toes—Morigan felt that she was a woman unaccustomed to rest. A woman propelled by incessant demands, orders, and duties, and rising to every challenge. Rarely had a person so instantly endeared herself to Morigan, and much of this was due to the similarities between the matron and Mifanwae. The two women weren't identical; this one seemed coarser in manner and lighter in spirit, yet the relation was present—the steel that ran in each from the same vein of responsibility. *She could be an aunt I've never met before*, mused Morigan.

"What's the story with you two, then? I've heard all manner of wild tales," said Mater Lowelia, putting her feet down so that she could lean in and hear what they had to say. "You're in love, that much is as plain as my dogs barking. How did you meet? How do you two know the great Sage Thackery?"

Morigan gave a small laugh. "Great Sage Thackery? I've only ever known him as a troublesome but affable fellow whose tower I clean. Just as my mother did before me."

"A maid! I can see that! A strange fit, granted, as you seem like so much more." Mater Lowelia reached out and stole one of Morigan's hands, turning it over for inspection. "You've managed to keep such supple skin, though you can't hide the wear around your nails. I can see the diligence in the rivers across your palm—from squeezing many a rag or gripping many a handle."

"Are you a palmist?" asked Caenith.

"Fortunes? Kings, no!" exclaimed Mater Lowelia, and dropped Morigan's hand to snatch Caenith's as it lay on the table. She examined it, as well. "Hmm...a workman's hands are these. Honest hands. They've seen blood and war—those are the callouses of a warrior. Old, though, quite old. And the slivers of metal or minerals, deep in the skin...I'd say you're a mason or a metal worker." Caenith eyed the woman with wryness and respect; she could sense that she was close, yet not exactly on the mark. "A smith! I can see the sparks in your stare! You are surely a smith," declared Mater Lowelia, releasing his hand.

"Impressive, Mater. You have a hawk's eye for detail and a keen wit to match," said Caenith with a tip of his head.

"We who toil often watch, and we are learned in ways that our masters are not," the mater said with a smile. "So a maid and a smith. I feel like I have only a crumb of the story here. There's nothing plain about either of you, aside from your jobs."

"What were you saying earlier about the great Sage Thackery?" asked Morigan, dodging any further shrewd insights.

"You know the man and you don't know what he's *done*?" gasped the mater. "For Eod? For all the free people of Geadhain?"

"I'm sorry," admitted Morigan, shrugging. "I work for the man, as did my mother, but he's never been more than our employer and—in some ways—caretaker. I know that he values privacy above all else. I knew that he had connections to the powers of Eod, though I never could have guessed how grand those ties were. A sage...a friend of the queen."

"There, there, love." The mater came out of her seat to give Morigan a hearty hug, and then ruffled her hair as if she was someone precious. "Up here in the land of the Immortal King, we often can forget that there are those on the ground who live very different lives from us. I think Thackery wished that kind of difference for himself. Anonymity, you could say. Perhaps just a comfortable sunny room to read in and wait out his days. My grandmum knew him—mater of the White Hearth back in her time, was she—and this Larson earned, not inherited, her present honor, let that be known. I cared for my gran when the twinkle of her star was almost gone, and on the better days, she told me the fantastic tales of the comings and goings of the palace. Stuff I thought I'd never see. Gran told me of the sage, spoke of him with the highest regard. He liked to read, she said. Always with a book, that one. And he liked his solitude, too. He ate quite late, apart from the other scholars, and Gran fed him on just about the very same chair you're sitting on, each night, as if he was her own child."

To prevent anyone from overhearing what was said next, the mater came right to Morigan and whispered in her ear, "My gran said he was a sad man, and that's why she cared for him so. I'm glad to see that he's being well cared for by one with a golden heart. I don't think there's a wrong bone in your body, love." That said, Mater Lowelia backed away, waving. "A pleasure to meet you each. I've really been off my feet for far too long. The kettles are singing for my attention! The pots are weeping from their filth! And it's a shame that with all this magik, turnips haven't learned how to wash and peel themselves! I look forward to the tales you two will grace these halls with. I am sure I shall see each of you again!"

Morigan raised her hand to stall the woman. "Wait! You never told me of Thackery's deeds!"

"His deeds?" In veneration, the mater touched her chest. "He's the sage of the Nine Laws. Penned them himself with our Everfair King!" chimed Mater Lowelia, and thereafter vanished into the crowd of workers, though her formidable voice could still be heard over the clangorous music of the scullery.

"The sage of the Nine Laws," muttered Caenith, impressed. "The very framework of freedom, ethics, and law in Eod." After draining the dregs of his mead, he said no more.

"How curious that he would never say anything," pondered Morigan. "Not a word of who he was. All this time, and he's been living like a recluse. A man who changed our world. Incredible. Perhaps the mater has it right, and he was crippled by his sorrow. He was only waiting to pass."

The bees sang that yes, this was true.

"We still haven't found what will inspire us," said Morigan. "Though apparently Thule—Thackery—found what he needed here. I would like to think we shall have the same fortune. Let's keep looking."

The two shouted a good-bye to the mater and went back to the web of hallways to see where Caenith's senses would lead them next. Hourglasses raced along with them as they discovered the hidden beauties of the palace. Caenith's ears took them to a concert hall, framed in a mesh of silver-and-glass plates that pulsed with lights and colors in concurrence with the orchestra that played in the pit below. They sat in the sparsely filled pews for a time, enjoying the music, and Caenith waved to the roof and told Morigan of similar displays made by nature that could be seen on certain nights, from atop the highest rocks in Alabion. *Faefire*, the Easterners termed the sight. *I would like to see it one day*, said Morigan, and Caenith swore that she would.

When they tired of the music—more of sitting still for so long, on Caenith's part—the Wolf sniffed his way down an invisible path of soil and leaves, and the two found themselves out on one of the terraced gardens of the palace. From Thule's remote tower window, Morigan had never discerned much detail, though she presumed that the gardens were beautiful. How pale an assumption that was to the truth, and even Caenith was quiet as they strolled through the sunny woodland—under the canopy of bird-chirping trees that seemed as old as the ones the Wolf knew in the East; down paths fenced in living bushes of ice, their veins and innards bare to Morigan as she bent to examine them; over root-woven bridges covering streams with crystal beds; and through pergolas of perfumed flowers with blooms of cold green fire that did no harm. They ambled by benches and hammocks strung together by twined saplings and occasionally occupied by contemplative scholars, folk so lost in thought that the lovers were unnoticed in their passage. Often the two stopped to bask in the shafts of sunlight or inhale the earthy spice of such bountiful life. All conjured from magik, yet so harmoniously cultivated that, to the Wolf, it did not reek of the sulfur of new magik. *You managed not to break Geadhain, not to whip her to your Will, but to soften her and shape her with kindness, Sorcerer King*, applauded the Wolf. As the noon sun peaked and faded, and their wandering wound them back to a grand stone arch, they were no closer to finding what they would create, though their spirits were calm and primed for invention.

Not long indoors, the sweat and clash of battle drew Caenith; he grabbed his Fawn's hand and chased the source. In a few sands, they emerged onto another tier of the palace, a long flat field of stone on which white tents and flapping banners of the king were set up. A training grounds, this certainly was, and Silver Watchmen bustled through the arch by which Caenith and Morigan stood. They strayed along the outskirts of the field, keeping close to Kor'Keth, and watching the spectacle of hundreds of His Majesty's army drilled by the shouts of legion masters. They saw lines of men sweeping into one another like silver winds. They saw rows of thunderstrike archers volleying electricity toward scorched sandbags, or sometimes upon circles of shrouded sorcerers, who would throw their arms out and bat the projectiles away with twisting currents. Across the stone field, there were obstacle courses of snares, hoops, and walls, which the Watchmen grunted past without complaint, not cursing even come a tumble, merely picking themselves up and forging on. The King's Cavalry pranced up and down the stone, too, and their thundering charges made Caenith's blood boil with passion.

Soon they discovered a rocky rim with a clear view of the field and the open sky—they were at quite an altitude, for the city was not on the horizon. They sat and enjoyed the exhibition of war until the men began to sparkle with the fiery light of evening. Although their presence could not have gone unobserved, no one bothered them, and few looks but the most fleeting were cast their way.

"I've never seen men and women so disciplined. So strong," exclaimed Morigan—the first words spoken since their arrival at the training grounds.

"Aye, it is impressive," agreed Caenith, and pulled his Fawn closer to his warmth as the chill of dusk crept in.

"I had a dream last night...where I was very weak," murmured Morigan, and her mind was lulled and sent wandering by the ringing sound of blades, the hoof-drums of horses, and the muffled thunderstrike explosions. "I wasn't myself...I was Queen Lila. As a young woman, no more than my age. A daughter of the Arhad. She had such a difficult life, Caenith. More struggle than I've endured, but I feel that I understand her, even empathize with her. To watch a mother die or to throw away your needs at the commands of another are only different sides of the same helplessness. Magnus came to her rescue and brought her into all of this, just as you came to mine."

Morigan slipped out of Caenith's heat and stood before him; she was as passionate and striking as the bleeding sun behind her. "It bothers me that I have to be rescued at all. That is not the sort of woman Mifanwae raised. The sort I want to be. I want to be able to protect myself, to protect *you*, should I have to. Reading souls and fates doesn't help much when a sword is at your throat."

She crossed her arms, looked out over the field of warriors, and admired their endless dance. Even the stripped-down bodies of those taking a break near the tents were rendered in sinew and strength.

"I think I should learn how to fight. Can you teach me?" asked Morigan.

"A noble aspiration," said the Wolf. "We shall make a warrior out of you. I can't teach you even a scrap of what you should know in a day, but I can teach you how to hold a weapon."

She turned to see the Wolf smiling his sharp smile.

"What is it?" inquired Morigan.

"You've found it, my Fawn. What we shall make together!"

"I have?"

"Something as graceful and piercing as its wielder." The Wolf pondered and frowned. "A mace won't do for your slender wrists, too bulky and unfitting. Perhaps a rapier? No, no, I don't want you burdened with a scabbard. A bow, then? Hmm, no, that wouldn't work, either, not in close quarters, and too much finesse for the point you are trying to make. What then? What then? What would be perfect for the hunter of my heart?"

The Wolf seized her and pressed her hand to his thudding chest. "Of course! The quickest way to any man's heart is with a light and deadly point. A needle of death you can hide in boot or belt that is as strong as any blade in the hands of a master, which someday you will become."

"A dagger!" they declared over the other.

The Wolf's smile grew larger, as if he would swallow her, and he dipped so that Morigan could climb into his embrace. Not even the most eagle-eyed scouts in King Magnus's army saw the pair move. One sand they were there, speaking intimately and close; the next, they had disappeared. Were anyone to look for them that evening, they would not be found in the palace.

✳ ✳ ✳

V

"Thackery, you could at least pretend to enjoy yourself," complained Queen Lila. "I called this feast in your honor."

"I never asked for it," huffed Thackery.

His mood was a foul, black storm today and nothing of White Hearth's splendor could cheer him. Not the music of the two delicate, fair-haired windsingers that floated above the feast and whose voices and fiddle-songs whirled through the chamber on silvery breezes, kissing ears, bending flames, and mussing hair. Thackery found the ruffling an annoyance, and the strings were a bit shrill. The watersculptors were twice as abhorrent and loud as they skated about—*schrrit, schrrit*—on sheets of ice between the tables, and he hated them, too. Even the exquisite food was flavorless as it passed Thackery's lips. He pushed it away and glanced to the two empty seats at his side.

"Is that where your misery stems from, my friend? Because she is not with us? Do you feel that she has traded you for this man?" asked Queen Lila, and laid her grip on Thackery.

The gesture appeared to cleanse him of his crankiness, and he sighed. "I believe it is. Yes. She is as much—no, and curse me for saying it—she is more of a daughter to me than my precious Theadora was. For I have watched her grow and stumble into womanhood. These pleasures I was never granted with my own child. I have watched her live. She has been my companion for over two decades now. Yes, I certainly miss her. And I am concerned at how suddenly she has surrendered herself to this...man. They have some hold over the other that I shall never be a part of. More than lust. I don't...bah."

"They are off trysting, I am sure. We shall see them tomorrow or the day after," said the queen. She patted her friend and then removed her hand. After a short silence, she added, "I rarely speak ill of others unless it can't be helped, but that man—Caenith—he worries me."

Delicately, Thackery suggested, "Are you certain it isn't simply his resemblance to Brutus?"

"No, it mostly is," replied the queen. She took a draft of her wine and then motioned for her glass to be filled. Once the servant left, she squeezed out the rest of her thoughts; though they were alone at the royal table, she spoke behind her hand, as if there were spies present. "There are enough differences, but there is enough that is the same, as well. It is highly unusual, impossible one could say, to meet a man who could be a cousin to the kings. I have not encountered one in my thousand-year rule. Mater Lowelia, Lady of Whispers, has told me that he is a smith, yet I do not see a smith when I look into his eyes. I see the other end of steel: *blood.* I know that taint well. It was the scarcely chained beast that rode Brutus before his surrender to darkness. Who is he, Thackery? What have you not told me?"

There is a growing chance that he could be several hundred years old? Or that he speaks in old and tangled ways like your husband does? Or that you might focus your attention upon him, and perhaps Morigan, too closely if I am to say too much? More lies, old friend. I am sorry. Hastily, Thackery spun a reply for the queen.

"He is a mystery. If it matters, I believe that he truly loves Morigan, and she feels as much for him. I think he would place himself in harm to protect her, and that right there is a man more noble than the Sun King, who never learned to love at all."

"Well said, I suppose," she said, shrugging.

She had more of her wine and watched Eod's finest scholars and soldiers cut loose from their responsibilities for the evening: clanging cups, chaining hands about their waists while crooning rudely over the windsingers, sliding themselves down the ice, and generally acting like irresponsible fools. *Good for them. They should celebrate each day as if it is to be their last. Soon, even the immortals might meet their end. One of them, I hope,* she brooded.

Thackery watched the queen's golden comeliness darken, and wondered if his small lie was the cause. He hated that he had to deceive her, but a selective avoidance of the truth was necessary, which also brought to mind the queen's task in that regard.

"Have you told the king of Morigan's vision?" he asked.

Bitterly, the queen said, "No."

As she had predicted, Magnus's wintry soul had visited her later in the evening, once his men had stopped the march for the night. It was a strange commune, far less vocal than anything they had shared in an age. A few faded images of a desert city built into a precipice like a honeycomb, and clips of broken conversation about his army's movement were what she was given. From the striking sight, she surmised that they were in Southreach, which meant that her king had cleared the most desolate of the desert and would soon leave Kor'Khul. *All right?* he asked her, many times over. Nothing more composed than that came out of him, and she assumed that he was inquiring about her welfare. *Fine*, she replied, as short and curt as he was. His frosty, pimpling anger—toward Brutus—died down after that, and that was the sum of their exchange. As close as she and Magnus were to the other, there were portions of their minds that were their own, and she spoke in her quietest place, the corner that was only hers.

Already our love is cracking. Why is your coldness becoming so weak inside me? What is happening to us, Magnus? Is this the cost of lies? First, the barb of deception pricks, then it bleeds, then it infects, and the rot sets in. I am sorry, Magnus, so sorry that we are now lying to each other. Thackery is right, an angry king is a motivated king. When this ends, and you have punished Brutus and his dark voice, will it all return as it was? I must believe that, and so I prick you again, and I shall not tell you what I have seen today.

Gently, Thackery tugged on Queen Lila's arm to gain her attention, as she was deep in thought with a face pinched in pain—not physical, but the pangs of betrayal.

"I have thought of a way that we could find out *who* this passenger—this would-be queen—might be. I don't think you'll care for my suggestion, though. Should I tell you?" proposed Thackery.

From his effacing tone, the queen could tell that she was not going to hear him suddenly pledge to undertake the quest to visit the three wise women of Alabion. A plan he had dismissed before the banquet began as *pure rubbish*. Apparently, he had designs of his own in mind. She should have known.

"You are going to, regardless of what I say," she replied.

"Indeed, you know me too well. Like a felhound, once I have a scent, I cannot drop it," admitted Thackery. "Hear me out, dear friend. If this thing that rides Brutus calls him its son, then it would stand to reason that our king is of the same relation as they are brothers. That much we can agree on."

The queen nodded.

"Good," resumed Thackery. "Perhaps all we need to do is examine those early memories, childhood ones, those as far back as our king can remember. If there is a mother or a father present, we shall know our true enemy. The kings couldn't have come from nowhere, and it's about time that someone investigated their mystery. Especially when so many fates are tied to their destinies. A seedling can follow a cycle through wind and fertilization that is difficult to track, yet it is still planted and grows the same as all life. There is an *A* and a *B*, which leads to a *C*. We need to find *A* and *B*. I suspect that the answer lies in the Hall of Memories, where our king ponders whatever he ponders, where all the knowledge of our kingdom is cataloged and kept—including his secrets."

Sternly, the queen shook her head. "Magnus has declared that he knows nothing, and I must believe in what he says. He contemplates within the Halls of Memory so often that he would know the answer you seek, of an *A* and *B*, and he would tell me if he did."

"Would he?" frowned Thackery. "Think back, dear Lila, to the sands and dawning of your years. Do you remember the red journey that brought you to Geadhain? Do you remember the face of your father? Your mother? Your sister or brother? Your first scream? Your first step?"

The queen did not answer.

"Precisely. One's recall is never impeccable. Does the king remember only what he is *capable* of remembering? Or does he remember all the details that the wonderful machine in our skull records without our consent? I want the details. The forgotten particulars. I want to see his first breath and what came after that. If I'm completely off base in my assumptions, we shall witness the birth of two beings from nothingness, which is an arcane marvel worth beholding, in any event."

Angrily, the queen whispered, "My bloodmate is not some experiment of yours. I see that the ties of your blood run deep." Thackery winced. "First you ask me to hide truths from my king, now you ask me to scour his soul for secrets. I outright ignore any insinuation that he might be deceiving me, and even if we entertain your theory that these memories exist past his recall, the deepest archives of the Hall of Memories are sealed beyond any magik you possess. You would lose yourself to even try."

Thackery allowed the queen to solve the quandary herself. She was correct that he would not be able to extricate what they needed from the maze of history and magik that was the Hall of Memories. Yet he was not the intended pilferer of this vault.

"The girl! You would use the mind-witch," muttered the queen, somewhat amazed.

"I would *use* no one. I would ask if she would aid her kingdom. Ultimately, the choice is hers to make."

"I must think on this," replied the queen.

Conversation escaped the old friends after that, as they mulled over their worries in silence. In due time, Queen Lila was as ill-tempered as her guest of honor was. As absorbed in themselves as they were, neither noticed the waiflike blond maid, who had tended the queen's goblet and who had been hovering around nearby tables, suddenly find an excuse to disappear from the banquet. As with most of the palace's great halls, the White Hearth was warded against poisons, farseeing, or espionage of the mystical variety. However, there was no protection in the world against a clever spy with foxy ears to listen and a serpent's tongue to whisper to her iron masters.

VI

"We've arrived," said the Raven, sighing.

The veil and the other trappings of an Arhad woman were removed from Mouse, and she saw herself in a clean, pleasantly furnished white-stone room with twin beds, a door leading off to a lavatory, and a sitting table circled with golden light from a small window. The madman of the Undercomb, her captor, and the six numbermen, dressed as Arhad traders with their kohl-rimmed eyes and heavy cloaks, would pose the greatest hindrance to her escape. She wondered how steep the drop was out the window.

"Still a bit of sand in your hair," frowned the Raven, as he fluffed Mouse's bangs and tidied her clothing with his chilly fingers.

The sand on her personage had come from their short trek across Kor'Khul after landing their skycarriage somewhere in the desert and proceeding to Eod on foot. At the gates of Eod, no one asked many questions of a band of Arhad traders or inspected the heavy bags filled with kings knew what sort of diablerie that the numbermen had hauled from the skycarriage. *Spices*, declared the Broker, his metal teeth hidden by a wrap, his Arhadic perfectly accented and convincing. If she could have, Mouse would have screamed and had them all captured or killed, but regretfully, the Raven's power over her muscles and bones had prevented this. For hourglasses now, since their early dawn march in the desert, she had been at the mercy of his black magik. So efficacious was his power that he had puppeted her as naturally as she moved herself, and she followed along as if she were truly a doting, silent, sewn-up wife of his. More frightening was that this measure of control proved to be not even the smallest inconvenience to him. The nekromancer chatted with her, with *Lenora*, or stopped so that they might kiss now and again. At least she had made use of her imprisonment to listen to the Raven's rambling and see what she could learn to help herself.

If I could just figure out who the fuk Lenora was, I'd have won half the battle, fussed Mouse. She had reached a balance with her repugnance, fear, and logic, and entered the realm of calculating coldness. Thus far, the Raven was content to molest her and fawn over her as if they were the most besotted lovers in Geadhain, though he was careful to dance around any memories they might share. *As if he doesn't want to recall them. A tragedy, yes...I get the same impression from the dead man. If only one of them would give me a morsel to chew on.*

As he adjusted her bustier, the Raven noted the twinkle of thought in his puppet. Perhaps the woman had remembered her manners.

"Speak, Lenora," ordered the Raven, and the cold claw of his magik unclenched itself from Mouse's spine. Last time, before disembarking from the skycarriage, Mouse had spit in the Raven's face, and that had earned her a day as his marionette. Diplomacy was the wiser course, for now. A friendlier approach could possibly benefit her, as a happy lunatic was a pliable one. *I shall play your Lenora, if that is what you seek*, she thought, and gave a strained smile.

"My...my love," she said.

Her greeting did not have the intended result.

Viciously, the Raven grabbed Mouse, turning her chin from side to side, appraising her countenance as he spoke. "You look like her. So very much. I am interested in what the connection might be, and we shall have to find out. But make no mistake, lost child of the Watchers." She was forced into a meeting of stares. "You are *not* Lenora. I am not as mad as my friend shuffling through our bags over there."

CHRISTIAN A. BROWN

Noting the comment, the Broker glanced up from the sack he was looting—removing and counting bags that spilled bits of black powder onto the floor—and waved happily.

"Allow me to explain how you are to behave," the Raven continued. "You are what I shall play with until the real Lenora returns to me. An object, a doll. You would be better off thinking of yourself this way: as property. I have bought you. If you will not be a willing dog, I shall cane you into obedience. Do not forget that. You may continue to play along as Lenora, in fact, I encourage it. Say her name, welcome her spirit to you. The more you invoke her, the more suitable your body will be."

"Suitable? For what?" squeaked Mouse.

The Raven's grin was as dark as murder. "I wouldn't worry about that. Not until we've finished up our business in Eod. I wouldn't have brought you along unless you weren't so determined to escape." He released her face. "A little bit of sunshine would do you good. Lenora had such a lovely complexion. You suffer from the pallor of Menos. Go sit and warm yourself in the light," he commanded, and Mouse's legs and arms moved according to his Will.

Mouse knew not to shout in distress, and was soon poised in a chair at the table like a proper lady: knees together, hands on her lap. The dead man, who had hovered somewhere behind her during the exchange, took the seat opposite to her. His side of the table was in darkness, and the sadness of his face was elongated by shadow. Now that she understood how helpless her outlook had become, her stomach crawled with centipedes of fear.

Help me, she mouthed to the dead man.

The Raven must have seen her plea. He flew across the room in a wind of rage and backhanded Mouse. She cried out but did not pitch to the side, as her body would not allow it.

"How dare you ask *him* for help! Is it my destiny to be betrayed by each of you?" accused the Raven, his eyes swollen with insanity. Mouse had the sense that he had forgotten who she was, despite his reminder a moment ago. He hissed into her face. "Wait, you filthy whore! You just wait, Lenora! How easily you escaped your guilt! Not again, not again. If you think he has suffered, I shall show you the beauty of pain. What it is like to live without your eyes, ears, or tongue. To neither see, hear, nor taste death, but to *feel*

176

the beaks as they tear and the maggots as they chew you from the inside out. Screaming, screaming."

Mouse spit a bit of blood onto the table. "You're right. I'm not Lenora, you fuking maniac, and you're twice as crazy as the Broker. If I ever get my hands back, I'll show you how to scream."

The Raven woke from his bluster. "Iron sages be cursed," he exclaimed. "I seem to have lost myself. Your likeness. Your expressions of sympathy. Even your anger. You are the perfect vessel. You could be her reborn. And soon you will be. So little stitching will be required."

Mouse attempted to make her next wad of spit hit the Raven, yet without being able to twist her body, it barely made it out of her mouth and dribbled down her chin. What's more, the Raven laughed heartily at her resistance, while the melancholy dead man did nothing but stare. She felt the regret rolling off him, though she could not tell if it was for her or a different sadness. Unexpectedly, the Broker interrupted their respective mirth and misery by calling for the Raven.

"The stone!" he lisped. "The stone is warm and wishes to speak!"

If Mouse could have followed the Raven as he went, she would have watched him stride to the Broker, snatch something from the man's hand, and hold it to his ear like a conch. Farspeaking stones were a valuable tool of a Voice's trade, however, and Mouse assumed that one was being used as the Raven demanded complete silence *while the stone delivered its message*. She didn't try to eavesdrop further, as the stones were as airtight as a wax-sealed jar. Mouse toyed with the idea of wailing and barking as loud as she could to ruin the message. But the realities of what would happen to her for her disobedience quelled the urge.

Not dead yet, old girl. Perhaps you'll live to see your thirty-third name day still, Mouse hoped.

Whatever the stone had shared with the Raven put him into a furor. Snippets of his hissing floated her way, and her trained ears caught what they could. *Mother's ears have found him. The betrayer is here, at the palace. A witch, too, whom Mother says we are not to touch. He can wait. No, she considers this one more important. No, I don't know why. Stop asking, I told you. We shall attack him where he feels that he is strongest. Not at the palace, you idiot, at his. At his...with...yes, I agree they make such sparkling music. We shall have to pick out one today. Mother said to take both targets if we are able, the witch above all else. I know, I know. We'll gut him if we can, and I'll deal with Mother. I agree. I had so much more planned for Uncle, so many faces of death. But this will have to do.*

After conferring with the Broker, the Raven handed out orders.

"The six of you will stay. Vortigern, too. We can't have too much attention. Watch our guest. Snap her neck before allowing her to escape. I can still make use of the body if it comes to that, though preservation in this heat could pose an inconvenience."

"Yes, Master," replied Vortigern.

Mouse held her tongue as the Broker and the Raven stormed from the room. In their absence, she sighed in profound relief, and also for reasons twofold. First, she noticed that the Raven's magik was immediately not as potent outside his presence, and she could already move a finger and a toe. She wondered how much more or how quickly the rest of her mobility would return. And finally, in his haste to exit, the Raven had neglected to reseal her mouth. She could speak if she wanted to and she intended to make use of that small freedom. The Broker's men remained about, hunched unseen in corners away from the light, though surely watching her as instructed, so she made the words without sounds to the only creature who might feel mercy toward her. She asked the question that brought him pain and to which she desperately needed an answer.

Who was Lenora?

Initially, the dead man ignored her and found a distraction outside to spy on, yet she could tell that he was pondering by the creasing of his brow. Once more, Mouse pressed the issue, in the slightest whisper, and the dead man turned to her. When asked a third time, the frown folded to the deep lines of time and memory. At last, something was returning to him.

"I...I knew her. Can't...can't remember," muttered the dead man. While staring at Mouse, he pulled out his pocket square and leaned across the table to dab at the drying spittle on her chin. He paused at their contact, his gray fingers skimming her swelling lips, and then dropped his handkerchief in shock. A shudder ran over him—not a normal reaction for one whose nerves were dead. The dead man retreated to his chair and clutched at his chest, trying to calm a spiritual thudding in his withered heart.

"I think...I think that we were in love," he gasped.

Mouse gasped, too, and one of the numbermen snapped at her to stifle herself or he'd slit her throat and drain her in the tub. From then on, she and the dead man sat in the sun, sharing glances—of curiosity, fright, and suspicion. One, grasping at the shattered mirror of thoughts in his head— memories that cut him as he clawed for them and cast bloody reflections that did not reveal themselves clearly. The other, realizing that finally she might have found her way out.

IX

BLOOD PROMISE

I

All through the night, Caenith's forge belched smoke, glowed with embers, and clanged metal tunes. Smithing was the hardest work Morigan had ever done, and surely the dirtiest. Before the first cast of metal had been filled, the forge needed a feast of coal, which left her soot-painted, sweating, and blistered on her hands. Such a helping was only to start the fire, however, and she had more to shovel while Caenith pumped the bellows into the pit. His dark-faced smile, like a creature of the night, gave her encouragement to continue, and she did not slow, not even as the blisters burst or the fire seemed unsatisfied no matter how she fed it. She would look to the Wolf for relief, just as he drank in her body as if it were a cooling tonic, and by nightfall, the long-neglected forge was finally hot enough to smelt.

That leg of the task proved no better, and often Morigan had to return to her stoking, and Caenith to his fanning, in order raise the cylindrical crucible's contents to bubbling. Morigan wondered what material could possibly withstand the temperature of the flames that they were creating, but there was no opportunity over the fire's huffing to ask. She remembered that she had another way, and she focused on the toiling man and sent her bees out to deliver some thought nectar. When the whisper entered Caenith's head, it startled him, and he stopped his pumping for a speck and then continued with a nod to his Fawn. *Grapharite, toughest metal one can forge, brought from the mines of the Mor'Keth,* echoed the bees in the deep timbre of Caenith's voice as they returned to their mistress.

While the sweat poured and the fire roared, she practiced more of her mindwhispering. Caenith, quite accustomed after her first invasion, was always ready with a reply. In many ways, it was more efficient than speaking, particularly in times such as this where conversation was hindered.

The sand is now; the metal wants to sing. Fetch the cast, my Fawn, he whispered back, not the answer she was expecting to her question on metallic simmering points, though she jumped to his charge. Without fear, with only his scorched apron and gloves to protect him, the Wolf squatted in the licking flames and thrust his tongs deep into the white-hot center of the forge, extracting the crucible, which itself glowed as if it held the sun. Morigan tried not to stop and gawk in awe at the Wolf, taking only short glances at his intrepidness, and was able to drag the heavy, black, iron-and-stone cast to Caenith in time for him to pour the liquid fire. Once the crucible was left to cool near the lowering flames, Caenith stripped off his apron and gloves and helped Morigan get out of hers. Even beneath their protections, they were tarred as two birds doused in oil. He held her filthy body to his, and they watched the metal for a spell.

"The making is not complete," he said suddenly. "Come, my Fawn. Metal does not wait."

He sat Morigan on the bench while he gathered his chisels, mallets, and a smaller anvil, arranging them before his Fawn, and then knelt behind her. Once set, they began to coax the radiant ingot to life. Many a time, Caenith wrapped his grip around Morigan's fist to give the hammer strength, and it shivered through them as a singular twitch of exertion. Or when it was his turn to draw and bend the metal with wrathful strokes, he did not realize that it was Morigan's hand that held the ingot steady between the pincers. He was her might, and she was his balance; together they were one set of hands, one body. If two beings could be any closer, Morigan crossed that final threshold, and the bees bore messages to and from their minds so as not to disrupt the song of the metal. She could hear it as they labored, the music of which Caenith always spoke: the clink of correctness, the hum of pleasure.

The spattering of their sweat was like a constant applause as the weapon was pounded into shape. Morigan's throbbing hands, cracked throat, and hunger dwindled. The hourglass was unknown to her, and there was only the song, smoke, and sweat.

Eventually, a creeping awareness came over her that the redness of the metal had left and that they were using different, finer tools and speaking less and less with the bees out of concentration. The song was slower now. Not far past that, Caenith repeated something several times, and Morigan woke from her dreaminess standing over a pail of black water. She was looking at a dagger lying in Caenith's scarred palm.

Knowing Caenith's work, she could tell that it wasn't purely his. It had a sleek hilt and an elegant blade, curved as a carving knife would be, but she spotted none of his flourishes, other than perhaps its balance and the airy heft that she found as she picked it up. Still, she discovered his artistry as she turned the blade over: on the spine and cutting edge was a calligraphy of runes and etched ivy.

"Exquisite," commented Morigan, though she could not read any of the letters. "What does it say?"

Caenith's fingers were too thick to point out the particulars, so he pointed along the blade as he described what was written. "In ancient Ghaedic, it tells our story. Here, of a wind that brought you to me. There, of a lonely smith, a broken wolf, a shattered man. You, the woman of fire and old magik. Our trip under Eod. The first time I tasted you...it's all there, up until this moment. It may seem bare, only because our story does not end with this day; it begins. I doubt that as the seasons pass there will be room enough on the metal to inscribe it all, though we shall try."

Morigan kissed the instructing hand and held it to her chest.

"What now?" she asked.

"Now I bind its hilt, find it a sheath that will fit, and you tend to those blisters on your hands. Cleanse the toil from yourself. My tub works...I shall join you when I am finished. So that we can consider a name," said Caenith.

"A name," agreed Morigan.

She wandered to the corner. Once there, she was amused and not terribly surprised to learn that Caenith's tub had none of Eod's modern conveniences—no faucets or taps, only an arm-operated pump. Thus, with more sweat and grunting, she got to work on filling the bath. At least the water she pumped was steaming and delightfully scouring on her skin, once she had undressed and slid into the tub's roomy ceramic embrace. She was reclining with her ears under the water when she felt Caenith's presence shadow her. For a time, Caenith watched the Fawn. He was holding their dagger and breathless at the nymph—her net of red hair, silky limbs, and lily-white breasts floating on the water. When he climbed into the tub, black-skinned and monstrously aroused, with his canvas of knots and veins coruscating in the sensuous light of dawn, Morigan was as terrified of as she was excited by what was to happen. Sex was not his intent, however, for they had not taken their oaths. Caenith set the dagger down on the rim of the bathtub, untied his hair, and doused his head. Then he scrubbed his beard and torso. After cleaning off enough of the dirt, he glided his hands up Morigan's thighs and pulled her near so that their softest parts touched. She could feel that he was no longer hard with desire. In fact, his features were weighed with remorse. Morigan cupped the sides of his face and waited for him to say what was clearly troubling him.

"You have cleansed yourself of doubt. You have put the pain of your mother in a box of memories, where you can honor and examine it as you wish. But I have yet to share my sadness and my wickedness with you," said Caenith.

"Your wickedness?" asked Morigan.

Shamefully, the Wolf nodded and would not meet her eyes.

"Tell me," she insisted.

"I...am old," he sighed. "I have wandered to many places on Geadhain. My tribe in the East has long fallen, or been driven to dishonorable ends to protect our kind. I have seen the Salt Forests of the West, the Land of the Sun King in the South, Eod in the North, and all places in between. And once, the Iron City, too."

"Menos?"

"Yes. Years, hundreds of years ago. I lived there. I...killed there. In the pits where men fight other men for the entertainment of masters and for coin. I was the greatest of that age. A...a monster, some would say."

Morigan could not claim to know much of the Iron City, only that its society was as barbaric as Eod's was righteous. She knew that one could find any pleasure in Menos, no matter how dark, so long as one paid for it. The sicker the sin, the greater the price. Nonetheless, nothing could sour her feelings for the Wolf. She needed to understand his state of mind, though, for she knew he was a hunter, not a ruthless killer. She wanted to know what had driven him to abandon his virtue.

"Why?" she whispered.

Caenith fought for justification himself. *What brought you to that pit? What kept you there?* he frowned. As tight as their bodies were, and as raw as the moment was, a few of Morigan's intrepid bees crept into the chinks in Caenith's armor, which they had yet been unable to penetrate. The nectar in him was sweet with sorrow and self-loathing. The bees drank, and Morigan blinked.

She is in a roaring coliseum, underground surely, for the noise echoes painfully in the ear, and the dankness of death is like a fog in this airless space. At the center of the ring, she stands, screaming to the vile masters who cheer her from what they think to be safe distances, though she could bound to every one of them and rip off their heads with the merest wish. Her body is impenetrable; she could not be stronger or faster if she were steel and lightning. She needs no armor, no sword; those are for the fleshy piles of sundered limbs and spooled entrails that warm her feet.

"I am death. I am the Wolf. Worship and fear me. You live only because I have not hunted you yet. I live because I am life. I am unbound by grief. I am alone. I am lord of all," she rejoices. Yet all that exits her mouth is a garbled howl.

In a breath, she returned to the world and spoke. "A wolf without a pack. A man whom time cast out. I can see the sadness that you carried with you. Too proud to die, too weary to live. You wanted to forget, as that was all that remained of you. You gave in to every black urge in your spirit. You surrendered to the Wolf. You let the beast ride you because the man was tired of living."

"Y-yes!" exclaimed Caenith. "Did you? Were you—"

"I was. Slipped right in. I think I am growing stronger, but that is not the point."

"No, it is not," scowled Caenith, and tried to look away again.

Morigan held his head. "Face this. Speak of this. This is what you must do."

"My Fawn, you must know that I would never again—"

"You can't say that, Caenith. The darkness is there, waiting, in all of us. Sadly, it is wilder and more demanding of its freedom in you than in most. How long have you carried this, Caenith? This terrible guilt? Is this why you now create in silence? Seeking to balance through discipline and art the crimes you feel you have committed? Is that not just the other side of the sufferance? It seems no better than surrendering to the Wolf."

"You do not know what you say. I feel nothing but regret for those years. I took many lives. Hundreds, possibly thousands. The red haze I was in does not permit me to recall how many I tore in twain."

Morigan was fearsome as she said, "Lives that chose to be taken. There are worse fates in Menos than offering up one's life to the sword, I hear. I am not one to lightly consider murder; every life is a loss. But there is a difference between death by choice and death by cold error or design. And what of your choices? If you are a man who can live many lifetimes, then be just that, Caenith. *Live another life.* You have already proven that you can. As a smith and a hermit. Now it is time to choose another. A life with me. Perhaps a balance of man and Wolf will bring you the strength that you need to tame each."

She could sense the conflict boiling under his twisting face in how his heart sped up and he suddenly wrenched her against himself, wrapping his grand limbs about her until she thought she might go numb. As he released himself of his ancient shame, his body slowly unclenched. He had not been weeping, although his flesh trembled with similar relief. He gazed upon his Fawn in wonder.

"You are a woman like no other. I feel as if each new day you become something greater."

Morigan blushed and smiled.

"I have thought of a name," she said.

"For what?"

"For my dagger. What is the old Ghaedic word for penance?"

Caenith pondered, then replied, "*Siogtine,* though it also means the freedom that comes after. The quest and the reward are as one."

"Then you have earned your penance, and I shall be your reward."

The Wolf's eyes caught the light of dawn peeking through the roof and flared it to glory.

"If you will have it, I would bleed myself and swear myself to you. Tonight," he declared.

"I would have it," answered Morigan.

As the sun invaded the den, they washed each other clean. Sometimes Caenith licked Morigan's pearly skin, as wolves do, and she accepted it, as she accepted him. Though their flesh was tempting to the other, any passion was restrained by the jittery excitement of what they were about to do. For Morigan, it was the final plunge off a cliff that began with exhilaration and had not relented since. For the Wolf, it was the elation of finding this most precious she-wolf and woman who could love him as not one thing but two, and whom he felt all the solitude of his life had prepared him to revere, honor, and protect. They dressed their glistening forms in what sooty clothes were about, having decided to see if the palace could provide them with finer attire. If not, they would make the blood promise as is. No petty mortal decorum would stop them. Tonight they would speak the oldest oaths and bleed their devotion into the other.

Tonight they would be one.

II

How quickly the day fled in preparation for their union. While the plan was for an unassuming ceremony, everything changed once the lovers appeared at Thule's chamber, invited themselves in, and informed him of their intentions to be wed by blood and ancient promises. The sage received the news with a pale bleak face, like a man who had been told that he had days to live.

"I should tell the queen, if you will permit me," said Thule. "A marriage of this sort—of blood and promise—is historic. These are not customs often seen, and I would like to partake in them, too, if there is room."

Caenith stepped forth and clapped the old man's shoulder as if they were comrades. "In the *Fuilimean*, the blood promise, one or each supplicant can be accompanied by a parent, mentor, sister, or brother. Any who loves them, wholly and truly. I have no one. She has you. The greatest honor among those gathered to celebrate the promise is with the one who binds us. I think that you should tie us."

"Tie you?" questioned Thule.

"With a braid woven of our hair," explained Morigan. "It's quite a simple ritual, as Caenith has described it to me: a binding, a sharing of blood, a trading of promises. I've never heard of so romantic and modest a ceremony. I can't think of a better way for us to be wed."

"To swear to each other," corrected Caenith.

Blood, spoken vows, physical binding. Sounds more like magik than observance. How much you've grown, Morigan. How scared I am for you. So brave and unflappable...and armed, too! Good kings, when did you get a knife? Or that fancy bracelet? You will end up a warrior queen before I know it, fretted Thule.

Caenith clapped the old man again, as he had not replied, his eyes glazed over in thought. "What say you?" asked Caenith.

"Yes! Of course. I shall bind you. I am pleased beyond words to have this duty." Thule bowed. "If there is to be a wedding, or promising, or what have you, we shall need to clean the two of you up. Proper attire! A lady should be clean, anointed, and dressed in more than rags. A man"—Thule appraised the hulking monster in the room, who hadn't worn a shirt in all the time they had been acquainted—"well, ideally a man wears clothes. Nice ones. Top and bottom."

"Oh," said Caenith, genuinely surprised. "I can agree to that. However, finding a tailor who can swath my frame could prove a challenge."

"The palace has many a skilled needle. You needn't worry about that," said Thule, and ran out into the halls to flag down a servant. As luck would have it, he happened to catch Mater Lowelia herself, en route to some emergency that required a belt full of solvents and rags. When she heard of a ceremony—which, despite Thule's mention of blood, she could not conceive as anything but a *normal* wedding—her cheeks lit up like candles.

"Deary mittens!" cried Lowelia, once she'd arrived. "We can't have you two together! No fruit before the feast or you'll spoil your appetites! I don't quite know what witchery the good sage was prattling on about—blood and nonsense—but I do know that good, honest suitors don't see their brides before the promised hourglass! I'll be taking you out of here, my rose. We need to dress you up right and pretty and burn those tatters you call clothing!"

Mater Lowelia swooped to claim Morigan's hand and tugged her out the door. Morigan waved to the Wolf.

"I'll see you tonight!"

"Tonight, my Fawn," vowed the Wolf.

"Does she know? Of Menos?" asked Thule, as soon as they were alone.

"I told her," declared Caenith plainly. "She has seen what I am. I shall strive to be the man that she sees in me, not the creature I have been. You, of all people, should be familiar with that journey."

Thule nodded. As for *what* Caenith had shared with Morigan, whether it was the details of being the ancient pit-fiend or secrets even deeper than that, Thule was unsure. He bet on the latter. Whatever the man was, Thule was no longer cautious of his aims with Morigan. He even respected the smith a little. Affably, Thule slapped Caenith's arm, and then winced as his hand smarted from the blow.

"Let's see if we can't turn you into a gentleman," said Thule.

"You can try," the Wolf said, smiling.

III

"What a vision!" cried Mater Lowelia.

Morigan studied herself in the oval looking glass, as agape as the woman behind her. She was astonished at what the mater had conjured up from only a bolt of fabric, a spool of thread, a pair of shears, and an hourglass or two. Absentmindedly, Morigan stroked the sensuously sheer crimson shift. She turned from side to side to admire its deep neckline and deeper back, and fidgeted with the plaited belt that cinched the garment to voluptuousness. She fiddled with the small sheath at her waist, Caenith's gold bracelet, and the snipped firebuds bound up in the woven crown of her hair. With the prick of her weapon like a thorn, the slimness of her form, and the bloom of her scarlet beauty, Morigan could have been a living rose. She had never felt so lovely; she hardly recognized herself.

"If you were a rose before, you are a queen of the garden now. Oh, look at how you shine!" exclaimed the mater, as she put a hand over her mouth and fought back tears. Mater Lowelia's emotion was infectious, and Morigan's eyes misted as well. A moment later, they found themselves in an embrace.

"As pretty as the queen herself," whispered the mater. "Don't you dare share that, now that it's been said, but it's the truth."

"Thank you, Mater," said Morigan, still holding the woman tightly. "I haven't had a mother in too many years to count, but you are certainly close to one. You will join us tonight, yes?"

"Of course."

Once they were done squeezing the tears out of each other, Mater Lowelia pulled back and fluffed the garment, and then lovingly tucked any loose bits of hair back into Morigan's crown—leaving a few crimson twists near her ears.

"You are a daughter to me on this day," admitted the mater.

The bees buzzed and stung Morigan's head with a vision.

She is a handful of life, made still and pale from death: an infant's corpse wrapped in white cotton, whose wood resting box is far older than its occupant. She was not even a year when she died, when that monster took her—

"She died. Your daughter," blurted Morigan.

Cannily, the mater eyed the young witch. "I was warned that you could sniff out thoughts like a truffle hog. Yes, my daughter passed well before she could ever grow into a flower like you."

"I'm sorry, I shouldn't have said anything."

"No, no, my rose, perhaps you should. I have not thought of my Cecelia in some time. Not remembering is almost the same as forgetting, and that is a disservice to the dead," she said, her cheeriness wilting to gloom. Sighing heavily, the mater padded over to the bed in this humble room; her living arrangements were as simple as what Morigan had slept in, if a little more untidy, with a loom and sewing board in one corner and a dresser in another. Morigan left the mirror and knelt by the mater. The older woman was wringing her hands, and Morigan took them, steadying the tremors of emotion in the woman. The mind-witch had to will the bees not to drink in this current of sorrow, and they unhappily droned at their confinement, but went no further. The mater tipped her head.

"It's an awful tale. I shouldn't spoil your wedding day with it."

"It's not a wedding, not exactly. And I've seen far worse than you might think," replied Morigan. "As Caenith has explained it, the cleansing of one's personal ghosts is an important step in the blood promise. Each of us has done this, and I feel that I am a wiser, stronger woman for doing so. If you have not thought of Cecelia, then you should. I am an ear, if you want it."

"You're likely right," sniffed the mater. "There is a wisdom to you that is not seen on younger faces. What a strange girl you are. I shall tell you, then, and I'd warn you not to make the same mistakes, but you seem much smarter than I am. When I was around your age, I made a terrible choice with whom I chose to love. My husband, Trevor Borvine"—her face crinkled in anger, and she spit on the floor—"well, that should give you an idea what I think of him. A wretched, worthless boor as poor and small in every way that your choice of gentleman is rich and grand. Came from an established line of failures. I should have known better; any woman would have."

The mater reclaimed her hands and hung her head in them; it was a while before she continued. "My little Cecelia must have been crying, as children do. I only stepped away for a speck to check on the laundry drying on the roof. Bloody stone that was Trevor never moved unless the ale ran out. I never allowed him to be alone with her for long. I worried that he might do...well, that he might do what he did. Shook her. Scrambled her tiny brains and then put her back in the crib when she went quiet. I don't even think he knew she was dead. I remember that sound, even though I was outside. Her tiny scream, then the coldest and longest silence." Both women shuddered. "A calm you know ain't right to hear."

The mater's eyes gleamed now, with tears and something else, too. "I wasn't myself after that. Even now, it's quite a haze. I can't remember what happened. I carved him up, I'm told. Almost killed him, but left him crippled enough to live on in misery. Some would say that is a fairer punishment. He'll never hurt another child again. He doesn't have the fingers to pick one up or the prick to make one."

Morigan swallowed; the bees were nursing off the waves of dark fury coming from the mater—a mother's love twisted into poison. While Morigan's silver swarm wanted to show her more, to show their mistress *everything*, she reinforced her desire not to see past the slivers of a flickering knife and spurts of blood that they fed her anyway.

"I was brought before the King's Court, as the Silver Watch couldn't decide what to do with me. Whether I was mad or a dangerous villain, they could not say. And neither could I, my memory being as fuzzy as it was. That was the first time I met the king and queen, though my gran spoke so highly of them. She was a mater of yore; I think I told you that. In any case, unless you're born inside the palace you don't live there. Too many concerns with persons coming and going, so folk lead double lives, to and fro, a month at the palace, a week at home. Even when her mind turned to gruel, Gran still recalled how fair and handsome our king was. Mooned over the man like she was sixteen summers young."

A reverence fell over the mater, and she held her listener in a long stare. "If you've never seen him, though, you don't know how short those praises fall. All covered in blood like a rabid lunatic I am, and he treats me as if I was a lamb tumbled down the hillside. Holds me as if I am the one who has died. You can sense kindness in him, a depth so old that he feels like a father, brother, and lover in one. Instant trust. He told me that he would help me remember...took me to the *Hall*."

"The Hall?"

"The Hall of Memories, my rose, one wonder after another that day. For that was a place as glorious as its master. Crystal and glass and *music*...but alive. I'm not enough of a bard to sing its miracles, so I won't try. I understand that it's a vault of a kind. Keeps memories and history. Pulls them out of people's heads, a bit like your tricks, I assume. He had me lie down, and I did, as I would have done anything for him—you don't know until you meet him how powerful his commands can be. It wasn't the kindest experience, what happened next. Quite like a hangover mixed with a pot banged on the head. When it was over, the king, the queen, and the Silver Watch had seen all they needed to see. They never told me what, but offered me pardon, stating that the murder of my Cecelia had temporarily cooked my noggin like a boiled egg. As if that mercy wasn't enough, their sift through my truths showed my relationship to Gretchen Larson, previous mater of the White Heart, twice removed at that point. One of the queen's favorites, Gran was! What marvelous luck! They offered me a new life, right then and there, as I lay on the floor weeping in sadness, happiness, and quite a bit of confusion."

Mater Lowelia clapped her thighs and stood. She crushed her downhearted mood with a smile. "Worked my way up from a scullery lass. We Larsons are like moths, a small nibble here and there, and soon we have the whole closet. There you have it, my rose, a tale destined for unhappiness with an end that not even I could predict. You certainly do have a good ear. I think it helps to confess to someone you know can pull the truth out of you if she wanted. Now, you have a wedding you need to be at—don't open your mouth, I'll call it what I do. Up, up, let's have a look at you."

Morigan rose for the inspection. Once the mater had spun her round, she kissed the young woman on the cheek.

"Perfect! This could very well be the perfect day. I wonder how handsome your smith is? Let's not keep him waiting."

Hand in hand, they were skipping toward the door as if they were giggling sisters when a stitch formed in Morigan's side.

"Ow!" she cried, as a pain shot into her abdomen and back. She wasn't worried or in agony, but the throbbing discomfort was familiar. "Really? Tonight of all nights?" moaned Morigan.

Being the orchestrator of hundreds of women each day, Mater Lowelia knew the signs. She rubbed the girl's back. "At least the dress is red, so don't worry if you've messed it. I've got some sanitary rags around. We'll dress you up tight as a master's dowry daughter. Nothing so sad as chastity on a wedding day. I feel for you, my rose. I truly do. I'd be rubbing myself like a heated puss every time that man so much—"

"The rags," snapped Morigan, whose mood was quickly spoiling.

Grimly, the mater strode off to rifle through her drawers, and Morigan rubbed her stomach and squeezed her legs together. Regardless of her body's rebellion, she was unfaltering in her conviction to go through with the ceremony. A bit of blood to the evening was appropriate, come to think, and there would be more before the night's end.

IV

A red sky, a blood king, and a scarlet bride all joined for a ceremony of blood, observed Thule. Had he known that Morigan was bleeding, too, the rain of signs would have been absurd to consider. An oracle was unnecessary to see that the couple's path would be as crimson as their union. At Mifanwae's grave, the promise seekers and their observers had gathered. A site of one's ancestors was required, and this was the nearest of either promise seeker's bloodline that would be found this side of Geadhain. Thule didn't have the time to investigate much more of Fuilimean, aside from what Caenith relayed to him, and the time for inquiry was over. Down the rise, the skycarriages were parked, along with pairs of rigid silver men—their backs turned in polite eschewal—while the queen, her sword, and the mater stood nearer to the promise seekers, rapt with interest. Thule was closest to the promise seekers, waiting for them to finish their weaving, consumed with fatherly fears and doubts. In Caenith's loose white shirt, leather cuffs, and polished boots, Thule had succeeded in grooming him to a person of correct appearances, but the nature of the man seemed unchanged. The transformation would be as temporary and successful as putting clothing on a wild dog, and it was unlikely to persist past today.

While the sun slowly surrendered to darkness, Caenith and Morigan sat on the ground and wove the talisman that was to bind them. He sat behind and around her, while she leaned into his strength, and their harmony was fascinating to behold. For such a large man, Caenith's fingers never got in the way of Morigan's nimble ones, and she threaded over and under the strands he held taut like a master spider. Not once did they appear to speak to each other for instruction. Not once did they make a mistake.

They are closer in habit than even my king and I were. One creature moving in two bodies, marveled the queen, and her gloomier impulses expounded further. *Perhaps this is the new order, and the old reigns are over.*

When the weaving was done, the couple stood and presented Thule with their offering. The sun was nearly spent, and the snowy shadow of the moon could be seen forcing its way into the world. A full moon it would be, and Caenith knew that this night could not be more blessed, more right, even if he could tell that they would not be together in the flesh, judging by his Fawn's metallic scent—a bother not to himself, but an embarrassment for her. Nevertheless, there were greater paths of unity than desire, and that is what they would find tonight. The bees were stronger now, and Morigan could taste his passion, his peppery fumes, and heat. As the lovers lingered in that moment, sniffing and examining each other with animal or extrasensory organs, Morigan was aware that what mortal trappings she had were quickly fading away. Her journey with Caenith had been one metamorphosis after the next. Surely, this was not the end to wonders, but the birth of them. There was only one last cliff to jump off, and a screaming, exhilarating journey to who knew where would begin. Everything she knew as a woman and as a normal being was about to be shed. All this, she intuited and accepted. She was ready.

Are you ready? she whispered into his mind.

The bees carried back a response. *Yes, my Fawn. I have never wanted anything more.*

Morigan took out her dagger. Caenith extended his hand to her, and she sliced a line across his palm from his pinky to his thumb. He didn't wince, and neither did Morigan as the dagger was passed and an identical wound was inflicted on her opposite hand. The couple slipped their hands over the other, interlaced dainty and massive fingers as well as they could, and squeezed. Blood pulsed, mingled, and fell. Then, the two turned to Thule. He was ready and tied their wrists with the talisman. With fortitude Thule spoke, hoping that he recalled the ancient Ghaedic words of the smith correctly.

"*Muad tairscinae gealfoi sigealoch!*" (We offer these promise-sworn to the Gray Man!)

Declared the promise seekers, "*Muad seach.*" (We stand.)

An invocation of the Gray Man surely, for the moon broke the skin of the night and rained whiteness over the rise. The queen shivered in her heavily furred cloak, which offered no protection from the chill of reminiscence.

In her head, Morigan had practiced the vows, and she uttered them along with the Wolf. However their strange union worked, she was never a step ahead or behind him, but perfectly matched, and as fluid with her speech as a native of the old world. If they were to consider where they were or what actions their bodies were taking, they would fail to draw anything other than the deepness of their silver and stone stares or the sense of tumbling together in warmth.

"*Dearthátyr, mo dearthátyr, siúl leh mae.*" (Keeper, my keeper, walk with me.)

A stillness claimed the night. Eerie and whole, a swallowing of sound. *Unnatural, this is unnatural,* Thule thought.

"*Sibh amharc ae dorchaedys.*" (Be my eyes in the dark.)

Was it a trick of the light? wondered Thule, for their eyes gleamed.

"*Tu claíom ae lámh.*" (Be the sword in my hand.)

As the promise seekers spoke, the moon pulsed brightly. Thule looked at the sudden, crisp shadow cast by Mifanwae's cairn, which was sharp and risen as a blade of darkness.

"*Dearthâyr mo dearthâyr, fulaing an fear seo maihrg leh mea.*" (Keeper, my keeper, weather this storm with me.)

A wind howled in from the east, rending the silence and blowing the dust from Mifanwae's cairn in a swarm of sand. The queen clung to Sword Rowena, and Thule bent his head in defense. Only the promise seekers did not notice, as they were warm and whirling and lost in the other.

"*Tu abyr ae ár síscéahl.*" (Sing of our tale.)

As the two spoke, the wind sweeping the plains went from a bluster to a whistle.

"*Dearthâyr, mo dearthâyr, siúl leh mae.*" (Keeper, my keeper, walk with me.)

The oath takers' pulses sped.

She is in a forest, brushed by pine fingers as she races. Laughing as the beast growls and pants upon her back. She hears it leap, feels its weight upon her, and tumbles in the leaves to see Caenith on top of her. He kisses her and then bites her tongue. She bites his in turn and their mouths fill with blood.

"*Goh an deireadh.*" (To the end.)

In a rush, the two were back in their flesh, though nothing was the same in either.

Away went the tired song of the wind, and the brilliant moon dimmed to a natural brightness. None of the observers on the rise spoke, as each was torn by private reservations toward what, exactly, he or she had seen. While there was no prickling of magik, there was little doubt that they were witnesses to mystical events. The expressions of wonderment were carved strongest on the bloodmates, or seen by the feathery touches they gave to each other, as if *feeling*—skin, hair, joy, life—for the first time. More than any, the queen understood the thrill of what they were experiencing, the bliss of knowing another inside oneself. Normal folks could make such promises, bind them in blood, and be left with sore hands and happy hearts at what they had done. But when the supernatural united and swore the oaths that the kings themselves once swore, impossible things were made possible. Feelings, souls, and magik all blurred.

And here I stand, as a mortal who was bound in blood to one who would not die. Think of how it changed me. What of you two? Pale Daughter of the Moon and creature who is not quite a man? What dark miracle have you birthed together this eve? pondered the queen.

All fair questions, and precisely what Morigan and Caenith struggled with: the sense of another within themselves. For the Wolf was truly inside Morigan—as a second heartbeat that raced incredibly fast with adrenaline and power—the throbbing cadence of a hunter. She didn't think she could run as speedily as he could, but she sensed the surety and confidence of a man who knew he could. Caenith was a river of heat, hunger, and craving all forded by unshakable control. He was a storm in a bottle, or a fire that could Will what it was to burn: dangerous, yet somehow balanced. And she found herself smiling, trembling, and sweating in fever as the river of her bloodmate washed her from head to foot. If Caenith was a river of passion, then Morigan was the ship to navigate his raging waters. Her courage was a wind to swell any sail, her compassion a light to shine away the dark. She was a virgin to her very soul, a creature untainted by sin or darkness. Like a white fawn, which not even the lords of fang and claw hunted, or the laugh of a child. Morigan filled him with a breath of cool light, making him brighter and kinder by its presence. She was a star to guide him, one to look to for hope. Not with Aghna had he felt this completion, this dazzling wholeness, and he was as stricken as the maiden was.

"My star," The Wolf gasped.

"My river," Morigan whispered.

Mater Lowelia was the least aware or most dismissive of the strangeness of the evening. There had been a bit of wind, things seemed quite dramatic for a speck, but that was over for a few sands now. She wanted a kiss, and she called for it.

"Kiss the bride!"

Caenith growled through the overwhelming tides pushing and pulling them apart, and he came to Morigan's mouth as if he might eat it. When they kissed, the star inside him pierced his head and eyes with brilliance. He could sense nothing but Morigan's brightness, rocking him like a child, just as Morigan was swept down the rapids of his passion, smashing against rocks of his hunger, lust, and strength, and swooning more with every impact. When the bloodmates parted, their senses faded back to them, and they immediately wanted another taste of the other's soul. A second kiss was too much, and the young woman was wobbling when it ended. Caenith had yet to let go of her, though, and he swept her off her feet, their bracelet of bloody hair snapping and falling to the sand, and then howled in ecstasy to the moon—for his bloodmate, for their unity, for the possibility that he would never be alone again. In that instant, everyone present, including the shaken men below, knew that they were in the presence of immortal beings. Caenith turned to Thule. The silver and stone gazes of the promise seekers were distant and frightening to behold, as if they held starry secrets that the old sorcerer could never fathom.

"We are one," declared the Wolf, in a growl that shook the soil and spilled dirt down the rise.

"The world will break before we do," said the lovers.

With that, the Wolf leaped from the rise, leaving only a cloud and a trail of dust to follow. Off into the desert they had gone, faster than any comet ever seen.

"King's mercy! Deary mittens! Holy shite!" shouted Mater Lowelia, running up to Thule. "He howled! Then he—" She made a series of agitated, sweeping gestures. "What the...? What was that?"

"That was a wolf's howl," muttered the queen, as she and her sword strode up to join them.

Mater Lowelia bowed. "Oh, do pardon my crassness, Your Majesty! I wasn't expecting such a fright. Will my little rose be safe? Should we alert the Watch?"

"No," sighed Thule. Now that the shock was over, he remembered he had hands and drew them over his face. "He would never harm her. And she is no frail flower herself. She is equally as strange as he is, I think."

"If that's the long and the short of it, then I'd like to go home," complained the mater, and stomped down the rise.

Before Thule left, there was a final task that Caenith had asked of him. He picked up the tacky plait of hair and placed it amid the stones of Mifanwae's cairn, burying it somewhat so that the wind would not steal it. The queen and her sword were patient and watchful while he tended to the grave. Mayhap it was the moon's waxy light, but Her Majesty appeared quite drawn when Thule approached her.

"Times are shifting, my friend," she said sullenly. "I feel for the first time ever that I am growing old."

The sage patted her shoulder. "That is an ache I know all too well."

"That you do. That you do."

With the sage on one arm and Sword Rowena on the other, the queen and her company started their descent toward the skycarriages.

"I have considered your request," said Queen Lila, when they were still out of the earshot of most. "There are far too many mysteries sprouting in Geadhain's garden, and if we are to root out the weeds, we must assemble whatever tools we can. I shall grant you and the young witch access to the Hall of Memories. I shall be present for the investigation, and if anything begins to go awry, we shall stop. Does this suit you?"

"It does, my Queen."

The matter was settled. For the journey home, Mater Lowelia decided to ride by herself in the vessel that had brought Morigan. The mater didn't want to speak or think too hard on what the night had shown her. She turned out the lights in the cabin and rode in darkness, though try as she might to spurn her worries, now and again her mind wandered to where the maiden was and if she was being mauled or eaten by her uncanny mate. A similar brooding occupied the cabin of the second ship. There, three persons stared out windows, watching the stars and mountains stream by, while they pondered rituals of blood, red skies, white moons, and howling men.

V

Is this normal? asked Morigan.

Nothing about us is normal...not anymore, replied Caenith.

The two were in their secret glade, lying on a nest of Caenith's old vest and his new shirt. They had been kissing and exploring each other, letting raw bolts of emotion tear into the other. Morigan couldn't say how long it had been, except that it was still night. Come a point, Morigan caught the large fingers that were playing with her hair. She could feel the Wolf's purring fascination at the softness and color of it, and not from the bees—who were no longer needed—but from a new channel of communication that was undiscovered before tonight.

Should we stop, Caenith? I'm starting to lose touch with what's happening.

As you wish, answered Caenith.

Speaking in their heads was more convenient than using tongues, especially when those organs could be used for better ends, which Caenith proved as he licked his way off his bloodmate. He hoisted her up. She smelled of every sacred and golden thing in the world—sunlight, meadows, sweet sweat, and honeysuckle—and it took great restraint not to taste her again. From her star, from her constancy, he drew the required self-control.

You've tamed me a little, and somehow made me stronger, he surmised with a smile.

Likewise, the Wolf's bloodlust and bravado was tingling its way through Morigan's nerves, pumping her heart and flushing her breasts and loins.

This is how you always feel, isn't it? This rush, this power? she asked.

Yes.

Well, since you can't have me, you can fight me, she brashly suggested, pulling out her dagger. *Show me how to use this. A part of me is Wolf now, and I would like to know how to scratch with my metal claw.*

Caenith slipped behind her, nudging her feet apart, showing her the arch and spring her legs should have to keep her mobile in a fight. After Morigan learned the basics of positioning, Caenith found himself a hefty branch and trimmed it to a small quarterstaff, which was more of a rod in his great hand, and the martial training began.

From then on, the lessons came and went quickly, for Morigan was an apt pupil. In her step, there was a new nimbleness, an extension of her natural grace toward more sinister motives. When she thrusted, it was as swift and well aimed as rifle shot; when she parried, she could riposte like a coiled snake. She wasn't the sort of fighter who would deal sundering blows, not a brute like the Wolf; she was a more elegant predator: a black cat stalking the shadows, or a swooping taloned bird. Soon, so much time had fled that the deep of night blushed with dawn. The two were sweaty and spent as if they had made love, and in a way, they had, tossing shouts and violent surges of emotion back and forth, or in moments where Caenith pressed his muscles against Morigan and manipulated her limbs through sweeps and drills. Once they realized the hourglass, the night's training ended, and Morigan stripped off her top, unbound her crown of hair, and joined her naked bloodmate at the pool to splash the perspiration from herself.

Once bathed, they dressed. She watched him struggle into his clothing, perhaps the only act he performed without dexterousness, and grinned at his awkwardness. For his incivility was a piece of her now, that animal in the skin of a man, that man who wrestled with his animal. And while she didn't feel any fangs or fur, she was irreversibly transformed. Wilder, yes. Braver, as well. Quicker, too, if she had to guess, for she'd never held a proper weapon before and yet she felt that she could carve up a man like a shank of beef, if she chose. Perhaps her nose worked a bit better than before, or was it just that Caenith's musk and sweat remained on her skin from all their closeness? When she licked her lips, she could taste the bitter salt of his sweat, and she could hear the whisper of the grass under Caenith's feet as he walked over to her.

I am a new woman. A new creature. I am myself and yet so different.

He offered his bloodmate a hand. They stood and watched the dawn rise to glory.

VI

It was a splendid day by the cave, a rare conjunction of cottony skies and gentle breezes rustling the green roofs of Alabion. Elemech and Ealasyd found themselves in the sunshine, blinking like moles, as it had been a while since they had last poked their heads outside, since Eean's passing. Everything they needed was within the cave: lichens, lizards, water, and moss. Mother Geadhain saw to provide them with resources never far from home. But Elemech was waxing maternal again, and she'd seen the beautiful weather in her pool and decided to take her younger sister out for some of Alabion's pine-spiced air. Sadly, the magik of the day could not improve her little sister's mood, and the girl sat near the cliff's drop, looking out over the woods with a frown.

"Come away, Ealasyd. You know we are to be careful when Eean isn't around."

The girl tramped from the edge and kicked her way across the grass toward her sister.

"I miss Eean," she complained, and shoved her rump next to Elemech on the rock on which her sister sat. Elemech held her, and they watched the horizon of foliage and clouds. A flock of blackbirds suddenly cawed and broke the tree line, flying west.

"An omen," declared Elemech.

"Of what?"

"Get me that rabbit, and I shall show you," said Elemech, pointing to a fluffy white hare that nibbled the discarded fruits of a blackberry shrub. Kindly Ealasyd, as innocent as a child's wonder, had a way with animals, and they never shied from her. She picked up the hare, kissing it and ruffling its fur, and brought it to her sister.

"Here," said Elemech, extending her hands.

As Ealasyd passed the animal over, she had an inkling of what her sister was to do by the coldness that ran through her features. In a single painless twist, Elemech broke the creature's neck, and then set its soft body on her lap beneath her budding belly, like a remorseless mother who had committed infanticide. Ealasyd fell to her knees.

"Why! Why would you do that?"

"Death, death is coming. Or something like it. You asked me a question, and I have given you an answer."

"Your lessons are always so cruel, sister," sniffled Ealasyd.

"You can't have kindness without the cruelty. The world has to balance itself out. We'll have rabbit tonight, with pepper and red willow root. It will be so lovely that you'll be thanking this white fellow once he's in your belly, and we'll sing a song about his sacrifice."

"You—you promise?"

"I promise."

The sisters helped each other up and headed into the viny curtain of their home. As they went into the darkness, Ealasyd discovered her cheer.

"I think I shall make something! Our walk has inspired me! I'm feeling the urge!"

Elemech smiled, icy and beautiful. "I'll let you play with your crafts until the hare is ready. Then I'd like to see what stories your crafts have for me. I have a sense they will be *grand*."

X

THE FORGOTTEN

I

"The Hall of Memories is just beyond," announced Thule.

After traveling familiar musty hallways and passing the spot where she and Caenith had fled during their first visit to the library, the five of them had arrived at the heart of the Court of Ideas. Here the dusty shelves parted to a natural cavern supported by limestone pillars and aglow with the same starry mesh that was rampant elsewhere in the palace. When cast upon the green rocks, the radiance was eerie. Their footsteps seemed hollow and echoing, and there was a humming of danger or magik that all could sense, regardless of their attunement to the Arts. Caenith prickled more than most. Since arriving at the palace, he had cringed at nearly every smell, whisper, and sight, all of which were grander than those to which he was accustomed.

Earlier on, they passed a serving girl whose dress was slightly rumpled and who shyly bowed to the queen in their entourage. While others might have noticed only that, Caenith saw the faint greasy fingerprints near the wrinkles on her clothes; he picked a strand of short brown hair from the collar at her neck; he smelled the sweat and saliva of a man who had rubbed his beard there and could identify a pungency of semen creeping out from under her dress. A flush was in the girl's cheeks, and if his ears weren't deceiving him, he thought he could hear within her a crackle of a second heartbeat, the first currents of new life.

You're with child, he realized, and quickly went on to explain his findings to Morigan. What exceptional senses he already possessed appeared to have been honed to microscopic degrees. He was sniffing under the skin, into secrets and souls. As he walked behind the queen and her sword, he might as well have been standing in a draft of the golden woman's emotion. Her mood was as plain to him as his own. Digging deeper, simply allowing his senses to wander, the queen's sweat had the vinegary sharpness of worry, and his lightning eye picked out the evocative way that she rubbed her palm—where there lay a scar so old as to be nothing but a pale wrinkle, which his eyes could see nonetheless—the place where Caenith and Morigan's scars still twinged. The queen was thinking about her bloodmate. About the ritual she had seen. About what she might see inside this strange Hall of Memories, where the wisdom of ancient sages and the Immortal Kings had been transcribed for eternity. She was worried that she might witness a truth she didn't find agreeable, a revelation tied to her mate, which is why she caressed and reminisced upon her long-faded wound.

All this he knew from the smell of her fear and the subtleties of her mannerisms. He wasn't sure if he could shut his omniscience off, nor did he find it all that distracting, having lived with a thousand sensations in his head at once for many an age.

I am myself, only better. He smiled at his bloodmate.

Once they crossed the cavern, they came upon a group of steel-bearing Watchmen. Around a dozen fellows were gathered outside a limestone arch that leaked light like a shuttered furnace. Most of these men Caenith had heard; they had chased Morigan and him from the Court of Ideas before. His new senses informed him of their familiarity by their scents. The Watchmen snapped their spears and backs to attention as Queen Lila approached and hindered no one as the company wove past them into the dim, narrowing corridor of stone. Caenith's ears twinkled with music—bells and xylophones of crystal—and the radiance was brighter to him than anyone as they emerged from shady confines into a hall of pure light. Once the spots sparkled away, Thule announced their arrival, though weakly, as he was struck by wonderment.

"The Hall of Memories."

They stood in a song. From the queer hum that shivered in the grand room to the vertical walls of open-ended tubing that whistled and burped puffs of magik, every aspect of this place was in musical motion. A tintinnabulation came from the pipes or was carried in the dew of the shimmering mist that rose to the top of the room, where more cylinders and convolutions were stacked like coral and the deepest heights were lost in a congestion of golden fog. Glass ran under their feet, and a universe of pale space and whiter constellations spun beneath it, drifting and pulsing in tune to the symphony of the hall. The company wandered in the musical cosmos, gaping and quiet, led by Queen Lila toward a crystalline bench in the center of the chamber that was nearly imperceptible in the luminance. Caenith spotted it, and he noted the mossy fragrances of extreme age that filled his nostrils like dander. This was not a natural smell, but his perception of it, of the conglomeration of magik, time, and history distilled in the smoke and sorcery of the chamber. *The spice of antiquity*, he decided.

"My king has always likened magik to music," said the queen as they walked. "Both are higher Arts; both arise from passion. When he created the Hall of Memories, it was to record the Art of the Wise. The memories of sages, witches, and fair rulers, as well as poets, philosophers, and heroes, so that he—and others—might ever reflect on their achievements. Those who would contribute each made the journey here at one time. Sometimes, it was the last journey they took, and their record would serve as their final testament."

Queen Lila reached the bench and settled upon it, with her sword standing over her. She patted the space beside her for Morigan. Caenith stood by her side, mirroring Rowena, while Thule floated around the company marveling at the hall's construction. Morigan and Queen Lila traded a long stare.

"Why am I here, Your Majesty?" asked Morigan. She and Caenith had returned this morning, knowing that they had left Thule in a state of shock and worry with their sudden disappearance. They had not anticipated any of this, as magnificent as it was.

Queen Lila waved her hand, her fingers looking as if they were solid gold in the light. "All this was created by our king's own magik and the knowledge of women like you."

"Women like me?"

"Yes. Enchantresses of the mind. Fugitives from the House of Mysteries. You are not the first witch of your kind to visit Eod, though certainly one of the most adept. Farcasters, seers, and mystics we sought. For a simple repository wasn't true to what Magnus desired to store our history. Any earthspeaker could craft that. He wanted a storyteller, a theater, and a museum in one. He wanted to create a mind."

"Is that what this is?" exclaimed Thule.

"Quite nearly, yes," nodded the queen. "A mind of metal and magik. With piped veins of thought and crystal cells of memory. I am a learned woman and a powerful sorcerer in my own right, but the genius of its making is far past what I could engineer."

While the queen was speaking, the bees were squirming against Morigan's Will, eager to drink the infinite emanations of the Hall of Memories. She was here for a purpose; she was here as a tool to operate this grand machine, to find something. A memory lost or forgotten.

"You need me to find something? A memory? A thought? Of what or who?" asked Morigan.

"The king," suggested the Wolf, with a sniff and a keen glance to the fidgeting the queen was doing with her palm again. Lila felt as if she was in the presence of two oracles, not one.

"That's exactly it," said Thule. He squatted before Morigan and clutched her hands. "But you must be careful. The Hall of Memories has its protections and can entrap the minds that wander too far. The king has memories for himself and himself alone. Those are the most dangerous to find—and the ones that we are after. Are you up for this task? I can only ask, and should you say no, our business here is done."

Morigan was a bolder woman than a week ago. The hauntings in her head, the voice that threatened her, she yearned to confront it again. She was beginning to see that she had a place in these many tangled fates; she would not have met Caenith without them.

"My answer is yes," declared the witch.

The queen nodded.

Morigan shut her eyes and unleashed her swarm. She smiled as Caenith's hand came upon her and his river roared within, knowing that he would be what grounded her, regardless of how the hall might try to snare her consciousness. In the thinness of reality inside the hall, her invisible magik was manifest, and those gathered gasped as she pulsed like a silver star and scattered the chamber with geometric butterflies and intricate equations of light. With the diffusion of magik, so too went Morigan's mind. Although a piece of it remained behind, swimming in a hot red stream of love, and she never forgot what awaited her, despite the spectacular journey that engrossed her senses.

She had entered a place brighter than the hall: a glimmering vastness without end, a nexus of threads of white light. Through the nexus, she soared, fleshless and carefree as a spring breeze. Her silver servants were all around her, crawling along the thrumming strands, nibbling trapped husks of memory, which dazzled her with recollections as they were eaten—none of which were her own. In an instant, she lived a thousand lives: a farmer tilling earth who recorded the soil composition and cycles of his plants; a seamstress in a black city who smuggled filthy, terrified persons to freedom trapped in great skeins of yarn. She was a widow and a mathematician. An ascetic warrior who cast aside his vows for love. She saw a choppy sea and felt the breeze of liberty on her face; she was on a journey to cross it, an explorer. She was once a mapmaker and, at the same time, a smith, a baker, and a philosopher living in a cave. Mother, father, sister, brother. She lived every life, every passion, thrill, and defeat that those who were honored in the Hall of Memories once experienced.

When Morigan was done being a wind, and none of these memories was what she sought, she knew she had to break free from the tide of memories, to move against the current. Not an easy feat, as the nexus was designed to loop and guide a traveler away from its forbidden channels. So she summoned her swarm. They surrounded her in brilliance, and she cut against the strongest tides of light, wanting to see what they were pushing her away from. A normal mind would have fragmented and dissipated, perhaps to be gone forever, but she was no mere consciousness, and she cleaved ahead as crudely as a warship through a creek, until the currents lifted and she drifted in a new region of the hall. Here, the nexus was dark and flickering with phosphorus patches as though she was in the heart of a storm.

Here we are, she thought, and cast her silver servants out into the storm to feed. The first morsel that her bees drew filled her unseen eye with a memory of love.

At once she knows the cold spirit of her host as the king, and the caramel beauty whose hands he holds and bleeds into as the queen. Their Fuilimean this is: done under the stars, alone, somewhere high up in Kor'Keth, where the coldest winds blow and the peaks are muffled in frost. A shadow is with them, a huge beastly thing that could be Caenith as a Wolf, though she knows it is a man—or something similar. She cannot look toward it to examine its curiosities, only ahead into the yellow eyes of her mate. What love her host feels for Lila, a river that is cold and drowning. His pull is inescapable to the woman who loves him, she knows. She pities the new queen then, for this woman is unaware of her doom.

A love to last a thousand years before it is tested, she thinks, and sees a mouth or three prophesying just that and hints of a sinister cave.

Yes, let's start with this, she decided, and the bees swarmed the memory thread and began to devour it.

Back in the chamber, a deathly silence had come over the company. No one had moved since Morigan's flare of light and shower of magik. Caenith did not seem bothered, but calm, for he could sense his bloodmate's travel in the unknown, her fluttering of a million sensations, no different from his twitching perceptions during a hunt, and he knew that she was safe and prowling. Suddenly, the chamber coughed and lumbered to motion, tooting and hissing steam from its pipes, filling the roof with vapors. Underneath the glass floor, the starscape spun, and a golden cloud descended upon them, a heavenly thunderhead, crackling with noise and power. Wonders unfolded within it. At first, there were too many impressions to distinguish anything specific—landscapes, battles, events, people of all sorts—and then the Hall of Memories stuck on a frame, engulfing them in a panoramic vision. From a man's viewpoint, the watchers stared into the face of the queen. Only she was far younger, far browner, and far more innocent in her eyes. The watchers knew this ritual, for they had witnessed it last night, though there was a question as to the enormous shadow hovering over the pair, blocking the soft light of stars.

"Brutus," Queen Lila said spitefully.

A violent red washed through the chamber, and the image folded away.

In the other realm, the place of music and memory, Morigan's bees were unraveling the threads at the speed of thought. Quite distantly, she heard a name spoken, *Brutus*, and knew she should hunt it.

More, more. Show me more, she demanded.

In the stone burrow of a cracked and blasted plain swept by sand and wind, she hides. Her host is the king, and this is his memory. He has made a small green fire to warm himself and is waiting for his brother to return. Somewhere out in the dusty turmoil, his brother hunts to bring them meat and the treasured roots that they can squeeze for water in this lifeless land. This is better than the Long Winter or the Wet Season, though, this Season of Dust. As time drifts by, he paces the cave, stitches up his skin cloak with a bone needle, and practices the tongues of the animals he has heard that stalk the Season of Dust or the ages that were endured before. He thinks he can do better than their caws and roars, and rolls the sounds on his tongue, making them prettier to the ear.

(One day he will hone and share these sounds with others. One day he will teach our world how to speak, Morigan understands in her absolute awareness.)

Sometime into his exercises, Brutus returns. As always, his brother moves too fast to be seen and is simply before him. While he is pale and transcendental, his brother is all things primal. Rawness is embedded in him; it can be noted in his unkempt beard and his luxuriously oiled black hair as curled as a lion's mane; or in his face like a mountain chiseled by lightning—carved nose, caved cheeks, and staid brow; or in the grotesque majesty of his body, a tower of twisted golden muscle, anatomically perfect, yet magnified to an obscenity of bulges and sinew. His sapphire gaze is the empty gaze of a hunter king: a remorseless stalker that has killed countless prey, and it does not soften even as it looks upon his frail brother, this dwarf to his giganticness. Nonetheless, the searing fire that consumes Magnus's chest tells him that he is loved and in no danger from this blood-crusted, naked titan. More than that, Brutus has brought what they need for survival, and throws down the crumpled skylizard that he has plucked from the heavens amid what water-roots he has foraged that day.

As they eat, they chat in their heads, playing with the sounds that Magnus was working on instead of their grunts and pulses of spirit, which has been all the language they have known thus far. Except for each other's names, which ring true in their heads.

(How? Who told you these names? wonders Morigan. And I'll be damned if that king isn't twice the size, rage, and shape of you, Caenith, with a likeness that chills my soul.)

Once the skylizard is gnawed clean of meat—not even its organs left by the giant's appetite—the brothers curl up. Large one over the small one, hot one over the cold one, and they sleep. Even at rest, they bleed fire and ice into each other and haunt the same dreams.

Quaint. It is good to know that Brutus was not always such a monster. Where did you get your names, though, you who had no words? This is not far enough back. I need to go farther, commanded Morigan. More of the thread was chewed, and another memory spilled into her consciousness.

This is an earlier age. A Wet Season. Her host and his brother are slogging through mire and bog, surrounded by hungry plants with serrated leaves and swatting off bloodsuckers as large as sparrows. The ones that land on Brutus, he is too lazy to swat, and they die by their own voraciousness as their stingers snap off on his brushed-gold flesh. But with impossibly agile hands he crushes the ones that would pierce his brother, or snaps the spines of the snakes that wind through the muck, and Magnus is left unharmed in a world that should kill his delicate self. Perhaps he is not so helpless as he appears, though, and when the greater dangers come, the floods and storms that not even his brother can beat back with might, and they are forced to hide in pockets of muck, he can steer the torrential waters off their burrow or ask the lightning to strike somewhere else. One such storm has just passed, and there will not be another for some time. The sky will tell him when it is angry, when it is time to hide, as is the way.

Lulled by this security, her host is not paying attention and he slips into a sinkhole clogged with thorns and sharp stones that rip his tender flesh as his brother hauls him from it. This is hardly the first occasion that his weaker self has been damaged, and his brother coos gently to stem the tears while he carries him to a patch of hardened mud. In a swarm, the mosquitoes follow them, and he wipes some of his brother's red essence on his back and shoulders to keep them busy killing themselves while he sets his charge down. The killer's stare in Brutus softens, and the fire inside her host goes wild as a forest of burning trees: *Magnus is sweating and shaking with the courage of his brother instead of the fear of his injury. Brutus treats him as he has always done, since the first scrape that festered, or the first bone that snapped and would not mend like his did. He chews into his palm with teeth that are suddenly sharp and clasps his brother's shredded shin with that hand. His rich purplish blood is immediately soothing to Magnus, and the fingers of fire and frost between them intensify to a whirling dizziness, a closeness where they cannot say who is wounded, who is strong, who banishes the thunder, and who tears the throats from their meals. When it is over, Brutus licks off the blood and dirt on Magnus's leg. He is satisfied that not even a scar remains. Brutus hoists his brother up on his shoulders and strides on through the bog.*

The Fuilimean, this ancient rite of sharing blood or being with another. So this is where it began. Without words, with the oldest of promises: to live and love the other. While it was interesting, this was not what Morigan sought. She was reversing time, though, going earlier and earlier into the ages, chewing up every one of the king's memory threads. *Almost there,* thought Morigan, and her bees tore ahead down the final fraying line of golden memory, arriving at a tangle, an axis where all such filaments met.

She finds herself in a snowy arctic hollow, cracked by a howling outside. Here in the Long Winter, the cold is vicious and unchallenged by sun. Her host shivers among the crystal teeth of the cavern; his brother's heat is gone, and he is a springling himself, unable to stay warm even under the heaps of pelts in which he has buried himself. So he quivers and waits for the giant to return. This is how time has passed; this is their life. Brutus hunts, they eat, they sleep. They are patient until the Long Winter's endless darkness breaks for a moment with sun and they race out into the tundra to find a new hole to house them before the snow comes down again.

Her host wishes that he could be stronger like his brother, even though the winds whisper to him when they will be calm; this is not a skill that is as valuable as raw might. To pass the time, he sings along with the storm, or makes a familiar sound that is not of the land or beasts of the Long Winter.

"Broo...tus."

(Yes, yes, that is the name. Who taught you that?)

Conjuring his brother's sound fills him with fire and hastens his pulse, and when the other knows that he is being thought about, it is not long before he is summoned from his hunt. Soon after, Brutus climbs in from the crack in the roof, swings from stalactite to stalactite without a care and lands before him; even as a youth, his brother is thrice the size of himself, hairy in places that he is not, unscathed by the cruel winter but for a melting glaze on his skin. Disappointedly, Brutus shakes his frost-beaded mane. No meat was found. Lately, the Long Winter has been a bitterer garden than they are used to; its sparse corners of green where furry things live to be hunted is shrinking and vanishing under ice. Brutus will have to feed him as he has since they were smaller still, and he bites his hand and cradles his brother, who begins to suck on the wound like a teat—mewling in pleasure.

(No one but each other...for how many thousands of years? No language, no comforts but love. Total dependence. Even acting as food for the weaker of you. One to hunt...one to guide. Have you ever been separate creatures? I wonder. For you seem like two halves of the same, my kings.)

Her bees were consuming every glowing drop of memory that floated around her as a rainstorm suspended in time.

She sees a landscape of split earth and magma, smothered under a cloud of ash. An Age of Fire. Her host is clinging to the mane of his brother, who crawls more than he walks, though is still large enough to ride. As young as they are, they know to rely on the other, and while Brutus hops over the scorching shale, Magnus leads them to murky pools that have whispered to him—deep down in charcoal shafts, where they can drink foul water or eat the tasteless, gelatinous fish that swim there. Failing that sustenance, they will bite each other and nurse of that nourishment. In these safer pockets, quiet from the rumbling of the world above, they sleep like sooty kittens and burble their name-sounds to each other.

Younger. Show me the moment. The first moment. The names, commanded Morigan, and the bees flooded their mistress with visions of lava seas, precipitations of flaming rock, and a sky torn with meteors. The bees peeled through age to that pinprick of recall, that one single memory that not even the king could remember, as his mind had not yet formed.

She is in a womb. If she could not feel the hardness of rock under her chubby infant flesh, she would have thought it to be natural cavity, so syrupy and dark the space is. For all the darkness, there is light. Two shimmers of movement. At first, Morigan cannot comprehend the details, and her host's budding eyes certainly do her perception no favors. But she hears the name sounds, though spoken by voices that are not mortal, but are akin to the crackling of earth or static. Elemental booms more than speech.

"BRU-TUS, MAE-GUH-NUS."

Dribbles of dirt fall from unseen reaches, loosened by the noise, and her host is dusted off by two sets of hands that are slickly black and silver as starlight. The touch electrifies and chills him, and as with the heat of his brother, these paralyzing currents convey what words cannot. Love, hope, promise, all the sentiments of a maker to its child. Magnus reaches for the fingers, clasps one, and it puffs away like smoke. Angrily, not wanting to leave, the Makers utter the names of their children in the earth-womb again.

(They cannot stay, knows Morigan. They are only Dreamers to this world.)

The shouts of the Makers fade like thunder, and no hands are there to brush away the rain of soil. The Makers are gone. Before her host can muster a cry, something grunts and burbles beside him. As it pulls him into its warmth, he feels its fire spread across his skin, then inside, too, and he knows that he is safe, that this is his brother, and that they are all that they have and all that the other shall need.

(There. This is what came before, thinks Morigan. Caenith waits for me with a fire of his own that beckons. I shall return to him.)

In the Hall of Memories, the pipes had trumpeted, and the memory-cloud roiled with scenes. The company's astonishment escaped in gasps as the history of the king was unveiled inside misty panes. First they watched Magnus peer out over a wind-blasted wasteland and fumble through the rigors of primitive language. *Is he? Could that be?* cried Thule, as the implications of this vision rattled him. Time continued to reverse itself, through a primordial swamp, a shrieking tundra, and a world of fire. Through each of these inhospitable torments, the brothers bled, fed, and leaned on the other for support. They were mother and father, caretaker and teacher. They were the sum of what the other knew. None of the observers, not even the queen with her king, had seen or known such intimacy, and the chamber throbbed with color and warmth, regardless of how grim was the scene on display. For the hall understood the kings' brotherhood, which was as unquenchable as the world was volatile around them. The queen was not jealous as much as she was cowed by how poor her love for the king was by compare.

What a fool I was to think that I could love only one of them, she despaired. *They are beyond love or lovers, they are the same man. And curse you, Magnus, for allowing me to believe that you could be mine.*

When the womb of shadows appeared in the memory-cloud, not a single member of the company breathed until the vision rippled away. Even as it passed, when the pipes sputtered out their last smoke, the mist sizzled away, and the starry floor slowed in its orbit, the companions found their breath but not their words. They had heard the sonorous voices of the kings' makers, seen the silhouettes of silver and deep starlight—skins of the cosmos, not mortal flesh—and knew that they were witness to the start of a mystery. Though as to what came next, no opinions were presented or even formulated in their stupor. Caenith heard Morigan stir and inhale, coming back from what fantastic spaces she had wandered; he caught her as she swooned from the bench.

"I'm tired," she croaked.

The metaphysical journey through the Hall of Memories had taken a fair toll on Morigan. She could hardly keep her eyes open and had pins and needles running from her face to her feet. Gathering her up in his arms, Caenith said, "My bloodmate needs to rest. We are done here."

As for the queen, she wanted to be alone, to find reason in what she had seen. As quickly as he had announced his exit, Caenith was gone. Thule lagged after him, muttering to himself and fidgeting with his fingers as if they played an invisible instrument. No doubt, he was burning with thoughts. Rowena stayed behind, quiet as she ever was. However, today she was not so inconspicuous and laid a hand atop her trembling queen's. They did not speak; there was nothing to say, no words to console a woman as old as any remembered age, yet younger, weaker, and more fragile than any of the prehistoric specters that had haunted the Hall of Memories.

II

I feel as if we are being given the boot, snickered Morigan, and behind her, Caenith nodded. How better to explain their sudden eviction from the palace the next morning, when they awoke to find an attendant knocking at their door. With polite smiles and obsequious courtesies, he explained that their stay was at an end. *Oh, the queen would see you off, but she is in court today, tending to matters of justice*, the lad had stated. With his new senses, Caenith could smell the milky-sour stink of a lie on him and knew this was not the truth, but what the attendant was instructed to say. *If she is to be shunned for revealing the black skeletons in Eod's royal crypt, then so be it*, spat Caenith. He wasn't the greatest admirer of Eod's sovereigns anyhow, as aloof and clandestine as they were. In the passageways, the glow-weave was still dim with early light. Serendipitously, they bumped into Mater Lowelia— always about, it seemed. The mater was distressed to see them go; she flung an embrace around Morigan.

"Deary mittens! Could my day be more soiled, I ask? My darling love-birds are out of the nest! I suppose you have a tree of your own to get back to."

"We do," said Morigan, smiling.

Although she hadn't thought over which house she would return to, now that she was bound to another, her tired suite in its noisy neighborhood felt inadequate to the rustic hole-in-the-roof den of her Wolf. At that, Caenith's river raged in her, agreeing with her choice.

"Oh, just look at the two of you!" cried the mater, pulling Caenith into the hug. "Goodness, you're a hard thing! Like a man of stone and bark!" After kissing each of their faces, she pushed the two away from herself. "Do come by the White Hearth, when next you're in the palace. I'll fix you up a proper feast, better than the one you missed."

"That would be lovely, though I do not see us in these halls again any-time soon," replied Morigan.

"Maybe not, maybe so. I have an eye for excellence, they say, and not only with what I spice my pots or how I can scrub a floor to shine your smile in. For *people*," winked the mater. "The palace is a place for greatness, and you each have a dollop of your own. You two found your way here once, and I hope you'll find your way here again. If not, I'll invite you as a guest of the mater herself. This I swear!" To stop the tears, the mater bit on a knuckle. "Shoo, my rose. Go on now before I get misty."

With heavy hearts, they parted. Of all their encounters in the palace, they would most miss the mater. As sad as their leaving was, the lovers quickly discovered cheer at the thought of finally being together, unhindered by responsibility or nightmares. Those were for the queen to sort out now, and Morigan felt no remorse for leaving this dark riddle with Her Majesty until she was doubtlessly called to involve herself in it once more.

A break, she excitedly panted to her lover. *From bees and kings and darkness. Only you and me and the current between us.* Whereas previously, back in their private glade, Morigan was apprehensive of losing herself to her mate, of forgetting where he began and she ended, she was excited to finally accept that surrender. Alone, in the privacy of their den. *I would like that*, growled the Wolf.

A winding jaunt had them out on the grand anchorage, with its many silver birds lifting off to parts unknown. In the skies were a scattering of unusually gray clouds, and the day was heavy with shadows. Gray and haggard, Thule matched the sentiment of the heavens and greeted the bloodmates with a nod as they approached the skycarriage set for their departure. Rowena was present and escorted her three passengers inside, seating them in a familiar cabin: in two groups across from each other, like before. As Rowena was to leave them to see to commanding the ship, she paused at the door. A skunky musk wafted to Caenith's nose—a warning of threat.

"It goes without saying that you are to keep your silences on all that has transpired in your time at the palace. Failure to do so would be treason. Punishable by the strictest means," warned the sword.

Rowena did not wait for a reply and left the cabin. The company heard the technomagikal engine cough and then settle into a purr, and in a moment, their stomachs dipped as they left solid ground. The vessel strayed beneath the clouds, and the cabin was hung in gloom. For a while, Morigan watched the shadows twist Thule's face into heinous frowns, and the bees buzzed the black nectar of his unhappiness to her. Caenith could smell it, too, like a rotten fruit that had been squished, and he was grateful when his bloodmate spoke up about it.

"Master Thule, why the long face? This is what you wanted, isn't it? To get to the root of these matters?"

"Thackery is fine from now on, Morigan," sighed the old man. "That name has a certain *repellence* to those with long enough memories to know it. I never should have kept the name at all. But we are bound and cursed and damnably drawn by our blood."

Repellence? she wondered.

Do you not know, my Fawn? Caenith held her closer as their minds whispered. *He is blood of one of the old ruling houses of Menos. The house of Thule. Among the masters of the Iron City, his lineage was feared for their brutality. I knew his grandfathers' grandfathers, and they were wicked men indeed. Spiders in the guise of men, weaving infinite webs. He has that craftiness, too. I can smell it. His story, and how it has taken him from the Iron City to a sage of Eod's Nine Laws is his to tell, though, and I know no more than that.*

Morigan's bees and Caenith's senses did indeed know more, despite his assertation otherwise, and their second senses brought them flickers of a black pit of sadness. Images of skin sacs dangling on curled fingers, cries carried in a rainstorm, and a dread name that Morigan could almost decipher the scratch of in her ear, trickled to the maiden. Likewise, the smell of charcoaled death, the ripeness of the fear that had driven the old sorcerer to Eod, and the carved lines of a hundred scowls of misery told the Wolf that Thule was never, not even for a speck, free of his torment. They knew he had a terrible tale to tell, one of love lost, and family, too, from how he treated Morigan. Wordlessly, the bloodmates seeped their pathos into each other, while the old man kept his watch on the clouds.

We should stay with him a spell, Caenith. As dark as certain hourglasses have been, we have each other, and he has no one but ghosts. He doesn't even have me anymore, my Wolf, at least not all to himself, whispered Morigan, and caressed Caenith's arm.

Caenith took her fingers and kissed them, tip by tip. *You, and only you, should stay with him a spell, then. I don't think he much cares for me, as much of an accord as he and I have reached. Be his daughter for a day. I feel that he misses one. And for you, my bloodmate, I shall prepare a den of fire-flowers and silks, a place so soft and welcoming that when you lie upon it, every piece of you will unfold like an eager mouth, and we can finally taste our desire.*

After the wave of his heat passed, Morigan straightened up. "I was thinking, Master—sorry, Thackery. Caenith has a few duties to tend to at the Armsman."

"Important duties," growled Caenith, sniffing the lily trail of perfume up his Fawn's neck and into her hair.

"Yes." Morgan shivered. "I was thinking that you and I might have supper together, like we used to, after Mother passed."

"You don't have to take pity on me," replied Thackery.

But I do, you stubborn old man, thought Morgan. Leaving her Wolf, Morgan tiptoed across the turbulent cabin with unexplainable dexterity. She sat next to Thackery, who refused to look at her, though he softened as Morgan stole one of his hands. Thackery continued his cranky charade for a while, pretending that he had work to do or tomes to read. *I'm very busy, you know. I'm a sage. I have responsibilities,* he argued. Eventually, Morgan's unrelenting grip and the sudden sunshine in the cabin as the skycarriage prepared for descent, dispelled his resistance, and he accepted that the young woman was sincere in her offer. Once he had halted his protests, the trip to Eod finished in silence. Both she and the Wolf could sense that a calm had blanketed Thackery's troubles, which neither wanted to disturb.

As soon as the skycarriage set down in King's Crown, the passengers were unceremoniously ejected from the craft. No fanfare or bows this time, only a stern, slicing glare from the sword of the queen—a reminder of what she had said earlier. In spite of her menace, the sword was no more intimidating than before, and Thackery gaily waved good-bye as he and his handmaiden, with arms linked, left the vessel.

"My regards to Her Majesty. I am sure we shall be summoned if we are needed."

Caenith's parting remarks were less genial, muttered as he walked down the glass-and-steel stairs.

"Do not threaten my bloodmate or the sage again. I can sense your strength, though it is not nearly enough to end me, or even scratch as a kitten would."

As speedily as the sword's hand shot to the hilt on her belt, she found the smith's boulder of a fist already there, blocking it. He had moved himself without her seeing him do so. She was a fostered daughter of the Arhad, rescued by the queen herself. She did not fear men, not any of them, but she was terrified of this one. Only she had exited the skycarriage; the other

Watchmen were a shouting distance away, which might as well have been the length of Geadhain. Caenith clicked his tongue in disapproval.

"Think before you do that again. Next time, if you forget that I am not your enemy, I shall take your sword and show you how to properly cut with it."

A hint of her bloodmate's hostility churned inside Morigan, and she turned to see Caenith walking away from the sword, who was sneering. *What was that, Caenith? That anger?*

He gave a small shake of his head as he came up to them. *Not anger, my Fawn. A discussion on the order of the hunt. I do not trust this queen. She reeks of desperation, doubt, and terror, and I think she might be as dangerous as the viper in her stare if she is pressed. Her sword certainly is eager enough to spit venom.*

In the short steps it took to reach Thackery's tower, the gust of the sky-carriage's departure had ruffled their backs. At the doorstep, they bid their good-byes. Thackery separated so that he and the Wolf could share a hand-shake and a scrutinizing appraisal.

"Thank you, Caenith, for making her happy. See that she stays that way," he said—a command.

"See that she stays safe," replied the Wolf.

As Thackery let go of the Wolf's hand, he astutely noticed the absence of a scar on a palm that had been deeply wounded the other night. Now that he thought of it, Morigan's hand wasn't bandaged or even injured, to his knowledge. She certainly wore no dressings. A correlation between this oddity and another that he'd recently seen floated tantalizingly in his mind, but refused to spark to a thought.

"If you two are done trading me like a prized sow, it's past midday, and we should get you a spot of tea before you fall asleep, Thackery. One in the morning, one in the afternoon, and you've already missed your first," Morigan said with a grin. "I wouldn't mind a proper bath, either, once we've dealt with that."

I shall return for you at dawn, vowed the Wolf.

They kissed. A tasting that lasted longer than was respectable, and had the prim umbrella ladies and suited gents of King's Crown stopping to exclaim.

"Find something else to peer at! It's love, you wretches! Love!" shouted Thackery.

The two parted with laughter. No spoken good-byes were needed, as they were never truly alone, not anymore. Caenith's river did not ebb in its force, and the Wolf felt no less full of light and balance, and they harbored that togetherness with them as she shut the iron door of Thackery's tower and he went off to prowl the streets.

Perhaps, were they not so immersed in their private wonders, they would have heeded the morbid stink and spiritual stain that had settled over King's Crown. Indeed, Caenith smelled death, but attributed this to an actual passing somewhere nearby, as no one living could surely be responsible for the *unwholesomeness*, the aroma of a week-old corpse left to fart its gassy rot into the sun.

But the smell had a source: a man so handsome and trimly dressed in black that he should have stuck out like a sore thumb on Eod's white streets. From the portico shade of a manse far across the square from Thackery's tower, the Raven watched, sitting in a metal chair twisted in lacy designs and sipping the apricot spirits that his host had provided him. Though the mistress who served him screamed in terror, this was only on the inside. Her powdered face and coif did not sweat, and she did not cry for help, as her body simply would not allow it. Nor would anyone help her. Her maid, Rosalie, was surely dead by now, lying in some closet in a pool of her jellied blood, chewed to pieces by that second maniac that had slipped inside the manse. After watching the handmaiden being savaged and dragged off by a man with metal teeth, the dark stranger ordered her to stop screaming and find some spirits. She did *exactly* as he asked: her body was no more her own. He then had her follow him outside. She'd been tending to the nekromancer since the morning now, watching him watch the square.

As soon as whatever he is waiting for has happened, he's going to kill me, she realized.

The Raven tapped the table he had his drink upon, and the mistress refilled his glass.

"After this drink, my dear, we shall take you away. Your life appears quite dull. No husband, no children, no sense of taste—this glassware is reprehensible." He dinged the crystal. "How unremarkable you are. But your life will end with a *flourish*. I promise you this."

"That was him, yes?" hissed the Broker.

Between the pillars of the elaborate portico were fragrant rosebushes in which the Broker hunkered. If the mistress wished for the one mercy in this nightmare, it was that her head was not locked in his direction: he was picking out scraps of what she felt to be Rosalie from his monster teeth and either sucking them off his fingers or spitting them into the flowers. A bit of vomit rose, but it never made it quite past her tongue and just soured the back of her throat. Fear didn't seem to squeeze her bladder, either, and she had never needed or wanted to piss herself so badly.

"Yes," answered the Raven, after a contemplative pause. "The young witch that Mother wishes us to retrieve is with him, too." He tapped his chin. "I don't know who that large brute of a man was, but I would fancy making a move before he decides to return. Before dusk, if we can. The dark hand of fortune has slapped us, my filthy friend, and we would be fools not to slap the bitch back."

"What if the young witch is with him?"

"Oh, she won't be. He won't allow it. He sees himself as a *protector*." Slamming back his drink, the Raven stood. "Cover up your face; we can't have you smiling at anyone. And you, my dear"—he carelessly flipped his hand—"whatever your name is. Time to go."

"A symphony of screams," said the Broker.

"It will be quite the show," promised the Raven.

III

Morigan sank into the scalding heat of the tub, allowing it to lap at her like a giant tongue. The whole room was a billow of steam, and she picked out shapes in it as if cloudwatching. Most of her fancies were impressions of the Wolf—his gray stare, his rumbling voice, his heat—and it was hard to contemplate anything else as his river ran so fiercely through her flesh. If she closed her eyes, she could smell his musk. When she ran her hand over her lips, she could taste his brandy kisses. And as she lathered up her breasts, she could feel his coarse hands on them. These were more than fantasies, she knew, for he inhabited her now. A welcome possession that did not take control of her, but filled her nonetheless.

Rap! Rap! Rap!

"Everything all right?" called Thackery. "You've been in there awhile."

"Everything is fine. I shall be out in a moment."

"If you say so. Keep in mind that you've been in there almost an hourglass. You'll be as pruned as old Miss Hattersham down the way if you don't get out soon." He became nervous. "Oh, I've left something for you outside the door. It's nothing special. I just...well...it's there, in any event."

Footsteps padded away.

Morigan forgot her fancies for now, as they would be real soon enough. She got out of the tub and didn't take much time throwing on her tired garments and a parting gift from Mater Lowelia: a fresh sanitary napkin, which the woman had slipped into her clothing like a master pickpocket. She threw open the door to see what Thackery had been talking about. Displayed on a silk cloth at her feet were two small twists of living fire: earrings, and exquisite in their make. Morigan was not wooed by material gifts, though she could sense the love and thought behind them, and next to her promise bracelet, she had not known a gift so pure in its giving. She hurried to the mirror to slip out the silver studs she wore and spent a few sands admiring the jewelry as it dazzled against her white flesh.

"You like them?" whispered Thule, peeking around the door frame. "I wasn't sure if you would."

The old man hastened away before she could reply—he was acting stranger than usual. Nonetheless, actions were weightier than words, and she thought of what she could do in gratitude, then rushed to the kitchen and rustled up a midday repast for herself and Thackery: smoked-fish sandwiches and a pot of white-thistle tea for them to share. If this was to be their final time to toast in memory of old, she would do it right and with all the things he enjoyed. While pouring the water for the pot, she paused, distracted by the buzzing of the bees. *Let us out. We need to feed. We have things to show you*, they seemed to say, and in that moment, the gloominess of the kitchen intensified: its hanging cast-iron pans a little blacker; its meek, solitary window a jail's slit of light. The feeling came and went like a wind, and the bees settled down after a speck. Morigan shrugged off the strangeness and took her finished tray upstairs, where Thackery awaited her in his study. Perhaps the glimmer of darkness in the kitchen was foretelling of his cheerlessness. For his hands were gnarled and clawed on the arms of his chair as a vulture's talons, and his face was black and pouting. He looked as if he was about to confess a murder or something worse.

"Thank you for the gift. They are lovely," she said. "I shall never take them out."

"I saw them in the market the other day. I thought that they would look beautiful on you and they do."

Her smile had done nothing to clear up his mood. Morigan walked to him, cautiously speaking as she went. "I could probably tell you what's gotten you so sour, though I'd rather you tell me. I'd like for this night to be one that we remember till our silver days."

Thackery sighed. "Sit down, dear girl."

Morigan claimed the empty footstool and set their meal upon the floor. She knew that she wasn't going to like what Thackery said.

"Is this about Caenith?" she asked.

"No. Though he is, in a sense, related to my contrition. He is an honorable man. He has come clean with you, and so should I."

While he took a pause, the bees grew angry inside her, filling her vision with silver spots. Morigan assumed that this was a new branch of her power, for it carried a sense of apprehension, a warning of events to come. She managed to shoo them away, but not before Caenith caught a ripple of her unrest.

What's going on? he asked.

Nothing to worry over, my Wolf.

"It is time to tell you what brought me to Eod. Of the sins that I ran from," Thackery said, trembling; he wavered between tears and rage.

"Sins?"

Thackery nodded and reached for Morigan's support. As she touched his hands, she had flashes of a black city, like an evil crown rising up amid jagged mountains. "I come from a long line of sinners. Wickedness is in my blood, though I have escaped my calling to it as best I can. I thought I could be forgiven if I helped others escape their fates."

She finds herself in the body of a spry Thackery, whom she remembers. He is in a shite-rank tunnel dripping and sloshing with filth. He glances back to the desperate grimy faces that follow behind him in a chain and offers them a smile of hope.

"Thank you, Whitehawk," they whisper. "We can never thank you enough."

"You smuggled people." Morigan's face wrinkled in recall. "And a black city, I could feel the stain of death thick upon it. What is that horrible place?"

At the realization that the witch was reading him, he did not pull away. He squeezed her hands tighter. "Good. This will be easier for the telling if you sniff what you need from my soul. You have seen true, Morigan. The black city is Menos, a distillation of every evil man has conjured on Geadhain. I was a shepherd to those who dreamed the impossible dream of living outside their station, of being more than cattle for the iron masters and sages. My dear Bethany was the first I saved. Though I did so selfishly, out of love, and I would be cast from Menos for doing so." Tears glimmered down his face now. "I disgraced my name; I damaged my sister's pride; I caused so much harm in breaking from my family. But what worth is a name soaked in blood? At least I had Bethany. She believed that I could be more than what I was born for, and she was right."

At the opening of light, shining like a door to the afterworld, Thackery and the refugees stumble into a pond and a clean starry night. Many of the refugees have never seen a sky that is not gray or streaked with poison. Some flounder and gasp at the sparkles of light—stars—that hang over them. Past the pond, under a shaded embankment of weeping trees, Thackery knows a brown-cloaked maiden crouches, as natural and invisible to the eye as one splash of color among the rest. He knows where to find her; his heart pulls him to the willow, beneath which she has hidden many times now. When they near, Bethany appears from the foliage like a nymph and embraces him.

"Twelve little birds," *she says, counting the folk splashing out of the water.* "Twelve you have given wings to tonight, Whitehawk. Twelve lives and souls."

He does this for his own justice, and for the crimes of his blood. However, most of all, he does this because he loves her. Because he believes no woman as special as she should ever be in chains.

"Who was she? Bethany?" asked Morigan.

"Bethany," muttered Thackery, and sneered the next sentence. "My wife and my pleasure maiden before that. I never touched her, I'll have you know. Not in Menos, not until she asked for it as a free woman. In Menos you can beat, rape, or kill your whores, but it is *unseemly* to marry them. I didn't want to do anything but. I wanted her to want me. And when I saw that what I thought I valued was of no worth to her, I threw it away. She called me Whitehawk, after the bird that takes over abandoned nests and raises any eggs it finds there as its own. That is how she came to see me, a Thule—the most vile of the vile—as a parent to the lost. As a person to be emulated. I never felt so proud as I did with her. She made me a greater man than I ever could have been alone. Braver. Stronger. Kinder. What price can one put on lessons like those?"

Morigan slipped her hands from Thackery's. She didn't want to steal his past; certain details were his pains to share. "What happened to her, Thackery? To Bethany and your child, of whom you never speak?"

Thackery fished for words, which did not come to him. In the long silence that followed, Morigan's bees buzzed in wild circles and pricked at the inside of her head. *Let us out! Let us out!* With their anxiety, the shadows in the room swam like eels, and the sense of dread returned in a throat-choking thickness. A premonition, surely, but a portent of what? Thackery's past? It couldn't be. Before she could calm her hive or make sense of the signs, Caenith's uproar added itself to her unrest. *There is trouble, Morigan. I can feel it in you. I know the quickening of your heart, the sickening of your stomach. That is instinct, Morigan. The hunter's compass. It warns and steers us from danger. You are in danger, even if you know it not. I am coming.*

As Caenith's river surged in her, adrenaline clenched her guts, and she bolted up, kicking over the tray. She fumbled to spin sense out of the alarms shrieking inside her. From outside, a woman's shrill scream of challenge came, shocking them both even more.

"Thackery Hadrian Thule! Fallen master of Menos! Bastard to your bloodline! Will you stand and answer for your disgrace?"

Aghast, the two ran to the window and looked down. Near one of the courtyard's grand fountains, with the statue of an athletic nude pouring a jug of water, stood a woman in a dark coat, her arms flung to the sky as if in prayer. They didn't recognize her immediately, though after much squinting, they thought it could be the white-haired old widow who lived across King's Court from Thackery.

"Mistress Hattersham?" exclaimed Morigan. "Why is she going on like that? How does she know you? The *real* you?"

"It's him," spat Thackery, his features contorting with hatred. "I don't know how he's here; how it's even possible. Stay here; the wards on the tower should keep you safe."

"Safe? Thackery!"

Alas, her shouts only trailed the man, who was gone faster than she thought he could move.

"Come, coward! Face your destiny!" shrieked the mad Mistress Hattersham, her voice so shattering that it was a stone to the glass cage in which Morigan kept her bees. Morigan stumbled and caught herself on the windowsill as her minions spun free, siphoning the dew of fate in the air, at last condensing the doom she felt—and its ties to the sage, to Menos, and to the dark lineage of Thule—into a substance that they could feed their keeper. As the bees returned with that nectar and infused their queen with it, Morigan tumbled from the world.

She is in the cabin again; the one where the shadows of Alabion's trees claw over the house. Never has she watched in this way before: floating as bodiless as a snake of air, circling a scene outside a host, observing as she sees fit. She was correct in saying that her power as a witch was blossoming. Casting aside this irrelevance, she looks to see what the bees have brought her. Little Theadora has just come running to her father after being scared by a man in her window.

(I remember this, yes. Show me. Show me how the fates meet.)

"Sorren," spits Thackery, with the same wrinkled snarl that she saw him do in the other world a moment past, only with a name this time. Breaking glass sounds, and from the milky shadows of Theadora's room steps a man: slender, handsome, and pale, dressed in black and with the cool blue gaze of a Thule.

Here, in the Dreaming, Morigan can see past his exterior charm to the tentacles of shadow that writhe about his soul and to the color of that soul itself, which is black. He is death and ruin and everything foul and wrong with a man. He is one who breaks the unbreakable order. Who twists life. A nekromancer.

"Uncle," he says, with a tip of his head to Thackery.

In what is unexpected from such a gentrified man, there is no preamble, no more dialogue before the violence. As a creature of spirit, outside time, Morigan sees the shadowy feelers lash out and entangle Bethany like a spider's treat, most heavily about her joints, which are then moved—as though she is a puppet—by the nekromancer's curling black soul. The black threads pull, and Bethany bats her husband away (while weeping, screaming inside at her uselessness) and jigs off to the hearth to fetch what the nekromancer has bade: a knife. While Thackery shouts at his wife to stay near him, he cannot see the immaterial or the black threads as Morigan can. He does not know if Bethany is mad or terrified. Regardless, he has his child to protect, and he calls to his Will—his love—and streams with white and gold light. In the cabin, the stars that Bethany and he were dancing to not so long ago are reborn in puffs of crystal light, though they are sharper this time, golden caltrops or angry suns, and they whirl about the cabin.

What happens next is blindingly fast, though Morigan perceives it all. First, the stars launch themselves at the nekromancer, only his aura of tentacles and wickedness blooms like a bubble of oil, and the galaxy of lights is gobbed in tarry magik. In specks—and she slows time down to observe— the globules stretch and vibrate and bristle with unlife: transforming into oil-soaked birds of pure darkness and filling the cabin in a cawing swarm. Immediately, in a torrent of blackness, the birds flock to Theodora and are pecking at her soft eyes and flesh. Thule is knocked aside by their rush, and Theodora's screams are muffled under a pile of shadowbirds; the child is so covered that she could be a black caterpillar, only Morigan dreads what metamorphosis has occurred.

"For Lenora!" cries Bethany, and Morigan can't decide what appalls her more: how Bethany thrusts and carves the blade into her gut or the pangs and wails of sorrow from her that rack Morigan's spiritual self. Unbelievably, this is not pain, only regret that her love has ended so cruelly. On the floor, Thule is sobbing and slipping for balance on the oiled guano of the shadowbirds that feed on his daughter. He watches his wife begin to pull out her insides and he careens into madness. The horror overwhelms his physical clumsiness, and he is buoyed up as the light of his rage inflates him and radiates throughout the cabin. In the center of the room, he hums like a star. Spears of sunlight blast from Thackery. With a piercing whistle, the nekromancer calls his shadowbirds to protect him, and they spiral about him and come together to form an inky cocoon.

Seeing the truth of Thackery's Art as she does, Morigan is lost for a speck in the intricacy and beauty of Thackery's star, shining so hot with love and anger. It could be a poem or a song written in light, with its golden runes and coronas and pulses.

The light fades.

With its drooping struts, raining shingles, and groaning frame, the smoky cabin will not support itself much longer. Before the nekromancer can strike again, Thule clutches Theadora's carcass and stumbles to his wife's hand; he does not stop to examine either of them, as that could destroy him. Morigan can see the black cocoon unraveling behind him; the tentacles are unseen no more but alive and snaking toward Thackery. Yet there is a wash of light, Thackery's star is born anew, and when the tentacles strike, they only collapse the corner and subsequently the roof on the precariously porous dwelling.

Thackery has transported himself, and Morigan does not stay to find out if the nekromancer has survived the trivial inconvenience of a house crumbling on him, for she knows he has. She has to move quickly through the Dreaming to catch Thackery, for spells of translocation, of moving matter through time and space, are the highest of the Arts; they rarely are precise and are only undertaken with the greatest precautions—of which none have been employed. She worries, then, where his terror and confusion have taken him, if they have indeed carried him and the remains of his family to a place where he can at least bury them in dignity.

Alas, the gray mist of the Dreaming parts to rainy weather on a dismal rocky plain, and there is Thackery, given no mercy. No reward for his service as Whitehawk, no justice for the lives he saved. The remains of Bethany and Theadora did not survive the transit. Perhaps in his crazed mind, he had thought they might still live enough to be saved if only he could get them away from Sorren's harm. Though clearly the bags of skin he holds, the hollowed-out faces, the fused puddle of bones, and the greasy crimson offal that are heaped on his knees tell a different story. There will be no burial; there are no corpses to bury, only meat. He has nothing. Only meat. He is nothing. He could not save his family, not even a piece of them. His worthlessness consumes him and gives rise to retching sobs. Horrible noises, stabs to Morigan's metaphysical ear that *singe the blackness of this moment into her soul forever. Morigan has a Will here, she is no more a passenger in the Dreaming, but a captain of its tides, and she does not want to see any more.*

(This is his pain; this is what he bears and what haunts him still. I must help him. He cannot face this alone.)

To leave, it is as simple as Willing it. The bees surround her and carry her through the Dreaming.

Morigan awoke, heaving and half draped out the windowsill. She collected herself and shouted to Caenith. *Thackery, his past. It's caught up with him. Here and now. A nekromancer. His nephew, I think. You're right, Caenith, something terrible is in the air, and I must—*

In the square, she spotted Thackery's tiny gray frame approaching the fountain and its mad keeper. *No! No! That is a bad idea!* buzzed the bees. Clinging to the windowsill, she screamed at the top of her lungs for him to stop, that it was a trap—even if she was unsure how. On the ground, Thackery plodded ahead, grim and set with the readiness for blood. Morigan was shouting that he was walking into a trap, and he was quite aware of that. But he needed only to find the hand that would spring it and cut it off. Mistress Hattersham's obscene ranting had considerably cleared out the square, and onlookers peered from gated gardens or darted for carriages to take them from the area. It was a chancy game that Sorren played, coming here to King's Crown, beneath the Palace of Eod. During his exile, neither the boy nor his mother had shown so bold a hand, which made Thackery all the warier.

How foolish I've been, to think that you would just leave me to rot in my sadness in a kingdom I thought you could not reach. Of course you can reach here. I forget the malice of the spiders from which I come. One never escapes the family web, cursed Thackery.

As he neared the fountain, he shooed off a few younger masters laughing at the madwoman. "Worthless Thule, a shame to the name," berated Mistress Hattersham when he was close. He kept a fair reach from her: she was grimly pale, seemed naked under her overcoat, and her abdomen was distended as if she were pregnant. Without a doubt, Sorren had done something horrid to her. The question was *what.*

"Where are you, Sorren? You spineless whelp! This is what you do? Kill women and children? Enslave the minds of helpless widows? Your Will was never strong enough to work your Black Arts on me! I have no one to defend, nothing to lose. How dare you blame me for the death of a woman who simply didn't love you! Who killed herself to get away from your touch! Can you blame her, you monster? You fight and whine as you always have, from behind your mother's skirts. A coward and a child you will always be! Face me man to man, and we shall see who survives!"

"I don't believe in fair fights," scoffed Mistress Hattersham. Her face was warped with the squint-eyed, teeth-baring sneer of Sorren. "That's a challenge for men who can't outwit their opponents. You underestimate the value of your holdings, too, if you believe there is nothing I can take from you. Know that before you die today, I will have claimed everything you love, everything you care for."

Sorren was quite communicative, which wasn't his style, as Thackery recalled: violence above parley. He scanned the deserted terrace for a black shadow. Sorren would have to be close to control his puppet.

"Why are you stalling, Sorren?"

"Patience," said Mistress Hattersham.

"The longer you stall, the faster the Silver Watch will arrive to have you in chains."

"Timing is everything," the puppet said with a smile.

What was the ploy? wondered Thackery, desperate. He had scoured every shadow in the square, seeking the one that was darkest. Nowhere did Sorren reveal himself, not in the shaded alcoves, or as a peering face from behind a half-drawn curtain. While Sorren gloated in silence, a silver shadow circled over the square: the Watch had arrived.

"Our bird has come," said Mistress Hattersham. "Time is up, dear Uncle. You're terrible at hide-and-seek. So eager to confront the villain that you've left your front door open. A hint: the best hiding places are *right behind you.*"

As Thackery whirled about, Mistress Hattersham began to unbutton her coat, freeing her bloated, stitched-up abdomen to the day. With shaky hands, ones that she knew were engineering her death, she dug out the small glass jar that held a red firebug and popped the container into her mouth: chewing on the glass, swallowing the sparking insect into her stomach. The sage was shining with power, ready to cast a spell, and she ran toward him. Sorren's hold at last broke, or he released a measure of it, and Mistress Hattersham was able to sob—but not to stop her legs—as she threw her arms wide and prepared to embrace the light.

Up in the tower, Morigan had given up on getting Thackery's attention and was dashing down the stairs when the damnable bees stung her with another vision. She staggered as her mind was torn open to a gruesome sight.

Mistress Hattersham is lying on a blood-soaked mattress, calm and still bound with a spark of life to a tortured body that has been emptied out like a taxidermy specimen. Organs lie in a tidy bundle beside her, and the nekromancer, this monster Sorren, stuffs her with pouches of a black powdery substance that mingles with the blood on his arms into a muddy paste. As he works, he whistles, as if he is a happy baker watching his bread rise. To him, this is as normal a chore as that.

"Put out the pipe, you imbecile! Are you trying to level the building? Do it again and I'll make another explosive out of you, fool," he snaps to someone in the room, and then gets back to whistling and filling Mistress Hattersham. He has left in her heart and lungs, buried somewhere under the little bags, and her eyes and all the skin bits that she needs to appear normal until it is time for her to detonate. The eyes, trickling tears, are the last Morigan sees as she spins from the vision.

"An explosive!" *Caenith! An explosion, they've rigged an explosion to kill Thackery!*

KABOOM!

What started with one cataclysmic explosion became a glorious chain of noises, fireworks, and tremors from outside. Each rumble and rip of the air sent Morigan skidding down the stairs. As she fumbled, she dodged debris dislodged from the walls or the flares of blue magik from sorcerous sconces that dropped; were it not for her newfound agility or the fire of the Wolf racing in her veins, she would have been struck unconscious. When the worst of the shocks was over, she was nearly to the bottom of the tower. She saw shadows moving through the dust and called out to them.

"That's the witch; seize her," commanded Sorren. She knew his voice without question.

Out of the smoke they came, swarthy men with cold steel and shrouded faces. She considered racing up the stairs, but her razor senses, as tweaked by nerves as the Wolf's, detected walls of fire and broken stairs that were unsafe for flight. A fight, then. She found her dagger and surely stunned her attackers by leaping at the first one to appear. Although he was heavier, she had the ferocity of a woman thrice her size and the advantage of height from her jump. When they clashed, her dagger skidded and sparked along the sword he raised and finally planted itself somewhere in his collarbone, close enough to a jugular to that she was showered in red warmth. She had never harmed a man before, but she didn't hesitate to dig the dagger in and ensure his passage. Perhaps the Wolf was to blame for her bloodlust; perhaps the shame of murder would come later. For now, rage was all there was. Morigan and her prey tumbled like acrobats down the stairs, and she used him as a meaty pillow to cushion her landing in the tower's lower chamber.

She wasted not a speck getting up. Caenith's river was turbulent in her, flooding her with a shadow of his strength and anger, and she sprang off the corpse and onto the back of the nearest attacker—who smelled of herbs and death—and gored him repeatedly along his spine. He should have died almost instantly. Instead, he merely stumbled, and by the time she realized that her victim wasn't dying, his cold grip had seized her and thrown her onto the tile with a strength that slammed the wind out of her lungs. By then, other hands were grabbing her, too many to slash, despite how slippery and spidery she was. In the struggle, her wrist was twisted free of its weapon. At that, she growled in defiance and managed to kick one man in the groin. She choked another with his necklace until that broke off with a flash and sent him flailing away, screaming and cooked by blue fire that ran over him as if he was an oil-soaked rag. She was dropped, and her hunter's instinct identified that her breaking of the chain had somehow killed her assailant. She wasn't clear on the details and didn't need to be. Without her dagger, as the shadowmen regrouped in the smoke-plumed antechamber, this knowledge was her only weapon. Escape was an option, too, she saw, for if she could make it past the men at Thackery's door, she could flee into the flames beyond. She had to shake her head, for she was seeing two Sorrens, not one, if differently dressed. A woman was on the arm of the more dapper twin. Morigan could feel fear rolling off the woman like a chill and understood that she wasn't an enemy.

"She's ripped off a ward and my magik isn't working on her! Brain the bitch!" screamed the twin on the left.

Sorren, she thought, and memories of Thackery's anger, of the defilement of Mistress Hattersham and everyone else he had despoiled clouded her sight, and she pounced for the nekromancer to rip at his necklace, his neck, or anything else she could get her hands and teeth on. She wanted to taste his blood. But as prey, even stripped of his greatest weapon, Sorren was far from powerless. His black Will flared, and a well of darkness gushed at his feet. The sticky magik coated Morigan like a jet of tar, gumming her limbs together and leaving her helpless and growling on the ground. Morigan caught a silver smile—a horrible caricature of Caenith's—and roared to her bloodmate before she was struck on the head and swallowed in oblivion.

On the edge of the blasted terrace, the Silver Watch had landed their skycarriage and were fanning out toward the billowing epicenter of the blast. Through the smoke, they spotted the black-garbed men and shouted for them to halt and make themselves known. Sorren did so with a flick of his hand that sent the men pulling their swords and wailing in confusion as they gutted one another. Once at the skycarriage, Sorren glanced to see if his uncle's corpse lay anywhere in the pitted courtyard. Unfortunately, he saw only the black crater where his puppet had gone off, still glowing as brightly as a fresh meteor site with embers and kisses of flame, and that satisfied him enough that his uncle was dead or crippled beyond even magik to repair.

Sorry, Mother; this revenge was mine. Not as sweet or as painful as I desired, but I still have Lenora for deeper gratifications, considered the nekromancer.

"Hurry, Master Blackbriar, before they realize we have stolen one of their craft," urged the Broker.

"Yes, we are done here," said Sorren.

Outside King's Crown, while racing toward the fingers of smoke going up into the sky, Caenith had discarded any pretense of normalcy and was startling the populace like a hurricane's wind: battering whoever was in his way, leaping and spinning through the streets as quickly as he could to reach Morigan. Her feelings had gone still, and the grimmest awareness in himself that he refused to accept—that she was taken—hammered into his gut as he reached the flame-stripped courtyard. Once, Caenith had seen a star land in Alabion and chased it all the way to its rest to see a scorched and glittering pit that had burned the woods around itself to kindling and soot. Whatever technomagik was wrought here was similar and just as devastating. Caenith paused, disinterested in the crying and wounded flung around on the flag-stones, wanting only a scent. That he found and followed across the fiery wreckage. He climbed to the top of Thule's smoldering, creaking tower and howled from its pinnacle when her trail vanished into the sky.

PART II

XI

THE FORKING ROAD

I

In the hourglasses that followed the attack on King's Crown, the foot of the palace was clouded in smoke, which told all of Eod that a dark time had come to the kingdom, that they were no longer invulnerable as a nation. Word quickly spread from frightened tongue to frightened ear, and the story became so distorted with speculation that each telling of it differed with a new enemy or plot. It was a sorcerer's experiment performed without proper sanctions and using dangerous elements. Or a mad firecaller come to burn his lover to ash. Many folk did not know that the reclusive sage of the Charter of Nine Laws had lived in King's Crown, though when that gossip rooted and spread, he seemed the most likely target of terrorism. For his ideals, for the freedom he preached—affronts to the Arhad or any number of secular nations. *Pay heed to the brown-skinned sand devils recently seen entering Eod*, whispered the gossipmongers. Indeed, all signs seemed to lean toward the sage being a target, and these theories were particularly compounded by the absence of Thackery Thule, who was not found during the careful inspection of his crumbling tower or in the charcoaled square thereafter. *Is that a* Thule? *Was that really his family name? Isn't that an old name from Menos? Who were those masters again? Descendants of the Iron Queen?*

King's graces! clucked the gossipmongers. More and more tangled the web grew until the city was drowning in paranoia.

Amid the chatter, only few suspected the most obvious of threats: Menos. With a grudge as old and rote as that between the Iron City and Eod, the people had grown complacent of Menos's animosity. Menosians were a gag in the common vernacular. *Wicked as a Menosian. Cheap as an iron master.* As enemies, they were never really considered. To believe that Menos had finally struck the City of Wonders was unthinkable. For in doing so, it condemned their entire realm to a bloody war, where each force would be matched by equal and devastating technomagik. No citizen of Eod wanted to consider that option, which ended in the destruction of their paradise.

II

"And he cannot be found? Nowhere in Eod?" exclaimed Queen Lila.

"Our earthspeakers have cleared the rubble and examined the scorched ruins of his tower, to where the fire from the witchpowder spread. We found neither bone nor flesh that could be his, Your Majesty," reported Rowena.

"How many casualties?" asked the queen with sorrow.

"Forty-six at last count, many of whom cannot be identified in their state. We can add a few more to that tally come dawn, I am sure."

Queen Lila turned and delicately leaned on the great yew in the Hall of Echoes as if it were whispering its consolations to her. The star-netting on the chamber above had a moonlike whiteness to its hue, and with her back to the company, the airy queen could have been a ghost. After speaking, Rowena stepped back in line with the four silver-armored masters of the Watch—North, South, East, and West—who had been summoned for this council. Among the stern older warriors, battle-scarred and broad as war chiefs of Alabion, was an epicene lad. With his flushed, freckled, and fair countenance, his golden ringlets, and hardly a shadow of stubble to call his own, one might question what such a green youth was doing in the company of his grizzled superiors. But the lad held his body taut as a shaft of iron, and his brown eyes peered with an acuteness seen in the sharpest swordsmen.

He bowed on one knee as he addressed the queen, and the timbre of his voice was clear across the rumbling music of the Hall of Echoes.

"My Queen, I think that if we look at the evidence, it is clear that we have been the victims of terrorism, deception, or some measure of both. What we need to decide now is how swiftly and to where the sword of retribution will strike."

"Galivad," sighed the queen, and it was a while before she indulged him further with a response. She was fantastically tired and seemingly alone to resolve whatever strife had shaken Eod. Whether it was a side effect of the spell that Magnus had used to stifle Brutus or there was another factor in play, her mindwhispering with the king had become like a broken farspeaking stone. A few words, faint breaths of his winter, no real dialogue over the past few days, and the degradation appeared to be worsening. She knew her share of magik theory and she suspected that you couldn't bind one body, when it was only half a man, without binding the other. Inadvertently, in shutting Brutus out, Magnus had damaged his second union. In this moment of crisis, she was truly by herself, and she would have to make decisions by her own prudence. Hard decisions, such as what must be done about Thackery and the young witch.

"Thackery would not betray us. Certainly not after fleeing to Eod and crafting the Nine Laws. I shall not rot my ear with any whispers that he is a traitor," stated the queen, and faced about to see the Watchmen cowed by her sternness.

"Not Thackery, Your Majesty," said Galivad, who was quite unshaken. "The girl. Or the smith. Either of them could be threats to our nation."

"Those are strong accusations to make," Rowena said, frowning.

"I would not make such accusations without forethought," replied Galivad. He stood and puffed out his chest. "While the destruction in King's Crown was being investigated this afternoon, I was tending to other affairs—"

"Yes, you were *missed*," interrupted Rowena with a tone that did not imply fondness. Much as she tried, Rowena was never sure what aspect of the master of the East Watch got under her skin. He wasn't arrogant, though he was sure of himself. He was as talented as he was young, and all his men spoke naught but the highest praises of him. As far as any would see him, the man was as polished in looks and virtue as a Watchman's medal of honor.

He seemed too polished, perhaps, for no man could be so flawless. She had seen the hideous bruises and scars on her mistress before they were healed, and if even the Everfair King was imperfect, then what hope was there for lesser men?

"I was absent with good reason, Rowena. I sent the men of the East Watch in my stead. There were many conversations to be had in order for us to unravel this mystery."

"Conversations were not needed. Hands to move rubble and tie tourniquets were."

"Who did you speak to?" urged the queen, ignoring their bickering.

"An interesting question, Your Highness," said Galivad, and threw a sideways glance at Rowena. "I regret that I was not there to aid in the efforts at King's Crown. However, a trail can grow cold rather quickly, and a man must hunt before the path is lost. In the hourglasses since the attack, I have met with the Watchers, as well as conducted my own investigation. This afternoon, I interviewed some of those who saw the explosion, and many of their stories corroborate one another, and speak of a ranting woman who set off the explosion. I propose that she was nothing more than the device, and one of dastardly Menosian design. The sort that only one of their black nekromancers could achieve. If I was to guess who, I would say Sorren, son of the Iron Queen."

The masters of the Silver Watch gasped, and the queen held up a hand for silence.

"How have you come to this conclusion?"

"From the use of witchpowder, which is impossible to find even in the darkest armories of the Faire of Fates. From the confusion among the eyewitnesses about how, exactly, the bomb went off. I spoke to one such witness in the infirmary set up in King's Crown—a sharp young page who was quite lucid despite the shock. He was quite sure that he had seen a Mistress Perriette Hattersham—the explosive—eat something and then run toward Sage Thackery. Or Sage *Thule*, as all of Eod now knows him. I don't know who the leak is in our palace, but it is wide enough to sink the ship. That is neither here nor there. Point is, right after she ate whatever she ate, she went—" Galivad flared his fingers.

A few of the masters of the Silver Watch made sour faces.

"That is hardly the end of the intrigue," continued Galivad. "When Miss Hattersham's estate was searched by the Watch, it turned up a dead handmaiden who might as well have been savaged by an animal. As well, elsewhere in Eod, in what might seem an unrelated atrocity, a blood-soaked mattress was found in an inn rented by eight Arhad. Two of these men, I believe, are the corpses found in Sage Thackery's tower, and among the gruesome relics that they left behind in the inn was a collection of organs: kidney, liver, intestines. Everything but the heart and lungs. Was there much of Miss Hattersham remaining, I would bet that our fleshbinders would confirm that those organs belonged to her."

"Are you saying she was hollowed out? How would she still walk and talk? Is that possible?" asked Rowena.

"I propose that it is. Hardly a difference between that and the corpse bombs that Menosians rig at one another's passages, where the death of one master can lead to the fortuitous passing of several more gathered in the pretense of grieving. In this case, the corpse walked. Or I pray to our Immortal Kings that Miss Hattersham was a corpse, for if she was instead kept in some sorry state of life for her remaking..." With a shake of his head, Galivad dismissed the thought. "A walking corpse would not be beyond the gifts of Sorren to animate, or to project a voice through, as she was heard to rant before her death, though no one seems to recall much of what she said, other than announcing a Thule to all of King's Crown. An old name, as you know, and long forgotten in the East or West until today. One that he never threw around, as far as I understand from his stay here as Sage Thackery. While the rumor mill is only idling at the moment, it will not be long before the people make the leap between the Thule lineage and the since-adopted surname of the Iron Queen."

"How can you be so certain that it was the Iron Queen's child who caused this mayhem?" asked Queen Lila.

"My meeting with a Voice confirmed this," replied Galivad. "Not precisely, as pinning loyalty on a Voice is like catching smoke, but in his cagey way, he let it slip that Sorren was in Menos no longer, but would not say where he was. I have drawn the appropriate lines. I believe he was here to set the explosive, to sow unrest, and possibly to claim the sage, who remains uncounted for in the dead or living, and whom I have been instructed not to consider a defector. A question for you, my Queen. Now that his identity is known, or will be shortly, how will you contain this? There will be outrage that a man of Menos has set the laws that rule us. And how was it that you kept his identity a secret for so long?"

Sinuously as a snake, the queen slunk closer to the master of the East Watch. Rowena, who knew her mistress's moods, predicted a measure of menace in her golden eyes.

"*How* was it kept a secret?" hissed Queen Lila. "Secrets are merely secrets when people try too hard to contain them. A truth that goes unnoticed is *not* a lie. When Thackery came to sit in these halls, he revealed himself as no different from the common scholars who roam the palace. He saw himself as no better, and oftentimes a little worse—I suspect—than those living here. He was quiet. He worked, he ate, he slept. He conferred with the king. Most people of that age are so faded in time and memory, and he never made the smallest impact on their lives or minds. At least not with his presence. His actions, grand and selfless as that list is, are legend. When living down in Eod, he maintained the same humility, the same reclusiveness. And back then, the Thule name was not one to be feared, for it was a house of ignoble birth. A house fallen from glory. Not until the Iron Queen's rule, many decades and a marriage to hide this lineage later, would that name spark curiosity again, and certainly not with our politics. As you can see, he hid nothing. If anything, he was too candid with the stain of his past."

Close to Galivad's face, Queen Lila inspected him, and he managed not to flinch. "You are brave and quite clever for your years, but you have not yet learned the temperance that accompanies greater wisdom. If the people make the tie between Thule and the Iron Queen, I shall deal with the matter the same way that I have done with you. I shall tell the truth. We have more important matters that concern our nation at this time, such as the sage's whereabouts. For if we have not found bones, then I cannot see how so resourceful a man could be dead. Which leads me to believe that he is in danger or has been taken. By Sorren, if what you say is true. He needs our help and not our mistrust."

"A mistrust that was never given, and I apologize for the affront," Galivad said, bowing. "The sage's unfortunate lineage aside, I am more concerned with the company he keeps. This smith and witch. A farseer, I hear?"

"You hear much," said Queen Lila.

"I do. Though to briefly revisit my earlier concerns over the security of the palace, a man can hear every whistle when his house is full of holes. No matter. I asked the Voice for the histories and whereabouts of these two, and while the girl's past was relatively banal, suspiciously bare of supernatural events for a *witch*, I'd say, the smith's was almost barren. Not even a blood-line to claim. I was the second person to inquire about this Caenith recently, and the information I was given was vague and nonsensical, aside from references to an old pit-fighter in Menos named the Blood King."

"Menos?" spat the queen. Thackery had said nothing of the sort.

"Yes. An interesting thread, you see? Since the attack, neither the smith nor his bride have been seen at their homes or around the city. Under my command, I ordered a search of their premises, and nothing of direct interest was found, though if you haven't seen the Armsman, Caenith's place of business, it is a wonder in the City of Wonders. The man is a savant with his craft. He can create items of greater delicacy than the most talented earthspeakers I know. Miracles of *engineering*."

"Stop prancing about your words. What are you insinuating?" demanded Dorvain, master of the North Watch: a bald, bush-bearded warrior as scarred and pitted as a training block, his skin tempered by the cold harsh sun of the peaks of Kor'Keth, where his watch surveyed Eod and the winter realms to beyond the mountains. When he laughed or spoke, he bellowed like a horn, though his laughter was reserved for only after a bout of drinking that would kill a man. While he wasn't an angry man, his once handsome nose had been broken several times in brawls begun when fools simply wouldn't quiet themselves—or prattled on, as Galivad was often guilty of doing.

Galivad turned to his fellow watch master. "If you know anything about exotic compounds, like witchpowder, you would know that magik alone is not enough to make it. It is crafted from shavings of truefire—crystallized elementum—from the Sun King's mines, and it requires a forge and exceptional delicacy to smelt the substance to a point where it can be cooled and scraped to powder. Chip too slowly and the truefire hardens again into a larger, more unmanageable mess than before. Chip too hard or fast, and sparks will ignite the truefire. You can imagine how that would end. You need to be a master of the forge to know the perfect tune that the ore has when it is ready to be worked or plied."

Glancing to Rowena, Galivad gave the woman a queer, penetrating look that she couldn't interpret. "You need to know when to stop and when to apply the gentle heat of a lover's touch. Not enough to bring the ore to a climax, shall we say, but enough to keep things hot and wet."

"For fuk's sake!" grunted Dorvain, bullish, as was his way. "And pardon that, my Queen! But I can't take his rambling floweriness any longer! What are you getting at, man? Do you mean to say that you think this smith has done the work for Sorren?"

"I am saying it is certainly a possibility. One worth investigating."

"The smith...he is a dangerous man," added Rowena. Her encounter with Caenith outside the skycarriage still shadowed her in fear.

Long sighs and longer stares were passed round as Eod's war council deliberated its quandary. Perhaps Galivad was right to suspect the smith of treason, considered Queen Lila; there was a darkness and savagery to his soul that she remembered all too well; an inkling of the brutality of Brutus. She debated what his strategy was, then. To seduce Thackery's handmaiden, so that he could make off with them? To disrupt Eod's peace? Far too many motives existed and the atmosphere for speculation was ripened on account of fear, so she would need to be wary before exercising any judgment.

"What do you say, my Queen?" asked Galivad.

The queen was not aware that a question had not been answered. "To what?"

"The Silver Watch has already been dispatched to track the missing vessel, though I am confident that should we find the skycarriage, it will provide us with no more enlightenment than our dialogue today. Shall we pursue the smith, then? Shall we see if his trail leads to Menos? It is likely that answers regarding the missing sage will present themselves during our search."

A queen could not be seen to waver. The watch masters needed a reply—a sign of confidence, the same unflappable decrees that their king would dole out to uncover injustice.

"Find the smith," decreed the queen.

III

In the corner of the First Chair's sleek office was a concealed panel that led into a metal chamber. Within was a surprisingly cheery space, bright with halogen spheres and a shelf of fuchsia, violet, and burnt-orange flowers. The rest of the small chamber was occupied by an aluminum cot, a neatly stacked desk, and a corner for one's daily ablutions. This room was the First Chair's sepulcher, where the *sacred treasure* of the First Chair was kept in cases of extreme emergency: a place warded against every known physical and spiritual element and impossible to crack without an assault of sorcerers. Gloriatrix had made it her home, though she was so immaculate that no signs of use were seen in the linens, washbasin, or anything else that one regularly touched. Today, she was pruning and watering the flowers, her face knotted in intense concentration.

Horticulture was not what the iron masters or lowly slaves would envision that the First Chair occupied herself with, yet that was precisely the activity that brought her the greatest calm after a trying day. Too often, the roads in Menos led to death, and she had her hand in many of these misfortunes. Tending flowers was a reminder to herself, then, that she was not only a heartless arbitrator, but also a bringer of order. Although it was a forest of black iron, Menos was the greatest garden in Geadhain—next to Eod, but that would soon change. That life could grow here, in a city spawned in barren mountains, was a testament to the Menosian attitude that creation was carved and won through progress and determination, much like her position. Growth was a part of creation, beautiful or cruel, green or iron, and she was simply a caretaker to its grounds. The *true* caretaker, if the Sixth Chair's scroll was to be believed.

She snipped the head off a dying flower and added it to the pile. The sick had to go or they would rot the whole plant. Dismally, she pondered if she or another would show her the same callousness when it was her time to be removed. Though who knew what wonders the Sisters had seen. One could extend life; why should a Black Queen not surpass it entirely?

She checked the elegant dark crystal chronex she kept in her pocket. It was almost time for her meeting. She hurried from the sepulcher, dusted off her hands, and was seated at her grand desk before her meeting commenced. She appeared more relaxed than her standard manner, as this guest was not deceived by pretenses.

"Elissa," said the Iron Queen, nodding as the white-and-gray woman glided into the room.

"Gloria," smiled the mistress of Mysteries.

The women weren't exactly friends, any more than two vipers in a basket would be, though when alone they addressed each other as friends would. In a city ruled by men and might, they were anomalies—women who had taken off the apron or garters to play in politics and masculine pursuits—there was a sisterhood they shared because of that. The examination of the Sixth Chair's scroll had drawn them into a deeper entanglement, making them conspirators now.

"Adder spit?" asked Gloriatrix.

Elissandra swept back her hair and rose in her seat like a preening swan; she was close to one hundred and fifty, but still had not a line to her face. Perhaps it was her magik that kept her young, thought Gloriatrix, as those with the gift of Mysteries tended to outlive even the most devout fleshcrafter aficionados: those sutured with fresh organs for every failing one, those outfitted in new skin at the onset of every wrinkle. Elissandra nodded, and Gloriatrix reached for a crystal decanter on her desk, pouring each of them a glass of black liquid. She slid the drink to Elissandra.

"How goes the work on the scroll?" inquired Gloriatrix.

"Very well." Elissandra took a sip of adder spit. "Mmm. Lovely vintage. You can taste the wood. Makes me think of trees...tall and black...and a shadow—vast and powerful—running through them."

The Iron Queen was familiar with her guest's mental ambling, and drummed her fingers on the table to get the woman's attention. "Elissa? Where have you gone? We were talking about your work on the scroll."

Dreamily, Elissandra blinked back into the room—she appeared confused about where she was for a moment. "I do apologize. I have been having the strangest dreams of late. I believe the sleeplessness is getting to me."

"What sort of dreams?"

"Dreams of a red-haired maiden." While she spoke, Elissandra reached out as if touching a misty shape. "A woman of fire and pearl being chased by a Wolf...the largest creature I've ever seen. The moon is full and full of promise. Yes...something to do with a promise. And the rust of blood. I smell it as strongly as the Wolf's scent. What a strange scent it is. Intoxicating. As if I would like him to..." The reaching hand came to her pale clavicles and stroked the flesh there. She shivered.

"That is a strange dream, Elissa," agreed Gloriatrix. She knew that it could be more than that. "Do you think it means anything?"

"I do."

Thoughtfully, they nursed their drinks. After some time, Elissandra shared her thoughts.

"I believe that it is a portent."

"Of what?"

"Death, fate, love. All three feelings I feel when I am in that dream. My bloodline is of the Far East, and while I have never seen the pines of Alabion, the soul never forgets its heritage. I believe that is where I ran in my dream: to the Untamed."

Greedily, Gloriatrix leaned forward. "Is this related to the scroll and the Sisters' prophecy, then?"

"I...would...say..." Elissandra indulged in a torturous pause, her gaze flickering with contemplations. Into the dark syrup in her glass she stared, as if it were a pool of secrets through which she could scry. Whatever inspiration she sought struck her like a thunderbolt, and she whipped her head up and glanced to Gloriatrix from under her loose cottony hair, which had gone quite wild.

"Yes...yes, it is all connected," finished Elissandra, and slumped back against her seat as if a weight had been lifted.

They polished off their drinks in silence. Elissandra did not need her gifts to know that she was not here for chitchat and spirits: Gloriatrix had summoned her because she needed a task done. Elissandra placed her glass back upon the desk and looked to the First Chair.

"The scroll. Work is progressing well. We can decipher a few of the words on the upper half, though we shall need the complete scroll to understand the whole of what the Sisters Three imparted to Malificentus. What remains of his skin could be between here and Alabion, though it was enchanted, powerfully so. The piece is out there, it is simply a matter of where."

Following the sentence of the Black Queen's rise, the Sixth Chair's scroll was jaggedly ripped in half, with faded or partially scrawled lettering along the tear. For weeks and counting, Elissandra and her farseers had been attempting to divine its location.

"That we haven't found it thus far means that it is powerfully warded or otherwise in a place where magik cannot pierce," proposed Elissandra.

"Alabion?"

"Yes. That is likely."

Gloriatrix drummed her fingers upon the desk again. "Well, that places it effectively out of our reach. Your ancestor could have passed clutching it to his chest. We were lucky enough that the Broker managed to catch our little treasure in the Drowned River. We should count our blessings with that. Regardless, I have another task on which I shall need you to focus your resources."

"What would you have me do?"

"My son will be returning in a day or so. He has brought with him a girl. A young witch, I am told, with powers much like those of the House of Mysteries. Perhaps even greater than yours, Elissa."

"*Really?*" muttered Elissandra, her smile a gash of hungry teeth.

Gloriatrix couldn't recall seeing such excitement in the woman before. "Indeed. My ears in the palace tell me that she and my late brother—"

"Late brother?"

Gloriatrix shrugged, scowled, and tossed back her adder spit. "Yes, Thackery is no more. A pity I wasn't there to plunge the dagger in myself. Or light the fuse, in this case. I thought that I would feel vindicated or celebratory, though it is mostly a disappointment that my son did the work his mother should have. I suppose your agents might be a bit slower than mine are, as mine were out doing the deed itself, and from your silence I take it that you haven't heard the news. It should be all over Menos by the afternoon. Giving the rabble something to cheer over as they scrub our toilets."

"News?" asked Elissandra.

"The war has begun, Elissa. I started it. King's Crown has been attacked by witchpowder explosives. *Sage* Thule is presumed to be suffering the curses of my ancestors. I've planted the rumors, my whisperers are seeding his name as we speak. There is no turning back now."

Elissandra's head was chiming with crystal bells of intuition at the mention of a myriad of events: the death of Thackery Thule, betrayer to his bloodline, inciter of a short-lived rebellion, philanthropist, and saint of refugees; the gauntlet at last thrown down to Eod. Behind her cold expression flashed smoky images of a white square streaked with sheets of fire, of shadows moving through woods, and of a crimson-haired beauty staring at her with stabbing silver eyes. *That's her. That is the maiden in the woods. The Daughter of the Gray Man. The one and only true. The loom on which the threads are woven. First and last. The snake that eats itself, the dawn of a new Age—*

"Elissa, you're very quiet."

"I applaud your success, First Chair," Elissandra said, and then stood. "If you will excuse me, I should return to my estate and prepare for the arrival of the witch."

Gloriatrix held up a hand for her to halt. "The witch? I haven't said what I need you to do with her."

"I thought that was obvious. I shall open her mind up and strip it of its secrets. You wouldn't have mentioned her to me otherwise, Gloria."

The women bid good-bye with sinister smiles. Once alone, Gloriatrix left her desk to survey Menos's dark vista through the tinted glass of her office. She was frowning in her reflection. Elissandra's actions today appeared more abstract than usual, and this dream of wolves and maidens was troubling. She sensed that Elissandra was withholding secrets, which was to be expected. What worried her was that the prophecy only spoke of a Black Queen. Singular. On the throne of Geadhain, there was room for only one ruler, one Black Queen, and that certainly wouldn't be Elissandra. Contingencies should be made in case their alliance ended, and the spider set her mind to spinning.

IV

Thackery groaned on the hard earth, more stiff and sore than he had been in years, and with what felt like a terrible sunburn. At least a cool hand of wind caressed his face and ruffled his clothing, which smelled of ash. No sooner had he made a noise than Caenith was upon him, shaking him and shouting.

"What happened? Where is she?"

"What! I don't—I don't know! Please, release me!" cried Thackery.

"Where is she!" growled Caenith.

"They took her!"

Caenith could smell the sharp stink of innocence among the man's fear, and he threw Thackery to the ground and stomped away. Carefully, Thackery righted himself. First to his knees until his head ceased its spinning, then up on trembling legs; he almost fell again once he took in his unfamiliar surroundings. They were camped in the shade of a lipped fold in Kor'Keth, somewhere along its endless range, with dunes rolling out in golden waves before them. Twisting eddies of sand swept the desert, but the horizon was otherwise bare. The baked desolation clenched Thackery's heart, and he rubbed his shoulders even though he wasn't cold, noting that the fabric there was tattered and burned, and feeling only more vulnerable. He turned to Caenith, who sulked in the shadows of their tiny stone pocket. In the darkness, the Wolf's eyes were cold glowing stones that watched him, and Thackery stumbled to find his courage.

"W-where are we?" asked Thackery.

"Kor'Keth. Spans from Eod."

"How did we get here?"

"I dragged you from the rubble."

Rubble, thought Thackery, and the jumbled fragments of his memory assembled. Sorren's taunts: *you underestimate the value of your holdings, too, if you believe there is nothing I can take from you.* Truly, the nekromancer had found what remained in life that Thackery valued. *Morigan, Morigan,* he despaired. He remembered an explosion from behind as he tried to transport himself to his tower. Miss Hattersham? It must have been. The force had surely propelled him out of his translocation spell while keeping his matter disembodied enough to live once it reassembled. He was beyond fortunate to be alive.

A shining object was thrown, startling Thackery. Glancing down to his feet, he saw that it was Morigan's dagger.

"This is all that I could find of her. No scents to the air. No tracks to follow. Only the smallest bit of sunshine, *here*." The Wolf pounded his chest and stepped from the shadows. Thackery saw that he was as dark as a furnace tender on his clothing and flesh, too. "That is how I know she lives. I *feel* it, for if she was to die, it would rip my heart in twain. Yet whoever has taken her has bound her, in fae iron or whatever you wicked magik-men use to stifle power in this age. I want their names, Sage. I want to know who I am to *hunt*."

Caenith spat the word from a mouth of teeth that were abruptly, dangerously sharp, and Thackery recoiled. As Caenith loomed over him, huffing and seething with rage, Thackery confessed a name.

"Sorren Blackbriar. A madman and an agent of Menos."

"Menos!" barked the Wolf. "Why would the Iron City have an interest in Morigan?"

Only two scenarios were feasible to the quick-witted sage. Sorren was out for revenge, or the Council of the Wise somehow knew of Morigan's gifts, and even worse, had an idea of how important the young witch was. If there were spies within the palace, the latter was possible, and the former was long overdue. He considered that Caenith might snap his spine if the wind blew the wrong side of his anger, and delicately chose what to say.

"I would guess that they learned of Morigan's power—through my carelessness in bringing her to the queen or another oversight—and that they intend to use it. She should be safe for a time; they would not harm her, not right away."

The Wolf sniffed him; the vinegar sourness of a half-told lie curdled off the old man. "You are not being completely honest with me. What you have not said is just as important as what you have."

"There...there is more, yes," whined Thackery. He closed his eyes, as the man's fangs—yes, they surely weren't mortal teeth—were terrifying him, and the rest of his confession spilled out. "Sorren is my nephew. It is possible that this was an act of revenge for something I did years ago—"

"I care not for your grudges or heartaches of the past," muttered Caenith with a menacing softness. "Where may I find your nephew? Is he in Menos?"

"I would think so, yes."

The shadow was off Thackery, and he looked to see Caenith stride out of the shelter and into the sun. Caenith pointed to his right, along the mountains. "Follow the range west for about a day in your slow-walker timing, and you will find Eod."

In what seemed like lunacy to the sage, the large man slipped off his shirt and began unlacing his trousers.

"Caenith, wait! What are you doing? We should return to the city! The queen—"

"Return to the city? Queen Lila?" scoffed Caenith. "Why do you think I took you so far out of Eod? No walled garden of man is safe, particularly not that one. I doubt your queen would hear my entreaty for aid as kindly as you imagine. In fact, I know she would not. There will be more questions raised than answered by my presence. My time in Eod has passed, and I must find a new life for myself—after I find this Sorren and drink the wetness of his death; after Morigan and I are united."

"What are you going to do? You...you can't just leave me here!"

"I can," declared Caenith.

He stepped from his boots and pants, naked in the sun as a golden idol to a spirit of masculinity. As Caenith stretched his grand arms to the light, Thackery watched the man's spine slither in a most unnatural way. Caenith howled and dropped to all fours; sweat or other secretions were glistening upon him almost instantly. Although Thackery was racked with a primal fear, one warning that he was about to witness something horrifying and magnificent, he ran up to Caenith anyhow. Morigan's fate was his responsibility. Sorren's involvement was, as well, and he would not see either left without justice.

"Wait! Please! Take me with you! I can't lose her! I love her, too! This is my fault! My burden to bear! I know the city! How to get in and how to get out! Ways that you have never heard of!"

When Thackery fell to his knees before the heaving smith, he wasn't prepared for what he saw: not the saliva-dripping, budding snout; the squiggling of the man's veins like little snakes; the sense that Caenith was flowering with bulbs of meat; or that his great shadow was growing ever greater and hairier. As Caenith swelled into something monstrous, he choked out commands distorted by a shifting voice box and wagging tongue.

"YOU...HECCCH...RIDE...TILL I STOP...HOCCH...ONE REST EACH DAY...HECCCH...BRING THE DAGGER...IF YOU FALL...I LEAVE YOUUUOOOWWWWW!"

The transformation ended in a howl, and it had happened so swiftly that Thackery could not reconcile the blurring and explosion of fur, flesh, teeth, and claws until it was over. Even then, his mind screamed, *No, no, no, no, no!* and all he could do was shake in disbelief while the Wolf panted not-quite-canine breath in his face. Impatiently, the Wolf stomped its paw on the quarried hill outside the shelter; so strong was the monster that smaller rocks slid down the range, and the sudden earthquake surprised Thackery to jittery movement. He scrabbled back from the Wolf, and it padded ahead, stirring more stones and dust, frowning at him with its gray eyes. Those eyes reminded Thackery of who this was, and he halted his retreat. Made no easier by the dizzyingly hot sun, his mind struggled to accept the madness of man and beast as one.

Again the Wolf pawed the hill with annoyance. *We need to go*, he was implying, and he lay his woolly head down so that Thackery could climb aboard his back. If Thackery had any longer to make a decision, he might have disputed his actions to no end. But fueled by a fear of being eaten for his indecision, he managed to find his legs. He found some sense, too, and quickly bundled up Caenith's trousers, boots, and promise dagger inside the large man's shirt in case he would, ideally, stop being a wolf. *A wolf! A wolf! A wolf!* his interior voice chanted, and he had to ignore it. Almost giggling in hysteria, he slung on the pack, climbed onto his heaving mount, stepping onto ridges of muscle like stirrups and clambering up between two mounds of knotted strength that were the Wolf's shoulder blades. Power hummed up Thackery's groin to his chest as he pressed his face to the soft, man-scented fur, and he had barely clutched fistfuls of pelt in his hands before the Wolf shot across the desert like the arrow of a thunderstrike bow.

While the wind tore at him with animal fury, Thackery laughed, he cried, he sobbed in madness. For the most part, he held on for all he was worth.

V

Poor lass. I wonder what the brothers grim have planned for her. All that trouble and all that death, and she is what it amounts to.

To the right of Morigan, and thinking these dire thoughts, was a brown-haired woman lined by evening shadows: a fellow prisoner on this craft. Akin to the prison marches of old, when slaves were herded into the mines of Menos to toil until they fell, the two of them were cuffed in black manacles with chains that connected their feet to their wrists and their wrists to each other. In the swaying, wind-rapped skycarriage, the heavy iron links beat against their bruised shins and shivered their bones with a song of hopelessness. The two were sitting hip to hip, though Morigan was mostly slumped on her fellow captive until a sand ago when she had groaned herself awake, out of an abyss of unconsciousness that had surely held her for a day, or longer. With her first gasp of awareness, she cried out for Caenith using her body and mind. But her communication was twice stymied: her mouth was muzzled by a cloth gag, and the bees never left her head; they only circled and buzzed. A power was restraining her gift, at least the far reach of it, and her instincts told her that the iron she was bound in had more of a burden than mere weight. Aye, it burned her wrists and ankles coldly, like the bite of frost.

She could still sense and hear the unseen by touch, however, and the proximity of her fellow captive was enough to catch echoes of what the other thought. This prisoner wasn't a warm woman; that much Morigan learned in only a short exposure to her. Which was good, figured Morigan, for the soft had no chance of surviving whatever was in store for them. The cool cunning of the Wolf or another boldness reined Morigan, and she counted her enemies. First, the grim men in fitted black clothing that stood steadied by an assassin's grace in the shaking cabin. Next, the dead man down the bench, who was calmly stitching an overcoat that Morigan vaguely remembered perforating with her dagger. The biggest concern with that adversary was that it didn't appear that he could be killed, not by any weapon she knew of, aside from magik, perhaps. The nekromancer and that silver-mouthed thing were not in the cabin, though she recalled them well. Calculating the odds of two chained women against seven very dangerous men left Morigan short of a solution.

Irrespective of her cunning, she would not get far in chains, not without help or an understanding of her fate. Morigan nudged closer to the other prisoner and was given a look of reproach.

Don't pull away, and don't show surprise that I am speaking in your head, whispered Morigan.

Little perturbed Mouse's steely demeanor, but the hollow voice, the shout in a mental room of her skull almost had her leaping to the ceiling.

She made a small noise of surprise behind her gag, and then shrewdly acted as if she was coughing when attentions snapped upon her. The dead man dropped his coat to the floor and was rubbing her back at once. Mouse made him stop with a glare, and he sheepishly chased down his thread and garment, returning to his task in a speck. When the situation had calmed, and both women were bleakly focused ahead like the preoccupied prisoners they were supposed to be, Morigan whispered again.

We need to talk, you and I. This is the only way that I think it is safe to do so. As long as we are touching or relatively close, you can hear my words, and I can hear yours. Respond if you understand me.

Mouse concentrated on what she was to say. *Can you...can you hear me?* A pause, as the message was relayed—and was that a tinny buzz, wondered Mouse—and then the woman next to her replied.

Yes. What is your name?

Mouse entered a short debate about how much to reveal to a woman who apparently could enter her head. Hiding the truth from a seer seemed a pointless endeavor, she decided.

Mouse. You may call me Mouse. And you, strange witch?

Along with Mouse's words, the bees returned with a few droplets of stolen memory nectar. Morigan was silent a spell while she sifted through images of a metal eye; the rank smell of a man's unwashed sexual sweat; a handsome, dark-haired face hidden in a hood—even with only his thin jaw showing, she knew this man was charismatic—and lastly, a gloomy manor with a rusted playground and scattered cricket set. Feelings of pitiful sadness tainted this final scene, and Morigan was stirred. This Mouse had lost something: her love, her innocence. After requesting that the bees behave in their travels, Morigan sent another thought to Mouse.

Morigan is my name. Where are they taking us?

Menos.

Morigan swallowed her distress. Every speck in this craft took her farther from the Wolf, though she knew in her heart of hearts that he was on the chase. The hope was there; she needed only to fan the flame.

Why have they taken you? asked Morigan.

The living one that looks like the dead man beside me, he's mad as a bull with a hornet up its ass. Master Blackbriar, he is. Sorren by first name. A nekromancer of the sickest kind, which is saying a lot for those folks. He stole, well, paid *my employer to own me, and I can only imagine what he will do to you or me after seeing what he has done to others. Stitched a woman—a living woman, ghastly as that sounds—with bags of powder, whistling while he did it. He thinks that I'm someone I am not.*

Again, Morigan saw the dilapidated black manor, its windows frosted with grime. She demanded that the bees stop their foraging. While Morigan's mind had slipped, Mouse had been repeating a question over and over, wanting it to be heard: *Why have they taken you?*

They want something from me, replied Morigan, and delayed before further explaining herself. Yet the same desperate trust that won over Mouse, that sinking reality that there was no one here to help them besides themselves, persuaded Morigan to be honest—within reason.

I have seen things, she continued. *I have information that I think would be of value to those who wanted to abuse it. I should have realized sooner that I was putting myself in danger, but I...well, I was distracted. I propose that what we think of next is our escape.*

Our escape? replied Mouse. This woman was as much guile as she was surprise. Cautious to her core, Mouse didn't fall into *like* with people, though she felt a curious tugging of respect toward this daring stranger.

Yes, our escape, Mouse. For I do not think I could do any of this alone and I don't need my gifts to tell me that you are as doomed as I. That look of creeping death, I saw it on your face in my master's smoking tower. Suddenly, Morigan remembered Thackery, and she swallowed before she could force the questions from herself. *There was an old man; I believe this Sorren had come for him. They have an ancient grudge. Did the nekromancer succeed? Or does my master, the old man, live? Please, what do you remember? Think back. Think as hard as you can. I need to know if he has survived.*

Mouse fought to recall the incidents in Eod. While under the control of Sorren, her field of view was limited to forward sight only, and she hadn't seen much. When the nekromancer was finished with his gruesome surgery on that unfortunate elderly woman, he wiped off his hands and doled out metal amulets—as plain as coins on a chain—to each member of his shadowy company. The talismans came with a warning that if they lost the amulets, they lost their lives. After dressing their bomb, they left the inn and took several carriages across town to the breathtakingly cultivated streets of King's Crown, where the beauty of the neighborhood rattled the bars of even Mouse's dismal prison. Only for a speck, however, for then the Raven's bloody orchestrations commenced. Thule—yes, that was his name—was called from his tower by the woman who was now an instrument of war. Safe and smug in the alley behind the tower, the Raven smiled as the old man ran out and took the bait, while they filtered into the sorcerer's sanctum with no more than a tingle of reproach from the wards. Mouse didn't see much from then on, only heard the Raven's quiet whispers as he channeled his voice into his puppet. Similar to when he was absent in the afternoons, his hold on her was weaker when his Will was split between more than one person.

Time is up, dear Uncle, the nekromancer had said.

Once proclaimed, there was a tremendous explosion that creaked the walls of the tower; heat licked her back and smoke clotted her vision. Her eyes stung and her sight became a smear, though she detected sounds of battle and hints of a reddish fighter causing mayhem among the men. The dead man left her for a speck and then returned, coughing—unusual for him—and suddenly Sorren was screaming for *the bitch to be brained.* Hope soared in her, though it was crushed momentarily when the dead man ushered her from the tower. A bit of shouting for their group to halt was heard, then the slicing of swords and gurgling of cried deaths. Another skycarriage awaited them, to take them to the one left in the desert. What she saw of Eod last was a pillar of smoke rising from its white majesty, like a signal along the mountains to herald war, which this truly would be. Through all these remembrances, Mouse searched for any clue regarding the fate of the old man, yet returned with nothing.

I don't know if anything could have survived the amount of witchpowder they packed that poor corpse-mule with. I am sorry, Morigan.

The Wolf in Morigan allowed her to devour the news of Thackery's death with cold compassion. The poetry of life lay in death, and that was an order to be revered even if the heart cried at loss. Later she would grieve, once the hunt was over and she had clawed her way to freedom. Then she and Caenith could sing to the moon together, and bury whatever piece of Thackery's memory they could find beneath Mifanwae's stones.

Morigan, are you sad? Don't be. We have the living to think about, namely ourselves, reminded Mouse.

I am angry, not sad. And my anger can wait.

Good, said Mouse. *I have learned a few things that might help us. Listen and see what you can make of my observations. The nekromancer's power has limits; the more he affects, the weaker the hold. Furthermore, it ebbs if he is away for too long, like a drug that simply loses effect when it cannot be administered. And he is tired after all the activity in Eod, which is why I've been bound to you in plain old iron.*

This isn't plain old iron, Morigan disagreed. *It has done something to my magik; otherwise, I could reach into the minds of every man in this room and rip out what we need to know to survive.*

Mouse frowned. *Ah, that would make sense. I remember him whining about how his power didn't work so effectively on you. We've been chained up in feliron, I suppose. It's what the Council of the Wise bind naughty sorcerers in who are awaiting execution. Still, the fact that you remain able to "magik" is certainly our greatest advantage once we get these chains off.*

Quietly as a young rogue, Morigan tested her restraints; they were tight enough to whiten her hands and surely impossible to contort oneself through.

No, that won't work, commented Mouse, noting Morigan's sly movement. *I've tried and I can slither from chains like a greased snake. We don't need a pick, either; we just need someone to let us out of them. The dead man might do it. I almost had the screws in him earlier before Sorren shut my trap for good. I don't know what the history is between those two, but it involves a woman named Lenora. The dead man was in love with her, and the madman was, too, I believe. As unlikely as it is, he is the only of our captors to show signs of consideration. I wasn't aware that the reborn could feel, but he surely does. He feels for this Lenora, the woman I bear a striking resemblance to. He doesn't remember her, not as he should for a woman he loved. I think I could twist him to help if only I knew the right words to say to him.*

The bees were sparking their stingers against Morigan's skull, eager as caged hounds to be released. They could smell delicious nectar wafting from the dead man: pheromones of sorrow and tragedy. However, she couldn't let them out if she wanted to. Not unless...

If I can touch him, as I am touching you, I can get into his head, realized Morigan. *I don't know if it will be enough to unlock his secrets, but I shall try. I shall hammer that lock with everything I have.*

Well, I'll be fuked! I think we have a fool's hope! Mouse laughed, but only in the space that she and Morigan could hear.

It seems that we do, replied Morigan.

The vessel rocked its way through the night. By dawn it would arrive in Menos. Without the smallest glance to each other, deadpan to their captors, the women wisely used every sand they were given to conspire. As light stung their tired eyes, and the skycarriage flew toward a new gloom—the black cloud of Menos—the captives readied themselves for the moment when they would convince the dead man to set them free. Even then, as the darkness of Menos's pollution wrapped the skycarriage, he glanced to the two prisoners with mournful regret, and Morigan knew he could be broken.

VI

At the edge of Kor'Khul, on the border between greenness and sand, Magnus told his soldiers the cause of their march. Shining and proud, the silver men assembled for the morning on the grasslands outside Meadowvale. Up and down the lines, his mare, Brigada, bolted like black lightning, and the king's voice, bolstered by sorcery, echoed like the thunder that followed.

Remember your oaths, men and women of the Silver Watch! he declared. *This is the time that all debts to your kingdom are repaid. I must tell you the truth of our journey, and what you have committed yourselves to do. My brother has gone mad! (No gasps from the men's cold faces, only frowns.) We ride south to see if he can be cleansed of his madness. If not, then we shall return him to Eod in chains of feliron. Every courage, ever honor is needed for this fight, and if you think that you are short on either, cast yourself from the Watch, from Eod, and never return. For the weak do not tread onward. The weak are not the cloth from which we cut the heroes of tomorrow. And against Brutus, we can have only heroes. Men and women with swords and even the smallest fear will not be enough: they will be ghosts before the battle is won. Ask yourself, are you heroes or are you spirits to be forgotten? Declare yourself now and ride onward, or ride back. The choice belongs to you.*

He stirred Brigada and plunged into Meadowvale. Come the counting of heads that night, not a single soldier had left their legions. With providence, a thousand warriors of stone wills could be enough to triumph against Brutus.

Meadowvale was glorious in the spring. It was a brocade of green fields and threading rivers ruled by weary, irregular hillocks, like ruined castles grown over with moss. Once, in an age that only the kings had seen, this was a land of fire and ash. Then, when the great inferno swept these vales no more and the land had cooled, life found the volcanic sediment to be a ripe bosom. As the king's legions moved south, the land welcomed them with arms of verdant beauty. The line of horses wound through great dales of pine and shaggy firs, trees so old that the king could hardly remember when they were saplings. In the trees sang throaty birds, and in the bushes rustled hearty animals for the Watchmen to hunt at night. Thus, the army's campfires were always satisfying and cheery, even if it was known by now that this was a march of war.

One night as they camped among the elders of the weald, these trees as imposing as a giant's emerald feet, the king found himself alone on a solitary rock. The army had covered much ground in a fortnight and they were around a day's journey from the Valley of Fair Winds. The king wondered how much the valley had changed in two or three hundred years. He'd last been through those lands with Lila, while on a retreat to the homesteads of Brackenmire, which lay beyond the valley. A realm of bogs and moss-bearded trees might seem a melancholy place for an escape, though he knew the secret pockets of loveliness that an avid or ancient explorer could find in Brackenmire—the pools where the moon shone clear through the trees and firebugs flew in the air like clouds of starlight. When this war with his brother was over, he would take Lila there again, and they could rise and sleep however it pleased them: making love, fishing, and living without responsibility.

Engrossed in the night, he did not hear his hammer approach. A tall, broad-shouldered warrior was suddenly in front of him, shaking him from his reverie. If a man could be an armament, then the hammer of the king was nearest to such a creation. With his chipped brown face and blue-steel eyes as cruel as a sword's edge, his curly beard, and his hairline branched with scars like the scuffs on a favored shield, he was all metal and mettle. His nose had been broken so often that its original shape was unknown, though it had settled into a ridged formation that was flat, if handsome enough. When he spoke, it was with a gruff indifference, as though the tongue of man was foreign to him. This was true twice over, for Magnus had found him in the Salt Forests of the West, where men spoke as he and his brother once did: in clucking, hoots, and burbles. And it was true because the hammer was more comfortable with the language of war, not words.

"My King," the hammer said, bowing.

Magnus nodded to a spot beside himself on the fuzzy rock. During the occasions where he and his hammer were alone or an importance need be stressed, Magnus addressed the warrior by his tribal name, not the more colloquial "Erik" that his fellows preferred.

"Sit, Erithitek," he suggested.

The hammer declined the offer. "No thank you, my King. I am here to watch and protect. Not to sit."

"You should take whatever solaces the fates bless us with, my friend. Few comforts are likely to be on the road ahead. At our pace, my brother's kingdom is less than a fortnight away. I do not know what awaits us there."

After considering the king's words, the hammer clanked his way onto the rock. Even though most of the army could be found around the campfires and stripped of their plate and arms, Erik was never at ease, and the king could count on one hand the number of times that he had seen the man out of uniform. Magnus suspected that the hammer's rest in this moment was really just another executed command: to *relax*. At least the man's helmet was off, if tied by its chinstraps to his baldric, should an enemy suddenly appear. On the contrary, the king was quite exposed, wearing but mail hose and naked to the waist; a vulnerability that surely made his hammer anxious.

"A beautiful night," noted the king.

"Yes. The air smells...different."

"Indeed, that is probably the perfume of the flowered terraces that lie past the woods. Stacked like potted gardens on shelves of rock and planted there by Mother Geadhain herself. Their beauty will warm even your stony heart, my friend. I have not seen them since the queen and I last had a moment to ourselves. That feels so long ago. You weren't even a thought in your mother's belly then." King Magnus gave a ringing clap to his companion's metal shoulder. "I am glad that you will see the Valley of Fair Winds, as it is a wonder not to be missed. At times, I feel like I have failed in my promise to show you this world. Peace does not require much travel, and many of your days have been spent in Eod and not abroad. Funny, then, how it is war that ultimately has gotten your feet to wander."

"You have not broken your word, my King," countered Erik, then spoke more loosely than he often did. "I have seen the reaches of Kor'Khul, the fords and dells of the East, and the bastions against the winter beyond the mountains. I have met the masters and lords of Geadhain. I have lived in the City of Wonders and witnessed miracles of magik and come to know what true freedom looks like. I have seen more of this world than any of those I left behind. You should not doubt your honor."

Is that what I was doing? pondered the king, and then realized that his hammer was right. Through the quiet march, as the queen's summer faded to a soft glow in his heart, and their speech became strained and harder to hear, he was more and more alone. Without his brother or Lila, fundamental questions of identity and security took hold of his spirit, and only he was around to solve them. Once he began to brood upon the chronicle of his decisions, the list was staggeringly long and riddled with faults. Ancient doubts as well as new ones surfaced. *Should I have spurned Menos all those ages ago when they pleaded for support? Was it ever right for me to live as a man when I am not? Should I find an heir? If not, what will become of Eod if I am to pass? Can Lila ever forgive me? Is our silence symbolic of the distance between us? Of a gulf that can never be crossed?*

"You read me well, my Hammer," confessed the king. "The past cannot be changed, and it serves me little to dwell in it, although my mind often does as it wants in that regard. I have forgotten who began this war. Brutus. I am merely responding to his challenge."

Erik gave a brisk nod. "I am glad that we are seeing eye to eye, my King. An army is only as brave as he who leads it. We must remember our enemy, our purpose, each day. As our king, you must remind us of that. Brutus is a force, not a man, and he has never faltered in his understanding of what he is or of what he is capable."

And yet I have, thought Magnus, and was again cowed by the hammer's insight. *I am the walker of the Long Winter. I am the eternal man. I am the voice of the skies and the fury of the earth. I shall make my brother and his dark voice suffer.*

The hammer could sense the change coming over his king: the shift in his leisurely posture to the erectness of a man on a throne, the glint of ruthless authority in his green stare. It was not his imagination, but the air around them chilled, as the elements tuned themselves to his king's mood. The hammer's next words came in puffs of white.

"Better, my King?"

"Yes."

Nothing more was said for many sands, and while the two men were outlined in the warm flickers of the distant campfires, they each somehow seemed cold as ice. Erik was shivering a little when the king asked, "Do you remember when we met?"

Erik needed no assistance; it was the clearest memory he held.

In the winter, although there is no snow, the winds ruffle the Salt Forests and they drift with white flurries. There are no green trees, but great pillars of salt with branching mineral extrusions all lined row by row, and many as tall as these bark-shod plants that travelers speak of, yet which the boy has never seen. Today, more travelers have come to the forest, and he watches them from his post in the trees. In his salt-stained cloak, he is as white and quiet as a spirit of these woods. One of the travelers, a pale man, rides a black beast so pure in its pelt that the salt does not discolor it past a graying of the hoofs. Immediately, by his carriage and appearance, he knows that the man is not quite mortal.

Power. He is power.

"We were headed to Carthac," reminisced the king, with a curl of his lip as the city and its petty masters brought him distaste. "The lordlings there were quarreling over some taxation or other injustice related to coin that could not be resolved by common sense. Brutus was never one for diplomacy, so I set out to box their ears, as a father should. As I am sure you have not forgotten, the Salt Forests are inhospitable to those unaccustomed to their dryness, and the elders of the Kree were kind enough to take us in, to share with us their precious stores of water and their cured meats—well, everything was cured there, I suppose. You earned your name that night, and your destiny, too. Protecting me as my brother did. From snakes, of all things, which have always had an unpleasant appetite for my ruin."

Curiosity is a weakness of the boy, and tonight is no exception. While the fires are low, and sleepy whispers are upon the village, he slinks through the caverns of his people, past small burrows dug into the side of a salt facade. No one will trouble him anyhow, as he is without parents; they were lost and dried out while hunting in the woods. The Kree call him wildborn, and they are right in that. He often sleeps away from the safety of the Kree cubbies and out in boughs of salt, clinging as the lizards do. He has learned how to hunt and kill and be strong so that what happened to his parents does not happen to him.

A predator's stealth takes him to the travelers' camp, which is in one of the largest pockets in the bluff. The space is necessary to corral the strange animals that the outsiders ride and to separate the tribe from the raucousness of these men, who are so very unlike the meditative personalities of the Kree. He watches their noisy union and frowns at their unusual metal skins and neighing beasts. Those creatures are pretty, but they smell odd and defecate on the pristine whiteness of the ground. Except for the black one with the set of horns made for goring; she (he sees no testicles) is too proud, perhaps. A circle of men is gathered around a bonfire that glows as green as some of the deep fungus that he knows shines at night. The fire mesmerizes him. He walks toward it and is seen, some of the smiling outsiders gesture for him to join them.

At the green fire, the pale man is present, sitting with the elders, speaking Kree as if he was born here himself. Erithitek is no longer captivated by the fire, but by this white creature: a ghost of ice and shadow, his eyes crackling with the same cold flames that roar nearby. Nanata and the other prune-faced elders are giving Erithitek scornful looks that he has shown himself, yet the stranger waves him to sit down. Every gesture of this man speaks of elegance, humility, and power, and Erithitek is infatuated with him in a speck, as hopelessly as a page chasing after a knight. As the cold fire licks the night, and their stares dance, he suspects that the stranger faintly feels that interest, too. He doesn't have the chance to sit or ask him, though, for his wildborn eyes have noted what those of his tired elders have not. In the Salt Forests, all things are white—its plants, animals, insects, and snakes.

"Don't move," Erithitek tells the man of power. From the fire, he fearlessly pulls a flaming log and swings it (like a hammer, the story would be told) while

the pale man watches him with more intrigue than fear, and his elders shout at his madness.

"One blow and that snake was dead," said the king. "Afterward, I had considered that you were trying to bash me, though at the time, I felt only trust. The eyes are windows to the heart, and I have always known yours, from that moment onward. It is a lump of obsidian with a diamond protected inside. Kindness wrapped in strength, both unbreakable. A balance of qualities that few men possess."

"Thank you, my King," replied Erik.

Affectionately, the king laid a cold hand on the back of Erik's neck. "Thank you, my friend. I cannot recall a man so born to be a warrior, so quick in action and set in virtue. You are the arm to strike when I cannot. The sense when I cannot find my own. You are my vigilance against the smaller threats that I ignore while blindly pursuing the larger. A bit of venom wouldn't have ended me that day, though it could have ended my journey. In a manner of speaking, it was you, then, who brought peace to Carthac. For no accord would have been reached without your intervention. A hero then and still...I confess, if not for you and Lila, I would be lost."

"Lila, yes," muttered Erik, and shrugged off the king's grip.

As the hammer of King Magnus, Erik had been outside the royal chambers when Brutus's rage had infected his master. Come the bleak morning, while the queen nursed her wounds in secrecy, Magnus explained as best he could what had occurred. Even after Magnus's clarification, Erik's imperturbable manner appeared unchanged. *I serve without question. I serve without judgment, my King*, was all that Erik would say. They had not spoken of the incident since, though Magnus felt that was hardly the end of it.

"I hope one day that you can forgive me for what I have done," said King Magnus.

"A man earns forgiveness. I believe that you will earn yours," replied Erik, and then gave a solemn stare to his king. "But that is not what you wished to speak to me about. You have something on your mind."

That earned a smile from the king. "You know me too well. Allow me to share with you my troubles. Before doing so, know that it is better that you listen now and consider what reply you might give later. Consider long and hard, my friend, but I shall need an answer before the week is through.

For if you will not commit to this undertaking, I shall have to consider other recourses."

Undertaking? wondered Erik. How suddenly the mood had shifted to dark, and a shine of despair was seen on the king's face as he continued.

"I have left Lila with instructions. Of what to do if we fail. She is a woman of grit and wit, but I fear that our dependence upon each other for so long has made her fragile. I worry what would become of her, and of Eod, if I was to leave this world."

"My King—"

"Please," insisted Magnus, holding up a hand. "I am immortal, but I can be harmed, made direly weak by the bite of a snake or the lethal poison of a scorpion. It is possible that I can be killed despite that limit never being tested. Brutus will see how much it takes to break me, I am sure. I must plan for every possibility. One such possibility, which I only entertain because I know I must, is that I shall lose this battle, or die. Whatever shade of failure I could suffer, I need to make certain that Lila is safe. She is the key to all that I have built. She is as much the soul and architect of Eod as I am. She will be a future, if I am not."

On the rock, the king huddled close to his hammer, whispering into his ear—not even the wind could hear them if it sought to. "The reason I shared with you the memory of Carthac and of our meeting is because I need you to remember what few places might be safe from my brother. Carthac is far to the West, reachable only through the Straits of Wrath—a journey only drunks and fools would make—and barring that, one must traverse the Salt Forests. A small company with spinrexes and many waterskins can make the trip, but an army would not survive there, no matter how fierce or dark. There is simply not enough sustenance to support the living, and to carry that much food for a legion has never been done. Only the Kree know the secret richness of the land: of where the meager springs can be found that hide even from watersculptors, of which roots can be eaten and which will drain the water from a man in an hourglass. Beyond the Salt Forests, Carthac thrives, particularly since our intervention there, now that men have learned how to behave themselves."

"What are you asking?"

"I hold more favor in Carthac than you know. Old debts even beyond the one you and I cost them, and I have made arrangements for Queen Lila's safety, should it come to that. If Brutus moves north, if Eod seems as if it will fall, she *must* be taken, hidden, and protected, as she will be the last and only royal of Eod. You must take this journey with her. I would trust no other man with her safety."

Erik slammed a gauntleted fist into his palm and metal cried out. He was furious at the king's many and wild implications, including the one that he would be cast from the march. Louder than was prudent, he hissed, "How? How would I play a part in any of your grim notions? I am at your side, my King! I am to serve you until the end! Would you have me leave this war to play escort?"

"Should you agree, it will be arranged when and only when the situation demands it. You are with me until that dark sand drops. I promise you this," the king swore cryptically. The king hopped off his rest. His stare was bleak. "Think on it, my friend. Think deep. Think of who you are to me, a man without children. I watched you sprout from a boy to a soldier to a champion of Eod. You are as much a son to me as I have ever known, and I would ask no other for this duty, nor do I wish to deprive you of the glory of this war. I have devised a way for us each to have what we want, to an extent, but first you must agree to help me if the tides turn against us. To help Lila." The king's voice faded into a farewell. "I should go to stir the men's courage now. Perhaps with a song. Good night, my friend. Do not watch over me. I shall watch for snakes myself this one eve."

Time passed, and the hammer did not move from the rock. When an enchanting vibrato that lowered to shivering depths or rose to tinkling heights—the king's voice—wended through the woods, the hammer plunged into deeper bush. As black as the hammer felt, the harmony did not soothe him. He walked until the noise was a haunting shudder to the trees, which swayed as if harking to the song. Then he walked farther still until only the crickets and rustling leaves were his company. Away at last from the tether of his kingfather, he could think a bit closer to a free man, for when the king sincerely beseeched him, his sincerity was like a spell and difficult to refuse.

With reason, he tried to think on what the king had said. Try as he might, Lila's glorious face disrupted any contemplation. *The king does not know what he asks,* cursed Erik. *I would protect her. Honor be damned, I would protect her above your own life, my king. Don't make me choose which.* Secrets, burning secrets chewed at Erik's ribs, wanting to be free, and he fell to the ground and bit back a scream. The king did not know how dangerous his proposition was, nor was he aware that Erik had been anything other than a silent collaborator to the queen's rape. Posted outside the door, never away from his master, Erik of course saw Queen Lila as she fled the royal chamber. His disgust at her abuse rose like a monster inside him. The queen had to stop him from—

"*Grraaaaah!*"

He let it out: his fury and disappointment, his shame and soiled honor, his loathing for the king's actions against Lila. He screamed to the woods until birds took flight. Then he stood, donned his tarnished duty, and returned to the encampment.

XII

AN UNFORGOTTEN DEBT

I

Riding on a giant wolf was a terrifying experience, even once the incredulity of the method of transportation had worn off. Thackery hadn't covered himself properly and could feel the sun searing his skin through the ventilated rags he wore, though he had not the slightest occasion to adjust his garments or fashion himself an Arhad-style wrap. All he could do was grip tightly and bury his head. Most of the time, he didn't open his eyes, as the golden smears of landscape he was treated to only disoriented him further. Thackery had no idea how long they bounded over the dunes, though his arms certainly had an opinion on how much longer they would assist him in holding on. Just as the pins and needles in his scrawny limbs turned to spasms of pain, the Wolf-carriage suddenly growled to a halt. The Wolf stood up on his hinds and shook its back free of its troublesome cargo. Thackery yelped as he landed on the ground. It was a softer landing than he had anticipated, and as he opened his eyes and let the black fog clear, he saw that the Wolf had brought them to an oasis.

Enticing them with shade were ferns and tall trees with peeling bark and wide fanning leaves, and across the grass, two boulders glistened in a sandy pool. The waters instantly sang to Thackery's cracking mouth, and he crawled toward them, shouldering off Caenith's pack. Soon he was up to his knees, refreshing and washing himself as gaily as a beggar in a King's Crown fountain. Caenith was along in a moment, wearing the skin of a man; he drank on all fours and then splashed his large hands and feet. Most of the ash had blown out of his hair, and it could have been his nakedness or primal masculinity, but he seemed as beastly in this as in his other skin to Thackery.

"I have read much, and seen even more. But I do not know what to call you," said the sage.

"A Wolf," grunted Caenith. "A changeling. A skin-walker. We have many names in many realms."

"Changeling." Thackery froze and played with the word, digging in his head for meaning and history. Not much came to him, except a faery story. One where a woman wed a fisherman, but could only be with him during the day. Come the starry hourglasses, she disappeared. Because she was so beautiful and caring, with the deepest brown eyes the fisherman had ever seen, he indulged in her eccentricity. Until one day, the fisherman's curiosity transformed into jealousy that she was being unfaithful to him, and he tracked her as she left their cabin and tiptoed to the beach. He could not believe what he saw there, as she dug out a leathery cloak, slung it over herself, and then dove into the sea. All night he waited and watched, and at dawn not his betrothed but a silky, deep-eyed seal returned to the shore.

He screamed when he saw her split from her skin, as a babe being passed from her mother, though his cry was more from shock than terror. When Dymphana knew that her secret was broken, she grabbed her cloak of skin, dove into the shores of Ban Loch, and was never seen again. Though often while the fisherman, who never took another wife, was on his boat in the White Lake, he would see on the horizon a lonely rock and a dark shape staring at him. But if he paddled toward it, the shape would disappear into the deeps. For he had seen Dymphana's greatest shame: the animal that hid inside her, and for that, she could never face her love again.

"Dymphana," muttered Thackery.

"And her seal pups, yes. They are the most famous of our kind. That tale is old, though, and not as romantic as what you might have heard. For the fisherman knew what she was, and hunted her on the beach as she sunned her breasts. He stole her skin and threatened to burn her hide if she would not submit to him, and then raped her for many seasons. One day, one of her three dark-haired children discovered a bundle of leathers that their father kept hidden in the rafters. She trimmed her skin and gave a piece to each child, and then took the children to the White Lake. When the fisherman returned, he was furious that she had escaped, and he pursued her. However, Dymphana had learned her lesson, as well as taking a few from man on *cruelty*, and she and her children swam to the choppiest waters of the lake and sang for the fisherman to hear. He harked to the cry, and his rage drove him onward. His vessel could not survive the voyage, and he died watching Dymphana and his children laughing at him."

Caenith threw back his wet hair and scoured Thackery with his cold stare. "The fisherman—whom we deign not to remember or honor with a name—was the one who brought malice to our people. His is a cursed tale to tell our cubs and pups. To warn them of man's desire to corrupt and break the Will of the Green Mother and her children."

"Quite different from what is said in the West," Thackery said, frowning. "I thought those were faery stories. As a learned man, I had not considered that they might be true."

"I tell nothing but, element-breaker," said Caenith candidly, and waded into the water to splash his groin. "Your kind is just as hated among the tribes of the West."

Embarrassment made Thackery look away. "My kind?"

"Element-breakers, skyrapers, earthbeaters, we have many names for men with your *gifts*."

"Sorcery is an Art," contended Thackery, coming out of the water. "An expression of emotion, just like painting, sculpture, or poetry. In fact, I'd say it's closer to the latter, a virtuosity of feeling paired with a monk's sense of control. Do you know what mastery and discipline it takes to feel so profoundly that your emotion can shape the world? Feel too strongly or without enough control, and the simplest of spells can unmake a man. Feel strongly and truly, and love—or hate—can become a glorious manifestation. We are the poets of Geadhain."

Thackery tore off the lower part of his tattered robe and fashioned himself an Arhad-style hood. He had assumed that the Wolf had let the issue lie until his mocking voice boomed, almost laughing.

"How highly you regard yourself. Hubris has always been a quality of your kind. What would you call a farmer who does not use the fertile spring to nourish his soil and plant what is to bloom, but only moves from field to field, stripping harvests? Or the shepherd who slays his flock to feed his fat self, and when their bones are clean, finds another hill and more frightened ewes to feed upon? *Sorcerers*," Caenith growled, "are what reap and never sow. That is why the Green Mother denies them their *art*—as you would call it—in Alabion. We of the East understand the sacrifice that every creation brings, magikal or otherwise. There is a scale. A balance to be maintained. For every act, a sacrifice. For every spell, a cost. That is the seed and water for the harvest. That is the proper order of magik. Not take, take, take, for which the magik-men of the West are famous. Eod's king is perhaps the only one I know of to ask, and not *command* life to do his bidding. There is a difference, son of Thule. There is a difference."

Thackery couldn't muster up a rebuttal to the Wolf's defamation of his craft. Whirling thoughts consumed him, anyway. Confusion and intrigue over the Wolf's strange lecture had him questioning the theories to which he and every other sorcerer adhered. *Takers?* he wondered. *Could there really be another way?* Leaving him to his uncertainty, the Wolf splashed out of the pool and was shortly back in Thackery's company bearing in each hand a furry brown fruit, as large as the skin balls with which boys made sport. The hard-shelled spheres might as well have been quail eggs, the way the Wolf punctured and cracked them with his thumbs, though their insides were not yolky, but filled with white meat and milk. The Wolf offered one to Thackery and then broke open another for himself. They squatted and ate like a couple of cave savages. The Wolf was as messy as Thackery expected, though he never found himself debating what Morigan found attractive about him, as his barbarity was so natural as to be charming.

"It is good that I had the foresight to bring you some clothing. You will have to wear it eventually," mentioned Thackery.

"It is good that I have a mule to carry it, then."

If this was a joke, it was said without a smile. The Wolf wiped his beard of milk; he had eaten the husk of the fruit, as well. "You have an hourglass to sleep. Some shade under the trees will do you well, and that meal should give you enough strength to hang on until we stop again."

"What about you?"

"I shall rest when Morigan is found," declared the Wolf.

His expression was so grim and frightening that Thackery did not inquire again. He hurried off to a nest of dry grass under the fanning trees and was asleep as soon as he shut his eyes. What felt like an instant later, he was being shaken awake by Caenith, who threw the pack of his belongings at him. He caught it with an *oomph* and tried to will his stiff and torn limbs to move, though they were as good as lead bones with throbbing joints of brittle, grinding glass. He could easily say that he had never been so sore in all his life.

How will I do this? How can I hold on? he thought bleakly. *Because you must. No matter the cost to this body, you must see that Morigan is found. If that is to be your final act in this life, so be it. At least it will be a noble one. Now move, old man.*

Using the tree as a cane, Thackery staggered up. He gave pause at the Wolf's gruesome transformation, nearly fainting from either the heat or his surprise at a sight to which he believed he would never be accustomed. Once the snapping, furring, and rearranging of flesh was complete, the Wolf pounded his way. Thackery put on the pack, shakily climbed aboard his mount, and clung his aching body to the muscled hide like a spider. His bladder complained, and he swore at not having tended to that need sooner, for they were off, and the oasis was gone in a blink. Either their movement was faster or Thackery was weaker, for their passage seemed twice as hard as their first ride together. His fingers were hooked, trembling, and felt as if they might break off as crisply as winter twigs; every ripple of the Wolf's body coursed bolts of pain into his chest and rattled his teeth. *Hold on, hold on, hold on*, chanted Thackery, and between the heat, the dulling wind in his ears, and the agony of his every part, he slipped into a state of numbness and delirium.

Tirelessly, the Wolf raced the sands, faster than a mare would, if not as fast as a skycarriage. When the panting beast finally lumbered to a trot, the desert had been embraced by a cool evening. Thackery whimpered as he turned his neck and feared that the fire in his limbs had left him paralyzed. Stars spun around him, in the sky or in his head, and one of the Wolf's shoulders dipped, worsening the effect. While this was an attempt at a gentle dislodging, the ground struck Thackery as sharply as a bed of knives. In utter discomfort, for many sands, Thackery lay without moving but for his quivering lips. He could tell by the disappearance of musk and heat that the Wolf had left him. How quickly then did the chill hands of Kor'Khul creep into his flesh. As the shivering intensified, he jittered to life, and groaned himself to his feet. Pain shot through his every nerve, locking his toes and fingers, and when the head sparks and vertigo calmed, he took a look at where he was.

Around him rose a canyon, grooved in wavy ripples by the water that had once flowed through the desert. They weren't in a mountain, as far as he could discern, for sand banked the tops of the stone walls, and whisking trails led upward into the dunes. On the bed of this dry river, the Wolf had laid him, and he could see large pawprints leading out of the canyon. He refused to despair and believe that he had been abandoned, and attempted to collect himself a bit. He started with a pee that sizzled and went on for sands, and then had a hobble about. There wasn't much in the way of sights or sounds other than the echo of desolation, so he circled a small area he had claimed for himself and tried to count the stars instead of heeding his hunger, thirst, or the burning of his heels with every step.

Falling apart...I'm falling apart, and this journey has only begun. A two-hundred-year-old man who takes up the life of a brigand! Ha! Better get your mind in order, old man. This won't be the hardest thing you'll face in the days or weeks or months ahead. The reality sank over him then, of the breadth of the peril and travel to which he had committed. He remembered telling himself earlier that Morigan's rescue could claim him. He was rather sure it *would*, and he didn't need the young witch's silver eyes to foretell that future. *It's all in how you look at it. Dying alone in a tower, perhaps in some embarrassing way, as the old tend to go: dead on a toilet or with a crust of bread hanging out of my mouth. Or on a grand adventure. I thought I was too old to have a child's sense of daring, but aren't we all just children in the end? The time we play as adults is mostly for show. I shall enjoy this, then, if I can. My last great journey.*

"Meat," said Caenith from behind him.

He was so pleasantly contemplating his end that the pain had dimmed and he had not sensed Caenith's regression to man or approach. He turned to a grisly if not altogether unsurprising sight of Caenith's naked flesh bibbed in crimson. The Wolf lofted up a lizardy corpse about the size of a hound, which Thackery recognized as a spinrex; he didn't ask where the rest of the herd was—in Caenith's belly, he presumed. Caenith handed him the lizard, and Thackery held it as one does with raw dead things, unsure of what he was to do.

"No water. Drink the blood and eat what meat you can. We move again in a few hourglasses," said Caenith, squatting on his haunches and surveying the canyon, the stars, and the desert with his twitching senses. Without any further instruction to go on, Thackery unslung his pack, retrieved the dagger within it, and then joined Caenith on the ground and tried to figure out the intricacies of the art of meat carving. Many stumbles with a blade later, Caenith took the messy carcass from him quite rudely and fileted the spinrex as deftly as a mariner gutting a fish, with painterly strokes that removed skin from flesh from bone in the passing of a sand. Caenith placed the juicy hunks of flesh on a bed of scaly membranes that resembled a gory salad. He then popped the organs into his mouth, slurped up the entrails, and tossed the bones, finishing with a red smile.

"Eat," commanded Caenith.

Thackery swallowed. *How rustic. An adventure, remember?* Embracing that adventurousness, Thackery consumed the rubbery chunks quickly. He tried to think of the oddly salty liquid as a fluid other than blood. The Wolf was wise, however, for the barbaric meal was as hydrating as it was nourishing, and it sat in his stomach with the fullness of porridge. That would sustain him for a time. The Wolf's dangling nakedness was making him uncomfortable, so he looked up to see unfamiliar stars.

"How far have we come?" wondered Thackery.

"About half of Kor'Khul," grunted the Wolf. "Another day and night and we should clear it. Morigan's captors are ahead of us, but not by much. Perhaps...perhaps she will awaken, or I shall feel her warmth in me again before then."

"Her warmth?"

"We are connected, she and I. In ways that you could never imagine. She is what I have hunted my whole long life for."

Lately, Thackery's imagination was being tested, stretched, and reassembled, and he could have guessed with relative accuracy at what strangeness united the Wolf and Morigan. Were he to draw parallels between what he knew—the king and queen's relationship was the most obvious, as incredible as it was—he felt that Morigan and the Wolf's bond ran deeper. *Deeper than a love that has lasted one thousand years? Do you really believe that?* He did. When he had been at the Fuilimean, he had even read a twist of jealously on Lila's golden self that told him this was true. *We shall find her, Caenith,* he promised. Glancing over to the Wolf, he saw the man sunken a little in his shoulders and majesty, and sought to change the subject.

"I would not question your skills as a tracker, but I am curious as to what road you mean to take to Menos. Past the deserts of Kor'Khul are the lordships of Blackmore, the fields of Canterbury, and the Iron Valley that precedes the Black City, though to get anywhere in the East, we shall have to cross the River Feordhan, which not even you could paw your way across with respectable speed."

Caenith looked over, scowling. With the animal in control, he had not given honest thought to the sensibilities of their travel, and it had been centuries since he crossed to the West. Remembering wasn't easy for him. "I took a boat last time. Landed at Taroch's...Taroch's..."

"Arm," finished Thackery. "Taroch's Arm is still where one catches a ferry, which takes a man to any number of docks in the East. We'll want Blackforge, city of house Blackmore. We're in a hurry, which is good, because we don't want to stay in either port for a moment more than we have to. I don't know what you recall, but as the bridge between East and West, those are two of the most dangerous cities in which a man can find himself. And while the Blackmore claim neutrality, they are thoroughly in the pocket of Menos, so we'd best not draw attention to ourselves. You will be needing your clothes once we get to Taroch's Arm, and tempting as it might be to *wolf* around the countryside after that, it is ill-advised, as Menosian Crowes patrol the skies and have instruments specifically alerted by signs of unusual movement. We shall have to proceed on foot."

"We can't afford the delay!" growled Caenith, slapping his hands on the ground.

"Would you risk our own capture? We'll be no good to Morigan then."

"I shall never be chained," declared the Wolf defiantly.

Thackery pursed his lips. "I would imagine every prisoner has said that before."

The Wolf calmed his pride. "What do you propose, son of Thule?"

Do stop calling me that, and I shall ignore your complete incivility in most instances, like your balls dragging themselves in the sand. Can't you feel that, you brute? Do you even care? Thackery thought, but managed to answer with decency.

"I have some bonds that I can call upon in Taroch's Arm from some fellows or their descendants, if I've outlived the debtor." Thackery waved away the thought. "We'll get to that when we get to it. Regardless, the bonds should certainly provide enough coin for the travel, and we can smuggle our way close to Menos on a caravan headed for the Iron City. That's the best I can think of for a plan."

Sparse as the strategy was, it was plenty enough for the Wolf; he stood and stretched. While it hadn't been an hourglass, Thackery's weariness cried out, for he knew that the beast-carriage would shortly be leaving. Agonizingly, Thackery trussed up the pack and placed his arms through the makeshift straps; they burned like pulled rope across his skin and fit into the red grooves on his flesh with familiar masochism. If not for his sleepless nights, he would surely have collapsed a dozen times over; he was still quite shocked that he had not.

He sighed. "Let's go."

The Wolf waved at him for silence and then darted up one of the sandy trails branching from the canyon. Thackery pursued him, climbing out of the windy channel to arrive on a plateau as lonely as an island in the wavy sea of the desert. At the edge of the island, the Wolf crouched and leaned into the night, sensing something that Thackery did not. Quietly, Thackery went to him and stood behind the man. He was no hunter, yet he could sense the tension in the night: the sudden stillness of the wind until the only scrape of sound was his hoarse breathing. Caenith pulled him down and covered Thackery's mouth—his head actually, given the size of the hand—to silence even that. A prudent notion, for Thackery might have shouted at what appeared next. At first, his eyes deceived him into believing it was a second row of dunes superimposed over the first or that he was seeing double. Out in the desert, something massive, something the length of a city street, undulated through the desert. How silkily it moved that only the faintest mist of sand announced it, and by that, Thackery could estimate its absurd size. How stealthily it swept under land, with at most a faint hum to warn—or mask—its menace. Once, a piece of the monstrosity exposed itself in a sinuous movement, and he saw a glimmering encrustation of shale and scurf. Had he not just eaten a lizard, he might not have made the comparison to scales. But his wonderstruck mind could not categorize what beast had scales of rock and gemstones, scales as large as the slab he trembled on.

What is the snake that eats the city...that swallows up man and house? he wondered. The answer struck him as the glittering coil descended into the sands, and the vast entity glided its way along a trail of starlight. Soon its movements could no more be tracked, not by his eyes, and when the Wolf felt that they were out of danger, he uncapped Thackery's mouth.

"I have seen it before," said the Wolf, still quiet. "A beast from another age. It is not the only descendant of its kind that I have seen in Geadhain, and but a babe to the elementals of old."

"That was a *wyrm!*" gasped Thackery.

"If that is what you call them, yes," whispered Caenith. "A predator not even I would cross. Children of the Green Mother are they. Powers that not even you element-breakers can tame. Monsters of earth, fire, wind, and water swim in the body of the Green Mother. The ones that live in the sand or soil like this can hear the smallest vibrations, and running feet are like drums to them. Your scream—had you made one—would have been a dinner bell, for they hunt without mercy. We shall wait a few sands more; I do not wish to test if I can outrun one of the true masters of Geadhain."

"I have never seen one. You hear of such things...read of them, even."

Thackery was unable to say more. He could not capture his awe and insignificance in words. As if he were a child seeing magik for the first time, he felt that innocent and new. He found himself holding the Wolf's warm arm and was pleased when the man did not instantly shake him off, as he needed the stability to tie down his soaring astonishment.

"Time is wasting," said the Wolf.

Thackery removed his grip and stepped back to watch the freakish transformation that was to unfold.

"We shall take a longer rest for you once we have left the sands behind us, Thackery," promised the Wolf.

Those were the last of Caenith's words that Thackery would hear for a time, though their sincerity infused the old man's limbs with the strength he would need to hold on to the Wolf again. For Caenith had addressed him by his name and with respect.

II

One quality that the Wolf never erred on was his honor, and true to his word, Thackery was allowed his first few hourglasses of solid sleep once Kor'Khul was a sandy memory. He was deposited somewhere softer than the last bed and twitched into a fevered sleep in specks. He dreamed of a wyrm of rock chasing him and eventually swallowing him whole. In that darkness he drifted; perhaps he was being digested, but he certainly wasn't dead.

Under the gloomy mantle of dawn, he awoke from the strange dream. The grayness of a threateningly rainy journey was a refreshing change from the desert's stinging light, against which he had squinted his eyes. In another welcome variation from the norm, Caenith had dressed himself in his sooty clothing and even tied up the wild nest of his hair with a strip of cloth. The third of the day's small miracles was a cooked meal that had been prepared for Thackery, and it was the succulent smoldering of a hare's gamy fat to which he awoke. He slapped his cheeks to liven himself and chewed on rabbit while breathing in the fertile mist of the lowlands that they had arrived at last night.

From their camp on a lightly treed hill, Thackery could stare east over a rolling valley. Deep glens glittered with water, and bushy dells dotted the green skin of the land. Here and there were piles of carbonized shale or half-risen cliffs that looked like tired old women in black robes and emerald shawls. From this dark stone, Ebon Vale got its name, and while the soil most immediately surrounding these deposits was not ideal for growth, pastures and farmsteads could be seen, their pens shuffling with fluffy shapes that Thackery guessed were sheep or cattle. After the blistering emptiness of Kor'Khul, these smoke-piped dwellings and their cozy comforts were exactly what Thackery needed to lift his spirits. Alas, he would be visiting none of them, he figured, judging by the pout on the Wolf's face. Surely, the strain of Morigan's capture was chipping away at even Caenith's great resolve by now.

He could feel the Wolf's impatience weighing over him as he ate, thus he did so quickly. Once Thackery finished his meal, he cursed and hobbled himself up. The Wolf stomped out their fire and was promptly leading the way. On their brisk stroll down into Ebon Vale, a castoff rowan branch called for Thackery's attention, and he picked it up and made a cane of it. Having the support of a third leg sped his huffing crawl into a limp that could almost keep pace with Caenith's stride. As the crisp air of the valley cleared out Thackery's fatigue, their last night of travel through the desert returned to him. His hands had finally unclenched from Caenith's fur and he had fallen, which explained one of the greater aches on his hip among his collection of miseries. He remembered flopping in the sand, completely spent of any energy to right himself, and sobbing for Caenith to go on, thinking that this was the end for him. However, Caenith had not abandoned him, but carried him like a babe for what remained of Kor'Khul, eventually laying him down to rest.

"Thank you for not leaving me last night," said Thackery.

"You love her, too," replied Caenith, without turning around or slowing his stride. "I have hidden myself too long from man's customs, and I shall need a guide in how you slow-walkers behave. We are in this together, you and I."

As the morning yawned itself awake, the temperamental skies teased with thick shafts of sunlight as well as bursts of rain. The companions stamped over great tiles of slippery shale and along damp trails wending through bracken and bush, trading sand for mud and scratches, though happy with the exchange. Often and with longing, Thackery stared toward the distant farmsteads that Caenith never led them toward and wished for a warm bath, a blanket, or even a patch on his vagabond's garments. While this unkemptness would do in the wilderness, they would have to clean themselves up properly before entering civilization. As if he had read the old sorcerer's thoughts, Caenith veered from his eastward path and took them down a mossy chasm to emerge into a dell. There, a brook sprang from the wall of black bedrock and bled out into a lily-spotted pond. Without speaking, the men drank their fill and then stripped, bathed, and scrubbed their clothes as clean as they could. Of the two, Thackery looked incomparably worse for wear when they were done, and Caenith offered him his voluminous shirt to wear over his rags, which made for a sort of nightgown.

"Thank you for the gesture," Thackery said with a sigh. "I feel ridiculous. But that's as presentable as I think we'll be until Taroch's Arm."

The Wolf nodded, and they were moving again. The land welcomed their travel, and the weather improved to a dampness that left a cool perspiration upon their skins as they hiked. Caenith continued his avoidance of farmsteads and people, and Thackery felt very much alone for their journey. Two explorers, perhaps, in a land yet unmapped and uninhabited. Soon he wasn't yearning for firesides, but celebrating the grunt and toil of his lungs, the aching of his feet, or the nose-tickling ripeness of soil and pine in the deeper paths they wandered. All pleasures that he had neglected in his silver years: the churnings and wonders of life within and without. Ahead of the contemplative sorcerer, the Wolf entered a similar solitude. He thought of Morigan, of her captors, and of the creative and horrifying ways that he was going to rend their flesh with his jaws.

By dusk, the silent pair had bobbed up and down the dips of Ebon Vale and paused on a shale rise to survey the area. To the west glowed the evening hearths of many farmsteads; there were fewer lights to the east. The going that way would not be easy, for the rock had surrendered to tangled forest. Thackery advised that they would be best to follow the path of the mountains, which would eventually open to scrubland and a grand riverbed, where Taroch's Arm awaited them, and the men plunged onward.

Indeed, as Thackery had forecasted, the land was a chore to traverse, trapped with fallen logs to trip upon or supple branches that were bent aside only to lash back at the offense as a whip. Yet Thackery blundered along, with Caenith helping him out of the worst of his troubles, and never once complained. Deeper and deeper they hiked, until hollow cries and strange birds made music to the moon. When the Wolf was satisfied that most of the farmsteads were at their heels, they stopped under great oak that glimmered as a tree of silver in the moonlight, and Caenith kicked off his boots and shimmed from his pants. Thackery knew what was to be done, and he gathered the discarded items while Caenith snapped and growled his way into new furry flesh. From out of a boot fell Morigan's dagger, and it shone amid the leaves for a moment before Thackery shakily retrieved it. He mumbled a prayer to whatever forces watched Geadhain that she was still, impossibly, safe and then wrapped everything up into a bundle made with his gifted shirt. He climbed aboard the heaving beast, held on tight, and was momentarily speeding through the woods. He knew that the Wolf's relatively casual stroll through Ebon Vale was so that the weaker of them could recuperate his strength—a kindness with an expectation attached, for he did not think that another stop would happen until they reached Taroch's Arm. And cry and scream as his muscles would at the trial being forced upon them anew, Thackery would not let go or slip from his mount again. Just as Caenith relentlessly pushed his body past sleep, need, or want, so too would he push himself as far and as hard as he was able, until Morigan was safe and Sorren was in the ground with the dead he so favored.

III

At a distance, Taroch's Arm hid its iniquity well. The city was grand and layered into a receding cliff of yellowed stone, with terra-cotta houses, circling gulls, and bountiful sunshine. Yet as they approached from the southwest, Caenith noticed a shadow draped over the regions along the waterfront. He saw bony peaks of what could be masts or the skeletal fingers of a giant beast, and a haze lingered there as if a fire were recently smothered. No fire was this, a playful breeze told Caenith as it bore scents to his nose; only industry and an abusive amount of that witchroot herb that folks who wished to forget often smoked. Past the indistinct harbor front crashed a choppy cobalt river that seemed born of the ocean. Dangerous rock islands dotted the strait, warning ships without steel-and-magik hulls that this would be their doom. Roads veined in many directions, high and low, to different areas of Taroch's Arm, and traffic filled them all. Folks here came from all corners of Geadhain, from the warm lands to the south or the snowy settlements north of Kor'Keth, eager for what could be bought or bartered.

Caenith and Thackery crept from the grasslands and joined the larger roads, walking along the wayside while caravans and howling idiots rode past. No one paid much heed to a shirtless giant and a dirty old man, beyond the brief and fearful stares that Caenith's size usually evoked. The road twisted on, and eventually the two men passed under a stone arch to enter Taroch's Arm: a city unguarded but for narrow-eyed men who clung to the shadows and carefully appraised every traveler.

IV

"Who are we seeking?" asked Caenith, frowning more than usual.

"Someone that I helped many, many, many years ago," replied Thackery. "She owes me a debt that a bit of coin will hardly repay, though it will be all I request of her. Hopefully, she has passed the obligation on to her kin, as I've outlived the lion's share of everyone I know." *But few of those I hate, sadly.*

"Well, let's find her soon and be on our way. This place is rank."

After living in Eod for so long, the Wolf had come to take its cleanliness and advanced technomagiks for granted. Most slow-walker cities stank, plain and simple. Few civilizations were afforded the benefits of Eod's sewage-disposal systems, so the undertone of urine sitting in pots in countless homes or splashed on alleys was as persistent as cat piss on a rug. Piss wasn't Caenith's only cause of distress; the sharp sweat of excitement and money lust had entrenched the stone beneath them, and nauseatingly sweet witch-root aromas were in constant supply from the shouting, pipe-huffing persons who swaggered in the streets. Again, Eod's civility had spoiled him, for he remembered slow-walkers as being drastically more respectful than the louts of Taroch's Arm. Here, he was jostled by the laughing crowd or rudely elbowed to move. His patience was quickly wearing to its last fiber, and he felt that he might snap if another inebriate nudged him; or worse, he might nudge back and send the man flying a dozen paces. The streets were too narrow for his wide self as well, and many of the houses had been converted into shops and encroached farther onto the road with greedy awnings and stalls. Caenith paid no attention to what was being sold, as no mortal thing on this earth mattered but for the dagger tucked into his boot. *Three days she has been gone. Three days,* his mind chanted. Despair was not clenching his chest as much as anger was. He wanted hot, hot blood and revenge upon his tongue, and soon.

Thackery was more attentive to their surroundings. Cities were his wilderness, and he led Caenith here. As Thackery inspected the clay houses, he could see little numbers hammered in iron faceplates near their door frames, and the streets were marked by crude arrowed signs placed at intersections. By following the signposts for the better part of the morning and scrambling to assemble the faded correspondence that he had read many years past, Thackery successfully toured them up stone steps and through shade-hollowed streets. He was confident that he knew where he was headed. He got lost only once, and never told the Wolf—who was too preoccupied to notice—and they successfully arrived at their destination.

A few knocks on the door of the dwelling and a brief chat with its burly occupant informed them that, sadly, this was not the case: the original owner had died, and her daughter had sold the home twenty years ago. Clearly, they had disturbed the man's afternoon drinking, and he wasn't partial to any further questions, leaving them with the suggestion that they should *fuk right off* before he fetched his blade. A twitch in Caenith's eye was all the indication that Thackery had before the giant seized the man and disappeared inside the home so swiftly that it was as if they had blinked from existence. Some clatters and thudding came from within the house, and just as Thackery was charging inside, Caenith filled the doorway.

"He gave me an address," said the Wolf. "One eighty-five Cordenzia Boulevard."

"You didn't hurt him, did you?" whispered Thackery.

"Nothing that won't heal."

Thackery pulled his large companion into the street and hustled him away. In a lane several blocks from the house, they stopped, huddled, and Thackery spoke in confidence. "I appreciate the information, let that be said. Still, you must be careful, Caenith. No undue attention to ourselves. People don't even know that I'm alive, and I would like to keep that confusion going for as long as we are able to. This city has eyes of its own, too, which we would not want upon ourselves."

"Eyes?" wondered Caenith. He had seen the slinking, shrouded men who prowled the streets. Perhaps Thackery meant those.

"Well, Fingers, technically," corrected Thackery.

An unusual slow-walker history was flitting back to Caenith. He didn't often delve into the details of slow-walker politics; they were always fighting, killing, and angry for one reason or another, and most tales were the same if with different players. Thackery reminded him of this particular insignificance.

"Taroch's Arm is so named for the warlord, Taroch, who once ruled the East between Kor'Khul and Menos. When he was deposed—unpleasantly, as warlords are—his quartered remains were given to each of those valiants who slew him. His right arm ended up here; there is a shrine that carries it to this day, in fact, as an object of historical worship. For while Taroch was a warlord, he was also a master sorcerer, tactician, and economist, responsible for half the currencies and markets that exist in Geadhain today. A ruthless genius, the man was, and most of Geadhain fell into chaos once his iron grip eased in death. Until the kings stepped in, that is. You have to wonder why King Magnus and King Brutus allowed the man to rule for so long—a century—if his reign was truly as vicious as the historians say."

Thackery was wandering off, chasing some runaway thought. Caenith snapped his fingers, which Thackery noticed had a bit of blood upon them.

"The point, Thackery? What is the point?"

"Right! The Fingers! Once the Hundred Year War ended, Taroch's Arm was brought home by a tongueless slave turned warrior. A great hero of the war who was given the name Glavius, after his weapon of choice. He learned to write and expressed his desire that men never be sold again. Which is why you'll find every desire under the sun for sale here, but not flesh. Indeed, for all its ties with Menos, this is probably one of the safest harbors for enemies of the Iron City. No single man, but an elected body of officials oversees the demands of Taroch's Arm, as decreed by the late Glavius. The Hand, they are called. And to enforce the will of the Hand, are those shadowy fellows that you've no doubt seen skulking the streets, the *Fingers*. In Taroch's Arm, there aren't any laws per se, but there are unspoken rules. Break those and you'll bring the Hand and all its Fingers in for a clench. This is a city of free exchange. You can deceive a man of his coin through words or bargaining, as wit is a commodity of its own, but you can never steal. You can punch a man in the face if he loses a bet to do so, but violence is otherwise prohibited. I'm hoping that no one saw what you did. I really should have forewarned a man of your temperament. We've already broken one rule, but I'm glad that you haven't been tempted to just snatch some coin and run. I know that seems the easy way; however, it will do more harm than good."

Since entering the city, Caenith had regularly observed that some of the fattest purses around hung with impunity from people's belts. He wasn't a thief, had never stolen in his life, and it was that honor alone that kept him from acting on the impulse to simply take what they needed to get on with this slow-walker-hindered pursuit of his love. It was good that Thackery had told him this, then, but no less frustrating.

"We have no time for these silly observances," grumbled Caenith. "Pray that this debtor of yours is honorable, or I shall take care of matters myself."

Two drunks swayed into the alley, kissing and groping at each other, and the companions took this as their cue to exit. As fast as he could step, Thackery hastened through the streets, passing earthen houses and their noisy smoking lodgers who bet on dice or bartered over merchandise—weapons, food, jewelry, games, or clothing—that was displayed for sale. Every house was a shop, every owner a proprietor of one thing or another. Thackery was leading them toward the port, and they descended via steep-walled byways, which offered brief reprieves from the crowds on quiet sidewalks speckled with sunshine and warmth. A regulation against trade must have been in effect along these routes, for they were traveled by foot only, and but a few whispering merchants dared to flash wares at passersby from inside the flaps of their cloaks, like perverts exposing themselves. Along these roads, Caenith spotted the first carriages and carts he had seen in a while, so presumably these were meant as routes for larger vehicles and were to remain uncluttered by commerce. Thackery took three of these byways, bringing them nearer and nearer to the salty breath of the Feordhan, and finally to the harborfront. When the byway ended, the men were deposited out onto a wider stretch of road that ran in both directions.

Across from them lay creaking grand piers with bobbing vessels of queer designs and origins: arrowhead-shaped, mastless ships that were made of metal, yet floated; the haunting white longboats of the Northmen with boldly blue sails, and other more commonplace wooden skiffs. Unsurprisingly, the merchantry had spread to the harbor, and men shouted in various tongues—sometimes impressively cycling through several—from behind cracked-open crates, shilling their wares without even leaving port. Along the side of the road that Thackery and Caenith stood on were rows of tall houses, taverns, and other dwellings that served for trade, habitation, or a mixture of each. It was quite a rush of activity to take in, and Thackery shook his head from it and set out north toward the mountainside, shortly taking them from sun to shadow again as they delved into a street off the main road. CORDENZIA BOULEVARD, read the signpost that Caenith passed.

"Cordenzia was a retired whore master from Menos," commented Thackery, who must have noticed his companion's turned eye. "One of the only women to have had that stature, and she gave it up so that she could live in freedom and no longer submit to others' rule or cruelty. She retired to Taroch's Arm and became a weaver, one of Geadhain's finest, I am told."

"You speak as if you knew her," said Caenith.

Thackery paused and spoke behind a hand; his expression was wistful and wrinkled by a hint of pain. "I did indeed. It is Cordenzia who owes me this debt. I was another person in another life, and I helped folks like her who wanted to leave the Iron City." *At the cost of everything I valued.* "Cordenzia was never one for adulation, which is why she never lived in the neighborhood named after her famed talents. Interesting that her family would return here. We can assume that she has passed since such a choice has been made."

Thackery continued down the lane. Cordenzia Boulevard was sparser of traffic, with a few one-man carriages and more inns than shops. Pleasant aromas of spiced meat and fresh ale lightened the Wolf's mood, and the people here moved at a more relaxed pace. They reached number one eighty-five in a few sands; the numbers were hammered into the facade of a tavern with a happily buzzing porch of red-cheeked patrons sipping drinks and nibbling on platters of game and vegetables that made Caenith's mouth water with their smell. The men walked up the wooden steps, and Thackery asked a busty serving girl where the owner could be found, as they had important news to share with him—or her, as he was soon corrected.

"She's inside," said the serving girl. "I'll show you."

Following the girl, they entered the busy tavern and waded through tables in a wide-beamed room toward a bar tended by a stout muscled man who blanched at Caenith's appearance.

The serving girl ordered them some watered mead on the house and darted off to find her superior, leaving the pair to watch the eclectic crowd that Taroch's Arm drew. Cloaked, wrapped, silent Arhad—men only, naturally—huddled in the corner, no doubt cursing the foreigners around them while indulging in delights that their desert palates should never taste. Cosmopolitan lords and ladies in their fancy formal wear and gowns peered toward the Arhad with reciprocated contempt. Northern brutes, with their blue-tattooed faces and white-and-blond beards as furry as the animal skins that hung off their huge shoulders, guffawed, drank, and slammed their tables. One of the Northerners saw Caenith and raised his mug to him, a gesture that the Wolf returned. The tribes of the North lived near to the tribes of the East, following old customs and natural ways, and he had a certain respect for them, even if they were slow-walkers. As he lowered his mead, he felt that they were not alone and noticed the serving girl conferring with a woman over by a staircase. The woman noticed him looking, as he was not shy about it, and motioned them over.

"Thackery, I believe we are being summoned," he said.

He left his drink on the counter and made his way to the quiet alcove, with Thackery hurrying after him. When they reached the stairs, the serving girl left them with a curtsy and a smile. The descendant of Cordenzia that they sought was a youthful but middle-aged lass in a simple cotton dress. She was wrinkled around her narrowed blue eyes from a suspicion worn over many years. Her features were thick, if pretty, and she had deep-sable hair. It was the crossing of her arms and her no-nonsense posturing that informed Thackery that she was surely a close relative of Cordenzia. They could have been sisters, though this was more likely a child or grandchild.

"Well," said the woman. "Maggie Halm, owner of The Silk Purse. I hear you've been asking for me. Let's hear what *important news* a beggar and a brawler think they can bring to me. Know this, I've smelled every sort of scam that one can sell in this city, so don't think that you'll be feeding me a shite sandwich and telling me its marmalade."

"Amazing," declared Thackery, touching his mouth. "You're just like Cordenzia. Was she your mother, or—"

Maggie stepped back and tightened her stance. "Grandmother. Don't think that throwing her name around makes me any more pliant to your tricks. As a matter of fact, it raises my hackles all the more." She snorted. "Are you implying that you knew her somehow?"

"I am," announced Thackery with all seriousness. "We should talk in private."

"Private? I think I'm well and good out here where everyone can see our conversation, including a kitchen staff of big men with knives, should you say something I'm not partial to." Maggie nodded toward a swinging door under the stairs that serving folk slipped in and out of, fanning them with the appetizing steam. "Say what you have to say, and I'll decide if it's worth further discussion."

This was not how Thackery had intended for their meeting to go; however, assuming that Cordenzia was faithful to her debts, her lineage would know of the code. They would know how to recognize the one who had given them freedom. At least Cordenzia had promised as much in her letters. *A debt never to be left unpaid, for you have granted me the wings to fly. They will know you as I knew you. Not as a Thule, but as a messenger of liberty. As a selfless man who gave his own love and life for the salvation of so many. They will know you by your true name: Whitehawk. Say it once and by my children or grandchildren, you will never be forgotten.*

Thackery beckoned the woman close. She hesitantly turned her ear.

"Whitehawk," he whispered. "I am he, and I am here to call in a debt owed to me."

Maggie's reaction was not materially evident. Yet the Wolf could smell the ripeness of her surprise—cinnamon and onions—and knew that she would believe the sorcerer. Her stiffness softened, too, and she wrestled with dozens of emotions. The Wolf tasted every nuance from fright to delight and was not shocked, as Thackery was, when she suddenly threw her arms around the old man and squeezed him tightly.

"Whitehawk!" she whispered to him. "That is a name that we Halms were taught as our earliest nursery tales! Tales never to tell to another child, for this was our secret story: of a Black City and a hero who led us from misery. I have never heard another besides my mother or Nan speak it. She said we would know you. Eyes as blue as a sapphire. Jewels of pain and wonder. The eyes of a man who broke himself to save others. I am sorry that I did not recognize you. I should have known."

Swiftly she parted, wiped her watering eyes and resumed her inflexible bearing. The busty lass was passing into the kitchen again. She had actually been loitering around, casting glances to the untidy brute meeting with Miss Halm, and spilling drinks from her neglect. She responded in a flash when Maggie flagged her down.

"These gentlemen and I shall be in my quarters, discussing matters of trade. We are not to be disturbed, but perhaps some refreshment," instructed Maggie. "You are hungry, I assume?"

Caenith nodded eagerly. The serving maid was off in a flurry. As soon as she was gone, Maggie began climbing the staircase. She muttered to her company as she ascended.

"I'll see what we can do about a bath, and possibly some clothes. No disrespect, but you look as if you've been in a fire."

More than a bit of Cordenzia's cunning had apparently passed into her kin, for Maggie hitched in midstep as somewhere in her mind, connections between men of great importance and blazing devastation was made. Cordenzia was a woman of poise and rarely faltered in her composure, and her granddaughter had inherited that trait as well. Thus she continued to climb without another word, and they strode down the landing and entered a chamber. However, the moment they were alone in her tidy apartment, she leaned against the door and gasped.

"By the kings...the attack in Eod...were the two of you there?"

V

After Thackery had convinced Maggie of the complicated avowal that *yes* they were present for the terrorism, and *no* they were not involved, and furthermore that they were to remain covert in their presence here, she still offered them aid. It hadn't been on her mind to refuse it, as disaster often followed men like Whitehawk and—she felt—the exceptionally large man introduced as Caenith, who was at once the most handsome and alarming person she had met. She had seen the sleek hunting cats of the woods of the Ebon Vale, and he reminded her of one of those, only far more dangerous. By the time the food arrived, the three were sitting in a room next to her bedchamber that was outfitted with couches, bookshelves, and a window, dazzling with bright sun. Once the serving girl had left the tray upon a table between them, Caenith gave up impatiently tapping his foot to dive into the fare. His pressing anxiety over Morigan was momentarily alleviated by the savoriness of the gristle and meat in his mouth. Messily he ate, while Thackery and Maggie sat on a couch and worked out the details of her assistance.

"Food, money, and clothing?" announced Maggie, and leaned across to catch Thackery's hand. "I would give you more, if I could. Anything, please, say it."

"A ship to cross the Feordhan." Thackery sighed. "I jest. The money should be enough to buy us seats on the ferry."

"Why would you need to cross the Feordhan?"

Thackery did not reply, and the light in Maggie's head flicked on all by itself.

"You're going to Menos, aren't you?" she said, her mouth twisted in disgust. "Why?"

"To rescue someone very important to me—to us—who has been taken to the Iron City," answered Thackery. Caenith stopped his chewing to pay respect.

"Grandmother said that you would never fly again, Whitehawk," muttered Maggie. "Certainly not to that black nest. I don't know if she would be happy or sad at this turn of events. Nonetheless, I shall do everything in my power to repay my family's debt to you. Not that such an act can be measured in gifts."

Maggie stood up and fluffed her skirt; she seemed as if she was readying to go somewhere. "You won't be taking the ferry, either. For a man who used to smuggle folks out of the Iron City, you seem to have lost your wits. The Hands require registry of every passenger who crosses the Feordhan, as they like to have their Fingers—pun intended—in every freight to and from

Taroch's Arm. If you wish to remain unseen, you will need a less conspicuous crossing. I can sense that you don't have sands to spare." As she said this, she looked to Caenith, who had eaten all on the platter that was brought but for a measly portion for his companion, and had returned to tapping his foot. "But if you give me an hourglass, I can arrange for a private, no-questions-asked voyage for the two of you. I have suppliers who would take on strange cargo for the right price."

"Thank you, blood of Cordenzia," Thackery said, bowing. "I shall consider the debt paid from these services."

"I shall not," she said, smiling. As she was leaving the room, she called back, "My lavatory is at your disposal. Towels and whatnot can be found. Don't worry about making a mess. Each of you probably needs a good scrub."

She was correct. Thackery had sand in places that one shouldn't have sand in, and while a bit of musk might suit Caenith, he felt as if he would leave a rump-shaped grease stain on Maggie's couch once he was off it. Distantly a door shut, and the companions stewed in their silences for a while, listening to the drum of the Wolf's boot—like a wagging tail, realized Thackery.

"I think I shall take a bath," announced Thackery, and rose. "I'll be quick so that you have time to trim up."

He was walking away when Caenith's grumbling voice stopped him.

"Earlier, and...in haste...I said that I had no interest in your story. I see that I have misjudged you. You are as scarred as an old oak on your heart, and those scars have come from doing good deeds in a world that generally favors the wicked."

A rare moment was this between them, where they were calm enough to listen to the other and not caught up in the chase.

"There is one more deed I must do," said Thackery.

He left the Wolf with a finality that lingered in the air. If Caenith were more of a mortal, he would have called out after the old man. However, as an animal, he accepted that when a beast knew its time, it often went off into the woods to die alone. Should it come to that, he would at least see that Thackery would not rot in some nameless grave. He would find a great tree, and stones as old as the land to place beneath it, and give him the burial of a man of honor.

✳ ✳ ✳

VI

Maggie returned well before the hourglass had dribbled out, just as Caenith was stepping from the steaming lavatory. He had washed, found some scissors to trim his beard, and after reclaiming his shirt from Thackery had scrubbed and lathered the last of the soot from his clothing. By the sink, he had found a collection of hair ties and pulled his mane back. As he appeared, his stateliness shocked Maggie, for she felt as if this was an entirely different barbarian than the one she had met. Still a savage, but perhaps a chieftain among savages, for so composed and powerful was the air he projected.

There's something very odd about you, big man, she thought, and handed him a black bundle that he fluffed into a roomy fur-trimmed cape.

"It's good that you tidy up so well, as this Northman's riding cloak was all that I could find that might fit you," said Maggie.

Leaving Caenith to sort himself out—he seemed puzzled over how to put his garment on—she walked over to Thackery in the sitting area, where he patiently waited in his rags on the edge of a couch. Thackery was hardly a man of fashion, yet he was rather excited at the thought of less aerated attire, and he made a girlish squeal as Maggie passed him a second bundle. Mayhap Caenith's exhibitionism had rubbed off on Thackery, and he didn't bother with modesty as he threw his ragged clothing on the floor and slipped into what Maggie had brought. When he was finished, Maggie turned around and clapped her approval. From his high black boots, tucked gray trousers, and tightly cuffed shirt, one could assume that Thackery was a man of moderate affluence: a merchant, perhaps. That was the intended disguise, which Maggie explained as she draped Thackery in a hooded dark mantle.

"I've taken a few liberties, but I doubt you'll find any of them disagreeable. A friend of mine is a spice broker from Sorsetta—far past the Sun King's land to the south—with business all over Geadhain. Ran into him down at the docks when I was barely one foot out the door, and it just so happens that he is having some troubles of his own, and plans on staying at The Silk Purse, staying low, for a while. He's a man that doesn't particularly want to be himself right now, which leaves the opportunity for someone else to fill that vacancy."

Maggie cinched the fabric at Thackery's neck with a silver clasp and then clutched his shoulders. "When I said he has business all over Geadhain, I meant that, literally: from Eod to the Iron City. With his papers, which he was kind enough to provide me with, you can walk right into Menos."

Part of Thackery wanted to laugh, but the dread awareness that he would be stepping again into the Iron City choked the excitement. He was somber as he said, "That's brilliant, my dear. You've saved us so much trouble. Ages ago, I took your kin out of the Iron City, and here you are returning me to it. A certain poetry to that, I suppose."

"Wait," said Caenith, and strode over to join them. He had figured out the cloak, even if it was a tad lopsided. "How will this work? Do these men even look the same?"

Maggie smiled. "I mean this as kindly as it can be said, but all old gentlemen tend to look alike. Jebidiah is bald and thin, and Thackery has a hood to conceal what differences there might be. As long as you don't go shaking hands with any acquaintances of his, I suspect no one will know any better. His vessel, which you'll be sailing on, is privately manned and the captain has been instructed of the ruse."

Caenith still wasn't entirely convinced. "If he is a spice merchant, who am I, then?"

"His muscle, obviously," answered Maggie.

She reached into the folds of her dress, pulled out a leather packet, and handed it to Thackery. "Jebidiah Rotbottom is your name. Unfortunate, I know, and I imagine he never had much fun around the playground. Well, that's not true, actually. Before turning to the spice trade, the Rotbottoms were herbalists. In the South, there's a rather famous disease called *rotbottom* where everything comes out the...you can imagine. Anyhow, it's Jebidiah's ancestors who put the sickness on the run through their herbs and remedies. That's how they got their name, and it's a prestigious one, so it will get you places that many can't go."

"Who is this Rotbottom on the run from?" frowned Caenith.

"A supplier in the South, with whom business arrangements have soured. Far south, in the Sun King's lands. No one you should run into from here and Menos, and I imagine you can defend yourself against a few thugs, if it came to that. He wouldn't say much more. In any case, speed and silence will be your allies. Don't stay in one place for too long, and don't go making any noise. You never know who is listening, especially in Blackforge or beyond, where the ears of the Iron Queen are plentiful."

Maggie rustled in her prestidigitator's pockets and removed a jangling purse. She passed that to Thackery as well. "There's some folds in your overcoat to hold all that. Along with Jebidiah's papers, you have one hundred fates and one hundred crowns, which should see to any expense. Don't worry about losing Rotbottom's papers; I'm sure that's not his only set or the only identity he values. The man sheds skins like a snake."

"I don't know what to say. It sounds as if you've thought of everything," exclaimed Thackery, and hugged Cordenzia's blood with gratitude.

Maggie's embrace was as heartfelt as his was. "I may not have done all the things my mum and Gran wished of me: never took a man, put down the needle so I could run a house of leisure, even moved back into the old neighborhood—good for business, having a hero's name attached." She chuckled. "But I never, not for a speck, forgot the story of Whitehawk. So I would thank you for giving a girl dreams and fancies to occupy her. For teaching her the value of maintaining integrity and honor, even if you never taught those lessons directly."

They held each other awhile longer, and knew that they were delaying an already late farewell. Finally, they pulled apart. Thackery found the pockets that Maggie had mentioned and placed his valuables inside them.

"Let's get you two on your way," said Maggie.

Down into the tavern they went. As they were leaving the loud room, the Wolf noticed a scrawny old man drinking by himself at a table. *That must be Jebidiah,* he knew, for he detected a comparable scent between the leather wallet in Thackery's possession and that man. *I guess all old slow-walkers do look the same.* Outside, the air was thick with afternoon heat and sweaty, packed bodies, yet being close to the waterfront brought relief in on-and-off gusts of wind. They did not talk as they walked, and Caenith allowed his heightened senses to rove a little off their leash: to teasing tangs of seaweed and fresh fish, the crisp calls of gulls, and the rocking lure of the waves. It was incredible how much his perceptions had grown since the Fuilimean, and while he had never said so to Thackery, his ability to cross Kor'Khul in days was a feat that he could not have accomplished a week ago. His great strength had been made greater through Morigan's blood. *Soon, my Fawn. Soon I shall have you, and I can thank you for how you have changed me. A man who thought he was too old for any change.*

When they had crossed the large promenade and come to the wooden planks of the harbor, Caenith's moment of tranquility was ruined by a twinge of familiar scent: metal and musk, the oily fragrance of a woman who wielded steel so often as to smell like it. His puffing nostrils took control of his head, and he stopped, turned, and scanned the crowd hundreds of strides deep. There, everything paused, and he saw an image as clearly as through a pane of glass. A woman. She wasn't in armor, but her broad carriage and stern brown jaw betrayed her, despite her heavy cloak.

"The sword of the queen," he muttered.

"Pardon me?" said Thackery, who hadn't quite heard.

Caenith pulled him aside and pointed down the boardwalk. At first, Thackery could not make out who or what he was looking for. However, Caenith's whisper of *Rowena* acted like a magik charm in assisting him, and he spotted the woman—along with a blond companion who appeared familiar—strolling toward them through the masses.

"By the kings!" he exclaimed. "What is she doing here?"

"Looking for us, I suspect," grumbled Caenith.

Maggie added herself to the huddle. "Who? Who is looking for you?"

At that moment, Rowena's gaze drifted in their direction and widened; although only Caenith could see this. She noticed the three of them crouched as conspirators and whispering, with the smith's size declaring his identity. Rowena elbowed her companion and the two broke into a run.

"They've seen us! The ship! Where is the ship?" demanded Caenith.

Maggie answered. "Three piers down! The *Red Mary*. Red as a whore's bottom. You can't miss it! Go! I shall delay them!"

With a pinched look of remorse, Thackery was hauled away by his large companion. Their pursuers were closing quickly, knocking over pedestrians in their haste, and she had few specks for a plan. *Think, Maggie! Think!* She saw some crates and contemplated knocking them over, as pitiful a delay as that would cause, when suddenly a dripping shadow fell over her. She looked up and grinned at the netted haul of the Feordhan, and then followed the arm of the rickety crane and raced toward its source. In a toll-booth-shaped cubicle, walled in glass and wood, she found the operator of the machine: a mariner so tanned and creased that his age was indeterminable. She rapped on the glass for his attention. He brushed under his bristly chin in the universal sign for *fuk off* until she produced from her bottomless skirt another purse and promised to give him all of it if he only did as she asked. Taroch's Arm was a realm of free commerce, where no good deal was denied, and even as she explained the ridiculousness of what he was to do, he did not back down from the bargain. Maggie whipped around to the crowd and found Thackery's speeding pursuers. She held up her hand, fingers spread— waiting, waiting, just a few more steps—and then snapped it into a fist. Somewhere in his booth, the mariner flipped a switch, and without warning or fanfare, the bulbous net, swaying like a fat cloud over the boardwalk, released its binding cords and dumped its slimy cargo. There were screams and noises of hysteria, which calmed to laughter for the most part, as people slid and flopped about in the fish pile as if they were fish themselves. The cloaked woman and the blond man were among the downed, though she was quickly hitching herself to stand using a shining blade. She reached for her sopping, cursing companion, and he ended up pulling her back into the mess, where they rolled about like jesters and Maggie lost track of them.

Maggie stayed a speck longer to make certain that the rain of fish hadn't injured anyone too seriously, and then left her coin for the cranesman and thought it best to disappear. While fleeing, she cast a look to the east and was happy to see a red shape cutting through the waters.

Safe travels, Whitehawk, she prayed. *May you bring another lost soul home from the Black City.*

VII

The waters of the Feordhan smelled of briny, ancient freedom to the Wolf: of years and secrets greater and older than his. He found the salty bluster an inspiration to their journey. It was like a wind pushing against his sails, encouraging him to move on, promising him that Morigan and he would be united soon. From the prow of the *Red Mary*, Thackery watched the river with his companion. They had not spoken after arriving on the boat, which was as easy to locate as Maggie had stated. Only the blind could miss a long steel ship, lacquered red as a concubine's fingernails and inscribed with the name *Red Mary* along its hull. Jebidiah had a proclivity for whimsy. They saw more of this as they were welcomed aboard by groomed seamen onto a deck that was clear of sailing apparatuses, rigging, or masts, and was decorated like a pleasure vessel with bolted benches and awnings for shade, and stairs leading to a second deck where lounging sun-chairs were set. Once the anchor was raised, the hirsute and handsome captain introduced himself to the *Red Mary*'s passengers and set sail without a single question as to the urgency that they presented to him. Since then, the deckhands had been mysteriously absent, but for a hale, often shirtless gentleman or two who would pop up and attend to any nourishment that they asked for, until even Caenith had his fill. After pacing, peeing off the deck, or lying about on the deck, the two eventually found themselves lured to the water. Enough time had passed that the sky was darkening and the stars were readying to prick their way through the firmament: mere hints of light now, but what a glorious night it would be on the Feordhan.

"An unusual ship, it carves through these rough waters like a sword," the Wolf said abruptly. "It was a good idea coming to Taroch's Arm. I thank you for that. You have brought wisdom into a head clouded with rage."

"Rage...yes," mumbled Thackery. "You should be angry. Perhaps at me, as well, for I remain burdened by thoughts that I am somehow responsible for Morigan's capture."

Caenith glared at him; not with cruelty, but harshly nonetheless. "You have said this before. Explain yourself."

Glancing elsewhere, Thule leaned over the railing and wished for the river to blow him the courage to speak. Someone had to know the truth. All of it. When he was ready, he turned to Caenith, though he was surprised by the manic, toothy grimace of the man and shocked more by the howl that he suddenly released to the skies. He forgot his confession and asked instead, "What is it?"

"Morigan," panted the Wolf, and tapped his temple. "She's speaking! She's free!"

✳ ✳ ✳

VIII

Back in The Silk Purse, Maggie helped herself to a drink. Jebidiah was still swilling his sorrows, though drunkenly bobbing along to a bard that had appeared near the hearth. Jebidiah could have been an old bard himself: once handsome and lean, now bald, wrinkled, and skinny, though the essence of an adventurous spirit clung in cold remembrance in his gaze, and his clothing was light and as gaily red as a performer's—typical, considering a Sorsettan's lust for color. The old merchant seemed amiable, more so than he had been in the morning, so she went to keep him company. He welcomed her without a word, and she ordered a meal and limitless wine for them each, which elicited a smile from Jebidiah, if still no conversation. The bard crooned an epic about a maiden pining for her love that went on for nearly an hourglass, by which time she was pleasantly drunk. Loose enough with her tongue to ask what troubles plagued the merchant.

"So, how much do you owe the man, Jebidiah?"

This provoked an immediate response. "Ssh! I am Myrtul. Myrtul Hawkins."

"Myrtul, then," she snickered, placing her elbows on the table to get closer to her companion. "You're as slippery as they come, and I've never seen you do anything but laugh in the face of threats. You must have royally pissed off this supplier of yours to come scurrying here. What was his name again?"

Her companion clutched his goblet, and his eyes darted as if he were a hunted animal. He wasn't scared; he was terrified. After a moment, he stopped trembling enough to stutter out a few words.

"I didn't...I never said a name." Jebidiah shook his head. "I...I...I may have overstepped myself."

Maggie waited for him to continue. It was a long wait.

"The spice trade, you see, it was never really enough."

"Enough?" she asked.

"Enough coin," said her companion. He tossed back his wine, hunched nearer, and the story began to spill. "Not to sustain my habits, which have grown ever more complex and expensive over the years. My jewels and silks are bitter comforts to a lonely soul. While I have no children, I have many mouths to feed. Many men who rely upon my caregiving and generosity. Expensive, so expensive."

Maggie knew of the merchant's predilection for hearty, able-bodied fellows who enjoyed the *brotherhood* of others like themselves. She had also been aboard the *Red Mary*, met its handsome crew, and watched how they fawned over Jebidiah like a gaggle of hens. Indeed, paying for a family of courtesans surely wasn't the cheapest vice, she considered.

"What did you do?" she hissed. "Who are you running from? You said that you were in a *pinch* of trouble. A pinch. This certainly sounds like more than that."

Jebidiah fluttered his hand. "As I was saying, I found that a ship as fast as the *Red Mary* was in demand to transport other, more lucrative cargos than perfumes and spices. Witchroot—still a spice, in a sense. Or Kurakik poisons for the black markets of Menos. That was definitely ignoble, I'll give you that. But never anything more than those small sins, I promise you. At least not until this last request." Jebidiah looked as if he might weep. "You have to understand that I didn't know what was being asked of me. What I would have to transport. I never would have agreed." Jebidiah stopped himself from talking and his stare went cagey. "Swear to me that you will not cast me out if I share this with you, for I have no one else to turn to. I know that what I have done—what I almost did—is a matter near and dear to your heart. A matter that you have certain sensitivities toward."

"Certain sensitivities," she muttered.

Jebidiah nodded.

Cordenzia and her daughter had raised a woman who could stand head and shoulders to their greatness and fortitude, and Maggie couldn't think of much that would unsettle her. Except...

"Spit it out. What was the cargo?" she demanded.

"Livestock, the master said. But I should have known."

A pause.

"People," he whispered.

Maggie recoiled, yet Jebidiah was quick to snatch her hands. Luckily, the bard and chatter drowned out his hectic pitch. "I didn't do it! I couldn't! All those trembling savages, penned and shiting themselves on my dear *Red Mary*! My lads gave me the most heinous stares, though I did not need their accusation to burden my remorse, which was crushing! I let them go... dropped the wretches off in the forested hills north of Blackforge. I have no idea what will become of the poor creatures, but I did justice's work in setting them free. I even gave them what arms my men could spare and a few days' worth of food, and then I headed straight here. For I knew I was marked. You do not defy a"—he spat the next bit with venom—"Menosian master, an *Iron sage*, and live in peace thereafter."

"Menosian master?" exclaimed Maggie, cupping her mouth lest she draw scathing glances. As much restraint as she showed, her mind was frantic. Inadvertently, she had betrayed Thackery as well as sticking the knife in herself.

"What were you thinking?" she whispered. "This is no petty debtor you've scorned! You've just endangered a hero! You should have told me that you were hiding from a master of Menos! I never—"

"Would have helped me," said Jebidiah, pouting. "I know. And you weren't listening clearly. Not a master, but an Iron sage, Moreth of El. Ruler of the blood pits. Those men and women were bound for death in the ring. What have I done? What have I done?" Jebidiah held his head and let out a quiet sob.

"You did a good thing," said Maggie, absently consoling him with a hand. "You are a stupid, lying fool, but you at least acted with honor when the choice was thrust upon you. We can keep you here for a time. But you are right, if Moreth calls for your head, nowhere between Eod and Menos is safe for you. Farther to the west, you might have hope. Your concern is the lesser of my problems, however, for I must think of how I am to get a message to the man that you have damned with your carelessness and lies. I hope it is not too late."

A fishy breeze came over her, like sardines left in the sun. Something behind her startled Jebidiah into clutching himself. She knew she was in trouble before the heavy hand clamped on her shoulder.

"That's the problem with Taroch's Arm," muttered a voice into her ear. "You can pay a man for any service, but silence on the deed is another fee altogether. You must not have made that part of your arrangement down at the harbor. Galivad and Rowena of Eod, here on the authority of Her Majesty, and we would have a word with you, tavernkeep."

XIII

THE ESCAPE

I

The glimpses of Menos that Morigan had seen in the minds of others did not capture the depths of its despair. Behind her gag, Morigan gasped at the Iron Wall with its barbed battlements that rose in a black tidal wave around the city. Unscalable and unassailable, it drove home the iron stake that Morigan was far from the white wonder of Eod and farther still from safety. Over the black belfries and steeples of buildings crafted like temples to unholy worship, the skycarriage flew, and through her fear, Morigan marveled at it all. Seizing her attention more than anything else, however, was a tower of gleaming dark stone or glass, for there was a diaphanousness to it similar to quartz. Morigan could tell that this was the heart of Menos, for it commanded the cityscape; it announced its rule simply by spanning from earth to murky sky, by being a glaring abomination amid an ocean of unnaturalness.

What is that? whispered Morigan to her fellow captive.

The Crucible, where the Iron sages hold their council, and the grandest schemes in Geadhain are born, answered Mouse. *Don't worry about that; we'll never see it. Just remember the plan.*

The plan. From what they had heard among the numbermen whom the Broker commanded, they were to be moved when they landed and then kept in holding at the Blackbriar estate until *certain parties* arrived for Morigan. Past that, their fates were dismal to consider, and they weren't certain how long they were to be kept manacled together, which left them a narrow sliver of time to pull off an impossible escape. Morigan was prepared for what they had discussed, though a measure of their success lay in chance. They needed a moment, however slight, with the dead man to themselves and without the interference others.

I'm ready, said Morigan.

Good, replied Mouse. *Time to grease up this hog before the roast.*

With a decade as a pleasure maiden under her belt, Mouse still possessed many of her charms, though she chose never to wield them. She was schooled in the silent seductions of a woman: the batting of eyes, how to puff out even a meager chest like hers, or more impressive still, a trick to knot the breath in one's chest and force a blush into her cheeks. In the gloomy cabin, she softly groaned and stretched. She could see the numbermen watching her with a particular interest, and doubtlessly the dead man was, too. After a moment she stopped, careful not to confuse the line between sufferer and temptress. Then the carriage was quickly descending, rattling against the currents, and she used the jostling to tip sideways in her seat and hope that the dead man caught her. He did, and set her right again with his cold but gentle hands. She mumbled something to him, and surely the softness of her expression entreated him, for he pulled down her gag.

"Thank you," she murmured.

The dead man dipped his head, woeful as a punished lover, and then went to place the cloth back into her mouth. *Not so fast. I need my tongue,* she thought, and bit the inside of her cheek. The pain filled her eyes with tears.

"No, please," she pleaded in a whisper. "It's hurting my face. I promise to be quiet. I shan't object, no matter the treatment."

Either the tears or her uncommon gentleness halted him, and he ultimately consented to her request. In the uneasy tension that followed, he continued to stare at her, advances that she did not refuse, but accepted with the subtlest smiles of her eyes. Shortly, the skycarriage creaked and then jolted to a stop. The dead man brought Mouse to her feet, with Morigan—attached—rising, too. The women were herded into the hull and then down the metal stairs into the miasma of Menos, into a foulness that swallowed them like a quicksand. Unaccustomed to the Iron City, Morigan found herself fighting for breaths against the dense air, and her skin was coated in greasy perspiration almost immediately. The stinging haze of a recent Menosian rain also wasn't helping Morigan acclimate to the conditions.

"Blink, a lot," advised Mouse.

The dead man escorted the ladies with his gentlemanly grace, as if they were not chained captives, but guests to a ball. Although Morigan only gaped at the black manor, Mouse recognized the gargoyle guardians, sneering their welcome, toward which they were being marched. The four numbermen were ahead, while beyond them were the Broker and the Raven, already climbing the estate's extravagant steps. The latter appeared to be having some difficulty and had to pause and grasp the shorter man's shoulder now and then.

Poor tyke, scoffed Mouse. *All tired out from his corpse-bombing and flesh-puppeting. Little fuk. I made a promise to gut you with my knives. And I'll keep that one day.*

"The stones are slippery," warned the dead man as they walked—the first words he had said in ages. "Be careful with your step."

We'll be quite the opposite of that, thought Mouse. She wasn't sure if Morigan was listening, but as the Raven and the Broker disappeared into the shadowy entrance and the numbermen showed a similar fleetness in approaching the estate, Mouse knew that this was their golden moment. She slowed a tad, as if cautious of the dead man's words, and tugged her chain twice—firmly and noticeably—as a sign to her companion. Quicker and more dramatically than expected, Morigan dropped like a stone. Mouse nearly went with her, yet was rescued by the dead man's reflexes. On the ground, Morigan moaned in pain and kept her face pressed to the disgusting cobbles; she wasn't imagining it: the contact was burning her skin.

"Hurry, help her up," insisted Mouse.

Being a gentleman, the urge to assist the fallen woman conquered any reservations, and Mouse's doe-eyed insistence tipped the last of the scale in

Vortigern. The dead man held up a hand to Mouse and then dipped to hoist Morigan under the armpits. He remembered coming face-to-face with her and, suddenly, her pressing into his flesh as if they were lovers, and seeing a queer smile and a stranger sparkle in her eyes, and then—

Go! she Wills her bees, as soon as their touch is made. They pierce their stingers against her prison, against the cold iron that traps her Will. They do not have far to go, passing only from skin to skin, from gaze to gaze, and they buzz deep into the soul to which they are connected. An empty space exists in the dead man, where things have been forgotten or locked away from a vacancy beyond mere absentmindedness. This is death, she feels, this blank and echoing void. He has been here, her host. This is why he cannot remember, because he has not crossed death with his mind, only his flesh. None but the most masterful traveler can do so, and in her silver cloud of Will, she soars from the darkness and into brilliance. Into recall.

Mouse, she thinks, at the woman in an ebony gown who stands in the gray light of a long window. Yet this is a misconstruction, for the nose is a touch larger, the hair fuller. This is not Mouse, but someone close to her. She bobs around the room—no more attached to the host, but to the memory itself—and watches a man enter the hall and take his place next to the woman. While it is dim in the hall, Morigan's spirit self can see the feelings that they share: they burn as white torches for the other, though nothing of this is expressed in the reservedness of their bodies. Morigan floats nearer, and is not surprised when she sees that the man is a harder-featured version of the nekromancer; rugged where the other is foppish. He is not as pale as the dark sorcerer is, and his vibrancy declares him as being alive. He is formally dressed and Morigan knows that he is a master.

("One of two," the bees hum, and Morigan apprehends that he is the brother of the nekromancer, of course. Twins, surely identical, given their extreme likeness to the other.)

"One more night, Lenora," whispers the man to the window, without turning his head. "One more night and Whitehawk flies for us. You must be ready."

"I am ready," says Lenora, and dares to touch her lover's hand.

Morigan quivers like a plucked harp from the yearning between them. They are fortunate that the servants have yet to catch them, as discreet as they have been for two people whose souls scream for the other. Not sexually, for they have only consummated their sin once, but spiritually. In the library was where it began, as they caught the other reading books of forbidden—Western—poetry. That was where the promise and trust was seeded. Thereafter, he would see her in the gardens, and they would walk with a shrub between them and whisper heretical ideas or prose through the branches. One day, he found Lenora tending to the broken wing of a sparrow, cradling it in her skirt and whistling to it, instead of crushing it, as a Menosian should. The speck that she placed the injured creature down, he kissed her, right there, and she did not stop him. She had a softness that he had never seen. She was a flower in the black garden of Menos; and his brother, who lusted for her, who had been handed her through a conceived marriage for their mother's ambition, had never seen her true beauty. He shivers as Lenora traces the veins on his hand, not with desire, but merely from a need to hold her, which he cannot.

"Where shall we go?" asks Lenora.

"Anywhere," he says, smiling. "My uncle will arrange for passage to anywhere in Geadhain. Bless him for pitying his cursed family. I did not think we would be given such mercy."

"It is only because we mirror his own torment, his own story," mutters Lenora. She touches her stomach, remembering a life that is no longer swimming inside it. "He has a child, too, does he not?"

The host scatters his caution and places his face to Lenora's neck, kissing it once. "Yes. Perhaps they will play together. Our children. Children of freedom."

"Sorren suspects nothing?"

"My brother is too full of his ego to see whatever does not fan it. He did not see the beauty under his nose, the light in your heart. He does not know that the babe he ignores is not his own."

"Good. I would die before I endanger her," says Lenora, a deadly and heartfelt promise.

"As would I."

So you will each, thinks Morigan, who understands more than the specters she visits do. The two pull apart, secretively slinking from the hall, and this memory is over for Morigan. The bees wish to take her elsewhere, and they swarm her consciousness and dive into the golden threads of memory. They swim like fish against the flow of this soul—going backward in time and space— and spill her out into another scene.

A child. The child of this union slumbers in a nursery as grim as a thorn garden in the moonlight. Lenora is at the metal crib that should house a beast and not a child, and the host of these memories lurks like an assassin near the velvet curtains of the window. He yearns to come close, though it is foolish for him even to be here; who knows what assumptions might be made? Lenora apparently cares not, for she beckons him to the crib.

"Come see our daughter," she whispers.

The host creeps forward.

"She is beautiful. She looks...so much like you," he gasps. "What have you called her?"

"Fionna."

Enough of this, declare the bees. No time, no time, and still much to see. Morigan is plunged into the memory river again and sent along with the current to the nearest memories. The ones before the darkness of death.

The host is in a deep rainy channel roofed in bridges and lined with grates of metal that reek of shite. Miserably, he wades in rancid water and shelters from the downpour under an overhang. As often as he wipes his wet face, he is certain to have stinkeye by now. But still he peeks and stares boldly into the rain. Lenora is late, and not by a few sands, but by several hourglasses. No matter, he will vigilantly await her, with the pitiful optimism of a man who will not consider reality. For they have made a promise. They love each other. They have a child who must see the world beyond these iron walls. He checks his chronex again for the hundredth time, as if it has stopped or has given him an incorrect reading. He waits. Shivers. Rubs his eyes. Then waits some more, until the chill and dampness has moldered his spirit, and he cannot deny that something is wrong. Desperately he scans the murky streets above, hoping to see a woman—any woman—and her bundle of a child appear.

A groomed figure looms atop the underpass, cozy beneath an umbrella.

"Vortigern," says the nekromancer. "How fitting that you should scurry in the sewers among the waste like the rat that you are. And here you will die, too. Nameless filth to be swept off with the shite and piss of our nation."

Braver than he should be, the host splashes out of concealment and waves a sword at his brother. "Where is Lenora?"

"She is mine! She was promised to me! My right! Our mother's will!"

"By the kings! You cannot own a person! You cannot force someone to love you! You are no man, but a child!" screams the host.

"Children...yes." The sneer is apparent even if it is not seen. "Shall we talk about those? Yours, I suppose. As I'm not the father I thought I was. Be grateful that I've picked a pleasant tree for her to be buried under."

Morigan watches the host collapse in the waters; sorrow wafts off him in a black cloud. He is shaking his head. "You wouldn't...a child? What have you done?"

"I simply removed what should not be. Well, Mother took care of it for me. Now Lenora and I can start over. Should be easier without you in the picture. It never mattered how smart or powerful I was, that I was the one with magik and you were only good with wit and a blade. Somehow, you always managed to achieve what I could not. You grew stronger and more handsome than I did. You could hold your own in a fight as well as a debate. Were it not for your treachery, I might never have seen the simplest solution to this problem. The problem of always being in your shadow. Killing you."

To Morigan's spirit eyes, the grief of her host veins with blackness: a manifestation of the darkest anger. He roars, flips his sword, and hurls it from the handle like a javelin. On his perch, Sorren's smugness turns to a yelp, and he throws out glowing white hands too late to stop the blade from piercing his gut and toppling him onto the street. Grunting in anger and shuddering with sobs, the conflicted host makes the climb onto the flagstones and stands over his brother's ruined body. He kneels and closes Sorren's gaping stare.

"Forgive me, brother. May you find the peace in death that you could not in life." He spits on the corpse's cheek. "But I shall never forget your sins. And I shall hate you, with my soul, for all time."

The host stands and walks away.

This can't be it, thinks Morigan. For Sorren, as she knows him, is quite alive, and his brother is quite dead. Faintly, she hears it then: a faraway whisper, a scratch of leaves over stone, the sound of a tomb from across the stars being opened. It is possible that the host senses an unnaturalness, too, for he halts and glances to the blood-pooled remains—a corpse and nothing more, to him. Only she sees what he does not. She sees the essence of Sorren's petulant malice clinging to his corpse, unready to leave this world. Great magik this one had, and his hatred is more than emotion; it is a force of potentiality. A Will.

Into the ether the black tendrils of his Will reach, toward the stars, toward the things that sleep beyond. The anger at being forgotten, at passing into decay and dust, at being dismissed and ultimately abandoned to nothingness, which comprises the whole of what drives Sorren, cries to the universe like a bleating child. And his call is answered. By an entity of like Wills and fears. A thing that should fade as a season, but refuses to pass into time. While this voice is light and as morbidly seductive as a funeral dirge, Morigan knows what sort of being this is. A shapeless mass of Will and power. A shadow from which the lesser creatures hide. A daunting presence that she would fear even more if this were not a memory. Nonetheless, she quakes in her metaphysical skin as it croons to the broken soul of Sorren. It is no Black Queen that speaks to the dead nekromancer, but a similar overlord: a queen of bones. A being who talks of the mysteries of flesh as if she wrote them herself.

"Hush, broken thing. Hush and be still. Your anguish has woken me. What a Will you must have to reach so far. So dark and furious. So weak and supple. You are perfect, but broken. Your meat has been split. The red tides leave you. I know death. I am death. If you will be my instrument, then I shall fill you with my wisdom. I shall show you the hidden pathways of bone, blood, and grub. How to stitch the meat, stem the blood, and make yourself stronger than you can imagine. Revenge? We shall make this offender against us rot and live and die each day. Punishment eternal. I promise you this: the darkest vengeance and knowledge that no man should have. Quick, broken thing. Decide now. That was life's final beat, and the tolling for your answer. Let me in."

The pact is made. On the precipice of death, Sorren accepts with his soul, and his body blazes in a black inferno. As the unholy fire crackles low, he steps out of the smoke toward his breathless brother. The sword is in the nekromancer's hand, and he carelessly discards it with a clatter of steel. While his garments are torn and bloody about his belly, naught but pale skin peeks through.

"Vortigern," he says, smiling. "Death will not be enough for you. My new friend has shown me a better way."

He raises his hands, mitted in cold fire, and Morigan watches the lines of black energy fly from his form like arcs of lightning into her host. The bees whisk her away as the host's flesh jitters electrically and begins to bleed ebony juices and distort from an abominable alchemy. The last she hears is a scream.

Abruptly, Vortigern and she were staring at each other, panting—mostly pretend on his part—and trembling. Evidently, the forced entry into his mind had snapped the lock right off, for he cast Morigan down and stumbled away from her while violently trying to toss the images from his head. Morigan wondered what he was seeing, how much she had released, and if she had hindered more than helped their situation. Anxious to know the same, Mouse threw her puzzled glares. However, no one had the chance to make peace with anything, for a few of the straggling numbermen had noticed the commotion and come running back to the three of them. By the time they reached the trio, Vortigern was on the flagstones, swaying and quiet. With pitiable moroseness, he stared between the two women, though mostly at Mouse.

"What happened?" demanded a numberman.

"She—" started Mouse.

"I fell," interjected Vortigern.

"Get them inside. We'll walk with you, in case your delicate self takes another spill," snickered a numberman.

"Useless things, you reborn are. They could have run. Though I fancy a good hunt," boasted another, and he pulled down his balaclava and tried to kiss Morigan's cheek.

She squirmed away. *So does my mate. I hope you meet him soon*, thought Morigan.

Into the Blackbriar estate, the three were marched. And try as she might to lean or stumble near, Morigan never had a moment to touch Mouse and thereby explain her spiritual wandering. When they were in the echoing foyer, the numbermen unlinked the chain that tied the two women and led Morigan off. She turned to the dazed pair she was leaving behind and shouted the truth she had seen from her muffled mouth, though it wasn't articulate and only laughed at by her captors. With any hope, Vortigern would recall the honor and love of the man he haunted and, more importantly, the promise he had made. For there was only one explanation, however extraordinary, as to who Mouse was.

* * *

II

Morigan's confinement was a nicer arrangement than any other mortal cargo would find in Menos: a paneled bedroom with an inviting bed, glossy furniture, and a padded chair that hugged her like a friend as she brooded in it, contemplating her dilemma. Outside it had begun to rain again, and she followed the intricate rivers that coursed over the windowpane. Her soothsayer's sense looked for meaning in the patterns, though no revelations stood out. Mostly, the rain was reminiscent of tears. She missed Caenith and could not ignore the burning sorrow in her chest that pulsed when she thought of Thackery.

It's all gone to shite. So quickly. I was so happy three days past. I want them back. Both of them.

The two numbermen who guarded her were near indiscernible against the black drapes, though their presence killed the tears before they began. She was a survivor. Tears were for the dead, and she wasn't that yet. *Think. Think,* she demanded. She wasn't exploring all her options. Would those numbermen have something in their heads worth breaking into? A vice or secret that she could exploit? She was willing to take the risk needed to find out. She moaned against her bonds. All dressed in black and draped in darkness, it was impossible to tell accurately if their heads were turning or attention was being paid, so she increased her writhing until she was rocking the chair and surely a nuisance.

"Feisty bitch," grunted the numberman who had tried to kiss her in the courtyard. "I'll go slap her quiet."

The larger of the numbermen left his post and went to Morigan. He didn't waste a speck in doing exactly as he said. He cracked Morigan across the face with his hand. Her head exploded with white lights, and as the man materialized, he was leaning over her chair. In his eyes was a gleam of sadistic pleasure, and he shook her manacled wrists as if she were a misbehaving hound.

"I shall need to show you how to behave."

Close enough, thought Morigan. Her eyes flickered silver, and the bees passed between them in a spark.

She spins into a cage filled with scrawny natives. For prisoners, they keep their spirits high, chanting and humming harmonies that tell of life and its

311

beginnings and endings, as if they are not fearful of their own. Her host is cling-
ing to someone, a woman, though that person's face is as gray as a foggy morn-
ing. He cannot remember her, and therefore neither can Morigan. She must be
memorable, however, for as the slavers bully their way into the pen and drag
him from her, they both scream until she is beaten to the ground.

Blackness clouds over Morigan's voyage, and as the bees dazzle it away, she
sees the boy chained in a dank cellar of a chamber—a place deep with despair
and rank as a sewer. The man with the metal smile is whispering lunacy to him,
telling him to escape, escape, that freedom is only his strength of will away.

"How badly do you want it? Enough to cost you pain? Enough to disfigure
yourself?" asks the glittering mouth. "Let us see if you can survive The Binding."

When the madman leaves him—to die and rot—the boy, who is a hunter
and a fighter, grasps the cruel test: he has seen how animals chew their way
from traps, and it is a cost of flesh. Tormentedly, for hourglasses, he wriggles
and howls as he snaps and squeezes his large hands through the chains. At last
he is done. His hands are shattered and limp as reeds, but perhaps they can be
fixed. At least he is free. Until the metal smile shines from the shadows, and he
knows that he is mistaken.

"Well done, you have passed the first of many tests, and the most impor-
tant. Let us see if you can earn a number."

"Twenty-two?" said the numberman by the window.

For Twenty-two had gone motionless. He held Morigan's hands tightly,
as if they were praying together, and the bees continued smashing the walls
in his head like delicate porcelain, each broken object releasing a memory.

Poor lamb, echoed Morigan into Twenty-two's mind. *You never had a*
choice in this, did you? Never stopped being a prisoner. Do you remember your
mother? You loved her so, though her face has been scraped from you. What
agony can make one forget those he loves?

As she thinks this, the bees carry her flashes of torture.

The boy is choking in a pit of excrement, trying to breathe, while faceless
numbermen piss on him. Then he is tied to a table and biting on a wooden bit so
hard that his teeth are cracking, while knives and whips lick his flesh. "Do not
cry. Endure and grow strong," demands the metal smile, who is always pres-
ent and watching, who is the one voice that resounds through the pain. After
a spell—weeks or years—it is all that the boy knows: this voice and its reason.

When the pain and abuse have ripped away what it is to live, the voice is his world and the will that he must obey.

Twenty-two was weeping, silently.

You are doing what has been done to you because you do not know better. You must remember what came before. Remember the lessons you learned from the mother and father you have forgotten. Remember what it is to love and care and be a man, insisted Morigan, and she pushed her ever stronger and bolder Will farther into Twenty-two, sending her bees for the sweetest nectar of his truth. Images whirled about their perceptions then, so vivid that they saw not the room.

The other numberman sensed an eeriness to his fellow now and moved to investigate.

She floats like a snowflake across a frosty winterscape with the white shadows of Kor'Keth to the south. Two hunters wander beneath her. By morning light, the boy and his father leave the tents and hike far through the woods to fish through holes carved in the lake. They share bits of seal fat, and his father tells him that it will make him strong, and that he will be a fine hunter one day. Come night, they count the stars on the way home and soon huddle inside a shelter: warm from fires, furs, and song.

Great storytellers are his people, a wisdom kept mostly by the women, who are the curators and leaders among them. His mother is the keeper of his tribe, the wisest of the storytellers. Her throaty songs drone on like a hummingbird's wings made to music, rising and falling, ever constant and mesmerizing. She speaks of the gifts that seal and fish have given them tonight, how they must be honored for the blood that has passed into the tribe's mouths. She sings of the Great Feast, this cycle of sacrifice, and how no sacrifice, from the lowly spider to the mighty bear, must be left unworshiped for their flesh and purpose in this life. Sacred, she calls this: the Will of the Green Mother. When the boy listens to her, he hardly thinks of her as his mother, for she is as captivating as the lights that sometimes dance in the north.

The next morning, the black ships and evil men come and her voice is forgotten. Her face drifts to mist, and all he sees, all he will come to know, is a metal smile and a voice that bids him pain.

The numbered man was upon them. But Morigan wasn't finished, not yet. Like Twenty-two, she was grieving at the boy's transformation from innocent to monster. She had been seeking a vice to manipulate, only to find mercy. She had one last gift to give him. His name, which the bees found nestled in the thorniest part of his soul.

Kanatuk, that is your name! The name given by your mother and father! Remember who you are! Remember the value of life that you were taught, and ask if you can call yourself their son!

Twenty-two was pulled away from her, and the bees prickled back into their mistress. The numberman was shaking his fellow.

"What is this, Twenty-two? Tears?" exclaimed the killer, who had never known one of his brothers to weep. He knew that something was wrong with his brother. He had watched them break before, and there was only one means to fix it. He reached for a weapon.

"I am Kanatuk, son of the Seal Fang!"

Kanatuk's outburst was as striking as his speed, and he had produced his blade and thrust it before the numberman ever touched his belt. With an expert's grace for killing, he held his hand over the man's mouth, twisted the knife upward, and then dropped the body and the blade once the shuddering stopped. He fell to the carpet and pulled off his mask. Morigan saw nothing but his dark hair and could not sense his state of mind. While this moment was a precious opportunity, it was also volatile; she would not risk it by pressing him further. She wasn't sure how much time passed, the moment felt drawn into forever, though he gradually, wearily stood. Even unmasked, the man was a mystery, shrouded in tumbled hair as dark as a raven's feathers. His eyes were exotic and his features thick and handsome, yet crooked and wild, not only from the scars that crisscrossed his beard, lips, and cheeks, but also from an inherent tribal quality. Here was a boy who had combed and run among the winter wastes beyond even where the Northmen made their homes. She could see that boy again, and not the murderer that had been beaten into his body. His tall frame was grander now with pride and respect, and Morigan felt that he would not hurt her. He assured her of this as he removed her gag.

"Thank you, mind speaker," he said. "The spirits of Estuuya and Tuuq—my mother and father—thank you, as well. I owe you an eternal debt."

"You're welcome," she croaked. "A key to these shackles is what I need most at the moment. Let's start with that."

"I do not have one." He threw a thumb to the corpse. "That one does."

He hurried to the body, rolled it over on the sticky carpet, and searched its pockets, returning with an unusual key that looked like a square peg of metal. It fit into a matching hole on Morigan's wrist clamps. With a snap and a fizzle of magik, the feliron chains sprang open and fell in clattering relief to her lap. While she rubbed her wrists, Kanatuk released the bindings on her ankles and then tossed the coils of metal aside. She was about to stand up when the bees suddenly buzzed in warning.

Crash!

Something moved with lethal speed into the chamber.

Though he may have just forsaken his life as a murderer, Kanatuk's muscles were still tuned for assassination, and he had thrown up an arm and pulled out a second, hidden dagger, which was driven upward into the throat of his attacker as two powerful arms came for him. His strike did not bear blood, but a spicy dust, and he was forcefully batted to his rump by a creature much stronger than he was.

"No! Vortigern! No!" implored Morigan, jumping up.

The dead man, empowered by nekromantic vigor, had shattered the door and rushed across the room as Caenith might. A hooded figure, whose wisps of brown hair and frowning face identified her as Mouse, peeked into the room while hanging off the splintered remains of the entrance. She slipped in as Vortigern extracted the weapon in his neck and calmly examined the scenario, from the body to the unmasked servant of the Broker.

"I see that you weren't in need of rescue," said Mouse. "You certainly know how to charm a man. Impressive."

"I am grateful that you came," Morigan said. She hadn't expected to see Mouse again.

Kings know I'm not going to drop a woman who can poke about in people's heads and convince them to do any sort of madness. What a dear friend you are, Morigan. At least until Menos is behind us. "I promised you that we would part ways once we were out of this," said Mouse. "And we're not out yet. I have a safe house, with money and papers. We should head there before we try our luck at escaping the Iron Wall."

Kanatuk stood. "We must move quickly before the avenues I know are closed to us."

Vortigern cleared his throat. "Can he be trusted?"

"Yes, as much as you," declared Morigan.

The two men eyed each other uneasily, and Vortigern cautiously handed Kanatuk back his weapon. Vortigern guided them down servants' passages and across dusty wings. Admittedly, Morigan had not spent much time with the dead man, yet she felt qualified enough to say that he was different, closer to the noble master she had known in her visions and not a specter without a past. Not a soul among them dared speak, for it was inevitable that they would be discovered as missing, and the slightest whisper might betray them. Sorren's neglect of his estate aided in their stealth, for much of the manor was untended and cobwebbed, ruled by spiders and faded memories. A mirror of this past caught Morigan as they raced down an abandoned corridor: a picture of Lenora—or Mouse wearing a curled wig—lay amid covered furniture. The image was torn as if in angry passion, and Morigan knew by whom. Seeing the painting raised questions about their current flight. Since they could not speak, she sent her bees into Mouse's head.

How did you escape?

Mouse stumbled a step. *Kings be fuked, that's unnerving. No warning at all. Whatever you did to him was enough. He unchained me as soon as we were alone in what was surely that Lenora's room. Pictures of her and clothing like this cloak. She looked so much like me...though I have no sisters, no family. Anyhow, I'm not sure what he wants, or what this other stray that you seem to have tamed wants. I know how he stares at me sometimes in that way that men do. And I shan't be bedding the man; I'll tell you that. I hardly do that with live ones and certainly not those without a pulse.*

I doubt you have to worry about that, thought Morigan, but she held that thought inside. Of course, a resemblance to a lost love and an inexplicable connection between the two might be expressed first as desire. Yet beneath that yearning, love had many shades, and the colors often bled together, so what was confused for lust was indeed another emotion. Obviously, Vortigern had said nothing to Mouse, or perhaps had still to untangle it all himself. Better that these secrets be tended in their own gardens for now, considered Morigan. Leaving the matter as it was, she had another conversation to have. She wrestled against her eagerness to speak until they had come to a mothballed pantry and descended into a webbed and hollow tunnel gleaming with dampness. Kanatuk produced a flameless sphere of yellow light that he used to illuminate the way. In these metal halls, dank as they were, Morigan at last felt the weight of oppression lifted from her. They were still prisoners in the Iron City, but no more bound to a cell. She would not shatter her Wolf with false hope if she called to him. And she did. While the distance or some other hindrance made it as if they were shouting to each other across a valley of wind, he heard her, and his whisper graced her in turn.

I am...not out of danger...but...I am not alone, she told him.

When he said that he was crossing the Feordhan with Thackery, she leaned against the wall to catch herself, mingled a cry and a sigh of joy, and then hurried along in the darkness. The Wolf pawed the confines of her chest and did not leave her ever after.

III

"What a cockup," spat Gloriatrix.

The trip from the Crucible to the Blackbriar estate was a few sands by skycarriage, and she came with her guard as soon as the news had disrupted her afternoon pruning. Disdainfully, she pointed at the corpse that had congealed on the floor.

"One of yours, I take it?" she asked.

The Broker was crouched on all fours on the carpet; he looked up and gnashed his teeth. "Yes, my Queen. Number Twenty-two is missing, though. He had better be dead, or he is a naughty, naughty boy."

"And Vortigern?"

Sorren, slumped in the room's only chair like a fainted woman, lazily answered. "Gone. I am sorry, Mother."

"Failures, each of you," she hissed.

Sorren clawed at the arms of his chair. "It is very tiring, what I do! To twist the flesh! To rule the bones! To make the blood boil! You do not know how tiring! The secrets, they ache as they are torn from me! You would not know the fever! The burning of it all! Like poison! Argh!"

She watched him rise and huff like a mad bull, stomping his feet and cursing, and knew that there was no way to help him in this state. The riflemen posted at the broken door peered in, but she waved them at ease and went to sit on the bed while her son calmed his temper.

Her son had not always been a lunatic. For most of his life, he was a soft-spoken, delicate child. The kind that would read as his brother climbed trees. After his strategic wedding to the Blackbriar heiress, she had expected that he would be a quiet, studious hermit. A man with a beautiful, wealthy bride who would dwindle in silence while she and Vortigern set to ruling the Black City. What a mind Vort had for chicanery, and what a waste that it was never realized. For some time, though, it appeared as if the fates would unfold as she planned. Through the marriage, she and her sons were given distance from the wretched mantle of Thule—for they *all* became Blackbriars, spurning the custom that the woman should take her husband's name—and she would go as far as to declare them happy: as happy as Menosians can be.

A cleverer mother would have seen the signals before her family collapsed—the cautious glances and smiles that Lenora and Vort slipped like schoolyard notes to each other. She was the one who had heard them plotting in the gardens. She was so furious at the mention of Thackery's name that she did not stop herself from telling Sorren. She was unprepared for his reaction. Being so gentle a soul, the darkness that possessed him in that instant made him unrecognizable. *Kill the child,* he commanded, this embarrassingly soft sorcerer who had never killed a creature in his life. *I shall deal with my brother, and Lenora, and you will never question what I have done.*

Sorren's innocence died along with his brother. Yet the fates demanded more blood, and Lenora disappeared the night that the pale walking ghost that was her lover returned with her mad husband. Sorren did not search for her until suspicions grew grim, for he wanted her to grovel for his pity. He was raging when they found Lenora picked and chewed by ravens several mornings hence, and he bitterly said, *It's too late to bring her back. I shall have to work on another vessel.*

Madness had taken him, and Gloriatrix left Blackbriar for the safer walls of the Crucible after that—walls warded in iron and magik, though she wondered if her son could breach them if he truly wished. The events of that murderous night had warped more than his psyche; they had changed his power. He'd gone from sorcerer to nekromancer in an instant. She did not ponder this, as she did not want to know what species of horror her son had become. No one could truly raise the dead. No nekromancer in Menos, Eod, or any in the history of magik. Once the fire of life was out, it could never be fanned again. What her son had done to Vortigern was an abomination, but she would not dare to tell him that, for who knew what form he might find more fitting for his mother. Particularly if he was to learn of how she, who had reprimanded him for his failures his entire life, had failed him in the act of blood that he had demanded of her: to kill the bastard child.

The tantrum finished after a spell of kicking the numberman's corpse so violently that Gloriatrix's skirt was splashed with blood. Spent, Sorren flung himself back in the chair. She waited a few more specks before attempting reason.

"I am sorry, my son. You try so hard to please me. Elissandra will be here soon. I am sure that there are footprints all over this manor. Ones that our eyes are blind to. A hair, a drop of sweat. That is all she needs. We shall find Vortigern and the witch soon."

"And the girl," added the Broker. He had remained in his position during Sorren's rant and was spattered in red whorls, which he did not seem to mind.

Gloriatrix found the freak as appalling as he was interesting. She shook her head to break the spell and asked, "What girl?"

"The one who looks like the lady in the pictures," said the Broker.

Finally, he noticed the gore and began the queerest ritual of licking a curled hand and then rubbing his face with it. It was animalistic, though Gloriatrix could not say from which bizarre species. She had to shake her head again to focus.

"Lady in the pictures? Who? Len—"

"None of your concern," interrupted Sorren, his voice tight. "A pet project of mine."

A pet project? Lady in the pictures? thought the Iron Queen. Threads were being woven outside her web. Dangerous threads. With secrets that threatened to disturb the deeply packed graves of the past. While she waited for Elissandra to arrive, the blood-soaked chamber became ever more stifling. And she had only a preening, metal-faced man and a son that was hollowed out and filled with wickedness for support. Should her fortunes turn, she realized, her own grave had been dug.

XIV

WHISPERS FROM THE EAST

The *Red Mary* left Thackery and Caenith upon the rocking wharf like two sailors come home from war. Only in what was a reversal of the tradition, men flamboyantly waved and cried from the bow of the ship instead of from the shore as it retreated into the waves. In the day it took to cross the Feordhan, Jebidiah's men had proven fine company, even if they were interested in Caenith in ways that he would never consider. Affectionately, he remembered the raucous feast and minstrel show they had provided while the *Red Mary* cruised along last eve. He gave an enthusiastic wave back to the seamen. His spirits knew no bounds now that Morigan had secured some measure of safety.

"They certainly liked you," smirked Thackery.

"I am likeable," said Caenith with a smile.

"Yes, you are."

With a nudge to his companion, Thackery turned toward Blackforge. From the corroded wharf that wrapped around a wall of grim rock, to the listless folk who shuffled, facedown, in drab gray habits, Blackforge was a stark contrast to the liveliness of Taroch's Arm. It stank less than Taroch's Arm did, too, yet what smells it bore were of iron and sweaty fear. A thick morning fog had coated the docks, and the sails on boats hung like heavy-shouldered mourners. As the companions started down the planks, the city on the hill forbiddingly revealed itself through tentacles of mist. Blackforge was a city of longhouses and cabins painted dark by coal-burning hearths, which grew up a casual stone slope like an unusual forest: one not unlike the steep vales of the Black Grove, a woodland outside the city from where the lumber for these buildings had been hewn. Overseeing the city was the grandest longhouse, which crackled with torches and fluttered with grim banners bearing the image of a hammer striking an anvil. Stone roads and steps snaked through Blackforge, and the companions soon found themselves off the wharf and climbing through sparsely populated neighborhoods. People were about, though the streets were light of steed or feet. Occasionally, Thackery and Caenith spotted pale faces peering from windows. At alehouses, bards plucked limp, out-of-tune melodies, and patrons kept to themselves and stared into their drinks with empty eyes. Thackery had always known Blackforge to be a despondent port, as the masters of house Blackmore were miserly rulers who taxed their fief to near poverty; however, its misery superseded its reputation. To divert his attention, Thackery struck up a conversation with his companion.

"Have you...spoken with Morigan again?" he whispered.

"Not as I am accustomed to," muttered Caenith. He strode beside Thackery for a while before stepping into an unused alley to explain himself. "Not with the same clarity that I should. I know that she is out of immediate danger, and I catch hints of where she is and of what she is doing. However, conversations between us are broken, at best."

"Conversations? You mean in your head?"

"Yes."

Thackery pondered over what might interfere with the sort of farspeaking Caenith was describing. He snapped his fingers as it came to him.

"The feliron! Of course! It's a mineral than dampens magikal aptitude, and the mines of Menos run deep with it. The bulwark of the Iron City is fortified with it, too: it acts as a repellent against spycraft or sorcery. Nullifies all magik within a certain range, come to think. While I doubt she is standing near the wall—or at least, I hope not—the feliron must be affecting the link between Morigan and yourself. Once we get within the iron wall, it should resolve itself."

Contemplating the trials ahead, Caenith's brow wrinkled with despair.

Encouragingly, Thackery cuffed his fellow's arm, and then shook his hand from the numbness, having forgotten how hard the man was. "We will reunite with her soon, I promise. First, let's keep our chins to the ground and get out of Blackforge. I expect that the sword of the queen and that other man—familiar, he was—a master of the watch, I think, though I can't recall his name. In any event, they're surely on our tails now." Thackery scratched his chin. "They were looking for one or both of us, though I cannot say why."

"They are seeking answers. Or someone to blame," said Caenith.

Surly and preoccupied, the companions slipped out into the streets again. As a man of odd customs and habits who did not age, Caenith had been run from many a settlement of man. When he became too reclusive, outlived one too many elders, or refused the wrong hand in marriage, the people's tolerance for his queerness predictably came to an end. He could well imagine what infamies were brewing in Eod regarding his name. With Morigan's consent, his next home might have to be beyond the great mountains. Perhaps in a land of snow, ice, and solitude, where loneliness was a part of life, he would be less questioned and more widely welcomed.

Striding fast, they were soon high upon Blackforge's hill among the grimy market tents and smoking outdoor kilns, ovens, and hearths that gave the city its reputation. At one time, metals surely simmered over these coals, yet today the travelers saw only bland foods, clayware, and the occasional jewelcrafter; no jolly bellows or aproned strongmen singing to the day with their hammers and anvils. As a city founded upon smithies, they were surely in short supply. Thackery recalled the rumors that in the last decade, Menos had bled the mineral veins under the city dry, and the absence of metal outside of scrap hauled by weary oxen in carts—*for what purpose?* wondered Thackery—confirmed this suspicion. More folk wandered around the market, though there were as many merchants as there were customers, which was not symptomatic of a healthy economy.

How far the iron hand reaches, thought Thackery. *Do you have any idea how much cruelty you spread, Gloria? All for an ambition that feeds itself like a monster. Do you blame our mother's weakness, or do you blame our father's sin? Do you still hold your husband's death against me? He was wicked well before you decided to outshine his evil. Either way, the poison stems from you. Into your children, too. Did Sorren act on his own? It seems unlikely, attached to your teat as he is. No, you share the blame as much as he does. I would pray to our Menosian ancestors that we do not meet, Gloria. For all my grievances flow back to you, and I shall see you pay for every one of your treacheries, wretched sister of mine.*

If he were a little less involved in himself, Thackery would have noticed the contingent of charcoal-cloaked warriors gathered before a table of poultices and tinctures before bumbling into the largest of them, who turned. The appalled sufferance with which the tall stranger beheld Thackery suggested that he was a man of mortal power, and his brocaded garments supported this thought. He was thick, but not fat, with a beard and hair that were sleekly groomed and a weaselly cunning to his eyes. One of the man's hands went to a hilt at his garish silver baldric and the other pushed against Thackery's chest.

"I would remove that, if I were you," cautioned Caenith.

The man sneered. "I am Augustus Blackmore, the master of Blackforge, and I shall do as I please in my realm. No wanderer or his oversized manservant will say otherwise."

A quartet of gruff whiskery warriors, all aged beyond their youth by scowls and frowns, attended the master of Blackforge, and they unsheathed their weapons in a flourish of steel that sent folks running and hiding behind barrels or under their tables, like the merchant tending this particular venue. As quickly as the blades flashed, Caenith's arm passed about him in a circle, the limb as vibrating and indistinct as a struck tuning fork: perhaps to key the chorus of yelps that followed. The men and the master all dropped their swords from his slaps. Caenith had moved too quickly for Thackery to interfere, and as the severity of the slight dawned on the old man and the astonished but rapidly reddening master of Blackforge, he stepped in to mitigate the worst of the offense.

"Do excuse my guard's swift hands," begged Thackery. "He is a martial disciple of the southern lands. A man of instinct, who only acts in the interest of my protection and is unfamiliar with the decorum of central Geadhain."

"He's rather large for a Southerner," said Augustus, pouting and nursing his wrist. "Rather dark of skin and heavy of frame for those reedlike yellow bastards. I could have him beaten for his disrespect."

Caenith's eyes darkly shimmered. *Try*, he thought.

"I would ask that you don't," said Thackery, who knew that such threats would end poorly for the master. "And that we put this unpleasant misunderstanding behind us. We have pressing business elsewhere and must be on our way. A thousand pardons to you, Augustus."

"Business?" asked Augustus. "What manner of enterprise are you involved in, old man?"

"Spices and exotic materials."

"Exotic materials? Sounds suspicious."

Having just retrieved and stowed their swords, Augustus's men were clearly debating whether to pull them again. Augustus nodded for them to still their hands.

"You are an apothecary, then?" asked Augustus, flicking a bundle of dried herbs off the table and into the muck. "With better goods than this hedge-healer's tripe?"

"I am a trader, mostly," Thackery replied, smiling shakily. "I do not practice the art of healing, myself. I merely provide the tools."

"I am at my wit's end, trader." The master sighed. "I have seen every physician and sorcerer passing or summoned to this realm, and I am still without a cure for the condition of someone I value. If I can borrow you for an hourglass or two, I would have you look at a patient and tell me if any *tools* you know of can assist in her condition. Perhaps that is where I have gone wrong, in seeking specialists instead of the medicines and their peddlers themselves. Perhaps the simplest midwife's draft will cure this problem."

"Oh, I don't know—"

"Your courtesy would make it easier to forgive the insult to my house," said the master, smiling without kindness. "I shall see you speedily set on the road afterward. You are not invited to feast with us, so you needn't stay."

After sparing a silent curse to Caenith, Thackery bowed his agreement. He was grateful when Caenith didn't simply sprint off to Menos and allowed the men to circle and herd them like livestock down the road. In fact, much of Caenith's manner was sullen and subdued, though what stirred under that cool mask was what worried Thackery the most. For the Wolf would not be indefinitely delayed in his quest. Soon the beast would tire of these games of men and would bite at whatever hands tried to thwart him.

"I never did catch your name," said the master from up ahead.

"I never gave it," replied Thackery.

"You should," said Augustus, again laughing without mirth. "Only a fool invites strangers into his home."

Only a fool trusts a lapdog of Menos, thought Thackery. "Jebidiah Rotbottom," he replied.

Only the barest pause was taken, though Caenith noticed it, and the odor of sweet strawberry mulch—the stench of corruption—around the man grew greater. Any ideas he had about knocking these wicked men around were stalled by the shadows gliding through the deepest clouds that Thackery, or most slow-walkers, could not sense: skycarriages of Menos. *Crowes*, patrolling the border of the Feordhan. They were not in familiar or hospitable lands anymore, and he must be wary—even if that meant bending to the whims of this insignificant slow-walker. Or at least he should wait until they were in a more private location to release any violence.

Folks shied away from the passage of their company, women pulled their children from the road, and the few who were caught in their path stopped their wagons and bowed their heads at Augustus. Beaten souls, all of them, noted Caenith. He pondered what cruelties they had suffered under the master's hand and felt a rare moment of compassion for slow-walkers, as these were so terribly broken. What, then, could break a man to a cowering dog? he wondered. Caenith received an answer as they came to the palisade that protected the master's longhouse. From beyond the wall rolled a sour wave, and Caenith's ears were teased by the faint bleating of mortal woe. With this forewarning, once they were marched past the churlish gatemen and into a mucky enclosure, what the Wolf saw did not surprise him. Thackery, however, gasped at the wooden platforms and their cluttered stockades: each prison filled with an emaciated figure, some dead for so long that the birds and flies had picked them to half-white corpses. The ones that were alive moaned, more of delirious agony than true pleas.

Augustus was mad, the companions realized.

So ghastly was the scene that Thackery's feet froze and he had to cover his mouth to catch the bile. The Wolf maintained nothing more telling than his usual glower. Gently, Caenith pushed his companion forward; he kept his hand to the man's shivering back for a time. The gesture and its warmth were comforting. The master's words were not.

"Criminals, all of them. Spare them no pity," said Augustus. "Do not think me cruel, for I cast the sentence that put them here, and I know the name and crime of every offender." He pointed to a skinny wretch on one of the platforms as they moved by. "That man there, Twyn Barlay: a bread thief, whose food allowance was not enough for his greed. Tough times are these, and the stores must be protected. War is on the horizon, and the people must be strong, lean, and ready to obey their masters. A hungry man is a willing man, and Barlay crossed the line between willingness and desperation. I make these decisions for the endurance of the house of Blackmore, and I bear the burden of these souls' penance as much as they."

Thackery was hard-pressed to believe that the master found any of this to be a *burden*, for such misery could only be gleefully inflicted.

"War?" asked Thackery.

"Have you not heard?" said Augustus, puffing himself up. "It seems you have been far away not to know. The Iron Queen has at last struck against Eod. An incendiary in King's Crown. Dozens dead. The first arrow fired, so to speak. The time of hidden alliances is at an end. All men must choose where to cast their lot. Who would you choose, merchant? The West or the East?"

"As a trader to all nations, it serves me best to claim neutrality," said Thackery. A heavy quiet fell over the group, until he added, "Yet as a man who must choose, I would side with those most likely to win. I would choose the Iron City."

Augustus clapped. "Wisely said. And even the simplest man can see the victor. A nation of peace-loving philanthropists and poets? Or a people who are born and bred to conquer without compassion? I know who is more likely to slay the other, sorcerer kings aside. Menos has its own technomagiks that can peel the soul from a man at a thousand paces or melt flesh like lard in a fireplace. I would like to see how a sorcerer king, mighty as the legends say, can withstand *that*. Legends are stories for children and campfires. History, however, is fact. Fact written by man. Immortal Kings have no place in our history. They should fade as stories, with the faeries, wyrms, and other relics of the past. House Blackmore will side with the Iron City. We shall make history. Already the Iron Queen extends the hand of their protection to our skies, and soon we shall—"

The master's boastfulness was running away with his tongue, and he said no more as they crossed the mud. They entered the longhouse, and the smells and oppression of the stockades were left behind a curtain of heavy pelts. Straightaway, the space stretched into a long wide corridor with many fires along the beaten floor. While much of the smoke escaped through holes in the roof, enough of it remained to haze the area. They walked through the dreamy mist, haunted by crying children and hushing wives, who were sensed but only seen as ghosts around the campfires or hidden in alcoves draped in hides. Whomever they encountered did not shy from greeting their master, but ceased whatever they were doing to honor him. Toward the back of the longhouse, steel screeched as it was sharpened or sparked as it was tested in drills between warriors. These martial activities were as vigorous—if far sloppier—than the graceful exercises of the Silver Watch, and Caenith sensed that there was a motivation to their training beyond the simple upkeep of a warrior's edge.

Thackery detected this readiness as well, though not as acutely as Caenith did. He considered that this was tied to what the master had abstained from voicing earlier about a war. *An outright alliance between Blackforge and Menos. Is it from this black port that Menos will funnel through into the West?* Strategically, he could think of no better place from which to launch a war. *And those oxen in the market...where were they taking all that metal? Is there another port I don't know of, one that builds ships or armaments? Perhaps the smiths have not left this town, after all. I wonder how long you have been planning this, Gloria, and how deeply rooted this plan is?*

"What fine swords your men have," praised Thackery. "Though I confess to being swayed by rumors that Blackforge was no longer the foundry for which it was famed."

"Do not believe henswives' gossip," replied Augustus.

"Where are the forges, then? I saw none—worth note—in the market or within the city."

To the far north, thought Caenith, who could hear the dim clangs and huffs of men toiling over great fires and machinery somehow within the earth, now that Thackery had planted the notion.

Augustus halted before a mighty rafter hung with sails of tanned flesh that swayed in sensuous ways and blocked off what remained of the longhouse.

"Metalcraft is in the blood of every man, woman, and child in Blackforge," declared Augustus. "We are nursed on bottles of molten milk. We are bred strong and stubborn with bones of lead, and our spirits are as honed as the strongest blade. Our greatness is not diminished simply because you do not see it. Soon the whole of Geadhain will know the song of our steel and the glory of our work. That is not why you are here, though. Come."

Now Augustus swept forward through the grand curtain, and the companions followed, caressed by layers of dead skin. Queer smells lured the Wolf from where they were headed: scents of freshwater lake mud and mint leaves that were incongruous with the hickory reek of Blackforge. He was anxious to see what lay ahead. Augustus's magnificent hall was an affront to the gloomy destitution of his city; that a master should live in such splendor or lecture about starvation while his people suffered was despicable to the companions. Especially in view of the huge stone table prepared with a cold and wasted feast; or the carpet of shining pelts, thick enough to keep any shivering wretch warm; or the chests spilling with wealth and jewels that were nestled among the furs. Among the treasures, Thackery spotted chronexes, astrology instruments, and a detailed globe affixed to a metal arm that could only be gifts from the artisans of Menos. Past the table was a splendid hearth. Here, the fire burned clean and the smoke was drawn out a wide gable. Beneath the opening was a pair of thrones made from polished pale wood, and a young lady as gray and melancholy as the light that fell upon her sat in one of them.

A tumble of black hair obscured the face of a girl so slight and small that she could be no older than twelve. Inexcusably, she was dressed in a sheer white gown made for a woman twice her age and with half the virtue. Blackmore's men escorted the companions all the way around the fire, had them kneel, and then stepped back so that their master could approach. As their shadows neared, the girl seemed to wake from her stupor, and her head snapped toward them. Her eyes were deep and intoxicatingly dark, and she did not look at Thackery or Augustus, but at Caenith. First with fear and then with awe, as if she knew who and what he truly was.

"*Mactyre* (Wolf)," she muttered.

"*Inan Dymphana* (Child of Dymphana)," said the Wolf.

Even as the words rolled off his tongue, the Wolf was astonished: she was the source of the teasing aromas of Alabion. He had not met another skin-walker in a thousand years or more. Before Morigan, he did not think he would see another creature of the old magik again. Yet here was a child of Dymphana. In Alabion, there was a natural order of supremacy, and this child would be but a lowly rung upon the ladder of his rule. Either Morigan's compassion had softened him, or he had discovered pathos of his own, for he pitied the tiny seal. *How did you get here, little wanderer from the East? How could you have traveled so far alone?*

Augustus strode between the two, breaking their line of sight.

"Do you speak her funny tongue?" demanded Augustus.

Caenith paid him no heed and continued to stare through him.

"That's the most I've heard out of her," Augustus said. "She won't utter a word to me. Her silence will do for a wife, though her infertility will not."

Shock at the master's words jolted Thackery to his feet. "Wife? Infertility?"

"Yes," snorted Augustus. He sat upon his seat and claimed his bride's hand, pulling it forcibly into his lap. "She is bound to me in marriage. We were wed two months ago and have consummated the arrangement many times since. She bleeds, yet she does not bear children. You're the apothecary. Tell me how to fix this. The physicians have told me that she is not barren, and I would not trade her for another wife, as she will be a fine beauty once she ripens. She is young enough to provide me with many sons, too. As an only heir, the weight of my lineage rests wholly upon my shoulders. So you understand my problem. I shall see that the faults of my father are not repeated with a single child, and that my seed is sown far and wide."

"But she is a child!" objected Thackery.

"And I am a master!" roared Augustus.

"There is no medicine that can make a child bear a child," spat Thackery. "I am sorry, Master Blackmore, but I have nothing to offer you."

Augustus smiled. "I disagree."

With a clap of his hands, men drew steel behind them, and more warriors rustled into the chamber. Caenith could hear the stretching of bowstrings and the heartbeats of at least a dozen of Augustus's guard. He calmly remained as he was, locking eyes with the sad seal girl. Like him, she was not concerned with this grotesque man and his abuses of flesh and power. She was thinking of Alabion or of another dream she had lost: a lullaby, as her kin had such beautiful voices; a mother and father, who had no scents upon her; or even her precious skin, which was also forsaken or lost, for no trace of it was felt by the Wolf. Nonetheless, past the sorrow, he could sense the longing in her eyes and heart, this joy at having found another, even if he was a predator to her. Somewhere beyond the cold Iron Wall of Menos, Morigan must have felt the growl of his empathy, for a rush of her Will was within him, supporting him in his decision over whatever wild act he was to do.

"Rotbottom," said Augustus. "A rather famous bloodline, not easily forgotten. It took me only a moment to remember that name, for I had heard it just this morning while receiving orders from the Iron Marshals. You are a wanted man, Rotbottom. The house of El will reward me for your capture. Had you not given your name, you might have slipped from the city unimpeded."

You know neither my real name nor what I am capable of, thought Thackery. He would be more worried if this man knew his true identity. Perhaps he would show him; it was time to cast off his failed disguise and shine as Whitehawk.

"Your fast hands won't save you now," gloated Augustus, stepping back · behind his throne, well out of what he believed to be Caenith's reach. He pointed to the kneeling man—still so unusually placid that Thackery could read a measure of his intent before it occurred. "You will die for daring to lay a hand on me. Know that you failed in protecting your master, dog."

"Wolf," corrected Caenith. He glanced to Thackery, his stare cruel as a murderer's knife. "Break the elements. Bring this whole chamber down. Burn them all."

"What?" exclaimed the master of Blackmore.

And that was all Augustus had time to say before twin furies, one of light, the other of wind, occurred. Summoning his anger at the venality and despair that they had seen was simple for Thackery. The hate and the tangled feelings surrounding Bethany and Theadora's ends never left him, never left anyone who had lost so deeply. Like monsters at the gate, they howled to be released, and he cracked open the prison with his Will and let it pierce and sear its way from his flesh. It burned as the magik of hate did. It felt as if he had swallowed the sun, but he bit the tears and tried to rein the white whips of lightning that lashed and charred all corners of the chamber. The great table was smashed by two crisscrossing lines of sorcery and blew into dust. Pieces of the wall blasted out into the day, and the roof lit up with a lattice of fire. *Not Caenith or the girl. Not Caenith or the girl*, he chanted, and tried to see through his blazing eyes what was happening around himself. Moving about the dazzling flames was an agile blur that he knew was Caenith.

When Thackery turned into a wrathful star and cascaded the room with magik, the Wolf rushed the thrones and snatched the delicate seal girl before any of that power came crashing upon her. Which it would have, a moment later, for the thrones exploded into sparks and fiery shrapnel, and Caenith danced among the bolts. To his regret, the master of Blackmore was thrown back with the scorching debris and lost somewhere; a shame, as Caenith wanted to rip out the man's throat. Approaching Thackery as he extravagated with electricity wasn't a clever idea, so he rolled like a master tumbler among the arcs of magik and waited for Thackery to restrain his power. During the gymnastics, his cloak scattered off him in a wave of ash. Stone dust was clotting the air, the rafters above were portentously groaning, and Thackery had not yet bottled his rage, so Caenith shouted his companion's name in a thunder that overtook the rattling of the room. At that, the light dimmed, the magik fizzled to sparks, and a space that was so bright was suddenly clouded to blindness from debris.

Screams cut the darkness, horns of alarm sounded. Thackery's tired old body tried to pick itself up out of the warm refuse so that he might find his companion. Caenith found him first, and he had never been so delighted to recognize the smell of a man. Up onto a mighty shoulder Thackery was slung, and he felt small hands holding on to his feet, which meant that the young girl was safe and possibly crooked in Caenith's elbow: it wasn't inconceivable that he had them flung together on the same limb, large as he was. Whatever the arrangement of parts, Thackery didn't give it much thought, as he was distracted by the dizzying leap that propelled them from the smoky chamber and into clean gray skies. The crumbling aperture of the gable they had flown through gave him a flaming wink as it collapsed, and he tried not to reflect on whether the heat-wavering longhouse was really as hollowed out as it appeared. But he only got the slightest peek at the destruction, and scenes were rather shaky after that as Caenith bounced along like a skipping stone from building to building. Once they stopped, however long from then, his only memento of the journey would be how bruised and sore his chin was.

So much for a stealthy entrance to the East, he thought more than once, and each time it brought him laughter.

II

The Black Grove was not deserving of the stain that came with the Blackmore's association, for it was a lovely weald. At night it was thick and flourishing with luminous blossoms that were sweetly fragrant, glowing insects, and many paths in which to lose oneself and streams to break pursuit by hounds. Caenith was an impeccable ranger, too, and he showed Thackery the softest peats and the most flexible twigs upon which to walk. Somehow, the Wolf was lighter than a bag-of-bones old man and left not the faintest imprint, compared with Thackery's stomping. The girl whom they rescued must have been exhausted in body or spirit. She slept in Caenith's arms, and only woke when he changed positions or if her head fell from the cradle he had made. In those moments, her eyes would startle and sparkle with what Thackery felt was fear, tremendous fear, at Caenith's great self. Then, a gentle look or an exchange of their Eastern tongue would settle her into sleep again. What an astounding change it was to watch, this reversion from ruthless wildman to doting father, and Thackery stopped to observe every instant of it. He had thought of Caenith as a purely passionate man, untamed and hot as a forest fire, and seeing him with a more patient affection broadened Thackery's opinion of him. When they paused at a creek so that Caenith could wet his sleeve and dribble water in the girl's mouth, Thackery's admiration compelled him to end the silence.

"We did the right thing," he said.

Caenith finished and blotted the girl's chin. He stared up into the pines, finding the white sliver of moon beyond and took many meditative breaths. When he was ready to speak, he did so with a bitter smile.

"I am glad that you feel that way. That man was evil. There was a stain on his soul. I can smell these things now, since the Fuilimean. I can feel with more than my physical senses. I felt how alone this child was, and how dark her future. I know that I have invited danger, yet she could not be left to her fate. We have given ourselves a burden, though I do not think Morigan would have forgiven me if I had left Macha there."

"Macha, is that her name?"

"Yes, that is what she tells me."

Considering the girl's use of ancient Ghaedic, and the unearthliness about her, Thackery asked the obvious question. "She is not a normal child, is she?"

"Normal like you, or normal like me?" the Wolf asked with a grin. He caressed Macha's face and stood. "She is no slow-walker, if that is what you mean. Although she is now an outcast from the East, too. A child without kin or identity. She will have greater troubles than what we rescued her from."

"What do you mean?" asked Thackery.

"I shall tell you as we walk," promised the Wolf, and began to splash through the creek. "I can smell the smothered fire blowing in from the west, and the Crowes over the Black Grove suddenly fly in flocks. If we are not pursued, we could be soon, and distance will be our only advantage now that I have ruined our false identities."

Quickly, Thackery snapped off a walking stick for his aching legs and chased after the Wolf. "I don't think that our aliases were all that sound anyhow, and rescuing that youngling was a choice that we appeared to make together."

"That we did," agreed the Wolf.

Each man had a private smile and was content with the quiet of the night. Caenith did not explain the girl's predicament immediately, and Thackery was in no rush for him to do so. The forest was calm and accommodating of the travelers and their solitary moods. Most of the underbrush had surrendered to a spicy bed of pine needles that cushioned the feet, and the trees grew far enough apart that there was no sense of entrapment. Indeed, they could have been wandering a vast temple of nature: each mighty pine an intricate pillar, each bird hoot the song of a worshiper. Stuck on temples, Thackery's mind rambled further, into thoughts of worship, of old voices and ancient kings. He intuited a meeting point of all these ideas, histories, and fates that he had been exposed to as of late, and tried to bind them into a single significance.

What could it all mean? The entity that has taken the Sun King? The ancient voice that demands to be honored through rule? What is this thing that is older than our oldest? Are there more like it? If so, then cosmologists, historians, and philosophers are blind to the greatest of truths, or they have chosen to forget so that they might rule as others should. If we are not the first children of Geadhain, what came before us? And more importantly, what will come after? After these entities have come or have gone again? Morigan's gifts...Morigan's fate...she is the center of this storm. What voice does she hear? What is her tie to this ancient past? For there must be one.

"Hmm?" said Thackery. Caenith had addressed him.

"Macha," repeated Caenith. "She is a skin-walker."

"I see."

From behind, Thackery watched Caenith's mighty shoulders slump with sympathy. "Only she has no skin to walk in. Hunters caught the girl and her kin out of their skins, lying with the sea lions south on the Feordhan. If I had to guess, I would say that they were taken for savages and were treated with the same kindness slow-walkers show to those who would live with nature instead of against her. Her father was killed, her mother raped and slain shortly after. All their skins—including hers—were taken. Once the beach was red, I doubt that the hunters knew what they had found. A few hides tossed in with the rest. I imagine they have since been sold and snipped up into the latest fashions for wealthy masters."

"She is stuck, then? As a mortal?" asked Thackery.

"Yes. She would need her skin, most of it at least, to ever swim once more."

Hearing of the girl's struggles brought Thackery a displaced anxiety. He rested against a tree for a speck. Politely, Caenith paused for his companion.

"How did she end up in Blackforge?"

"Sold," grunted Caenith. "The men used her for pleasure, found she was good at it—as she never struggled. '*Mea leatach socair, an said doch ni tabhair tinnaes,*' she told me. 'I lay there quietly, and they did not hurt me.' She learned that lesson quickly, and it's good that she did, for her complacency is what kept her alive. The hunters pillaged the shores all the way to Blackforge, and it was there that they traded her for more competent whores to Augustus, who was conveniently seeking a young, unblemished bride. Her chasteness must have been less important than her youth. Who knows with men so ill."

As the insects cheeped their songs, the men chewed on bitter silences. At length, Caenith turned to Thackery.

"I respect you, element-breaker," he said with fierce passion. "I do not know what torments you, though I see how you fight against it. As we all must do: challenge the darkness of our natures. I commend you for your strength. Know that I do not idly fan the ego of another, and I have never called a slow-walker a friend, yet you are close to that in my mind. As for Macha, she is one half of her nature and without a single guardian in this world. We can be this for her, her guardians, until we can find a place of safety better than the arms of two dangerous men. I shall not ask if you have committed to this, for I knew your answer when you called your wrath upon that vile master."

That said, Caenith was moving again. Inspired by their candid conversation, their professing of honor and sentimental responsibilities, Thackery chased the Wolf down.

"Wait," he requested.

Penitence was heavy on Thackery's face when Caenith turned round. The stink of a confession was all over the man.

"If we are to call each other comrades," said Thackery, "I must tell you of my ties to Menos. Sorren, my sister...all of my shame."

Caenith did not ask what this shame was; his presence was as dark and spiritual as those of the veiled priests of Carthac who counted and forgave sins. Thackery continued. The truth was easy to tell: it wanted to get out.

"A woman...I fell in love, and I disregarded everything a Menosian master cherished in order to be with her. We helped others like ourselves. People who wanted to break the chains fate bound them in. I still had money to my name, a gross amount of coin, though not the infinite resources of my family, and I used every crown toward this venture. We saved so many. We lived as free as a man and woman could...near the Untamed, where we believed ourselves safe in the shadow of Alabion. We had a child. A beautiful girl named Theadora, as lovely as the one you're holding yourself and magikal in her own way. Perhaps even in my way, for I felt she was special..."

He had faded off, and Caenith had to focus his companion's attention.

"They died?" he asked sharply.

"They did."

After a silence, and much shuffling on the pine needles, Thackery went on.

"My family, you see. We are cursed. No matter what we do, it seems that blood and madness is what we were made for, what we excel at without effort. We used the Watchers to communicate with those who wanted our aid. An unreliable ally, I know, as they are agents to the highest bidder. I can't accuse them of betrayal, for that would be to project upon them virtues they do not have. They acted as one would expect rogues to do. While I am sure that they never openly gave our exact names or locations, they gave enough clues for us to be found. I think, however, that it was my willingness to help another Thule, another soul trapped in our family web, that truly called the hounds. You see, my nephew reached out to me."

"Sorren?"

"No, his brother, Vortigern. He and Sorren's wife had fallen in love, and they wanted to escape the Iron City. I was suspicious of helping them until their pleas grew desperate. Moreover, until..." Thackery was rent by twisted emotions; his frown looked painful. "I learned that they had a child. I had the Watchers confirm this, and knew then that I had to aid them. Therein was a critical error, for the information returned to my sister. How much, I do not know, but she made use of whatever scraps wisely and wickedly. Sorren intercepted his brother and killed him, though I am told he keeps the corpse around as some sort of grisly trophy. The boy's mind is all filth and death. I have never been so close to such madness."

"Sorren's wife? And the child?" asked Caenith. Unconsciously, he brought a hand to the chest of the small life he cared for in his arms.

"Lenora was her name. Heiress to the Blackbriar fortune and from a family of great prestige: technomagikal-engineering magnates. The sort of valuables my sister desired and connived her way into attaining through the marriage of her son, Sorren. She had plans for Vortigern, too; I can only imagine what. Strange that my sister never chose to remarry herself." Thackery caught himself wandering. "Lenora, right. I have seen cameos and portraits of Sorren's wife, and she was as fair as they come. Noble, too, for she was willing to leave it all for love and family. Vortigern's passing and the loss of her child threw her over the edge of sanity. Quite literally, I suppose. She tossed herself from the highest roof in Blackbriar, only her body slid into an easement and never made it to the ground. It was almost a week before the corpse was found and only because so many ravens were feasting on it. In Menos, you may remember, those birds are ravenous vermin that shame the gulls of the Feordhan or the vultures of Kor'Khul. As I think back on it, her desecration was likely for the best, or Sorren would have brought her shambling back into some state of unholy life. There wasn't enough of her to do that, bless whatever powers control these things. Sorren tracked me down after that. Blamed me for his inability to have a heart or give a woman love. And the cost..." Thackery bore into Caenith with the rawest hatred—this was the Will that had summoned the fire in Blackforge. "What he took from me can never be replaced."

"Vortigern and Lenora's child?" asked Caenith a second time.

The old man's anger crumbled into glimmering sadness. "I have dodged the question...it seems my heart does not want to share that. Yet you should know what sort of monsters hunt us and the ones we love. So I shall tell you the bitter end. My sister, well, she is the teat from which Sorren has sucked his evil. She disposed of the child, I was told. What particular end is unknown, but it is best not to think of how children can pass."

Caenith's instincts would not let Thackery slide into sorrow. He smelled a rotten truth, as old and settled as an aged stain of wine upon wood.

"Who is this woman? Your sister?" he asked.

Thackery muttered a reply as if it were of no consequence.

"Gloriatrix Thule, now Blackbriar. The Iron Queen of Menos."

Silence.

In what was a fortunate interruption, Macha whined and then squirmed against Caenith, and the men attended her at once. The familiar moment where she was terrified of her guardian came and went, and Caenith set her down to stretch her limbs. While Macha tiptoed around them, burbling old Ghaedic to the night birds she spotted camouflaged in trees, Caenith and Thackery soaked in the other's grim stare, considering what had been said.

"Now you know everything," declared Thackery.

"Yes."

Unpredictably, Thackery tossed away his walking stick and hunched to make grinning overtures to Macha. She wasn't clear on what the wrinkly gentleman wanted, but he reminded her of an old stone that she and her kin once lay on: all lined and gray with the blue of his eyes like a splash of the sea. So she went to him, to the memories he represented, and he picked her up and carried her into the woods. Thackery wouldn't be able to navigate them anywhere but in circles, so Caenith quickly took the lead. The sun was beginning to thread through the pines, but neither man was weary. Invigorated from the release of secrets, Thackery felt as though he could walk for spans. While the well of secrets was dry for Thackery, Caenith had one of his own: a part of Macha's tale that he was still trying to untangle. The matter of why she and her kin had come so far west into the deadly lands of man. Alone, for that matter, without even their clan.

Why did you leave the safety of the Untamed? he had asked in one of their exchanges. Macha had appeared confused by the question, so he asked it once more.

Safety? she had said, finally understanding. *It is not safe. The lords of fang and claw have united under a terrible warmother and the clans that do not bow to her are hunted. Alabion is at war.*

III

Augustus sighed with pleasure as the compress was placed upon his throbbing face.

That fuking merchant and his oaf. They should have stayed to stick a sword in me, for I shall hunt them to the ends of Geadhain.

"How bad is it?" he asked the muddled shape that was tending to him. The burns had eaten the flesh around his cheeks, forehead, and right eye. The eye was unsalvageable by even the fleshcrafters and had been removed. He assumed that he looked hideous, and the delay in a proper response by his maid only deepened the speculation. Furiously, he clawed for his tender and seized a wrist.

"Answer me, you cunt!"

"I...am a man, Master Blackmore," confessed the tender. "The wounds are...I am no physician. Should I fetch the fleshcrafters?"

Augustus wrenched the servant close to him, so close that they panted like lovers across each other's cheeks. At an old maid's distance, he could see a bit more of the dopey, unremarkable lad; mostly, he could read his horror.

"How does it look?" he hissed.

"T-terrible!" stuttered the tender.

His wrist was twisted by Augustus, and he was thrown somewhere into the cloudiness of the room. Augustus heard him scramble away. In misery he lay, the room fading in and out like a daydream. Deceptively delectable, the air reeked of roast hog, and the smell began to nauseate him because he knew it was his own cooked flesh. Over time, the tincture that the flesh-crafters had given him had fluttered into his fingers and toes like tiny but-terflies, taking most of the pain away. He was only semi-aware that he was in a cordoned-off, salvaged section of his longhouse, or that he had been so viciously humiliated by Rotbottom and his oaf. Dark urges and wincing memories haunted him. He thought of slapped hands. Of the denouncement of his rights as a master. What had the oaf called his master? That shout... when the walls were falling in fiery waves and he was crawling on the burn-ing soil. Tack? Tackry? Tadackry?

"What are you mumbling, man? I see that the palliatives have taken effect," said a cultured voice.

Now Augustus noticed the subtle woodsy cologne. A master this was—somewhat familiar, too—and Augustus slouched over in his cot to see him. Master Moreth of the house of El sat by his bedside, preening his handsome beard with his gloved fingers. He had a countenance as frozen as a mask: eerily skeletal and wide-eyed, with hardly a line of expression to be seen of either smiles or pouts, and in Augustus's altered state, he seemed glossy and fishlike. Even his lacquered hair could have belonged on a wax statue. While the master's bowler hat and cane rested across his lap, this was an indication of class, not patience, which was a quality Moreth did not have.

Impassive, Moreth managed to sneer using only his words. "Please, I would rather you do not look at me. I've seen a man's face scraped off in the pits, but yours truly is a dog's breakfast."

Augustus snorted in disdain and lay back down upon his cot. "What do you want?"

"I was in the neighborhood, as it were, delivering some fresh workers to our operation in the fort when I heard the news. Well, I saw the fire, too, though I wasn't particularly inclined to investigate it until the Iron Marshals handed me their report. Jebidiah Rotbottom was responsible for this? He's causing quite a bit of mischief lately. How much witchpowder did he use? And how did he manage to slip away from a fully armed...well, this shitebin isn't quite a keep, is it? So a fully armed encampment, shall we say, being generous."

"Magik," grumbled Augustus. "His guardsman is a touch unnatural as well; moves like a spitting snake."

"Pardon me? Magik?" exclaimed Moreth. "There isn't a dash of sorcery to be found in the Rotbottom lineage. That's not possible."

"I know what magik is and what it looks like, and that is what he used."

Following a quick debate over Augustus's lucidity, Moreth put on his hat and got to his feet. "Thank you, Augustus. The Council of the Wise has acknowledged your work. Please recuperate with haste. I shall leave you to your Thack/Tak anagrams, then."

Moreth's suggestion inserted the puzzle into Augustus's mind anew. As Moreth was prodding aside the hides with his cane—not wanting to touch them with a hand, even gloved—Augustus recalled the name screamed during the inferno.

"Thackery," he muttered.

"What did you say?" asked Moreth, whose ears were sharp.

"Thackery. That is what the servant called him. I remember that. I feel as if I have heard that name before," said Augustus.

"You very well could have," whispered Moreth with a genuine and rare frown. "He is the cursed blood of Thule. The cast-out brother of our Iron Queen and the one who sought to unmake the order of Menos."

Slinking back to his seat, Moreth asked to hear the master's entire account, and listened to every word from Augustus's misshapen mouth with the greatest severity.

XV

WELL OF SECRETS

Menos was the coldest place Morigan had known at night. Although the winter realms that Kanatuk had come from were certainly colder, the spiritual chill could not have been greater. Staring out the windowpane into the man-made nightmare valley of black peaks and feeble yellow lights—less than a mole would need, surely—it was a wonder to her that people chose to live in this place. Or that they would stay and not choose to flee, though perhaps Thackery's misadventures had put an end to that. To leave, one had to get past the Iron Wall, which dared the brave with its ever-present horizon of blackness, no matter where she looked across the city. It was as permanent as the Crucible, but all the more daunting because she knew that she would have to challenge it.

With a whisper, Mouse left them, saying something about a contact and that she wouldn't be long. While she was out, Morigan explored the musty chambers of the manse, slinking through ghostly dormitories, hollow classrooms, and chambers that stirred her head with flashes of children. In a dilapidated studio, she saw dancing phantoms, as plumed and marvelous as exotic birds. Later, she saw a line of children practicing their makeup before mirrors in an empty lavatory. Chased by these ghosts, she hurried to find attire less red and more subtle to wear than her promise gown. Between a bedroom here and a closet there, she discovered some bloomers, a blouse, a cape, and even a pair of boots. Moth-eaten and a pinch small was most of it, but she beat it free of age and mites and made do. When she returned to the classroom where her companions were waiting, Vortigern and Kanatuk were studying the cobwebs and inextricable spirals of dust on the blackboard as if it were a profound equation. She could tell that they had hardly, if at all, spoken to each other. She returned to her watch at the window.

"What is this place?" asked Kanatuk, who was more comfortable speaking with Morigan around. Living under the whip of the Broker allowed one to see many places in Menos, though he was not quite certain how this building was used.

"Menos's attempt at mercy," said Mouse.

Unseen, unheard to even the acute senses of an assassin, reborn, and seer, Mouse had manifested in the doorway. Her fancy dress had been discarded for sleek black garments and a sweeping cape. Mouse glided over to the abandoned desk at the front of the room. Textbooks were concealed under a gray blanket of years, and she brushed off their covers and examined them.

"The children that lived here were taught mathematics, sciences, and the languages of Geadhain," she continued, her head down. "Along with performing arts and lessons in society and grace, skills to make them sophisticated and intelligent companions."

"Companions?" asked Kanatuk.

"The finest courtesans in Menos," said Mouse. "In a city of only slaves and masters, an indentured life is the nearest one will find to freedom. Work long and hard enough and you can—theoretically—buy the chain off your neck. More often than not, this is a dream to distract from one's prison, not a reality that can be attained. Most indentured never make it. If disease doesn't kill you, one's master or clients are the next surest bet."

A flash of insight stung Morigan. *An old man with a gold-capped smile is leering in the vision; the glint of the knife he holds complements the malicious sentiment of his smile. He is going to cut Mouse with it, somewhere lower, for he traces the cold steel tip down her abdomen. And scream or struggle as she might, she is bound and gagged as a slaughterhouse pig and there is nothing she can do about it. "Bear it out, Mouse. Swallow the pain. One day it shall be you holding the knife," the host tells herself.*

The first warm thrust is so excruciating that her head floods with stars and she blacks out.

"I'm sorry," said Morigan.

As if sleepwalking, the seer had drifted from the window without any recall and was standing by Mouse. Morigan put her hand on Mouse's shoulder and could taste the sour nectar of her despair. That despair suddenly festered into anger, and Mouse grabbed the hand that was upon her and pulled Morigan close. Mouse's stare was hollow as she whispered, "I see you've been poking about, and I don't need your sympathy. I am one of those who *won*. I earned my freedom in this shiteheap of a world. I saved every crown; I abstained from every indulgence that pleasure folk drown themselves in. I thought only of who I would be, not who I was. I paid my debt to my master. The first in my lifetime to have done so, I am told. I am a survivor, and if you pity me again, you will see how strong that has made me."

The rage fell away and Mouse released Morigan.

"Back to your question, Broker's man," she said. "These orphanages never worked as well as they were intended to. A few generations after the Cost for Freedom Charter was penned by the *philanthropic* Gloriatrix herself, it was dismantled. Masters quickly realized that it was cheaper and more efficient to purchase hopeless slaves than to deal with the blight of optimism in their houses. Furthermore, the taxes paid by indentured servants were better thought to be in the greasy hands of their masters, who could obscure these costs more efficiently when the money was not monitored by the city. Thus, no more indentureship contracts were drafted, charterhouses like these were left to fade into history, and I would think that if one has not earned his freedom by now, he never will."

Gloriatrix wrote the law on indentureship? thought Morigan. *She couldn't possibly have seen that far ahead, could she? No, surely this was a welcome coincidence. Though why spare the child? A queen of iron and mercy?*

Mouse rolled out the schoolmaster's chair and sat upon it, obscured by dust for a moment. "That should settle any questions on where we are. Now we wait."

"Wait? For what?" asked Kanatuk.

"A former associate of mine," answered Mouse. "He has helped me before, and I believe he will again. I left word for us to meet at one of our contact points."

In a swirl of silver, Morigan is transported elsewhere. To a gloomy rooftop with chattering cages and a carpet of pigeon shite. Mouse is present, skulking near one of the aviaries. She does not claim a bird to convey her message, but stoops and scrawls a tiny pattern at the speckled base of a cage: a pigeon print with five, not four, toes. An ambiguous mark, yet this is how she and her mentor communicate—through signs that do not appear as signs—and it is all she needs for Alastair to reach her.

One of Mouse's talents was the reading of lips, and she noted the shape of Alastair's name as Morigan mouthed it, as well as the distant cast of the other's face. *For fuk's sake, stay out of my head!* she wanted to shout. Mouse was frightened and a bit annoyed at how loose and fast the witch's powers were, once she was out of feliron. *Too bad we don't have a spare set of chains at the charterhouse. I thank you for your contributions to my freedom, but you certainly need a leash.*

Morigan caught a hint of this attitude, and she left Mouse and her scowl at the desk and went once more to the window. Kanatuk came from his seat and followed her like a dark-eyed puppy. There was an affection that he had toward her that was platonic and tickling to her extrasensory abilities, as if feathers were brushing her heart. He stopped beside her, and they were quiet for some time, making ivory clouds on the windowpane and brooding together over the Iron City's grotesque grandeur.

"Where will you go, once we have left the Iron City?" he asked.

Back home, she nearly said, when she realized that her home would no longer accommodate her—not without many compromises.

"I don't know," she replied. "I shall see what my bloodmate thinks. I cannot make decisions for us both. We should decide together."

Earlier, Morigan had shared what she knew of Caenith's progress into the West with those who were not informed of his journey. *My bloodmate, Caenith, and a powerful ally of mine—a sorcerer—are en route to the Iron City. If we have not found a way out by the time they arrive, I am certain that they can show us how they got in.*

Kanatuk squinted. "Bloodmate? Is this the man you say is coming for you?"

"Yes."

"What is a bloodmate?"

"When two people who love each other swear a covenant in blood, they are bound as bloodmates. It is an old and sadly forgotten ritual," explained Morigan, as if teaching a young man, for aspects of Kanatuk were childlike.

"That sounds quite special."

"It is. Caenith and I are together forever. In our hearts and minds."

Kanatuk pondered this. "Is that how you can tell where he is?"

"Yes. Though there is something in Menos that hinders that awareness."

"The wall."

"Yes, the wall."

"How will *he* make it past the Iron Wall?"

"He will. He'll leap it if he has to."

"Leap? How can a man do that? Leap over a wall?"

She smiled, and Kanatuk puzzled over what kind of man—or sorcerer—this bloodmate of Morigan's was. Morigan turned the original question back to Kanatuk.

"Where will you go?"

As he said *north*, a drift of white washed over her vision, and she saw the frozen veins and woolly vales of the North. More striking than the imagery was the sense of wholeness among the cold: a furious regard that the Broker's abuse had concealed but never really smothered in Kanatuk.

"The North, yes," she agreed. "I think that is where you belong." She waited a speck before tactfully adding, "Do many of your people remain there?"

"Possibly," said Kanatuk, and his scarred face lit with the gleam of happiness. "We never know what the spirits will bless us with. If those of the Seal Fang still hunt the North, then I shall find them. If not, then I shall discover happiness down another path."

"I think that you will find them," she said. "Or this other happiness."

Her hunch was deeply gratifying for Kanatuk to hear. Particularly from the woman who had pulled him from darkness and returned his name to him. They weren't looking at each other, but Morigan could see his contentment reflected in the glass: an unshakable optimism, the spirit of a child. *I found that spark,* she congratulated herself with a humble enjoyment. *I helped him remember who he was. This gift is far, far from a curse.*

In the smog above the city, a star pricked the darkness and glimmered like a silver bead. The two wished upon it for good fortune, although neither said for what. They were pleasant and quiet company after that, and sands upon sands trickled away along with their worries. In this state of tranquility, then, Caenith's clear, loud shout to her soul struck her without warning. She understood that he was somewhere in relative danger and that there was a sad, precious child—her sullen and beautifully pale face revealed in a shimmer of sight—whom he wanted to help. She Willed a reply to the Wolf. *Save the child. What we save today brings us salvation tomorrow.* How many of her words made the distance to her bloodmate, she did not know, though she felt that the essence of her feelings, at least, was conveyed.

As the panting subsided, she tried to relay the strangeness to Kanatuk. "I am sorry. That was unexpected. It's Caenith, and he's stirring up equal amounts of mischief and virtue somewhere. I don't think he's far away. A few days, perhaps? He may arrive before Mouse's friend can."

No one else had come to her side except Kanatuk, and as she mentioned their sly companion's name, she realized that Mouse was gone. The dead man had joined her in absence.

"Where did they go?" she wondered.

"We should find them," suggested Kanatuk.

The bees disagreed with his advice and stung their mistress in protest.

"No," she winced. "I think that they are meant to be left alone."

II

The dead man's fixation on her—his eyes like two pins of coal—while Morigan and the Broker's man were talking drove Mouse from the room. Even the most secret of the charterhouse's hallways were well-traveled paths to her, and she took forgotten stairwells and poked up through hidden accesses as she moved higher and higher into the building. Memories surrounded her:

whispers of laughter, suggestions of footsteps walking alongside her, even once the sound of her name being called by young female voice.

Adelaide was the caller's name, a friend of hers during her years here, and it was Adelaide she was chasing, in a sense—as much as one can chase the dead. Mouse made it a point to honor the girl whenever she came to the charterhouse. One would be hard-pressed to find the strings to Mouse's heart, yet they were present, if hidden under callousness, and Adelaide's string was one that thrummed a melancholy tune when plucked. Her memory of Adelaide was not tarnished by the years, but polished through handling, like a favored pocket-chronex. She didn't think of the girl as often as she should have, and that she regretted, for Adelaide was such an important part of her life.

You were like a wave sparkling in sunlight. Or like leaping into that wave perhaps, as your very presence was refreshing and bright, she thought, and missed her friend achingly.

She climbed a constricting hallway and its precipitous steps and came to a grand crawlspace, empty and echoing as the belly of a ship's hold, with the circular windows being cloudy portals to a dark sea outside. The rain began when she arrived, splashing down the windows and pelting the roof like hail. Curious shapes were about, which Mouse knew were merely sheets pulled over sharp-angled furniture or crates, though in the dimness an active or young imagination might confuse them for horned ghosts. Today, she fearlessly walked among the specters and amusingly recalled how Adelaide and she used to clutch each other when taking these same steps. This was the only place in the charterhouse where the masters never looked for them; it had been their sanctuary. She was smiling at these memories as she came upon the tribute to her friend: a nook with a brass-framed picture on the floor and bouquets of dead flowers around it.

When Mouse was alone, in the rarest moments, she allowed herself to cry. She was misty-eyed as she came to her knees before the portrait. Mouse had commissioned the picture from memory, and paid a pretty crown for the service in order to get it exactingly correct. Adelaide had been captured in watercolor, so there was an aqueousness to her appearance that was right at home with the girl's Carthacian origins. Persons of the sea and surf who dared the Straits of Wrath to fish and plunder the ocean to the west, those of Carthac, had the paleness of the sun to their complexions and the dazzle of blue water to their eyes. It didn't matter how far one ended up from Carthac—and truly, Adelaide had drifted far—the ocean never left them. Salt was in their blood, and their heads were full of the free-blowing will of the ocean. Mouse had never learned Adelaide's history, and the girl herself was far too young to understand how she had been carried to the Black City. Without the truth, they indulged in fantasy, at which Adelaide was marvelous. She could be a master's bastard daughter, or smuggled princess lost in the West: they did not consider the reality of their situation unless they were forced to do so. Such cheerfulness is what drew Mouse to the girl at first glance. She remembered that time.

"How can she be smiling? Does she not know what's in store for her?" thinks Mouse.

A blond girl in little more than tattered clothes has been prodded into the dormitory at rifle point. She thanks the men for her escort, and waves to the other children in the room, who are silent on their wooden bunks, practicing their makeup in mirrors along the wall, or simply turning their faces to wherever the soldiers of the Iron City are not. Many bunks in the room are empty, and the girl skips over to the unclaimed bed next to Mouse and pleasantly asks, "May I?"

Mouse has no idea how to reply to this chipper dolt, who is surely a few wires shy of a properly connected brain. So she snorts and ignores the newcomer like the rest of her dormitory mates. Such ostracism scarcely dents the girl's liveliness, for she whistles while she fluffs and remakes her bed. Mouse lies upon her bed and from the corner of her eye, she watches the stranger: entranced and suspicious of her. Every time the girl catches her, she breaks her whistling to offer a smile, which only adds to the redness on Mouse's face. While the newcomer is tucking in her blanket, she discovers something under the mattress, and Mouse tries—without appearing to try—to see what has been found. No investigation is needed, however, for the girl strolls over, plops herself down near Mouse's hip, and then disturbs her even more by poking her for attention.

"You there, what's your name?"

Mouse rolls over and faces the wall. "Mouse. Now leave me alone. You look like trouble, and trouble doesn't last too long around here."

"My name is Adelaide, not trouble. Nice to meet you, Mouse."

"It is not nice to meet you," huffs Mouse. "Now go away."

Adelaide brushes her golden hair behind one ear as she whispers, "Well, that's a shame you want me to go, as I found something interesting that I'm not certain what to do with." She waits a few specks for a reply, which does not arrive. "Something very interesting," promises Adelaide.

Still Mouse holds out, though her curiosity is tweeting like a trapped bird.

"I guess it's all mine, then. Pity, as I like to share," Adelaide says with a sigh, and is off the bed.

"Wait!" hisses Mouse.

Begrudgingly, she sits up and makes space for Adelaide to join her, then has the girl reveal what she has cupped between her small hands. It appears to be a thin rectangular box.

"I think I know what these are," mutters Adelaide. "But I couldn't tell you from where. Gamblers' toys. Demon decks. I think older folk used to play with them around me."

"Play with them?" says Mouse.

"Yes, let me show you."

With a charming theatricality—a white smile and the sweeping wrists of a riverboat con man—Adelaide holds up a pack of cards. Whatever illustration was on them is faded, but they bear bits of teasing colors and shapes that belong in a carnival. Adelaide wastes no time in opening the pack and fanning the cards with that same practiced grace as before. Of all the glossy numbered pictures, Mouse cannot pick a favorite, as they are all magnificent: images of scaled monsters and bird-winged men, of sorcerers and warlords. A glint of black suddenly hooks her attention, and she pulls out the card of a beautiful dark-haired king. She knows he is a king, just as she knows who the pale man wrapped in green fire is.

"Fates and Crowns," whispers Adelaide. "That is what they called it, the game you play with these. That fellow there is the Everfair King, and most powerful in the deck next to the Wildman, Brutus."

"Who taught you this?" asks Mouse.

"Who knows?" shrugs Adelaide.

Any concern is banished with another of Adelaide's infectious grins, which Mouse feels twist her own lips, too. Mouse stares past the girl's shoulders to *the slouched orphans in the room; they are keeping to themselves now, but would sell out this daft girl and her contraband cards in a heartbeat if it spared their hides in any small way. Mouse tidies up the cards and places them back in Adelaide's hands.*

"Listen, Adelaide," she coaches, "you can't flash these around or you'll meet the whip for sure. Hang on to these, keep them somewhere safe, and don't take them out unless I tell you that you can."

"All right."

Adelaide searches her ratty gown for a place of discretion to hide the cards. Her fingers poke through her pockets and she frowns. Now, Mouse is a savvy child; she has learned the lessons of obedience and observance, and knows how and when to apply these traits for her benefit. Poor Adelaide has none of this wisdom, and her bumbling would be laughable if it wasn't kind of endearing to Mouse. She has never wanted to help another besides herself, as there is nothing to be gained from such a transaction. Yet she wants to help this girl before she trips and kills herself from clumsiness.

"No, no," says Mouse. "You can't do that. You've just arrived, and they'll be taking those clothes and giving you a young woman's frock like mine in a few sands. Here, just give them to me and I shall look after them."

"Very well," replies Adelaide, without the merest reluctance.

Mouse is handed the deck. She shuffles back to one of the posts on her bunk and tells Adelaide to "cover her," which Adelaide does by making a Y with her arms and acting as conspicuously as a bibbed fox in a henhouse. Again, Mouse feels the urge to chuckle. She represses it while she slips them into a slit cut in the side of her mattress, where she keeps a sharpened spoon and a couple of other items she has picked up in the charterhouse. She likes to take things, and she has yet to be caught. She finishes in a rush so that she can push Adelaide's arms down and caution the girl that there are better ways to act discreet.

"I thought I was," declares Adelaide with utter seriousness, and Mouse erupts with laughter. Even if Adelaide isn't in on the joke, she throws herself into it anyway, and the two girls cackle in escalating hysteria until their sides hurt. As it is so scarce a sound to be heard in the charterhouse, their joy draws the heavy footsteps of a warden, and Mouse shoos Adelaide from her bed.

As they part, Adelaide whispers, "We're going to be friends, you and I. You'll see."

And we were, thought Mouse.

Out came a tear, then another, and still more. Mouse wiped them away roughly, as she was not used to weeping. *You're here to get the cards, not for a memorial,* she reprimanded herself, and with that, her grief was bottled back up. With great consideration, she lifted the flaking bouquets around the tribute and set them aside: there were three bundles of flowers, representative of each of her visits. Lightning pranced about the attic, and the faded jacket of the pack was momentarily as vibrant as it once was, lurid with the outlines of snakes, twisting things, and men, all embroiled in a terrible battle. She paused before grabbing the deck—not from the picture, but from acknowledging the finality of this act. Once the memento was hers, this was her farewell to the charterhouse, to Menos, to that whole segment of her life. Not all of which was worth forgetting—particularly Adelaide—though she felt that she might.

"I shan't forget you," she promised, taking the cards.

Vortigern's rich, layered voice crept through the stormy attic. "Forget who?"

What dastardly stealth the dead man had, though Mouse smelled his potpourri cologne now that he had announced himself. Acting as if she had been caught doing an unmentionable act, she slipped the deck into her pocket and quickly threw the bouquets over Adelaide's picture. When she stood and faced Vortigern, it was with a scowl of contempt. She could not tell his expression, for at his back were flashing windows, though once he spoke he sounded sad.

"You lost someone, I see."

Mouse ignored his observation. "Why are you following me?"

"We are due for a talk."

After they had arrived in the Blackbriar estate and she and Morigan were separated, Vortigern had taken her to Lenora's bedroom. He had appeared airy and distant, and she was questioning how, if at all, the witch had affected him. He sat her down, shared a deep stare with her that made her shiver with discomfort, and then smashed her doubts by twisting the bindings off her wrists as if they were made of foil. There was no room for gentility in that moment, for he was moving and instructing her that they had to find the witch.

"I never did thank you," she realized. "Please accept my thanks. We should be returning to the others. I am done here."

The dead man was blocking the small alcove and he did not move. "If you would pay me for your freedom, then do so with a conversation."

Since Morigan's tampering, a shift in character had occurred in the dead man that Mouse was noticing more and more. He possessed a surety and steadiness to his manner—a lordly presence that was cultured and commanding. Mouse was usually immune to the charms of men, but she found herself warming to his demand.

"Very well," she sighed. "But our sands are not unlimited. I am expecting someone."

"I understand," said Vortigern.

The dead man stepped aside and eased onto a dusty construction that must have been a chair, for it fit him like one once the sheet upon it was depressed. He was mournful and slumped, and looked off to study the storm. Mouse did not sit but tapped her foot from anxiousness.

"Why do you call yourself Mouse?" he asked.

An interesting question. Mouse smirked. "Magpie is too generic but that is what I am. Or was, for certain. A taker. A five-fingered patron. A thief. I squirreled my goods away in cubbies, floorboards, and mattresses. When I was caught, which wasn't often, the name just seemed to fit. I wasn't given much in life to call my own. But a name...that's mine and mine alone. I chose it; I own it."

"I suppose you were very young when you were brought here, so you wouldn't recall any name that you were given."

"Given?" scoffed Mouse. "By whom?"

"By your parents—they who surely named you."

"I have no parents."

With a piercing sadness Vortigern said, "Even I, as a man no longer living, cannot claim that. Have you never wondered where you came from? Or sought those ties of blood?"

"No," declared Mouse.

That was a lie. Her pursuit of the truth of her abandonment had taken many years of her life. Once she was welcomed into the Watchers and became aware of what resources were available to her, she spent every sand of her free time trying to find her parents. Yet each trail ran cold, and there were walls erected to hinder the deepest forays of her investigation. Political barriers, obstacles that could be nebulously traced to the Council of the Wise itself but without any actual names or facts to which to tie these obstructions. She knew that someone had left her at the Eastminster charterhouse, though she had no idea who, be that person male or female, relative or compassionate slaver. Years of inquiry and that was as far as she got before finally throwing her hands in the air. That the dead man would provoke her thinking on the matter again was an offense, and she was nearly done with their conversation. Following the uncomfortable silence to the drum and drip of the storm, he spoke again. His next question was equally stinging.

"The girl you were mourning, you were close to her?"

"I was not mourning."

"You were," asserted Vortigern. "I have seen grief. I am grief. This cursed body gives me senses and strengths that a sane man would never wish for, yet I have them regardless. I can smell the salt of tears upon your cheeks."

Mouse would not be pitied; she proudly strode ahead. "My past is none of your concern. I have been gracious enough to indulge your questions, and you will hear no more from me."

"Sit down," said Vortigern.

While there was nothing threatening or malicious in his tone, Mouse obeyed the order instinctively, as when a master barked a command to his servant. Another shrouded heap was across from the dead man, and she sat on a gently rounded surface with hard metal bits, which she presumed was a chest. In the presence of Vortigern, she was aware that she was influenced by an uncanny patience and that her actions were unusual, while having no willpower to change any of it.

"You were mourning her, so she must have been important to you," said Vortigern once she was settled.

"Yes, she was all that I had...family. I suppose."

"Family."

Vortigern slipped off into some gloomy memory, and Mouse—by whatever queer intuition—was afraid of what he was revisiting. He shared it with her in a speck, when he returned with his swallowing black stare from which she could not draw herself.

"I had a family...when I was flesh and blood, not this thing that you see before you. I was a rich man. Not with coin and power, though I had those, too, but with true riches. Love. Hope. A future as bright as the skies Menos has never seen. I had a woman who stirred my soul like a song. I had a child who was...so beautiful. Yet here we are. Everything was lost, and I am a gray and dead monster." Vortigern bared his teeth as if a wave of pain ran through him. "You do not believe in pity, I can see that. Neither do I. Thus I would ask that you understand, without pity, as I explain to you this nightmare to which I have woken. What can be worse than an eternal emptiness, you might think? What is graver than a fog over the mind, where pain is felt, but its source never remembered? Such is how I existed, for so long. Haunted by phantoms without name or shape. Only now...I see what I have lost. I *know* what I have lost. At times, that can be worse than a walking death."

Mouse was taken by the unprecedented urge to reach for and console the dead man; she had to sit on her hands to stop.

"The witch," continued Vortigern, his face lined even heavier by regret. "She returned that knowledge to me. All of it. Whether that was her intent, that is how she left my head. In shambles mostly, as each piece is like handling a double-edged sword. The memories cut no matter how I try to hold them." Vortigern fumbled with his large pale hands as if to catch the intangible.

Mouse could no longer restrain her sympathy. "I am sorry about your loss."

"It's not all grim," said Vortigern. His fathomless eyes reflected a strange twinkle in the sudden lightning.

"It's not?"

"My daughter, Fionna. She *lives*."

"She does?" whispered Mouse.

"Yes."

He rose from his chair and slowly strode toward Mouse. "She couldn't do it, Mother. The Iron Queen is not so *iron* after all. I would not have believed that kindness existed in her, but perhaps even the blackest soul shines once with light. By whatever frail virtue, she could not finish the deed. Though I might never have guessed what became of my daughter until you brought us here."

"M-me?" stammered Mouse. "What have I to do with any of this?"

Vortigern was before her now, and time slowed to a heartbeat. Vengefully, thunder and rain shook the attic, and yet this moment, which should have been terrifying to Mouse, was not. Indeed, the tension was made calm by the dead man, who knelt and caressed Mouse's face with his icy fingers. She did not flinch, and the way he touched—with utter delicacy and care, as if she were a painted egg—told her that she had mistaken his affection entirely. While it was the touch of love, it was not the touch of a lover, and instead the touch of...

Mouse quivered.

"You are beginning to see," the dead man said with a smile, his yellow teeth no longer hideous to Mouse. "Even before the witch restored my truths, I had wondered who you could be. Who this young woman was that looked so like my Lenora. How do we know each other, you and I? For there is a pull, and I alone do not feel it. Why do I burn to watch you and hold you? This is the flame of love. Here." He laughed and tapped his chest. "In a dead heart, I feel it. While time has taken much from us, it can never take the love one has for his child. I remember you, Fionna."

Mouse was shaking her head, as if the truth could be banished so easily. When that didn't work, she tried to bolt upright, but the dead man caught her and held her in an embrace. She struggled, much weaker than she could have.

"Please do not run from me," he pleaded. "Not when I have waited so long to see you."

"F-father?"

What came from Mouse was a pitiful sound, and it broke each of them like a hammer to glass. The dead man could not weep, but he shuddered still, and Mouse sobbed enough for them both. Her hands, which were limp and trapped, clung to the dead man, and they held on to each other as if they could fall or fade away. As if all could be lost again. On and on the thunder played and the world raged. But they had found an anchor to cling to while the world spun to chaos; they had found family.

✳ ✳ ✳

III

Mouse and Vortigern returned to the classroom wearing uncomfortable, guilty smirks that had Kanatuk thinking they had been fooling around in a closet somewhere. Although Morigan could sense the change in their demeanors, she did not ask about it, and left them to their quiet fascination, where they shyly sat together at adjacent desks like schoolmates, and traded not notes but glances that were more telling than words. *He told her, or she figured it out*, thought Morigan. At times, the dead man would slip a humbled look to Morigan, which warmed the witch as she kept her post by the window.

Kanatuk stayed faithfully beside her, and appeared amused enough watching the storm. Although he was not a simpleton, there was an innocence to his being, and a less perceptive observer might easily mistake him for an imbecile. But to Morigan, the bees were humming to the hidden songs of Kanatuk's mind: drums around a campfire, throat music that cut into a blisteringly cold and snow-torn sky, and the pummeling of rain outside, all blending into the rhythm of a giant heart. He saw the world as one grand, connected organism. As far as Kanatuk knew, there were differences, but only cosmetic ones, between the white woods of his home and the black peaks of Menos. If one listened hard enough anywhere, he would hear the one beat of Mother Winter: the essence of Geadhain. Kanatuk was a calming tonic for Morigan's mind, and she permitted her bees to harmlessly suckle on his meditation. Time floated onward, Morigan the leaf on the stream of consciousness that was Kanatuk. She only momentarily considered the strangeness of her sharing a state of being with another, as she had done so—on a much more intimate level—with Caenith. As the Wolf entered her thoughts, her river wound down a course of its own. Something hotter and wilder.

"How quaint. I don't know who your new beau is, Mouse, but we have to move."

Morigan and Kanatuk spun to see the speaker. Mouse was already racing toward the doorway, where a black shadow was leaning against the frame.

Aside from his skinniness and the scruff of red hair upon his chin, details on the stranger were scarce. Nonetheless, Morigan had a tingle of recollection that if not herself then someone close to her had met this man before. The notion bore flickering memories of fanfare; she cast them away as she strode to meet him.

"He's not my beau," said Mouse. "He is—don't worry about that."

"I am aware of who he is: the dead son of the Iron Queen," said the pithy stranger. Then he pointed toward Morigan. "Here we have Eod's finest act: the girl who picks men's minds. I know of you, and of your dark lover. Not as harmless as your master would believe. You keep ever more dubious company, Mouse."

All of the group had gathered around the stranger by now, and Mouse and the man were exchanging hissing discourse like a couple of serpents.

"This is your associate, I presume?" interrupted Morigan.

"Yes, this is Alastair," Mouse said, and pointed around the circle. "Vortigern, Morigan, and Kankut."

"Kanatuk," corrected the Seal Fang.

Mouse waved away the inconvenience of his speaking. "Sure. Sure. Alastair, tell them what you told me."

Alastair droned out a reply. "Skycarriages, several of them with riflemen, have landed a block or so away. We can assume that they've come for any number of you." He pulled out an elegant crystal chronex on a silver chain. "I'd say...hmm...five sands before they're storming the building."

"We can't be taken again," said Vortigern.

"Brilliant observation," replied Alastair. "I see that the Thule acumen has not been lost through reanimation. I suppose we should be off. You can take this as my favor to you, Mouse. Although I know you were hoping for false papers or shuttling, I'll give you another hole to hide in, and that's about the last of what I can do for you before your stink rubs off on me and I, too, reek of shite."

"Fine," said Mouse.

Not too kindly, Mouse pushed him from his leisurely pose and into the hallway. As he spun, Morigan saw a glint of heavily browed blue eyes, and felt a flutter of the man's person waft off him like pollen. He was inexplicable and murky, evasive to her bees somehow, though she sensed a jocularity to his spirit, as if life was all a fantastic game and the odds or prize never mattered. This lightness made her trust him enough to see them out of the charterhouse. For as Mifanwae was fond of saying: *a man without humor is a man who can't laugh at himself, and that is not an honest man.* While they hurried down flickering corridors and descended staircases—headed somewhere low—Morigan wondered if this was to be her life for the foreseeable future. Escapes punctuated by the briefest instants of meaning, laughter, and love. If she had Caenith with her, she thought, the chase would certainly be more gratifying. While it was an inopportune moment to miss him, she did so anyway. She called out to him, hopeful that he would somehow hear past the Iron Wall.

I miss you.

You don't even know me, dear child. But you will.

Caenith had not answered, but a woman's sultry echo, almost a slowly spoken song. Whoever it was that had spoken in her mind tripped up her feet from the shock. She drunkenly slipped a few steps on the staircase before Kanatuk had her by the arm. From the landing below, Alastair tersely asked what was wrong with her. Kanatuk did so with far more concern.

"Can you walk?"

"Yes," she said.

Morigan was given a railing to hang on to, and they quickly went to the others.

"A woman just spoke in my head," she explained.

With a foxy, handsome grin, Alastair said, "What a commodity you must be, Miss Lostarot, to have the Iron sages throwing themselves out in the rain to see who can catch you first. Gloriatrix, now *Elissandra*, mistress of Mysteries. Whatever little tricks you do are but cantrips to her. Don't be fishing for thoughts or you just might reel her in with one. We should definitely be hurrying."

With that, he was bounding down steps like a long-legged stork. The others expediently followed but could never quite catch up to the lanky shadow, who was always a flight ahead. In short order, they arrived at a lower landing that was dark and cluttered with old furniture and possessed with the dampness and fungal spice of a basement. A buckled metal door was present, so corroded that it would not budge as Alastair wrenched on it.

"I am a quick man, I am a clever man, but I am not a strong man," he said, sighing, and stepped aside for someone else to try.

Vortigern rose to the challenge. He grabbed the handle and gave it a hearty tug. Unfortunately, his efforts were a bit too enthusiastic, and with a sharp *tang*, he tore the metal bar clean off.

"Drat," he complained.

For the first time, Morigan noticed, Alastair's unflappable humor darkened. He was a shade pale as he said, "We can't go any other way. Certainly not how I came in. Get the door open. Now."

Vortigern attacked the door anew, pulling at it from a bent corner. The metal protested with screeching and a showering of rust, and the noise of the labor echoed high up the stairwell. Even without her prescience, Morigan could have guessed that the disturbance would serve as an alarm, and she was correct. The warning stings came as the shouts resounded from above, followed by the thundering of boots upon the stairs. She did not fear conflict as she should, but anticipated it, and had to harness the impulse to race toward the Ironguards and tackle them with her fists. These were the Wolf's instincts as much as her own, and she was fighting their allure even as Kanatuk pulled her through the bent opening.

On the other side, her feet splashed into puddles that reeked of swampy stagnancy, and she set them to running across a wide dark chamber of poured stone that was supported by metal columns. As the company sprinted through the murk, it was difficult to perceive any more than the dim silhouettes of her blackly dressed companions. Nevertheless, she felt that she was seeing clearer than she should have and running faster than her usual pace. Rage was not the only gift that the Fuilimean had bestowed upon her, and she grimly recalled her lethal acrobatics in Thackery's tower.

I'm just about done with running, she thought. *These fools that are chasing me will soon know the bite of a bride to a lord of fang and claw.*

Her bloodlust attracted the mind that wandered the charterhouse searching for her, and it pierced her skull once more.

Bride to a lord of fang and claw? How interesting. You speak of old dreams of the East. And this passion in you. This violence. It is almost...animal.

Morigan stumbled but managed to maintain her pace. *Get out of my head.*

I don't think it's so simple, the seeker said with a laugh. *You have power, child; you shine it like the brightest light on a deep winter night. But you don't have the skill to rebuke me. I know the secrets of the Daughters of the Moon, the Arts of dreams and the immaterial that you fiddle like a fat-fingered child to grasp. I know the path into your mind now, and that door cannot be shut. The Ironguards are closing in. We are not enemies, but sisters. You should surrender, or I cannot promise safety for those who protect you.*

Shots of zinging blue fire lit up the gloom: the Ironguards had breached the doorway. That was warning fire, Morigan knew. The next rounds would be made to maim or kill.

Surrender, demanded the seeker.

More blue pellets glittered in the darkness. The only one to strike its mark hit Vortigern, running beside her, though he didn't falter a step, and merely patted out the flames on his shoulder. While the dead man could brush off their peril, the rest of them could not. Each speck, the blood of the Wolf grew hotter, and she became angrier. Caenith's pride and majesty were taking hold, blurring Morigan's perceptions. How dare they try to capture her again: she who was meant to roam and rule the Untamed. How dare they herd the hunter, or invade the sacred spaces of her mind. Violators and fools, all of them. She would not be taken. She would not be claimed. If they wanted to know what it was truly like to tame an animal, she would roar like one. She stopped, hunched, and released her rage.

"Begone!"

Although it was said as a word, to Morigan at least, it came out as something else. The oddness that came from her throat could have been a song, as there was a melody to the undulations, though for now the notes seemed distressed. Kanatuk had heard the noises that the great swimming beasts under the frozen sea made: hypersonic and hypnotic when they were peaceful, shrill when they were not. This reminded him of the latter. A cry from a cornered and dangerous monster. Across the chamber and up through the ceilings and walls the spellsong wavered, unhindered by matter. When the sound reached the Ironguards—wherever they were—it drove into their ears like swords. They dropped their weapons and fell, screaming, to the ground. A speck later, they were snoring in heaps upon one another like spent pups.

Far above Morigan in the charterhouse, Elissandra sensed the ripple of tremendous power approaching, and her smugness wilted as she realized that she had underestimated so much of what this maiden was capable. She had time for a shout of surprise as the invisible energy speared her head. The agony lasted only a speck, and then the mistress of Mysteries was slumped and dozing on the floor.

The darkness seemed eerily calm when Morigan looked up. Her Wolf-sharp eyes could pick out the pale faces of her companions, gathered and staring at her.

"What the fuk was that?" exclaimed Mouse.

"I don't know," muttered Vortigern. "But I do not hear our pursuers." Try as he could with his nekromantic senses, the sound of footsteps had faded in the charterhouse. Replaced by the sound of...Snoring!" he said, astonished. "I hear snoring. Plenty of it. I think every soul in the building beside ourselves is asleep!"

"What did you do?" gasped Mouse.

Morigan thought of an answer for a circumstance she could hardly explain herself. She was angry at their chase and filled with the passion of the Wolf. She tapped into something: emotion and force. Was that Will, as Thackery had spoken of? Was that magik?

"Magik?" she squeaked, uncertain.

"I misjudged you, Miss Lostarot," Alastair said with a smile, ever foxier as his white teeth flashed in the dark. "You are every bit the party. We'll have time to ponder our little miracle later. The sewer access is just ahead. We can be spans away by the time Elissandra wakes. What a delight it would be to slip her fingers into a glass of water, but alas. Hurry ho!"

The felicitous nature of their escape was lost on no one, and the miracle as proclaimed by Alastair was at the fore of their minds. Well after they had entered the slippery stone intestines of Menos and were almost blindly sloshing among filth, the question burned. For Morigan, it was a slightly different conflict, however, and what she did not tell her companions was that if she needed to, if she was pushed, she could do whatever that inexplicable act was again.

✳ ✳ ✳

IV

"Mistress Elissandra."

Heavily, the mistress of Mysteries stirred from what felt like the winter sleep of a bear. She was numb with comfort until she apprehended that one whole side of her body was asleep and her chin was wet with drool. Men were upon her: large faceless fellows with cross-shaped slits in their helmets and full dark armor that fit with leathery sensuousness. They took her to a chair while her swimming consciousness pieced together events, times, and places. Thinking was quite hard at the moment; she could not recall having been afflicted by such grogginess or a pressing desire to sleep. Outside the rain had stopped, and a shy beam of moonlight had squeezed through the pollution and was casting a pale pall over the classroom in which she had fallen.

That's right, you fell, she remembered. *She did something, that witch. Old magik. An invocation of the moon. How could she? Is she the one Malificentus spoke of? The child of the Fates?*

Elissandra pushed off the hands of the two Ironguards who had found her and stood up. She regained her composure with a toss of her head and a smoothing of her garments. The Ironguards were anxious for orders. There was an escapee on the loose who had yet to be detained. But Elissandra issued no commands. She paced along the line of moonlight on the floor and appeared wandering in thought. After much time had passed, one of the Ironguards took the liberty of addressing her.

"Should we go after her?"

Elissandra shook her head and looked to the moon, as if it were speaking.

"No. I am to see her again. Alone. Please understand that there can be no witnesses."

The luminance of the moon seemed to pour over Elissandra, and she whitened to a dazzling saturation. At first, what the Ironguards were beholding was lovely, made more so by the feathering of magik over their skins. That was until the feathers began to scratch and itch, and a terrible heat began in their stomachs. The Ironguards only snapped fully from the enchantment when they realized that they were on fire. By then it was too late to raise their rifles, for their eyes had popped in their sockets and their fingers were scarcely matchsticks.

Elissandra left the smoking corpses and drifted from the room. She had an appointment with the Daughter of Fate.

XVI

CHASING DOOM

I

After hearing the king's extensive praise of the flowers in the Valley of Fair Winds, Erik was a little disappointed. As the army rode between the great mossy crags, the hammer struggled to spot any blossoms above them. Nor did he see any flowers along the rock-strewn path. The wind was sweet as the king had promised, though perhaps not as *sweet as a mist of honey*, and not as cool as a clouded sky should permit. In fact, he found the air quite hot and tugged often at the straps of his armor. Looking around, he could see that many of the Silver Watch had removed their helmets or gauntlets entirely. He didn't care for this laxness and the ragtag air it conveyed, and those soldiers he caught with his reproachful stares put on their armaments at once. At war, a soldier was never to remove his protections, not even when he believed himself to be safe, for death held no courtesies or pardons toward the living for their unpreparedness. With that vigilance in mind, he focused his watch upon the king, who rode beside him.

The king had engaged in no more communication than was necessary today: a series of hand waves, nods, and short answers. The deeper tension to the king's austere self could only be noted by those who knew him as well as themselves. A distance to the stare, the faintest wrinkle on his marble forehead. Erik wondered if this was the same weakness that he had addressed in the woods rearing itself again or another concern altogether.

"My King, may we ride alone?" he asked.

Magnus responded by moving out of the line and into the shadow of the crags. Erik followed, and the two riders trotted around tall fractured stones; the echoing of their mounts' hooves made the silence between them thicker. While it was only a suspicion, Erik sensed that his king was angry.

"You are preoccupied," he stated.

"Yes," replied Magnus curtly. "We are nearing Mor'Khul. My stomach winds itself in knots when I consider the choices that must be made there."

"Choices?"

"Of how viciously I shall punish my brother. The line between love and hate is thin, they say. Yet with Brutus and me, the emotions bleed and confuse themselves even more. Even the hate is a passion."

The lone wrinkle on the Everfair King's brow pronounced itself further. "I have been contemplating dark, dark torments, Erithitek. Artistries of pain. I won't tell you the sickness that I dream, for it would taint whatever innocence remains in you. I shall tell you that in these fantasies, I am there with Brutus for every scream and every plea. I weep and I laugh. And when he is so miserably broken—a heap of meat and tears—I feed him my blood to heal him. It continues like that, the delicious cycle of horror, of me unmaking and making my brother."

Here the hammer had worried that his king was sliding into the doldrums of mercy, when the opposite had occurred. He had sharpened his hate to a vicious edge. This was good, thought Erik, the king had finally become a weapon.

Clip-clop, clip-clop. At the pace of their masters' phlegmatic moods, the horses trotted along. For almost an hourglass, the skies darkened with them, and when the king's cold voice came, it was as unsettling as the first peal of thunder.

"Have you come to a decision on my proposal?"

Erik had not. The mystery surrounding the king's plan did not sway his opinion for the better, either.

"No."

"Do you not think yourself up to the task?"

I can protect Queen Lila. I would take a sword for her, thought Erik. He and the king had no secrets but one, and he was gruff with his reply.

"I have sworn my soul and service to you, my King. However, it is difficult to accept a duty that has not been explained. You are asking me to leap blindly, which is unwise for any man to do."

"I am asking you to have *faith*," the king threw back.

Magnus's cold emerald eyes almost tossed Erik from the saddle, and it was no trick of the mind, but the winds grew fiercer and the clouds rumbled on high. The men stopped their steeds, and the king asked his question a second time.

"You have faith in your king, do you not?"

Erik huffed in his saddle. "I do."

"Do you have faith in yourself?"

"Yes."

"Of course you do," Magnus said, grinning. "Therein lies your true value as a man and as a warrior. You are not some trained beast, soullessly obedient to my commands. You are a thinking, breathing extension of my wishes and your Will. When I am lost, as I was in Meadowvale, you led me from my gloom. When I am cruel, you remind me to be kind. When I am mad...well, you do not fear the madness of an Immortal King. You pick up steel and come at him."

He knows, thought Erik.

Both Magnus's smile and the wind grew colder. "I know, Erithitek."

Yes, but how much? worried Erik.

"You stood outside my chambers," continued Magnus. "You would have heard Lila's anguish. A weaker man would have run. A stronger man would have run. A man of duty, who defended the king's virtues even as the master himself forgot them—*that* is the sort of man who serves me. I saw the shine of your steel in my doorway, and in that moment, I might have accepted your justice. For your impudence, I could just as well have blasted you into a thousand splinters of ice."

The emerald stare flickered, and a ripple of lightning ran overhead. Against his thighs, Erik's mare strained like a penned colt in a flaming barn. Erik was no more immune from the weight of this moment, from the crushing perceptions that the king had laid upon him. The king resumed talking with a sinister softness.

"Still, as time fades the scar, and I think of how I am to protect my legacy and of who would care for the queen without me...I see one man. I see you. The only mortal in my lifetime to have come at me with true grit and steel: an ally, a son, and a friend. Only the ones that we love can hurt us so deeply. The paradox is as bitter as it is beautiful. For a father is to be outdone by his child—it is nature, even if I am not a part of that cycle. Thus, when I ask you to do what I know is in your heart to do, and you do not leap at the prospect, I begin to dwell upon your hesitation. The hourglass is dark, and my mind weaves constant conspiracy. Do not give me a reason to doubt your faith in me, or in yourself. Here and now, there can be only one answer to the question that I shall ask you." Magnus paused, then said, "If I am to fall, and if Eod thereafter is to suffer the same fate, will you protect Lila? Will you see her safely to Carthac?"

Despite the lightning and thunder, the sky had yet to crack and weep. For the elements were bound by the king's feelings, and the storm would come when he had his answer. Perhaps a bolt of fury would fly to smite the man who had nearly treasoned against him.

"I shall," vowed Erik.

The rain began.

Without a second glance, the king urged his beast and rode off through a torrential curtain to join the wavering line of white riders. Erik allowed himself to lose track of his king, which was easy in the downpour. In wet solitude, he examined himself so somberly that he could have been another gray stone in the valley. He thought of honor and mercy, and whenever flashes of the pale golden queen rose, he took those monumental virtues and smashed them upon the images. He buried his shameful lust. Magnus had offered him redemption, and he would earn it with his duty. His king had shut out love and made himself into a weapon, and so too would he. When Erik was empty and ready to serve, he nudged his steed forward. He found the king's shadow through the rainy veil and fell in beside him, looking south with the same ruthlessness as his master did.

✳ ✳ ✳

II

She's a flower in the sunshine,
A wonder to behold!
And if I drink 'nuff courage
Den I may be so bold!
To take 'er hand,
Would be so grand!
No more chores!
Though I'll keep my whores
And remind the Miss,
That dem potatoes do need peeling!
These 'ands do need some 'ealing!
It's tough to till!
And tougher still,
To get off my behind
Bless my life!
I 'ave a wife!
Oh Gods, she 'as a knife!

As annoying as Rowena found him, Galivad had a smashing voice: strong, medium-timbered, and capable of sustaining long notes. In another time and place, he could have been one of Eod's finest performers, and he certainly had the grimy bearded miners that rode in the rattling wagon with them cheering as if he were a master bard. Hourglasses ago, before he started, one of the workmen had handed him a weary lute—all busted strings and sour notes—which he tuned to perfection in sands. There was skill in him, and it behooved Rowena to know from where.

The occasion to ask him did not come till far later in the day, after the cart had bounced its way far down the Iron Road and stopped for the night. They made camp on gravel beside the road and fetched kindling from the nearby copses of ash that cast their swaying shadows over a witch's moon. Fires were built and roaring, small game hunted and roasted—*nothing quite like skewered badger*, thought Rowena—and kegs were cracked open. Those who labored hard relaxed with equal vigor, and soon bard Galivad's songs were no longer needed, for the night was roaring with a drunken chorus. Eventually Galivad, his feet heavy from drink, stumbled over to Rowena. She was sitting with a few other folk upon the blankets that would be their bed for the evening. Galivad gave Rowena a rosy-cheeked smile that failed to charm her and dropped himself like a sack of potatoes to the ground.

"Fine singing, fair sir!" applauded a merry plump chap who was beside Rowena. "What is your name, sir? For you are surely famous."

"Corybantes Thorpe. Though you may call me Cory, good sir," beamed Galivad, and he slapped Rowena on the back. "This is my sister, Merriweather Thorpe. Merri, she prefers. A bit darker than my fair self, but Mother did fancy men of different port and call, so this is what she got. We are not artists, but procurers for wealthy masters and their queer tastes in the Southlands. Merri, well, she performs quite the dance with that sword of hers. My instruments are those of more subtle charismata: the gifts of gaff, haggling, and song."

The story continued, growing more embellished and fanciful. It was a miracle to Rowena that anyone believed Galivad's rhetoric, though his golden looks and rakish smile seemed to win any skeptic over. Again and again, Rowena shrugged off Galivad's broad hand, which had a tendency to linger on her when given the chance. While Galivad was enjoying himself and the ruse, at least he appeared to have remembered the identities Maggie had given them, which was one less bother for her to worry about. Already the ferry had taken a detour from landing at Blackforge, as the lookouts claimed to have spotted smoke in their telescopes. That inconvenience had cost them a day's pursuit, then more time still as the ferry was forced to dock south at Riverton. One of the strangest places Rowena had seen, Riverton was a mash of bilge parts and ship hulls that people somehow lived in, poking out like little moles from naval compartments or hosting their shops and taverns on slosh-ing, slanted decks in a topsy-turvy parody of what was normal. Still, it was in Riverton that luck finally graced them, and they learned of a convoy of feliron miners headed to Menos. Not long after that, they had paid their way onto the wagons, using Queen Lila's generous fates. *We all have armor that hides who we are and different masks for different occasions*, thought Rowena many a time, as she looked at these free men who were to toil alongside whipped slaves. Out here, they were gay, while in the dark hollows of the earth, where their skilled fingers could do what a slave's could not, they were surely as grim as the masters of the mine were. She knew that sense of duality well, and even as she smiled and idly chatted with those who would bend her ear, the soldier in her was ever focused on the mission. Regarding that, Queen Lila had yet to be notified of either the smith or the living sage, and that weighed on her mind. Still, she had but one farspeaking stone to use, and she would not waste it until she had spoken with the men she and Galivad pursued.

"What are you thinking about, my dear Merriweather?" asked Galivad.

He must have finished speaking a while ago, for the portly fellow had rolled over and gone to sleep. Others around them were curled up in blankets as well, and the revelry was fizzling out to sloppy laughter and snoring.

"All that frowning and you will wrinkle such a beautiful face," said Galivad.

She could not tell if he was serious. "The hourglass is late. We should sleep," she replied.

Rowena lay down and wrapped herself in her cloak. With a sigh, Galivad placed himself beside her. As Rowena's eyelids were growing heavy, Galivad began to hum a soothing tune: something about a girl chasing a falling star. He sang it often, and it had become the final sounds that would sweep her off to dreams. Tonight she resisted the pull of sleep and forced herself to ask the question that she had been nursing for days. Rowena shifted so that they were facing each other; Galivad stopped his music from the surprise.

"Where did you learn to sing?" she whispered.

Galivad's brow smoothed, and a gentle sincerity effaced his bravado. He said, "From my mother."

They were quiet a speck.

"Where did you learn how to use a blade?" he asked.

"From Queen Lila."

Rowena left the matter to die, though their twisting faces told that there were layers unrevealed to their stories. When it seemed that no one was ready to part with truths, Rowena went to turn her shoulder.

"My mother was a minstrel," hissed Galivad. "From the hearth fires of Heathsholme."

The name of the village was familiar to Rowena, though placing it eluded her. She returned to their huddle.

"I wasn't entirely fabricating in the little history I've been weaving for us," continued Galivad. "Not about my mother, at least. She made her way to many towns, and many beds, and one day came home with me in her belly. Her songs...I still remember them, every one. And if you fancy my voice, hers was a true delicacy for the ear. You might think me a liar, but I tell you that in my childhood memories, I recall birds roosting on our windowsill with their tiny heads cocked to hear her melodies. A song maiden. She could have been one of those legendary enchantresses of music from the East. At least, that is how I remember her."

Down the memory path he wandered and encountered something dark that twisted his comeliness. Rowena did not ask what it was, though the allusion to his mother in the past tense was telling enough, and Galivad was speaking ere she could have asked him.

"The sword. You say the queen taught you? Why did your father or brother not teach you the blade?"

"Those are not only a man's pursuits," snorted Rowena. "A woman is just as capable with a blade and with twice the sense on how to use it."

Eod had many a female conscript to its army, and Sword Rowena was twice the thickness and muscle of Galivad—a lean brown virago. Galivad realized how foolish he had sounded and apologized.

"You are right, of course."

"I had no brother or father to teach me," confessed Rowena. Her eyes were hard with anger and pride as she went on. "Do you know how the Arhad treat their women? It is despicable. The milk-lizards are given better considerations. How they treat their children is worse. You can imagine, then, what standing is given to young girls. They are excess. *Khek*, they are called. The liquid splatter that spinrex dribble from their arses. Shite, as I learned when I came to Eod." Rowena took a breath, which worked to soften her voice to a growl but did nothing to calm her nerves. "If there is a poor season and not enough meat or milk to go around, the weak are trimmed from the flock. The khek are left in the desert with the rest of the shite. The chieftains claim that this is a mercy, for if the child is strong, she will survive in a wasteland—by herself, without tools or skills—and she will return to the tribe with the strength of the desert itself. From khek to blessed wife, as if the reward is better than the punishment."

"*You* were one of those children." Galivad was aghast.

Out of compassion, Galivad's wandering hand had crept its way onto her forearm. He had very large hands for such a slight man, and Rowena wasn't sure why she noticed that or why it made her so uncomfortable. She pulled her arm away.

"I was."

"Yet you survived."

"I did," she nodded. "Destiny, some might say, though that is what the star-watching elders of my people would call it, and I spit on all that they believe. I walked and walked and I would not die. I pushed myself raw and somehow I was found before the breath of life fled from me. By the queen's escort, en route from diplomacy in the West. I remember her."

Are these spirits? she wonders. Have I died? What else could these silver-shelled men on their scaleless ivory lizards be? And yet there is a golden spirit among them who disturbs what is understood of the afterlife. Women are not among those who ride the deserts of eternity. Yet here she is, this breasted rider, brighter than the wavering sun and free of her trappings, rudely but exquisitely exposed with her curves, sinfully thin dress, and flowing hair.

The spirit woman is the first to reach her, floating from her mount like ribbons of light, or perhaps it is only the girl's distorted, delirious perception that makes the shapes so stretched and dazzling. As she falls, the spirit woman has her, cocoons her in light, and murmurs in the tongue of her people.

(There, there, my dry flower, you have nothing to fear. We shall wet your roots and see you bloom again.)

"She took me in as if I was born of her loins. From khek to sword of the queen. I spit on the Fates, but there are nights when I thank them instead."

"I thank them, too," said Galivad.

The moment hung between them: a nakedness of feeling, of two lost children in hard adult skins recognizing another of their kind. Abruptly, Rowena turned her back to her companion and mumbled a good night. With such a troubled telling before bed, she had to fight for sleep. Galivad might have seen her fussing, or he might have simply decided to resume his song, but soon the tale of the star-chasing maiden was being crooned into her ear. At once her eyelids were heavy, and in another breath she was out and drifting down the river of dreams.

✳ *✳* *✳*

III

By nightfall, the rain had stopped, and a quilt of fog covered the valley. The oblong markers that littered the road had taken on a fearsome consistency in the mist, as if they were eggs in the nest of a giant horror. To the first legion the gloomy king and Erik rode, and pushed the army to keep up with the pace of their grunting steeds. When at last they rested, the king did not warm the men with ballads, but deepened the chill that had set beneath their skins with a fierce and short speech on valor and death and then left them to their meager fires. The fanciful orations were over, the army realized. The king would waste no more sentiments on rousing their spirits, but on tempering them.

Around the king's fire were those with the hardest expressions: the legion masters and Erik. The ten grave warriors watched the flames like ancient seers. They discussed reserves and strategy, though for seasoned veterans of war, the council spoke with very little depth. For they knew nothing of what Brutus had prepared for them, and the truth was that this war would not be contingent upon the steel and magik they had brought. As soldiers, they were superfluous to the clash between the two kings. Stormy thoughts of that magnificent destruction sent the legion masters to bed early. One by one, they bid bitter partings and drifted from the fire to toss and turn on their damp bedrolls. Before long, the final good-bye was made, and it was only Erik and the king sitting together on the same stone. As close as they were, the emotional space between them was a gulf. Erik expected a continuation of their silent game of punishment and forgiveness, so he was surprised when the king addressed him.

"It is warm for the season," said the king.

Once the cooling rain passed, mugginess had set in; for many an hour-glass Erik had been sticking to his armor. This was the sort of clammy itch that too much time in a steam house would bring. Nor had the heat abated after the storm; it seemed to be getting worse the farther they marched.

"I remember you speaking of fair winds and fairer flowers, of which I have seen none," muttered Erik.

"Indeed, there should be," the king said, frowning as he slicked back his sweaty hair. "In the fall, there should be gardens on every knoll, and petals fluttering into the valley like butterflies. This place has an incomparable beauty before winter sweeps upon it. Yet if I listen to what the soil and stones tell me, I feel as if spring, summer, fall, and winter, has already come and gone. Come, look here."

The king left the rock and knelt. He swished his fingers about in the dirt, scooped up a handful, and began to pick through it. Erik was promptly squatting at his side to see what the king was investigating. A white and wormy thing was pinched from the dirt and held up to Erik: up close, it seemed to be a small twist of paper.

"A petal," said the king. "Long since cast from its flower. The seasons are confused, and the valley has suffered for it. Without the softness of fall rot or the protection of winter frost, whatever seeds were loosed are squandered. Geadhain is a delicate organism, and I have watched her elements and moods shape the very road we stand on. This is unnatural."

Wistfully, the king rolled up the petal and followed its descent to the ground. Then the cold emerald stare found Erik.

"I am concerned for what awaits us in the South. There is power at work here, a power not unlike my own. One that can twist nature and warp the seasons. And that heat." The king wiped his brow. "I was right in confiding in you. I believe that my brother has something wicked planned, though I have not yet gathered what. Listen now, my Hammer, for you may well be the salvation of Eod and everything that I have built."

The words felt tight as a noose around Erik's neck.

"Come close and give me your hand, Erithitek," commanded the king.

Erik obeyed. Like a trickster, the king pressed their palms together, and when he lifted his fingers, there lay in Erik's hand a fragment of green crystal, no larger than a coin. The crystal was as deep as the king's eyes and as cold as a chunk of ice. Erik's hand shivered merely from holding it.

"W-what is it?" he chattered.

"My gambit. A bit of magik. More than a bit. Hundreds of bits infused into matter throughout our travel here, done so slowly that it would not shatter such a delicate casing. It holds enough power for a tremendous act of sorcery once it is broken."

"Broken?"

"Indeed. The stomp of a boot should do the trick."

"And what is the trick, my King?"

The king clasped his hammer's metal shoulder and beheld his friend with sympathy. "If the hourglass grows darkest, and we have lost, break that stone. It will see you to safety, farther and faster that any skycarriage. A blink and you will be there, for I have filled that spell with my love and hope."

Translocation. Erik had heard of this type of sorcery before, though never on so grand a scale. For him, the king had prepared an escape from an inescapable situation.

"Place it somewhere out of sight. If the Fates are willing, you will never have to use it."

So ended their parley. The king stood and went again to his rock where he would keep a lonely vigil. As his second shadow, Erik would join him in a speck. Though first he caressed the cold piece of magik and pondered the responsibility that this tiny stone held. His freedom from death and his punishment all in one.

I shall not fail you, my King. Nor shall I sully my honor with thoughts of she who is not mine. I shall protect her, true as my own sister, and think no baser thoughts, promised Erik. *Please forgive me for having ever raised arms against you. You who are a father to me, you to whom I owe my life.* When he looked up from his small prayer to his kingfather, the dark and haunted man was observing him. They stared, deep and true, and Erik clutched the farstone tighter, for it was as if the king could hear his promise or read the deeper guilt upon his face even through his helmet. What astonished the hammer most was the slow nod of Magnus's head: a blessing or acceptance. He wondered if any mysteries, futures, or fates were ever safe from the Everfair King.

He had a padded pocket sewn into his linen under-shirt and he placed the farstone within it. Once that was done, he buckled up his plate and stood behind the king so that they would not cross stares again. More than ever, he was beginning to sense that the king doubted their odds of success. For the looks and exchanges between them these past days, as passionate and hard as they were, felt like final sentiments. The last words of those who know they are doomed.

XVII

THE LONG NIGHTMARE

I

After they were through the thinning pines, Caenith knew that their real danger was beginning. For the skies were busy with flocks of Crowes, cruel black arrowheads that slunk under the veil of gloomy skies, and they had spans to go across the fields of Canterbury before they reached the Iron Valley. Yet Caenith's senses were growing grander and grander, and the wind whispered to him when the black shapes would come. He knew then when to hunker in the brush and when to hasten across the exposed countryside. Thackery informed him that the Crowes had high-range telescopes and other technomagikal instruments for scanning the ground, so Caenith stuck to whatever wooded belts he could. Without the sun or chronexes, the hourglass could not be ascertained, but Thackery felt that it was afternoon when they huffed their way into a verdant ravine, like a half-laid pipe festering with coniferous growth. Cheerful birds tried to stave the pregnant skies from raining with their songs, and a brook ran through the narrow valley. Their feet had been slapping the soil since Ebon Vale, and Thackery hated to be the weak link in their number, but he felt as if he could go no farther without a moment's rest. Little Macha, who was insistent to be carried no more, had kept a brave pace with these two determined men, and she was dark about the eyes and dragging herself with weariness, too.

"A break. A sand to catch our breath. Please," he requested.

When the Wolf turned to see the seal in her muddy, torn dress and his scraggly bearded companion weaving despite a sturdier walking stick than the last, he realized how indefatigably he had pushed them. Quickly he spotted a circle of hedges shaded by the drooping hands of leafy giants that had appeared among the pines of Canterbury. The ground in the small dell was as comfortable as a bird's nest with bracken and twigs; one could even lay his head down and sleep a spell if he chose, and the pebbled shore of the brook was nearby to quench one's thirst. He led the company to the spot.

"Rest here," he said. "I shall see what can be found for food."

The Wolf was off as a breeze, rustling the bushes and unheard beyond that. Although they had traveled together for a while, Thackery's communication with Macha never progressed beyond gestures and smiles, so he used a few of those to coax the girl over to the brook. She drank rather oddly, with her face in the water instead of bringing the liquid to her mouth. When she was done, she stayed kneeling by the brook; trailing her fingers through the currents or sometimes harking to the chirps and calls of creatures. *Lost*, thought Thackery. The poor thing was so very lost. The sensibility of her being along for their journey stabbed his heart and mind in different ways: they could not leave her, yet they certainly could not keep her. And there would come a time where they would have to surrender her. But to whom?

"We shall find a good home for her."

Thackery had smelled the Wolf's—not unpleasant—woodiness before hearing him, so he wasn't as surprised as he should have been. Macha noticed the Wolf and made noises that a girl should not make: *uroo, uroo, urro*! Friendly, happy even, but utterly strange. They did not glance to each other, but continued to watch the child.

"A mortal guardian could be a problem, considering her eccentricities," noted Thackery. Like the wise old man he was, he stroked his beard and pondered further. "Orphanages would not take her or give her the sort of care she deserves. I suppose the queen could find a place for her. Whatever your opinions of the queen, she is a saint toward those less fortunate. The palace is full of those whom her charity has touched."

"She would still be an outsider," contended the Wolf. "I have said my piece on the queen as well, and I would rather we find another caregiver. Moreover, while I do not follow slow-walker politics, the signs of war are all around us. The grass shivers in fear, the winds carry scents of smoke and riflepowder. I do not know if Eod would be safe for Macha. Or you, should you choose to return."

A chill gust swept the ravine, as if Geadhain were in agreement.

"You are right. The signs are all around us, Caenith. So many Crowes in the sky—more than there should be. I suspect that Augustus and the Iron Queen are brewing something vile in Blackforge, as well."

The Wolf thought back to Augustus's city. "Grease, grunt, and fire. Hammering and the screech of metal being shaped. I remember these things. I have been a smith long enough to know the sounds of a forge. Many forges. A war camp. Somewhere to the north of the city. Somewhere underground, from the echoes."

"War."

"War."

With their agreement, and their bleak acceptance that these events were beyond their control, the conversation was closed. Macha was up from the bank of the brook and headed their way, too, pointing to something on one of them and muttering in Ghaedic. Thackery turned and saw that the Wolf's shirt had been removed and made into a wet bundle. If Thackery had to guess, by the dampness of the man's hair and trousers, he would say that Caenith had been swimming and that those were fish—caught with reflexes and not rods. His supposition was validated once they were back at the hedges eating smelt off Caenith's shirt as if it were a picnic blanket. Macha had quite the appetite for the fish and tended to swallow them whole, again reminding Thackery of her displacement in the world. Not that Caenith ate with any more refinement. As Thackery nibbled, he smiled at their animalism.

Well, you're in it now, old man. The strangest of the strange. I seem to have more unusual friends than normal ones.

Once they were finished eating, they rested for a spell. Caenith washed and donned his shirt and took watch over his companions. Macha was soon slumbering on the bracken, and Thackery attempted to shut his eyes as well. In and out he blinked, seeing claws of foliage above him, or flickers of Macha, as pale and helpless as a white prawn out of water. Flashes of the Wolf as well: vigilant and frowning and staring up through the leaves for Crowes. *Does the man sleep?* pondered Thackery amid his dreary state that was neither sleeping nor waking. Sometimes he almost went out, and he would begin to see a misty woodland that slithered with shadows and had trees thrice as tall as the ones that should be around him. He knew this place, and the innate fear of it startled him awake every time. After a while, he gave up on resting and shuffled around in the leaves like a fussy hen.

"I thought you were tired," said Caenith, who was crouching nearby in his predatory way, with his hands between his legs and his head cocked.

"Shouldn't you be?" replied Thackery grumpily.

"I shall sleep when Morigan is found. But we should let her rest until dusk," declared the Wolf.

Thackery didn't think on how a man could go without resting for days, not when his own body needed tending. He groaned his way to his feet and stretched. Such cracking and aching he made, though it was possible that he was getting used to their constant exertion, for the pain was not as terrible or as noticeable as he had anticipated. He had been a spry man once, perhaps his body remembered a bit of that. Regardless, he was holding up better than he had predicted at the outset.

Macha suddenly bolted out of her sleep. She was gasping and fish-eyed as if from a nightmare. The Wolf crawled to her, and they whispered ancient Ghaedic to each other; Thackery interpreted the expressions as he could. Nothing the gentle Wolf tried would lull Macha back to slumber, and in a sand Thackery was told to grab his walking stick, for they were to be on their way.

Another hourglass lay between them and the concealment of night, yet with the land darkening, they took greater risks. From the ravine, they hurried across a sward—delayed a bit by Macha's distraction over the silver butterflies and early nightflies congregating there in clouds like faery creatures. Before the next flock of Crowes whooshed through the clouds, they were down in a muddy cleft, as if the earth had simply cracked and dropped in a spot. They followed this passage until the path rose into more plains, hills, and forested ravines. The mountains fenced their side as a line of black teeth, hungry and intimidating, and the land ahead appeared endless, disappearing behind a fog as night fell. Yet the three pressed on, if primarily because the Wolf set their stride, and his was determined. Even as the stars winked and shone, Thackery did not ask for rest. With every step nearer to Menos, his concern over Morigan's fate increased. A day in the Iron City was a lifetime anywhere else and plenty of time to find one's grave.

Thackery asked once after her welfare, to which the Wolf answered him vaguely and without breaking.

"I felt her once. She was in trouble; now she is not. I think she has found allies."

Allies? wondered Thackery, and he was given much to occupy his mind with as his legs churned out steps. If she had discovered people to hide her, that was a promising development; even if friends in Menos were simply folks who hadn't found a knife to stick you with yet. Night seemed to darken Thackery's thoughts as well as the land, which sprouted with tanglements, deeper vales, and taller trees. Come the final coat of darkness, the birds surrendered their tweets to the hooting of owls and the growling of vicious hunters. Now and again, these beasts came, ruffling thickets or clawing their ways up trees, yet they never attacked the company. A fortune owed to their guide, no doubt, who stamped fearlessly ahead: kicking his way through bush, snapping back trees, and hacking a trail through the land as if he owned it, as if he were its king. Thackery was no naturalist, though he understood that the Wolf's scent, and moreover the primality of his presence, was keeping any predators at bay.

Here I walk with monsters, roars and claws and teeth. Here I bow before the lord to offer up my meat. The grisly lines entered Thackery's consciousness more than once as he watched the Wolf hewing ahead, and he wasn't sure where he knew it from or of what greater work it was a part. Another bit of prose from Alabion, perhaps, as those were always rife with references to death and lords. *Alabion!* he thought, and while it wasn't ideal, perhaps they could arrange for someone in the East to care for Macha. Properly, among the culture of her kind. While they were crossing what looked to be one of the last broad stretches of land before a rising wave of forest, he brought this up with Caenith.

"I think I have a solution, or at least part of one."

"To what?" the Wolf called back.

Thackery glanced to the child shivering by his side; he had given her his cloak as the chillness of night set in, but it didn't seem to be enough. He squatted and warmed her shoulders with his hands, and she rewarded him with a tiny smile.

"To our fellow traveler," said Thackery. "We should return her to Alabion. What better home could there be for a child like her? Would you like that, Macha?"

What Thackery had said was interesting enough to stop the Wolf's unyielding stride. However, he was already shaking his head as he turned around.

"Do you remember her nightmares this afternoon?" asked the Wolf.

"I do."

"Macha was dreaming of Alabion."

"I don't understand," replied Thackery.

Quite rightly, the Wolf was annoyed at this conversation and delay, as every speck was teasing doom. Until Macha impulsively ran toward his heat and wrapped her arms—as much as she could manage—around his leg. At last, then, some of the callousness and pain that Caenith had layered upon himself like a scab finally fell off. The Wolf knew that he had been driving himself past what should kill a man. Willing himself to stop only to piss, shite, eat, and then to continue at all costs toward the Iron City. In all the long years of his life, he had never tested his endurance so violently, and a razor of hurt ran through his every nerve with each step forward, as if he tread on a bed of nails. Agony was its own stimulant, and it kept him awake and even transcendentally aware: smelling, hearing, and feeling to extrasensory heights. But these two who traveled with him, with their slow-walking and fragile selves, could not be forgotten, or he was no better than the masters who had taken his Fawn.

Realizing his errors, he unclasped Macha's cloak and handed it back to Thackery, whose shivering indicated that he needed it just as much. When that was done, he picked up Macha, and she sat sidesaddle on his forearm and eagerly hugged his neck. Thackery tried not to take offense; it wasn't that she didn't want to be picked up, it was that she didn't want to be picked up by him. Caenith motioned his companion ahead and ambled for a while so that Thackery could take less labored breaths.

"Macha speaks of Alabion as if it is no longer safe," the Wolf said grimly. "Such is why she and her family fled. The forest changed many centuries ago, after I left it. I hear that she became unkind to those who used magik, and many of the old clans left, as it was the only way they knew to survive. Still, many skin-walkers and the oldest creatures of the woods remained, as they were the least affected. I thought that the change in Alabion's kindness signaled the fading of my kind: an end to magik. That those who stayed on, those with fangs and natures unfit for the world of man, would drift away like morning mist. I believed my kind to be safe in their silver sanctuary. I was wrong—Macha says that the lords of fang and claw have risen from their gentle decay and bound themselves to the will of a warmother."

"Warmother?"

"Aye. *Ban Mactyre*, she calls her. The monster in her dreams. A white wolf. Though in her dreams, which I believe are as much memories, the white wolf is often red with blood and dancing as the oldest witches once danced around sacred stones and fires." Caenith's eyes sparkled. "I have known a white wolf before, and they are fierce but deeply spiritual creatures. This one, this warmother, sounds mad or possessed of a passion for conquest. If we sent Macha to Alabion, it would be from one terror to the next."

"Another possibility will present itself. They always do!" Thackery clapped Caenith's arm—yet again, he forgot the hardness of the man. "Like slapping a stone! By the kings, I need a pair of mittens if we are to be proper friends."

"Come, friend," said Caenith, smiling. "I hear the birds of Menos moving west again. We must make those trees within a few sands. Are you up for a sprint?"

"I don't need you to carry me. Save that for the women and children!" cackled Thackery, and he was off.

Caenith raced after him, and had no trouble overtaking the old man, though he chose to match his gait. Once they reached the shadows of the forest, the warmest of their camaraderie cooled while the coals of it remained. Burning in each man was a spark of unanimity. It fueled their spirits as much as Caenith's pain did. They climbed through the forest, which grew ever steeper and as tangled as a yarn of vines and bush. Using only a single hand, Caenith ripped through it all, without waking little Macha, who had fallen asleep again against his grunting flesh. They were each wet with leafy blood and heaving when they came to a summit in the woods on which the trees were few and far between across a hump of mossy bedrock. It offered a sweeping sight of the valley beyond. To Thackery it seemed like they were about to tread into another day of forest, for the fuzzy shadows rolled on and on, so thick that he imagined walking across the canopy. They had left the fields of Canterbury, and the constellations above told him that they were north, quite north. He was not able to say where.

Caenith, however, saw much farther and understood their location better than his companion did. In his sharp sight, Kor'Keth's range had tumbled down like an old dry stone wall that would no longer keep the cattle in, and the glistening line of water past even that was to their side, while ahead was a day's hike till they tested themselves against the last leg of their journey. He could see that challenge, too. At the end of the wood, where the land gave itself to rubble, a haphazard arrangement of rock was piled in slanted tiles, which made for a second mountain range, heading east. The whole formation appeared teetering even if it was ancient and fast, and could have been made by a messy giant, for it had the appearance of building blocks left unfinished. Into the dark winding tunnels that ran through that rock maze they would go. Caenith squinted until the stars faded, the forest folded away, and he had only a sliver of sight. A black cloud plumed beyond the Iron Valley: Menos.

Two days at most, until they reached the Iron City. They were nearly there.

II

"Tread carefully," warned Thackery.

Barring any cautions from the sage, Caenith could feel the prickle of menace and sense the extraordinary dankness of the Iron Valley. An ancient death. That is what he smelled—the powder and must of bones—and sensing deeper and further with his uncanny perceptions, a corruption, too. For a charcoal stain crept up toppled pillars of gray rock like wicked ivy, dyed the dusty slabs that were tossed about, and infested the greater crags of the range. So dark was the shadow of the valley that it could have been dusk and not the warm day from which they had come. And so strong was the sense of wrongness that Caenith's iron stomach curdled.

Macha was awake and clinging tightly to Caenith, and he distractedly murmured to her while embroiled in anxieties of his own. Even though there were aspects of the Iron Valley that nudged him with familiarity, nothing was as it should be. When he looked about expecting grand, clear roads, these trails were so overgrown that it was as if no roads had ever been there. Granted, his memory was fuzzy at the best of times, yet he seemed to recall the quarry in which they stood as a great junction. He looked to the monolithic heap, expecting tall rectangular tunnels, and saw none of those, either. Truly, it was as if his memory was deceiving him. He sought an answer from his companion, the man whose idea it had been to take this cursed path.

"What happened here? These were the gates to the South and West. The axis of trade and travel from Menos."

"Indeed they were," replied Thackery. "I wouldn't expect you to be up-to-date with your—what is the term—*slow-walker* histories, so I'll pardon you not having heard this terrible tale."

"Terrible tale?"

"Most terrible."

Thackery waved for Caenith to follow him and began caning his way through the stones like a tired old well-weirder: he seemed to have a path in mind.

"Greed," announced Thackery. "The curse of Menos. Those who once had nothing, crave everything. Greed is built into our values, bred into our children. For the masters, there is no food or pleasure that can satisfy us; for the slaves, there is an endless craving to be free. We all hunger for something in this world. But Menosians are prey to this vice more than any. You could blame the kings for this, for their refusal to give us mercy in some dead and bygone age over which my people forever hold a grudge, but really, the venality of a Menosian is a *disease*, passed from parent to child. I doubt that the kings' mercy would have healed any of that. If I were sage and advisor to Magnus back then, I would have told him to let the city starve and fester with plague, too. Had I the foresight, I might have cast death upon my own people."

Switching roles with his companion, Thackery now skillfully led them up a slide of rubble. Caenith suspected that the old man had taken this path before, as his stride was ever sure. Onward and upward they went, moving into stretches of difficult terrain, huffing around jagged stone talons and hauling themselves over fallen stone logs made to trip and maim. The shadows grew colder and the rocks darker. Even the wind had a subtle hiss and brought only more of that dusty stink. The land did not want them here. The land did not want any living thing here, thought Caenith, for he had seen no birds in the bleary skies, not even a spider scuttling amid the rocks. When they had made fair headway from where they started, Thackery continued his tale.

"There is iron in these foothills, the tremendous vein that fed Menos for centuries, perhaps a thousand years, even. Now, wherever there is iron, if one digs deeper to where minerals and the invisible energy of Geadhain mingle, one might—rarely—find feliron."

Caenith knew the metal by a different name: *witchburn*. For that is what it did when used upon witches or magikal creatures.

"They did not have the magik of the kings, so they built weapons and walls to withstand such powers," said Thackery. "Their rifles, their ships, even the great black wall of Menos. All ingenuities that came from the metallurgists and mad alchemists of my people. Here, well beneath where we tread, is the greatest lode of the material that has ever been found. It runs from where we started to the peaks that surround the Iron City. Though the deposits there are weak compared with the richness of what is under us. A tributary of the river below, in a sense."

Thackery tapped the chalky slate he was walking on, as if to remind himself of something. "Greed, yes. That was the point. The Menosians built up extensive operations. Tunnels and buildings beneath us, and roads—as you recall—for hauling and transporting materials and ore. They were pushing into the West, you see. Establishing settlements and battlements, of a mind to rule from Menos to Blackforge. A success they seem to have achieved, though not as openly or as quickly as their old masterminds envisioned. For their ambitions, they needed feliron, an obscene amount of it, and I am sure if you listen with your curious senses, you might still hear the screams of the slaves whose blood wet these stones. I do not believe in ghosts, though even I feel that this place carries a particular foreboding: a chill that cannot be placed or blamed upon the weather."

"A taint," agreed Caenith.

"Yes, that is it."

Thackery's telling was interrupted as Caenith noticed the sudden screech of metal wings slicing wind. *Crowes*, he muttered. In the Iron Valley, there were no shortage of places to find cover, and they walked a few paces to huddle under a stone tent. They waited for the skycarriages to pass. Macha, who the two men had discovered had a sensitivity to the particular frequency of the Crowes' movements, covered her ears and hid her face against Caenith. Within a few sands, the vessels appeared, dark shapes that rumbled overhead like rolling thunder. When the Wolf could no longer sense the vessels, he nodded for Thackery to continue. Which the old man did, both in hiking ahead and in resuming the cursed history of the Iron Valley.

"The decision to conquer westward took an immeasurable amount of resources. I believe that the Council of the Wise's ambition exceeded its common sense. More slaves, more tunnels, more feliron. The slaves who fell were *reborn* by sorcerers of the dark arts. Slower laborers they made, these corpses, and, it is said, the mines buzzed and reeked with decay. Understand for a speck how horrid that is, toiling beside the corpse of your fellows."

Thackery shuddered and sadly hung his head. "As the strata started to deplete, they had to dig deeper, into the veins that beat close to the heart of Geadhain herself. In order to break these crusts, they required explosives and other Menosian magiks. But like any organism that is under assault, Geadhain repels those that try to harm her. She has the elementals, these wyrms that I have been blessed enough to see during our journey together. To those who would poke at Geadhain's flesh, she defends herself with cave-ins and pockets of deadly gas, which when struck by the faintest spark, light a fire that cannot be smothered or extinguished by water. Nonetheless, my clever ancestors were prepared for such complications. Therefore, they made their bombs of air, not flame, and were delicate about their placement. What they did not foresee—which no one could, as the depths of the Iron

Valley were a survey in progress—was the massive fault that spread along this entire range."

"Fault?" questioned Caenith.

"Like a crack down low that you don't want to touch. Make it bigger and it affects everything above itself in the most unpleasant ways. Less hasty and more diligent eyes would have noticed the indications on the surface: rockslides, tremors, striations, and even rifts in the Iron Valley. I imagine that the masters of Menos spat with scorn upon any who presented these facts to them. They wanted the feliron, and quickly; they ignored any contrary voices. With that in mind, and little else, they blasted lower and lower, and eventually they hit what they should not have." Thackery softly sighed. "Still, that was not the worst of their folly, for at the bed of this deep, earthen river, was something else that they had not the caution or care for which to plan: a vein of truefire. A small one, though that's all it needed to be. The fault, and the explosion, together—"

Remembering the tragedy made Thackery pause. He was a child when it happened, and with all that had dulled since then, he still recalled the day that Menos was shaken by the hand of Geadhain.

Buildings fall like sandcastles, pulled from their bottom and funneling to oblivion upon themselves. Screams, there are so many screams amid the rumbling, and so much dust that he cannot see from where. He is too hysterical to be as terrified as he should be, perhaps from whatever injury has made his head hum and blood trickle over his eyes. Gloria and Mother are about, somewhere in the storm of filth, and he adds his cry to the racket.

"Mother! Gloria!"

Nothing answers but destruction.

While the cobbles turn under him, he stumbles through more of the dusty obliteration. His determination is rewarded, and he sees a pale hand that he recognizes. A moment later, the smoke parts to his sister's wan face. She is coughing and partially buried in the remains of the carriage, and the rush he has when seeing her enables his small boy's body to heave debris—great panels of wood and smoldering wheels—off his sister. When she is up and they have hugged each other, he asks where Mother is. To this, Gloria shakes her head and points to the rubble from which he has extracted her. From the smoky pile, a broken axle of the carriage rises: it is red and gleaming as a freshly painted pole. Red with blood.

"We'll be all right, Gloria. We have each other," he says.

As the world continues its disintegration around them, they weep, hold each other, and promise to survive together.

Thackery came back to his friend. "The smallest touch, the tiniest spark—which with truefire can come from two motes of dust—and the whole range tumbled. Buried everything for spans and bore its vengeance all the way east to Menos. Twenty thousand were estimated to have died in the mines, another half of that claimed in Menos. My mother, Isabelle, was among those taken. She died pushing my sister and me to safety. My mother was mourned, along with the other masters lost in the disaster, and for a whole week, the city wore shrouds of black. Then we moved on, without memorials or testaments, as grief is the crutch of the weak, and we are people of iron."

"We?" questioned Caenith quietly. Repeatedly and in many conversations, Thackery had identified himself as a Menosian. All this regardless of the how much that affiliation had cost him.

Dourly, Thackery smiled. "What unites a man with his country—and his guilt—if not shame or tragedy? I cannot separate myself from the sins in my blood any more than you can separate yourself from your bloodthirstiness. Nor should I, and nor should you, for it is these struggles that define us. We are what we are, Wolf, though we can always try to be something better. I know that you understand this."

"Aye."

The men held a moment of silence with each other. Once it passed, Thackery waved his stick toward the heights.

"Let's keep climbing," said Thackery. "I'm almost finished the story, and it is important that we get to the end."

As they ascended, the stone heaps grew taller and more tottering, the footholds shakier, and the paths thin as thread. Thackery's lead was impeccable, however, and he saw routes that the Wolf himself might have missed. Thackery took them into whistling, constrictive chasms that could have been fissures in an arctic glacier if not for the absence of snow. He showed them where to step as they entered a wide field of rock so broken and sharp that it was like navigating a basin of shattered crystal. When they were safe on the other side of that particular hazard, and walking like mountain goats along a slim path on a steady incline with an echoing drop to their sides, Thackery—fearless, apparently—chose to speak again.

"After the destruction, Menosians' plans for expansion stalled until they rebuilt their resources and empire. Now, tens of thousands of deaths was hardly a deterrent to the Iron war machine, and at first, they thought to start again, as the truefire vein was now spent, the fault-line was now known, and enough of the tunnels and infrastructure remained intact. Yet that plan was more difficult in execution than in concept on account of the...*occurrences*."

"Occurrences?"

"Disappearances. Unwholesome noises. Accidents whenever reparative efforts were made to the tunnels. It was not uncommon for entire dig sites and crew to simply vanish: gone like flatulence in the wind. Technomagikal equipment functions erratically in and around these ranges, and if you had a chronex to check, you'd note that the time would be off, or frozen entirely. As steadfast as Menosian tenacity is, they ultimately gave up and sealed the Iron Valley, opting for safer deposits of feliron elsewhere. A decision made from fear, yet also so that their enemies could not sneak into the hollows and set off another city-damning earthquake. Here we are, then, treading over the largest grave in Geadhain. I told you before that I don't believe in ghosts, and that still holds true. However, even you, at first instinct, sensed the *wrongness* of this place. A shadow of death that no amount of time seems enough to wash clean."

Caedentriae, thought Caenith. In Alabion, when great acts of sorcery mixed with blood and tragedy, dark and persistent enchantments could result. Spells where time and reality themselves were scarred and twisted. A sacrifice on this scale could power the blackest of nightmares.

"What you describe, I would call the Long Nightmare," said Caenith. "A sacrilege against the Green Mother, where there is so much blood, death, and magik that it troubles her innocent mind, filling it with terrors. Only what she dreams, we live, and thus we live in her nightmares, too."

"An interesting theory," mused Thackery. "A sound one, too, considering the balderdash that I've heard from supposedly learned men. Not a haunting, then, but a memory. A terrible memory conjured within the mind of the great green creature that we crawl upon."

389

"Yes."

"Be that as it may, I've been up and down the Iron Valley more times than I can count and have yet to see anything more terrible than this depressing atmosphere. A test on the nerves, but not much else. We should hurry and outpace the darkness, though. Accidents can happen in the dark."

Soon the two men were off the ledge and on a harsh incline. The heights of the range were ahead of them, crashing upward in twists of black rock like a gravity-defying wave. Here they traversed slowly, for the black stones were brushed with fine and slippery dust that would send them tumbling down the rise to the left or right and into the shadowy crevasses there. Only one path was open to them, and that was ahead. Caenith's incredible fatigue chose now to harangue him: his feet were throbbing, his thighs were searing, and his spine had knotted above his hips, sending starbursts of pain into his groin. *You shan't stop. Not until she is with you. Not while you hold this child*, willed Caenith. A punishing wind came over him, gagging his senses with the ash of the Iron Valley. Thackery heard his companion grunting, looked back to see the sweat and unsightly paleness on his overly tanned face, and understood that he was fighting a battle with his spirit.

"I never told you how I know this place, if you haven't already guessed," shouted Thackery. "Bethany and I, this is the secret road that took many to freedom in the West. We traveled the paths that no one else would dare. Yet before any of that, we had to learn these roads ourselves. We had to force our feeble flesh to sweat, bruise, and scrape its way from one end to the other. There were times, many times, where we thought it could not be done and that we were to die together: more bones for the Valley. You, Caenith, are the strongest man I have ever known, and as much as you ache, as much as you burden yourself with responsibility, this trial will be a footnote to your ordeals. You will not break, not now or ever."

"I shall not break," declared Caenith.

Thus spoken, the fire of determination flared in the Wolf anew, drowning the meager flicker of doubt that had poisoned him, and he assuredly stomped after the old man. The wind was nothing against his hide now but a petty distraction; the agony of his legs, a trifling concern. Not long after, they were up and striding the peaks of the Iron Valley. The air was thinner up here, and their tread still quite unsteady, so they spared the expense of speaking and lugged themselves across the bluster while the sky began its surrender to night. *Hurry, hurry*, they each thought, but could not force this race without recklessness. Time deteriorated into task without measure: foot after foot, handhold to handhold, and cranny to cranny. All this, Caenith did with a single hand, for to allow Macha to test herself against these elements would have been murder. If he needed any more fire to drive him, the little seal—hanging tight—would whisper into his neck, *Mo riderae* (My knight).

He would not disappoint her with his service.

Another heave, another pull, a thousand burning breaths, and abruptly the Wolf became aware that they were descending. Although a grand gorge pitted with shadows and cruel holes still remained to be challenged, they had beaten half the range. Night was racing to hinder their travel with darkness, and the wind was a bitter slap to their faces. Thackery quickened their pace. *Accidents can happen in the dark*, he reminded himself, and on nearly every trip across the Iron Valley, this dire prophecy had fulfilled itself.

The sun has been eaten, and there are no stars to light their path—not that there has ever been starlight in the Iron Valley. The group's progress was slow today, as one of the refugees is with child and has a boy and a girl already brought into this world that travel with her. Ten of them started this journey, and now only he, Bethany, and six others remain. On top of the range, one man was taken into the abyss by a violent breeze; later on, another unfortunate wandered off the path and slid amid a rockslide to his doom. Yet the worst of the journey has ended, and they are in the foothills that will guide them to freedom. They dare not make a light without it calling attention to the Crowes, so Bethany soothes their trembling souls with the humming of her voice.

A girl's scream interrupts Bethany's music.

Oblivious of his own security, he spins and pulls Bethany to himself. Commotion has broken out along the line, and he is counting heads and faces in the gleaming dark. Two are missing, and he can tell from the girl sobbing near a coughing hole, who has met their ends. "My mother! My brother!" she cries, and her words quickly devolve into sobs. While Bethany pulls the girl from the pit, he helps the other folk around the obstacle, which is still crumbling and looks as if it is ready to give way some more. Once they are back on the path, huddled like scared cattle, he leans over the yawning grave and wishes for the mother, her unborn child, and her son to find peace in the mystery that comes after this.

As he turns, he sees it: a glimmer of something blacker than the night up the hillside. He can't be sure of what it is, now or when he will look back on it in future years, although it could be a figure. If it is a person, it might be one of those he thought they'd lost. However, he does not call out to it. The words freeze in his throat, and his heart plays a frantic drum. He knows in that place of intimate knowing that this is not something he should reach out to, but a presence to be left alone.

Bethany is shouting his name, telling him to hurry. He blinks and the wrinkle in the darkness is gone. A figment, he tells himself. A figment and nothing more.

He had buried that story within himself, and how odd that it should resurface at this moment. His mind had done him the charity of clouding over a lot of what transpired in the Iron Valley. No escape from Menos was free of casualties, and no trip across the Iron Valley came without the cost of more bones for the hungry darkness down below. Forgetting was the easy part, he realized. Remembering was what brought the uncertainty and fear.

There are no ghosts, he scolded himself. *Only darkness, which is just as dangerous, and a lack of caution. No ghosts.*

From behind stirred a grumbling that Thackery strained to hear over the wind. Perhaps Caenith had spoken. "Pardon me?" he called back.

When no answer came, Thackery whipped around. Neither the Wolf nor his tiny charge was there, and a dusty rip in the mountain, a wound into darkness, was where the two had certainly been.

III

A person. Or what approximated one. That is what had drawn Caenith's keen eye on the dusky peaks. From a great distance, the figure rose from between two rocks: it shuddered to uprightness in a jerky way, and its appearance was so immediately shocking that Caenith stopped. *What are you?* he wondered, and could not pry himself from solving this riddle. What is dark as the immanent night and man-shaped? What has misty flesh and blurs like a shadow brushed between two rocks on an oil painting? What are those glistening accents where a face should be? Did he really want to know?

Pinning an eye on the aberration, he stepped forward quickly, trying to signal Thackery without raising an alarm. Had he not been so engrossed, he would have noticed it sooner, the step into nothingness, and next, the sudden pitching of his weight forward. He was falling, and without a moment to scream. He tossed out his free arm, yet anything to hook his fingers into was well out of reach, and his body somersaulted over itself. While he could have spread his limbs and flailed for handholds, that would have come at the forfeiture of Macha's life—something he never once considered. Instead, he held the whimpering child closer, shielded her with his enormous arms, and then did his best to straighten his body as he plunged through the shrieking void. For a man plummeting to his apparent death, Caenith was rather composed. Concentration was essential to the mastery of his flesh, and to achieve perfection, one had to fade out the world: the rattling darkness, the slash of air to his ear, the boom of his heart, and the panting of poor Macha. As a youth, when he had first discovered his uncanny resilience and power, he had jumped from the foamy heights of the Weeping Falls and landed without even a red mark from the water upon his skin. He could be harmed, yes, but he had still to find anything in Geadhain that could kill him. Macha's survival was another matter entirely.

The chasm did its best to end him, bouncing him against ledges and outcroppings in ways that would shatter a slow-walker like an egg, while he somehow held straight and true as a rod of steel. He hardly winced from the pain as his body was carved into. Abruptly, the ripping at his meat ended, and he was soaring through cavernous space. To his nose came the reek of stagnant water, and he tensed his every muscle, and cast out his every nerve and sense. In one broad net of sentience, he absorbed every drip and creak of the space he was in, tasting currents and calculating impossible mathematics—though he would never perceive them this way—information that was fed to his consciousness as mere instinct: a single miraculous effort of muscle and movement. In the air, he leaned and twisted acrobatically, realigning himself for a softer landing than rude stone.

I shall not break, he thought. The Wolf took a hearty breath.

Macha screamed at last, and suddenly her mouth and lungs were filled with filthy water. It was not her destiny to drown, however, and as quickly as she was submerged, she was up again, retching fluid out and dragging air in. Her tireless knight was then paddling like a man in a sling, and before she could make sense of the madness, they were out of the soiled lake and onto dry land. Her knight staggered a bit—he was surely wounded—and finally rolled onto his back. His arm slowly loosened about her, yet she continued to lie against him, and whispered for him to stay awake, for she could feel him slipping away. He was the only grace she had known since the slow-walkers had ripped her parents from her, and she was not about to lose him. Fiercely for a child, she slapped his face and pleaded with him.

"*Cos ni fiag, Mactyre!*" (Do not leave me, Wolf!)

When that had little effect, she did what seals do in their most abject moments. She bit him, right on the neck.

"*Mae creach na fiag tu* (I shall not leave you)," groaned the Wolf.

He was far from dead. Aching like a hundred-year-old man thrown off a tower, lacerated across his shoulders, back, and buttocks, with bones that felt wrapped in barbed wire and a gong in his head that resounded with pain, but he was most certainly alive. He healed many times faster than a slow-walker did, and by dawn, these wounds would be but small pink memories on his skin. Fatigue was his greatest adversary at the moment, and he cursed his body for its ponderous size as he tried to move. First, he lifted the delicate child off himself, and then he hauled the rest of his sluggish mass up to sit. He waited a speck for the fireworks to fade, and with his gleaming sight—tuned for darkness—he began to discern the silvery details and outlines of their surroundings.

From what he could tell, they had fallen through a crack in the roof of a domed excavation. He could see dust still raining from the black spot, and he was confident that they would not be returning that way. The space was huge and hollow, with a ringing silence disturbed by his breath and the faint pattering of debris down into the body of water that had cushioned their landing. It was not quite a lake, Caenith realized, but a flooding of water from an unthinkable depth and age that was as black and befouled as oil; the stink of it clung like pond rot to their clothing and hair. The pool filled a good portion of the room, and the shore to which he had dragged them was a twisted beach, where broken carts were buried in dunes of filth, rusty pickaxes and shovels were discarded with abandon, and hints of metal tracks lay muffled in gray sand. If he followed these tracks, he saw them lead to wood-framed tunnels. These, he was interested in, for one would hopefully bear them to the surface.

He remembered how they had fallen, the creature that had distracted him into this trap, yet could not sense its presence in the cavern. Still, it was doubtful that was the end of their encounter, and he wasn't in the best state for a fight, if it came to that. They needed to move. He knew his share of field medicine from the blood pits, from the years of maiming and watching the maimed, and he hastily checked Macha for bumps, breaks, and bruises. She was intact, if completely terrified. Standing up was a bigger chore for Caenith than it should have been, and it took him a sand and much staggering and panting. Once he was on his feet, he reached for Macha. She wouldn't have his gallantry; she crossed her arms and politely refused him.

"*Nae, masiúl. Canna ma iompair tu gualach cannamo.*" (No, I can walk. I would carry you if these shoulders were able.)

"*Si* (Yes)," Caenith said with a smile.

He offered her his giant hand then, and she took a finger, which was all she needed. They set out. Since the back half of the chamber was inaccessible without swimming in the lake, and the tunnels there were likely to be flooded anyhow, Caenith aimed for one of the shafts to the south. He was sure of their direction, for even at this depth his compass was unerring, and south seemed a good way to go. In all his years and vocations, Caenith had never taken an interest in prospecting on this scale: he sniffed out the lodes in animal caves or the veins that hid in waterfalls, but never went too deep into the earth. For Geadhain's body was a sacred place; a living entity with a plodding, almost undetectable heartbeat of tremors, shifts, and grumbles. Yet here, the silence was deafening. It was as if the Green Mother was asleep or even dead. Acute as his senses were, they did not hear the clacking of rats that should live in dark places, nor the fluttering of bats or the chittering of crawly things. Nothing lived here; not even the smallest mite scuttled from his boots as they waded through the ashy sand.

Green Mother, why have you forsaken this place? he wondered.

Kuuuheeeeeeee.

Or had she? His ears perked up to a sound coming from one of the tunnels, though it was dispersed as if from all directions and not one. He could not say what it was, that noise: a warbling whisper of wind, an instrument, or the quavering of a watery throat. Before he could puzzle over it further, the sound faded, though it left a chilly prickling of sweat upon him. Macha had heard nothing. She tugged on him and asked why he had stopped. *Faech* (nothing), he assured her, and hurried on. Macha frowned, for she had not made it so far in captivity without reading the whims of men and knew that her knight was lying to her.

A dozen tunnels awaited the pair when they reached the end of the beach. Some were collapsed entirely; others were split along their beams and sagging from the weight of stone atop them; none of them looked safe to travel. To make his decision of which route to take, the Wolf gently tossed his head and filled his chest with air. Most of what he inhaled was that distasteful, dry mildew and putrefaction that he had come to expect, yet hidden in the corruption was a tease of fresh air. No other nose but his would have found it, and the source was spans and spans away. Where there was air, there was freedom, and he followed that scent.

Kindly as a father, he helped the young seal step over the rubble of the mine shaft he had picked. On the other side of the obstruction, as he guided them into the winding passage, he exhibited the same care. He spotted tools under the dust that she might trip on, or places of the floor and ceiling around which they needed to tread warily. Each of them could tell that they were the first in many hundreds of years to walk these paths, and they moved ahead as cautious explorers of this great tomb. *Where are the bones?* wondered Caenith. For as they wandered this grave of twenty thousand souls, he saw carts, tools, even garments discarded under the ash, and yet no sign of the bodies that once wielded or wore such items.

At forks in the path, he would stop and smell which route was desirable. And although the tunnels appeared to continue indefinitely and without distinction, as if they were trapped in a nightmare, he always sensed the correct way. While they did not speak much, the grim and gleaming smile of the Wolf came to Macha often, which was all that she needed and almost all of what she could see in a space so dim. These smiles warmed the Wolf as much as they did his charge. How this child, with her sordid history, had ever come to trust a Wolf and another strange fellow was a miracle of the Green Mother's compassion. He was anxious for Morigan to meet Macha, for they shared a determination against adversity that he felt made them kindred spirits. He also wanted Morigan to see that he could care as mortals do, and not only for her. He wanted her to recognize that he was not simply a beast masquerading as a man. She knew this truth about him already, he felt, or she would not have committed herself to him in blood and promise. Nonetheless, it was validating to understand this lesson himself.

"*Ta mae ageanch feach tu, baeg rón* (I am lucky to have found you, little seal)," he muttered unexpectedly.

"*Ta mae ageanch tu feach mae, Mactyre* (I am lucky you have found me, Wolf)," Macha replied with a grin.

Hand to finger, they continued down the mine shaft. Time had separated from meaning long ago, and there was only the march. One foot and then the other. Onward into the wet shadows while the relics of a damned civilization peeked at them from heaps of ash. Neither could have said how much time had passed when the cry came again, echoing out of the murk behind them.

Kuuuheeee.

Caenith had not forgotten the sound, pushed it to the back of his mind, perhaps, as it was a sound that one wanted to ignore. Hearing the cry again, he could not dismiss it as anything idle: it had come from a mouth or some approximate opening. As he was still quite weak, and not in the state for a fight, he did what was prudent and picked up Macha and their pace. He managed a fair speed, certainly faster than Macha could run by herself. He sniffed the air wildly, hunting their freedom, and while it was not quite open sky that he caught the tail of, he sensed them approaching open space. He kicked a clouded path down the mine shaft toward a gray chamber and emerged into less suffocating confines.

However, he felt no relief, and his slapping feet slowed to a stunned shuffle. After a dearth of landmarks, here was a section of the old undercity that was remarkably intact: a tremendous stretch of housing that spread to either side of him. These homes were from an era that he remembered, which meant that they were old. Square boxes with decks and oxidized-iron roofs. They were the sort of dwelling that a frontiersman would live in, only in a place without prairie sunshine or anything bright. For every window frame was fanged in broken glass and ready to bite; many of the porches or roofs had crumpled, as if from a great blast, and spilled their insides out onto the large causeway on which he stood; and the collective emptiness of so many abandoned households was as chilling as screaming into a void. Carriages lay toppled in the street, while others were perfectly stuck in time: their doors opened, as if someone was to step out. Children had lived here, too, he noticed, for toys and wooden swords were mingled in one sandy bank that poured from a nearby dwelling. A rag doll winked at him from the spill. It was wondrously preserved for fabric, like all that he had seen in the Iron Valley, as if mold itself could not even thrive as an organism here, only dust.

If Caenith needed any motivation to stop staring and find his feet once more, another *Kuuuheeee* trilled in the air. He couldn't ascertain from where, which was quite annoying, given his perceptiveness. He hustled down the large avenue. Streets ran elsewhere into derelict neighborhoods, but these he ignored. His nose, his instincts were telling him to continue down the main road. He was worried about many things at present: what that noise was, the less-than-acceptable condition of his strength. Thackery was worth a concern, as well, for he had no idea how the old conjurer was doing, though he suspected that the man had enough tricks of his own to endure this dark night, at least for a while. Amid the uncertainty, little Macha was a welcome weight to tether his anxiety. She held on, nuzzled his neck, and once or twice called him her knight.

The shadowy road was reaching its end: a facade that sloped upward into darkened heights that Caenith could not make out. *How deep are we?* he worried. *And how much farther to go?* In the bottom of the wall, small as mice holes, were more mine shafts running off to unfathomable ends. He thought to pause only to check the scent, and then held his tread when more than sweet air came to him. A musty, mucky smell, as if the lake had followed them. After he sniffed himself and Macha, and cleared them of fault, he looked for the cause. No lesser eye would have noted it, and even his was strained to see the sliver of darker darkness that lurked in the opening of the tunnel he was to take. He approached with caution and then stopped cold once enough of the creature was revealed.

Kuuuheeee!

Whether it was man or woman, he could not determine. Nor could he make sense of the jet-black membranous skin in which the creature was tightly wrapped. Or the caul that clung to its head. Or the warped bones, the pulsing sphincter of a mouth, and the uneven eye sockets that could creatively be deemed a face beneath the shroud. No matter how it shivered and twisted, it could not straighten itself past a hunched mockery of standing. He thought of persons consumed in flame, their bodies scorched and fused. He thought of roaches squealing from their egg sacs. A thousand horrible things, he thought, and none of them could capture what stood a hundred strides from him, reaching with its palsied fingerless limbs.

The thing dribbled its noise again. *Kuuheee!*

He could detect it now, the edge of pain in the call, and what he could not perceive, his extraordinary senses explained to him. *This is a creature that once had a mouth to cry with and a soul to weep for. This is a creature that was once alive.*

"*An Ochrach* (The Hungry)!" hissed Macha.

The brave child could not keep herself hidden against the Wolf and had looked to see what stalled them. Her assertion was correct, and had he gotten a good view at the one up above that had tricked them here, he might have been better prepared. Every whelp, pup, and slow-walker of Alabion knew tales of the Hungry: those that would not pass, those who lingered between the veil, bound by selfishness or torment to a life they were denied. The Hungry could take as many shapes as hatred had expressions—violent, sad, sinister—with flesh or without. The ones with flesh could be harmed, but not by steel, tooth, or claw, only by magik.

Urgently, he scanned the ashes and sand for something with which to defend himself. A tipped miner's wagon caught his attention and he ran for it, dropping to his knees as soon as he arrived. He set Macha down, barked at her to be still, and then began shoveling through the spillage like a mad dog after his bone. Tongs, hammers, chisels, picks, and all the tools of the excavator's trade that were deemed unfit were tossed over his shoulder. He was seeking whatever instrument would blister the palm of a creature as magikal as himself: anything cast of feliron, which would not be unheard of in these depths.

Hurry! Hurry! he huffed.

Kuuheee! Kuuhee!

Not a single cry that time, but one bleat to another. When he looked up from his foraging, he saw that the Hungry had slithered alarmingly fast down the road, closing almost half the distance that separated them in specks. He had to rip himself from the hideous spectacle as it lurched again. *Kuuuheee! Kuuuhee! Kuuuhee!* The warbles were flying like flocking birds now. They were coming, the Hungry, alerted by their kindred's call, drawn by the hateful brightness of two souls in their lightless purgatory. Macha had not the Wolf's sight, though she could sense the movement in the darkness, the sloppy shapes rising from shadows or dragging themselves lamely as hobbled warriors onto the street. She could smell the nauseating stink of the Iron Valley's damned: something earthy and sickly pungent—prunes and clay, perhaps—that made the glands salivate and the gut roil. Macha fought to contain her stomach as the stench and shambling Hungry closed in. She tried to restrain her screams, for she knew that wouldn't help. Nonetheless, she could not hold them in as the first Hungry that they had spotted abruptly manifested in a quivering motion above her knight and joined her in a shout.

"Aaaaah!"

Kuuuheee!

"*Calliachtine* (Witchburn)!" shouted the Wolf.

He was not unaware of his jeopardy. He felt the cold rush over his back, smelled the rank despair of the Hungry, and saw the warped visage reflected in the blade of the pick he had retrieved. The instrument sizzled as he touched it—not that he minded his pain—and he swung it in a swift arc. Now, the horror was soft, and he was strong, and he cleaved the Hungry from hip to shoulder. As if a watersculptor's spell had been broken, the creature fell into a slop of darkness. Although this one nightmare had ended, the undercity had only begun to stir. Caenith snatched up his charge and bolted into the unprotected mine shaft. Vibrating figures threw themselves toward him, and he bashed one with his feliron tool and was too quick to be caught by the rest.

I shall not break, he chanted again. That, the life he protected, the friend he had made of the old man, and the bloodmate toward whom he raced were enough to power a body far beyond collapse.

He sniffed and ran, hunting the taste of freedom that was growing closer and closer. All around them now, the Long Nightmare was churning itself to unlife: the forgotten souls of the Iron Valley were waking and raging at the desecration of their rest. The Wolf dashed through black corridors, sprang over splintery pits, and felled any glistening, hideous apparition that appeared in their path until they were coated in slaughter. Once more, time escaped the Wolf. There was only the race, the thunder of heart and foot, and the wash of rancid blood over his face, which sometimes he licked off: eating death. Ruler of the Hunt. His wounds were forgotten, and he felt unstoppable. How long their imprisonment beneath the earth had lasted could not be gauged, though in these moments of pure carnality, he could have gone on forever.

When the darkness secreted a sound to his ears other than the cries of the Hungry, the Wolf was drawn from his trance. That was *Thackery's* voice, cascading toward him from a space up ahead. He sped toward the noise, clipping scores of the Hungry that oozed from the walls or popped up like weeds before him. As a rush of wind, he blew into an airy expanse, and only his fantastic reflexes stopped him from skidding over a cliff. On one side of him, a shrieking fall to oblivion; on the other, a broad ledge that wound upward along a steep wall. In what was the sweetest sight next to Morigan, the sage was above him. Against the ravenous darkness, the twist of glory, the staff that he held shone like dawn itself. The sage walked down the slope and held it before himself as a holy prophet would: issuing judgment upon the keening black souls in his way that boiled away to gas or threw themselves off the precipice. A line of the damned clogged the ledge, souls surely drawn by Thackery's shouting and magik. Caenith mustered his fury and roared through the rows of the Hungry. The foes were so thick, and his maneuverability so hampered that he could not fend off every freezing cold touch that stuck to him and peeled away flesh like it was hacked. Striped with red and black as a hunting cat, swinging murderously with a single arm, and screaming with every motion, Caenith climbed the path of pain. Macha screamed with him, and he prayed to all the spirits of Alabion that it was for valor and not out of agony. As long as she screamed, she lived, and it was this dark thought that carried him to Thackery's bosom of light.

"Begone!" shouted the sage.

In the chamber of Thackery's Will, his feelings condensed: the desperate joy at his companions' appearances, his sorrow at the state of the great Wolf and Macha, and guilt at his foolishness in treading the Iron Valley. What tore into the world was a radiance to melt the coldest darkness. The Wolf dropped his gory pick to shield his eyes as the sun rose inside the Iron Valley, and what straggling damned remained upon the ledge were scattered into stardust. Thackery was spent and fell upon his staff; the light in the wood dulled to a warm ember. He wheezed out merciful gratitude.

"I'm so blessed to have found you. All night wandering and scouring the Valley, until I discovered a way inside. That was when I encountered them, the faceless lurkers of this place. But I knew that you two were not lost! I can't believe that we survived this nightmare."

"We have not, until we see the sky," replied Caenith.

The keening had receded, not vanished, and the Wolf went to the edge of their footing and cast his senses down into the endless dark to see where the voices had gone. He could hear the Hungry in the depths, more cries than he could ever count, and he was shivering as he stepped away from the ledge. His fright mounted as Macha's arms slipped from about his neck, and he had to react in an instant to catch and cradle her.

"*Baeg rón! Baeg rón* (Little seal! Little seal)!" he cried.

Thackery came over to examine her. She would not wake to shakes or names, and too much of her condition was obscured by filth. Perhaps Thackery could mend her, even though fleshbinding wasn't his forte. He would try when he had more strength. At least her chest rose and fell, if a tad erratically. Apparently, this cursory assessment was good enough for Caenith, for the Wolf was staggering up the ledge.

"I can smell the day," he grunted. "We must hurry. I doubt the Hungry will follow us into the light."

Thackery rushed after his friend. He gasped as he saw the Wolf's raw crimson back, the hide of a flayed man, yet he never considered a suggestion to slow on behalf of these wounds. For the Wolf was right: their danger had not ended. They were climbing higher, limping through shadows that had begun to ease to brown, when a cacophony rose from the abyss. A cauldron of something wicked had boiled over below, and the chamber shook with cold, steamy belches and a wailing that cut into their temples like a knife.

"We've woken it!" hollered Caenith. "We've caused too much noise! Too much light! Unchained the Long Nightmare! Run!"

Thackery ran.

From the ripping at his cape, he could only guess that a tempest chased them. He didn't want to confront the stupefying horror that the wind was really the hateful breath of twenty thousand dead souls: the wrath of slaves free of their chains and flesh. Through clouds of sand and piles of stones they battled, as the cavern was steadily swallowed by whatever dreaded mouth was at their backs. A mouth it surely was, or an orgy of slavering orifices, for all the wailing that it did. Blind and deaf in the tumult, the unstoppable Wolf somehow hefted the two of them—while holding dear Macha—against the storm and toward a pinprick of light. Once, Thackery glanced back, and not then or evermore would his mind grasp the madness it saw: the deteriorating ridge, the billows of destruction, boulders flung to and fro like marbles. What riveted him most was the twisting maelstrom of vestigial limbs and gelatinous bodies; the gobbling darkness, wherein every stretched, irregular mouth inside the mess was making the same wretched *KUUUHEEEE!*

He would have held that stare all the way until the Long Nightmare consumed him, but the Wolf would not permit him so stupid a death and was tugging him along like a troublesome brat. As they raced through a small opening and into the golden grace of the sun, Thackery cast his staff along with what power he could muster into the cleft. Fear is what he Willed and charged the wood with, and it was simple for him to produce. With a crack of thunder, a gust of smoke, and a blast of light that bowled them to their arses, Thackery sealed the shame of his people for what he hoped would be forever.

He picked himself up and scoured the craggy foothills for his companions. When he saw the ripped figure of Caenith, prone and slung over a rock, and near his reaching hand—trying to clutch her even in insensateness—the still and skyward-staring Macha, despair squeezed a whine from his throat. *No! No! No!* He ran for them, dreading what final price the Iron Valley had exacted for their crossing.

XVIII

AN UNIVITED GUEST

I

Morigan was deeply asleep when the cold hand of horror reached into her guts and twisted her awake. The bees were at her at once. *Terrible things afoot!* they warned, and weren't any more specific than that. She had wisps of a dream to cling to: of being lost and wandering through a dark subterranean web, while fingerless terrors groped at her. She had no idea what it meant, but it sickened her with anxiety.

Kanatuk's scarred head appeared.

"You were making strange noises."

"I was having a difficult sleep," she rasped.

"Here, some water," he offered.

With Kanatuk's assistance, she sat up. She nursed the rusty can of water that he passed to her and tried to flush the fog from her head. The cold helped to wake her, as did the dissonance of the dripping roof, the rattling of wind against boarded-up windows, and the squeaking of rodents—some of which she was certain had crawled over her in the night. *Beggars can't be choosers, I suppose,* she scowled. A derelict atelier, fit not even for vagrant habitation, was surely one of the last places their pursuers would look.

Condemned for its mad master's dabblings in plague craft, Alastair had gaily informed them, as if they were passengers on a gruesome sight-seeing tour. She did not spot his lean shadow amid the covered crates or age-caked workstations, and assumed that he had slipped off in the night. Whether he was to return, anyone could guess. Although he had fulfilled his obligation to Mouse, from the interest he expressed in the *Curious Case of Morigan Lostarot*, as he termed it, Morigan felt that his involvement was merely beginning. Her other companions were across the long, cluttered room and conferring upon twin boxes. The meager grayness of a Menosian dawn that filtered over Mouse and Vortigern could have been as bright as the brightest sunshine, so convivial was their chatter. Still, a certain shyness persisted to their manner; a nervousness to their laughter, as if they were unsure of the happiness they shared. Quite understandable behavior, she acknowledged, for family members who never knew each other to have met through the means that they did.

"Is it true?" whispered Kanatuk, who was crouched beside her. "My ears have heard the words *father* and *daughter* enough times for my head to accept it, but I do not."

"It is," declared Morigan.

Kanatuk clapped her on the back. "I would not want to interrupt, but we should speak to them. We have been in the Iron City too long, and if Elissandra could find us once, she can do so again."

Elissandra. Morigan chilled at the recollection of that woman creeping around in her head. She left her tatty blanket and followed Kanatuk to the others, who pulled out crates to accommodate them. Morigan tried not to think of why her seat was marked with a black *X* and a skull. The four exchanged pleasantries, which quickly ran their course. In moments, the conversation turned sobering.

"Your friend, he has left us?" asked Kanatuk of Mouse.

"Alastair? I would hesitate in calling him a friend. He's an acquaintance with vested interests in my existence—I don't know what those interests are." Mouse pointed to Morigan. "I believe that he's added you to his *collection* now, as well."

"Collection?" asked Morigan.

"If he's given you an alliteration, then yes. He has them for all his interests. *The Mighty Mouse.* That's mine," she said. "He drops it from time to time. I don't think he even realizes it when it comes out of his mouth. At least yours has a certain flair. Could be a thrilling book, even."

"However did you meet so strange a man?" asked Morigan.

"He was the one who transacted my freedom from indentureship. A neutral party is often delegated for matters between Crown and common folk—rare as those are—to ensure fairness. The Watchers do most of this work. Anyway, he said it had never been done, commended me, and then asked what plans I had as a free woman. None, of course, as a slave dreams of escaping her chains, not of the reality that comes after. I was soon to see that I had exchanged one imprisonment for another." Mouse frowned as dark memories rattled through her of times and torments she would rather forget.

She is repulsed that it has come to this. Sitting in smoky taverns, powdered, and painted in makeup. Smiling at men who only return the happiness until their seed is emptied. Sometimes they pay her less when they see the scars between her legs. She does not blame them, as she is a broken good. As she sips her wine, she tries to mask her bitterness, for that is not the fragrance that men desire. Yet the internal voices will not be quiet. The shame and self-revulsion grows with every grunting body that she pushes off herself, and no amount of wine can wash down her disgust.

What have you accomplished? What have you become? You are still a whore, she spits at herself. How long until you buy the rope to end your miserable life? She has the money to fetch herself a proper rifle: that would be quicker, if messier. She is contemplating her suicide and wearing her grimace of a smile, when a thin stranger dressed in black sits down at the bar next to her. In what is a twist of convention, he does not slide a drink to her, but takes her glass and dumps its contents on the floor. Furious, she turns to him.

"My Mouse, my Mighty Mouse," says the red-bearded man. "How meek you have become."

"I was quite lost and quite poor when he found me again," she continued. He offered me what I could not find myself: purpose, a true vocation. Such is how I became a Voice. All that thriftiness and cunning amounted to something, after all."

"It amounted to much more than I see you giving yourself credit for, Fionna," said the dead man.

Either from the use of the name or her own misgivings, Mouse blushed.

"Can he be trusted? Is this place safe?" pressed Morigan.

Mouse pondered the question. "While it is true that information is brokered to the highest bidder, I do not think there is a price that can be paid to Alastair to betray his own odd principles. None that I have seen."

"When will he be back?" asked Morigan.

"That I cannot say," replied Mouse. "He is out on an errand, and his comings and goings are unpredictable."

"Errand?" said Morigan.

Mouse beckoned them into a huddle. "Since he didn't immediately disappear after taking us here, I thought I would test his patience and ask him to fetch us some supplies for a trip underground." She waited to see if any of the blank stares resolved themselves into realization. When they didn't, she resumed. "We've been attacking the problem of the Iron Wall with all the wrong ideas. That's the challenge of the Wall: it's insurmountable. You can't get through it, and even if you bore a hole into it with the rage of Eod's king himself, you'd have the Ironguards to deal with. We can avoid all that by simply going *under* it."

Kanatuk was the first to perceive her plan; he waved his hands in dismissal. "Too dangerous. The Undercomb is the Broker's realm. He has eyes and ears everywhere. We would never make it to where you intend to take us."

Mouse corrected him. "Where *you* intend to take us."

At this, Kanatuk flushed red and trembled with anger, and he stormed away from the group. Morigan called to him, but Mouse only sighed as he left.

"He seems to listen to you. You will need to make him see reason," said Mouse.

"Reason about what?" exclaimed Morigan.

Vexed, Mouse exhaled loudly and leaned back on her box. "I suppose this all came out in a messy way. The plan. I was thinking about it all night. Along with Vortigern. He's quite good for bouncing ideas off of."

Proudly, the dead man flashed his yellow teeth while Mouse continued.

"I've been in the Undercomb. Deep in its passages, and there are roads that lead out of the city that men do not use. One-way roads, most of them. Pipelines and such. Most lay beyond the Broker's *nest*." She spat the word. "I never wanted to see that place again, but we may have no choice. Dealing with a few of the Broker's foot soldiers is certainly preferable to battling the armies and Iron Wall of Menos. Wouldn't you agree?"

Morigan did not agree, not immediately. She sullenly pondered the proposal until sense bled its way into her. What Mouse suggested had merit, though they would need Kanatuk's assistance if they were to navigate the realms beneath Menos safely.

"I shall speak to him," huffed Morigan.

Wasting no time, Morigan left the two to explore the atelier, trying to find where Kanatuk had so quickly and stealthily retreated. She whispered into corners, checked behind stacks of boxes, and coughed her way through dusty curtains into a surgical chamber that racked her mind with gory splatters of unwholesome, unconsented operations. She was ill after stumbling from the room and almost done with hide-and-sneak, so she sent out the bees to do what her eyes and ears could not. The buzzing guided her to the back of a storeroom. She bumbled about in the darkness, knocking her shins on things and cursing, and ended up near the one window that shed some of its sulking light into the room. In the murk there, Kanatuk was a ghost, a shade that peered through a boarded window. His eyes and heart sparked with anger. Morigan went to him.

"You are quite good at not being found," she said.

"You are quite good at finding," he replied.

"Have you thought about what Mouse asked?"

"Yes."

"Will you do it?"

He did not answer.

"I used to believe in coincidence, not fate," said Morigan. "Now I could not tell you the difference between the two. In this world, there are hidden rules that few, if any, understand. Perhaps it is our destiny to storm the Iron Wall and die in a blaze of glory. Perhaps that is written in the ledger of the one who scribes our fates. However, I am starting to think that if we learn these rules ourselves, we can influence them. We are the scribes. We give life meaning; we create our fates. Was it luck that brought us together? Luck that carried you from beyond Kor'Keth and me across the world from Eod? To meet as captive and captor and somehow break the bonds that chained each of us?"

She had Kanatuk's attention now, and he turned his face toward her.

"A remarkable accident that would be," continued Morigan, and a bit of the Wolf's passion for prose flushed her heart. "If we were looking at only ourselves. Yet we must look at how far the entanglements spread. Caenith, my bloodmate. Thackery, a fallen master of Menos. Mouse and Vortigern. Four fates, all entwined, and this can be no accident. But I declare that it is not an invisible caretaker, nor random chaos, that has thrown us into one another's lives. It is our choices. *Powerful* choices, which have powerful consequences, a painting in which each of us is a willful stroke. In the end, the choice of whether you will take us into the Undercomb is entirely yours. It belongs to no one else. Weigh the power of that choice as you consider, though. Think on how bound together these other souls are to your choice. And remember that you decide the fates of not only us four, but all the unnamed who have yet to add to our picture."

Throughout her speech, Kanatuk's anger ebbed. When she was done talking, he was trembling with pride, humility, and happiness. He bowed upon a knee and hung his head.

"I would have done what you asked, only because you wished it," said he. "Now I understand that I must, and I am privileged to make that choice. I would like to see what we create together, too. Where my strokes land on the great picture."

After sands of silent prostration by the silent warrior, Morigan became uncomfortable and asked her friend to rise. He emitted a harmoniously ringing melody that the bees found enticing. *Duty*, this was, and he was brimming with it.

"I shall tell Mouse what I know," he promised.

"Thank you."

Kanatuk began to slink away. He turned when he noticed that Morigan was not following him.

"Are you coming?"

"I think I shall stay for a moment," she replied.

Although she never heard his footsteps, she sensed his departure. She was relieved to have only her silence and not the worries of another to manage. From the day her gift had awoken, there had been so little time inside her own mind, or to think of things as an individual. Even her joining with Caenith was a small sacrifice of herself; though for him she would make it again and again. She thought of the Wolf, clawing his way toward her, and wondered how near to the Iron City he and Thackery had come. If all went as planned, she might cross the Iron Wall before they did. As wrenching as their separation had been, there were positives to their distance if she chose to see them. As she had explained to Kanatuk, she was beginning to identify the patterns in their destinies and had found—or created—reasons for her existence. She now had some rather extraordinary goals, which she would not have had the inspiration or courage to set for herself before, mostly on account of their seeming impossibility. *I want to know my mate, every secret, beauty, and darkness of his soul. I want to see this great world from end to end and make my place in it. I want to meet my father, if he lives, or find the stones that bury him if he does not. I want to be a warrior, a poet, a lover, a mother. I want more experiences than I can fill a lifetime with, and I swear that if I am given more years, or if I steal them from fate, I shall not waste a single day.*

She had not the slightest notion if her life would be as spectacular as she portrayed it to the Seal Fang. Yet she was excited to discover where her choices would lead her and eager to make more, no matter how daring. She wondered what had become of her fear, and laughed at its cowardice.

As brave and untamed as the rivers of Alabion, echoed the voice of Elissandra in a conversation that only they could hear. *To think that I believed I ever had the right to tame such power. I would ask you not to scream. I am not here to harm or thwart you. Your Sight will tell you that.*

Shouting for her companions was indeed Morigan's first impulse. However, Elissandra was either weaving a spell of deception or telling the truth, for the bees were calm. Cautious still, Morigan peeked past the planks and into the gloomy city. Nowhere amid the ghetto of broken fences and abandoned dwellings did she spot a spectral woman wrapped in gray—she knew that this is how Elissandra looked, even without ever seeing her.

Where are you? I do not speak to spirits, she said.

Then I shall appear, announced Elissandra.

There came the tiniest rip, and then the faintest breeze tickled Morigan: a wind risen from inside, not outside. Morigan spun to see a white and fair woman in a flowing gown and cloak. Surely as alarming as the woman's inexplicable appearance were her delicately lined eyes that flashed with a hint of silver. Not as sterling as Morigan's, though with the same twist of light to them. The hostilities flew from Morigan.

How did you do that? Where are your men? What do you want?

Too many questions, and I cannot answer them all, Elissandra said, smiling. *The greatest lessons are those we learn on our own.*

Tell me or I summon my companions, demanded Morigan.

Elissandra was displeased. *Direct your anger elsewhere, child, we are closer than you would care to know. The Ironguards who were with me were dealt with, personally, so that our privacy could be assured. No one can or will know that we have met or spoken. I am as much in jeopardy in being here as you are. What I did is an Art that you have not yet been trained in, the Art of shifting through the wrinkles in Dream and reality. It is no crude propulsion through time and space, like sorcerers do, but a true mastery of what is real and what is not. Such power is not beyond you. It is, in fact, beneath you. And that is why I have come. Our time is finite, and you must trust me and listen true, for what I have to say will change everything you know.*

Trust her? thought Morigan. An Iron sage? A woman who just confessed to killing the men who serve her? Maddeningly enough, the bees were complacent in the company of this cold-blooded murderess.

Do not judge me, stated Elissandra. *Death without a purpose is senseless. What I have done was a blood sacrifice for our meeting. Those men would have traced a connection to our fates. You have tasted blood before, and you would taste it again. I'd say that you like it.* She waved her hand in the air as if defogging a wintry window and seeing some invisible sign through the pane. *Ah yes, the lord of Pining Row. The Blood King himself. You are promised to him. You are so deeply rooted in our traditions and yet so blind to what you are.*

Morigan held a final debate with herself about alerting the others, yet her daring was rapidly outgrowing her caution. She sighed and leaned against the wall. While she was willing to hear this woman's words, she kept a fair distance between them, and felt ready to call upon that strange somnolent power again at the merest hint of aggression.

Good. You are listening, said Elissandra. *We would need hourglasses for me to tell you all that you desire, and we have only sands.*

Sands?

Sands, said Elissandra with finality.

As Elissandra started speaking, she glided around the small space behind the boxes. She did not cross the unspoken boundaries that Morigan had placed, not for the moment at least. Some of what the Iron sage spoke of Morigan already knew, though there was much to pique her mind with interest and disgust.

We come from the East, said Elissandra. *Those with the blood of the Gray Man: the ancient spirit of the moon. Daughters, mostly, but there are sons, as it is a brother and sister that we are descended from—they were the first of our kind. Our people came West when the forests turned against us and have not returned to Alabion since. The wisest of our ancestors found favor with the masters of Menos, who would pay to know whatever paltry fate. Here we thrived, though elsewhere in Geadhain you will find those with the blood of the moon reading fires or palms, hearing whispers of fate, and as ignorant as you as to how noble their lineage is. They are not true daughters or sons. They are mongrels.*

Mongrels? That is a harsh characterization for those of your blood, countered Morigan.

The derision was thrown back by Elissandra. *My blood? You are not listening, which I instructed you to do. My ancestors, those who settled in the Iron City, ensured that no slow-born mongrels were bred into our line. Brothers to fathers, sisters to wives. My blood is pure.* She paused and hooked a finger at Morigan. *You, however...you should not be. You who call down lost Arts. The Song of the Gray Man? Do you even know what you have done? We speak of that in our legends. Of the spell that can lay all of Alabion to sleep. A melody unsung since the earliest ages. How has this power come to you, and not to me? That is the question, and I ask it without jealousy and with genuine stupefaction. For there is no unbroken circle to be found outside Menos. No pure womb that could bear a creature like you, and you are surely not a bastard child of the House of Mysteries. The Voices I have courted say that you came from a slow-born mother—*

Morigan clenched her fists. *Do not insult her!*

Elissandra was gliding again, and the threat rolled off her like water off a duck. *She is what she is. Just as you are what you are. Which is a mystery. To some, but not to all. I believe I have figured you out.*

Instead of revealing this mystery, Elissandra wandered into another topic. *Do you know who Malificentus Malum was? Of course not, you wear your ignorance like a badge of pride. I shall tell you of this legendary man, then. The male children of the moon, they're not as good with the Arts as you and I. Better made to physical and intellectual pursuits: extraordinary warlords, hunters, and masters. Malificentus Malum was the great-great-great-grandfather of my house, and a brilliant tactician. His dream was to undo the reign of the Immortal Kings.*

Morigan was certainly paying attention, but the darkening logic of this woman was tearing at her nerves.

Yes, I can sense your opinion on that. Without warning, Elissandra spun and passionately hammered a fist into her palm. *You think like a slave to the teat of Eod, and you see me as an enemy and a Menosian, when I am neither. My spirit, your spirit, and the loyalty of souls like ours belongs to Alabion! That is what my forefathers protected, and why we have and shall always stand against the kings.*

Why? I don't understand, when they have done so much for us, refuted Morigan.

Have they? questioned Elissandra, stepping closer to her company. Her eyes were daggers of silver and her voice was a serpent's lisp of rage. *Such powers do not exist in isolation of all else. One cannot be a storm and move through a forest without uprooting trees and slaughtering animals. That is what they did. Well, one of them, at least, and in a manner of speaking. When the Everfair King came to Alabion a thousand years past to consult with the Sisters Three. We, the oldest families of the woods, know what history does not. The selfish reason for his quest. He sought a bride, or the truth of where one "worthy" of his love could be found.* Elissandra spit upon the floor in contempt. *He got his bride, but he twisted the woods. He broke the covenant of our people with the land. Intentionally or not, it was done, and he is to blame for the lifetimes of culture and harmony that he shattered. The woods would not have us, and what Alabion doesn't want, it turns against, and it destroys. We could no longer live in our home—no longer weave spells or make the music of the moon. All the ancient orders were destroyed. All so one man—who is not even a man—could have his love. Malificentus did not fight for the petty grudge of Menos, but for a far, far more noble triumph. For the protection of us all, really, from the immortal masters—crueler than any here in Menos—who break the world simply by walking through it. Better that they stay in their mountains, breathing storms and farting earthquakes, than to ignorantly sow disaster through the lands of Geadhain.*

With a snap, Elissandra's mania morphed into sanity. She stayed where she was—standing close to Morigan—and continued with a measured and airy tone. *To save Geadhain, Malificentus went east, into the Mother that did not want us. He braved Alabion to consort with the Sisters Three on how the kings could be ended—once and for all removed from this world, along with all that they influenced. Alas, that journey ended him and his ambitions, or so we of the House of Mysteries always felt it to be. But our magiks cannot pass the green walls of Alabion, so even our strongest Sights could not see that while he himself had died, his legacy had been preserved. A scroll he left behind, one scribbled with the Sisters' words and ripped of his own flesh. What guile he had, for he protected the treasure through time by rites of blood, which is the only sorcery that one can work in Alabion since the Exile. While the woods, the spell, or the surgery to create the scroll ended Malificentus, the Fates have seen this message delivered to those who would complete his mission. I shall tell you what it says, dear Daughter of the Moon.*

Elissandra was close enough to kiss Morigan, and the madness and passion once more possessing her implied that she might do it. Impossible, was all that Morigan could make of the witch's ramblings on chains of incest, the true loyalty of the House of Mysteries, scrolls of flesh, and the great exile from Alabion. She was waiting for the bees to sting her with vicious admonition at this woman's lies, and yet they were illuminating with their silence. Elissandra resumed her mindwhispering.

Brother will rise to brother...a black star will eat the sky...the old age will crumble to the rise of a Black Queen. Those are three of the four lines of the Sixth Chair's scroll, and that is all that the slow-born bitch who rules this Iron City or those who bow to her need to know. For you, my sister of soul, I shall tell you the rest. For the scroll is actually complete, and you are the final piece of the Sisters' prophecy.

Morigan's bees were ecstatic: *this* was the nectar for which they had been patiently waiting. The room began to whirl.

Brother will rise to brother.

(She sees a field of flame writhing with shapes. All she can smell is scorched meat. All she can hear are screams and the triumphant laughter of a man like a bassoon.)

A black star will eat the sky.

(The constellation is above her: pulsing like a heart, unfurling like an ebony anemone. Even its dark light blinds as a sun would, for it is an abomination.)

The old age will crumble to the rise of a Black Queen.

(Again, the ageless voice of the void is chasing her. **Flee, little fly. Flee and await the coming of my reborn son, the Sun King. Await your turn with his gift and worship me as I rise to the throne of Geadhain.***)*

Night falls for Geadhain, and only the forgotten Daughter of Fate will shine the way. Elissandra and the bees grew so clamorous in Morigan's head that her knees gave way. Elissandra was there to catch her, and she whispered, *I am as blind as any in the dark night that will swallow us. But I have Sight sharp enough to see that you might guide us through. To the end of an age, the end of the kings, to a victory over this Black Queen who would rule us and cast our world into darkness. How do I know that this is you? Because you are forgotten, because you should not be, because I know, just as you know, the truths when they are thrust into our heads. All these threads that lead to you, this spindle of fate. You have no idea of your own importance.*

Elissandra caressed her as though she were a precious newborn child. For the mistress of Mysteries could see the countless patterns of possibility: these magnificent incantations that floated about Morigan as snowflakes of magik and silver, and she had never seen an object, a person, so resonant with destiny. Without question, this was the Daughter of Fate.

You are shining like a torch, if only you could see, murmured Elissandra, awed.

Morigan allowed herself to be fondled by Elissandra until the woman's actions turned uncomfortably sensual, and then she pushed her away. She had forgotten who this woman was. A maniac. Not a friend.

We are family, said Elissandra, perceiving Morigan's distaste.

Morigan had no retort to that, for as with all that Elissandra had told her, this grand confession was enough of a truth that the bees did not contest it. As valiant as she had been moments before Elissandra's appearance, ready to tackle every possible trial with bared teeth and grit, this was too much: too much importance, too much weight, as if the protection of the world was her responsibility alone. She shook her head against the absurdity of it, while the bees hummed *yes, yes, yes*, affirming her destiny.

I said that we had sands, and that time is almost up, said Elissandra. *I know that you will remember all that we have spoken of.*

Morigan would, everything.

Good, nodded Elissandra, and she stepped away from Morigan. *I am glad that we had this chance to know the other, fellow Daughter of the Moon. The future echoes with sounds that I shall see you again, though you will be a woman so very changed from the child before me when that time comes. I look forward to that meeting. You should hurry back to your slow-born friends, for I am not the only one with senses to track you. And while the hounds of Gloriatrix are slower, the one with the sharpest nose and sharpest teeth has caught up. Beware of him; he is not what he seems.*

"Hounds?" exclaimed Morigan.

But Elissandra did not explain herself. She reached up and took hold of something that could not be seen: a handhold of reality, an invisible curtain. Whatever the mystery was, she pulled on it and the air before Morigan split. Starry matter floated in the fissure the enchantress created, and Morigan glimpsed misty, cosmic things. In a speck, the tear had manifested; in another, Elissandra had glided into it; and in a final instant, it winked shut. By the time Morigan stumbled out of her surprise, desperately fumbling for this strange woman and her revelations, the wrinkle and Elissandra were gone. She hit the floor with a thud.

Daughter of Fate? A black star? A Black Queen? Our time is up. The last line was the most significant, and it slammed Morigan from her whirling doubt and shoved her to her feet. *Hounds*, she thought. Elissandra had left · her with a warning. As she raced across the storeroom and into the atelier, the bees stung her with a premonition. If only she had a bit more training as Elissandra had suggested was necessary for these gifts of hers, she might have known of what. In the absence of knowing, she shouted for her companions as she ran across the atelier; yet there were so many boxes, stacked high and deep as a warehouse, that she could not be certain that she was heard. *I can reach them first*, she hoped. When the crashing and screaming began up ahead, she realized that she would not.

A shadow leaped to the top of the crate canyon. Morigan didn't get a good look at the clacking, slavering shape above her—a dog, though wrong in every way—but shoved the nearest box with a ferocious she-Wolf strength that sent the whole stack falling upon itself like a game of tiles. That wasn't enough to kill whatever she had stalled, and it scrabbled and barked from the dusty cloud that concealed it, splintering wood and breaking glass in its bid for freedom from the mess. She had mere specks to act. *A pole*, she thought calmly, looking at the rusty shaft that pronounced itself against the boxes opposite the chaos. She pounced for the weapon and snatched it up. The shadow sprang from behind her. She spun and charged with all her might, and the two forces met in the middle, flesh invariably softer than the thrust of metal. Triumphantly, she roared while spearing the pole about, until her fists were wet with blood. As the bloodlust lessened to a haze, she saw that she had killed a felhound: a limp and massive beast, patched with iron about its leprous hide and with yellow slitted eyes that belonged to another animal before being inserted into its head. She had gored the felhound just beneath the throat and right through to the rectum, and she wouldn't be getting her weapon back without laboring for it.

No time for that, she knew, for shouts were rising. She seized a pipe that came rolling to her from nowhere and rejoined the hunt. Commotion was breaking out over the atelier now, dusty landslides were all around her as men and felhounds tore up the building. She knew what she had to do, and hoped it would work, but she first needed to see if her companions were safe.

Another shadow tried to tackle her. She faintly identified it as a number-man and whacked it as if it were a naughty mole. *Good luck catching me now that my chains are off*, she cackled, the Wolf in control of her sanity. How astutely Elissandra had ascertained her nature, for as the pulpy thing that had been a man fell away from her, she was heated with satisfaction. Off she loped, moving like a true bride of a lord of fang and claw, her bloody pipe thumping like a happy tail behind her.

Somewhere a fire had started and smoke was reaching black fingers through the room. The least primal part of her realized that a catastrophe was imminent when the more volatile substances in these crates were exposed to flame. This inspired her to run faster, and she soon passed the desk and her crumpled-up bedroll, jumped over roadblocks of ruin, and came to a trail of man and beast bodies. She had an instant of relief when she saw her companions were nowhere among the dead, and followed familiar shouts to spot Vortigern's pale face in a melee that had broken out at the end of the atelier. Apparently, the Broker wanted them alive, which was proving problematic, and besides hamstringing his forces, her companions had thrown together a barricade of heavy tables. They were beating at the heads, swords, and snouts that appeared. Alas, for all the casualties they had inflicted, there were only three of them with a line that could not be held and no place to go once it was crossed. Even as Morigan arrived, more felhounds and numbermen lurched from the shadows and flung themselves at her companions.

Enough! screamed Morigan, though it was not a word, but a Will that left her. A shriek as beautiful and as piercing as a siren's call. The spellsong pulsed from her in a single silver current through flesh, wall, and floor. Next came the clatter of steel as numbermen dropped their weapons. Then there was clownery as they bumbled into one another or swaying felhounds, and finally there was hard slap of bodies upon the floor. Cheers rose from her companions, who had felt the tingle, seen the flash, and known that Morigan had saved them. They began to kick down the barricade. Their victory was short-lived, however, for a hungry spark had at last found a crate in the atelier that was hemorrhaging incendiary blood.

Boom! Boom! Boom!

The explosions erupted around them like cannon fire, and Morigan was pitched in several directions before her head connected with a sharp surface. She groaned and looked up, squinting through the blood, smoke, and wavering orange light for a friendly face. She saw a metal smile instead.

"Nice trick," hissed the Broker. "But tricks don't work on me."

The bees were screeching in alarm, and with hardly any senses to defend herself, Morigan wildly swung with the pipe she had managed to hang on to. But the Broker was faster, faster than her Will, faster than a man, as fast as Caenith, and he caught the weapon, ripped it from her hand, and clubbed her soundly on the skull with it. His strike didn't even hurt, it happened so quickly. There was only darkness.

✳ ✳ ✳

II

During the explosions, the company had seen the Broker abscond with Morigan: watched him toss her upon his shoulder like a merry traveler and disappear into the walls of flame while they struggled from their barrier. Even Vortigern, with his speed, could not catch the Broker. The three scoured the flaming building for as long as they could—until their faces and clothes were as dark as chimney sweeps' and they were wheezing Morigan's name in the choking blackness. Thanks they owed to Vortigern, who hauled them from the atelier when the living of their number were sapped of strength. From the porch of a deserted house, the three watched the atelier burning: it was a cathedral of flames now, in which no living thing could possibly exist. Kanatuk pounded his fist into the bricks.

"He took her!"

No one spoke. They didn't know what to say. For every triumph, it seemed that fate was ready to smack them down with a defeat. Kanatuk would not have it. Morigan's last words echoed inside him. He still had choices to make, choices that would bear powerful results.

"I did not see the nekromancer, so I know where he has taken her," declared Kanatuk. "Where he takes all his prey. I am going after her."

"I shall come, too," said Vortigern.

At first Mouse chewed her lip, not ready to throw in her lot. She was uncertain of how to treat this instant compulsion to help the witch. Yet her father's smile—yellow and dead as it was—and the seedling of compassion that wriggled in her heart told her simply that this is what she must do. *I promised to be with her, even if only until we are free of the Iron City.* In truth, the sentiments ran deeper than that, though she was reluctant to admit them.

"L-lead the way," stuttered Mouse.

Crowes were hovering in the smoky clouds above the atelier. The alchemically fueled fire had only begun to burn, and Ironguards would soon be swarming the ground. They had not a speck to tarry. They did not set out on their journey with bravura or promises, as they understood what was to be done and what the stakes were. Three against the Undercomb. As they descended, they accepted that they would not see this dark sky or any other again without the company of Morigan. Kanatuk knew the paths into the Undercomb like the lines upon his palm, and in sands, they had delved beneath the city.

III

Just like that, more fates flock toward her. Incredible. She is an axis of possibility, mused Elissandra. The three who escaped the flames had not seen her as she hid behind the wrought-iron gates of a nearby garden, peeping out through her tiny window in the bushes. They moved into an alley, and she lost sight of them there, though she was certain where they were headed: to the Broker.

Over many nights now, she had been having the same dream, and with each dive into that other world, she returned with a larger fragment of the story. Before she understood the importance of the visitation, she had slipped Gloriatrix perhaps a bit more information than the Iron Queen should have. Nonetheless, she always shared a *bit* of what was necessary with Gloria, and she kept the juiciest morsels to herself. Such as how the dream of the Wolf and maiden ended. With a storm.

The maiden is in the woods. Hair as red as fire, clothes as white as winter. Chasing her is a wolf: a king among the lords of Pining Row. He is important, as important to this mystery as the maiden is, she feels. Has he been hunting her? Is he hunting her? She senses that the answer is yes to both questions. And he is nearly upon her. Nipping closer and closer. Trees fall as if felled by invisible axes, and in their place rises a barbed thicket as tall to the sky as the white moon itself. In the dream, she can smell the tang of metal—iron—and she understands that this is Menos. So they are racing through Menos, then; the maiden and the king.

They each slip unhindered through the great obstructions before them. Their charge cannot be stopped. Not by the dangerous burrows laid in trenches to snap their feet and paws, traps they simply skip over. Not by the broad-winged crow that swoops at them and is barked away by the Wolf. Not by the parts of the thicket that are as tangled as yarn; these, the maiden bypasses in a gust of whiteness, these the Wolf tears right through. With her otherworldly wisdom,

*she knows these obstacles by their names: the Broker, Sorren, and Gloria—the
great web herself.*

*In time, the maiden and the Wolf break the thicket and are free in a clearing
blessed with stars and the full, glowing grandeur of the Gray Man. Here stand
timeworn stones—faintly green and dusted in blue moss—and a slab bedded in
ivy. If she looks about, twists the dream as much as it can be bent at different
angles, she can read names upon the stones. Thackery, Vortigern, Fionna, and
more. Even her own, she sees: all written in the stick scrawlings of the oldest
written tongue.*

*The maiden goes to the ancient table, where she lies and waits for the Wolf to
climb upon her. When he does, he is a man, handsome and virile, and Elissandra
watches them kiss and then grease their hardness and softness against each
other for what could be forever. A magnificent forever, and as a dreamer, she
wants to watch nothing else. The moon swells, the two roar their passion, and
as their release comes, so sounds the peal of the storm. The land shakes, clouds
coat the moon, and when the cutting sheets of rain begin, the maiden and the
Wolf only kiss and resume their lovemaking. Fuking as the world is torn into
whirling dirt and disaster around them.*

Elissandra was always flushed after thinking of the dream and the lovers' contortions, and now was no exception. The dream was mostly allegory, aside from the names upon the stone-pillars, which were quite clear.
Without a doubt, these were the people marked by the Daughter of Fate. At
her manor, she had begun compiling a list of them, and it would be best to
return there to examine this mystery further. For the end of the dream was
not ambiguous. Once the maiden and the Wolf met, which her Sight told
her would be *soon*, there would be a storm: the sort to shake the world. She
wanted to be home in the most fortified of all spaces—a danger room that
had been built by her forefathers after the Iron Valley quake—when that
occurred.

After the storm, she would see how much of her city remained and who
survived to rule it. With the darkest luck, there might be eleven seats to fill
on the Council of the Wise. She wasn't opposed to being queen of Menos
until night fell on Geadhain. Elissandra watched the atelier burn a little
longer and tickled herself with her moody thoughts. When that no longer
amused her, she ripped open a tear in reality and slipped away.

XIX

THE END OF ALL ROADS

I

Brackenmire was not as it should be. When the mouth of the Valley of Fair Winds opened, it was to a rocky plain that swept in gray steps down into a greener land populated with hanging trees, reedy patches, and shaded pools. In another age, King Magnus and Queen Lila had camped in one of those glades, and made do with nothing but the warmth of their bodies and the simplest supplies for hunting and gathering—tasks, they discovered, much to his chagrin, at which Lila was better than he. At night, they had counted the fireleaf butterflies that blazed about like comets, and he told her whatever ancient poem came to him as he caressed her naked beauty in the moonlight. Through the march, he had sharpened the edge of his hate to shining perfection, and he had done that so efficiently because somewhere, beneath the rage, these memories endured. These things remained for him to fight for and protect. And yet, as the cavalry thundered down the stone road, he began to see that like Lila, what he cherished was changing and being stripped from him faster than he could save it.

First of what he noticed was the stink. No milk thistle and willow breezes, but a sour stagnancy to the air. Soon, as the days grew hotter and hotter, the green drained from the land, and the refreshing pools clogged and dried up into muddy scabs that were picked at by buzzing insects. The grasses withered to straw. Trees turned brown: their fruits withered and ignored by the feral animals that hunted amid them. Misery had claimed the land and thrown the ecology out of balance. Come the evening campfires, the animals were vicious and bold from starvation. Not only the wildcats, but also peaceful creatures—badgers and even squirrels—charged the supply tents and had to be killed for their determination. Slaying them was a mercy, really, considering how scrawny and desperate they were.

What have you done, Brutus? King Magnus asked often as the march went on. He was at a loss, for he could think of no magik but his own that could do this. Now and again, his frustration boiled into such a storm that he himself contributed to this imbalance, and whole sections of their march were turned into muddy slogs, as rainclouds conjured by the king's leaking Will followed the army. With the rain, the animals, and all of nature against them, it was a wretched journey. Each man started to feel the thud of his horse's hooves like the drops of sand in his life's chronex, and that he was, indeed, marching toward doom.

Reaching Willowholme, then, at the heart of Brackenmire, should have lifted the army's spirits. But the willows for which Willowholme got its name were as hung and dry as an old maid; the quaint houses that nestled in the trees like a city of birds' nests and the rope bridges that connected them were lifeless when they should have been busy with light and the famed music of the river folk; and the few people who finally stirred from their holes came shyly and without the cheer or the hospitality for which they were known. Whatever wretches were bold enough to approach the army would cry and plead for food. Mostly, the people of Willowholme watched from the roadsides with the same long pitiful stares as the animals of Brackenmire.

In any event, the army needed to pass through Willowholme to reach the bridge that crossed Lake Tesh and connected to Mor'Khul; thus, there was no way to ignore this plight. Not that the king would have anyhow; he wanted to know what evil his brother had caused these people. He called a halt to the march, and the army settled along the road. No tents were raised, for they did not intend to stay, only to delay their journey. Upon his request to meet with the ruling council, a thin beggarly woman was brought to Magnus, his hammer, and his legion masters, as they gathered in the shade of

CHRISTIAN A. BROWN

the city's tallest and oldest trees. How sad it was for Magnus to witness these weeping, sickly giants: plants he recalled from when they stood no higher than shrubs, before Willowholme was even a thought in men's minds. He was involved in this reminiscence when a woman bowed and greeted him.

"King Magnus."

She tried to hide her face behind her dirty scarf, so unkempt did she feel in her rags while in the presence of this unspoiled immortal and his chosen warriors, who gleamed like men of light. She was shocked when the resplendent king himself joined her on his knees in the mud. He tilted her head and captured her brown eyes with his emerald ones. She would be as pretty as a sunny-haired, freckled barmaid, if not for the hollowness in her cheeks and the despair and famine that had eaten her flesh. Despite this, a glimmer of determination shone in her like a flash of steel. The woman had grit still.

"What is your name?" he asked.

"Tabitha Fischer," she replied.

If memory served the king, the Fischers were among the first settlers of Willowholme: tillers with strong backs and stronger wills.

"I have heard tell of starvation and sickness, and I can see that the land has not been treating you well." *Crack!* He slapped a hungry blackfly just as it pinched his neck for blood. "I asked to see the masters of this village, and you are all that has come forth. Please tell me that you are not all that remains to guide these people."

"That I cannot do," said Tabitha with a shiver. "I *am* the council of Willowholme. Or all that has chosen to stay. I could not abandon those who have deep roots and no families elsewhere, as this is my one and true home. Many of our other families fled north when the winds changed and the waters sickened."

"Waters sickened?"

"You do not know," said Tabitha, her face waxen. "I shall show you, King Magnus."

The king and his legion masters strode after the woman, who hobbled ahead with praiseworthy vigor—a dash of the Fischer spirit remained, it seemed, and would not be crushed. Out of the sticky shadows of the willows and into the sweltering day, she led them. They were shortly away from the village and wandering the dry fields preceding the shores of Lake Tesh.

Blowflies ruled the stagnant air, and what wind wheezed toward them was foul as a belch from a rotten mouth. As they descended a gentle hill, whisking through brittle reeds and staining their armor with mud, the smell became a permanence, and there was no mistaking its source—the lake. Once the ground leveled out, they stopped in the shoals and were up to their calves in muck. They went no farther. There was no need, for they could see the lake many strides beyond: its brown waters churning lazily as the sloppy contents of a chamberpot; the greasy film upon its skin; the upturned fish—bellies to the sun—floating upon this feast of rot like scores of maggots, fish that even the pecking gulls along the shore deigned unfit to eat. Far off into the blinding glare of the sun, the disaster stretched along this lake of endless death. *Has the whole of Lake Tesh been destroyed?* wondered Magnus. Unwittingly, Tabitha answered this for the king.

"We've taken the rowboats out, all the way south until the waters get so hot that steam and carcasses can make a man pass out."

"Heat?" whispered the king.

"Yes, Your Highness. You could dip your hand in the water—though I'd advise that you don't—and find it warm as a bath. Hot as a kettle the farther out you travel. It is good that you've come from a desert, for I imagine another awaits you on the other side of Lake Tesh. That is why you're here, isn't it? Not for our mercy, but for business in the South."

"We are paying a visit to the South, yes," the king said guardedly. "When did this begin?"

Tabitha turned to the king. She was torn with sadness. "A month past. I remember. It all happened so quickly...I can think of only one force that could wither beauty so fast. Magik. Perhaps it was longer, when the first signs came, and the odd dead fish popped up. But it was in the third week of Lunasa, when things became quite serious, when the lake became a grave. Around then when folks took ill, too."

"Ill?" questioned the king.

"From drinking from our wells," said Tabitha. "We thought that those were safe and we could wait out this blight. But it's all spoiled, King Magnus. Not just what you see here, but the soil beneath where we stand. The fish or some other rot crept into the streams that fed our wells. People were drinking death for days and never knew it." Tabitha shook her head.

"We don't have the medicines or magiks here that you of the North surely do, only family-recipe poultices and remedies. Those will do for a fever, but not for a plague. We figured out boiling the water made it bearable to drink, and we traded our rods for spears and bows to hunt. If you've seen the wildlife, though, you'd know that it's not enough to support all the starving bellies in Willowholme. Not when the animals are no better off than ourselves."

"Why have you not sought aid?" asked Magnus.

Pain and anger passed over her face like a dark cloud. "Aid? Oh, but we have. From your brother himself. Two parties went to Zioch; the first with my husband and my son. I wonder what they've found on the other side of Lake Tesh that has kept them. Maybe you could ask your brother where they are when you see his kingship. He who we fief and fish the land for, the man who is supposed to help us in times like this. Where is he? Why is he so silent while the land cries for relief?"

She had raised a fist to him, and Magnus could sense the slick hands of his company already upon their hilts. He stood them down with a glare, and then took the shaking fist and spoke to Tabitha with a cold passion that calmed her.

"My brother will answer for this, to me. This I promise you."

Frightened from his intensity, the cruel apathy of a snake—though not toward her—Tabitha pulled from his grasp. She wasn't imagining it, but her wrist was rimed in frost. She dusted it off and begged his pardon.

"I spoke out of turn, and quite a bit too much. Please forgive me."

"You said nothing that you were not right in saying," replied the king.

With a glower, he turned to Lake Tesh again. He allowed the atrocity to consume him: the decay, the utter waste of life. None of this could be repaired without sorcery, and not until whatever magik had taken hold was banished. Brutus was to blame for this. Brutus and whatever diabolical force he had partnered with. *I share everything with you, my dearest brother*, he spat. *Including your guilt.* Restitutions for the mistakes made by the other of his blood could begin today. After the heavy stillness, he addressed his company.

"Masters."

The warriors and the hammer jumped to military alertness.

"We shall stay the day and night and help these people in all the ways that we can. Seventh Master, your sorcerers can provide clean water for the people of Willowholme. Eighth Master, the duty falls upon you to organize and dispense as much of our provisions as we can spare. Zioch is less than a week away at a breakneck pace, which is how we shall ride on the morrow. We can worry over our stores once we have finished *speaking* with my brother. The rest of you masters are to help where it is needed. We have many hands and much need to fill them with tasks. If there are to be tears, let us make them tears of joy. Show Willowholme that there is no war against tyranny on the battlefield or the tyranny of suffering that cannot be won by the Watchmen of Eod."

The nine legion masters barked their assent, saluted, and were stamping up the hill. Tabitha was stunned by the whirlwind of what had been said and done.

"Tabitha," continued the king, who was not yet finished with his orders, "while your pride does not want to hear this, I need you to organize your people for a march."

"King Magnus—"

"I know what you have said, and I would not lightly ask you to leave what you love and have known." Bitterly, the king gritted his teeth, and a waft of cold came from him. He spoke with the rawest candor, and Tabitha was magnetized. "Seasons are changing. We are all to lose things that we hold dear. That is the nature of life: that it cannot exist without death. A lesson that you might think a man who lives forever does not know. But I know it all too well. I have seen more that I love pass than you or all those you know will see in your lifetimes. I know when the seasons are turning, and that time is upon us. If you stay here, a terrible summer or a terrible winter will come. And whoever remains in Willowholme may not survive it."

The king was talking in metaphor, and while she was no poet, he was not difficult to decipher. A king did not secretly herd an army south for an exchange of peace or pleasantries. Whatever was to occur in the mountain ring of Mor'Keth would have consequences, and the king was fairly warning her of that. Stay, and there would be more loss. Go, and they might have a chance to return to Willowholme one day when the seasons had calmed between the kings.

"I-I shall do as you ask," she promised.

"I thank you," said the king. "If you head east to the River Feordhan and follow its shores past the smaller settlements, you will reach Bainsbury. Speak to Gavin Foss, elected lord of Bainsbury, a man whose forefathers and I have a history back to when they were camping in huts. Tell him that the king of Eod has ushered you there, and he will take you in. Your people are legendary for their skill in charming a catch from the waters of Lake Tesh, waters that few can tame, for the fish swim deep and are as canny as snakes in how they hide. You will be welcome for your trades. And your music, too, which is wonderful, and I regret I shall not hear."

"Tonight! We shall play for you and your army tonight," pledged Tabitha. The weeks had been unbearable, and she was near to tearing up and embarrassed that she had nothing else to offer for the king's generosity but songs. Yet he nodded, and she noticed the slightest smile, which told her that this was enough. There was much to be done, and the day's wick was shortening, so she bowed to the king and the strange silent suit of armor that followed him, and then slogged away. King Magnus called after her with an unusual question.

"Your husband and son. What are their names?"

She paused. "Their names? Why?"

"Because if they do not return to you, then I shall ask my brother where they are to be found. In his lands, he should be aware of all who enter. If he is not, then I shall seek their fates myself. One way or another, you will have peace."

In a day of euphoria and surprises, more of the king's compassion was almost too much to bear for the beaten leader of Willowholme. She spoke gushingly about her family, and perhaps bent the ear of the king more than a humble woman should have, but this pale and glorious man's compassion prodded her onward past her usual discretion.

"Beauregard...well, I would have said he's about the most handsome man I've seen, until I met the Everfair King. He's dark-haired, but fair in the face, and with a spot of freckles and a birthmark on his cheek that looks like the one true star of the North. I feel he is a great man, and I hope that he is alive to see that destiny through. His father, Devlin Fischer, is about as tough and tall as those changelings in a faery story: a bear, perhaps. My bear. You'd know him to see him; just look for the largest, hairiest man in the room. If you hear of them..." She was unable to finish, and embarrassed now that she had prattled on for so long. She turned to hurry off. "Don't mind my troubles, please forget what I have said," she muttered.

"I shall not. Neither their names nor their fates," swore Magnus. His statement made her buckle at the knees, though she did not look back and was choked on a sadness.

"We are nothing if not the value of our word," said Magnus to his hammer. "I do not make promises that I cannot keep. You know this, Erithitek."

"I do."

Then the king's mood shifted, and Erik felt as if he were standing next to a block of ice. On the one hand, this was not an altogether unwelcome change from the heat. On the other, Erik understood where the king's temperament was and could not stop his mind from slipping into thoughts on seasons. Winter particularly, and he was certain that he would see the king's before all was said and done. He wondered what mark it would leave on the world. Another Lake Tesh, only frozen? All of Mor'Keth imprisoned in a glacier? Or a third untenable, imaginative devastation that would scar Geadhain beyond belief? Although he had never truly feared this man, as he shivered in the cold that grew greater and greater and flurried the air about them with snowflakes, as he saw the black winter storm brewing in Magnus's eyes, he felt that he should.

II

As the king had told Tabitha, the Watchmen of Eod were a force to be reckoned with, and a battlefield of mortal strife was no exception. When Tabitha returned to Willowholme, it was to a flurry of fastidiousness: silver men shouting her people into orderly lines and dispensing waterskins from sorcerers; these shirtless, sweating men—and shirted women—who stood over buckets and squeezed liquid from the air itself as if it were a sopping cloth. Tabitha had not met many sorcerers, only the ones who discovered their craft and quickly left for cultured cities to train in, and she paused to watch their miracles. After a speck, the itching frostbitten ring around her wrist reminded her of another sorcerer, a man whose very touch could bring winter, and she hurried off to the responsibilities he had imparted to her.

Everywhere she went in Willowholme, the Silver Watch had arrived beforehand, and it was far easier to inform her kinfolk that they were about to become refugees once they'd been plied with food, blankets, and the care of fleshbinders. This uncanny art, fleshbinding, fascinated her as much the conjuring of elements: how these sorcerers reached under people's skin and moved bits about like putty was equal parts grotesque and fascinating, and she tried not to become distracted by it. As she bustled along the ground and under the latticework of the trees above, delivering her message and witnessing wonders, she often returned to the king's words. His insistence that change was imminent—and catastrophic, from the sound of it. The more she considered their meeting, the more pronounced his melancholy became, as well.

Throughout the day, in fleeting moments, she saw the king around; removed from his armor and dirty as a common man in wear and work. He was always fixing something: a person, a cart to be readied for the mortal migration, even the shoe on a child's foot. No task was too small or too far beneath him, and while she respected this, she felt that much of it was penance. Whatever he spoke of back on the shore of Lake Tesh, these seasons and promises, the reason for his army marching south, it would end in tragedy. And she pitied him for it. She didn't know why, and more than once she stopped to hold her tears as she thought of his sad, stormy beauty.

With evening's kiss, the heat reduced itself to a muggy sweat. All the people of Willowholme, from the smallest to the eldest, had learned of their new fate and agreed to it. The wagons were loaded and drawn in a circle down the stone road from the king's snaking camp, and Willowholme was darker than it had been since Lake Tesh was untouched in the wilderness. Tabitha had promised the king music, and that he would have. She rallied her kinfolk and their lutes, harps, flutes, and drums, and made a procession from their encampment down the stone road. King Magnus had been humble when praising the musicians of Willowholme, for here was the birthplace of some of Geadhain's greatest minstrels. That night, they showed the Silver Watch what sort of magik they could weave: a miracle without sorcery that coordinated hands, voices, and hearts. Up and down the stone road, the people marched, so that all could hear them. And while war had not been mentioned—not by Tabitha or anyone—they sang songs of victory for the king's men and songs of glory for when men fell with a sword.

In the morning, when Tabitha woke, it was to the earthquake of the legions heading south. Along with the other survivors of Willowholme, she raced to the road and shouted and wept for their safety in the South. As strange as the sentiment was, as implausible the notion that her family's fate was somehow intrinsic to the mind and motives of the Everfair King, she felt that he would keep his promise. That he would bring her husband and son home. Once the dust faded, and even as the night fell on the caravan's first day north, she held this promise to her, wishing upon it like a star, and certain that it would come true.

III

Even for men born in the desert, the heat was unbearable. As their horses made a dusty drumbeat over the fractured and ancient stones of the Bridge of Summer, the army's mounts and soldiers huffed to make use of the syrupy air that stuck to their throats. Tabitha had been fair in her warning about the nauseating smell of Lake Tesh farther on, and the king and his sorcerers had to weave nets of wind to push the foulness away. Even so, the undercurrent of rot lingered, and the sight of sun-split fish coating the lake like scales on a dead leviathan left a taint in the mind that was just as unpleasant. The army crossed the bridge as the sun began to set, yet they were not granted the cool respite of evening, and against what they understood of nature, the land continued to stoke itself hotter. In the wavering heat, the desiccated grasslands took on the illusion of a savannah. Many men among them did not know how green and lush this land should appear, and it was simply another misery to add to a long, growing list. But the king knew the land differently, and saw dust instead of loam, dry veins instead of brooks, and insects and snakes, with not a furry creature to be found. Since they had committed almost half of their remaining provisions to the people of Willowholme, hunting in this wasteland would be a challenge, and the going from here on would be a hungry march, indeed. Magnus worried not so much over this as he did over what was causing the land's dehydration. He was not, therefore, paying attention to material matters, certainly not as much as the unceasingly vigilant Erik, who noticed the wisps of smoke in the distance before the king, the scouts, or anyone else did. When Erik alerted his master, the king waved him away to investigate, and the hammer and a dozen other riders charged toward the signal on the horizon.

They rode hard and fast to the east of the king's line, aiming for a cluster of hills to which a haze clung like the smoldering of a dead campfire. This was an old fire, Erik realized, the remains of a blaze long burned out, but so fierce at its height that it had polluted the area with ash. From across the stale air, it summoned them with promises of doom, and it did not disappoint as they cleared the hills and descended into a scorched valley of matchstick houses. Whatever village had been here was once grand and quite verdant, if judging by the withered trees that remained. The scouting party trotted through the wreckage, covering their mouths with their cloaks, shaking their heads, and wandering without much direction, for even their steeds could not make sense of the destruction. Among the black silt, they found puddles of cooled metal or tangles of wire, but nothing with the frailty of paper, leather, or wood had survived the temperatures of the flames. No bones, either, and Erik could not decide whether it was a relief that these people were still alive, or a sadness that they were still alive and had been stolen for a darker fate than death. *Magik*, was Erik's thought for all of this, for nothing but a sorcerer's flame smelled so strongly of sulfur or burned hotter. Those with the hammer shared in this silent observance. He could see their concern over mystic powers at work carved on their faces like cruel scars. Once the scouts had dwelled long enough to paint themselves and their white steeds in soot, they rode from the ruins. The king had not waited for Erik and his riders, and it was not until dusk that they caught up with the nighttime fires of the army. The scouts rode through the camp bearing dark tidings with their stained presences, and while men wondered what the message was, they did not ask for fear of the answer. At the warmaster's circle, the riders broke apart, and Erik approached the nine warlords and their pale king, all wise and still as owls upon their logs around the fire. Erik removed his helmet and bowed to his liege.

"What did you find?" asked the king.

"A village," he replied. "Burned to the soil it was raised upon. Only magik could have laid waste like we saw."

"Survivors?"

"I cannot say, my King. There were no bodies for me to make a claim for or against the living."

"No bodies?"

"Not even a tooth."

"I see," said the king. He stood and dumped his cup onto the fire, which rose and sparked gloriously. "There are bodies, I am certain: able bodies, working bodies, bodies for foot soldiers, slaves, and whatever other meat cogs Brutus needs for his war machine. If they are not dead, those people are elsewhere. I believe that I have underestimated my brother. I had believed him to be a rabid beast, loose and mad. Yet he seems to be more cunning than I expected. He is prepared for us, likely more prepared than we are ourselves."

Walking away, Magnus abandoned his warmasters with that chilly notion to tuck into their bedrolls and guarantee them a restless sleep. Erik ran after his master and found him reading the stars of the South, looking for a meaning or sign, perhaps, to tell them how doomed they could be.

IV

The days fled while the army marched farther south. There was no end to the heat, to the furnace they had entered, and when the men looked up to the shimmering skies they could imagine themselves walking upon the sun. What had begun as a plain became a wasteland where the dusty soil split like the lips of a desert castaway, and no life but the smallest and many-legged crawled. By night, the land was so viciously heated that just as relief would come, the dawn returned. For the army, there was little rest, less conversation, and dwindling food to quiet even the despair of their stomachs. They were hard men, though, and brave men, and it was their spirits that kept them moving ahead.

Each day this mettle was tested, though, as they passed another deserted and scorched tract that had once been a village. Whatever culling the mad Sun King had commanded, it had taken all the fiefs in his lands. Before long, the scouting parties were sent out no more, and if someone spotted a black haze, he turned his stare back to the road ahead and mentioned it to no one. Alone the soldiers marched, through sand and blistering heat, as if they were the sole wanderers in a primeval time that only Magnus and his brother had seen. Magnus thought of these earlier eras often; with every hoofbeat closer to Zioch, he slipped deeper into his state of waking memory. In those vast silences, where even the shuffling and clank of the army faded to a meditative hum no different than the thrumming of rain, Magnus lived amid the glories and strife of his long, long life. He was looking for the thread that had unraveled his brother, looking for whatever weakness had turned Brutus into this defiler of life, and yet he could not discover a single cause. Only a multitude of smaller signs precipitating the decay into madness.

We who slept like cubs in the Long Winter, you who nursed me like a mother with your blood. When I left you for Lila, any man with a head outside his bliss could have foreseen how you would have perceived my choice. Betrayal. Here I thought we were being men apart, learning to live above our natures. But you never wanted that, did you, Brutus? How long has that hate festered in you? That jealously and abandonment? How much has it worn down your spirit to let the dark voice in? I still hate you, my brother. I shall still rip you raw with thunder and ice for what you have done, but I shall do so with love as well as fury. We have drawn this line, and we shall cross it together. I made a terrible mistake for choosing to live as man. When this is over, if we cannot die, if you are to suffer for all eternity, then I shall do what I should have done a thousand years ago. I shall never leave you again.

Again and again, Erik watched his master sparkle with frost under the dreadful sun and knew that terrible broodings were taking place. But he offered the king no counsel, as he knew that this mood could not be broken by words. Erik's own miseries kept him occupied anyhow, for the black villages and enervating march across a lifeless landscape were tipping the scales away from victory. What awaited them in Mor'Keth was uncertainty, and there was a chance that he would have to use the king's gambit. While he knew he should not, he fondled the cold talisman the king had given him—playing with it when the camp was asleep or the king was lost in one of his trances—and pondered his responsibilities, each of them more than a man should bear himself.

Warn a kingdom. Prepare for a war. Protect the queen.

The third thought repeated itself more than the rest, and with the delirious heat, he found himself reflecting upon the queen, even though he had vowed to abstain from such fancies. His feelings were a weakness, and he should not be indulging them so near to battle. And yet he was no worse than the men and women whom he would see from time to time caressing a locket with a cameo of someone they loved back in Eod. *Only she doesn't love you, you fool,* he would spit to himself. *She was only kind to you in the most innocent of ways, and you have distorted her kindness into something it was not.* But the mind played tricks of that fated instance, and no matter how many times he played the scene in his mind, he was no less convinced that he had imagined that spark, that connection.

He isn't happy with the assignment: playing porter to Queen Lila while her Sword Rowena is away on unexplained business that he is told does not concern him. A woman's troubles, he thinks, matters of which he is as innocent as a schoolboy, for he does not seek the company of women or know much about how they work. He does not seek the company of men, either. He has himself, which is enough, and a few quick sands of tugging when the desire boils in him like a kettle of lust that needs to be poured out. But otherwise, sex is a distraction from duty; release is a necessary oil to one's armor, and it should be done as efficiently and frequently as the weekly hammering out of the kinks in one's plate.

The presence of gyrating women in silk shawls is what has brought on these odd, distracting thoughts. He squints them away and makes note to tend to his desire tonight, lest it continue its imbalance in his humors. The Faire of Fates is busy today: Carthacian traders bickering over the value of their rarities, rivermen from the Feordhan all but throwing salted fish at passersby, the well-fed urchins of Eod doing tricks like trained dogs for fates. Still, danger can come from any shape, young or old, and he watches them all as if they hold a knife in their hands. His great feliron hammer might be upon his back, but it is a speck's reach and a cat's reflex away.

In an hourglass, they have completed whatever mysterious womanly duties the queen has set out for herself—visits to silk shops and perfumeries and bakers—and they are leaving the Faire of Fates when they pass the most obvious threat: a platform on which a wizened, manic-stared man rants about the injustices brought on since the Nine Laws. Since it has been only a decade since the Charter was written, not all of Eod's citizens are happy with the decree that all men are equal. Some would have things return to the simpler state of master and lesser men, and it is known by the court that the Iron sages of Menos secretly funnel coin to Eod to feed these dissenting voices and organizations, which the king has not cracked down upon, as the divisiveness of opinions is a quality of a free nation. After this incident, Magnus's perception and ruling on radical voices will change.

"We are not the same! Not equal, not by blood, name, or right! None of us!" screams the anarchist. For a frothing madman, he has drawn a considerable crowd: the drunk and angry poor—men who can no longer use the excuse of class disparity for their failures; haughty masters and their trembling servants; and rough strangers in cloaks, who would be the sort upset when the Silver Watch did checks on their skycarriages to find people in chains.

"Why, then, do we still have a king?" continues the anarchist. "If all are supposed to be equal? Why do we not tear down the palace, tear down King's Crown, and see this dream of privilege for all fully realized? Why am I—and you and he and they—made lesser than what we were yesterday, while our king rules the same as before? No charter, I say! No laws! No king to rule and certainly"—the anarchist has spotted the regiment; he points toward it and roars—"no queen!"

A roar is met by the crowd around him, and the hateful stares turn to the queen and her company. This is the perfect storm for violence, an alignment of forces and fates that could only have been arranged by the wickedest Menosian mind—although this will never be proven. Foolishly, the queen makes matters worse by halting her procession and trying to beseech the madman for calm. But her charm will not work on persons so filled with hate, and before she has even made a small pardon, the first stone is tossed. As the hammer, he is vigilant, he is a living weapon, and he sees the cruel old woman in the crowd reach into her kirtle and rear her arm back. His reflexes have moved faster than her malice, however, and he has spun his steed and intercepted the stone with his body. That act shatters the delicateness of the situation, and violence crashes out in a tidal wave: a wave of shouting bodies and fists and weapons drawn from hidden pockets.

Chaos has seized the marketplace, and the mob is upon them at once. One of the Watchmen tries to raise his whistle, but he and his steed are pulled to the ground. The others of the queen's guard cluster around their precious sovereign and cut at any hands that draw too near, painting their white horses in freckles of blood. With his savage instincts controlling him, Erik grips the reins of Queen Lila's mare in one hand; in the other, he wields his trusty hammer, sweeping men away like dust to a broom. He is doing his best to guide the regiment out of the vicious bog of treason and toward the panic-stricken streets where they might break into a canter. Suddenly, he smells the ozone of magik and through the glaze of blood and movement, he sees the anarchist upon the podium crackling with red light like a powder keg and likely about to go off much the same. He realizes that they need a distance they may not have time to make, so he does what duty would have him do: he casts away his weapon, saddles up next to the queen, screams, "Trust in me!" and then throws the two of them to the ground with his body over hers.

The blast heaves the earth a speck later: vomiting destruction, tossing horses, people, and stones like paper cutouts. Yet while shrapnel and flames shower down, the queen is safe beneath her metal mountain. The explosions have dimmed to screams, and he removes himself from his charge, drags her to her feet, and stumbles through the smoldering vapors that have become the Faire of Fates. He needs to get the queen somewhere secure; no other concern matters—not his limping leg or the bent shards of armor in his back. Like an angry mule, he kicks aside whatever hindrances of wood or flesh present themselves. He is frenzied and not particularly heeding his surroundings beyond finding something calm.

"Stop," says Queen Lila. "You must stop."

She is not the one whose commands he obeys, not the father who found him in the Salt Forests, and yet he cannot deny her request. Not with his body, anyhow, for whatever toll he has taken in shielding her is too grave, and he spins and falls on a hard stone floor with glimpses of rafters and the scratches of hay at his fingers—which have lost their gauntlets during flight. While the queen mumbles, he blinks in and out of darkness. He can feel his essence bleeding *out of himself as if a warm towel has been laid over his back, though the pain itself is too strong for him to feel. Sliding, sliding into numbness and darkness, walking down the long black stairs to oblivion he goes. At least the queen has been protected. He will visit his ancestors with pride and is glad that he has not failed his kingfather. He so easily accepts death. He does not fear it, not as he fears failure. His eyes close, and there is only the dark staircase. He wants to see where it leads, what mystery awaits him.*

And then the light fills him: his heart leaps, his eyes flick open, and a groan of ecstasy breathes him back to life. What is this that has awakened him? What is this that strips raw every nerve in his body and swells every sense tenfold? Magik. The soul of another has touched his. He sees the stable where he is risen—the horses, sunshine, pails, and other insignificant things—but more than those he sees the woman who saved him before taking that final step. He sees her fretting gaze of gold and her sympathy that pains and elates him with a rush like fire up his spine. Is it inappropriate, his sudden urge? The desire to touch the face of this woman? He does not consider decorum or stop himself, but reaches to the queen and cups her face in a rough manner that her shiver indicates she is clearly not used to. Yet she does not retract herself from him. Time drags into eternity, though eventually the alarms and the besmirching of the queen's beauty with his grimy prints awakens him from the moment. He remembers his duty and discovers his shame.

"My Queen," he says. "We must get you to the palace. The king will want to know that you are safe and sound."

She said nothing, not even a thank-you for her safety, as if she was embarrassed to speak. Nor was he ever to see her again, more than in passing, until the day she fled her bloodmate's chambers—when she begged him not to bring his sword upon the king, and he listened at once, for he would have done anything she demanded. However distant their crossings between those two points in time, he had thought of her almost every night for many years. He remembered the warm honey of her sorcery, the touching of their souls, and he could sense in moments when they met, where he bowed and she smiled, that she had never forgotten it, either. Whatever that was, that moment of theirs away from the world, he did not deceive himself that it was anything more than illusion. A fantasy, an image for when the rod needed to be oiled, which he found himself doing more and more since that union. Still, when thoughts of Lila and sex intertwined, the result was guilt, as she should not be thought of that way by any man, ever. He had married himself in spirit and commitment to the bride of his king. He had damned himself from love. Nonetheless, when he reasoned with himself, if that one memory of the queen and him was all that he would ever have, it was enough to last him a lifetime.

"The Fangs of Dawn," said Magnus.

Days had it been since the king had spoken; Erik sat up in his saddle and dropped any thoughts of the queen into the wasteland. He looked for what the king spoke of and saw a range of mountains rising up like the teeth of a titanic snake buried in sand: the tips of Mor'Keth, chewing at the red sun of dusk. Into massive canyons they descended, through bleached steeps and walls that should have been hummocks and gullies of the deepest green. Still, they had come too far and seen too much to let the Sun King's new sorcery daunt them. The pass between the Fangs would take them toward Zioch, and that was all they cared about. With renewed vigor, they rode ahead, and would camp one final troubled evening outside Fangs of Dawn before moving onward to strike the heart of the Sun King's realm.

V

"Riders!"

The cry came from ever-watchful Erik as he surveyed the land from beside his master, and was confirmed by a scout rushing into the warmaster's camp a sand later to tell them what they already knew. A red sun, a warring sun, was upon them, and the king was shortly seated on Brigada and racing to meet their visitors in the darkness of the Fangs of Dawn. Accompanying the king came three legion masters, a small cavalry, and the hammer, who rode at the head of the line with Magnus. The hammer darted his suspicious eyes to the three mounted figures that they approached, as well as to the tumbled spires of stone and the shadowy canyon beyond them, watching for signs of an ambush. When they arrived at the mouth of the Fangs of Dawn, the riders did not approach, and the king reined Brigada from going farther. For a while, the two forces held a cold silence with the other. The king was the first to break this.

"I am King Magnus, brother to the master of the Summerlands. Come forth and announce yourselves."

The riders did not move, but stayed draped in the heavy gloom of morning shadows. While details of the trio were evasive, their hunched and thorny shapes—one quite smaller than the others—bespoke of strangeness. Their steeds, too, for they did not neigh or hoof the sand as horses should and could have been a nekromancer's reborn; only the king did not sense any of the icy magik of death clinging to them. Another power was present, however, crawling in the shadows, webbing the three in menace, which, while the king could not name it, was far more chilling than any nekromancy.

"I ask again that you present yourselves!" he commanded, afraid of neither Brutus nor his tricks.

At that, the third and littlest of the riders detached itself from the others. The king's men drew their weapons as it slowly trotted forward into the crimson morning light. At first, the Watchmen were taken by pity, for this was a child, as young as those the fathers among them had sired themselves. Though as it continued to near, they noticed the black greasy pits where it should have eyes, the arcane scars carved into its hairless forehead, and the tarnished armor that had been affixed through fleshcraft to its skin: a metal jaw, a pauldron of razors, a golden cage fused across the ribs and groin. Once, this armor had been a whole suit of the bladed, gilded plumage, like rays of sunlight and the feathers of a metal peacock, in which the Sun King's men would preen and strut proudly. Now, it had been reconstituted and perverted, the same as this child. Before it stopped and addressed them, the king knew that this child was nothing more than a mouth for a Will that was elsewhere.

"I bear a message from the Sun King and his master, the true queen of Geadhain," said the child in a sexless, rasping voice that upset the mounts of the king's cavalry as though a snake were loose among their hooves. The child's gray colt was unmoved by its rider; though from its oily stare and the black froth spattering from its muzzle, it was clear that the beast was also infected by dark magik.

"I recognize no queen of Geadhain!" challenged the king. "Nor do I bow to faceless cowards who would hide in the skins of children!"

"You think yourself virtuous. You think yourself a defender of life. I shall show you how wrong you are, my son."

My son? thought the king.

The child slid off the horse and walked ahead a few paces, causing the king's retinue to bear their arms. When it saw their defensiveness, its face jerked into a grimacing display of teeth, as though it was a marionette. The child did not move farther forward, but knelt before its mount.

"What is a child but meat that has not matured to flavor?" said the Black Queen. *"What are any of you but grains of sand in the desert? Meaningless. Each of you. As passing as the leaves in the seasons of death, the seasons of my Name, for I am Change and Chaos. Quiver in your metal skins, warriors, for you are nothing to me. Except for you, my son. You are a vessel of promise, and I shall give you purpose. I shall fill you with my Will once you surrender to me, and we shall remake the world."*

"Surrender? I shall never surrender!" exclaimed Magnus, and a spiral of winds rose about him, pushing his cavalry away.

"You will surrender," said the Will inside the child. *"If it makes you feel better to choose, then choose to come to Zioch and stand against the armies of your brother. Come to your defeat. It will be one of many that will smooth away your hard wall of ice until it is too weak to stop me. You will surrender. You will be mine. Greatness awaits, and you will have greatness, willingly or not. See how little life means to me, how insignificant these meats are, and you will begin to comprehend the glory of the designs that I have for you."*

After it was finished, the child threw back its arms as if to welcome the wrath of the wind-wrapped king or the lightning that had gathered in single black cloud above. Yet the king had a heart of mercy and could not strike this creature, no matter how foul. He hesitated, and the choice was taken from him. In a blitz of violence, the dead gray mount was suddenly wrenched by an invisible bridle up onto its hinds and came pounding down upon the child beneath it like mortar blocks on a bag of wet tomatoes. The child was killed almost instantly; however, that was not the end of the Black Queen's malice, and as soon as the execution was over, energy twisted the horse from within and it toppled in a heap upon its victim. Unceremoniously, efficiently dead, each life as worthless as the Black Queen had promised.

In a gasp the king's swirling wind and anger left him, and he and his men had only disgust in their stomachs. Fear as well, from the knowing that what they faced was an entity worse than Brutus, any enemy without body or emotion. The Black Queen drove the spike of terror deeper as she spoke through her new mouths: the twin riders that had remained behind in the Fangs of Dawn.

*"**Your mercy is your weakness, my son**,"* they said. *"**Once you are hollowed out, I shall show you the glory of a life without pity. Enter to Mor'Keth and accept your destiny.**"*

The riders turned and made dusty trails into the canyon.

"Do not pursue them," commanded the king. "Return to the camp. I shall speak to the men once we have crossed the Fangs of Dawn."

Which was all he was to say on the matter for the moment. No words of reassurance, no explanation for the inconceivable events they had witnessed. No denouncement of the entity's lies, or truths. Only cold rule. Nonetheless, this is what the soldiers needed, not more confusion to muddy their resolution. King Magnus raced back to his troops and the Watchmen followed: faithful, brave, and unquestioning in their march toward death.

VI

Tanned backs, golden tracks, the paths wend to and fro.
Into dales as green as the Northern King's gleam
Streams where the fish leap right to your dish
And fields are as chaste as virgin lace.
Bring your drum, bring your voice,
Leave your sorrow and rejoice
For frowns cannot abide the golden hair of dawn,
Nor can sadness hide from chase and kiss of fawn.
Here the wind is sweet, and time is sweeter spent
On soil untouched by winter's lament.
So bring your song, and clap your hands
For you have come to the Summerlands.

Kericot, the famed bard of Carthac, had penned that tune upon taking his first breath of Mor'Khul: or the Summerlands, as he had coined it. For there was only one season in Brutus's lands; it was never winter, hardly wet enough to have a spring, and fall appeared only as a shedding of leaves that even then filled Mor'Khul with an apple fragrance and not the faintest tinge of decay. Kericot had never returned to Carthac, and whittled out his years wandering Mor'Khul and composing poems of its beauty, as in love with the land as if it were a maiden fair. When the bard looked out from the higher points of Mor'Khul, from the mossy nipples of these great breasts of rock, as he was fond of poeticizing, he would speak of the wavy land beneath as an emerald woman. Of the gold and green mountains as a spine he would caress; of the misty folds as pools of sensuous sweat; and of flocks of colorful birds as dreams taking flight. All sights comparable to the woods of Alabion, which he had also seen, though without any of the darkness or fright. Often, he waxed passionate on the smell of Mor'Khul as a woman; and in more lurid poetry, the earthiness was her sweat and the honey-rose, sugar blossom, and all the other saccharine-termed flora were the waft of her womanhood. Magnus had always found Kericot's poetry accurate in describing his brother's kingdom; in capturing the raw essence of life that radiated from every rock, leaf, river, and breeze. While his own kingdom had flourished inward and born springs of magik, intellect, and ingenuity, Brutus's had come to reflect his opposite nature. In the Summerlands, the trees grew taller, the animals meatier and wilder, and every color from glorious green to harlot's red saturated the land with his brother's furor. Mor'Khul was the product of millennia of his brother's passion feeding the soil, flourishing all growth for spans and spans, and there was not another realm in Geadhain that could claim to be as beautiful or bourgeoning. Or at least that was how Magnus and Kericot had remembered Mor'Khul. What he was looking at now was a nightmare that could not be.

Past the escarpment where the king and his closest stood, the land plummeted into a vast smoldering basin. An ocean of lava had once filled this space for sure, and had since cooled to a mottled igneous skin that belched torrents of hot ash onto the faces of the men who gaped at the destruction. Across the land, glowing crevices and spits of fire remained, telling of a great heat that persisted under the ground. They stared and stared, enthralled at the scale of Brutus's madness. They stared and stared, and could not see a scrap of green from their vantage point until the highest humps of Mor'Keth: mountains that were no longer gray but black as heaps of charcoal. Coal to feed the furnace that had become Zioch, once a City of Gold, now a City of Darkness. The city could not be adequately captured through the fog of smoke, but an intimation of its sheer sprawling majesty, its chronex-shaped towers of gears and metal, or its great wall of scaffolding and stone could be sensed. The fiery apocalypse had not spared the city; in fact, Magnus believed it was at the epicenter, so dense was the smog. Ghosts of that infernal blast still haunted the Summerlands. They painted the firmament like a storm with clouds of soot and despair, hiding what should be the morning sun. All this gloom, and yet there was no change to the wilting temperatures that bathed them in sweat, or the heat that they gagged like gruel into their lungs. Nor was there cotton enough to wad their ears from the howling wind or the grumble and constant grinding of the earth as if the land were sick. Not one among them had ever beheld a more cursed place. Except the king, perhaps, who had lived through the Age of Fire.

If the elements were not enough to make them cower, or the mountain of smoke and menace that was Zioch did not cause their legs to quiver, then these men could no longer be broken by fear. King Magnus stayed at the edge with each of his legion masters, forcing them to look ahead with him until he was certain that they were unshakable. When he could feel their obedience, pert and hungry as attack hounds, he turned to his commanders and hammer and inwardly smiled at their dirty, determined countenances.

"I shall save my motivations for those not made of pure steel, as you lot are," he said. "We must decide how we are to wring victory from this travesty. Your ideas, men! Do not wait your turn, speak!"

The warriors and their king conferred in a tight circle. Magnus had a sword, more for show, though he could use it, and he carved a map of the Summerlands and drew the strategies they presented. Smart men, ruthless men were these, warriors of a thousand battles and scars, and there was no wanting for hard tactics. While they had yet to see the Sun King's army, confronting it head-to-head on the lands outside Zioch would be foolish. Who knew what traps lay under the hot black earth or how dangerous that terrain would even be to cross? They would lure Brutus to their encampment, then; bury themselves in the Fangs of Dawn like bandits in a pass, and force their enemies through a narrow gauntlet. Many times, the men of the war council steered themselves from discussing how overwhelmed they would be, or the nature of the foes they would face. For after the incident outside the Fangs of Dawn, there could be no doubt of the fate of all those empty villages and missing villagers—of all the merchants, wanderers, and even spies who had failed to warn the world of what Brutus was conjuring here—tens of thousands of men, women, and children surely made into unwilling conscripts for a colossal mindless army. Such a force had been cultivated for a single purpose: the reaping of Geadhain. But again, this they did not consider beyond a trifle lest it invite doubt and weakness. They could not and would not say aloud the stakes if they failed here and the Sun King's monstrous army was allowed to swarm the land. Nor did a single head raise issue with the king over the dark power driving Brutus, or its mention of Magnus as its son. None of that mattered on the battlefield anyway, not to these steel souls who spoke only in terms of victory and defeat. That was their role, as soldiers. What came after—punishment and rebuilding, they hoped—was for the king, councils, and sages to debate.

Without chronexes or transparency in the bleak sky, the war council broke around what they estimated to be noon. Each of the legion masters saluted and then hurried to his post; so much needed to be done and they had no idea when Brutus would reveal his hand. The king hailed the last of the legion masters as he left.

"Leonitis, stay a moment."

The Ninth Legion master and leader of the king's retinue turned on his step. He was the younger brother to Dorvain, master of the North Watch, and they shared the same apparent mother of a mountain and a cinder block. For he was as broad and stoutly muscled as his brother, with custom-crafted armor that still barely fit his girth. Mayhap his position was less stressful than Dorvain's, for he had managed to keep a full head of brown hair, woven into braids against his scalp. Certainly, his job was less dangerous, for his wide refined face was not as scarred or beaten as his kin's was, though he shared the same twinkle of metal to his stare as Dorvain. Brother blades they were, though one a chipped great sword and the other a polished broadsword.

Leonitis's advice had been exceptionally helpful during their strategizing, but the king had a final set of instructions that were for select ears only.

"How may I serve, Your Majesty?" asked Leonitis, as gruff as the hunting cats for which his parents had named him.

"Keep a hundred horses back behind the lines," said the king. "The men of your legion will trade lance for sword. We need you on foot. Too much cavalry and we shall do little but clutter the pass."

"My King—"

Magnus smote the big brute with a glance like lightning. "This is not the time to question. Do as I say."

"I shall!" said Leonitis.

The king dismissed him with a nod and went back to pondering the shadows and ash of his brother's kingdom. After he and Erik had been alone for some time, the hammer voiced some of the worries he had been harboring.

"Your order...was it for their escape, my King? The horses?"

"I cannot think only of your safety or of the importance of your duties. If there is a chance for others to avoid certain death, then it must be arranged. Even if those men are too brave to hear of exigencies beforehand. If I fail to stop my brother when he and I finally clash, that should be the push that any sensible soldier would need to see a horse and leap upon it. Leonitis is the most level-headed of my commanders; he thinks of others before himself, and not in a cowardly way. I am sure that he will remember my couched intent in a dark moment of decision."

"Should it come to that," contended Erik.

A beat.

"Should it come to that," replied the king.

Erik knew the king well enough to worry over what the pause meant. What bothered him more than the outcome of this conflict was how ambiguous their enemy was. *What do we fight? Brutus? A bodiless spirit? Both evils united, is what it seems, and if so, to what horrid end?* As he stared over the impossible desolation, the questions that he had for his king were as endless as a deep-water spring, which, if he tapped it, might never run out. Unexpectedly, the king allayed many of these misgivings by simply placing a gauntlet upon Erik's back.

"Son of the Salt Forests," he whispered, "no matter what remains after the storm of this battle, I am proud that you have come this far in life with me. I have few centuries that I remember, the memories blend like water on glass, but I see our years together with the brightness that parents speak of, or with the camaraderie that soldiers only feel. You are, and always will be, my *son*. Blood will not change that."

Erik's black makeup was cut by a tear. "As you are my father."

And while the encampment behind them bustled with the clangor of war, and the land ahead of them began to tremble from a second drum, a new rumbling—the march of countless synchronized steps—and the hourglass of death dropped its final sands into the chronex, the hammer and his kingfather had their silence; their calm in the storm, their memory of the other before the knowing of how precious that memory would be.

VII

Brutus had acted according to the king's prediction; the Sun King was a hunter, and not the patient kind that hid in the bushes, but a predator who bashed down the woods while chasing his prey. *He wants this fight and he will come for it*, the king had advised his legion masters, and not long after the council had disbanded, the smoky, unseen gates of Zioch opened. With their shaking spyglasses, scouts could see what approached, wave after wave of people—part metal and part meat—each as unique as a fleshcrafter's mistake, with no real conformity to their make. There was no end to the freakishness that churned from Zioch's factory of horrors: rows of cavalry; the knights like pincushions who rode on ebony-stared horses; firecallers who had been pulled from the flames they conjured, somehow still alive, with charred skin, red coals for eyes, and staves of crimson magik in their hands; persons made into golems covered in sheet metal and golden nails; swordsmen and pikemen whose weapons were fused to their fists so that they might never be dropped, their only purpose to kill. The scouts could not believe what they were seeing, how effectively living beings had been turned into weapons, but they were steady in their flow of reports, if not entirely in their nerves and trembling voices, as they told the legion masters what was coming. *Blackeyes* and *Redeyes*, one clever scout coined them, for a name had to be found for their enemies, and their unearthly stares were the one aspect they shared.

In a few hourglasses since the meeting on the escarpment, the thunder of the Blackeyes' march shuddered the valley like a heartbeat, and the scouts were relieved to tend to other matters once all could see the dark wave rolling in. Brave, so brave were the king's men and so set in their valor that the imminence of war and death set their feet and fingers working faster. Weapons were counted, honed, and checked. The field of battle was cleared and trenches were dug. Tents and bedrolls were shredded to make ladders for access to the bluffs of the Fangs of Dawn; from there the thunderstrike archers and sorcerers would rain ruin upon the Sun King's horde. An advantage perhaps, for the scouts had spotted no artillery among the Blackeyes except for the deadly crimson conjurers; though a more pragmatic opinion shared by the king's army was that Brutus had no intention or subtlety to the warfare he proposed, and that it was his intent to pulverize them in a swell of bodies. He certainly had enough men to do so, and as the river of Blackeyes swayed toward the king's camp, it was apparent that they were outnumbered ten or even twenty to one. Still, none of that was important. Every man knew that a victory through force was unreasonable well before the endless stream of foes appeared. Their role, as explained to them by their legion masters, was to dam the tide long enough to give Magnus an opportunity to defeat his brother. Only then would this battle be ended—if the head was taken from the snake.

The Blackeyes were nearly across the valley when the king summoned his men. He would not leave them without words to inspire them, or thanks for the lives that they would dearly pay today. On the field of battle, he met his army, all nine hundred of his fellows as quiet, stiff, and ready as a crop of swords and gathered in half-circle ranks about him. Beyond their king, the sky darkened with evening, and yet the black dawn of Brutus's army rose and shimmered at his fore. The army's thousands of footsteps rumbled the land, and they made a fearsome, unified chant of the mad king's name: *Broo-tus! Broo-tus!* But none of this frightened Magnus's army, for they had passed the threshold of terror, and they shared in a silence with their fellows that shut out any distraction. King Magnus rode along the line, shouting to his warriors.

"Men! We stare into a nightmare! Look at this plague my brother has conjured to ravage Geadhain. Look and feed your anger and pride! For who else has seen this danger? Who else will protect our lands, our children? We are alone; I shall not lie to you. We are the single star in a sky of darkness. Therefore, we must shine ever brighter; we must blind the darkness with our deeds! No matter the cost, our line must not be broken! If a new age is to be born from the blood of our sacrifice, then we shall boldly go into what comes beyond! I shall lead that charge! I do not fear an end to my long years as much as I dread my brother's madness bleeding into the world. If I die, I die for you! For tomorrow! For Geadhain!"

A roar went up through his army, and the king unleashed his blade, which fumed with green power as he threw it into the soil. Where it landed, there was a *whoosh* of flame that spread as if on oil along the length of the escarpment. In specks, the fiery strip had writhed into a wall, and the wind that flickered the tall emerald flames blew frosty, refreshing air onto the army—while cold, that fire would sear whatever passed through it. Quite literally the line had been drawn. With this signal, the footsoldiers went to their ditches, spearmen clanked their shields into phalanxes, knights raced to their mounts, and thunderstrike archers and sorcerers climbed to their perches. The king ascended with them; after his daring speech, he would not sit this battle out, but he needed a bird's-eye view to find his brother in the horde if their plan was to work. Brigada was left in the care of Erik, and she behaved under him as if he was the king himself while he trotted to join the other mounted men who would lead the charge.

Then came the waiting, along with the dying of whatever cursed sun was hidden. They chanted their own rallying cry of weapons on metal, and a chorus of *For Geadhain!* that while sung by voices many score less than their enemy, was somehow all the grander and louder from hope. *We are the line between chaos and life*, they all thought in one manner or another. Watchmen said their prayers to the fates, or the more learned ones to the Sisters Three, who wove them. And Erik glanced more than once to his kingfather while pressing the lump under his armor that was the king's testament. He could not say how, yet he understood in that moment what the talisman was. Magik, yes, but a specific sort of Will: a condensation of love, the Will of a father wishing his son to safety. He was stung by the beauty of it, and he would have hurried to the king to say one more thing that had yet to be said; however, a horn boomed from above. The war had begun.

VIII

Brutus's horde surged out of the valley and spilled onto the escarpment in a tide; the chanting did not slow or end as the smaller were trampled by hooves or boots and died praising their king's name: *Brutus! Brutus! Brutus!* When the Blackeyes and Redeyes reached the barrier of flame, they paused to organize their numbers and herded the skinnier and smaller of their kind—women and children—through the inferno first. Magnus did not wait to watch them get consumed, but sang to the sky with his anger, the bitterness of an eternity of brotherhood ending in this atrocity. The heavy evening clouds grew blacker than the ash could make them and then dazzled with white. Forks of lightning roared from above and landed in the swirling mob outside the barrier; wherever they touched, the land exploded into potholes of ignition.

Up in the nooks of the Fangs of Dawn, the thunderstrike archers wiped their sopping brows and added their bolts to the fray. Then followed the sorcerers, who unleashed arcs of fire onto the earth. A symphony of destruction had commenced, its music crisscrossing the sky in crimson and white power. The whole of the land shook, scattering rock upon the gutsy soldiers who held their ground under the rain of magik; men who watched with awe the starry detonations that made whirling torrents of bodies beyond the green flames. Wonder fled to nerves as, despite the destruction, the chanting horde was successful in snuffing the wall of sorcery with sandbags of their cindery dead, and in many places, the horde was trickling in. An initial wave of piecemeal Blackeyes that made it through were skewered by countless glowing arrows, but crawling over their remains came more and more of the cursed things, and handfuls of viciously barbed riders who wasted not a speck kicking their mounts into a charge. Behind the dread riders, the accursed firecallers followed, glowing in their auras, and they threw back at the rain of magik and arrows with pyrotechnic explosions and lashes of flame that toppled handfuls of archers and sorcerers from the cliffs surrounding the king. The line had scarcely held for sands, and behind stretched the tail of the horde deep into the valley. The king found him then, his brother, felt him more with his heart than located him with his eyes. At the tip of the tail was a glittering warband that had not lost the luster of the Sun King's regalia: he was convinced that his brother was there.

Good luck, Erithitek. Hold them as long as you can, and I shall end this, swore the king.

Mortal sorcerers could rarely translocate without assistance and mechanical computation. However, Magnus was not mortal, and he when he closed his eyes, he saw the strings of brilliant patterns that composed all things—and arranged them into an invisible passage through which he forced himself. Agonizing, but when the pain left him, and his body resumed its shape, he knew that he was successful by the granite voice that called his name.

"Magnus."

Magnus looked up from the heaps of hot ash into which he had fallen. An enormous float was passing by, one carried on the backs of man-golems and naked slaves, and atop which a parade of feathered male and female concubines swayed in a trance around a huge golden throne. Magnus dismissed other details, like the paint of blood that blemished the abundance of gold, or the repulsive mortal trophies—faces, limbs, and garlands of genitals—that hung off the banners. He was interested only in the massive shape that was rising off the throne and tossing whatever bodies were in its way off the platform. The shape leaped to the burned earth, landing with a tremor, and in the flickering light of war, Magnus gazed upon this heaving giant dressed only in a warrior's skirt and slathered with spirals of gore, as if they were strangers. Savagery had overtaken him, as violent as the thick musk of death, sweat, and sex that wafted off him. Brutus's regal beauty, the charisma and pride of a lion, had been warped into hideousness; with his luxurious hair and beard all matted and entwined with bones, his rock-carved, handsome face now twisted into a wolf's wrinkled growl, and his bulbous, veined musculature made more threatening from a primal hunch, as if he was an ape.

The line between beast and man had been erased, that battle had been won, and Magnus could recognize nothing of Brutus, his brother of forever. For the first time in eternity, their hearts and minds did not reach out to each other, and he saw nothing in his brother's stormy blue eyes but hunger.

"Hold, Brutus!" shouted the king, and stood. "You are a wild and wounded thing. I would hear your confession before I end your madness."

Brutus laughed at that, booming bellows that added to the concussions going off in the darkness. While he amused himself, his army slithered on, heedless of this conflict.

"This is your chance to ask for forgiveness," spat Magnus.

Brutus whipped from his laughter. "Forgiveness! You would dare to speak to me of that! My brother of the long seasons! The cold half of my soul! My partner in eternity! You, who left me for the sniff of a woman's legs!"

"Is that it?" Magnus threw back derisively. "Jealousy? You would wage war on Geadhain because you could never find a woman, or man, who could bear your bestial lust? Pathetic. How far you have fallen from the man I knew. Look at what you have done to your accomplishments, to the people that trusted you, to the land that you swore to nurture! Do you remember when this was green? When we picked and named the saplings that would grow in the garden of your kingdom? Look around at what you have wrought and you should feel only shame. If you can admit that, then your punishment may be less cruel, but still more painful than you have ever known. This is my mercy for you. As for the dark spirit that haunts you, the one that you have cursed yourself to for this despicable power, I extend no kindness. I shall cast it back into bottomless filth where it belongs."

"Your mercy?" Brutus bit his lip with a fang and spit the red mucus on the earth. "How little you understand. I do not need your love, your forgiveness, or your mercy. For I have *hers*, and it is vast and warm as the rush of blood and milk in the throat. Hers is a river of darkness without end, an appetite that can never and needs never be sated. She feeds me as you never could. As only a true companion can."

"Of whom do you speak?" demanded Magnus. "To whom have you pledged this horror?"

"Our Mother, Zionae," growled Brutus.

While Magnus anticipated some or all of that answer, he was no less confused by these associations that he could not recall, and there was no time to contemplate them. If Magnus had not been his brother since it all began, he might not have recognized the twitch of violence in the other's face, even hidden under all that beard and mane, which told him that he was about to be attacked. Like a smear of grease across the eye, the giant was upon him. Perilously late, Magnus hurled up his arms and threw forth his Will, and a jet of crackling ice tore up the ash around him. Brutus crashed into the wall, snarled, and then vaulted over it. Brutus called his Will—the magik of the jungle, dominion over flesh and fang—and his arms twisted with brilliance into ragged blades that took the place of his forearms and hands and could rend a stone in twain: his claws. He descended upon his brother, who looked up, stunned, so slow compared to the agility that coursed inside him. Easy prey.

Yes, my son. Make him bleed. Bleed him to love him, it is the only way, hissed the Black Queen inside him.

In the instant that Brutus's blade flashed before Magnus—so near that he could see his face reflected—the Sorcerer King lashed out with his Will. His gaze blazed with emerald energy, and the giant was blasted away from him in a smoking arc: plummeting to a stop far away. As quickly as Brutus was down, he was up again, a golden lightning bolt across the black land, and Magnus used that precious instant of distance to shut out the pounding of war and fall deep into himself. He sought the arctic vein of power that ran within him, the magik spawned in the tundra where they were born; forever had he carried an essence of the cold of that place. He broke the skin of memory, and the sum of his great life's emotions rushed out. He screamed as the power tore through him: from the shredding physical agony, from the rage of Brutus's betrayal, from the torment of his love for Lila and Erithitek. He screamed as well as Brutus's bull charge shattered the frozen cascade that he hunched behind, and those golden blades sank somewhere into his flesh. But that pain only made the magik stronger, and Brutus's slavering grin was wiped away in the nova of retribution, light, snow, and the ripping noise more hateful than the coldest night of the Long Winter that blasted from his delicate brother and consumed the valley.

When the light and devastation eased to a howl, Magnus floated back into himself. He was shivering in a hollow of ice, with frozen waves and twisted spikes radiating outward from him and a veil of whipping snow over the land. His hip and shoulder were numb and rather useless, and he realized that he was in some state of hypothermia or shock. Sloppily, he dragged himself over to a glassy crest, lightheadedly watching the red trails he made on all the whiteness. His wounds were surely grave, though he did not have the Will to repair himself: he needed to rest a speck. The war might have ended, though he could not hear much over the screeching winter he had called. *Is it over? Have I done what I set out to do? Lila, Erithitek, those who taught an immortal creature how to love, this is in your name.* Was he to feel triumphant? For in his stomach there was only merciless grief. Had he ended his brother? The significance of that choked a sob from his bloody lips. *Please forgive me, brother, please forgive me.*

"Do not weep for me, little brother," thundered Brutus in the storm.

Magnus rolled from his support and swayed to his feet. Strides from him, slumped against an icy finger, was his brother, and in no better shape than himself: his war skirt had evaporated, and his naked flesh was minced and prickling with ice that not even his tremendous heat had melted yet. Astonishingly, or perhaps not so for a man who had endured the Long Winter, Brutus had survived. His fight was spent, though, as empty as Magnus's reserves of might, so a victory could hardly be announced.

"Damn you," said Magnus.

Brutus laughed and hauled himself up, huffing as he spoke. "Your strength fills me with pride; for with so much passion, there is surely love. You cannot kill an immortal. Not even you, little brother. You cannot stop what is coming, either."

Magnus had a sense of what that was: a Black Queen and hordes of men with their souls sucked out for her Will. He cared not for what this monster was, if it was a mother as Brutus said—he wanted no mother that was so vile. With no magik to call upon to defend himself, he used the one remaining weapon that might pierce the madness of his brother: he undid the seal that shielded him from Brutus's mind and soul. The spell blew away like dust. The wall between them fell. The wildfire of his brother's spirit roared within him, while Brutus doubled over and whimpered as the winter returned to his chest. Magnus stumbled toward his brother. He would forgive him if it would bring peace. He would not leave him alone again.

Brutus, end this. Please, there has to be another way, he begged. *If it is loneliness that has sickened you, then I shall cure that with my company. I shall give everything that I have built to the hands of others and never leave you again. Please, take my hand, and we shall go away. We shall leave the world of men and live as ghosts to the ages.*

Those words were the weapon he had hoped for, and his great brother cringed as the sword of Magnus's cold love was driven deep. He would surrender it all, as he had said, and live as one beast of two bodies again. The idea was not unappealing to Magnus, either. Losing Lila would be the hardest part, though in a sense that loss had already started, for with the connections between blood-bound souls restored, his first and only sense from her was terror. Erithitek would be a proper king for Eod: virtuous, hard, and strong. He would leave those he loved before he and his brother hurt them more. Brutus would have him. They could sleep as cubs and speak in grunts and whistles without worrying about the courtesies of a world that was not made for them. Magnus slogged ahead toward the fire that was his broken brother, craving that heat and weeping tears that froze on his cheeks. He fell before the trembling giant, a mouse in his brother's shadow, and offered his hand. He was not afraid of Brutus, not anymore.

It is time, said Magnus. *Time for us to go.*

Brutus bowed his shaggy head, as docile as a lamb. *I've been a monster... the things I've done...yes, take me away, little brother. Away from this world I bite at. I need your silence and your cold love and nothing else. In another age, I shall remember how to be noble again,* sobbed the giant. He reached to Magnus.

WEAK!

The Black Queen's denouncement split the skulls of both brothers. Magnus reeled, and Brutus clamped down upon his wrist, shattering metal, bone, and meat. But the pain was secondary to the passion of the Black Queen that gripped him: the black and throbbing lust, the gurgling illness that made Magnus want to shite, vomit, and fuk all at once. Connected to Brutus's mind and flesh, Magnus could sense that now, her indomitable hold on his brother. With her whispers, she had poisoned his brother, and her venom was not so simply cured. He had flashes of her nattering insinuations, her goading to feed his bestial urges—to eat the meat, drink the blood, and pump his seed with abandon—and he reeled from revulsion as well as from the crippling regret at how fantastically he had failed Brutus. Centuries of this torment, this secret madness had his brother endured, and he had known nothing of it while living as a man in Eod.

Brutus! Please! We can still—

No, grinned the giant; his teeth all fangs and the wildness again in his stare. Magnus had lost him.

He is mine! As you will be soon, my son. Once you are stripped down. Once I have eaten your Will. Then, and only then, will you be ready for my gift.

Magnus roared at the thought, and his rage puffed the flicker of his magik to a flame. In a humming blast of white-cold sorcery, the brothers were scattered strides apart. Magnus was exhausted afterward, as chilled as the snow he lay and bled upon, but he staggered to a knee. Brutus was striding toward him, empowered by foul whispers and smiling sadistically; the fragments of ice that were embedded in his muscled hide sizzled away into steam. The giant stopped as his brother found some untapped reserve of power—his love, perhaps, and his wish to be together beyond all these struggles—for the magik that shone from him was as pure and glimmering as a crystal in the sun.

Mother warned me of your magik, shouted Brutus. *She said that I would not have the strength to break you on my own. But there are forces in Geadhain that not even your winter can still. Powers as untamed as each of us. Only Mother has shown me the leash, the old whispers to tame the wildest beasts. How much strength do you have, really, brother? How strong is your winter? Enough to stand against the power of fire itself?*

Fire? thought Magnus, his mind scrambling. *Impossible.*

But the impossible was made possible in that moment, and Magnus's darkest fears were realized. Brutus mouthed a word, an ancient sound, the sort that could not be attributed to language and yet was language still: a groan, a growl, a purring in the throat from which few mortal syllables could be fished among the notes. *Eeeegh...niiii...faaaa...ks!* Magnus now understood how Mor'Khul had been scorched and ruined, and the source of all that unendurable heat: the firefather. His brother had chained the eldest of the elementals, the Great Wyrm of Flame itself. None of this knowledge would serve him, however, for the ground had already begun to split and glow with red light, steam wavered his vision, and the ice was running like a full season of spring passed in a single speck. Brutus was howling in mad glee as plumes of fire, rock, and ash heralded the rising of the monster that shook the world from below. Magnus called to his light, his love, though he knew it would not protect him.

IX

Once the horde had snuffed out the king's green fire and begun cascading over the embankment, the mounted Watchmen and infantry had charged ahead to form a new line. Erik was among the first to meet the enemy with his hammer, and he cheered with every soft body that crumpled under his blows or every Blackeye knight that he batted from his saddle. Brigada was unstoppable, and trampled or kicked whatever hands or blades came for her and her rider. For however many moments, as Brigada bucked, the blood sprayed around him, and more and more of the chanting damned were beaten back, he felt invincible. Alive in the purest way a warrior knew, connected to body and to the transit of life and death: balancing one, delivering the other. He came out of this state on occasion, and could tell that the battle was not going as well for others as it was for him. Of the five legion masters who rode the front lines with him, his darting eyes could spot only two that had not been pulled from their mounts or were otherwise unseen. When Brigada spun, he caught a look at the Fangs of Dawn, where the Blackeye horde had pursued a similar tactic to its crossing of the king's flame, whereby they piled themselves against the taller reaches of rock and climbed over the crispy remains of those blasted by a fusillade of arrows and sorcery. There, the artillery was still under a second assault from the cursed firecallers and their lances of flame, too. He could not tell how many of his men remained clinging to the cliffs. In the pass itself, it was equally difficult to make out much past the stacks of the dead, though Erik noticed the shining tips of Watchmen's spears, and that gave him hope that the phalanx held. Still, it would not do so for long. The Watchmen barely clung to the land they had begun with, and beyond their small stake, a wave of the damned, as unctuous as a sea of ants, continued to roll out of the valley. A few sands at best, and he and his men would be pushed back; a few more after that and they would all die.

Hurry, Kingfather! he thought, as the king was their only hope. By now, King Magnus had surely cast himself into the thick of Brutus's army. Translocation was always a gamble, but Erik had faith that the transit was safely made. He clutched at that faith and drew power from it when heaviness began to burden his arms and his swings became messy. He believed in his king despite the rising, unitary chant of *Brutus! Brutus! Brutus!* and the dimming of the war-cries made by his allies, who were dying now, undoubtedly. *You will save us, Kingfather!* he trusted, even when the horde shoved Brigada against the scattered phalanx, and sorcerers and archers were falling from the Fangs of Dawn like victims of mass suicide.

His faith was rewarded.

Winter came. Somewhere out in the valley, a storm rose like a flower of whiteness. When it opened, there was a purity of light so bright that it seared the eyes to blindness and spots. A wrathful wind followed: sharp with slivers of ice and snow, and if not for Brigada's footing and his grip upon her bridle, Erik would have flown off. The whistling quiet was what he noticed first; the song of the Blackeyes had ceased. Erik and his mount bumbled for a bit, Brigada as sightless as he was. Though in the blinks and freckled visions that he had, he saw the miracle of Brutus's horde, dusted in frost and as still as a portrait of war: their strides and swipes paused, their heads hung like stringless dolls. His wonder did not end, for the escarpment had been made slippery with a gloss of ice and snowy dunes, while in the distance winter reigned. In the valley, none of the black despair of Mor'Khul could be seen, and there ice ran rampant in spirals and spines as tall as trees. *A forest,* thought Erik. His fellows were finding their eyes again, and astonished cries echoed through the glittering wasteland that his king had conjured. While he gaped, Brigada guided him among the desolation, butting over stiffened Blackeyes in her way.

"Have we won?" a soldier whispered behind him.

Erik twisted in his saddle and saw that the speaker was Leonitis. The legion master was pink across his punctured armor with frozen blood, crazy in his stare, and had the look of a lunatic dervish: bearing a Blackeye hatchet—ripped from the arm of an enemy and with shreds of flesh still attached—and his broadsword. Other men were kicking through the snow behind him.

"I think...I think we have," replied Erik.

Relief fell from him, and then came the emptiness of purpose that a warrior felt when the battle was over, and lastly the leaden fatigue of a body pushed for weeks and finally realizing its rest. The cold came in as the heat of battle left, and Brigada carefully plodded over the icy terrain, still directing herself, while Leonitis limped along beside her. They were headed toward the howling lip of the arctic valley without a clear sense of why: to see if they could find the worker of this miracle, perhaps, their king. Even in the biting wind and surrounded by the hideous mutated bodies of Brutus's horde—each twisted specimen more freakish with metal fusings than the one beside it—the warriors found their first smile in a very long time.

Suddenly, the earth lurched, and their smiles died.

Brrooooootuuuusss...came the murmur from the lips of the countless damned, who were not frozen, it appeared; only motionless without their master's Will: a Will that had returned. Again the land pitched, and out in the valley, the crystalline forest began to crumble in shattering explosions.

Erik jumped from his mount and shook the reins at Leonitis. "Take the king's charger, round up who you can and flee!"

"We do not flee!" barked Leonitis.

"Your king has commanded that you do! Think of what he had you hold back!"

Brruuutuss! hissed the horde.

Slowly the damned were moving now, like elders stretching from their beds, only with clattering daggers instead of arthritic hands. One of the abominations sluggishly reached with its sword-arms for Leonitis from behind, and he stuck his hatchet in its head without turning around. He would not unlock himself from the hammer's stare. Not until Erik shouted at him again, abandoned Brigada, and ran forward through the writhing fields of the damned. He hoped that Leonitis took King Magnus's steed and saved whomever he could, for a babe of horror was kicking in his belly, and his instincts told him that the darkest hourglass was now upon them. Magnus had failed. Brutus and his dark ally would ravage Geadhain. The war of all wars had begun. He knew this as truly as a dying man could count his final breaths, and the passion and anger he felt at his kingfather's defeat turned him into an engine of goring death as he hurtled down the battlefield. The Blackeyes were shuffling into his path, trying to throw their lazy bodies upon him as if he was another fire to be smothered. It was to his favor that the horde was still so sleepy, for he would not have cleared a hundred strides were they not. He still did not make it far enough to grant his wish and learn the fate of his kingfather.

GRAAAAAHHHHHCCCHHH!

A high-pitched explosion of incredible magnitude ripped through the valley and hurled him back. On the topsy-turvy earth, he slid and danced, not only the patches of ice, but the tilting and jostling of the land itself working against his coordination. Blackeyes tumbled into him, senselessly biting at him before he tossed them off. The titanic bellow shook reality once more—*GRAAAAHHHHCCCHHH*—a noise that could be an earthquake's passion and that Erik irrationally accepted had come from something with a mouth large enough to cause such uproar. Then came the rain of fire, the powdery cracking of the ground, the brume of embers that throttled all of Erik's senses, and the boiling heat that seared his metal plating into his skin, so swiftly had the apocalypse descended upon him. He was lost in a realm of fire. *Brutus! Brutus!* the damned sang, their swaying choir a whisper to the symbols of destruction ringing out even as the crimson landscape devoured them in tongues of flame.

Please live, Kingfather. Please, somehow be alive.

That was his final wish.

Hysterically, Erik tossed away his gauntlets and tore at his chest plate, which was soft and pliable, almost ready to be poured back into a mold. Then he wailed as the clothing underneath went up like cotton in a kiln. But his clawing hands found the cold stone he needed, and he squeezed it as if grasping at life itself. He didn't have the stomp of a boot, as the king had suggested, but the fear and sizzling of his burning flesh made his hands just as hard. The fragile vessel broke, leaking numbing, soothing cold over him: a blanket of the kingfather's love. Away from the land of fire he spun; to somewhere safe, somewhere calm, somewhere with the sound of waterfalls and echoes.

XX

THE STORM

I

The thickness of the air before rain, the feeling of walking into a dark room and knowing that something awaits you there, a tingle of lightning along the spine: all the sensations of forewarning that Mouse possessed were going off at once. She wasn't an oracle like the woman she sought, and she didn't need to be to understand that grand events were circling about her like dark water in a drain. Every time she glanced down through the grates they trod over into the filthy, loud streets of the Undercomb, or forgot to breathe through her mouth and could smell shite and tangy fear, she asked herself what she was doing here. Scampering with the rats in piss-rusted ducts, following a man who had abducted her a day ago and a risen corpse that was the father about whom she had never known. Yet whenever Vortigern turned his ghastly white face to her and gave her his creepy yellow smile, she found her rude reminder for this journey. *I am here to save Morigan, the mind witch who brought my father to me. I am here to honor that gift,* she thought. These notions of honor, trust, and family were exciting if foreign to Mouse—as thrilling as hearing Alastair declare her freedom for the first time. While she had been cautious about so many aspects of her life—never trusting, never believing in the promises of others—she had faith in Vortigern, Morigan, and that strange northern lad, too. So whenever her doubt arose, which was often, she reminded herself of these truths.

Kanatuk was as skillful as a rat in navigating the Undercomb. The speck that they had descended, he took them off the Blood Road—the great reddish stone path that traveled through the Undercomb—up some metal steps and into an access that he quickly opened with a picklock. Despite Vortigern's insistence that he couldn't *hear anything* on the other side of the entrance, they prepared for an ambush. For hourglasses, they had bustled through thin windy hallways that circulated the necessary air to keep the Undercomb from suffocating itself. They would stop only if Kanatuk, or more often Vortigern, detected noises coming toward them: sounds that turned out to be rats or a creaking, rattling fan on every occasion. Kanatuk had expected more of a reception from the Broker, unless the madman believed that they had all perished in the atelier's fire, which was unlikely. A more reasonable explanation was that the Broker did not think that a hodgepodge of scoundrels cared all that much for the fate of a single woman. How wrong he was, for they each owed Morigan a debt: the kind that could never be repaid.

Sometime into their skulking, they paused at a four-pronged junction while Vortigern strained his ears to a dissonance.

"Hmm...screams. Coming from beneath us, I think. Up through the vents," he said.

"We are near the meat markets," replied Kanatuk. "You will hear many, many screams."

"That means that we are getting close," whispered Mouse.

"Yes," agreed their guide.

He was about to move onward when Mouse hissed for him to hold. "Wait! I am all for charging in boldly and hoping not to get gutted, but we really should discuss some sort of a plan. No matter how trivial."

Kanatuk frowned. He wasn't keen on wasting sands, though they had not considered any tactics for raiding the Broker's stronghold. Rushing in would lead to swift defeat, and Mouse was right in stalling him before his headstrong ways carried them into danger. Sighing, he called his companions into a circle.

"Right now, I assume that we have the element of surprise," he said, quickly taking charge. "That is good. Now, if we follow these vents all the way to the old reservoir, there are ladders leading down into the shore of the Drowned River—"

"River?" Vortigern was a Thule, Menosian born and bred, but he had never heard of a river.

"What the Undercomb folks call the tides that run out of the reservoir," Mouse explained. "They flow in from Alabion and out of the city to the falls on the east side of Menos. To freedom, if one can swim them. They never do. And so—"

"As I was saying," continued Kanatuk, "off the river are paths leading into the nest. They will be guarded, and these men are like me: difficult to see unless they want to be seen and as deadly as poison." Kanatuk firmly gripped the dead man's shoulder. "You move faster than them or me, so it will be up to you to silence them."

Vortigern flashed his yellow smile. "Consider it done."

"Good."

Seemingly, that was the extent of their strategizing, for Kanatuk was striding off into the shadows. Mouse whispered after him.

"Really? A little sparse on details, don't you think? She is wanted by the Iron Queen! Hunted by that dreadful"—*uncle*, her mind whispered, but she shook it away—"that dreadful nekromancer and that Elissandra, who is no treat herself. What you've proposed—rushing in and hoping for the best—is mostly a terrible fuking plan. Do pardon me."

"Then we must hurry, Fionna," called Vortigern, also moving into the tunnel. "Before the witch's other enemies find her. I do not fancy seeing my brother again. Even if I were to twist off his head, I doubt it would do much good."

Mouse couldn't argue with that, and hearing her father speak her name had the same effect on her as it did on many a child: she listened and followed. Determined and grave, the three walked for a time past thrumming fans, catching whiffs and cries of sorrow from the streets they skirted above, with only the occasional glimmer of yellow bleeding through a grate to guide their steps. Even the rats were surely lost in this lightless misery, and yet Kanatuk appeared to know precisely where he was headed, and could have done so blindfolded, judging by how quickly he moved. There wasn't much opportunity for them to speak, though Mouse did tug on Vortigern's sleeve at one point and ask him about something that had been nagging at her.

"What did you mean earlier, when you were talking about your brother? I would think that twisting off a man's head would settle most arguments."

Vortigern paused and debated for a speck how much to share with his daughter. When Morigan had unlocked the tumblers in his head, every memory had returned to him, and those that he had of Sorren's later years were despicable. His brother was mad, his plans for Fionna were heinous, and worse than that, the man was *immortal*. If not in the sense of time, like the kings, then in a way that defied death regardless. *I remember killing you,* he thought. Likewise, he remembered his brother rising afterward, and a glimpse of that dark fuming shadow that his brother had unleashed upon him. The touch of that darkness, as it raped his soul and scrubbed away every precious thought he possessed, was unforgettable. He was certain that it was not magik. It was a force: a living presence on a cosmic scale. A chill as if he was basking in the shadow of the moon, gazing upon this heavenly body and frozen by his crippling insignificance: that sense that he was so small to that grand whiteness. He could not say as to what that power was, but it was tied to his brother, and he was not eager to face it a second time.

Mouse tugged on him again. "Vortigern?"

"He is more dangerous than you can imagine," replied Vortigern.

"How? He is just a man. A man of power, but a man still."

"No." Vortigern placed a cold hand upon his daughter's cheek. "I hate that I must tell you this, yet you should know. You should know what he really is and what he wanted to do with you. Only then might you fear him as you should. My brother is not a man, not anymore—though I remember him as an innocent child, as once he was. Now, he makes pacts with dark powers and darker spirits. He cannot die, not by any weapon I wield. He wanted to bring her back." Vortigern sneered from disgust at the knowledge that poured from himself. "He thought to place her soul, your mother's soul, into new flesh, so he could punish it eternally, as he punished me."

He made several...vessels, my dear Fionna. But none was quite right. They weren't close enough to the original flesh. You, however, would be perfect for his designs. You are Lenora's child more than you are mine, it seems, both in beauty and spirit. And he will do it, too, my daughter, if he catches you. He will empty you out; he will do the unspeakable and pervert life for his vengeance. He has the power to make and unmake the living, and I doubt that you, I, or anyone can stand against it.

Vortigern sneered and was unable to finish his warning as the images of thrashing maidens—their cavities opened with chains and hooks like frogs ready to be dissected—disrupted his thoughts. He could not bring himself to tell her the worst of his brother's lunacy.

My mother's soul? "I don't...how...how is that possible?" exclaimed Mouse.

Vortigern only shrugged. Suddenly the darkness was stifling, her cloak knotting like a garrote around her neck.

"We should hurry. Kanatuk is right," urged her father.

Mouse agreed, and they did not stop another speck inside the tunnels for fear of what might catch up to them.

II

Caenith woke from his forced sleep of unconsciousness roaring like a poked beast and nearly hit his head upon the lip of rock under which they were camped. With haste, Thackery was upon his groggy friend and assisting the man with his bearings. What sobered the Wolf most was the sight of Macha, who was bundled in Thackery's cloak on the dusty ground and wrapped in tourniquets made from what looked to be remnants of his missing shirt, which was in tatters anyhow. While Macha was clean of most of the filth of the mines, her sweaty slumber, her shivering, and the thatching of sores across her body, red as the lashes from a hundred whips, told of her health.

"She's not dead," claimed Thackery bitterly, with an edge that said he had been at this desperate bedside watch for hourglasses. He hustled over to Macha and knelt to check her fever. "I am no great healer, but I can mend what needs to be mended. I tried every art I thought would help, but nothing seems to work. I don't understand it."

The Wolf came over and squatted behind his friend. Thackery could feel the man's weighty pensiveness adding to the burden of his failure. After some consideration, Caenith spoke.

"Aye, there is nothing you can do for her. My kind is slippery to magik. What injuries she has cannot be healed by your hand. We need the magik of the East. No other power will mend these wounds. Now more than ever, we must find Morigan."

"Morigan?"

"Yes, she is a Daughter of the Moon. Those enchantresses have many gifts, and the sun is not the only power that brings life. Night has its own mystery and magik, and miracles can be made to happen if one Wills it hard enough."

"Can Morigan save her?" gasped Thackery.

"Possibly," answered the Wolf.

Possibly was enough. Caenith pushed past his friend and lifted the limp child into his arms. They set out immediately into the rubbly foothills. The gray-cotton sky grumbled with the threat of a storm, and another night was nearing, yet the two were strong with the fire of hope. Rarely had Geadhain seen creatures with faces so weary or worn to their souls as these two, and perhaps it took mercy on them by not raining. Not that any downpour could have slowed them, nor could any obstacle have been too tall for them to transcend. The pleading of Thackery's bones for him to stop—aches worsened since dragging the Wolf to shelter—and the wind that abraded the still-healing lesions scoring Caenith's flesh were meaningless annoyances to these men. They had crossed from West to East and would go as far as it took to find Morigan, and now to help the child they had sworn to protect. Theirs was an unbreakable determination, the stuff of which the greatest legends were woven. But here, in this moment, they thought not of heroism or bravery, only of their duty.

In time, the foothills flattened and the Iron Valley was cast as a shadow to their backs. They followed the impression of the old road, once grand and now effaced to little more than a trail between shelves of aged stone. Now and then, they were deterred as the Crowes flew overhead and they were forced to find cover, or they paused so that Thackery could squeeze some water from the air to wet Macha's lips. Nothing woke her, and she did not drink. While creating something from almost nothing was exhausting, another stone on Thackery's shoulders, he ploughed on without complaint. *Once they're all safe, you can rest*, he told himself, and it was that promise that pushed him onward.

At last, the narrow pass opened, and the travelers were rewarded with a sight that thrilled and frightened them. For across a scrubbed plain there rose the grotesque majesty of Menos: a girdle of black iron around a city of pointed spikes so grand that it blocked most of Kor'Keth's expansive range behind it. Busy roads converged upon the black wall, and formations of Crowes swooped through the flickering smog that wreathed the city. As thunderous as those clouds seemed, the untainted skies closer to the companions had turned darker still. A great storm was imminent, and one that hackled the Wolf's hide with the tingle of power. Beyond the pending deluge—which would be spectacular, he felt—there was a second prickle of warning: a telling of something worse than a storm that he could not shake from his fur.

They hid in one last haven of rocks before braving the open plains, waiting the short while for night to fall and speaking in broken whispers to each other; Thackery mostly describing where they were headed, while the Wolf answered in crude grunts. *To the aqueducts on the east side. There will be a waterfall, but if we climb up from there, you come to shallower pools and a forgotten access to the Iron City. I was amazed it had never been discovered and I hope that for our fortune it has remained the same.* A willow tree would be there, too, haunted by the ghost of his wife, but he did not mention this to Caenith. He was lost in fleeting images of Bethany, made vivid against the canvas of night that had fallen, when Caenith prodded him and said, "It's time."

Looking to the Wolf, he wasn't surprised by the other's nudity—something he was more or less used to by now. The fields of Menos were watched, not only by Crowes but also from spyglasses along in the Iron Wall, and there were few gaits fast enough to avoid the all-seeing eyes of the Iron City. They had discussed how they were to approach, and in this instance, the Wolf's speed might be the only thing that could take them swiftly and unseen to the other side of Menos. Caenith had to move quickly, yet not so quickly that the abnormality of his movement would be detected by the more sensitive instruments of the Menosians that Thackery had earlier described: technomagiks devised to capture the activities of carriages, skycarriages, projectiles, and the like—all speeds that the Wolf was not far from matching himself. While the Wolf snapped and stretched into his furrier skin, Thackery kissed Macha's clammy brow and trussed her up as delicately as he could, binding her like a little caterpillar with a knot of fabric that the Wolf could slip into his jaws like a bit. He was hardly comfortable with this arrangement, and even less so when the huge beast pounded its way over to him and opened its mouth as if it were going to eat the nicely wrapped meal.

"Be gentle," he urged.

To that, the Wolf made an endearingly innocent whimper. Once Macha was secure in his jaws, the Wolf bobbed his head up and down. As unsuitable as the image of a small child in the mouth of a monstrous wolf was, the bundle hardly moved. Thackery gathered up Caenith's pants and shoes into a pack and then mounted the changeling. With two fistfuls of fur and a prayer that he would not fly off, they were moving. The Wolf did not travel with the swiftness that he could, but a constant running pace. They avoided getting close to the roads, skulking across only the one that led to the new mines north of Menos. Here and there, when spotlights cut the night sky from the turrets of the Iron Wall and swept over the land, the Wolf stopped to plant himself like a great black boulder while Thackery struggled to breathe under his mass. Then the old man would climb back up and the game of hide-and-sneak would continue; deadly if they were to lose, for Thackery knew of the technomagikal bombardments that could rain from the Iron Wall—he had invented a few of them himself. Thackery wondered what awaited them in Menos: tragedy and death, surely. He was excited in a foolhardy way. Even if one of those deaths were to be his own, he would ensure that Sorren would join him in oblivion. Death was an end, after all, and that is what the saga of his past needed. Finality.

Perhaps we'll see each other again, Gloria. A family reunion, he laughed. *I would like you to watch your son die for all the pain you have caused me. Sorren is brilliant, but not so much for social engineering and duplicity. That was always your forte. I know you had a hand in Bethany and Theodora's ends. You simply can't keep your hands out of things. That's always been your problem. And you will suffer, just as I have. If there is any justice in this world, we must all pay for our sins, and your price will be great indeed.*

By the time his brooding ended, they had already circled the Iron Wall and had entered a deep misty cleft that crashed on one side with water, and where the only safe ground was a beach of shattered rock as slick as an ocean's front. At least in here the scouring lights of Menos did not seek them, and Thackery dismounted; in a roar and a twisting of flesh, Caenith joined him in his body of two legs. Thackery handed the man his clothing while he tended to Macha. She had survived the trip comfortably, though she was pale as a white worm in the darkness, and her breathing was but a flutter. Her injuries were a concern, as they were pustules, and there was a sweetness and sourness to the girl that was some kind of infection. Caenith came over to cradle the child, and he and Thackery shared a knowing look: a warrior's and a physician's understanding, respectively, of a body close to death.

Thackery led the Wolf. Old trails are never forgotten, and Thackery recalled the pocketed faces of certain wet stones he stepped upon. Occasionally, he pictured Bethany racing ahead of him and had to halt to shake the memories from his head. *She is dead, and Morigan might be, too, if you don't hurry.* In time their path curved around the waterfall, and the land continued in a quiet foggy canyon that narrowed and narrowed, ending in an incline that ran steeply upward. Pressing on, the journey became slippery and tedious. However, even as Thackery hunched and fumbled for handholds, the Wolf's hand was ever there to hold him up—despite having a child to bear and his own balance to worry about. Repeatedly, Thackery cursed his age, which was all the more evident from this climb, as well as rejoiced that Caenith was here with him. If he had the breath or time to spare, he would have thanked the man for countless compassions, for this was a trip he would never have survived alone. Together they made it out of the wet darkness and onto a deeply shadowed plateau beneath the Iron Wall. Trees were abundant here; the sad shapes of willows and tangles of bushes and wildflowers gasped their perfume toward the travelers. Although this was some of the first real verdure that Caenith had seen since the woods west of the Iron Valley, and it was quite unexpected in its appearance, they did not need a reminder of their cause and hurried into the overgrowth before the lights of the Iron City discovered them. On the other side of the small copse, there was a pool exactly as Thackery had said, and at the end of that was a screen of reeds and a cloistering of vines that dripped with water. Caenith had to look twice with his incredible eyes to note that a metal tube behind the vines extruded from the base of the Iron Wall: an entry into an impregnable city. As they waited for the flurry of lights and Crowes to die down,

Thackery read the puzzlement on his friend's face and told the Wolf how he had found this place.

"It's an old access tunnel, built by my father to use in cases of emergency. Father told me about it, as I was the eldest male of our family. I doubt Gloria knows of it; if she had, it would have been sealed or heavily guarded for her own personal use. The architects that my father hired for its make were all… silenced. The passage leads to the Drowned River, near the old reservoir, and I am pleased to say that it appears my gamble was not in vain and that it has not been discovered. I suppose we shall confirm that in a speck. The lights are no longer hunting us for the moment. Let's move."

They darted out into the night and splashed their way toward the wall. Once through the whipping reeds, the two men ripped at the vines—Caenith's one arm moving faster and doing more than both of Thackery's—and soon revealed a heavy black gate, like that of a prison cell. Just as the watchtower lights swooped past, they hauled themselves up onto the rim of the pipe and pressed their bodies against the bars. As soon as they were in shadow again, Thackery turned and clutched the lock that sealed the gate. Caenith would have simply kicked the metal in, but Thackery muttered something—a woman's name, *Bethany*, heard the Wolf—which opened the lock with a crisp click. The gate screeched as it swung into the dripping tunnel beyond.

"We should cover up the entrance in case it is spotted by the patrols."

Thackery had to ask again, for the Wolf was distant and staring into the pipe. While he still could not feel his bloodmate, her scent of wind and flowers and the soils and sweetness of the West was somehow wafting toward him. She was close. His heart stirred from the rush of the chase.

"Morigan, I can smell her," he said.

Thackery didn't ask what miracle this was, or how it had come to be, for he had learned never to question good fortune. In a flurry, he pulled the greenery over the pipe and then waved the Wolf on. With that, two men and their tiny fading charge sped into the bowels of Menos to find the one woman who could right almost everything that was wrong.

They fled before the storm began, though Caenith absently heard the drumming and thunder echoing after them. He did not see the magnificence of the weather: the sky as it ran black as ink, the droplets as large as stones, or the winds that clawed hunks of earth and hacked the green from the sanctuary of the trees they had recently left. The land was angry; the land was in sorrow. A sadness greater than either of those two could have guessed had occurred, and Geadhain was about to mourn.

The storm had started.

III

He's coming, the bees whispered.

Morigan rattled her chains when the message was delivered. She hadn't meant to; it was the surprise that made her do it, and she had been pretending to be quiet until this point with relative effectiveness. Or so she believed.

"It's about time we ended the charade, no?" said the Broker. "I don't get many guests, and my sons don't tend to converse much. I wouldn't say I'm lonely, but I'm certainly lacking for an ear. Well, maybe not an ear, per se—I have a collection of those. C'mon now, let's have a little chitter-chat. I imagine this will be the last civil discourse you have before the Iron sages take you. They're not the convivial sort. You won't much care for their conversation, I'd say. Go on. Open your eyes. Don't be scared."

"I'm not scared of you," declared Morigan, and she meant it.

Inside her, the spirit of the Wolf growled, and she sat up as dignified as she could while being chained by the wrists and ankles—more of that feliron, she could tell, from the way it aggravated her skin with itching and chill. A bit of the Wolf's senses were with her, and she could construe the particulars of her dingy imprisonment: the strange stucco walls made of metal and trash; the high roof and its dying yellow lights; the tables and their piles of coin, weapons, and instruments heaped with a mad child's incompetence for organization; and the sugary decay of the withered things—bodies—hanging from sets of chains like her own along the wall. *More children like young Kanatuk. Only they were spared the disgrace of a life in his service*, she thought with solemnity.

"Sons. Weak sons. Failed sons. They didn't survive The Binding," the Broker said, sighing, when he noticed her staring.

Morigan was having difficulty finding the man's voice in the shadowy chamber. Whenever she thought she spotted him, it was only out of the corner of her eye. He moved with a serpentine slipperiness, and the bees warned her with a sting that there was something unusual about him.

"They are not your sons," she challenged. "I've seen what you do to these poor boys, how you nurse them on cruelty. How you beat their flesh until their souls scream. You are the weakest kind of creature. A parasite that feeds on pain and fear. When that is all you have, it is all you are, and that is an empty life, indeed. I do not fear you because you are pitiful. I do not fear you because you will shortly meet your end."

In a black sweep of motion, the Broker was before her, clacking his teeth in her face. Still, Morigan did not cringe.

"You are right," he hissed, and licked his scarred lips with curiosity. "You do not fear me as you should. Which means that you have either foolishness or power in abundance. I'm betting on the latter, as I know that you did something to Twenty-Two. He was a favorite son of mine. So strong and diligent, and you *ruined* him. You took him from his father."

"I did not ruin him. I freed him. If there is a soul to be salvaged in you, perhaps I shall free you, too."

Morigan smiled, wolfish and dangerous. The Broker had placed himself perilously near—close enough to touch. Ferociously she sprang at him, and while her chains limited her, she was still able to reach and grasp one arm as he pulled away. As soon as contact was made, she called her Will and sent her swarm to attack the man. *Show me your secrets! Show me your sins!* she commanded, and the air rippled with invisible force. But the bees could not penetrate their target, and silver sparks scattered in the air as their stingers bounced off the hard soul of the Broker, his spirit somehow resistant to her magik. While laughing like a tickled man, the Broker viciously slapped off Morigan's hands and then cracked the witch across the face. He stepped back, creating a distance that she could not cross with her chains, and took a sand to finish his spell of humor. When he was done, he had to wipe the tears from his eyes. Morigan did the same, though from pain. Despite this development, she was no more afraid than before and twice as angry that her magik had failed. She didn't have to wonder why, for the Broker's ensuing rambling explained plenty.

"I told you that your tricks don't work on me," the Broker said, snickering. "I see now exactly what you've done to Twenty-Two. Went into his head like a technomancer with a wrench and jiggered all the bolts you shouldn't have. No fixing him now. Should he pop his head out of a hole again, I suppose I'll just have to lop it off and add it to my ears." Pensively, the Broker stroked his beard, and his beady eyes worked furiously upon thoughts. "Yes. What power you have. A touch of the East. The lost Arts of Alabion. A Daughter of the Moon? Perhaps, perhaps, though I wager Elissandra doesn't have the tricks you do. It's a shame that I must surrender you, for we could have such interesting play together."

The Broker sauntered over to Morigan and slithered his thin fingers over her neck and bust; she thrashed away from some of it, but by the king's, his hands were fast.

"What are you?" she spat.

"It has been a while since anyone has asked me that." The Broker grinned. "These slow-walkers here, they don't remember the truth to the old legends, only the stories. Of the things that crawled under the bed, gutted their wives and cows, and ate their children. You should know what I am, for you have encountered my kindred before." The Broker darted his head toward Morigan and sniffed. "A lord of fang and claw...his scent is all about you. Rank as an otter's piss. How special you must feel, being a mate to such *majesty*."

Mockingly and with foppish flair, the Broker bowed to Morigan. She understood then what she had been missing thus far: his speed, his animal senses. Of course. Morigan blurted her realization aloud.

"A skin-walker."

When the Broker looked up, his metal smile was shining. "Cleverness. Wise as the winter owl, you are. A skin-walker, yes, but not like your *noble* lordling. No, not all of us are born to royalty. Some of us are not meant to be born at all! We are abominations. The sins and surprises of two who should not mate. A ratling and a catling. A badger and a bear. We have no clan that will house us, no place in the East. Though Alabion is a wicked mother to her children now—not fit for any but the strongest claws and teeth. I have those, but I would not stay where I was not welcome."

"You left Alabion?" asked Morigan.

The Broker nodded; he continued quite sulkily. "I tried to make friends, but you know how slow-walkers can be. They buy you a drink, you tell them your sorrows, and the next thing you know they've got you in felirons and performing for scraps of meat. Many names, many cages. Gorgo the Swallower. The Jaws of Doom. Kashar the Gnashar. The slow-walkers all thought that I was an experiment gone sour. Always sour, always wrong! Ghaaa!"

Morigan decided not prod the man's lunacy further, afraid of what she had already stirred. Also disturbing was that he had unfastened his cloak and was now unlacing his shirt. She assumed that he was undressing himself.

"I had many names and many masters, dear daughter. Until I'd taken my last whip. They should have thought better of Gorgo's jaws. Even in our slowest skins, we have many times the power of a fleshling. It took me all night and shattered every tooth I had, but perseverance wins the race, and I chewed those chains to pulp. The masters and handlers then made for a better meal. These new teeth are just fine, just fine. Now I rule. I command. I mete out life and death. That's what you were after, isn't it? My story? A little pathos that you could use to *heal* me? Therein lies your mistake, in thinking that I need your compassion, when I am beyond those sentiments."

With his clothing in a pile, he approached Morigan again. His sinuous body glistened with a sweat of excitement, and the heat of his repulsive desire was thrust upon her not only from his throbbing member. This lust wasn't for her, not entirely, but directed more toward the things he spoke of: domination, pain, rulership. She knew that the Broker would never find salvation, by her or anyone else. He was a monster, and he reveled in that as a pig among the mud and filth.

Very near to her face and reeking of an animal's heavy musk, he said quietly, "Do you fear me yet? I feel you fluttering. I am a nightmare. I am the sickness of the seed. I am...*Jabberwok*."

One of Mifanwae's grimmer Eastern tales rose in her mind and would not be silenced. She could almost hear her mother reading the poem to her while tapping the horrible depiction on the page: the sketched charcoal image of a pit scattered with bones and twined with the body of a great wriggling lizard, its mouth ragged and distorted as a clown's messy smile, its talons long as swords.

Beware the Jabberwok, dear one.

In darkling coves and slithering groves,

> *it hunts with coruscating eyes and trilling cries.*

Running is fair, though death has its flair,
    and is the enviable endebum to the affair.
For you cannot bescramble, and are better to amble—gleefociously
    into the curlivanting claws and the goobering maw.
A mouth to eat yer toes and feet,
    to swallgag you down like a soup of meat.
In the bellybosom it's warm,
    and there you shall warn
with every belch of your bones,
    those of bravery prone,
        who dare the bloodscotched dark of the Jabberwok's home.

"This has been nice, our chitter-chat," said the Broker, and turned his heated passion away from her. "Mice—yes, one Mouse in particular—appear to have gotten into my lair. I can hear them scampering about. My sons are out looking for them; seems that they were looking in the wrong holes. You and your friends cost me so many of my boys. Spread too thin, too thin. I shall have to take care of this matter personally. I haven't stretched from my skin in a slow-walker's age. This will be enjoyable. Once I deal with the mice, maybe we will have an occasion to speak again before the Ironguards take you. Or after, I suppose. There won't be much of you left when the Ironguards are done, but I'll ask for the scraps, lovely as they are."

Mouse? Mice? Did he mean Fionna? wondered Morigan. No sooner had the hope alighted than her skin crawled in horror. *Jabberwok,* she reeled, not quite understanding the monster, if in full appreciation of its menace. *Jabberwok, Jabberwok, Jabberwok* was all that she or the bees could natter—as the Broker suddenly hunched and groaned before her in the throes of a grotesque transformation. Whereas the shedding of Caenith's skin was a shocking yet natural molting akin to a butterfly's emergence, the Broker's metamorphosis was like watching maggots festering in a wound. From within, he was viciously squeezed and twisted. It must have been excruciating from the cries he made, and he arced and spun and gurgled sprays of crimson and clear plasma. In specks, he swelled and bloated, he pimpled with scales, and bristles tore from his flesh. And when she believed that the shuddering mass could grow no more revolting, what rubbery trappings of skin remaining upon him flew off in splatters, and one such salty treat landed in Morigan's gaping mouth. She spit the disgusting thing out, but could not abide the unwashed stench or the gagging heat of the grand shadow pacing the chamber, and the vomit burbled its way out of her. With watery sight and a heaving consciousness, her perception of the monster was fantastical and farcical. Surely, it could not be true, she prayed.

For no creature could be so terrible. The slobbering crocodile jaw was jumbled with tusks and puny silver teeth. The swinging tail as mighty as a giant's club battered furniture around as its massive body turned itself on stumpy legs—two clawed, two finer-toed and black. Was she imagining the webbed wings, these atrophied things useless for flight that were misplaced all over the creature? Or the black pearls of its eyes under a spiny crest of a brow? Or the long fluffed ears? These qualities belonged on a bat. No, this was actually happening, she grasped, and the upturned, mucus-huffing nostrils that snuffled at her spew affirmed this freakish reality. She jumped away from the head, which could swallow her to the waist as the legend said, and pressed herself to the wall as much as her chains would allow. The Broker had read her well: she was terrified past all reason, quailing and bloodless, not only for herself but also for the others that were rushing to her rescue. *Go away! Please just go away!* she Willed, as if magik or wishes could save her.

Mercifully, fate or another hand intervened, and the Jabberwok trilled a roaring screech, stomped its monster feet, flapped its many vestigial wings, and then vanished as quickly as a foul wind. She could breathe when it was gone, although the air was still polluted with its stench. She used her first breath to scream.

IV

After his episode, Sorren had calmed, as he usually did. Gloriatrix had returned him to his room and ordered the Ironguards to fetch him night willow tea—a nanny's task, which they frowned at, yet knew not to question. The curtains were drawn, candles lit to flicker on the ominous and overwrought woodwork of the room, and he slept as overexcited children do, which is to say all night and into the following late afternoon. During that time, Elissandra and then the Broker had come and gone, and Gloriatrix had been taken with the affliction of nostalgia and found herself staying at the Blackbriar estate while her son rested: a situation and place that she tried as often as possible to avoid. When she came in the following afternoon, Sorren was finally awake; up against his headboard, dark-eyed, pouting, and clutching his sheets as though he was naked underneath, although he had slept in his clothing.

"He's betrayed us," complained Sorren.

He was referring to Vortigern, of course. Gloriatrix sighed and pulled up a chair to the side of her son's sprawling bed; the seat was embellished with studs of onyx that uncomfortably poked at her. In a strange burst of sentimentality, she wondered if this wealth had ever done her family any good: driving a rift between Thackery and her, teaching her to love power over people, isolating every member of her family from one another, and ultimately ending in the death of her husband and one of her children.

"Mother, are you listening? He has *betrayed* us. Twice now!"

"Yes, I am thinking of your brother, too," she said, and threw her emotions back in the cell that kept them. The *iron* for which she was famed stiffened her features. "While you were resting, Elissandra confirmed his disloyalty through whatever airy conjurings she uses to determine these things. The Broker, too, has suffered treachery in his ranks and lost a man to this witch you caught."

"Who slipped away! With my prize!" shouted Sorren.

Wary of any accusations that might prompt another fit, Gloriatrix was less reprimanding and quite cosseting as she asked, "Your prize? A Voice, I am told. There is easier flesh to buy in Menos, particularly for the price you paid to the Watchers, from whom I did not know bodies could be had. You could have bought a hundred girls for that. Why such an interest in her, my son?"

He was sheepish with his reply. "She reminds me of someone."

"Lenora?"

"Yes."

Likely because that is her daughter, who should have died years ago in a pleasure house. If she is alive, let that be a miracle, and a second miracle that you should never see her again. She is my mistake. Do not pursue this path,

Sorren. Truths, these bones of the past, can never be placed back once they are dug from their graves, worried Gloriatrix as she wrung her hands.

"I can see that it is bothering you," said Sorren, startling her.

"I...indeed."

"I would shut him off if I could. Snap the cord that brought him back like the spine of the weasel that he is," sneered Sorren, clenching the bedsheets in angry fistfuls. "But it doesn't work that way, the magik. Life flourishes, even in a garden of death; it puts down roots and grows. That cold body is as much his as it was before. Now I feel that he has his mind back, too, and he will no longer listen as a proper empty reborn should. I cannot control him. Now, if I could get close to him again..."

The nekromancer's hands squeezed to whiteness, and his gaze twittered with black thoughts. After thinking for a moment, Gloriatrix was jolted by something he had said amid his rambling.

"My son, are you implying that Vortigern has remembered who he was?"

Sorren slapped her with a look as if she was dense. "I'm not implying anything. That is precisely what has happened."

While Gloriatrix chewed deeply on her ever-complicating issues, Sorren rambled on. Speaking of Vortigern dredged up his most unwanted memories, but also many of his favorite ones, and he waxed bitter while reminiscing.

"I remember when Vort and I were young. We would play out in the gardens among the thornbushes and climb the highest trees we could find. We pretended to be conquering masters, gone to herd the savages from abroad to the mines of Menos. Mostly, we scraped ourselves terribly. Well, me more than Vort. I never fared well with the physical disciplines, as you know. Yet I always tried to keep up with him. I wanted to win his pride, as if that were a glorious trophy that I could put on the mantel of my achievements: Vortigern's respect. Harrumph...do you remember the day I fell?"

"Hmm? What? Oh, yes, I remember," responded Gloriatrix. "That was a mother's worst fear realized: the screaming of children with not a head in sight. I thought that an assassin had come for you both."

She is chasing the cries of her children through the clawing hedge-maze. Madness has seized her, instinct has hold of her every sense, and she is moving so quickly that the Ironguards are puffing somewhere behind her, calling for her to slow and be wary. But she will not slow, she cannot, not until she finds her boys. It is storming and slippery. The rain burns her eyes, and she stumbles into thorns. The thunder trumpets, yet her calls sound louder than the elements. Please, please, she begs, to whatever forces heed the prayers of mortals—even the cursed kings, if they will court her pleas. Then the bushes part, and her sons are painted in lightning: small Sorren is being held by his wailing brother. Her child is not dead, but glazed and placid, perhaps in shock, judging from the angle at which his leg is twisted.

"You shouldn't have been playing out there, especially not in a storm. We had the physicians putting those awful drops in our eyes for a week." The Iron Queen's mask split with an awkward, much unused smile. "Climbing trees like the apes of Alabion. Really, you two. I knew that one of you would slip, and I'm not surprised that you did."

Sorren and Gloriatrix saw each other then as they scarcely ever did. Not as nekromancer or queen, but as people. As a child and his mother. Sorren's honesty welled up, untapped and raw.

"Would it be odd if I said that moment when you found us was the happiest occasion of my life? Even the pain faded for a while. You may have thought that it was both of us screaming, Mother, and I tell you today that it was not. Vortigern was my voice. He was my safety. And when you appeared, that fury, that cold armor that you always wear melted like so much snow in the rain. There was the three of us, and the storm, and yet somehow a peace that no thunder could shake. I would take that moment and frame it, if I could: a phantograph of eternity. That would be all I could ask for, to see, live, and feel that time again and again. How strange you must think I am," confessed Sorren, and turned away from his mother's drilling stare.

"You are not odd, my son. It is a lovely memory to hold on to, and we have so few of those," Gloriatrix said.

They smiled, privately.

Rap-rap-rap!

After the succession of knocks, the door to Sorren's chamber was opened and an Ironguard made his way in.

"Iron Queen, noble Master, I did not mean to interrupt."

"You've interrupted nothing," snapped Gloriatrix, once more in her armor. "What news have you?"

"One of the Broker's men has delivered a message."

479

For a speck or two, the Ironguard hemmed and hawed over the scroll in his hand until Gloriatrix ordered the paper from him.

"His words, not mine, Your Eminence," the Ironguard said, bowing as he exited the room.

Already she was reading the simple missive: *I have the witch. I shall hold her here, where it is safe and warm, in chains of cold iron until you wish to collect her. We do not need any further ineptitude in her keeping.*

"Filthy scoundrel," she cursed, and was swiftly standing. "It seems a trip to the Undercomb is in order to gather our tool against the West. Come, Sorren, your presence and power is needed in matters like this. Sorren?"

He was not hearing his mother, but a dim and rusty whisper, like leaves blowing over a tombstone. He was heeding the one from beyond who seldom spoke, and always did so with wisdom. In a way, this was his true mother, for her icy love had birthed him into this world anew. Gloriatrix sensed this, not merely his separation, but the wintriness that crisped the air, the chill that ate at her marrow, and the candles that sputtered out and welcomed darkness. A shadow had entered the room, cast from something immense and unseen.

Said the winter whisper to Sorren's ears alone: **Find her, take her. She is the Daughter of Fate. She is the instrument of our war. We cannot rise against the Black Queen without her. She must be controlled. She must be ours.**

"She must be ours," repeated Sorren.

When his reptilian eyes found Gloriatrix in the gloom, she gasped and shuddered. She did not recognize the stranger who beheld her.

V

Reading the tea leaves was among the oldest of soothsayer traditions; it felt appropriate to Elissandra in light of the confluence of events and powers happening at this moment. Even in the sanctuary of her cement-and-feliron bunker, the ripples of an environment in turmoil still carried: in the pressure in her ears, the vibrating of the bookshelves, the flickering of the sunny globes ensconced about the quaint studious room, and in the rattling of her porcelain teacup set upon its saucer. The world was trembling. And if it shivered this deeply in the earth, she wondered what racket was occurring above. Before going into seclusion, she had warned her immediate family; told them to take their children and most trusted servants belowground. As for the rest of the masters and Iron sages, they could fare for themselves; such was the way of the wild. With every disaster, Geadhain purged herself, and Menos was a city long due for a cleansing.

Tonight, the tea leaves were being coy. They said nothing of the catastrophe, of the Daughter of Fate, or of anything that transpired outside this refuge. *As if the future is unwritten,* she mused, and was twice as intrigued. *The prophecy of lifetimes past is coming to fruition. I wonder what it will bear. A new world, we are promised, and yet the outcome eludes my sight. Darkness or light? Where will you lead us, Morigan? Back to Alabion, I would hope. If anyone can heal the wound left by the Everfair King, you can.*

Right when Elissandra was about to push the teacup away, a stunning image manifested: a cloud like a dark claw reaching over the hemisphere of a world and a starscape of sorrowful eyes. She had only a flash, and then the picture shifted out of focus, and she was staring at black meaningless spackle. *A Black Queen,* she thought of the greedy hand. But who were the watchers in the sky? They could be any of a number of mysteries: the Sisters Three, the Immortal Kings, an unnamed queen. Too many mysteries and not enough answers; no wonder future had no clear divinations. Who were these creatures, these forces? Where had they come from? And what more lay buried in time?

Suddenly, the shelter groaned and spit a bit of dust from the ceiling. Her children woke from the noise and called out to her immediately. Putting aside her enigmas, Elissandra rushed to her younglings. Two pale youths, one male, the other female, both with their mother's lean features and silvery eyes, were sharing the bunker's only bed and stuck to each other in fear. She peeled them apart and fit herself between the two.

"Tessa." She kissed the little girl's head. "Eli." She kissed her other child's crown. "There is no need to be afraid. We could not be safer here."

"What of Papa?" asked Tessariel.

Elissandra had used a farspeaking stone earlier to advise their father— her third cousin—to find the sturdiest cellar he could and hole up in it. He would know when it was time to come out. "He is doing business in Carthac. He knows to find shelter. Do not worry for him, my lamblings."

The bunker shook again; a book slipped off one of the shelves and onto the floor.

"A story," said Elissandra cheerily, and ran to fetch the volume. The book was one of her favorites from a childhood a hundred and some years ago. A collection of classic tales from Alabion that she had not seen since she was a youngling herself: *The Untamed*. Fondly, she caressed the stippled green trees on its cover and took a short breath as the tingle of foresight came over her. She settled back into bed with her children and selfishly thumbed through the pages of the book, reading accounts of beguiling enchantresses, speaking bears, ageless sisters, and the saddest story of a lord of Pining Row who buried his bloodmate and then left Alabion forever. *The Wolf*, she realized, and could not look away from the great beast upon the page.

"Mother, I thought you were to read to us," complained Elineth. "You seem mostly to be reading to yourself."

"She's *seeing* at the moment, you dunce," said Tessariel, and slapped her brother's shoulder. "You wouldn't understand. You don't have the gift."

Quick as a striking snake, the boy slapped his sister back.

"My lamblings," exclaimed Elissandra, and put a stop to their fighting with some firm hands of her own. "'Tis no time for quarreling, but a time for unity. Your sister speaks truly. I have been in the grip of many a vision today. Yet even the fates can wait. For here I am with my two lamblings, as snug as any winter beast in its burrow, with food and comforts for weeks, should we need them."

"Weeks!" the children complained together.

"It shan't come to that," clucked Elissandra. "Now listen up and listen well, for I shall tell you the stories of where we have come from. Of a land that we may one day return to. I shall tell you of Alabion."

The children gathered close and gave all their attention as asked, as pert as two tiny birds to the beak of their mother. Flipping back to the first page, Elissandra began at the beginning of *The Untamed* with the story of the Lady Dymphana and the wicked fisherman who forced her to be his bride. Even as the chamber steadily rattled, and other books and breakable things began to tumble to the floor, Elissandra's melodious voice managed to keep her children calm. For there was nothing to fear, all things—fair or foul—had their season, and the best one could do was to weather the worst. Wars would come and wars would go, and this one would be darker than any other. But fussing over inevitabilities was for another day. Down here, in the shuddering dark, she was not an Iron sage or even a seer. She was a mother.

On she read without a care, while above her the storm ripped Menos to its foundations.

VI

After crawling on their hands and knees out of a moldy sewer pipe that barely accommodated Caenith's size and onto a slippery ledge, the two men carefully came to their feet. Falling would be deadly, dangerous even to Caenith, for under them a pummeling rapid crashed off rocks of metal, damns of splintered wood, and bolls of wire that would shatter bodies like ceramic dolls. The Wolf held Macha as the most precious of cargo. He would not lose her to an accident after coming this far, even though the thread that tied her to life was almost frayed to snapping. Cautiously as cavers, the men spread their backs to the wet stone and crept forward with their hands and feet. Darkness gave them a cover that would have otherwise left them completely exposed, and they followed the ledge until it met with a beach and then climbed down into dunes of refuse.

"To think that you made this journey as often as you did," said Caenith, in praise of steadier ground.

"I was a younger man, clearly," wheezed Thackery. "I could not have done this without you, Caenith."

"Nor I, you," replied the Wolf.

They celebrated their brotherhood with a nod, and then Caenith was sniffing after the scent of his bloodmate once more. Centuries of the waste of a wasteful nation had accumulated on the shores of the Drowned River: toys and knickknacks, broken bottles, sheets, torn paintings, spoiled food, furniture frames, and springs. Every imaginable permutation of junk did they see, as well as mounds of pure rot, the decay of which they had to shield their mouths from. Regrettably, they stepped in buttery matter once or twice. For the most part, though, the thin roads threading the heaps were free of debris in accordance with city mandates. An order was in place here, as inconceivable as it might be for an outsider like Caenith to construe. Above, the profligates of Menos dropped their shite, piss, and whatever else was the by-product of their all-consuming whims down toilets, or into larger repositories, and left it for the pipes below to sort out. Into the reservoirs it went then, vast drums drawn from the sweet lakes and streams of Alabion, to be filtered through machines and magik. What was deemed drinkable enough was given back to the system, while the larger, less digestible—even by Menosian alchemy—pieces were shat into the Drowned River. Sanitation slaves were supposed to tend to the mess, though it was a bit like shoveling a sandbank in the desert; there was always *more* sand. In truth, the shore of the Drowned River was mostly abandoned until the garbage reached critical masses that threatened to block the circulation of water out of Menos or had summoned enough rats to cause a dread plague. During such times, enormous teams of slaves would dig in these putrescent piles, wetting themselves in rubbish until their backs broke or fevers claimed them—then they would be thrown into the river to drift away with the fruits of their labors. Thackery kept an eye out for these operations as they slunk through the flies and filth, and saw neither workers nor persons of any sort. The Drowned River's shores were quite abandoned.

Caenith, on the other hand, understood nothing of this unpleasant infrastructure and thought only of the strange flotsam that would sometimes lodge itself on the banks of Alabion's streams, back as far as his days there. He shook his head, appalled by the excess of these people. Luckily, Morigan's sweet trail of incense was all the easier for him to track amid the greasy air, and it was growing riper by the step. *Almost, my Fawn*, he huffed. *I shall take you away from this. Somewhere silent, where the voices and fates cannot reach you. Only you, and I, and Thackery—anyone you choose to invite into our pack.*

As the first sounds of existence came to him, the Wolf traded his ebullience for vigilance. Odd sounds those were: whispers, shuffles, snapping, and choked air. To novice ears, those noises were innocuous. To Caenith, they were the music of murder.

"Trouble precedes us," he whispered to Thackery.

The cluttered hills alongside them became small rises, and patches of stone flooring could at last be seen. Soon the garbage was too loosely dispersed to hide behind, which did not matter, for Caenith could see where Morigan's fragrance was leading him. With the river rushing behind the compost to their right and a wall in the dimmest distance, the only way off the beach appeared to be the large sphere bubbling out of the darkness many, many strides to their left. He noted holes in the structure, which seemed to have been made of much of the detritus found in the area, although with an architect's care. Something lived there, and a gloomy nostalgia claimed him—as if there was an echo of Alabion here, albeit one that had ill tidings. *A lair*, he thought, but his ancient mind was filled with too many recollections to find the one he needed. The quandary did not give him pause, though, and he was quickly moving toward the building. He picked the deepest darks to slip into, even though he did not feel that they were being watched.

When they were almost upon the looming mass, Thackery hissed, "Wait."

"What is it?" asked Caenith.

"Shouldn't we take precautions? I have no idea what this place is, and it gives me an eerie chill. It was certainly not here in my days."

"Precautions are unnecessary. The path has been opened for us, and there can be only danger ahead. Look," whispered Caenith.

He didn't have the Wolf's sight, but as he squinted into the murk of the nearest hole leading into the sphere, he saw a tumble of darkness. "What is that?"

"A body," replied the Wolf.

Caenith was darting ahead before Thackery could begin any of his frantic questions. He followed Caenith into the dank passage, stepping over the corpse of a man wrapped in black like an assassin. From the way his limbs flopped, he seemed broken in many spots.

"What did that to him?" muttered Thackery.

"I don't know." Caenith took several long sniffs and then frowned. "But it's still here. I smell Morigan, too. Twice. In two different places. The nearest isn't far. Whatever killed this man is with her. Here, take Macha. I need the freedom of movement, and your magik could bring this construction down on us." Before handing the girl over, Caenith kissed her sweating forehead. *"Ta mued rachaidh mea mionghàire gan mhoill, cén uair ta leaghas."* (You will smile for me again, once you are well.)

Macha fell into Thackery's arms as weightless as a bag of down; she did not have much time remaining in this life. A number of urgencies drove the Wolf ahead: his need to reunite with Morigan, the drumming of water far overhead, Macha's dribbling chronex, and the confusion of scents that threatened to turn him around in this place. Among these, the reek of these tunnels was the most prominent, overpowering all other smells. It was the muskiness of an animal's unwashed loins. This was the stink of a creature that, again, he felt he should know. Had he hunted this monster before? No, that didn't seem correct. Was it a hunter itself, then? *Aye,* his instincts told him, but how muddled was the mind of the ageless Wolf that he still could not recall from whence. He needed his concentration to pursue the scents of his bloodmate, so he refocused himself upon that. For the tunnels had no real order to their arrangement, unless that layout was meant to confuse, and the paths sloped up and down, left and right, often meeting at the queerest junctions with passageways both high and low. Discouragingly, the walls were sharp with objects, and the lights were few, far apart, and dull as dying embers. But they were never lost, not with the Wolf's guidance, and they found a macabre trail of bread crumbs, more bodies of the shadowmen, to tell them that they were tailing Morigan's captors. The Wolf heard footsteps and susurrations well before Thackery ever could. He made a *hush* gesture and stalked off ahead, leaving Thackery to sneak up as best he could. As soon as the commotion started, Thackery ground caution under his running feet and hurried into the tunnel where the Wolf had gone.

In the terrible lighting, it was hard for Thackery to see what he had blundered into. Down past the grand shadow of Caenith's back was an athletic, darkly dressed woman doing the shouting and bearing glinting arms. "Release them!" she was screaming, while taking swipes at Caenith, who snapped and bit at her attacks. The Wolf was too occupied to outright smack her away, for he had a hand and knee upon one figure on the ground, and with his strong fingers he had caged another man up against the wall.

"Where is she? Where is Morigan?" he snarled.

"M-morigan!" exclaimed the woman.

The man with the wild hair and exotic features crushed against the wall was pulling at his prison and desperately trying to wheeze a reply. Caenith heard enough of what was being said to loosen his grip.

"Blood...*hech hech*...mate," coughed the man. "You're her bloodmate."

"If you wouldn't mind getting your rather large self off me," said the struggling gentleman under Caenith's knee, apparently unbothered by the weight. "This is really more of an annoyance than anything productive."

Thackery had the mind of a spider, and he spun the connections quickly into reason. "Caenith, wait! Allies, remember! You said she had found allies!"

The Wolf's fury simmered. "Allies. That would explain why you smell like her. Is this true?"

"Yes!" the three answered.

Caenith released both men. One collapsed sloppily and was helped to stand by the cloaked woman. The other sprang upright as a spring daisy—the most notable aspects of him were his incredible paleness and the solid blackness of his eyes. His spicy aroma was not the stink of an undying thing, yet it wasn't the freshness of life, either.

"You're not quite dead," said Caenith, a bit surprised.

"You're not quite a man," replied Vortigern.

"We have no time for this," snapped Mouse. "Your bruiser has no doubt rung the dinner bell through the Broker's lair."

Thackery swallowed. "The Broker's lair?"

"Yes."

That said, Mouse quickly pointed about and lastly at herself. "Vortigern, Kanatuk, Mouse. Introductions have been made. Lovely to meet you, Caenith, and whoever you are. Let's go."

"Thackery," he answered, hurrying to catch up with the rest while carrying Macha. He and the snappy young woman continued a bit of conversation as they hustled along.

"Thackery, hmm? I think you're my great uncle. That there is your nephew. You may not have recognized him, being a bit dead and all."

Thackery almost tripped from the realization. "I am?"

"Yes."

"I am."

"Who is the child you're carrying?"

"Macha."

"She looks unwell."

"She is."

"Hmm."

A few strides forward and the Wolf elbowed past Kanatuk's lead. Frantically, he sniffed for Morigan; almost hunched to all fours was he, in full spirit of the chase. His Fawn was close; he could hear her whimpering, her noises more thrilling to his blood than the gasp of any prey he had ever hunted. He wasn't sure where he was leading them. His head was in a haze; his limbs were mindless of his body. Tunnels blurred by, and there were only two pulses throbbing and beating together: his and hers. At last, he sped into a chamber wider that the constrictions of this foul maze and strewn with insignificant articles, and there was the pearl and crimson sliver of light that was his Fawn. How bright and glorious she was among the filth. How fragrant a flower among the toadstools.

"Morigan!" he roared.

She had known where to look for him. She had felt the heat rushing upon her, inside her: the passion of the Wolf. In his warm wind, he swept to her, seized her restraints, and pulled them apart as if they were yarn. They did not kiss, but touched each other's dirty cheeks in teary wonder. For their journey had taken them into the need and trust that came with true hardship and devotion—a faith that they would find each other, a bond forged against the strongest separation. Without the feliron, they could speak into the other's mind, they could bask in the other's fire and light.

Do not fear that you will walk this world alone. Do not fear the kings or nameless monsters. I shall stand with you, and you will stand with me. Death will not separate us, said the Wolf.

She had heard these words once, long before any of this terror began, and she believed them more than ever now.

And I shall stand with you forever, she said.

Forever, promised the Wolf.

No truer a vow had been made in this world. They knew it, they felt it, and they embraced and held that moment for as long as they could. Then the unusual trembling of the room—something was happening above, Caenith was sure of it—and the watchful presences nearby drew them from their peace.

I see you've met my friends.

Morigan glanced past the arms of her bloodmate to the tired folk gathered by her—Vortigern being the exception. For a speck, she smiled at them, and then the vestiges of her euphoria dwindled, and she recalled the terrible danger they were in.

"By the kings! We have to get out of here! A jabberwokargh!"

Pain stretched the word into a screeching note as the bees violently attacked their mistress. Nothing she Willed would stall them, nor could the heat of the Wolf deter their assault. The bees were uncompromising. They were free, and they had something that she *must* see. Morigan went slack in the arms of the Wolf; she heard his howling voice as she faded into elsewhere.

Into the milky dark she tumbles, helpless and bodiless on the silver cloud of her magik. No! Return me to Caenith! she demands. Yet she has no control. The reins are broken, and the horses run wild. Through the shapeless tides of time and space, she is hurtled, roughly, erratically, and with the greatest of insistency. A trip that should cross a thousand spans takes her a mere speck.

SEE! boom the bees.

At that, the darkness breaks, and she is swooping over a scorched land with the chaos of war welling under her intangible wings. Immediately, she forgets the thrills and terror of where her flesh casing lies. She is engulfed by the horror of what the bees have revealed to her. The smoke and death, the screams of noble men, and the malevolent chanting of an endless swell of man-things—men, women, children, and beasts alchemized with metal, made with sword hands and needle teeth—that pour upon a faltering bastion of white warriors and sorcerers casting desperate magiks from peaks heaped in the dead. Two armies, two kings; this is their war, she realizes. Though it is more of a slaughter, for the doom of the white warriors is fated to arrive in moments. As magnificent as the carnage is, the bees pull her away, toward the rear of the battle, toward the source of the unholy river of the damned. A shimmer of white and gold is there, two men whose greatness can be seen like stars in the sky from any distance.

The kings, she gasps.

"Her eyes!" cried Thackery.

After the stunning flash of light, Morigan had fainted. When her companions gathered round the angry Wolf, the radiance still had not gone out, only dimmed. For the light came from within Morigan, streaming through her mouth and stare in misty rays, as if she had swallowed a torch. In the throe of a nightmare, she clawed at her bloodmate, and he had to restrain her tightly.

"What...what am I seeing? What is wrong with her?" demanded Thackery.

Caenith could sense Morigan's remoteness and fear; he understood that the fates had taken her as a witness. He answered crossly, "She's away. Very far away from us. Watching something dire."

Mouse, the eternal survivalist, wasn't particularly interested in the lightshow happening with her companion or what it meant. They needed to flee. Morigan had been warning them about something prior to this spell taking her. The oddness of Morigan's word inspired a cold dread, and Mouse ejaculated it like a bug in her mouth.

"Jabberywoka! Or something! That's what she said! And to run!"

Caenith rose a bit to his senses. Suddenly, the stinking musk and nest of regurgitated garbage began to chime warning bells in his head. The legends were old, but easily remembered for their wickedness. All pups were cautioned of the deformed bastard offspring of two skin-walkers, these hateful abominations who deplored their miserable selves and the world that created them and dwelled in depths unfit for the living. Nests of bone, shite, and rotten meat. *Or refuse*, he thought, glancing around.

"Jabberwok," muttered the Wolf.

"What are you two talking about? What is a Jabberwok?" asked Thackery.

Morigan moaned, falling deeper into her nightmare, and her sight flared and pranced among the shadows in the room. Revealed upon the roof was one shadow: lumpy and enormous, swishing with lizardy sinuousness. They saw it. They were terrified by it and flushed from its tremendous heat. Its curdled sweat—the piss and blood and grease that it rolled in, the *fear*—made them cough.

"Jabberwok!" screamed Caenith.

"HAROOOOOGH!"

The Jabberwok trilled its cry in return, showering them all with powdery rubble, and charged. In the quaking dusty chamber, the monster was as fleeting and vicious as a hurricane. Reeling in shock, the two armed among them—Mouse and Kanatuk—crazily thrust weapons at the blubbery snapping snake that was instantly upon them. *Don't think about what you're seeing!* counseled Mouse's inner voice, lest the madness paralyze her. There was madness aplenty to reflect on, should she survive: the iron jaw, the disarrayed teeth, the flapping wings, and beady eyes of glorious hate. Relentlessly it fought, biting them into a corner and dissuading any escapes with its thrashing mace of a tail. Mouse shrieked as she thrust her daggers through any bit of scaly fur that she could, while Kanatuk was steelier in his focus and cleaner with his strikes; he opened a few gashes upon the creature, though nothing that would kill it. Vortigern and the others had not joined the fray, and Mouse called for her father. A howl rent her back, and she cowered from the force of it; even the Jabberwok faltered in its nerve. Then Vortigern was pulling her, and her weapons clattered away. Kanatuk had thrown his weapon at the monster and was stumbling along at her side. Everything was happening so fast, she didn't understand where her father was hauling her, or what the immense black shape was that flew past them, smelling of dog and roaring loudly enough to weaken her knees. Whatever it was, it shot into the Jabberwok like a bullet of darkness, and the two monstrous shapes tumbled away in a blur of claws and a thunder of growls.

She tripped and had to turn away, finally looking ahead. Thackery seemed to be jogging at the lead; her father had her in the cold vise of a hand; the strangely glowing seer was slumped over Vortigern's shoulder and clutching and biting at him—still a victim to her dark spell; and Kanatuk huffed at her side. So all were safe, except for...Caenith? A fantastic howl, triumphant and raw, followed by a gurgling trill of the Jabberwok rippled up the tunnel at their backs, and in the absolute hysteria, Mouse drew the conclusion that Caenith was somehow all right. Perhaps even making that first call. She had lost the plot, surely. Dread and fire rode them ragged, as they floundered over themselves through passages that had begun to shiver and creak threateningly. Their peril wasn't only behind them, but where they were headed, for the Broker's nest was losing its cohesion. *The whole place is falling apart*, thought Mouse, another fear to be added to the lunatic's cauldron. More howls and trilling echoed, metal and gobs of trash fell on her and in their path. She did not consider that she would die here and be buried among garbage; she ran with purpose and that steadfast fire that had always warmed her. *I shall live! We shall live!* Mouse had found a new voice to motivate her, and that was the only one she heeded now.

In that tunnel of focus she found herself, and when it suddenly expanded and rushed with stale but plentiful air, she knew that they had escaped the nest. Safe, or safe enough, and upon the destitute shores of the Drowned River. But why was the land still shaking? Why was trash bouncing like ticks off the stone? What was the pounding of a hundred drums in her ears? All fair questions, and she had some of an answer as a splitting crack rang out, and she was swiftly wrenched aside by her father and saved from a chalky explosion. *A slab*, she realized, as she and the others staggered upright. A gigantic tile dropped from above. While waving away the smoke, she peered for the source of the accident. Yet as with many events at the moment, there was not the slightest pause for voyeurism—which could be fatal—and her indelibly caring father was tugging her hand anew. However, she did see a swirling window of red and blue light up through the fissure in the ceiling. Was this a window to outside? she wondered, and if that was the case, what strange fires were lit in Menos? Again, mysteries and mysteries, with no time to solve any of them. Running, running was all that there was.

She had never felt so hunted and so trapped in a nightmare as she did right now. The collapse of Menos upon itself became a dreadful strident noise louder than her heart or any of the shouts her companions were making as they dodged more crumbling meteors. Persistence was in all of them, though, these men and women hardened and bitter against death, and they were nimble and alive to the dangers. *We have come too far; only a little farther to go*, Mouse imagined them saying.

They reached the larger dunes without being crushed, and Thackery wound onward—Mouse saw him whispering madly to the little girl he held, the child she had yet to see move. Here, they had greater worries than Thackery's sanity. For the piles were unstable, teetering, and toppling, transforming into fetid sludge, and water had risen from the Drowned River and arced in gouts that could batter them away like passengers on a sinking ship. While they splashed through brown water, the trills of the Jabberwok and the howls of the second monster resounded in the caterwauling. Even above the din, she could hear it, and knew that the monsters were close. Still, this was hardly the end of their peril. The company tripped round a shifting mountain and were slammed by surprise.

"Thackery!"

Sorren hailed them from atop a metal platform swimming in garbage. In attendance was the Iron Queen herself. She clung to her son on the unsteady stage; she expressed none of the nekromancer's bravura, though she possessed a similar sparkle of ire in her gaze toward the sage. A foursome of Ironguards stood beneath them, wading in filth, but with their rifles dry, cocked, and tipped with blue flame.

"Always the rat!" ranted Sorren. "Sneaking off to some tunnel, no doubt! So eager to get to wherever you think you're going that you ran past us like a frightened herd! Well, I am the hunter today! I shall have my trophy! Your heart! And with it, my *vengeance!*"

Another roar and trill contested this, but it went largely ignored in the groaning of the world and the smashing of boulder-sized objects around them. Although this was a confrontation that Thackery would need to put his soul at rest—this resolution between himself, Sorren, and Gloria—it would not be a fair exchange if he was to lose Morigan and Macha in the process.

Bitterly and with fury, he spat back, "Gloria! Curb your fool son! See how the world turns to ash! I would settle this here and now was Menos not about to drop on our heads! Our debts are old and soaked in blood; they will endure like the mountains of Kor'Keth. Our hate will shine brighter and longer than any love! For we hate with passion! We hate with our souls! But this moment is not the time for us and our violent resolution! Lay down your arms and let us pass, or we shall die in senseless rage together! Crushed under garbage, buried, and lost!"

"Are you asking me to let you go?" exclaimed Gloriatrix.

"I'm asking you to consider your own life! The life of that offal you call a son, even!"

"Never!" shrieked Sorren, losing all control. "You will die! You, as well, Vortigern! And you, Lenora! A hundred deaths, a hundred times for each of you!"

Thus spoken, the nekromancer burst into maniacal laughter, and his figure beamed with rays of shadow. In that instant, Thackery could have ended everything without raising a finger, could have let fate determine the punishment and outcome of his familial war. For the vaults above were gaping with cracks, whole segments of buildings and roofs, carriages, and wailing folk were falling into the Undercomb, so many bodies and bricks splattering the sloshing junk heap in a deluge of chaos. Flames were among the cascade, and shards of ice fell. What could be seen could not be totally understood; reality was out of order. One grand accretion of street signs, burning shingles, furniture, and walls, all packed in hunks of snow, was plummeting toward his darkly fuming nephew. He could have said nothing and let the landslide erase Sorren, Gloria, and all the tangled sins they shared, yet out of a sickening kinship or a need to squeeze the blood from these wretches himself, he called out.

"Gloria! Above you! The roof!"

Snarling, Sorren looked up and saw the barrage of elemental death descending, and he knew that he could have only his vengeance or his mother—not both. His power blazed into a black sphere of hungry sorcery about himself and Gloria. The pitiable Ironguards, outside the ebony shell, screamed for their makers as they were interred in tombs of scorching, frost-burned wreckage. A puff of snow and licks of fire flushed the area, and the stunned companions were dumb as mules for a speck until they threw off their astonishment and remembered to run.

Did they live? wondered Thackery fleetingly. Who knew? He hoped that they did, so they could finish their pledge of murder to each other. Mouse, at this time, had fully descended into a river of disbelief. *The sky is falling and raining fire and people. Ice and streets and lampposts. Ha-ha! Ha-ha-ha-ha!* She and Kanatuk were guided on like gawking tourists by the only two men who had yet to drop their wits. The waters were deepening, the world rocked and slid out from under them, obstacles floated and flung themselves at them. Somehow, they reached a delicate precipice and were told by the barking old man to climb along it. *Don't look down, not down,* Mouse cautioned herself, as the rising, frothing maelstrom under her was commanding of her fear. But looking to the storm they were creeping away from was no better, and twice as surreal, as though someone had crushed up toy houses and thrown them into a furnace and a snowstorm.

"HAROOOOOGH!"

The Jabberwok's trill nearly pulled her off the ledge, too, as it wasn't far off: down on the submerged shore from which they had come. Two shadows rolled into the mire there, and she was gripped by their conflict. A ball of fur and teeth and a fatty, hideous worm. She paid heed at a critical instance, for the battle that had been raging this whole while was brutally decided, and the Wolf—yes, it was a giant, hulking wolf, she saw—clamped his fangs upon the Jabberwok's tail and then thrashed it to and fro. First, the Wolf smashed the Jabberwok against the rock wall on which the companions climbed, and it misted the air with blood. Then, as the Jabberwok dribbled out a mewl, the Wolf mercilessly tossed the beast into the Drowned River. Mouse and the others watched it scrabbling against flotsam, bleating and despairing to live. But they gave it no quarter and only a black pity, as the devouring currents eventually pulled it under. When Mouse glanced to see what had become of the Wolf, it had vanished, although a naked and familiar man was now speedily ascending the ledge many strides behind them: Caenith.

What remained of sense in the world dissipated after that, and there was only the trek up the shuddering rock, and the anxiety over every opportunity to fall, which somehow none of them did. The old man, even burdened and one-armed, was admirably agile and well ahead of the rest in reaching the pipe into which they all soon crawled. Twisting and turning through the grating metal guts of Menos they went, ever afraid that the thin walls would suddenly buckle. For a time, Morigan acted as a torch in the darkness, and then her light eventually ran out; she stopped her moaning and struggling, too. When the tubes were tall enough for standing, the naked man ran up to claim his bride from Vortigern. As he brushed by, under the stinking grease and gore of the Jabberwok, she could smell the animal that he had been, as well. She mumbled a dazed thank you to the Wolf, but it may not have ever left her mouth, and he did not act as if he heard. He was too engrossed in the care of the woman he carried. How strong their love was. She could sense it like the heat of his body. If she were a painter, there would not be enough colors to capture their passion: red, if anything, the deepest crimson, a love of blood and sacrifice. Deliberations on her place in this tale—for she felt she inexorably had a role to play—wrestled in Mouse's mind as the dark trek continued.

Light came at last, though with it not the succor of freedom, for the red and blue glows that glimmered in the tunnel foreran the phantasmagoria beyond. Outside, it was day and it was night and nothing was as it should be. The clouds were a red sunset that had not fallen and were lambent with twists of whiteness. There was rain and sleet, a whipping wind, and a hail of embers. With the vines that had concealed the aqueduct burned away, they could observe the apocalypse in quiet awe. Although they had reached the point in their flight where escape was presented to them, the company could not move past the gate. They waited. For what, exactly, no one said. Only the naked Wolf detached himself and approached the exit: there, he stood as dignified as a tattooed war chief in his firelit wounds and stared with his knowing gaze out into the end. This was an end; he was certain of it. The close of an age. The dawn of something darker.

I saw it, whispered Morigan to him. He had felt her spirit wake a while back, her light trickling into him, though she was still too spent to stir.

What did you see, my Fawn?

I witnessed the End. I saw one king fall and a shadow take them both. When the Everfair King broke, he broke the world. I saw fire and ice...tears of the Geadhain. How the Green Mother grieves and grieves. Tell me that it is not true.

The Wolf could not.

The storm will pass, as all things do, he said. *And you and I shall go on.*

He kissed her cheek, so gently and indifferently to the profane tempest, symbolic of how unshaken he was and would always be, and then he sat. Duly, the others became braver and came forward, as well. They huddled as a pack to wait for the storm to blow over. Then, and only then, would they explore the new world that awaited them.

XXI

THE ROAD AHEAD

I

"Menos," announced Galivad.

Off in the dark it gleamed, the stronghold of all sins on Geadhain, as black as the hearts of its masters, with white lights streaking from its ramparts like the spirits of the pure seeking to escape. Both of the weary companions had grimaces upon their faces, though Galivad's was rather intense. Rowena knew the cast of hatred, and he wore it.

"Have you been to Menos before?" she asked.

"Once. To find my mother's killer."

After slapping her with that disclosure, he strode ahead. A storm was brewing on high, and the warmth of the miner's caravan was sorely missed by Rowena; they had parted at one of the roads wending north. The whistling darkness and desolation of this stripped and rocky place kept the travelers on edge. Moreover, while it wasn't more than a frightened fancy not worth mentioning, Rowena thought that she had seen a large shadow bounding by them in the fields not too long ago. So there was wildlife hidden here, the ferocious kind, she wagered. Perhaps the beast was hunkering down for the impending weather. The menfolk were surely sparse and hurrying on their steeds and carts toward the city. She and Galivad were mostly alone.

KRAKKLL!

When thunder and lightning suddenly tore up the sky, and the first drops of rain struck them like pellets of ice, they knew that they would not make the city in time for shelter. Fortunately, a flat jut of stone off the road availed them, and they ran to it: soaked as drowned rats and shivering once they arrived. With the rain falling in sheets and unlikely to be relenting anytime soon, the pair settled in on a high cold stone and watched the water slowly swamp the soil about them. Since his cheery farewell to the miners that morning, Galivad had been quite taciturn, and Rowena found herself missing his loquaciousness enough to start up a conversation herself.

"Your mother's killer...did you find him?"

The question hadn't come out as she intended; her social graces were as blunt as a mallet, and words never ceased to stumble in her mouth. While the thunder and lightning continued, her companion sank deeper into his sodden cloak. He did not look at her, but at the storm, and Rowena suspected that she was not about to get an answer. Galivad's quiet response was a surprise.

"*Her,*" he whispered. "My mother's killer was a she."

"A woman?"

"You seem amazed," he laughed. "Women are capable of the worst cruelties. You cannot be a bearer of life without understanding the opposite side of that covenant, without knowing death. Some women indulge in this darkness. They become as drunk on evil as my mother was on good. Look only to the Iron Queen to see a woman who has disowned herself from everything noble about her sex. Beatrice of El, the wife of Iron Sage Moreth, is a woman wickeder than any Iron Queen, I say. For while the Iron Queen throws away her virtue for power—a pursuit that I can understand—the mistress of El is an epicure of pain. Her husband might rule the flesh of thousands, but she has cravings for their minds, their light. She can take things from people. Possessions that one should never be able to claim: beauty, hopes, dreams, an artist's touch."

"She is a sorceress, then," muttered Rowena.

Galivad snorted at the notion. "She is a thief. A vulture of souls. There is some magik involved, I shall grant you that. But to call her anything more than a witch is a disgrace to the lowliest conjurer. If she has any spells, it is only the one: a spell of reaping. Beatrice took something from my mother, and not only her life. I would see her burn for it, the whole of Menos, too."

Rowena did not push to discover what the mistress of El had stolen, nor how far along Galivad was in hunting her. Being a wise listener, she could sense that he had attempted revenge before, probably coming as far as Menos, and failed.

"I hope you find justice one day," she said. In what Rowena thought was a kindly tone, she added, "Do remember that we are not here for vengeance."

"I do not need to be reminded of my duties, Sword," snapped Galivad.

Huffing, Galivad shifted on the slippery rock to face away from his companion. Soggy arses and soggy sentiments were all that they had to share until Rowena pulled out the bit of bread the miners had given them and offered half of it as a token of apology to him. He was red from regret as he accepted the food, and he gave fluttering glances to Rowena while they ate.

"I would never place my wants over the responsibilities of our kingdom," he mumbled between bites. "We are here to find the smith, the sage, and the silver-eyed girl. I have no greater priorities."

"I know. I do not always express myself with delicacy," admitted Sword Rowena.

"That you do not! However, there is a certain delicacy to you, Rowena." His brown eyes were sparkling with reflection. "One would not say that you are a womanly woman. Not a waif in need of my or any other man's protection. This is rare in a world where women so often seek the arms of men. Indeed, you shun many of the ideals of Western society, and there is courage in doing that. In being what you feel and not what you are told. If I had to liken you, it would be to the title that the queen has so aptly given you, a sword. Yes. Fine, crafted to perfection, glorious to look at, and deadly to be on the receiving end of. My mother had that same edge, and Queen Lila possesses it as well. I think that women like you will be needed in times ahead. Women who appreciate life, yet aren't afraid of death. Women of pride and mettle who challenge the walls we have built around ourselves."

Rowena had to consider the man's words for a spell before deeming them a compliment. She had been given few of those, and it caused an unexpected blush. She might have found a voice to thank him, yet the storm had its say.

KRAKKLL!

When the light and fury did not end, the two became concerned. First, they ran to look out of their shelter, and then quickly splashed back to the rock as the winds beat at them. They each knew storms, the barrages of sand that could shear the skin off a man's face in Kor'Khul or the tempests that could flood the River Feordhan and sweep entire villages into the mud—disasters after which the king's forces had been dispatched more than once to assist the displaced. But what wailed and whirled around them, what shook the stone over their heads like a cheap ceramic plate, was a force that neither could define. Soon the gusts were so great that they could not huddle upon the rock and had to cower behind it in spuming water. For safety's sake, they clung to each other, and Galivad could not have been more grateful for the strength of his companion. She was the anchor in this storm, already proving what he had declared about women of her ilk. She spit at the slashing rain as if it were any other enemy who would seek to down her. Not even when the drops came streaked with fire and ice, and the whole of the world outside their rattling stone roof was aglow like a madman's painting of sunrise did Rowena wane in her fortitude. She was the oak whose branches he clung to, she was the shadow that he would peer out from behind once the storm of storms had ended.

In the moment that the chaos finally screeched away, she was so beautiful to Galivad that he almost kissed her.

II

How haunted the world was afterward: a realm of smoke and glowing fires, of mist risen from steaming patches of ice. The clouds and smog over Menos had been shredded, and dawn was bleeding into the sky. Walking in the eerie redness strengthened the sensation that Rowena and Galivad had entered purgatory. "What happened?" they whispered to each other. So many times the question was posed, and always without an answer—most often gaping disbelief sufficed. At least the alarms tolling in Menos broke the illusion that they were the sole survivors of the world's end, and they wandered toward the noise as drearily as ghosts chasing the cries of the living.

With morning's light came a greater appreciation for the power of the event, for how deeply the land had been purged. Far and wide, east to west, the storm had come and gone, leaving tracts of charcoal and frost behind. "It is like a field swept before the harvest," remarked Galivad once. Which was the logic that suited him best for the moment, for everything was stripped and raw, as if the weeds and chaff had been pulled and cast aside to make way for new growth. Is that what they were witnessing? The turning of a cycle? The tilling of nature's crop? Where was the place of men in the season that came after the fire and ice, wondered Galivad, and he was worried for the philosophical results of that line of thinking. The shells of skycarriages and road wagons caught in the storm smoldered in heaps along and off the road, momentarily distracting him from this debate before strengthening the argument that mortals were increasingly irrelevant to the events on Geadhain.

However, all was not death and despair. Not every heap had cindery bodies twisted into the wreckage. Animals were braving the new world. Galivad saw a mouse and nearly cheered. Stragglers, too, wandered ahead of them in the road, mortals who had found a sanctuary solid enough to fend off the storm. They could have been the vilest masters or criminals, but as Galivad and Rowena came within greeting distance, muddy faces broke with smiles, hands were clasped and pumped, and soon-to-be-forgotten introductions were made. Such were the exchanges of people who had danced with oblivion and returned, and for the moment, they were all brothers and sisters of the end. Galivad, who expressed himself best through charm and music, could find no outlet for his euphoria but singing, and the groups scattering the fields mingled into one another, drawn like happy moths to the fire of Galivad's voice. In time, a rowdy clapping band of dozens marched toward Menos. Although this went against Rowena's need for discretion, she restrained herself from interrupting her companion's music. Admittedly, she liked it, and this was a time to be joyous.

So it was that the merry troupe came to the caved-in arch of one of the black city's entrances. Once there, the sour Ironguards posted about killed their glee, and the company dispersed into its smaller original parts, though they all paid an honored farewell to Galivad and Rowena. When it was their turn to be admitted, the Ironguards did not bother with the typical Menosian interrogation; they simply took their names—Cory and Merri Thorpe—and waved them through the valley of darkness that was the Iron Wall.

"Nice people, those folks we took the road with," commented Galivad, when they were nearly into the light again. "They're not all bad. I take back what I said."

Too late, and it seems that you got your wish to see the city burn, thought Rowena. Destruction marked the wide street they traveled, with soot or puddles in every step and whole tears in the road that were fenced off. Many of the black houses were burned and tumbled like ruined gingerbread. Yet cranes and technomagikal machinery were present at roadblocks or ruined sites, clearing rubble or conjuring new stone into place. Off in the distance, the Crucible dazzled in its perfection, unscathed by the storm. Rowena got a chill from seeing this, yet could not quite say why. Much like their tower, the Menosians were shockingly unfazed by the destruction, and the crowds were thick. Galivad and Rowena stuck tightly together so that they would not be separated. Triages appeared in the busiest areas, and tents were erected on the sidewalks or within the collapsed frames of buildings. For so many in need, the lines before the fleshcrafters and ration stations were impressively calm. Patiently, these people held their bleeding limbs or continued to tend to their master's hair and clothing if they were slaves. As foreigners, the two were impressed that such aid was being bestowed and that the populace was so orderly in the aftermath of a disaster. While the Ironguard patrols found at every station and at many spots along the promenade were surely the main deterrent against unrest, there was another directive influencing these people that puzzled Galivad.

"I did not know that Mother Menos cared for her chattel," murmured Galivad behind a hand. "From a military perspective, it's a bit concerning how efficiently they've mobilized."

Rowena muttered into his ear, "A weak slave is a useless slave. They only starve them to death in the pleasure houses or pits of blood. Or so I hear. And yes, their readiness is frightening and worth a certain praise. We must not forget that they are a people of iron, and I doubt even that terrible storm has done much to dent their ambitions."

"We should find a Voice," whispered Galivad. "A tavern might be our best bet for contact—I'm not hunting down a bloody carrier pigeon in the mess. I know of a place."

The need for haste was implicit. For the ateliers and factories that remained with fires to stoke were burping smoke skyward again, and clouds were thickening around the Crucible. In no time at all, the sunshine would disappear, the darkness would be restored, and the city would be as it was yesterday. Some things, the most stubborn, the most *iron*, could not be transformed by catastrophe and were only hardened by it. Rowena hoped that Eod had the same resilience, as the storm they had endured would not be the last, and another—one of iron—was coming from the East.

III

Sshh, my Fawn, you are safe.

Morigan stopped her clawing. Whatever had been chasing her in her nightmares ended as the warm presence of her bloodmate enveloped her. She couldn't remember anything, only bumping along as though being carried and fading to and from the darkness. She breathed in Caenith deeply: he was woodsier than normal, and she could hear the tweeting of birds nearby.

No more separation. No more running, she sighed.

No more running. We can rest, my Fawn. But first, a final task.

The days had weathered her into a harder element than she could have predicted: a woman of nerve and steel. Another duty did not bother her, and the sweltering fire of Caenith's spirit declared how important this was to him. Truly, the nectar he was emitting was delectable to the bees, and they drank all that they could, and in an instant, she understood everything about the young skin-walker whom she had never met: her name, her story, Caenith and Thackery's promise to her.

Macha! she exclaimed.

Groggy but determined, Morigan struggled to a stand, assisted by Caenith's strong hands. Soon she was up and gulping the thick air in astonishment at where they were. Even Caenith was startling to her, as he was wild, many days unshaven, and attired only in a loincloth. Still, the chattering forest that nearly surrounded them was worthier of her fright—from its gargantuan trees with their stringy manes of vines and gnarled trunks that stared at her as if they were ancient green witches, to the unwelcome musk of predators, the acridity of earth that was so old and pure that it reeked of raw clay, and the ferns and thornbushes that shook as if a beast was waiting to pounce in every one of them. One glance, and the woods were made to dissuade all passage. *Danger for ye who enter*, the hissing wind seemed to whisper, or perhaps that was merely the snakes slithering inside that Morigan imagined made the sound. Morigan had never been here, though she knew · this place, remembered a poem of it even. *A weeping sky, a sea of trees that eats, what foolish hands and little feet. Do poke and tread upon its fright. Do dare to brave its darkest nights.*

Alabion, she gasped.

Yes, my Fawn. Thackery led us here, said it would be safe. Put aside your wonder and fear for the moment. There is a child that needs you, reminded the Wolf.

Others needed her, too. Thackery appeared as if from a puff of sorcery and startled her with a hug. He cried a little, as did she. Past his shoulder, the trio of those who had risked themselves for her in Menos rested in trampled grasses around a campfire. Mouse and Vortigern hailed her quickly and then went back to tending something on the ground, while Kanatuk leaped up and threw himself into her embrace.

"You are safe!" he said. "We are all safe. I don't know which spirits to thank: Crow for her cleverness, Eagle for his bravery, or Seal for her luck. I don't know who to thank, so I have thanked them all."

A seal...a final task, recalled Morigan, if the Wolf's fiery insistence stirring her wasn't enough to goad her ahead. Unfailingly, the bees told her where to go, and she separated from the two men and wandered over toward the fire. On the other side of the flames, closest to Mouse and Vortigern, a child was lying atop the bracken. She was wrapped in what cloaks the company had among them—minus the one that had been spared for Caenith's loincloth—and was as pale and pretty as a princess of ice, even with the welts upon her skin. The child appeared to be sleeping, though the Wolf's anxiety, the long face of Mouse, and the even deathlier expression of her father told that this was a slumber from which she could not be stirred. The last sleep, the long blink before the darkness. As Mouse daubed Macha with a rag, Morigan could almost hear the girl's life sliding away like the beads of water over her flesh. *Drip...drop...dead in an hourglass*, the bees lamented. Morigan refused this prognostication. After seeing Macha's truth, after knowing how this child's life was merely a transit from one tragedy to another, surely, this could not be a proper end.

Morigan went to her. Absorbed in the girl's care, Mouse did not immediately acknowledge Morigan; the bees murmured of a delicious sympathy flowing from nursemaid to patient. *What did she see?* wondered the witch. A cast-off child like herself? Morigan did not interrupt, and after a while, Vortigern took his daughter's hand and gently pulled her away.

"The big man says that you can help her," said Mouse. "She deserves to live. Even if she doesn't want to."

Morigan nodded.

Her words are wise, whispered the Wolf. *Daughters of the Moon were not healers as the West would know them, they could not play with flesh and bone like clay; their curatives ran deeper. To the soul, my Fawn. For what else keeps us in this world but that desire to live? Macha's desire, her flame, is weak, almost out. If you can rekindle it, if you can remind her that this world still has love for her, then her flesh may mend itself.*

I shall try, promised Morigan. *Even if I don't understand what you are asking.*

Oh, but you do, contended the Wolf, and his shadow was suddenly behind her. *You were my reason for crossing Geadhain; Thackery's, too. You lured us as naturally as the moon calls to any wolf. You are an enchantress, though when a magik is as deep as yours is, it is no longer a talent but a characteristic of what you are. I understand you now, my Fawn. Perhaps better than you would see yourself. You find what is special, what is secret, what is sacred, and you bring it out for the pain and betterment of whom you touch. You healed me of loneliness, a curative no magik or fate has ever brought. You gave an old man the inspiration to discover his greatness again. You broke the chains in that Northman's mind—as rusted with blood and murder as they were—and discovered the man inside. You found the withered tie of family between a man long dead and a child he thought he had lost. Your very actions are miracles.*

You weave and bless the spirits of those around you into a radiant music, as sweet as the summer winds or freshest scents I have chased, and you do all this without realizing your own wonder. Look to these souls that you have touched. Look, my Fawn.

A strange fear stalled her, an unwillingness to accept her own power. From face to face, her silver stare flashed, and even in the cagiest of her companions, she beheld gratitude. Five souls, each from the unlikeliest of places, the most jaded and dark of histories, all somehow drawn into a circle of fellowship.

Did I do this? she wondered.

Aye, insisted the Wolf. *Whether you see this now or will see it later, Macha is here by your Will. Another note in your song...acting through me, or through a pity you planted, for I was not the man who would have saved her before you, but an angry Wolf. Go now, finish your song.*

A song?

A song.

A song, agreed the bees, and they burst through her skin with stingers of light, chiming as they went and washing the fire, the woods, and even her bloodmate in silvery brightness. What the companions experienced was a sky that went swiftly dark, a woman who glowed pale and white as a newborn star, a prickling breath of bells upon their ears, and a choir of ageless high voices. How many sang or what words were used would never be understood; there was only harmony, a humming peace that froze all thought and instilled rapture. Caenith kept a hint of his senses and held the warm radiance that his bloodmate had become, feeling the woman inside shivering from the vibrations of her glorious magik; she was not quite in this world, and he would not let her slip from it.

She is in the Dreaming again: the neither here nor there of everything. Like a foggy sea, the grayness parts and there lies an island, small, white, and bare, and upon its shores, a child much the same. Hastily, her bees courier her to the island in a silver cloud; the island is distant and then it is present, the child now before her. If she has a body here, she cannot see it, though she sits on the ashy sand as if she does, and the child looks at her as if she does, too.

"You are bright," says Macha.

Here, there are no words or languages, yet their souls speak fluently. Morigan replies, "You, too, are bright, though the darkness eats at you."

For this is an ageless soul she speaks with, one of the oldest and wisest of the great cycles: a spirit that has been in and out of many bodies, each of them destined for magnificence. Not what mortals would claim to be greatness, but the true acts of virtue: a mother who has sacrificed herself in a fire to save her children; a man who died in the iron mines getting others—slaves and masters—to safety; a contemplative of the Southlands beyond Brutus's kingdom who would not raise his hand to violence even as the sword of a man black with fury came for him. Selfless acts, in every iteration of life in which this soul has manifested. What calls herself Macha is so dazzlingly pure, and yet this last tortured existence has dulled her light.

"I am tired," says the girl, and pulls her glowing legs up to herself, withdrawing. "No more pain. No more watching what I love die. No more dying, either. I want to go. I want to forget. I want to fade."

In her omniscience, Morigan knows what the girl means. Of the endless sleep, the great mystery into which all things can go. If Macha heads there, she will never return; she will be gone forever.

"But there are ones who care for you," she puts forth.

"And I care for them, but I cannot stay only for others. That is the story of my soul. You know that."

Macha smiles sadly. Her features are blurry, as if she is many persons at once—tall, short, bearded, smooth, old, young—all of them smiling, though. The soul stands and waves to the traveler. She reaches for Macha, but her hands are not hands, only nothingness, and she cannot hold the soul here if it chooses to leave, not with any of her power. This isn't right, she thinks. Not another death, not when so much has been lost. Where is this soul's happiness? Is that all they are meant for, to live and suffer, to never know love without sacrifice?

No, the bees whisper, and her headless head fills with a premonition: a stare of green ice, a cold kiss of passion, a frosty blanket that is a man's arms around her, and the sense of perfection in that moment, even as all else descends into ruin. Short and quick is the vision, like a dagger to the gut, and just as effective.

"Wait!" cries Morigan.

"What is it?" asks Macha wearily. Bits of her are sparkling away.

"Stay! I have seen it! A reason! If you remain in this life and the many others to come, if you persevere in this cursed journey you have been living, I promise you glory! You will have a reason, a destiny that will fill you wider than the greatest sea, will stir you more than any pleasure you have known!"

The spirit stops fading; half in, half out of time. "What reason?"

"Love. A love as treasured as mine. A love that the world will honor. A love to last for always."

"You promise grand things, witch."

"I am the Daughter of Fate, the weaver of destinies. I know what I have seen. It is no mistake that our paths have crossed, that our souls have met. They will meet again, in a time when Geadhain is at her weakest, when I am an aged memory, and it will be you who must right her wounds."

"Me?"

"Yes."

Even with her omnipotence, Morigan cannot assure herself of what she witnessed, and the vision is crumbling into vagueness. Only she knows that it is important, perhaps the most important thing ever. This soul cannot go into the great mystery. It must stay.

"Stay, and you will know bounty and purpose. Stay, and one day you will save us all and live to share the light with one you love, in that one blessed life. I promise you this, if only you endure."

The soul of many faces is crying with each one, its glittering tears falling like stardust. Momentously, it considers her words, weighing the cost of any future loneliness against the dream of this distant time. Yet it is a brave soul, and a dreamer's soul—it had to be to suffer as it did—and it accepts the witch's offer. The soul gives its hand, now solid again, to the witch.

Morigan knows that the words must be spoken. She asks, "It is sworn, then?"

"It is sworn."

With that, the soul-pact is made, that these two will forever be entangled until the ordainment—of an icy man's love and a calamitous time—comes to pass. The soul is in Macha's shape once more, and it hugs the body that Morigan feels and cannot see.

"Shall we return?" suggests the witch.

"Yes."

Now they can hear the enchanting music to which their companions out-side the Dreaming listen. And the bees gather them up, as tightly as they hold each other, and whirl them into the grayness, through tides of space and time, and into the circle of the bright souls who pray for them.

Cruelly the light and song ended, leaving Morigan's audience stunned and mournful. She was again in the dark spooky outskirts of Alabion, with the heat of her lover behind her and the salt of his tears—which the bees could taste—upon her shoulder. For a time, they were all at a loss. Each of their memories was inconsistent, as if they had fallen asleep with their eyes open and had a beautiful and melancholy dream. Morigan was particularly afflicted by forgetfulness. She remembered a flash of a white island, a girl who was and yet was not Macha, and words that made no sense to her at the moment. Was there a vision? A dream within a dream? she speculated, as the truth was not so clear.

Macha's whimper snapped them all from their reveries.

"She stirs!" exclaimed Mouse.

The company rushed to the child, who was not awake or miraculously free of scars, and only a little less pale. Though at least she was making the sweaty squirms one made when a fever was breaking, at least she was showing signs of life, which was more than she had done in the last few days. When she thrashed in her throes and clasped Morigan's knee, the witch recalled a fragment of her travel in the Dreaming: a promise for hap-piness and love had been forged in the gray lands beyond. She cupped the hand, kissed it, and whispered to the sleeping child that this promise began today.

IV

While the rest of Geadhain recovered from the storm, the company camped in the untouched shade of Alabion and finally found a moment of peace to savor. Alabion could be frightening, yet it was also quite enchanting. Full of harvest and game to those who knew how to brave its entanglement, and there was nary a secret that Caenith appeared to have forgotten in his thou-sand or so years away. Indeed, without venturing too deeply, he showed the companions the safest of mushrooms and plants to eat before leaving them with the dead man to sniff out beasts to roast over the coals at night.

Once the gathering was done and those who stayed behind had eaten their fill of berries and roots, Thackery suggested taking a constitutional. He proved to have a bit of a woodsman in him, or was familiar with the area, as he was only a little lost as he led them along the forest's edge. With Macha resting in his arms, he and the others headed northward; they cheered with joy as they came to a babbling stream spilling out of the woods. Thackery left Macha in Mouse's care, and the two groups—men and women—washed and refreshed themselves at opposite banks. Morigan noticed the old man glancing off rather often, and followed his stares to a misshapen mound like logs or stones long ago taken over by moss, plants, and time.

Or a cabin, the bees whispered. She knew then how Thackery had found this place, and of the home and its cozy hearth that once lay over yonder. She said a prayer for Bethany and Theadora's souls, and absently addressed Thackery after they had filled their water skins and were walking back to the encampment.

"This is a lovely place."

"Yes, it is," he said, his eyes sparkling.

Morigan gave him an embrace that needed no explanation, and then laughed as Kanatuk elbowed his way in and asked, "What are we all hugging about?" Macha woke up right then, bothered by all the noise, and though she was feverish and gummy-eyed, she was met with tears and smiles that cut through any crabbiness. By the time a freshly lit campfire wriggled a smoky finger in the distance, Macha was back on her feet: scampering and chattering in Old Ghaedic, which most of the companions were hopeless to understand, but overjoyed to hear, nonetheless.

Inevitably, night wrapped its arms over Alabion, and the woods hooted with husky birds that weren't owls and glowed with hungry stares. But nothing was to be feared about their happy campfire, where a stag had been placed on a spit and roasted with curious piquant herbs, and their faces each strained with unaccustomed grins. Once they were sated, the demand rose for a performance. Stories were told first by Caenith, who knew many more legends than there were hourglasses to spare. When his throat needed water, he ousted his bloodmate into the cold by pushing her to sing. She did so reluctantly, though the unsteadiness of nerves in her voice was unnoticed by her admirers. For them, the music was as magikal as they remembered, the same tingling experience if without the apparent sorcery and lights. Caenith redeemed himself by recognizing the folk tune she sang and adding his voice to hers. Together, their harmony of light and dark notes, of airiness and heaviness, was a heart-pounding perfection that brought an ovation from the company and a stillness to the beasts lurking outside their campfire's light. The song felt like an end to the evening, and the company broke apart into hushed conversations.

Sometime later, while reclining against her bloodmate, Morigan sleepily let her eyes wander around the fire. Macha had formed an attachment to the Northman; their languages were similar, if his being a broken form of the other, and they had been communicating throughout the night. The girl had fallen asleep with her head upon his shoulder, and he kept himself up and watching the stars to the north so that she would not have to be disturbed. *He will love her, though as a sister and not as the love that I promised her,* thought Morigan as the intuition hit her, though the details of that promise were increasingly obscure. Mouse and her father were similarly snug with each other; she dozed in his lap, and he did not study the heavens, but the shining gift that was his sleeping daughter instead. Only Thackery was by himself this eve, yet he was not wanting for company. The fire he slumbered close to was warm, and he could surely sense the serenity around him, for Morigan noticed that the carved-in-stone worry upon his face had actually eased to the simple tired countenance of an old man.

I am not a solitary hunter anymore, said the Wolf as her sentiments moved in him. *Because of you, I see that I have found a new pack.*

Morigan twisted in his arms and kissed him. They ached for that contact. It had been forever since they were able to touch or taste the heat of the other. Quietly, they slipped away from the company, and the Wolf raced north, following some invisible scent, or even a phantom impression from his bloodmate, and in sands they had arrived at the brook near Thackery's ruined home. He took her into the water, knelt, and returned the dagger he had kept so long for her. *Siogtine,* they said, and were overcome by how much significance that word held. They kissed, sniffed, and pawed at each other as animals would. Yet passion was not their intent, and soon the grunting softened to sighs, the grasping to embraces. With how hard their journey had been, how desperate and unsure, they simply wanted to feel flesh to flesh and mind to mind. At times, they held each other so ferociously and spun in the stream so dizzyingly that they could not tell who was who: they were a moving, whirling force. They were one. When lust faded altogether, Morigan washed her handsome Wolf with handfuls of water, anointed him with kisses from her red lips, and then they went to the bank to sprawl on grass and count the flickers of whiteness above, feeling small and yet not insignificant beneath the vastness of the universe.

Will you tell me now? asked the Wolf, at the moment of their greatest relaxation. He meant her dream. The one that had stricken her in Menos, which she had not mentioned to anyone, and that he felt roiling in her.

Tomorrow, she said, and that was good enough for the Wolf.

He buried her in bites and kisses, and they fell asleep listening to the cheeping and howls of Alabion.

V

"Come to haul us off to your mistress, eh? I am not to be chained, and I dare you to try!" roared the Wolf.

So angry was he that a hint of his transformation had begun, distorting his jaw and sharpening his teeth. He and his hunting partner had caught the interlopers skulking through the ferns toward the camp, as quiet as cats in the dusk, but not stealthy enough to escape his and the dead man's senses. He threw one of the three trespassers down on the ground near the fire, and he almost rolled into the flames—his hood flew off as he tumbled, exposing an angularly attractive man with mussed red hair and a groomed goatee.

"Alastair!" cried Mouse.

"You know him?" Caenith asked, frowning.

"She certainly does." Alastair spit out a bit of dirt and threw irritated glances to the faces around him; he recognized them all. "The sage, the fire-haired witch, I know everyone at this gathering—except the little whelp. I saved many of you in Menos. Open your mouths and vouch for me, you scoundrels."

"He's fine, Caenith," urged Mouse.

Morigan concurred with some unspoken gesture, for the Wolf looked to her as if she had spoken. Meanwhile, Thackery kept his silence; the last time he'd seen the man—as the Voice in Eod—was nothing but an annoyance. While Alastair straightened himself, the two other prisoners were thrust forward by Vortigern and had their hoods pulled back. Thackery found his voice when the faces were revealed.

"The sword of the queen and the watchmaster of the East! I didn't recognize you back in Taroch's Arm, and almost failed a second time today, as unkempt as you are."

Casually, Galivad scratched his beard. "End-of-the-world sort of storms and weeks spent chasing a highly mobile and elusive old man will ruin one's refinement."

"How did you even find us?" asked Thackery.

Alastair tipped his head to Mouse. "Check your boot."

"My boot," she said, and squatted to examine her footwear. "I don't... how would you even? I'll be fuked!" After much fondling of the leather, she had found what felt like a tiny pin slid into the folded top of her boot. She removed the object, which was a sliver of cold black metal—feliron, presumably. The metal could bind the powers of others as well as keep an enchantment bound to it, such as a spell of seeking.

Mouse threw the sliver into the grass. "I don't appreciate being tailed."

"I do need to keep an eye—or witchneedle, as it is—on my most exciting prospects," countered Alastair. "Besides, I'm better at watching out for you than you seem to be. By the kings, I was gone less than half a day before you burned the hideout down. It was one of my favorites, you know."

"Blame the Broker, not me," huffed Mouse.

"All very interesting stories to hear, I'm sure," said Galivad, and sauntered over to the fire to smell one of the hares that roasted there. He seemed completely nonplussed by this circle of rough strangers. "However, we have more dire matters to discuss. As you are no doubt aware, my companion and I were sent at the behest of the queen to find and question the crimson witch; yourself, good Sage; and that exceptionally large man with whom you ran off. Mostly him, until we learned that you were alive. It was around then, after the unfortunate fishy incident in Taroch's Arm and a chat with the woman responsible for it, that we began to realize that the men we chased might not be foes and were, in fact, acting covertly on a mission of rescue. This Voice has confirmed your motives, and I no longer see either of you to be terrorists."

"You could have come to the queen, Sage," said Rowena. "The Silver Watch could have helped you."

Swiftly, Thackery managed to interject himself over what was to be a growling response from Caenith. "We were pressed by the need for speed and secrecy. Any arrangements with the king's army would have been hindrances for both. Particularly when there are spies within the palace."

"Yes," said Galivad, frowning. "I had thought the same, myself. Espionage is the only way Menos would have learned of the crimson witch so quickly. I am glad that we have come to this accord with one another, but still I must ask what it is that you know that has Eod and Menos making war."

The blond rogue was pointing at Morigan; she sat and gazed at the flames, and then motioned for the others to rest, as well. Now was the time to tell the company of her vision in Menos. For the sky had rained fire and ice, and she knew *why*. Perhaps she should unburden herself of her other visions as well: of a Black Queen, a black star, the Immortal Kings and their love and hate, and her uncanny connections to the very folk around her. When all was quiet and the company was pale with anticipation, she spoke.

"Fate has chosen me to witness terrible things. I shall not ask why, for my dark destiny has come with many blessings." Caenith had settled in behind her, and she pulled his strong embrace tighter. "The war between Eod and Menos is not what we should worry ourselves over. Magnus's war with his brother is what will shape Geadhain. If you look to the lands apart from these woods—protected by the Sisters' magik or their own resilience— you can see that the shadow of their war has reached far, indeed. I saw their conflict. A clash of ice and fire, beautiful and horrifying. I saw Magnus fall to his brother."

Many about the campfire winced as their spirits were wounded by the news. They did not shed tears, for grief could not be found in the cold river of shock that ran through their hearts. Night layered them in shadows, their faces growing darker and darker, and no one spoke for many sands.

At length, Morigan continued to the stony crowd. "This is not the end of my dark foresight. Nor should we grieve a king who I do not know is yet dead. We have more enemies to consider, the true threat in the south. For Brutus has made pacts with ancient powers: a beast of pure fire, like a snake—if a snake could be the size of a mountain—and a bodiless menace that seeks to call herself queen. She is more dangerous than Brutus or his pet, this spirit that defines wickedness. I can see the truth of the world when I wander the other realms, and what I have seen of her is *hunger*. For life, love, light, everything that makes Geadhain green and pure. So much hate and anger...she could be pitied in her obvious despair if she wasn't so merciless. She wants it all, and she will break the kings and the order of nature to have it. She has already taken Brutus, and I admit I do not know the fate of Magnus after his fall."

"Who is this dread queen?" whispered Mouse.

Morigan shivered out a shrug. "I don't know. Something old. Something that comes before the memories of men or any who could recall such a monster."

Not all memories would be so foggy, mused Thackery. Beguilingly, the woods called him, and he drifted away from the conversation and into its muddled darkness. Deep inside, he wondered if the Sisters Three watched from a cauldron or whatever scrying surfaces those ancient witches used. He marveled at the synchronicity of fates all drawn to their realm, remembering the suggestion born by Lila that he was to seek their wisdom should the worst befall Eod. How ridiculous the idea had appeared back then. Yet, the worst had come, and here he was. Led by Morigan, joined by a man who knew these woods, for he had once ruled them. He had even brought them to the shelter of Alabion without realizing the obvious lure. Was he even a person or simply another pawn in this game of destiny?

"Thackery?" Morigan waved for the old man's attention. "This is not a time for silence. We could use your counsel."

"Yes. Where were we?" he asked, apprehending that time had escaped him.

During his lapse, the stunned faces had been replaced by shaken fists and animated discussion. Morigan had stood and was pacing about the fire, as bold and in command as a warmaster. Thackery almost wandered into whimsy again, remarking at how much she had grown.

"If there is any light to cling to," she declared, "it is that Brutus's army will need to be rebuilt after the battle. I watched most of his forces die in the storm that the brothers made. Brutus's army is nearly wiped out, I would say. So there is time, at least, to prepare for his coming. I do not advise diplomacy. I have seen the red madness of his twisted mind, and he speaks only in blood now."

"While Brutus cannot be ignored, the West must guard itself against Menos as well," advised Thackery. "I shall tell you of what Caenith and I saw in Blackforge."

From there, the company threw itself wholly into the conspiracies threatening Geadhain. Thackery explained the operations under way north of the Blackforge, which were worrying, given Galivad's description of the Iron City's incredible rebound from calamity. There would be no stalling the Iron engine of war; on it would march to Eod, immortals and their blood feuds be damned. Word must reach Queen Lila, then, so that she could entrench her city for battles on two fronts. To this end, Rowena produced a farspeaking stone, which solved many of their concerns over how to communicate the grim news to the West. Quickly then, the sword moved to find privacy and make contact with her mistress. Rowena returned to the others more troubled than when she had left. "Queen Lila knows," she confessed, and the misery and sighs made their rounds. Already, Her Majesty had been informed of Magnus's defeat. Lila had sensed it, of course. Rowena had felt a depth of pain in that revelation that could not possibly be conveyed in the short whispers of speech from a magikal stone. She yearned to be with her queenmother and hated that she had to be spans away from a woman who surely needed every compassion. Not all was dark on Eod's horizon, however, for the king's hammer, Erik, had made it back from the battlefield through an act of tremendous magik, and he had not stopped for praise of his survival, but immediately started with the city's repairs from the great storm—which had spared no corner of Geadhain, it seemed—and its subsequent fortifications against the next. Thus, while Eod was imperiled, it would not be caught unaware. Such tidings brought the first rush of relief to the company, and they could pick at the well-done rabbit after that.

In more measured tones, then, and with the pleasantness of food, the company deliberated where they themselves would fall in this web of events. Rowena and Galivad's orders were clear: they were to head to Blackforge and investigate the extent and power of Menos's forces there, and then report to Eod with haste. The others around the fire were not as set in their decisions. Although physically present that eve, Kanatuk could not have been more absent from these grand discussions on kings and wars. The stars caught his attention more often than any of the talk; his gaze followed the shining heavenly paths to the North, and Morigan could feel his longing like a tidal pull. His desire to return to a quieter place. *He will leave*, she realized. *And I cannot ask him to stay.* The old soul with whom she had communed in the Dreaming was no less afflicted with wanderlust. Macha stayed near to Kanatuk, attracted to his withdrawnness and giving leery stares to the woods. *She will go with him, for Alabion is no place for her, and she is terrified of it. He can make them a home in the cold bright reaches of the world where they might never see darkness again*, remarked Morigan. Prophecy was spilling from her like water from a broken well: these were not guesses, but probabilities. Next, the silver eyes cast their perception upon the father and daughter playing with a deck of brightly colored cards by the fire. *I think you have more caring and honor in you than you know, Mouse. You have discovered family, and that tiny flame inside you—love—will grow grander than you can imagine. You will be fierce and fight for what you have found. You will walk with us, for we are a part of what you cherish now.* The bees buzzed to Thackery after that; he was huddled with Queen Lila's agents and shaking a rabbit bone at them as if they were learning a vital lesson. *You, my father from Eod, you will follow me to the end of all this. I wish you would not, for I fear that the journey may claim you. Do not go there, my silver servants*, she had to warn her hungry bees. *Some mysteries, like the hourglass of a man's death, are sacred. But I shall not steer another's fate. All choices are our own, even if the pattern of destiny seems preordained. Come with me, then, and if there is to be a passing, it shall be one bright from the memories we have made in togetherness.*

Morigan watched the lively old man for a while until tears blurred her vision. She was nearly done with her reflections when she spotted the slim shadow of the foxy man wavering through the flames. For the entirety of their council, he had been silent, and it had been quite easy to forget that he was even among them. They had spoken with reckless freedom in front of this man, this Voice, and yet she did not fear for his keeping or selling of their secrets. Curious, her swarm migrated across the flames to feed on this enigma. Yet past her base instincts, he was as elusive as the twists in the fire, and the only thing that they returned to their mistress with was that same sense of amusement that he had exuded when she had met him before. *And who are you, trickster? What hand do you have in all of this? For while I can attribute myself for drawing these fates to this fire, you are a shade responsible yourself. What are your secrets? Whom do you serve?*

Alastair winked at her, as if he knew what she was thinking, and the startled Morigan pressed against the flesh of her bloodmate.

You are filled with suspicion and a delicate sorrow, my Fawn, said the Wolf. *I feel you grieving and questioning the world around you. There is no need for confusion. There is no need to stare into the future if it troubles you.*

Morigan tensed. *But I know where we have to go.*

Alabion, yes. All roads have brought us here, no clearer a path could there be. My past, your past. Thackery's cottage lies just through the bush not far from here. He led us here like an old dog finds its home. Many fates, all woven on the looms of the Ladies of the Wood. Patterns that have seemed so tangled are really only formed by a master Will. We shall answer their summons, then, these Sisters. We shall see what they say, and if we do not care for their answers, then we shall make our own.

Yes, we shall, Morigan decided.

For she was no more a slave, no more an idle chronicler. She was the Daughter of Fate, and if she could partake in destiny, then she could shape it, too. The Sisters could not be alone in that power. The light of her surety was a golden surge: a tickling wind that passed through and over Caenith.

At last, the animal that Geadhain should fear, praised Caenith. *The Queen of Fang and Claw.*

There are no queens in Alabion, replied Morigan, smiling.

Tonight, the first has been crowned.

As the night thickened, and the woods of Alabion pressed over the small campfire with their eerie calls and long shadows, the company sought what fellowship they could. Even though they were so different in purpose and spirit, they scraped up every enjoyment to be found. They banished the darkness with their laughter, for Galivad was a rousing and comical storyteller. Songs came out again, funny ones at first, the sort of tavern slang not appropriate for a child, so it was good that Macha could not understand them—she clapped and smiled anyway. They did not address the hollow gleam in one another's eyes. They brushed away the dim ache in their stomachs that rabbit and fruits could not fill. They did not dwell on these maladies, which were not sicknesses but a knowing of this fragile moment before the coming uncertainty. When they went to lay their heads, though, these thoughts and others could not be quieted and haunted their minds. For in the morning, paths were to be committed to, and partings were to be made.

After the morning, some of them would never see one another again.

EPILOGUE

"Ooh, settle those feet!" cursed Elemech.

Little Eean was restless today, kicking her mother's womb and tugging on her cord. Even in her unformed state, Eean must have sensed the spinning of destiny's threads and was reacting to them. Ealasyd delicately placed the spider she was playing with on a leaf of the nearest bush and went over to her sister, who sat on the rock she so often favored and was squinting into the morning. The youngest sister placed her hands upon Elemech's stomach, whispered to the life inside and then looked to her elder.

"She should be quiet for a while," said the girl. "I've promised her a story later."

Elemech stroked Ealasyd's golden hair. "Thank you. Now a bit of silence from you, too, while I speak to the woods."

At those words, her spirit was already flying like a golden shimmer along the rays of sunlight, dancing over the eaves and then swooping down into the earthy mist of the woods, where it skipped as a fluttering presence from flea to tree, bear to leaf. She soon had crossed uncountable spans and slipped into the tight skull of a hawk. From there, she could watch the borders of her lands, where a company was breaking. *Two shadows to the North, one bright as the star that rules there—we shall see her again. What a glorious soul. Three shadows to the West. Five facing our woods: a wise man, a thief, a dead man, the lord of Alabion, and our errant sister—*

"What did you say?" demanded Ealasyd.

Elemech was flung back into her flesh by the disruption and gentle shoves of her sister. She must have been speaking her vision aloud. However much she had uttered, it was enough to upset Ealasyd, and the girl's face was red and knotted. Mothering had given Elemech a wealth of patience and taken all her cold retorts away; she realized what was wrong and would address it. Kindly, she explained.

"My youngling, you are confused, when really you have only forgotten. Such is the curse of ever being a child: your mind is always hither and thither. Chasing butterflies and daydreaming. Reality runs out of your ears like warm honey. I do not blame you for not remembering."

"Remembering what?"

"Your sister."

"I count three sisters, and all of them are right here," said Ealasyd. "You are speaking out of tune like that nattering sparrow that comes here from time to time."

"I am not, dear one. You have another sister. Half of our blood, half of another's."

Fast as a flipped coin, Ealasyd's anger transformed into joy. "I do?"

"Indeed."

"Oh, tell me about her, Elemech! Please!"

Up she came into Elemech's strong arms and cradled herself against the hard, stirring lump of her unborn sister, who, too, was interested in a tale and had been promised one. Elemech began her story, and the birds and mice flocked round to hear, the bugs froze on their leaves to listen, and all around the Sisters were still. What a grand tale did the ancient sister weave, so thrilling—and sad—that the mice were upon their hinds and squealing, the birds were flapping their wings, and the bugs were cheering with their clacking teeth. Ealasyd applauded, too, even though she would forget most of it in an hourglass. Though not her new sister's name. *That* she would trace in the mud of the cave and make songs of so that it would never flee from her mind again, and so that they could greet each other when soon they met.

Morigan.

—Fin—

ABOUT THE AUTHOR

Christian A. Brown has written creatively since the age of six. After spending most of his career in the health and fitness industry, Brown quit his job to care for his mother when she was diagnosed with non-Hodgkins lymphoma in 2010.

Having dabbled with the novel that would eventually become Feast of Fates for over a decade, Brown was finally able to finish the project. His mother, who was able to read a beginning version of the novel before she passed away, has since imbued the story with deeper sentiments of loss, love, and meaning. He is proud to now share the finished product with the world.

www.christianadrianbrown.com

51428830R00330